Alfred Seelye Roe

Rose Neighborhood Sketches

Wayne County, New York - with glimpses of the adjacent towns - Butler, Wolcott,

Huron, Sodus, Lyons and Savannah

Alfred Seelye Roe

Rose Neighborhood Sketches
*Wayne County, New York - with glimpses of the adjacent towns - Butler, Wolcott, Huron,
Sodus, Lyons and Savannah*

ISBN/EAN: 9783337314064

Printed in Europe, USA, Canada, Australia, Japan

Cover: Foto ©Andreas Hilbeck / pixelio.de

More available books at **www.hansebooks.com**

ROSE

NEIGHBORHOOD SKETCHES,

WAYNE COUNTY, NEW YORK;

WITH

GLIMPSES OF THE ADJACENT TOWNS: BUTLER, WOLCOTT, HURON, SODUS, LYONS AND SAVANNAH.

BY

ALFRED S. ROE,
A NATIVE OF ROSE.

"What's in a name? that which we call a rose
By any other name would smell as sweet."

PUBLISHED BY THE AUTHOR,
WORCESTER, MASS.
1893

PREFACE.

This volume represents summer vacation work for eight years. Born of ancestors who were among the very first to redeem Rose soil from the wilderness, I cannot remember the time when the story of early adventure and hardship was not heard. Grandparents and great-grandparents filled my childish ears with anecdote and incident, so that when they had passed on, it seemed fitting to give the narrative a more permanent form than that of mere legend and tradition. This was the prompting to write, for the *Clyde Times*, in 1886, the first of the series, taking my native district, No. 7. When that was ended, friends and relatives in adjoining districts said, "You must tell the story of Nos. 5 and 6 also." Accordingly, they followed in successive issues of the *Times*. In this way the beginning was made. When they were finished, the idea of going over the entire town began to take shape, and the eventual visitation of every home in Rose was the result. Having gone through the more or less ephemeral shape of a newspaper serial, and having been read by many, through a wide extent of country, I was told that the matter deserved the lasting form of a book. Obedient to such advice, the book was projected, and here it is. In securing data for these pages, I have walked and ridden above one thousand miles in and about the town. Were I to include the distance covered in reaching Rose, from my Massachusetts home, and in visiting New York places, to some degree connected with Rose, the aggregate would nearly exceed belief. Very few persons write more than one town history. Such a work needs the whole heart of the writer. He must have grown up thoroughly imbued with the ideas of the town, and its story, he must have drunk in with his mother's milk. Then, he must have a certain amount of leisure for investigation, and, above all, he must be able and willing to write out the results of his birth, rearing and searchings. These necessities prevent his undertaking more than one such venture. "My native town!" There is only one, and its progress from the forest primeval to cultivated fields is told in the following pages.

Hilly countries are filled with clannish people. The ranges of drift hills, so characteristic of Wayne county, have formed excellent boundaries for school districts. Had the town, as in New England, rather than the county, been the unit of political organization in this state, the people throughout Rose had been better acquainted with each other. The youth reared in District No. 7 was wont to have in mind, as *terræ incognitæ*, such sections as "Over East in Butler," meaning the land beyond the Loveless range of hills; "North of Wolcott" was to him as remote as was Gaul to the ancient Romans; "West of the Valley," for all reachable purposes, might as well have been west of the Rocky Mountains; while "South of Clyde" meant a region as unknown as is the Antarctic continent to the navigator. Fortunately, common church relations brought the most of the people together, as a rule, once a week, though every one of the neighboring towns has claimed, from the very beginning, some Rose citizens as church members. Then, too, the acquaintance of residents on the borders of school districts has prevented absolute crystallization and complete non-intercourse. Spelling schools, husking and paring bees, brought the young people of a wider area than one school district into intimate acquaintance, an intimacy that frequently ripened into matrimony. In fact, intermarriage in Rose has been so extensive, that were every family, resident in town for thirty-five years, to be represented by a ring, while the ring on the eastern side would not be very near that over on the Lyons border, yet were these to be interlocked in marriage, the taking up of one would involve the whole number. The truth of this statement can be easily ascertained by any one who chooses to follow out the marriages given in this book.

As the school district, in its political and social relations, comes nearer than the N. Y. town to the principle of self-government and to intimate acquaintance, I have made that the unit in my story. The dates at the head of each chapter tell when the matter appeared in the *Clyde Times*. To comprehend fully the time involved, the reader must have the sliding temporal scale in mind. All changes, since the first writing, are indicated by parentheses. In making the book I have had to leave out much. It has been a choice of materials. Anecdote and incident that would add a fourth to the volume, have been elided. The genealogical data have been given in passing rather than in separate chapters. I have aimed to make the narrative one of to-day, a series of events now passing, rather than one of yesterday, all in the buried past.

The story is told with the heartiest good-will towards everybody. Having no axes to grind, nor grudge to pay, I have made the book, possibly unduly *Roseate*, but this is a matter for each reader to settle with himself. If some families are given more in detail than others, it is because said data were more easily forthcoming. When facts were given, I have aimed to use them. In embellishing the volume with illustrations, I have, as a rule, abstained from the use of pictures of people now living, save in the case of my own family and in that of town officers. The most of the pictures of individuals, have been secured with great difficulty, and many have had to be copied before going to the engraver. Obviously, the results are not the best pictures in the world, but they do serve to show us how the first settlers looked. Rose abounds in scenery worthy the painter's brush, and my camera was used in many places that are not shown in these pages, simply because the sun and the plates did not respond to my efforts. In other words, the negatives were not good.

This book should not go forth without rendering thanks to all those who have aided in its preparation. As every one who has written a letter or answered a question has thus contributed, I hereby thank each and all, not only for helping me, but for their zeal and affection for the township, which is or has been home. As these pages are read, I hope the thought will be constantly in mind that the silent sleepers in our cemeteries fought a good fight, that we of to-day might enjoy what they suffered for. Let us not forget the first settlers who, in house and field, toiled unceasingly that the comforts of civilization might follow.

Hoping that the story of Rose, thus told, may bind us yet more closely to the scenes of our childhood, and that our common regard for each other may hereby be intensified, this volume is submitted to any and all who care for the town in which they reside, or which was formerly their home.

ALFRED S. ROE.

WORCESTER, Mass., Nov. 20, 1893.

CORRECTIONS AND ADDITIONS.

Page 21. Wm. Sherman died in Butler, and his son, Henry, was in the 111th Inf.

Page 28. The Martin Saxton place is now owned and occupied by Robert Weeks.

Page 47. Wm. Hallett was married Sept. 13, 1893, to Miss Ida Bovee, of Wolcott.

Page 52. For Sally Bump, read Bundy.

Page 57. Mrs. Ida (McKoon) Wickwire died Sept. 22, 1893. Ernest O. Seelye and family have returned from Dakota to the home farm.

Page 62. For Mary Champion, read Champney.

Page 67. Add to Oaks family, Charles G. Oaks, Jr., of North Rose.

Page 113. John W. Vanderburgh is living in Des Moines, Iowa.

Page 115. The farm house of Geo. Catchpole was burned Oct 19, 1893.

Page 185. Mr. Jeffers Dodds sold his farm in October, '93, to Mr. Loren Lane, formerly of Rose.

Page 195. For Alonzo, read Lorenzo Snow.

Page 203. Mr. Geo. H. Green died Sept. 26, 1893.

Page 311. For Mrs. John, read Mrs. Joseph Phillips.

Page 391. Add John Sherman, Feb. 6, 1864; H, 111th Inf.; Sept. 10, 1864.

THE TOWN OF ROSE.

—

LOCATION.—This town is about three miles north of the village of Clyde, a station on the N. Y. Central R. R., midway between Syracuse and Rochester. It is about eight miles south of Lake Ontario, and is east of the middle line of Wayne Co.

GEOLOGY AND TOPOGRAPHY.—In this town are extensive ledges of lime-stone that have been worked both for building and burning purposes. At Glenmark, the ledge outcropping produces a very interesting waterfall, shown in the illustrations. Here, too, may be found fossils peculiar to the Clinton group of the Niagara period, to which group and period the town geologically belongs. Among the cobble stones, or hard head rocks, with which a large part of the surface is covered, may be found many conglom-erate shell petrifactions. They are water worn, but, as a rule, show their composition excellently. Obviously they came here by the same agency which produced our many ranges of hills, viz., the ice march or movement. The late George S. Seelye found several specimens of *orthoceratidæ*, which showed admirably both the fossil and the cast. Farmers' boys have turned up these specimens for years, exciting usually no further remarks than "I wonder what they are." There is not a stone wall in the town which has not some of these fossils, remnants of a Palæozoic age, doing the ignominious service of field defending instead of gracing a college cabinet.

The hills of Wayne have formed the theme of poet and of scientist. The late Dr. Lawrence Johnson, of New York City, himself a native of Sa-vannah, found in them a never ceasing source of interest and enjoyment. Upon them he prepared a valuable monograph, "The Parallel Drift Hills of Western New York," read before the New York Academy of Science, Jan. 9, 1882. In this, he shows that our long ranges were formed under the immense glaciers that once overspread this section, naturally taking the direction of the ice stream. When the ice disappeared the hills were saved from denudation by the resulting water, which formed a vastly greater Ontario. He says, "This lake undoubtedly discharged its waters southward through the valleys in which lie the small lakes of the moun-tain ridge. During this period the parallel drift hills were in deep water, and hence beyond the reach of denuding agencies, though they doubtless received the *débris* of melting icebergs, particularly the large boulders of crystalline rocks which here and there dot the surface, but are not now present in the boulder clay." The traveler along the line of the N. Y. Central R. R. cannot help noticing these elevations, pronounced and of a singular regularity. If at all given to surface observation, he cannot readily forget the impression. Wayne, and to some extent Cayuga county, are noteworthy for their ridges. They are nowhere mountainous nor exactly precipitous, save, possibly, their northern terminations, which are steeper than elsewhere. All of them are cultivated, but it would doubtless be much better were the western sides allowed to grow up to woods. The eastern slopes invite the early sun and fairly laugh in wonderful fertility. To the farmer no finer sight can be had than the fields along these morning sides, for instance, those of William S. Hunt, lately Colonel Briggs', or those of the John B. Roe and Roswell Marsh farms. Of these hills, Rose has twelve well defined illustrations, viz., south from the Delos Seelye farm ; that extending into Galen from the southeast part of the town and the one immediately west ; then there are two ranges, including much of the old Finch and Benjamin farms: leading north, from a point back of William H. Griswold's farm, is a ridge which, to some extent, shuts off the view of that forming the western boundary of the Town district ; still further to the north is the high hill, the highest in town, one hundred and forty feet, back of the Roseview or Sherman Brothers' farm ; immediately to the westward is the long range leading down to the Valley: southwest of the village is found, first, the hill on which once dwelt the Drowns, now owned largely by George Milem ; west of the Valley, on the Jeffers road, is the hill on whose summit lived the Dodds and Glen families, while last of all, looking off towards Lyons, is the range long held by the Ways, Worden and Weeks people.

In the southeast the drainage is in that direction, reaching finally the Montezuma marshes and Seneca river. In the southwest, water flows toward Clyde river ; in the northwest, through Mudge's creek, the flow is into East bay, while west of the Mirick or Closs hills, the water finds its way into Great Sodus bay. The surface, for many square miles northward from Clyde, is as level as a tennis court, and until the Sodus canal was undertaken, there seemed to be very little inducement for water to flow in any direction.

SOIL AND PRODUCTS.—Men who have wandered far have returned to Wayne county with the reflection that no part of the country can produce, in abundance, a greater variety of objects which contribute to the good of mankind than Wayne. Fruits, vegetables and grain in almost limitless kinds and quantities are here produced from tree, bush and soil. The latter is a gravelly loam, mingled with clay in places, and in the swamps the blackest of mud abounds. At any rate, this is true of Rose, for in the county no township more thoroughly merits the application of the introductory remark than this. The early settlers found immense trees—beach, maple and hemlock, with ash, cedar and tamarack in the swamps. The legend still lingers of a buttonwood or sycamore, near Wayne Centre, so large that a section of it was used as a dwelling house after it had fallen down and proven to be hollow. In fact, one of the interesting stories of the late Simeon I. Barrett was that of putting up at the Buttonwood tavern early in the century. The late Hiram Church of Wolcott said that in 1808 three families, numbering fourteen people, young and old, put up at this same inn for the night and were well entertained. Osgood Church, his father, was one of the guests. He also says this was on one of the Jeffers farms. Maple trees furnished a large part of the sugar used by the first settlers: beach, hewed and mortised, formed framework for buildings that yield to no destroyer save fire, while hemlock afforded material for tanning, and siding for house and barn. The swamps were dark, luxuriant and almost impassable. In fact, as late as the forties my father once wandered several hours in the tamarack swamp, now the Osgood onion fields, thinking to make a short cut to the Valley, only to emerge, at last, near the point of entrance, viz., near where Stephen Chapin now resides. When the late Linus Osgood discovered the onion-raising qualities of this black, vegetable mold, he added scores of dollars per acre to its valuation. Something in soil and atmosphere has made this county the peculiar home of peppermint. Rose dwellers remember how rank it grew by the springs in early days, and how it was gathered and hung up for winter's use. Early in the century, says Anson Titus, Phelps' historian, a certain Andrew Burnett of Deerfield, Mass., who had gathered mint along the streams of his native state, came west in the effort to dispose of his distilled product. He found the plant in greater abundance here than elsewhere, and so settled, following his vocation. The farmers, quick to discern a good thing, began to cultivate, and from Lyons the growing eventually worked into Rose. Latterly, the raising and evaporating of blackcap raspberries has proved a paying industry, experience having taught Rose farmers that they cannot compete with the western wheat growers. After all, probably, the crop that promises most to the careful husbandman in Rose is that which comes from his apple orchard. Barreled green or in a dried condition, this fruit is as necessary as wheat, and the world must have it. No part of the country raises more to the tree or better in quality. Each year will see additional orchards planted, till, in a sense, the town will return to woodland. The census data in this volume show what have been raised: already

> " Round about them orchards sweep,
>   Apple and peach tree, fruited deep."

INDIANS AND RELICS.—It is probable that the territory included in our town once formed a part of the Cayugas' possessions. Still it was on the border of the Senecas' lands, and may have been an almost neutral section, thus accounting for the limited finds of relics. While in some parts of the country arrow-heads and hatchets are found in abundance, any such memento is rare in Rose. Relics in the possession of George W. Aldrich, in North Rose, and of Abner Osborn, in the Valley, are noteworthy examples.

Mr. L. H. Clark in his Military History narrates the finding of a piece of a cannon on the old Collins farm, in the Valley, about fifty years since. Chauncey B. Collins, now living in Clyde, was his informant, and he describes the relic as eighteen or twenty inches in length, having a bore of about two inches. The place of finding was north of Wolcott street. Unfortunately the item was lost, else what an interesting beginning it would make for a Rose museum. A little further north, on what is now Fisher land, then that of Thaddens Collins, Jr., was found an old axe, of shape and make indicating French origin; near by also was found a bit of ancient pottery. Arrow-heads have been found along the ridge where now lies the road north from the Valley. These facts to Mr. Clark suggest the existence, years since, of a line of forts or fur trading posts following the old Indian trail which led from Crusoe lake along Marsh creek into the plain west of the Valley and so to Sodus bay. Pertinent to the foregoing is the finding in 1889 by Dwight Flint, just over the Rose line, at the head of Sodus bay, of a large quantity of lead and bullets. Though Mr. L. H. Clark, H. H. Wheeler of Butler and Mr. D. M. De Long of Rose all took part in discussing the how and when the material came where it was found, it does not seem that the supposition is disproven that the bullets may have had to do with early times. In 1891, July 5, Mr. Stephen B. Kellogg found in his corn field, on the old Aaron Shepard farm, an exceedingly well-preserved silver coin of the value of an old shilling piece, having this inscription: "Ferdinandus VI., D. G. Hispaniarum Rex. 1751." Older far than the settlement, it may have been lost by some early explorer, French or English, passing through these parts from one post to another. Of course it is barely possible that a settler may have possessed and lost. At any rate, the coin remains.

ORIGINAL OWNERSHIP.—The early charters of Massachusetts and Connecticut included all the land between certain parallels from the Atlantic to the Pacific. At the same time, New York, through her charter, held all now included within her borders. Accordingly, New York possessed what two other states claimed. This was especially true as to Massachusetts. Before the Revolution it is supposed that the Bay State agreed to New York holding sway over all that territory between the boundary of the two states and the extreme western line of settlements made before the War. After the War the dispute was reopened, both states claiming jurisdiction over western New York. Instead, however, of appealing to arms, as the Michigan and Ohio people did in the thirties, these parties, with whom the memory of battles against a common foe was still fresh, left their case in the hands of commissioners, who met in Hartford, Conn., Dec. 16, 1786. These officers were Oliver Wolcott, Richard Butler and Arthur Lee, all being men revered in American history. They confirmed the sovereignty of New York over all the territory in dispute, but to Massachusetts was conceded the preëmption right of the soil from the native Indians of all land lying in the state west of a line drawn due north to Lake Ontario, from a point in the north Pennsylvania line eighty-two miles west of the northeast corner of that state, excepting a territory, one mile in width, the whole length of the Niagara river.   Also, they ceded to Massachusetts a tract equal to ten townships, each six miles square, between the Owego and Chenango rivers.   In 1800 an amicable agreement was effected with Connecticut, whereby the latter state received from the general government lands west of New York, and thereupon relinquished all claims upon the future Empire State.

Massachusetts, then, had to secure a title from the Six Nations, whose hunting grounds and homes she had acquired from New York.   There were sharpers in those days as well as later, and efforts to negotiate with the natives were frequently frustrated by the nefarious advice of these companies of men, who had united to rob the Indian and to cheat the white man.   In 1787 Massachusetts contracted all her claims to the land west of the Pennsylvania line, about 6,000,000 acres in all, to Messrs. Oliver Phelps and Nathaniel Gorham for $100,000, to be paid in three installments. Here is the origin of the famous Phelps and Gorham purchase.   Canandaigua was the headquarters of the new project, and here in July, 1788, was effected a treaty with the Indians, prominent among whom was the noted Red Jacket.   After opening this great tract to settlers, the purchasers in 1790 sold all remaining lands to Mr. Robert Morris, a man of great wealth, a resident of Philadelphia and a signer of the Declaration of Independence. He it was who loaned to the government, in its distress, more than a million dollars, yet late in life he lost his fortune and spent some time in a debtor's cell.   The price paid by Mr. Morris was about eight pence per acre, but he soon turned his contract over to a syndicate of English gentlemen, viz., Sir William Pulteney, who held nine-twelfths; John Hornby, two-twelfths, and Patrick Colquhoun, the remainder.   The chief capitalist was the first named.   Hornby was a retired East Indiaman, having been governor of Bombay.   He also was a capitalist.   Colquhoun was a statesman and philanthropist.   The London agent effecting this sale was William Temple Franklin, a grandson of Benjamin Franklin.   They paid £75,000 for the lands, and passed their management over into the hands of Captain Charles Williamson, who had been a British officer during the War, but who became thoroughly imbued with the American spirit, and managed the business of his principals with great success.   At that time foreigners could not hold landed interests in this country, hence the vesting of titles in Williamson, who took the oath of allegiance in 1792.   He was a native of Balgray, Dumfriesshire, Scotland, and to that country he retired when through with his labors in America.   The property was known as the Pulteney estate, with land offices in Geneva and Bath.

However, the territory included in Rose did not fall into this allotment. Its connection therewith came about thus: When the preëmption line

HON. ROBERT S. ROSE.

was run out it touched Lake Ontario some distance further west than was expected, but no complaint was made, till some years later it was discovered that an apparently intended deflection had been made to the west, far south of Geneva. To obviate this fault a new line was run, that known to-day reaching the bay at Briscoe's cove instead of three miles west, as run at first. Again, to compensate Revolutionary soldiers for their services. New York had promised a large tract of land along her western border, or near the preëmpted Phelps and Gorham purchase. The northwest township in this allotment contained more land than some later counties. Through Romulus, Washington, Junius and Wolcott, we come finally to Rose; but in the early assignments it was found that the state had disposed of land included in the Gore that triangular strip having its acute angle near the Chemung river, its base Lake Ontario and its sides the old and the new preëmption lines. To compensate, there was made over to the Pulteney estate all the land now embraced in the town of Huron; in Wolcott a strip on the west side, about two miles in width, the same boundary line extending through Butler, touching Savannah near the residence of H. H. Wheeler, Esq., and all of Rose save three lines of lots extending across the town and into Butler to the above-named line, said lots being known as Annin's gore, though they really make a rectangle. In other words, these compensating lands extended from Annin's gore northward, taking certain portions of Rose, Butler, Wolcott and all of Huron. This was known as Williamson's patent.

Early in the century an extensive purchase was made by Messrs. Rose and Nicholas of Geneva. This land, 4,000 acres in extent, lay on both sides of the Clyde and Valley road from Annin's gore, or near the farm house of William H. Griswold, to within three-quarters of a mile of the north line of the town, or to the northern boundaries of the Lyman and Corell districts. There was a western ell included between a line drawn from a point just north of Isaac Campbell's house and the northern line, a little beyond the home of Mrs. Charity Stearns, and both running to within less than a mile of the western limits of Rose, or a trifle west of where the widow Messenger now resides.

The Rose and Nicholas purchase suggests certain names that should have mention here. Robert S. Rose and John Nicholas were Virginians by birth, and through marriage, brothers-in-law. Nicholas came of an old Virginian family, born Jan. 19, 1764, in Williamsburg, Westmoreland county, and was elected to the 3d, 4th, 5th and 6th Congresses from that state. After settling in Geneva, in 1802, he became prominent in all local matters, devoting himself largely to agriculture. In 1806-7-8-9 he was a member of the State Senate. He was presiding judge of the Ontario county court. He died Dec. 31, 1819.

Robert Selden Rose was born in Henrico county in 1772. In coming to Geneva he made very extensive investments on the east side of Seneca lake. Both families brought slaves with them from the Old Dominion. Mr. Rose's wife was a Lawson. He was a member of the New York Assembly in 1811, '20, '21, and was in Congress during the sessions of the 18th, 19th and 21st Congresses. He died suddenly, while about to get into a sleigh, in the village of Waterloo, Nov. 24, 1835. He had long been apprehensive of a sudden death and had kept his affairs arranged for such an end. As his picture amply shows, he was a man to be revered and honored. Said a little girl, when looking at it, "How much he looks like George Washington." His extensive possessions, in the very heart of Rose, secured for the township his family name. Descendants of both of these gentlemen are prominent citizens of Geneva.

TITLES AND AGENTS.—Titles to farms in Rose ran from the Williamson patent through the Geneva agents to those purchasing. It was in 1790 that Morris sold to the syndicate. Captain Williamson managed the affairs of the estate till 1801, when, worn out with his arduous duties, he surrendered his position to Robert Troup, then of New York City. He visited the section repeatedly till 1814, when he became a resident of Geneva. He died in 1832 at the age of 74 years. Troupsburg, in Steuben county, was named for him, and an old map, 1838, gives Sodus Point as Troupville. He was a distinguished soldier during the Revolution. Williamson returned to Britain and there died in 1808. As sub-agents were John Johnston, John Heslop and Robert Scott, till we come to Joseph Fellows, who was by far the most important factor in these early sales. Many local agents were employed, and the first settlers in those parts transacted their business with Osgood Church of Wolcott. Associated with Mr. Fellows for some years was an active little Scotchman by the name of Andrew McNab, and he was accustomed to go about the towns looking after payments, etc. "You won't drive me off," said a delinquent to him on one of these visits. "Oh, no," was the ready answer; "the weeds and briers will do that soon enough." He frequently remained in Wolcott a week or two, keeping in sight the interests of those whom he served. By the side of an old church in Geneva I find this inscription, which tells about all that is now to be had about him: "Andrew McNab, a native of Scotland, died at Geneva, Oct. 26, 1829, aged 46 years." In 1862 Mr. Fellows associated with himself Mr. Edward Kingsland of Geneva, and in 1871 Mr. F. retired, leaving the latter in care of what is left of the former great interests.

From a grand-nephew of Mr. Fellows, H. C. Heermans, I am enabled to present the following facts: "Joseph Fellows was born at Redditch, Worcestershire, England, July 2, 1782. In September, 1795, his father and family, then consisting of his wife and seven children, of whom Joseph was the oldest, emigrated to America. After a brief stop in New York, he pushed on to Luzerne county, Pa., where Scranton is now, leaving Joseph in New York to study law with Isaac L. Kip, the indenture being made June 24, 1796. He served his time faithfully and received his cer-

JOSEPH FELLOWS, ESQ.

tificate July 2, 1803. In his work for Mr. Kip he came in contact with Alexander Hamilton, Aaron Burr and other distinguished lawyers of the day. Here he met Colonel Robert Troup, and at the age of twenty-one was offered a situation at the salary of $600 per year, which he accepted instead of entering his profession. Subsequently, as stated, he became in 1832 principal in the management of the vast property of the Pulteney estate. When 89 years old he gave up the trust. In 1873, April 29th, he died in Corning, Steuben county, N. Y. In his own affairs, he began by saving a portion of his scanty earnings, even in his apprenticeship days. In his agency work his salary was increased from time to time, till on succeeding to the full direction he received $5,500 per year. This income during a long life, with his habits of economy, afforded a continued surplus, which, being invested in lands and otherwise, made him a millionaire. In his agency his strong point was his strict, unswerving honesty. With millions of money passing through his hands, there was no effort on his part to make money at the expense of his employers. While not a member, Mr. Fellows was a liberal supporter of the Episcopal Church.''

SURVEYS.—Colonel Hugh Maxwell, who has been called the ''hero of Bunker Hill,'' superintended the first survey of the Phelps and Gorham purchase, beginning in July, 1788, and completing the same in the next year. To accommodate certain parties who had settled at Geneva, the subordinates of Maxwell deflected their north and south line so far to the west that Geneva was left out. In 1791-92 Adam Hoops directed another survey, which relocated the preëmption line, leaving it as it is today. The land included between the two lines amounted to about 84,000 acres. Still, all of this was west of the Williamson patent, in which Rose was included. These lands were not opened for actual sale till (Hiram Church says) June 16, 1808. As to the surveys of this tract, I am indebted for the following data to John C. Bishop, of Lyons, though a native of Rose. Valentine Brothers began his surveys from the vicinity of Sodus bay, where, at Port Glasgow, the Helms had located, being the first settlers in those parts, they coming a little before the close of the last century. He made his surveys to suit the settlers who were already on the grounds, thus laying out 17 lots, and the beginning of the numbering at this point is thus accounted for. Mr. Bishop says, '' Then proceeding easterly he laid out lots 18, etc., following the old ' Sloop Landing ' road and numbering on each side till he put in the large lot, No. 50, in the east bound of the district (where is now the village of Wolcott) ; thence south along the east line of the tract till he reached the southeast corner, having by this time scored 63 lots, with very little regularity as to sizes, shapes or positions. So anxious were the parties to sell they would lay out a lot anywhere, of any size or shape wanted, and the numbering was continued in the order of date. I think more than thirty years elapsed between the beginning and end. This work was done by Valentine Brothers, George

Matthewson, John M. Gillespie, Elias R. Cook and others." The Rose and Nicholas purchase, of 4,000 acres, was sub-divided by the owners to suit circumstances. As to Annin's gore, the strip in the south part of the town, Mr. Bishop says: "The surveyor general, Geddes, in an attempted 'smart trick,' caused a map to be made, allotting the original town of Galen. It was submitted to the Legislature and approved, and an appropriation made to pay for the labor, the representation before the Legislature being that the work had already been performed, while the fact was, only a few base lines had been surveyed. The next summer Joseph Annin and others were sent to survey the tract according to the map. They found the territory larger than the map, both ways. As they could not (very well) move Seneca river, they changed the numbers and filled out the Gore on the west, making a very long lot for No. 1, between the map as constructed and the new preëmption line as it really existed. On the north, the overplus strip was known as Annin's gore. The next year Annin surveyed it into lots as laid down in the map. Joseph Annin, together with Humphrey Howland and others, were in the employ of the state, under the direction of the surveyor general, for several years. They laid out a large part of the military tract, and, so far as I know, the whole of it." This Joseph Annin was a conspicuous figure in Cayuga county ; from 1803 to 1806 he was a state senator, and in 1799 and 1800 was sheriff, in fact the first one in the county. His home was in Genoa. The accounting for the peculiar western boundary of Galen and the queer parallelogram in the south part of Rose is exceedingly interesting. Eron N. Thomas, in his Rose sketch furnished to Everts' "History of Wayne County," makes the exact dimensions of the town to be six and one-half miles east and west by five and one-quarter miles north and south, and the area to be 21,849¾ acres. It should be stated that Mr. Hiram Church, in his valuable articles on the old town of Wolcott, contributed to the *Lake Shore News*, several years since, said that the surveys and allotments were made in 1805-6 by John Smith, to whose maps early deeds make frequent reference.

SETTLEMENTS.—Exactly when the first settler came, or who he was, will never be clearly known. No record, however, is had of any dwellers before Alpheus Harmon and Lot Stewart, who came in 1805. Very likely Caleb Melvin came at very nearly the same time, to a point south of the Valley. In those days the spirit of unrest was, if possible, more rife than it is to-day. Besides, for several years it was difficult to secure perfect land titles. Hence the migrant halted for a brief time, and if a breath of trouble arose, hastened toward the ever inviting west. Inevitably the first comers were squatters. They built wherever they found a good location, naturally selecting a spot by the side of a spring. When surveys were made, some early comers bought, others moved on. The very earliest data at hand are those furnished by the late Hiram Church, from his father's book. Osgood Church's record gives 117 contracts. Of these, those falling within our bounds were as follows:

Alpheus Harmon, lot 169, 113$\frac{1}{10}$ acres, at $3.50, June 21, 1808; now the Chester Ellinwood farm. Also, same date, lot 170, 114$\frac{9}{10}$ acres, at $3.50; now the George Steward or Jones place.

Pendar Marsh, lot 205, 50 acres, at $4.00, Jan. 11, 1811; the John B. Roe farm.

Epaphras Wolcott, lot 160, 100$\frac{6}{10}$ acres, at $4.00, Jan. 30, 1811; the Brockway and Munsell places.

Seth Shepard, lot 187, 40 acres, at $4.00, April 1, 1811; now Hopping and Collins.

Daniel Lounsberry, lot 206, 106$\frac{6}{10}$ acres, at $4.00, April 3, 1811; now Chatterson, McKoon and Lockwood.

Jonathan Wilson, lot 140 (south half), 50 acres, at $4.00, April 3, 1811; Eustace Henderson place.

John Wade, lot 185, 107$\frac{1}{2}$ acres, at $4.00, April 16, 1811; now Joel Lee.

Asa and Silas Town, lots 212 and 213, 150 acres, at $4.00, Nov. 11, 1811; now Desmond and Town.

John Burns, lot 153, 108$\frac{6}{10}$ acres, at $4.25, April 8, 1812; the Jonathan Briggs farm, in part.

Abram Palmer, lot 140, 102 acres, at $4.00, April 22, 1812; now Lovejoy and Henderson.

Thomas Avery, lot 154, 103 acres, at $4.25, May 4, 1812; in part the farm of Charles Harper.

Demarkus Holmes, lot 187, 101$\frac{5}{10}$ acres, at $4.32, June 25, 1812; long the Joseph Seelye farm.

Nodadiah Gillett, lot 132, 101 acres, at $4.00, Oct. 2, 1812; now Barrick and York farms.

Eli Wheeler, lot 188, 99$\frac{7}{10}$ acres, at $4.00, Nov. 13, 1812; now Hopping and Hendricks.

Jacob Ward, lot 140 (in part), 60 acres, at $4.25, Nov. 12, 1812; possibly Buchanan farm, in part.

Elijah How, lot 167 (east side), 50 acres, at $4.00, Nov. 18, 1812; the Samuel Osborn place.

Jonathan Wilson, lot 161 (south end), 31 acres, at $4.25, Dec. 29, 1812; Lawson Munsell farm.

Asahel Gillett, lot 155, 50 acres, at $4.25, Mar. 10, 1813; Avery H. Gillett farm.

Thaddeus Collins, 1st, lot 141, 99 acres, at $3.50, Oct. 23, 1809; farms of J. S. Salisbury and E. Jones, in Butler.

After 1813 the work of sub-agents ceased, and thereafter all business was done with the main office in Geneva, which became the Jerusalem up to which the early settler had to make his yearly pilgrimages; frequently the road was a *via dolorosa*. The books of the Geneva business are not at present in accessible form, so that a continuation of facts like the foregoing is impossible. Much of the land was bought on speculation, and for longer or shorter periods was held by men who never came to these parts.

ROADS, ETC.—It was not until 1810 that regular surveys were made. Till that time roads ran anywhere, at least they found the settler, or he made them in going from his home to that of his neighbor. In time it became desirable to straighten these paths and to make them passable at all seasons of the year, hence their official location. Osgood Church's old record book gives the first Rose road as that leading east from Stewart's corners, and the date is May 10, 1810; next is that north from Clyde to the Valley and Stewart's, June 29. 1810; from Port Glasgow to the Valley, March 20, 1811; north from the corners, at George Rodwell's, to Stewart's, May 11, 1811; east from Shear's corners, Dec. 25, 1812;

from Glenmark to North Rose, April 1, 1814.   Mr. Church was himself
the surveyor.   This ends Mr. Church's record, and the burning of Wolcott's
first data precludes further early facts in this direction.   To-day the roads
are as good as the average in western New York.   Perhaps that from the
Valley to Clyde is much better, succeeding the plank road, whose tolls
necessitated considerable care on the part of the stockholders.   It had a
good beginning and the dwellers upon it have kept it very well.   The material for making the roads of Rose well-nigh perfect is yet lying, more or
less a nuisance, in the fields of the town, in the shape of cobble stones, so
annoying to tillage ; but when the stone crusher has been purchased, and
the principles of McAdam are better understood, Rose may have thorough-
fares that will be a pride and a delight.

Our town is among the "might-have-beens" in some respects.   As
early as 1841, General William H. Adams, of Clyde, secured a charter for
a canal to extend from that village to Sodus bay, and its location was to be
very near the Valley.   Everybody knows "Adams' ditch," and it is frequently referred to in the following pages.   In 1827 a preliminary survey
was made, but Oswego was clamoring for connection with Syracuse and,
through superior wealth, won.   General Adams' devotion to this dream of
his lifetime was touching.   What he wrote upon the subject would fill
volumes.   His letters are clear, earnest and pointed.   Possibly, some day,
the wheels of time will develop the fact that he was not altogether a
dreamer.   Joseph Fellows was one of the promoters of his scheme.

Then there was the project for a Pennsylvania and Sodus bay R. R.   The
charter was granted in 1850, and there were numerous share takers in
Rose, the matter reaching its climax in 1870.   In 1853 was printed the
engineer's report, and from it the following words are taken: "Starting
from Port Glasgow the railroad was to follow the margin of the bay, or
nearly so, till it came near the town line.   Thence it was to pursue a little
more westerly course, till it neared the Valley, which it was to pass, only
800 feet west of the main street.   Its course southward is nearly direct,
crossing the Clyde and Lyons highway, the Erie canal and then turns and
runs parallel with the Central R. R. to Glasgow street."   Eron N. Thomas
was treasurer and a Rose director.   The others from this town were Henry
Graham and Chauncey B. Collins.   William H. Lyon, of New York, was
also a director.   There is extant a letter from Joseph Fellows, in which he
pleads the infirmities of age for not embarking in the enterprise.

However, what water and steam have failed to do, there is little doubt
that electricity will yet accomplish.   His reputation as a prophet would
not be greatly imperiled who should predict that the year 1900 will see a
line of electric roads connecting Clyde and the Valley ; thence diverging,
one part will extend to Wolcott and beyond, while the other will pass
through North Rose, Port Glasgow, and will terminate at the Lake.

MAP OF THE TOWN OF ROSE.

ROSE NEIGHBORHOOD SKETCHES.

SCHOOL DISTRICT NO. 7.

Oct. 21—Dec. 2, 1886.

In presenting these articles, it is my purpose to note the ownership of the farms ; the families and the buildings that have for years past been associated with this section, confining myself, for the present, to that part of the district embraced in Rose.

No. 7 lies three miles east of the Valley, as old residents call the village of Rose, and includes a slice of Butler, *i. e.*, that portion of the town lying along the border road, second in number, to the westward of the Loveless range of hills, running south from Spencer's Corners, a locality better known to "ye inhabitants" as Whisky Hill. The district itself includes one long line of hills, or at least one side of it, the east, from the former residence of Delos Seelye, deceased, to the farm of Roswell Marsh. Two roads crossing have made, at the home of the late George Seelye, a four corners, noted for many miles around on account of the hospitality of Col. Seelye and the eminent respectability of the neighboring residents. A few rods to the eastward stood for nearly or quite forty years the cobble stone school-house, wherein the children of the vicinity received the essentials of an education, and whose homely figure gave to the section a distinguishing feature and a name.

Having, then, our bearings, let us go back to the remote past and learn what the early names were. Starting from the extreme northern part of the district, we have, on the west side of the road, first, the home, or what is left of it, of Joseph Seelye, who died February, 1854, an old man of seventy-seven years. He was born in Kingsbury, Washington Co., N. Y., of Connecticut ancestry. He early married in Stillwater, Saratoga Co., N. Y., Elizabeth Carrier, of an old Sharon, Conn., family, and, with her, essayed a farmer's life in Sherburne, Chenango Co. Here all his children, save the youngest, Delos, were born. A desire to better his condition prompted him to go still further west, and in March, 1815, he moved his young family to this then an almost unbroken wilderness. Blazed trees formed the chief means of tracing the roads through the forests. One Holmes had taken up the farm on which Mr. Seeyle located, and a small log house with a few acres of cleared area formed the only improvements on what was to be the

2

"homestead." The willing hands of his two sturdy sons, George and Ensign, contributed not a little to the success of the venture, till the younger, Ensign, at the early age of nine, was killed by the fall of a tree which he was engaged in cutting down. The place of the lad's death was the field just north of the barn, and nearly in line with it. The log house gave place, about 1820, to one of the most commodious structures in the vicinity, and in point of comfort it may be doubted whether it has ever yet been excelled. Large fields in time surrounded it, and they, with their owner, were well known for leagues around. "Uncle Joe Seelye" was a character well remembered by middle aged and older people as a man of most marked peculiarities. Kind-hearted and generous when his feelings were touched, he was, nevertheless, choleric and opinionated. Of vast proportions physically, he found summer's heat almost unendurable, and frequently sought consolation and comfort in the coolness of his cellar. In winter, while others grumbled at the cold, he would sit in his shirt sleeves upon his porch and laugh at their discomfort. For years, the people entering his yard saw resting against his red horse barn a slab of marble having the inscription, "Sacred to the Memory of Joseph Seelye," he having thus providently made preparation for his demise. His coffin, too, he had provided and stored at an undertaker's. He boasted that he had his tombstones and coffin ready, had hired a minister to preach his funeral sermon, and he is known to have offered a neighbor a pig if he would agree to dig his grave. Amusing anecdotes are still told of his eccentricities. It was "Rate" Barnes whom he sent into a cherry tree to pick fruit and compelled to whistle all the time he was "up the tree," so that he might waste no time. "Uncle Joe" threatening him with the most terrible caning if he abated his music for a moment. I sorrow now over the terrible pucker into which that poor boy's lips must have gathered. He long had in his employ a lad who is now one of the most respected citizens of an adjoining town, but who in his youth fairly put nature to her test in devising schemes of mischief. It was a never failing source of delight to H. to do something which would arouse the old gentleman's ire and cause him to attempt a pursuit, ending always in his falling, and, owing to his rotundity, remaining prone, until some one, usually his wife, came to his rescue. Prompted by some older people, the boy once performed a wanton act, for which "Uncle Joe" determined to pay him in full, and so bided his time until one luckless moment — luckless for the boy — he was caught in one of the stalls of the barn. The immense form of the irate farmer filled all the space. Escape was impossible, and for once H. felt the full weight of the cane and the strength of Mr. Seelye's arm. Back of the house in the orchard was the first cider mill of this vicinity. It was made in the true "down east" style. A huge sweep was moved around by horse or cattle power, and diligent industry might run through seven or eight barrels a day, provided the apples were reasonably juicy. The great wooden screws used in the press were in existence only recently, though the mill has not been used for nearly fifty years. Back of the main structure once stood a smaller house, in which Mr. Seelye's son, George, lived for a time, but in 1856 this was moved away to become a corn crib for his youngest son, Delos. The great red barn, erected near the road, also went up the hill. In time the shed and wood-house disappeared; the wide, shady piazza fell away and the old house stands only a suggestion of its former self. After Mr. Seelye's death, in 1854, this portion of his estate fell into the hands of his son. Delos, and the old house became a sort of caravansary, in which abode, for a season only, a long line of tenants, the mere enumeration of whose names would make many lines of this article. The noble walnut tree, one of the largest in the town, still stands in front of the house, but there is little else to remind one of the beauties of the past. The great cherry trees have grown old and fallen. The Isabella grape that clambered over the cherry tree has also gone, and everywhere we see proofs of the truth that man and his works are perishable.

Mr. Seelye was twice married. His first wife dying in 1833, he wedded, in 1834, Miss Lorinda Clark, of Waterloo, but a native of Connecticut. She survived him many years, dying in 1880, at the advanced age of 92 years. Many changes have been wrought in the years since 1815. Then the howl of the wolf resounded at night-fall from the hillside, and Mr. Seelye's favorite diversion was deer hunting. A black bear once ambled across the garden where he and his son, George, were at work. Forests covered nearly all the surrounding country, and to procure material of the proper kind for his house he had to go to Pineville every day — he and George—to draw logs to Wolcott, to be cut into boards. He left two sons, George and Delos, and a daughter, Mary Louisa, who married Dudley Wade, and was long a resident of the district.

Passing to the southward along a road on whose sides apple trees still grow, the result of Joseph Seelye's thoughtfulness, we come, on the corners, to the place where for more than fifty years George Seelye greeted his friends and dispensed free-hearted hospitality. Coming to the country in its newness, he had marked all the changes in his surroundings from 1815 to the date of his death, December, 1885. What constituted his original homestead was a lot of ten acres at the cross roads, obtained by way of trade from his father. He had erected a modest house, set out an orchard of apple trees and surrounded his house with cherry trees, for many years the most prolific fruit bearers in the vicinity, and making his place one much thought of by all the boys in those parts. Many a tumble have luckless youngsters taken from those branches, but no one was ever seriously injured. On the death of his father, Mr. Seelye was able to extend his farm to the northward, making his estate very compact and valuable. He had early wedded Polly Catharine, the younger daughter of Aaron Shepard, the first settler in the district; but he never took his wife to his new home, as she died in 1829, leaving a daughter, Polly Catharine, who married, in 1843, Austin M. Roe, the youngest son of Austin Roe, one of the early comers to the neighborhood. In 1834 Mr. Seelye married Sarah Ann, daughter of Dr. James Sheffield, of Sherburne, Chenango Co., who survives him. His son, James Judson, who served in the 9th Heavy Artillery, married Frances, daughter of Artemas Osgood, long a resident of the district, and now resides just north of the "old home," on what is known as the Aldrich place. His second daughter, Eudora, married, in 1865, Lucien, elder son of Artemas Osgood, and for several years lived north of her father's, on one of the Lovejoy places. She died in 1870. The third daughter, L. Estelle, married, in 1878, Merritt G. McKoon, a schoolmate, born and reared in the Butler part of the district, and with him retains the "old place." Mr. Seelye enjoyed the confidence and esteem of his fellow citizens, was a life-long Baptist, and in early life was very active in the state militia, holding, in succession, the offices of adjutant, major, lieutenant-colonel and colonel of the 186th Regiment. The titles of colonel and deacon are indifferently applied to him.

Just opposite the Seelye home, on the south side of the road, was, years ago, a log house which Mr. Seelye, in the early part of his married life, used as a barn. Before that, it was occupied by one Ransom Ward, who afterward moved to Whisky Hill and ran a potash factory. Again, diagonally across, near where James Armstrong's dwelling stands, was another log house, built by a Mr. Eaton, a would-be settler from Connecticut. He came up with Mr. Shepard, but, at the period of moving, his courage failed him, and he gave his possessions into the care of Mr. Shepard, who finally became the owner in full. Also on the north side of the road, a little west of Mr. Seelye's, was a log house once occupied by Mr. Savage and his family. These humble houses, I have been told, were built upon the lands of certain parties for the occupation of wood cutters, who labored in clearing up the country, and whose wages, I learn, were oftentimes quite one-half paid in whisky, of which the proprietor was wont to lay in a plentiful store. Long since, the very last vestige of the houses disappeared, not even so much as a currant or lilac bush, nor sprig of tansy, remaining to show where families lived and children played.

Proceeding to the east, just beyond the school-house, on the north side of the road, were we to look sharp, I doubt not we should find the remains of an old log house already old as long ago as the oldest inhabitant can remember. Passing over the long line of early occupants, it will suffice to state that its last tenant was Edward Stickles, who married Sarah, oldest child of Abram Chatterson, of the same district—No. 7. This house was on the farm of Dudley Wade, who for many years lived in the large white house still further to the east, on the south side of the way, and is now the home of Oliver Bush. (Sidney P. Hopping, 1893.) The farm originally belonged to John Springer, who sold to Mr. Wade and went further west. Dudley Wade, who was born in Paris, Oneida Co., in 1806, was of excellent Connecticut parentage, his father being Dudley, son of Dr. John Wade, who died in Oneida Co. in 1803. His own father dying when he was very young, he was brought up by his uncle, John Wade, a brother of Mrs. Aaron Shepard, wife of the first settler. Before getting through with these sketches, it will be seen that almost every permanent settler in this neighborhood was, in one way or another, related to his neighbor. Mr. Wade's wife was Mary Louisa, the only daughter of Joseph Seelye, a most estimable lady, now residing with her daughter Imogene at South Butler. His son Joseph married Emma, daughter of Artemas Osgood, and lives in Rose Valley. Ensign married Lucy, daughter of Kendrick Sheffield, and grand-niece of Mrs. George Seelye. He is a farmer on one of the Ellinwood places just east of the Valley. Frank, a promising boy, died in 1875 in Boston. Imogene married Chester Irish, a native of Indiana, but of a Cayuga county family. She is now a widow, as is also her only sister Emily, who married a Mr. Cushman of South Butler. Mrs. Irish has three daughters, Lorena, Dora and Maud. The large house, so long Mr. Wade's home, was erected by Mr. Springer, he having bought a few acres of Aaron Shepard for this purpose. For some reason, inscrutable to us, he was unwilling to have his home on the same side of the road as his barns, which were and are now quite extensive. In one of these barns was a stationary threshing machine, to which the farmers carried their grain to be threshed, just as now they take it to the mill to be ground. Columbus Collins, a native of the district, was, when a boy, severely injured by falling into the machinery when in motion. Geo. Seelye has been heard to say that this was the worst place for threshing that a man ever suffered in. For some inexplicable reason Mr. Wade was prompted to sell his farm during the War to Messrs. Abraham and John Phillips of Wolcott. They, however, held it but a short time, in turn selling it to Hudson R. Wood, who had married Catherine, daughter of Thaddeus Collins and grand-daughter of Aaron Shepard. He, too, soon passed the place along to Oliver Bush of Oneida county. Mr. Bush keeps up the relationship traditions of the vicinity, being a cousin of Mrs. John B. Roe. Mr. Bush's wife was a Stone before marriage, and her mother, an aged lady, lives with them. They have four sons, Leverrier, Fletcher D., Lavello S. and Edward. He has held the estate for nearly twenty years, and has introduced many improvements, both in the house and upon the farm. He is one of the two farmers of the district who have made hop growing a specialty. Just now, in addition to hops, he is giving much attention to berries. (Mr. Hopping has still further improved

the place, repairing house and barns, making them among the most attractive in the town.)   His eldest son, Leverrier, married some years ago, and
resides in a new house erected recently on the north side of the road and a little further to the east. Near this spot there stood many years ago a log house,
among whose early occupants was Philo Saxton, father of Martin Saxton
of Butler. An earlier tenant was a Mr. Brewster, whose son Samuel married Experience, a sister of John Kellogg.   John Ogram, long a well known
resident on the plank road south of the Valley, was her second husband.
Brewster, the tailor of Wolcott, and his brother, once proprietor of the
Clyde Hotel, and Decatur B., are her sons, and there was a daughter, Polly,
by Mr. Ogram.   She was the mother of Priscilla, who is Mrs. Wm. Wescott of Syracuse; and James, who lives in the north part of the town. (In
1891 Mr. L. Bush sold to Frank A. Hendricks, who, Wolcott born, married
Eva Vought of the same town. They are Rose Methodists. Mr. Bush and
family went to Syracuse. There are 44 acres in the farm.) Nearly opposite, in years agone, was another log house, in which at one time lived Mr.
Goodrich, the Baptist minister. This house, with the ten acres upon which
it stood, was given to Geo. Seelye in lieu of one hundred dollars, the stipulated compensation for one year's labor given by him to Aaron Shepard immediately subsequent to his marriage to the old gentleman's daughter. He, however, never lived upon the place, but traded it with his father
for the place upon the corner. Returning, for a moment, to Dudley Wade,
it ought to be said of him that he purchased, after leaving District No. 7,
first, the old Fuller place, near Rose Valley, and afterward the Ellinwood
farm, just east of Fuller's. Here he died in 1876. The name Dudley has
been prominent in many successive generations of the Wade family, or
ever since Jonathan Wade of Medford, Mass., married, in the 17th century, Deborah, daughter of Gov. Thomas Dudley of that state. I hope
others may yet bear this cognomen as honorably as the Dudleys of the
past. It is safe to say that no man in the town of Rose was ever more
widely known ; whether as auctioneer, speculator or marshal at a county
fair, everybody knew " Dud. Wade." There may be cases where he was
beaten in repartee, but few of them are recorded. The man who tried to
get a joke on Wade usually retired from the contest dejected. His merry
joke and his hearty laugh will linger long in the memories of those who
knew him, and instinctively we ask, "Why couldn't such men live longer?"
A quarter of a mile beyond Mr. Bush's, on the same side of the road and
on the Butler side of the town line, about thirty years ago Frank Rice, son
of Jonathan Rice of the Butler part of the district, was killed by the kick
of a horse. He was one of the merriest youngsters that ever delighted a
parent's heart, or worried a school teacher. He was returning from
school, and, in his frolics, going too near the heels of a lively team driven
by Stephen Kellogg, was kicked so violently that death ensued in a few

hours. For several years a board erected, having a picture of the boy inserted, served as a warning to all children.

Returning to Seelye's corners we will journey westward, pausing as we go to note the disappearance of the woods that, till recently, filled the valley on the south side of the road, and to lament the dwindling of the brook at the foot of the hill, which, through climatic changes, has become a mere suggestion of its former self. The hill we have before us is no ordinary one, but years of working have rendered it a little more easy of ascent. At the left on the slope of the hill, half way up whose sides we are, stands a house repaired about thirty years since by Sheldon R. Overton, now of Wolcott. Daniel Soper built it. Since Mr. Overton disposed of it to Henry Klinck, who married Caroline, eldest daughter of Artemas Osgood, the place has remained almost unchanged save in owners. Mr. Klinck sold to Homer Stone, a brother of Mrs. Oliver Bush, who in time sold to Edgar Armstrong, who now resides there. He married Libbie, adopted daughter of Oliver Bush, and their three children are Morton, Lullavine and Virgil. Mr. Armstrong has long been a resident of the district, having lived with his father, James Armstrong, for many years upon the Dr. Dickson place. (Mr. Armstrong has recently completely renovated the house inside and out.) The first note of this place that we have, is its occupancy by a Rhodes family, who lived away up on the very top of the hill, to whose log house led the road which yet runs up the side of the almost mountain, and which serves a very useful purpose now as a farm way. When at home these people certainly had a most breezy outlook. In time, however, they wearied of their elevated home and moved the frame additions to their house down to the road, or near it, and this was the building so long the abode of the Lewises and Sopers. In time the father died, the widow married again and moved away, and the place became the home of a family named Lewis, whose stalwart sons are yet recalled by the older residents of the neighborhood. They were from the east, Connecticut, I think, and only paused here a while on their journey westward. After them came Daniel Soper, an industrious man, brother to Brewster Soper of Rose, who reared here a very large family. His mother died Feb. 19, 1865, at the age of 79. Daniel, the eldest son, is still in the town. Robert and William, with a sister, Phœbe, moved years ago to Berkshire county, Mass., and there married. Deborah married a Mr. Saulsbury and lives at the Valley. Annette is the wife of Asahel Colvin of Wolcott. Delia died young, while Emma and Alfred are unmarried. (The latter has since died.) During Mr. Soper's residence upon the place, it was held by the General Adams Agency, a corporation that purchased everything that could be bought, as some will remember, at the time that a canal was contemplated from Sodus to Clyde. The melancholy traces of this venture still exist, west of the Valley, in the shape of its channel, still called Adams' ditch.

Eron Thomas was long the agent for this and other farms, and from him Mr. Overton purchased in 1855. Still further along the ridge of this hill, perhaps a half mile south, was another log house, still marked by the apple orchard which stood near it, where dwelt a family named Gould. All that I can learn concerning them is that Mr. Gould taught singing school, and that they all long since moved away. The place was once in the possession of Milton Town, who sold to James Benjamin, the present owner.

Crossing the road from Edward Armstrong's, we shall find the comfortable home of Joseph Roat, whose wife, Angeline, is the eldest daughter of Delos Seelye, for many years the owner of these fertile acres. They have two daughters, Nellie and Inez. The first resident here carries us back to a log house, standing some distance from the road in what is now the orchard. This resident was a certain John Holloway, who married the widow Rhodes, and moved, I am told, down near Clyde, but just when and where I can't tell. He sold to Zach. Esmond, of whom I know nothing save that he had a nickname of "Ishmael," and that he was a Protestant Methodist in religious matters, not over enterprising either physically or spiritually, and he in turn sold to Delos Seelye. Mr. Seelye was a native of this district, being the youngest son of Joseph Seelye. He married early in life Almanda, daughter of Erastus Fuller, one of the oldest dwellers on the road leading to the Valley. She was in all respects a most worthy helpmeet, and by hand and counsel assisted Mr. Seelye in securing a competence. There was a small frame house standing near the road when Mr. Seelye purchased, and in this he and his family resided till along in the fifties, when he instituted the changes, making his home one of the most pleasant in the vicinity. No one who ever knew Delos Seelye could forget him. Nature had endowed him with a physique such as seldom falls to the lot of man. During his youth and early manhood it may be doubted if he knew what fatigue was. From dawn to twilight he could lead in all the labor that then made up the farm routine. He laughed at any mention of rest. When he wished to push matters even more strenuously, he would secure the services of a Mr. Stickles, a Mohawk Dutchman, who lived a mile or so south of him, and who was the only man in the vicinity capable of keeping up with him, and together they would crowd each other in the harvest field from sun to sun, accomplishing as much as four common men could do in the same time. He made very little difference in his work on account of the weather. A thing to be done must be done, rain or shine. At the table he was just as energetic as in the field. Great stories are yet told of the work that he could do and of his feats of strength. All this could have but one ending, and before he was fifty years old, broken in constitution, he retired from his farm to the Valley, where he lingered out a few years of invalid life. He died in August, 1870, at the early age of fifty-four. Kind-hearted and generous, he passed away lamented by a wide circle of friends. As already noted, his oldest daughter married Joseph Roat of Steuben county, and now holds the old place. (Now owned by Ransom Jordan of Lyons. The Roats are in Clyde. Nellie, married, lives in Watkins.) His second daughter, Annie, married Felton Hickok, a Rose boy, who served his country in the 9th Heavy Artillery, and who lived many years on the old homestead, in fact succeeding her father and remaining till followed by Mrs. Roat. Mr. and Mrs. Hickok now reside in the Valley. The youngest child, Elnora, is the wife of Valorus Ellinwood and lives just south of the Valley. At her home, in 1883, died her mother, Mrs. Almanda Seelye, a lady of no ordinary mental ability, as all will testify who have argued with her on topics in which she was interested.

Going to the west, we next come to the place where Thomas Smart, an industrious Englishman, long had his home. His particular trade was and is that of a ditch digger, acquired, I believe, among the fens of Lincolnshire, England. No man in the town could make so perfect a trench as he, and, I suppose, very many miles of tile of his laying now underlie the fields of Rose. At one time he was blind, but always he was the soul of industry. His home he located on a swampy corner of Lyman Lee's farm, adjoining that of Delos Seelye's. This land he tried to reclaim by his deep and excellent ditches, but in spite of all his care his surroundings were, to put it mildly, damp. During the present season he has yielded to the inevitable, and has moved the house to a sandy acreage that he has for some years possessed, nearly opposite the home of Kendrick Sheffield. Mr. Smart's sons — George, John and William — have grown to be, like him, worthy and industrious citizens. His only daughter, Mary, takes the place at home of the mother, who died several years ago.

Nearly opposite the late site of Mr. Smart's abode is a modest house erected by Egbert Soper, a brother of Daniel, mentioned already. The first family of whom I can obtain any trace upon this farm was named Hodge, and they lived in a log house just on the side of the hill to the west of the present location. Mr. Hodge sold to John Pierce, who for some time resided here. He had three sons, at least, and a son of one of them, Eugene, married Emily, daughter of S. R. Overton, and lives in Huron. John Fairchild, Baptist clergyman, also lived here a while. To the Pierces and Fairchilds succeeded Mr. Soper, who, for many years, lived in the log house, and there reared his children, of whom Theron, early deceased, will be remembered as a young man of rare promise. Mr. Soper's wife was Margaret, a daughter of John Deady, a respected farmer living about one mile south. Charles and James Deady, of Rose, are brothers. After Mr. Soper left this place it was occupied for a time by Nehemiah Seelye, son of Benjamin and a nephew of Joseph Seelye. He afterward went to Michigan and there died. His sons—Royal, Alfred, a member of the 9th Artillery, and Frank—accompanied him. He had one daughter, Mary, who now lives in Michigan. This property passed into the possession of Joel Sheffield, of the Valley, who still retains it, the house being the home, in succession, of so many families that it would be difficult to enumerate them. Josie Way, the daughter of one tenant, is recalled as a very pleasant school girl. She subsequently became Mrs. Heman Shepard of Galen, and died March 1st, 1892, aged 38 years. Upon the level ground beyond the ascent we come to the home of Kendrick Sheffield. I am under the impression that the house was erected by William Briggs, who long retained it. He had a lively family, some of whose members are yet remembered with pleasure. Their names were Sarah, Mary and Harriet. There were sons, John and others. Elder Graham, a Baptist minister, came next, who had a son, and a daughter Louisa. Afterward succeeded Elder N. Ferguson, pastor of the Baptist Church of Rose. He believed that contact with the soil was conducive to excellence in the pulpit. He had children, who were entertaining members of Rose society during their father's pastorate. Clark Ferguson was a scholarly boy, who afterward became a minister himself. The daughters were Emma, Minnie and Mary, the latter of whom were school teachers of note.

Kendrick Sheffield, who purchased from Elder F., is a nephew of Mrs. George Seelye. His father, James, moved from Madison county early in the fifties, and located on the place now owned by Gleason Wickwire, he buying of Hudson Wood. Mr. Sheffield married, in Madison county, Mary Ann Chase, sister of Mrs. Wickwire. He has reared a family of children on this farm, and they having left the homestead he is again alone. His oldest son, Judson, married Ornie, daughter of Peter Harmon, of the Valley, and is now in the employ of a Rochester firm. His second boy and namesake, whose black eyes few who knew him will forget, died several years since, just as he was blossoming into the manhood which everybody said he would ornament. The youngest, James, is a promising lawyer in Lincoln, Nebraska. Of his two daughters, Lucy is the wife of Ensign Wade, as stated before, while Mattie married Chas. Osborne, and lives in Oneida Castle. Mr. Sheffield has long been noted for his taste and success in the care of horses. Perhaps no man in the town has done more to improve the quality of this kind of stock than he. So far as I know, he was the first man in the town to cultivate hops, and with Mr. Bush the only one to keep up the culture through a term of years. (Mr. Sheffield died July 10, 1892. Chas. Osborne, now on the farm, is a graduate of Colgate University, a son of one of the professors. By him the house has been much improved and many salutary changes have been made on the farm. Mr. and Mrs. Osborne have two children, Kendrick N. and Lucy E.)

Just west of this place, on lot 193, once stood a house bought by Chas. Sherman from George Seelye, and in it the older Sherman children were born. It was afterward moved to the northward, and is now the home of Henry Decker. A little west of opposite is the pleasant house where live Thomas Smart and his children, George and Mary. Thrift and neatness here reign supreme.

The next place on the south side of the road is held by the widow of the late Linus Osgood. Years ago it was the property of Chas. Sherman, who, with his first wife, Lucina Allen, reared here many children, whose names are well known in town. His second son, Willard, married Permilla, daughter of John and Betsey Kellogg, of Butler, and has lived for many years in Clyde. The other sons were George, married Sybil Wilson and living in Rose; Charles, killed a year or two since upon the Hudson-Central R. R.; Frank, the oldest, who married a Moore, of Spencer's Corners; and Ezra, who (a member of the 111th, N. Y.) was taken prisoner and died in the hands of the rebels. Their only daughter, Lucy, married Putnam Sampson, and lives on the old Mackie place on the Clyde road. After the death of his first wife he married Miss Charlotte Tyler, of Butler, who, with her sons, Chester T. and Ezra A., manages the farm one mile east of the Valley, to which he moved after selling his first home. Mr. Sherman was a man of great energy and perseverance, and is well remembered as a valuable and patriotic citizen. During his holding of the farm it belonged to the Valley district, but, at the request of Artemas Osgood, to whom he sold, it was set off as a part of No. 7. Mr. Osgood moved into Rose from Hamilton, Madison Co., and was, with his large and interesting family, an exceedingly worthy addition to the town. Mr. Osgood is of Massachusetts birth, and has ever manifested the sterling qualities so characteristic of the land of the Puritans. His wife, who died in 1870, was Harriet Pierce. Many will recall her mother, a gracious lady, who spent her last days here. His older son, Lucien, married first, Eudora Seeyle, as already stated. She dying in 1870, he afterward married Matilda, daughter of Gleason Wickwire, and resides in Rose. The younger son, Linus, into whose hands the farm passed, married Sarah Sheffield of New York City, a grand-niece of Mrs. George Seelye, and, till his death, Oct. 9, 1886, maintained one of the most successful places in the town. The tamarack swamp, in the rear of his farm, has proven to be the very best onion grounds in Rose, and it is most thoroughly utilized. He left two daughters, Iola and Mabel. (His widow, as Mrs. Ellsworth Klinck, and family still occupy the place.) The marriages of Artemas Osgood's daughters — Caroline, Frank and Emma — have been noticed already. Of the other two, Nannie married Joel Sheffield, the third son of James Sheffield, and resides in Rose, while Mary, the youngest, is the wife of George Catchpole, well known in Rose.

The last place to the west in this district is situated a little back from the road, and at the earliest accessible date was the home of Lucius Ellinwood. To him succeeded, as owner, Dr. John Dickson, though I think he never lived there. Andrew Bradburn and family were here for several years. For a long time this was the home of James Armstrong, who now lives near Seelye's corners. One fact alone should make Mr. Armstrong's occupancy noteworthy, since he was the first to introduce the culture of mint in this neighborhood. Mr. Armstrong's children, several of them, grew here to manhood and womanhood, and from this passed out to homes of their own. George lives in Lawrence, Mass.; Edgar we have noted before; Duane lives in Rhode Island (Now Brockton, Mass.); his twin brother, DeWitt, in the southwest (Now Creete, Colorado); James is at home (Syracuse); Alice married Harvey Ferris, but died several years since ; Ella is the wife of Ephraim Wilson, Jr., and lives in the Valley; Carrie and Minnie are still at home. Mr. Armstrong came to this town from Lewis county and is a relative of the Armstrongs, of Butler. His wife, a Miss Sweet, is a member of the famous Rhode Island family of Sweets, bone setters. No more sturdy and straightforward man ever came into the neighborhood. To Mr. Armstrong succeeded Harlan P. Wilson and he still resides here. His wife was Miss Carrie Snow, daughter of Alonzo Snow, from Chenango county. Their children are Harriet, Charles, Frank and Lewis, (Mrs. Wilson has since died).

Again returning to the Corners we will go south, and first, at our right and near the cross roads, we shall find the home of James Armstrong, whose family we have already described. His house is a new one, taking the place of the first building erected here, which was destroyed by fire in 1882. This farm was first Eaton's, then Aaron Shepard's, from whom it passed to his son-in-law, Thaddeus Collins, 2nd. He sold it to his son, Josephus, who built the house early in war times as a convenience for his hired man. I think its first occupant was Charles Rice, long a resident of the Butler part of the district, being a son of Jonathan Rice. He married Mary Holcomb, also of the Butler portion of No. 7. Her father, those who used to go to school-house meetings will long remember for his fervent prayers and eloquent experiences. After Rice came John Crisler, a brother-in-law of Mr. Collins, his wife being Ruth Livermore from Oneida Co. She is also a sister of Mrs. John B. Roe. He now lives on the Butler side, on the old McKoon place. Wesley Livermore, Mrs. Collins' brother, came next, remaining several years. He now resides near Clyde, following the trade of a carpenter. The place was finally sold to Chauncey Darling, who built a barn and cleared much of the forest back of the house. His successor was Mr. Armstrong, as already stated.

Over the elevation to the southward, we shall find the burial ground, but this, with the school-houses of the district, we shall reserve for the closing article. A little more than half a mile from the corners, on the west side of the road, is the house of Stephen Kellogg. This marks the former abode of the first settler. Aaron Shepard. He was a native of New Hartford, Conn., and there married Polly, daughter of Dr. John Wade, who afterward moved to Paris, Oneida Co. His trade was that of a blacksmith and traces of his Connecticut shop can still be found. Catching the western fever in 1811, he came to this new country and took up two sections of land lying on both sides of the road, though there was no road then. This land extended from the western border of S. Kellogg's farm to very near the first north and south road in Butler. Just under the hill, back of Mr. Kellogg's house and a little to the south, is a spring of pure, cold water, and here he built his log house, preparatory to bringing out his wife and two girls. His boy he had already laid to rest in the old Town Hill burying ground in New Hartford. Moving in those days was no trivial matter, for the transit was made with an ox team. This was done in the following year, 1812. What a long, tedious journey: staying, when possible, over night in houses; when not possible, camping. A brother, Seth, accompanied him and settled on the farm now occupied by Isaac Lockwood, in Butler. Deacon Shepard, as Aaron S. was usually called, and his wife had peculiarities that will be long retained in memory by all who knew them. He early built a shop, the first in town, and was the horseshoer of the vicinity. I think pieces of forge slag can still be picked up near the road, marking the site of his anvil. When he built his farm barn he hewed planks out of logs to make the floors. These planks, showing the gashes of the scoring axe, still serve their original purpose in Mr. Kellogg's great barn. In fact, the barn itself is much as it was when built, seventy years ago, though it has been moved from its first location. As a deacon it was necessary for him to maintain great strictness in demeanor, and he was anxious to secure corresponding staidness from all about him; but he had in his family once, a lad who tried his deacon's soul in no ordinary manner. This young man would parody "Watts" in this heathenish way:

"When I can shoot my rifle clear
To pigeons in the skies,
I'll bid farewell to pork and beans
And live on pigeon pies."

How distressing this must have been to the good old man, to whom the hymn book was second in sacredness to the Bible only! However, it was left to the deacon to devise a way of keeping "Young Dud." out of mischief during church time, that for originality has no equal. Taking the lad to the shop, he would back him up to the vise and screw the slack of his trowsers therein, taking care to properly secure his hands. I am afraid the boy's ruminations were not on things sacred while he thus stood out the deacon's hours of worship. The old gentleman was one of the original members of the Presbyterian Church in Rose, and long stood high in its councils. He first joined the old church located at Port Bay, but which, finally, became the Presbyterian Church of Huron. He died in 1839. If the deacon was peculiar, his wife was more so. The boys of the neighborhood, to this day, when forced to the monotonous employment of pulling daisies, will say : " There wouldn't be any of these things here if it weren't for old Granny Shepard." Legend has it that mindful of her surroundings in the Nutmeg State, she thought she must have daisies about her in her new home to make it look natural, and so carried with her a quantity of seed, which she sowed broadcast, and behold the result. Tansy yet grows luxuriantly in the corner of the dooryard, marking the place where she planted the first seed, seventy years ago. Once when her husband was away from home, she directed the hired man to fell a large quantity of timber through the swamp or swale, in order that she might have an unobstructed view, from her pantry window, of the hill-side beyond. How strangely history repeats itself, for I find that the first pastor, Jonathan Marsh, of the church in New Hartford, Conn., directed his parishioners to do just the same thing, that he might, from his parsonage, see his church. The reputation of being the best cook in the neighborhood, I have never heard disputed, and she trained up her own girls and those who lived with her to be equally deserving of praise. She was determined and pertinacious in her ways, and when a Mormon missionary sat up all night endeavoring to convert the deacon, she sat up, too, and effectually counteracted the poison of the enemy. She was liable to spells of hypochondria, when she would send word to her daughter, Mrs. Collins, opposite, that Mrs. C. must come right over, as she was going to die right away. Likely as not, Mrs. C., who knew her mother perfectly, would reply : " I can't, for I am going visiting." Just as quickly as the messenger could return, would go the message : " Just wait a few minutes and I'll go with you." This story is told with much glee by old residents : A certain man in the neighborhood was much disliked by nearly everybody—possibly feared. The old lady shared the common feeling, and seeing him coming one day, she had her screams all ready ; but contrary to expectation he walked directly by. Not to be cheated out of her fright, she sallied forth, shouting: " Zekiel, Zekiel, don't you come in here, I am afraid of you." After a few years, the old log house was given up, and the family moved into the first framed building in the district, constructed before 1820. The town road had been located, and it lay, or ran, some rods east of the house by the side of the spring. There are still living in Rose and Butler very aged people who can recall childhood memories of this pioneer cabin. The new house was a marvel of comfort and elegance for those days. Painted red, it stood with its gable facing the road. The interior was divided into a front room with a wide fireplace, a stairway leading aloft, a pantry and a bedroom on the north side, with a back parlor. The chamber was unfinished. An immense chimney, while necessary in its day, took up about one-quarter the space of the entire house. In this shape the building continued till 1855, when it was re-covered, an addition put on the north side and the entire interior altered. The frame is the one put together by the deacon. This change was effected by Rev. A. M. Roe and his wife, a grand-daughter of the first builder, and then the owner of the place. Just south and a little back of the red house stood an unpainted building, some years younger than its more pretentious neighbor. This was built by Mr. Shepard as a residence for his daughter, Harriet, who married Thaddeus Collins, 2nd, of Rose. After their leaving it, it formed a very convenient house for tenants, till its demolition in 1855. The orchard just south of the house and fast going to decay, was the result of seed sown by Mr. Shepard many years ago. The marriages of the two daughters of this family have been noticed already. To the daughter (Polly) of Catharine Seelye the place passed on her marriage, and was the home of herself and husband till he became a clergyman. Only once afterward did they reside there, and then for a single year. (They are the parents of four children, Alfred S. of Worcester, Mass.; G. Mortimer of Cincinnati, Ohio; Charles M. of Syracuse; and S. Addie, who, the wife of the late Dr. Lawrence Johnson of New York, died March 31, 1893.) It was then sold to Thaddeus Collins, who conveyed it to his younger daughter, Harriet, the wife of Stephen Kellogg. For nearly thirty years they have lived here, seeing their three boys—William, Levern and Frank—grow to manhood. (Will, married, lives in Manango, No. Dak.; Lavern died in 1887, and rests in the burial ground just to the north; while Frank resides in Covell's Dist.) It should be added that, after the death of her husband, Mrs. Shepard married Azel Dowd of Huron, and lived, till his death, with Watson Dowd, a son. Afterward her home was with her daughter, Harriet, till her death, which was in 1859.

Nearly opposite is one of the largest, perhaps the very largest house in the district. It is that of Josephus Collins, who inherited from his father, Thaddeus. The first knowledge that I have of the house is that it was built by Charles Richards, who, very likely, purchased of Mr. Shepard. At any rate, Mr. Richards lived here for many years, and managed a distillery located near the spring in the pasture, some rods east of the house. This institution was destroyed by fire before the farm passed out of Richards' possession. Just south of the distillery, in what is now a rich meadow, general trainings were had in the "long ago." The juxtaposition of distillery and training suggests the motive power so common in those days. Near the road was a cider mill, long since dismantled. There were in the Richards family a son and daughter. The latter was courted and married by a Mr. Olmstead, and I have been told that all went to Canada. Thaddeus Collins, 2nd, who purchased of Richards, was born in Vermont, the son of Thaddeus Collins, one of the early settlers of this town, and at one time the owner of much of the site of the village of Rose. The latter died in 1828, and is buried in the Rose burial ground. The family was originally from Massachusetts. Thaddeus, 2nd, was born in 1792, and died in 1865. He was a man who always excited and retained the liveliest esteem and regard from all having him in acquaintance. There is now many a man who recalls his boyhood's delight over Mr. Collins' recitals of his own youthful adventures with bears and wolves. To be sure, the boy might seek his trundle bed, with hair fairly erect with fear, fancying that the sighing wind was the howl of the wolf, and a chair in the corner, possibly, a bear,—he always came back to the same old stories with unabated zeal and interest. I suppose I have heard him tell a hundred times how he took a stake from a sled, standing near the site of the district burial ground, to repel a possible attack from wolves whose howls he heard when he was on his way home from courting his future wife. A thrill of sadness comes over me as I reflect that husband and wife have long slept, side by side, in the inclosure over which crept, years ago, the prowling wolf. They are alike oblivious to the howl of the ravening beast and the tears of their mourning friends. Mrs. Collins survived her lamented husband nearly nine years, dying July, 1874. As I recall them, they were almost my ideal pair. I cannot forget Mr. Collins' testimony in the old school-house meetings, when, rubbing his hands together, he would say : " I feel that it is good to be here." Then, too, his wife's recital of her own conversion is vividly recalled. They were of the salt of the earth. Perhaps people have gone from their doors hungry, but I never knew an instance. An amusing anecdote of Mrs. Collins' discernment is told as follows : A short time after her husband's death, an aged widower, quite infirm, called on her, obviously with the intention of proposing marriage, thinking no doubt that her home would be a very comfortable haven in his decrepitude. Finally, after beating about the bush, he presented his cause, having absolutely nothing to offer but his enfeebled self. Mrs. Collins, readily discovering his object, sent him to the right-about quick, saying that she had enough to do to take care of herself without taking in any cripples. Gathering up his crutches the old gentleman made haste to carry his wares to more favorable markets. Four children grew to maturity. The oldest, Columbus, married Lovina, daughter of Joel Lee of Rose, and, a farmer, lived at different times in Rose, Butler, Huron and Wolcott—dying in the latter place several years since from a most distressing accident. Catharine married Hudson Wood of Butler, and was a most efficient companion to him for many years. She died in 1884. Her second daughter, Frank, is the wife of George G. Roe of Clyde. Josephus married Polly Livermore of Oneida county, and has successfully managed his farm during these many years. His oldest child, Ida, is the wife of Rev. Wm. Winget of the

Free Methodist Church. (Now of Buffalo, N. Y.) Mr. Winget is Huron
born, just on the confines of Rose, at York settlement. Newton is a prominent physician in Rochester, while Jimmy, a lad, is yet at home. Harriet,
the youngest daughter of Thaddeus, has already been mentioned as the
wife of Stephen Kellogg.

The next place is that of Henry Chatterson, received from his father,
Abram, and he inheriting from Betts Chatterson, the first comer of the
name. This name, in its Dutch purity, was Chadderdon, but Aunt Laney,
as everybody called her, a sister of Abram, determined to charge it, and
to compass this transformed the d's in the old family Bible, considerably
more than a hundred years old, into t's and s's. Early in the century this
place was the home of Daniel Lounsberry, who, going west, sold to Moses
Wisner, whose three daughters — Sarah, Elizabeth and Charlotte, it is
noteworthy, married three brothers—Austin, Willis and Brewster Roe, of
Butler. Wisner sold to Isaac Mills and moved to Penfield, Monroe Co.,
and there died. Mills went west, after selling to Betts Chatterson. This
family was from Columbia county, and was of great originality of speech.
Commenting on the Scriptural statement that when the iron is blunt then
must he put to more strength, Mr. Chatterson said: "Strange that he
didn't know enough to sharpen the knife." He died in 1851, aged eighty-
seven. "Aunt Laney" (Helen) was one of the most peculiar characters
of the neighborhood. She had in her girlhood learned how to make
artificial flowers, and this formed her chief occupation through life, though
she was joint inheritor with Abram of the farm. When very aged she
went once to Glenmark to have some wool carded. The mechanic, meaning no discourtesy, but still desirous of knowing her age, politely asked
her the question. Her ready reply, snapped out in her quick speech, was :
"Old enough to mind my own business." For some time before her
death she was totally blind, but it was not till near the very end that she
would grant that her sight was seriously impaired. As she was born in
1785, she must have been nearly ninety years old at her death. Her
brother, Abram, was a genius, as all who knew him will concede. How
he did like to play upon the fife, and into what ecstasies, almost, would he
pass when, with closed eyes, he would extract those ear-piercing notes
from the little wood instrument. Old Yankee Doodle himself, at Bunker
Hill, was not half so enthusiastic. I should like to see the boy of the
neighborhood who has no pleasant remembrance of "Abe" Chatterson's
fife playing. He, too, was quick in speech, and his replies were often quite
out of the general order. Not satisfied with acceding to a request with all
of his heart, he would, quite likely, generously throw in a piece of his
liver. Born in 1803, he died in 1881. He was twice married: 1st. to
—— —— ——, and 2d, to Ruth Goffe, the mother of his sons. His
children were: Sarah, who married Edward Stickles; Josephine, Wm.

3

Olmstead; Louisa (Mrs. Spencer), John P.; these three live in Greene county, and Henry, the older of the boys, who retains the old place. During the Rebellion he was for two years in the 27th N. Y. Regiment, and then going west served till the end in a Wisconsin regiment. He went with Sherman on his march to the sea. Perhaps no Rose boy has a better military record. His wife is Addie Waldron, whom he married in 1870. (Mrs. Chatterson died Dec. 27, 1891, aged 43 years, leaving two sons, George and Louis.) As tenants, for a time, Isaac and Abram Phillips have lived in the Chatterson house. They were cousins of Abram C., and came from the Hudson river country. Isaac had three sons — William, Horace and Frank—all residents of Wolcott. William was postmaster during President Cleveland's first term. Isaac Phillips died in Wolcott, Nov. 1, 1889, in his 75th year.

Going back a few rods to the west side of the road thirty or more years ago, we should have seen a little unpainted building with no land to spare about it, yet every inch utilized. Across the road, the wonder of every school boy, was a cellar built above ground. The edifice itself was the old district school-house, which became a dwelling house when the stone building was erected. Let us enter. There is a very small, narrow entry, from which, at our left, a door leads into the single room constituting the interior. In one corner we shall find a shoemaker's kit, and, pegging away most diligently, old "Uncle Tipple," who, with his neat Dutch wife, is a dweller here. On a tombstone in the burial ground, I read the following: "Jacob Tipple, died April 1, 1853, aged 66 years." Yet his wife is living to-day, the oldest person, I suppose, in the town. On the 30th day of last July, she was ninety-nine years old. A few days before, it was my pleasure to take her by the hand and to recall the days when I, a small boy, thought her a very old woman. She lives west of the Valley with her daughter, Mrs. Abram Phillips. Though bowed with the weight of years, her mind is clear and her eye bright. I confidently expect to see her pass her centennial mile post. How she laughed when I described my boyish impression of her home in the old school-house. Those two beds so high and smooth; so high that I couldn't see how any one could reach them, and if, by any means, he should get to the top, how could he dare to muss or rumple such immaculate surfaces. What a pattern of neatness! Uncle Tipple always furnished early cabbage plants for the entire neighborhood. The Tipples had two children, Eliza M., to be met later in the Covell district as Mrs. Abram Phillips, and Philip, who died many years ago. Following Mr. Tipple's death in 1853, his widow went to dwell with her daughter, and the house became the property of Mr. J. B. Roe, who moved it away and made of it one of his out-buildings. (In 1887, July 30, many friends helped Mrs. Tipple celebrate her centennial at the home of Mrs. Phillips, west of the Valley. She survived till July 7, 1888.)

JOHN B. ROE. AUSTIN M. ROE.

AUSTIN ROE.

ALFRED S. ROE. GEORGE G. ROE.

Near at hand, on the south, is the home identified with the name of Roe since 1833. Before that time, it was the property of Pendar Marsh, who, with his brother, Amos, on the adjoining farm south, came with the Shepards from New Hartford, Ct., descendants of that clergyman who wanted the forest cut from his home to the church. Pendar Marsh, for a time afterward, lived on one of the Briggs places further south, and then, with Seth Shepard, went to Michigan. Austin Roe, a younger brother of Daniel Roe, one of the pioneers of Butler, was born in Connecticut in 1782. After the death of his mother, in 1832, he made haste to move his family, by the process of river and canal travel, to this, to him, remote region. For generations his family had lived on Long Island; his own birth in Connecticut being the result of Revolutionary broils, as his parents were driven thence by hostile Tories. Island farming was not encouraging, and having discharged his filial duty to his parents, he moved his family of wife and six children to Wayne county. Devotedly religious, it was a source of great pleasure to his relatives after his death to find his exhorter's and local preacher's licenses, extending over quite forty years. Hard of hearing for many years, he makes a very pleasant part of one's mental picture of the services in the old school-house. The minister in his desk was not more prominent than Father Roe, as he sat in a chair, close by, that he might lose no word of the discourse. Then, when the sermon was ended, how he commanded the rapt attention of all listeners as he recounted God's love to him and his. He died, full of years, in 1864, though he would doubtless have lived much longer (his Butler brother died at ninety) had he not given way to excessive grief over the death of his wife, Sarah, who died the preceding September. She was his own cousin, a native of Long Island, and had most faithfully attended him along life's pathway. Recently meeting a gentleman on the Pacific coast, the writer was much pleased to hear him say that Mrs. Roe came nearer the perfect woman than any being he had ever seen. Through years of acquaintance, he had never seen her temper in the least ruffled. After the marriage of their son, John, they, for a time, lived in a house nearly opposite, a little south, standing where Merritt McKoon's house now is. Afterward they returned to the old home and formed a part of J. B. Roe's family to the end of their lives. When Mr. Roe bought the farm, there was upon it the usual log house. This was supplanted, in 1838, by the present roomy and pleasant structure. The great butternut trees in front of the house, the largest in the vicinity, were set out by Mr. Marsh; but one or two of them have succumbed to the tooth of time. Daniel J., the eldest son, married Ann Tillow, a sister of Mrs. Isaac Mills, the neighbors opposite, and soon removed to Michigan, where he now lives at the age of seventy-four. Catharine married Sheldon R. Overton, for years a near neighbor, but who now lives in Wolcott. (Died. 1887.) Eliza married

George Stafford and resides with her daughter, Sarah, in Ohio. (Died, 1889.) John B. was twice married; first, to Roxana Soures of Huron. Her children were Merwin S. of Syracuse, and George G. of Clyde. (Who besides managing his extensive carriage business, has been, since 1890, the highly successful postmaster in that village.) His second marriage was to Eunice Livermore of Oneida county, who survives him and manages the old farm. Her children are Alice C., the wife of Henry T. Lee of Clyde, and Ottie E., the wife of Stephen Soule, also of Clyde. Mr. Roe was a model farmer and a most respected member of the community, but whose ambition was in excess of his strength, bringing him to his grave at the comparatively early age of sixty-six. Rev. Austin M., already stated, married Polly C. Seelye, and lives in Fulton, N. Y. The youngest child, Fanny, is the wife of Timothy R. Smith of Clyde. Their only surviving child is Duke, a teacher of music in that place. Chas. Freeman, born in Rose, became a member of Austin Roe's family at an early age, and remained so till nearly or quite of age. For the past twenty-four years he has resided in Portland, Oregon. He is now cashier of the Oregon R. R. & Navigation Co. (For several years the farm has been cultivated by Charles W. Hurter, a native of Rose, whose wife is Delilah Barager, born in Canada. Their only son, Willie, has marked musical talents. The family, like that of Mr. Roe, is connected with the M. E. Church.)

Across the road a gate opens into a lane separating the Chatterson and McKoon farms. This was once a public way; but to my knowledge there never was more than one house upon it. This was the log home of "Sammy" Jones, a stone mason by trade, whose deep and lasting potations few neighbors can forget. One of his daughters became the second wife of Dr. John Dickson. Jones' first wife was, years ago, buried in the district cemetery, and when afterward he took to himself another spouse, it gave rise to the most noted "horning" that ever took place in the town. All the young men of the vicinity united to do the business up in style. Before beginning their concert, they called the roll, and no little amusement was created at the names to which somebody vociferously responded "here." The worthy names of Roe, Collins, Seelye and Kellogg were all answered to, although Austin, Thaddens, George and John little knew the liberty that the boys were taking with their titles. Such discord was never in town before nor since. Horns, horse fiddles, guns and yells made the night dissonant. Finally, the house itself was attacked and entered, the frightened inmates fleeing in utter terror. The house was not razed, but there was left scarcely one whole piece of crockery on the premises. He laughs best who laughs last, and when the "boys" paid the bills engendered by that night's fun, their smiles came, as we say, out of the other corner of their mouths. Several years ago Mr. Jones went to Michigan to live with a son, his farm being merged in the McKoon place. He has since died.

The last place in the district is just south of the lane before mentioned. Years ago it was owned by Isaac Lounsberry, a brother of Daniel, his nearest neighbor on the north. He sold to the Gen. Adams' Land or Canal Co., supposed to represent a certain capitalist, Pompelly, by name. It then passed into the hands of Austin Roe, as before noted. He sold it to his son-in-law, S. R. Overton, who retained it for many years. Mr. Overton, a native of Long Island, was born in 1800. His children are Laura ; Clarissa, the wife of Wm. Finch ; Howard, living in Huron ; Lucilla, who married and lives on Long Island ; Emily, Harriet and Everett—the last two died just as they were leaving childhood behind them. Mr. Overton sold to Wm. Sherman, whose power in prayer and love for a horse are well remembered. His wife was Clarissa (Thompson) Ellinwood, born in the Butler part of the district. An adopted son, E. Wallace Blackman, went to school in the old stone school-house with the rest of us, and, going into the army, like a patriotic boy as he was, died in 1862. Mr. Sherman sold his farm and went with his family to Michigan, and there died. Another son, Henry, enlisted from the west, and died in the service. There were other children. Wm. Haney of Boonville, Oneida county, was the purchaser of the farm. He was a Scotch Irishman, of great presence and power, and is still, in Seneca Falls, an important factor in all that goes on about him. When he came to the town he had two sons, Albert and Victor. Two daughters—Emma and Clara—were born here. Death, however, removed Victor and Clara to the other land. As his teacher for a season, I can safely say that no brighter, better boy ever responded to a teacher's efforts than the curly-headed lad whose body has long slumbered in the cemetery on the hillside in Boonville. After the death of his children, the place ceased to be attractive to the surviving members, and he, accordingly, sold to Hudson Wood and moved to Seneca Falls, where Albert is now in business. A niece, Anna, was the first wife of Merwin S. Roe. Mr. Wood did not live on the place, but his son-in-law, Leonard, managed it for a time. He soon sold the place to Isaac Lockwood and Merritt McKoon, in whose possession it now is. Shortly after their purchase the house was destroyed by fire, making the second conflagration in the history of the section. The present edifice was soon afterward constructed, and in this Mr. and Mrs. McKoon lived till they moved to their present residence at the corners. (George, oldest son of the late Isaac Lockwood, married Lina Chappel of Butler, and for several years has occupied this place. They have children, Ambrose, Maud E. and John C.)

The history of no American community is complete till we have the story of its schools. I cannot find the time when there was no school in the vicinity. District No. 7 was once a part of a school patronizing section, covering what is now given up to five or six districts. The first building was a log one, standing on or near the site of the present edifice at

Stewart's corners. An interesting souvenir of this first school-house is yet in existence in the shape of a great iron used over the fireplace to support the chimney. It has for more than sixty years performed the same office in the old Seelye mansion. In this building the Seelyes, Shepards, Smiths and Ellinwoods obtained all they had in the way of education. School records of those days would be hard to find, and I am certain of only a few names of teachers. There were Eli Ward, Messrs. Knapp and Sherwood. One of the latest was George Salmon, who afterward married Lorinda Welles. He subsequently became a very prominent business man of Fulton, Oswego Co. He died a few years ago, a man much respected in the community. His second or third wife was a Leavenworth, of Wolcott. I have often thought, as I saw him walk into church, that his looks and manner were not unlike those of the great Washington. In time, as settlers became more numerous, a division of the district was necessary, and, about 1830, the old Tipple house was built and opened. Here followed the usual routine of school life, under the care of masters in winter and mistresses in summer, till about 1840. In this edifice, among other teachers, was, in 1833-'4, one Squires, who had a strange way of drying the boots and shoes of his pupils who came into school with wet feet. Taking the foot in his hand he would, with a ruler, give it a terrible beating. Any one who has ever tried this method of getting transmitted force can imagine what the torture was. He had a queer way of grinning as he made or mended a quill pen, and many a luckless youngster, thinking the master was laughing, would laugh, too. Alas, what a mistake! The boy who laughed, soon had occasion to weep. In 1834-'5, George Seelye taught, and they do say that he prayed but once a week. Doubtless he thought it best to give his time exclusively to instruction. Darius Clark, a son of "Priest" Clark, and a brother of Col. Emmons Clark, of the N. Y. 7th Regiment, was one of the early pedagogues. The story is told that he pronounced the word "yelp" to William Marsh—Amos' oldest son, who went to California in 1849—to be spelled. The boy did not understand what was wanted and nearly suffocated himself in his efforts to yelp. The more he tried the more the master shouted "yelp," till the boy nearly fainted. The master thought it funny, but the pupils were indignant. Another teacher was Sloan Cooley. The stone building came in 1840, and the first teacher was Arvine Peck. Among other masters, in the long succession of years, were A. M. Roe, George Stafford, Martin Blynn, Marvin Wilbur and many, many others. Mr. Stafford, who married Eliza Roe, could scare a boy out of his wits, nearly, by one loud exclamation. For continued whispering he would threaten to cut off a boy's tongue, and would produce block and knife, to the lad's excessive horror. But he kept a good school. I have heard grown boys say that Martin Blynn, afterward major in the 10th

N. Y. Cavalry, was the best teacher they ever had. "There was no use talking, we had to learn any way." When, in 1865, the writer taught the school, he found, out of something more than forty pupils, that thirty-five were, in one way or another, related to him. This illustrates pretty well the consanguined character of the district.

It was near the centennial year that the old stone house gave place to the present wooden edifice. The stones were tumbled into the space enclosed and the new building rose on the ruins. The serrated benches and desks with the recessed windows, deeply scarred with well-known initials, are in the irrevocable past.

While articles like these have little to do with the religious proclivities of the people, I might state that, almost without exception, for many years, the residents have been faithful church goers; communicants of the Baptist and Methodist Churches. It was long customary to have union afternoon services in the school-house. Till comparatively recently, there was not an individual in the district who did not trace his ancestry, directly or indirectly, to New England sources. In well deported lives, I think, these people have well sustained the long accorded New England reputation of honesty, sobriety and piety.

We have followed the early and late inhabitants of this locality through many years, but the paths of obscurity, as well as those of glory, "lead but to the grave." Where sleep the forefathers? The first burial place in the neighborhood was near Stewart's corners. Probably fifty persons were buried there, among whom was Jerusha, mother of Deacon Shepard, who died soon after his removing from Connecticut. However, in the twenties, the present cemetery, south of the corners, was opened, and has been added to once since, a small portion of land being taken in on the east side. Here are buried all the forefathers of the hamlet save John B. Roe, who lies in the cemetery north of the Valley.

> "Oft did the harvest to their sickle yield,
> Their furrow oft the stubborn glebe hath broke.
> How jocund did they drive their teams afield;
> How bowed the woods beneath their sturdy stroke."

There is very little of the famous elegy that will not apply to the enclosure. Each year marks a new grave; some pilgrimage ended, a new life begun. And so it will be for years to come. When the present has become "the old time," the tale will still be told. The first interment was that of a son of John Springer. This is the inscription: Died, December 2, 1828, James P. Springer, aged 8 years, 9 months and 18 days. The second and third to enter this final home were Catharine, wife of George Seelye, who died in 1829, and her infant son. Mr. Seelye himself, fifty-six years afterward, has just been laid by her side, and the scene is ended. "All the world's a stage," says the chief of writers, "They have their entrances and their exits." Here sleep, side by side, so many who together fought life's battles, and now rest from their labors. "Under the dew and the sunshine," indifferent alike to summer's heat and winter's cold, they await the glorious resurrection promised all the children of God. "After life's fitful dream, they sleep well." *Requiescant in pace.*

THE BUTLER PART OF NO. 7.

Aug. 11—Sept. 1, 1887.

The eastward limit of the Rose portion of the district was reached when we wrote of the property of Dudley Wade and of certain log houses, in which various parties, as Brewster, Saxton and others, had lived. Just beyond the town line and at the foot of the hill is a small house, which has had numerous occupants. The first owner of whom we have any trace was Jesse Woodruff, who sold to William Olmstead—brother of Mrs. John Wade, of Rose—who, with others of the family, came from Connecticut. He is supposed to have built the house. He sold to William Sherman, whose name we find in connection with many farms in the near regions of Rose and Butler. He was a son of Elias D. Sherman, one of the most conspicuous of the early pioneers of Rose. Mr. S. built the barn on the hill, intending to move up the house, but instead the barn went to the house. After him came Daniel Burgess, a son-in-law of Philo Saxton, who had himself occupied the house. He, Burgess, had two daughters, Alzina and Phœbe—named thus, I suppose, from his two wives, both Saxtons. Selling his place to Dudley Wade, he moved to Red Creek, and now lives near Westbury. The house then became the home of several tenants, prominent among whom was John Pitcher, an Englishman, who finally moved to Allegany Co., and there died in 1887. Mr. Wade sold to John E. Jones, more familiarly known among his townsmen as "Erv" Jones. He was from Saratoga Co., and married Permelia, daughter of Benjamin Kellogg, of Butler. His children were Harriet, who married George Voorhees, and died several years since. Henry married Julia Toles, of Rose, and now resides in Wolcott. Mary is the wife of George Dowd, of Huron. Isaac married Eliza Lovejoy, and lives on the lime kiln farm, near Butler. Adelbert married Lillie Weller and lives in Huron. Mr. Jones was a good citizen and made the most out of his farm. He dug out the spring, on the opposite side of the road, and conducted water from it to his house and barn. Finding the farm too small for himself and sons, he sold, as he supposed, to Mortimer Calkins, of Chenango Co., but in reality to Dudley Wade. Mr. J. always thought this a sharp trick on the part of his neighbor, to whom he would have made a considerably higher price. But buyer and seller are alike beyond the world's bargainings, for Jones, after buying a farm in the northern part of the Stewart district, died in 1877, and was buried with his former neighbors in the Collins burying ground. After holding the farm for a short time, Mr. Wade passed it along to his eldest son, Joseph, who, with his newly wedded wife, Emma Osgood, began housekeeping here. The young people of the neighborhood enjoyed rare sport in the long winter evenings, when they gathered round "Joe's" hospitable fireside and helped him and his wife kill time. Is it possible that the youngsters of to-day have half as much fun as we did ? What a pity that there was no "chiel" among them taking notes in those semi-remote days. No one who passed a winter's round of home festivities can ever regard them with aught but the most intense pleasure. But "Joe" wearied of farming finally, and he sold to Cornelius Marsh, a native of the Town district of Rose. Mr. Marsh's wife was the Widow Leaton, a daughter of Mr. Whitehead, an industrious Englishman, well known in the vicinity. Her daughter, Alice, became the wife of Geo. S. Seelye, and is now in Dakota. Marsh made many improvements in the buildings and worked hard for many years. He finally sold the farm back to J. S. Wade and now lives west of the Valley.

Ascending the hill, we turn to the north, and the first farm at our right s that of Elias Taylor. The original proprietor was Jesse Woodruff, who, vith his brother, Charles, was joint proprietor of a large four hundred acre farm. The brothers were sons of Lambert Woodruff, who came from the east in 1806 to Wolcott. Jesse sold off his acres in sections, and finally, having built the house, burned some years ago, moved to Newark. This part, what we shall call the Taylor farm, he sold to N. W. Tompkins, who, a native of Waterbury, Conn., had moved with his parents to Oneida county, and thence, in his early manhood, came to this place. After leaving the farm, he went to Wolcott, where he engaged in milling and mercantile business for many years. Retiring from these he went to a fine farm south of Wolcott. Next came E. Y. Munson, who, after several years of occupancy, sold to Abram Moore and went to Wolcott. After Moore, the farm was owned jointly by T. J. Lampson and Mr. Andrus. The story is told of one of the owners, about this time, that becoming badly chafed, he asked his hired man what was good for him, and was answered 'turpentine." He went to the house, presumably to apply the remedy. Smetime afterward the amateur physician followed and found his employe sitting in a tub of water, and thus doing his best to allay the torments into which the medicine had thrown him. James Jenkins, a Methodist minister, followed, and to him succeeded Jonathan Rice, who held the place for a number of years, and here reared a large family of children. Mr. Rice came originally from Massachusetts, and now, in his old age, is a resident of Huron at Sours' Mills. His oldest son, S. Decatur, who used to be one of the big boys in the old school-house, married Lydia Taylor and runs the grist mill at Sours' Mills. Lavina married Jackson Terbush and lives in Wolcott. George married Emma Bump and is in Peterboro, Madison Co. Charles married Mary Holcomb and lives near Watertown. Hattie is the wife of Ethan Kellogg, and they, too, are at Sours' Mills. Jared wedded Frances, another daughter of Harrison Holcomb, and is a miller in Mexico, Oswego Co. Frank, as was stated in the Rose articles, was killed in childhood. It is an interesting item that all the above sons, and at least one son-in-law, are millers. Mr. Rice sold to Crandall Loveless, who, in time, sold to the present proprietor, Mr. Taylor, who came from near South Butler. His wife is Martha, daughter of Joel Bishop. After his moving upon the farm, his house, the one so long standing, was burned some years ago, and then his barn followed in like manner. New ones have taken the place of the old. Mr. Taylor's daughter, Vesta, is the wife of Washington Loveless, of Butler, while another, Eliza, is at home. Before leaving this farm, it will be in place to state that among its many owners was one who liked very much a drink of whisky, but he scorned to take his liquor without paying for it. So, getting a small keg of the ardent, he, with a sympathetic neighbor, managed to open a bar, and with a single sixpence the two would buy out the establishment. To keep up the illusion—for no true American likes to take his liquor in any other way than standing—one would saunter up to the improvised bar, plank his sixpence and get his drink. Then, by the way of fair turn about, he would go behind the bar and the late tender would become purchaser. Thus each one had the pleasure of buying and selling, of drinking at a bar and of getting as drunk as a lord, with no great expenditure of ready money. How often this sort of play was had deponent doth not state, but it is claimed that the game was never over til the supply was exhausted.

Nearly opposite is the home of Patrick Burke; but older people will recall it as the residence for many years of Widow Kellogg. The farm itself is a part of the Woodruff purchase, and after having been held by N. W. Tompkins, was for a time in Wm. Sherman's possession. From him it passed to Columbus Collins, who built the house. C. C. Collins was the son of Thaddeus, of the Rose part of the district, and very soon after marrying Lovina, daughter of Joel Lee, 1st, of Rose, came here to live. Though his children were not born here, it may be stated that at his death in Wolcott, he left May R., a teacher in the Wolcott public school, and Julian, who now lives in Rochester. (Torrington Ct.) C. C.'s widow is in Wolcott. Perry Jones then held the place for awhile. Jones is a son of the "Sammy" Jones mentioned in a former letter. His wife was Drusilla Saxton, daughter of Philo. They now live in Michigan. Charles Kellogg, his successor, was a long time resident of the neighborhood, a son of Benjamin K. His wife was Mairetta, daughter of Wm. McKoon, and a native of the same school district. Mr. Kellogg died in the winter of '53-4. For years Mrs. K. held the place, and by the aid of her sons managed the farm. She was a most industrious woman, and in her life time must have made many hundred pairs of binders' mittens, a pursuit in which, I think, she never had a rival in the near vicinity. Of her three children, Ethan B., 2nd, married Hattie Rice, as already stated. In 1862 he enlisted in Company H of the 9th Heavy Artillery, but was discharged therefrom on account of disability. John C. married Mary Fisher of Wolcott, and afterward Effie Terbush, and now lives in Rose. Lucy's first husband was John Reynolds of Butler; her second, J. Byron Smith, now of Wolcott. Several years since, the whole family moved east of Wolcott, where Mrs. Kellogg in 1879 passed to her reward. Jonathan Rice was the next owner, then Walter Maroney, who sold to Peter Van-Buren, who, an ex-soldier in the Rebellion, belonged to an old Butler family. He is now in Lincoln, Neb. Cornelius Marsh was then for a time the owner, then Joseph Wade, who sold to the present occupant. Patrick Burke and his wife, Catharine Dunn, are from Waterford, Ireland. Their children are Wm., Edward, John, James, Ella (Mrs. James Whalen of Galen) and Anna. The town has no more industrious people than this family.

Everybody, far and near, knows " Mart " Saxton. His home is next, and the house is reached just before taking another turn toward the inner part of the town. Again we are on the old Woodruff land, though Saxton began his farm by a purchase of one acre from Mrs. Kellogg. He built a house and barn, and has added to his estate by purchases from the Benjamin property, north, and the Wade place, south. His first wife was Rebecca Marsh of Rose, who died in 1877. She left two daughters, Rosa A. (Mrs. Edward Klinck) and Mary E. Mr. Marsh's second wife was, before her first marriage, Sarah A. Leonard of Butler. " Mart's " father's family was a large one. By his first wife, Philo Saxton had three children, one of whom, Albert, married Jane Knapp, and was one of the first owners of the first farm east. He afterward moved to Wolcott and died there. By his second wife, Drusilla Parish, he had eleven children, all of whom grew up. Drusilla married Perry Jones, as before stated, and now lives in Quincy, Mich. Two daughters, Phœbe and Alzina, were successively wives of Daniel Burgess. Lucy Jane married Samuel Pomeroy of South Butler, and is the mother of Mrs. Abel Wing of Butler Center. Mr. Saxton died in 1859, aged 77, and his wife followed in 1866, at the age of 71. This family came to Butler from Otsego county, where Mr. Saxton's first wife had died. He had a good reputation as an industrious man. His wife was large in stature, and the quality of tallness she gave to some, at least, of her children. In my childhood, I thought " Mart " Saxton the tallest man I had ever seen. Either he has shortened, or my notions of longitudinal extension have grown. Father and mother sleep in the neighborhood cemetery. (Martin Saxton died 1891.)

The furthest point eastward in this district is reached when we turn to our right and come to the farm now owned by Dr. T. S. Fish, of Wolcott. As with the other places thus far described, in this vicinity, this farm was once the property of Jesse Woodruff. There has been a bewildering array of owners, of whom perhaps Harrison Holcomb held it longest, and for this reason it is often called the Holcomb place. Albert Saxton bought of Woodruff, and built a shanty on the north side of the road and about thirty rods from it. In 1850, or thereabouts, he sold to Charles Wright, son of Jacob Wright, well known in Butler, who built a small house south of the highway, and also put up a barn on the north side. This barn, some years ago, was destroyed by fire. Harrison Holcomb came from Galen in 1854, and built the house now standing. Mr. H. enjoyed the respect and esteem of his neighbors, and his children were among the other happy ones that sought knowledge in the old stone school-house. His daughter, Elizabeth, became the wife of Charles Tegg, and lives at Bay Bridge. Mary and Frances have been mentioned as wives of Charles and Jared Rice, respectively. Hattie married Mr. Johnson and resides in Kirkville. The only son, William H., married away from this neighborhood. The subsequent owners in order have been Ransom Loveless, C. Baker, Loveless a second time, George Talcott, who built the barn now on the place, E. Snyder and Dr. Fish. Not very long ago, while digging a well on the premises, the earth caved in and buried a boy who was at the bottom. Fortunately, some boards, in the caving, so placed themselves as to somewhat protect him. His frantic cries for help could be heard, but no one would endanger his own life to save that of the lad, until his father, who had been summoned from Wolcott, appeared. "Johnny" had been admonished to say his prayers, for a rescue was deemed impossible; but the father threw himself into the well, and prompted by a father's love, regardless of personal peril, worked till his boy was drawn from his living tomb, but the rescuer's hands were torn and bloody, the nails worn far down into the quick, through his frantic efforts to save his child.

We must now return to the road where we turned to the left, or north, after leaving the Joseph Wade place. People forty years of age will remember a log house which nearly faced the road, perhaps a little south of it. This house was the home of Ebenezer Pierce, who built it about 1835 and lived in it until his death, in 1854. His second wife was the widow of Benjamin Kellogg. Mr. Pierce had served in the Revolutionary army. He is reported to have run away from his home in Massachusetts, at the age of sixteen, to enlist. Many reminiscences are told of his soldier days.

It is said that he was detached by Gen. Washington for service near him, and it was the old man's boast that he had repeatedly shaved the father of his country. His first wife was Mary Ballard, also Massachusetts born. After the war he was for a time a boatman on the Hudson river. He had three children: Dr. Jeremiah B., late of Lyons ; Elizabeth, wife of Judge R. Root of Buffalo ; and Matilda, who became the wife of Simeon Barrett, now one of the oldest residents of Rose. She died twenty-four years ago. Subsequent to Mr. Pierce's death, the house was occupied by Gamaliel Sampson, who, from Cattaraugus county, had married Harriet, oldest daughter of Benjamin Kellogg, and his own first cousin. Of their six children, Sally married Darius Lovejoy and resides in Rose ; Betsey married Harlow Peck, and is a resident of Butler, north of Spencer's corners ; Warren married Rhoda Myers and went to Illinois. Alsifine is the wife of William Calkins of Savannah. A. Putnam married Lucy, daughter of Charles Sherman of Rose, and lives in Galen, while the youngest son, Ethan B., married Ædna Burch and lives at Whisky Hill. (Sodus, 1893.) Mr. Sampson, who died in 1870, was a soldier of the War of 1812, and his widow, past four score years, draws a pension from the government. Her home is with her son, Ethan B. (She died Apr. 25, 1891. Had she lived till the 30th, her age would have been 87 years.) The old log house was torn away by Wm. B. Kellogg. The farm itself was purchased from Fellows & McNab by Benjamin Kellogg, who came to these parts from Salem, Mass. His first log house was just east of the present Colvin house, and here he lived until his death, in 1829. Ethan B., his son, succeeded to the owner-ship of the farm and built the present frame structure. Benjamin K., whose wife was Pamelia Trask, had eight children—four sons and as many daughters. His oldest son, William, born in 1800, married Rebecca Brewster, is yet living in Cattaraugus county, N. Y. Ethan B. married Matilda Allen and resided for many years east of Clyde, and there died, in 1881. (Mrs. Kellogg died Apr. 16, 1889, aged 75 years.) They are buried in the Collins neighborhood, as is also their son, Lewis, who had married Emma Livermore, niece of Mrs. John B. Roe. Their daughter, Rebecca, became Mrs. Ketchum, and Maria, Mrs. Peckham. Their son, Henry, married a Pomeroy of South Butler, and lives on the Clyde farm. Charles B. has already been mentioned, as have also Mrs. Sampson and Mrs. Jones. Mrs. Experience Brewster, afterward Mrs. Ogram, was named in the Rose let-ters. This leaves only Betsey and John. At the former's marriage to Willard Peck, there followed one of those long-to-be-remembered horning scrapes for which this vicinity was, in years agone, famous. In the midst of the uproar one of the participants, Richard Garratt, now of Rose, was wounded by the bursting of a gun. He had to be carried home and the fun came to a premature end. Mr. Peck moved to Clyde, and on a visit to Michigan several years ago was killed by the falling of a tree. John Kellogg married Betsey Westcott of a prominent Butler family. Following Ethan B. Kellogg on the old homestead came Willard Peck and then Wm. B. Kellogg, John's oldest son, who here began his married life. He sold to Oliver Colvin, the present owner. Mr. Colvin is a native of Kingsbury, Washington county, and his wife, who is Jane, *née* Seelye, was born in Morean, Saratoga county. She is an own consin of the late George and Delos Seelye. Mr. Colvin's brother, Dr. Nathan, was for many years a noted physician in Clyde. After several removals, he, Oliver, settled upon a farm south of Clyde, where he resided till 1855, when he was struck with a migrating fever, which prompted him to sell and go to Virginia. This trip he made with his family in almost old-fashioned emigrant style, in that he drove there, though they did not camp when night overtook them, but sought the shelter of some hospitable roof. He located in Spottsylvania county, where his youngest child, Clara Virginia, was born. His place was two miles from Fredericksburg, and, had he remained there, his home would have been in the very theatre of the late war. As it was, life in the south was distasteful to himself and all his family, so, after a three years' trial, he returned and soon bought where we now find him. Mr. and Mrs. Colvin have reared a very large family, only one member of which has died, and she, Cornelia, a wife and mother. As Mrs. Stratton, she had lived some years in California before her death. The two older sons, Thomas and Augustus, have long resided in the Golden State. (Augustus died March 3, 1892, aged 56 years, in Jacksonville, Oregon.) Sidney, who was a lieutenant in the 9th Heavy Artillery, after the war was over married Electa Powers and went to the Pacific coast. He now lives at Lake View, Oregon. Elizabeth is the wife of Clark Sanders of Waterloo. Narcissa is well known in Rose as the wife of Eugene Hickok. Asahel, a good soldier in the 111th N. Y., lost an arm at Petersburg. He married Annette, daughter of Daniel Soper, and lives in Wolcott. Pitt, now a druggist in Rochester, has been twice married—first to Mary Ann LaDue of Wolcott, and second to Alice Seelye of Brockport. Frank married Giles M. Winchell of Wolcott, who now manages the farm. Clara is the wife of Harvey L. Dickinson, once of Rose, now of Idaho, though just at present, for his health, he is in Salt Lake City. (Later in Washington.) For fifteen or twenty years Mr. Colvin made cider for the people in Rose and Butler, averaging, he tells me, one thousand barrels a year. No resident of the district ever had a merrier nature, or drew more enjoyment from life as it passed. His amiable wife has kept him excellent company in all this journey. Time would not suffice to tell all his pranks, but one that he and Mrs. C. often laugh over was his bringing home, soon after they were married, a small owl, which he handed to her, saying: "Here, Jane, is a bird I have brought you for supper." "It's a nice one," says she; "a partridge, I think." So she proceeded to fricassee the same, much to Mr. Colvin's delight. It required long boiling, and even when cooked, Mrs. Colvin remarked the exceeding blueness of the meat, which she could not induce her liege lord to taste, and before she had eaten much he enlightened her as to the character of the bird she had been stewing. Query—Is this incident the origin of people claiming, when blue and used up, to feel like a "biled owl?" In early life Mr. Colvin rode on the packet that formed a part of the triumphal progress through the state, on the opening of the Erie canal. From Lockport to Troy, he was one of those who accompanied Gov. Clinton on his way from Lake Erie to tide water. He states that cannon were stationed every ten miles to signal the starting of the boats. When the firing had reached the Hudson, the return salute was fired back to Buffalo, the time employed being four hours. Few of Mr. Colvin's acquaintances can fail to tell of his quaintness in repartee, and I am reminded of the reply he made to old Mrs. S., who, always anxious about what didn't concern her, once said: "La, Mr. Colvin! why, where have you been?" "To the Valley." "What have you been there for?" "To see a pig shaved with a hand saw." Exit old lady in a hurry. As the shadows lengthen, these two old people watch the sunset of life, seeing in the past more of pleasure than sorrow, and complacently contemplating the life beyond which awaits us all. (Mr. Colvin died Oct. 9, 1892.) (Mr. Winchell is of a Hannibal family, and is an excellent farmer. To him and his wife have been born two children, Fred and Laura.)

Toward the south, on the west side of the road, we find a house fast going to ruin. It is many years since the owner dwelt in it, and during this time a long line of tenants has moved in and out. The first owner whom I can find was Joseph Brewster, whose wife was a sister of Uncle "Sammy" Jones, and he sold to Samuel Thompson. The latter's wife was Abigail Wainwright. Mr. T. died in 1852 and Mrs. T. in 1851. Both are buried in the district cemetery. They had six children, who married as follows: Clarissa, William Ellinwood, who lived but a short time and she afterward married William Sherman; Cordelia married Charles Warren; more than thirty years ago George Thompson went to sea and no trace of him has ever been had. What unwritten tragedy this long silence covers, we can only conjecture. He was a young man of stalwart frame and great physical strength. Eliza married Horace Peck; Edwin, noted years ago as a musician at country dances, married Emeline Cobb. He is now living with a second wife in Watkins, N. Y.; Camilla, a maiden lady, in whose name the property stands, lives in Wolcott. Edwin and Eliza Thompson were married on the same evening by Elder Ladd, of the Valley. Then followed the very worst horning spree that ever this region had known up to that time. The boys were mounted and the line extended from the Colvin farm to Thompson's. The clergyman begged to be let out, that he might get away from the din and noise. Among the dwellers in this house, after the death of Mr. Thompson, may be named Charles Warren, George Rice, Jackson Terbush, Daniel Soper, Ensign Wade, Giles M. Winchell, John Meehan, George Lasher, Murrill Burch and, lastly, William DeVoe. The first owner, Brewster, finally died in Clyde. He was doubtless from Saratoga county. Patrick Burke now leases the farm.

Crossing the road and going a few rods southward, we find the house of William B. Kellogg. The farm is a part of his Grandfather Benjamin's purchase from Fellows and McNab. John Kellogg bought it in 1837, and here lived until his death in 1876. His wife has already been mentioned as Betsey Westcott. To the neighborhood she was known as "Aunt Betsey," and when she made a visit she was always welcome : then came merry times. Her prevailing characteristic of jolly good nature she imparted in no small degree to all her children. Full of years she died, after a brief illness, in the fall of 1886. Her oldest child, Almira, married Alonzo Hubbard, of Butler, and died at the early age of twenty-eight. William B. married, in 1853, Eliza Tyler, and lives upon the old place ; his only son, John, married Anna Valentine and lives in Clyde. Stephen B. married, in 1854, Harriet Collins and lives on the old Shepard farm in Rose. Permilla became, in 1843, the wife of E. Willard Sherman, one of Charles Sherman's sons, and resides in Clyde. Paulina died at the age of sixteen, in 1851. Allie married, in 1877, Duane LaDue and lives at Warner's Station, Onondaga Co. When John Kellogg bought this farm it was a dense wilderness. He gave seven dollars an acre for it. Clearing up the land he built a log house, and in it all his children, save Allie, were born. He afterward built the present house and barns. In the possession of the Kellogg family from the beginning, let us leave the farm with the wish that it may remain with the same family *in perpetuo*. (Now the property and residence of Patrick Burke and family.)

The very last farm to be noted in this school district is that across the road, just to the south. Here, early in the century, 1817, came Wm. McKoon and his helpmeet, Lucy Cole. Mr. McKoon was born in Rhode Island ; but when an infant, in 1794, his parents came to Columbia, Herkimer county. Thence he made the trip with ox team to Wayne county. When he reached what was to be his future home, he had just fifty cents. With this he purchased an axe and a half bushel of Indian meal. He was a true pioneer, and brought his farm up from the very beginning of primitive forest. His log house stood some rods back of the present house, and after his building of the framed structure, it passed through the usual degradations of barn and pig pen to final dissolution. To grind his corn, he cut down a tree and hollowing out the stump, had a samp mortar of the most substantial character. He had but three children. Mairetta has already been noted as the wife of Charles Kellogg. Jairus married Rachel A. Merritt of Savannah. Rhoba married Elihu Spencer of Butler, and

moved to Appleton, Wisconsin. Wm. McKoon is one of the most noteworthy characters who, in the early days, settled in these parts. Always
a man of sterling integrity, he became a minister of the Methodist denomination, and for several years preached under the direction of the presiding
elder. At the time when anti-slavery excitement ran high, he left the old
church for the Wesleyans, but finally affiliated with the Disciples, in
whose communion he died in 1870. Mr. McKoon had a remarkable
ancestry, being sixth in descent from Roger Williams, and twelfth from
Martin Luther. For some years previous to his death, he had lived in South
Butler; but his body was brought to sleep with his kindred and friends in
the Collins cemetery. Many years ago, he planted five Lombardy poplars
on the road-side south of his residence. They can be seen, located as they
are on the top of a ridge, from points many miles away. There is scarcely
a hill-top within a radius of ten miles whence these five mighty fingers,
pointing heavenward, may not be seen. I have noted trees of this variety
in all parts of this Union, but my eyes never rest on the long tapering form
of a Lombardy poplar without having my thoughts revert to this row on
the hill, and I think how proudly they stood out between me and the
morning sun, and when the western sun was hastening to its setting, how
glorious were these trees gilded with golden light. No one fortunate
enough to have been born in sight of these trees, will ever forget them,
nor cease to be grateful to Wm. McKoon for planting them. Jairus
McKoon succeeded his father upon the farm and here reared his family of
four children. Merritt G. married L. Estelle Seelye, and lives in the old
Geo. Seelye homestead; Hattie, who married Isaac Lockwood, died in
November, 1885, leaving five children, Lida, Ada, M. Burt, Irene and
Hattie; Charles married Jennie Terry and is now in Michigan; Ida became
the wife of Jarit Wickwire, and lives in Rose. About 1865 Jairus McKoon
sold to his sister, Widow Kellogg, who thus came back to the home of her
childhood. Mr. McKoon moved to the next farm southward, and there
died in September, 1885. His widow is there now with her son-in-law,
Isaac Lockwood. (Mr. L. died December 19, 1887, being supervisor of
Butler at the time.) Mrs. K. sold to Josephus Collins, and he to his
brother-in-law, John Crisler, who now holds the place. His wife is Ruth,
née Livermore. Their only daughter, Mamie, is now a pupil in the State
Normal School at Oswego. By his first wife, Mr. C. had Cora, wife of
Daniel Harper of Rose; Nelson, who married Mary Stone, and Evander.
(Mr. C. died January 17, 1892, aged 68 years. Mamie was married June
29, 1893, to Melville Terwilliger of Walden, N. Y. Nelson lives in
Wolcott, and Evander in Rose. The place is now occupied by Chauncey
Darling and family.)

4

Thus we have traversed the district, running the record through fully seventy years, and there yet remains only to mention some of the peculiarities of the school which the children of this vicinity constituted. All were farmers' progeny, and all except the families of the Dudley Wade and George Seelye houses brought their dinners in pail or basket, and he who has never generated an appetite, sitting on the hard benches of a country school-house, can have no idea of the flavor of that same dinner now so carefully packed away by mother's hands in that two-quart pail. Many a time during the forenoon his eyes stray from book to shelf, where his pail with scores of others reposes. At recess he treats himself to an apple lunch, but when noon comes, how he throws himself outside of that nice bread and butter, the hard boiled egg, the small piece of cold meat, and then, reserved to the very last, how that triangularly shaped bit of apple pie disappears down his throat. Then putting the pail back upon the shelf, he drinks long and deep from the old wooden pail standing on a bracket just between the end of the desk and the door. The dipper is rusty, but he doesn't care. He is not at all fastidious. All drink from the same dish, and then, with a whoop and a bound, they are out of the door and ready for play. What fun the youngsters had at recess! Summer afforded excellent facilities for playing horse, and many a nailless, bleeding toe attested the speed and carelessness of the gait. This sport was for the boys of course; but the girls were not idle. Sometimes, in spells of unwonted gallantry, the boys would bring boards, rails and brush, to build for their sisters strange and fantastic houses, in which the sweet damsels would arrange large quantities of broken dishes which they had brought from home. Future generations will wonder if once there was a pottery in the vicinity, and all this went well for the girls until their brothers, returning to their native barbarism, would make a fierce incursion and level to the dust the result of many hours of labor. A steep bank with friable soil afforded the children of both sexes excellent opportunity for grist mills, a chance which they were not slow to embrace, and with sticks thrust through the soil they sawed away, sending down a stream of sand flour, until Uncle Thad. Collins' farm seemed in danger of running into the road. Winter brought a merry season. The boys still played horse, but they loved better to divide into rival parties and to snow ball, claiming for their respective sides those who were hit by the pasty mass. Then, too, they threw balls over the school-house, accompanied by a stereotyped cry of "Aily, aily over," and this the schoolmaster within would hear during the moments of recess or noon. Over the fence, in Dudley Wade's field, they would mark out paths for "fox and geese," and here the boys and girls could play together. Further still down the lot was a low place where a little skating and more sliding were afforded, and clear over the hill, close by the fence, were several elm trees, whose slippery bark afforded material for hours of rumination. Occasionally, some daring boys would steal away from the school-house to get tamarack gum from Sherman's swamp, where now I suppose so many onions are raised, and on their return would stand, like Trojans, the threshings which the irate master was sure to give. The gum they passed around among the girls, in whose eyes these truants were heroes. By way of variety, when the school-master had gone to dinner, the boys—and it is strange how near the average boy-nature lies to the savage state—would set upon a certain necessary building and tip it completely over. Then getting it in position, they would roll it over and over, accompanying this mischief with yells that would have done credit to their brother Comanches in western wilds. If, at this time, Uncle Dudley Wade or Uncle Delos Seelye should happen along, then was the fun fairly bewildering, for, added to the devastation, was the impotent rage of the wrathful tax-payer. Divided as the district is into two nearly equal portions, it was a common thing for the Butler boys to array themselves against those of Rose. Then Greek met Greek and fierce was the onslaught. At the close of school, how dinner pails were banged against offending heads! How missiles of all descriptions flew, while timorous sisters stood around and tearfully begged their irate brothers to "stop and come home." Strange that with so much fighting there were so few hurt. Occasionally, self-appointed champions would undertake to settle deep-seated, long-standing wrongs, and the tales of the encounter long stirred the blood of the boyish listener. There were few boys who did not have their turn at the foe; but perhaps no battle was fiercer than that which the Butler Hector, J. R., waged with the Rose Achilles, G. G. R. Just what the provocation was, the careful historian has not chronicled, but of the fact of the battle there is no doubt. Long and fierce was the fray—sanguine, too, for noses and faces bore witness to the earnestness of the warriors. Their respective parties, or shall I say armies! were ranged in admiring, not to say awe-struck, silence. The air was full of hair and active combatants. It was said that it was impossible to tell east from west, so close and vigorous was the fray. Unfortunately, either the return of the teacher, or the calling of school, put an end to this terrible contest, and I can not record a victory for either side. So, in the school history, it must go down as a drawn battle. All this was in the days of the stone school-house. It is possible that in later days, since the advent of the wooden building, many of the asperities and hardnesses of the olden time have disappeared with the edifice in which they generated. Let us hope so.

SCHOOL DISTRICT NO. 5.

Sept. 8—Oct. 13, 1887.

This district, located to the south and west of No. 7, is known in home parlance as the Town district, from the families of that name that have from the very first settlements lived in the neighborhood. It lies mainly along a north and south road, running at the foot and on the west side of the long hill just south of the old Delos Seelye farm. As we turn into this road, we soon find a small house with barn near at hand. Here lives Stephen Chapin, who, several years ago, came from Huron, bought a few acres of the Egbert Soper place, and put up these buildings. He also ran a blacksmith shop for some years. He has a family of five daughters. (Mr. C.'s wife was an Eldridge of Butler. Their daughters are Hattie [Mrs. Gardner Harper], Mary, Irene, Blanche and Kittie.)

Still further along, fairly nestling under the hill, is an abode, which, with its predecessors, runs back nearly or quite fifty years. In a former series, reference was made to certain houses built upon the very summit of the high eminence. One of them, that of Rhodes, slid, as it were, down to the site of the old Soper house—the other, Mr. Gould's as gracefully descended on the other side and rested where James Benjamin now resides. Following Mr. G., who went down to the Clyde road, came a Mr. Swift, who sold to Sheldon R. Overton, son-in-law of Anstin Roe. Here several of Mr. O.'s children, as Laura and Clarissa, were born. Mr. Overton, who, we may remark in passing, died in April last in Wolcott, sold to Isaac Curtis, a Long Islander. His wife, a Soper, was a second cousin of Mr. Overton. Here Mr. Curtis died, and Egbert Soper, a brother of his wife, succeeded. Mrs. Curtis, with her three children, returned to Long Island. Mr. Soper, as a dweller on the Pierce place, we have already mentioned. Once more we find Wm. Sherman in possession, and then Milton Town followed. He was a son of Silas Town, and married Clarinda, daughter of Lyman Lee. They began here their married life, and here their only son, Lewis, was born. Mr. Town, some years since, sold his place to its present owner and moved north to the Philetus Chamberlain farm. From there he moved to the Valley, and, in 1882, died. He is buried in what is called the Ellinwood burial ground on the road to the village. His widow and son reside at Rose Valley. James Benjamin, who is one of the family so long identified with the south part of the town, although his father, Henry, did not move here, married Mary Comstock, and has two children, Grant and Grace, both at home. Mr. Benjamin was a good soldier in the 111th. (Mrs. Benjamin died in 1887.)

The next farm has buildings upon both sides of the road, and the farm itself is divided by the road. The house, that of Charles Deady, is on the

west side. To this place came, many years since, John Quackenboss
Deady, from Cambridge, Washington Co. He first located on the Lackey
farm toward Clyde, but, buying out a claim here, he made his payment to
the Land Office, and so may rank as an original proprietor. His wife was
Susan Waters, who, at the age of two years, had been brought by her
father, James, from Maryland. He died near Alloway, town of Lyons.
Mr. Deady reared a large family of children, one of whom, John Henry,
met a violent death, one of the few recorded in this quiet neighborhood.
His team ran away on the steep hill-side and he was thrown out, receiving
injuries so severe that he lived only a few moments. No incident in the
history of the district or vicinity ever gave a more terrible shock, and still,
old people warn younger ones to be careful, by recounting this untimely
death. His oldest son, Thomas, married Esther A. Garratt, and died in
1847, aged twenty-seven years. Elizabeth became Mrs. Van Dusen, and
died in Alton in 1886. James, living west of the Valley, took for his wife
Carrie Swift, of the family that once lived on the farm to the northward.
Margaret was named in the former letters as the wife of Egbert Soper and
lives in Westbury. Mary married Henry Decker and lives in Stewart's
district. Charles holds the homestead and has been twice married. His
first wife was Henrietta Swart, of Detroit, Mich.; his second, Louise
Guthrie. He has four children—one by his first and three by his second
wife. (June Deady is Mrs. Wm. Barrett in Montana; Edith, Mrs. Edward
Martin of Rose; Estelle, Mrs. Merritt Bennett of Wolcott; Grover C. is the
boy at home.) The youngest member of the family is William, and the
resident in Rose who does not know "Bill" Deady must be entirely devoid
of enterprise. For many years he resided in Rose Valley; but recently he
has taken up his abode in Lyons—his business, that of a speculator. A
summer home at Charles' Point affords him and his a pleasant respite from
harvest heat. His wife is Jeannette Jeffers, who has made him the happy
father of three boys and an equal number of girls. John Q. Deady was a
man of great energy and industry. This was evident in his twice paying
for his farm. He was one of the unfortunate men who committed themselves to the Clyde Bank, founded on the farms of the adjoining towns, and
which went to the wall. Men who had been considered independent found
themselves poor. Instead of repining and sinking under his misfortune,
he manfully went to work, and before he died beheld his acres again free
from incumbrance. (Well known in this part of Rose, Mr. Frank Sager,
a native of Albany county, has been for several years an aid to the farmers
on this street. His latest home is with Mr. James Benjamin.)

All the farms along this road are divided by it. They run eastward just
over the ridge of the hill and to the west, well up to the summit of the
range of hills whose westward slope takes us down to the Clyde and Valley
road. The next place is the one that Silas Town reclaimed from the

wilderness. Asa and Silas Town came to this section from Paris, Oneida Co., but they were natives of Winchendon, Worcester Co., Mass. They were accompanied by their sister, Lavinia, who many years ago returned to Oneida county. She was the last survivor of a family of eleven children, reaching the great age of more than ninety-three years at death. The least age attained by any one of the children was fifty-nine, while the average age of all at death was beyond seventy-six. They were of the very straightest sect of the Puritans, and from the father, Absalom, down, nearly all the children had Bible names. An ancestor of the Towns had lived in Salem, Mass., an 1 there in the troublous days of witchcraft excitement two of his sisters were hanged as witches. Another was accused and escaped only by the allaying of the delusion which had so long possessed the people. Mr. Town's children tell me that he often told them stories of witchery, and when we reflect that his mother, who died at the age of one hundred and six, was born in 1747, we see that her childhood was within sixty years of the excitement itself, and eye-witnesses of the horrors of Gallows Hill must have narrated to her the infamies of Cotton Mather's day. By these long lives of two individuals, we bridge over the interval of nearly two hundred years. The brothers, Asa and Silas, took up their land, one hundred and fifty acres, from Fellows and McNab, and cleared away the forest. This must have been about 1817. Silas married Polly Seelye, a daughter of Lewis Seelye, and niece of Joseph Seelye, in whose family she had lived many years. Their children were Emily, who married William Vandercof, of the Valley, where, with her son, Clarence E., she still lives. Her husband died in 1885. Milton, as we have already seen, married Clarinda Lee. Sarah married first John Vandercof, brother of William. He died in 1861. Since then she has married Asa Plumb and lives in Macedon. Her only son, Elvin, lives in Rose on the Joel Lee farm. Mary married Joel Lee and lives on the Lyman Lee place in Stewart's district. Lewis, who had engaged in the mercantile business in Clyde, died greatly regretted, in 1853, at the early age of twenty-three. Lucy married George Howland, of Rose. He died in 1869. Eugene married Ellen Norris, of New York, and succeeded his father upon the farm, the latter dying in 1873, aged eighty-seven. His wife died in 1882, at the age of eighty. Eugene followed his father, in 1881, and his widow, who subsequently married Ellery Davis, now lives on the place. Her two children by Eugene Town are May Evelina and Norris. (May E. is Mrs. Wm. Graham of Galen.)

Asa Town built the next house, using cobble stones as his material, and though there are several buildings in the town thus constructed, I never could see that any stones were missing. Certainly, hoeing corn time revealed all the boys cared to turn over. Mr. Town's wife was Hannah Stacey, whom he went down Utica way to find. She died in Chippewa

Falls, Wis., in 1873, at the home of her eldest son, Henry M. He had married Malina Chamberlain, sister of Hamlin T. Chamberlain, from Monroe county, who, by way of reprisal, had wedded Mary Almanda, the only daughter of Asa and Hannah Town. Another son, David H., married Cornelia Valentine, sister of Jackson V., at the Valley, and lives at Strong's Prairie, Wis. These two brothers had placed their log houses near a spring, and the houses themselves were separated by scarcely more than a walk—being in all respects, like their occupants, brotherly. One enthusiastic narrator says, " I shall never forget the sweet flag [near the spring, nor the sweet gooseberries in the garden. There were no yards nor gardens like them in these parts." In time, the first houses disappeared, and then came Asa's stone house and Silas's framed structure, which he placed further north than the old one. Asa died in 1848, and lies over the eastern hill in the Collins burial ground. Before saying " good-bye " to this family, I must echo the oft repeated praises of "Aunt Polly Town." No one can remember when she was not a remarkably handsome woman, and her beauty of face was fully equaled by that of her character. She kept her house a model of neatness, and trained her family in the most exemplary manner. Skilled in all the necessary accomplishments for house-keeping in those early days, she taught her children to be virtuous and industrious, and when her girls went out to other homes, they carried with them, in addition to great quantities of linen woven by their mother, the ineffaceable impression of her womanly example. "Aunt Hannah," Asa's wife, went from the neighborhood years since to dwell in the west with her sons, but she left an excellent memory of intelligence and worth. Some people, in these too practical days, affect to sneer at the Puritans and Puritanical ways. I, for one, could wish that their tribe might indefinitely increase. After the decease of Asa Town, his widow managed the farm for a time, and then sold to William Desmond, who came to this neighborhood from west of the Valley, though his name proclaims him from one of Ireland's proudest families His first wife was Lucy Ann Way, who, in a period of temporary insanity, committed suicide, leaving one daughter, Agnes, who now lives in Clyde. Her husband is Alexander Weeks. Mr. Desmond's second wife is Lucy Toles, from the Lovejoy neighborhood. They have three sons—Albert E., Truman T. and Charles H. (December 28, 1892, Albert was married to Aurilla Transue, daughter of the Rose M. E. minister. They are at the old home.)

We next come to the corner and to the school-house, where the children of the district are taught. The present pretty, white building is a great improvement on its red predecessor, which was the first one built after this part of the town was set off from the eastern district. The old red house was not beautiful, but it was useful. Like all other similar edifices

in these parts, it had its weekly and Sunday use.   Here preaching was
often heard, and at times Sunday schools were maintained.   The middle-
aged citizens, and older ones too, could tell of the days when the spelling
school was a delightful occasion, and the singing school also.   What
facilities for seeing the girls home, and what life-long intimacies were here
begun!   To enumerate all the teachers who have held sway here were a
task too great; but suffice it to say that almost every amateur user of the
birchen rod in these parts, at one time or another, has here taught the
"young idea how to shoot."

Across the way is the house of Richard Vedder.   The place has changed
hands often.   The earliest occupant whom I can recall, was the Mr.
Stickles, who was Delos Seelye's favorite farm laborer, though doubtless
the house long antedated him.   Henry Decker lived here for a time, as
did Major Wm. Snyder.   Very likely the original founder was Hiram
Van Dusen, who had married John Deady's daughter.   (Mrs. Vedder,
born in Saratoga county, died, 1893.   Her first husband was a Leaird.
Her daughter, Ida E., is the wife of Wm. H. Sowls; a son, Charles Leaird,
though better known as Vedder, now lives here with the Sowls family.
The Sowls children are Charles E. and Marion E.   The parents are
natives of Saratoga county.)

Across what was once a lively stream, which we shall call Marsh creek,
is a small estate of nineteen acres, on which, nearly or quite thirty years
ago, George Calm, an industrious Englishman, built a small house.   His
wife was Mary Smart, sister of the brothers Smart, who lived just south
of him.   Mrs. Calm's parents, William and Mary, lived with them, and
here the father died.   The mother survived to a great age, dying December
30, 1864, aged 82 years.   A familiar sight, in the early sixties, was that
afforded by Mr. and Mrs. Calm riding comfortably on the only seat in their
wagon, while mother, sitting upon a stool or board, hung on behind; but
the old lady asked no odds of teams and vehicles.   She made nothing of
stepping off at a lively pace to the Valley or Clyde, and returning in a
way that would discourage many a pedestrian.   She bore good evidence to
the virtue of her English training.   A Lee intervenes, then Josephus
Collins held and sold to a German, John Wyke, who was noted hereabouts for the fervor of his religious manifestations.   The story has never
been contradicted that when John was married, and reached that part of
the ceremony where the minister prays, John and his frau knelt also, but,
being led away by the words of the clergyman, he forgot all about the
business of the hour, thought it was a prayer meeting and prayed on himself, till the gentleman of the cloth had to inform him that the marriage
was not yet over, and he must attend to one thing at a time.   I am fearful
that another yarn is somewhat apocryphal, but I give it as I received it.
It is to the effect that some years subsequently, he was not pleased with

the character of his better half's prayer; and she refusing to stop on any milder plea, instead of flinging a stove lid at her, *à la* Jerry Cruncher, he incontinently stopped her mouth with a hot potato. John had always claimed that the Lord told him to marry Margaret Nusbickel. Whether the hot potato incident altered his opinion or not I cannot state. After Wyke came Maurice Cleary, the present possessor. (Mr. C. is from Cork, Ireland; his wife, Mary Cavanaugh. Their children are Mary, a graduate of Geneseo Normal School, teacher in Long Island City; Nora, a nurse in the Canandaigua Insane Asylum; Julia, at home; John, educated in Clyde, a teacher; Nellie, also a teacher and educated in Clyde; Michael and Edward, at home; William, died at the age of five years in 1880.)

We next find, west of the highway, several substantial barns, but the house is wanting. It, a log one, once stood opposite, and was constructed by Martin Van Buren. The only trace of Van B. in the vicinity now, is a child's grave in the cemetery. It bears the date of 1831. He, with his brother-in-law, Henry Ferris, had taken up an extensive possession in the immediate vicinity. After him came James T. Vandereof, about whom more will be written when we reach the Stewart neighborhood. Ananias Smith then bought this portion of the farm, though his home was on the Andrus place, further east. The next possessors were the brothers, William and Newton Smart, who, after a few years' ownership, sold to John Finch and moved to Illinois. John Finch was a son of Jeremiah Finch, about whom there will be more anon, and he lived here till he built his brick house, twenty-six years ago. His wife was Deiademie Chapin of Wolcott, but she had lived for some years in the home of Thaddeus Collins. Their children are Harriet, who married Abram Vanderburg, now in Selma, Kansas; Loania, married Warren Drury of Wolcott; Mary, died in 1859, aged fifteen; Frank, married Mary Jordan and has three daughters and one son. He is the present owner of the farm, succeeding his father, who died in 1874, aged nearly fifty-nine. His mother's home is here. Mr. Finch was one of the most energetic and progressive of the second generation of the farmers who, early in the century, sought this farming region. The next house, standing well back from the road and, long since, painted red was John Finch's early home, and is now a tenant house belonging to the farm. In addition to managing his farm, Mr. Finch is an extensive dealer in garden seeds. (He now has a family of four girls and one son.)

Nearly opposite, and on the corner of the private way, leading up the hill, forty or more years ago, Henry Snyder bought eight acres of land of the Finches and Deadys and put up a log house. Here his numerous children—four girls and seven boys—were born and reared. Mr. S. was originally from the Mohawk valley and settled first in Conquest. His wife was Margaret Rose, from Schoharie county. She is now living in

Sidney, Neb., with her daughter, Margaret, while Mr. S. died years ago and is buried in Conquest. His oldest son, William, was a valiant and efficient officer during the war, coming home with the rank of major in the 10th Cavalry; his wife is Melissa, daughter of William Benjamin. They now reside in Clyde. The place passed into his hands at the death of his father. He sold to Manly Benjamin, and finally it came into the possession of William Desmond. There is not a vestige of the house standing, only a few apple trees serving as a reminder of earlier days. The other children reared here are Harvey, who married Julia Blood, and is a resident of the Valley: he also was in the army: Charity C., as Mrs. Ruger, lives in Cortland; Mary J. married an Olmstead and dwells in Seneca Falls; Wilbur, as will be seen, later was drowned; Charles H. married after going to Michigan; John W. and Azro C. both migrated to Missouri and married there; Amariah is in Nebraska. His wife is Eliza Moore of Conquest. Margaret Ann, as Mrs. Worden, lives near Sidney, Neb. When families like this crowded the old school-house, there must have been lively times. Modern customs will render school-houses almost useless in some localities yet, and through their lack of material, districts will have to be merged. Outside of the village of Rose, probably there is not a school in the town as large as it was twenty-five years ago.

Pursuing our way up the hill, we come to a building that enjoys one of the most sightly outlooks in the town; but our road terminates here. To the northeast of the house and nearer the foot of the hill, I think there must be a spring hard by, there was once a log house, in which lived a Mr. Burgess. Afterward Pendar Marsh lived here, and subsequently built the house near the top of the hill, though the house has been ascribed to one Crampton. Philetus Chamberlain also lived here, but whether he followed Marsh or not I cannot state. Col. Briggs, also Millard Olmstead, were owners before Major Wm. Snyder, who held it for a time, from whom it passed to James Benjamin, who rents it to various tenants. A private way leads over the hill to a place owned by Wm. Matthews, where once lived David Benjamin and possibly others.

Coming back to our north and south road and going further south, we come to what was the south part of the Van Buren-Ferris purchase. Here Ferris built a log house, and after some years of occupancy sold to a Mr. Van Amburg and moved to Cayuga county. Following him came Lorenzo Dow Thomas. He was the youngest son of Charles Thomas, one of the very first comers, and was familiarly known in town as Dow Thomas. His wife was Hepsie Andrews. It is more than thirty years since he sold to George Aurand and moved to Illinois. After Aurand, Harry Shepard and his wife, Mary Barrett, lived here. They had one daughter, Libbie, who died when her parents lived south of the Valley, one of the prettiest, merriest girls ever born in this town, noted for its beautiful maidens. Mr.

and Mrs. S. never recovered from their loss, and died several years ago. In his business as a buyer and seller of cattle, "Hack" Shepard had a wide circle of acquaintance, and everywhere was known as one of the jolliest men who ever drove a herd. He belonged to the large family of Shepards who live in Galen and on the Clyde road. Asa Traver followed, and after him Wm. Jordan was the next possessor to live on the farm. He came from near Lyons and still remains. Since his holding the place he has had the misfortune to lose his house by fire, but this has been rebuilt. His family, a large one, consists of twelve children. One daughter, as we have seen, is the wife of Frank Finch, next neighbor toward the north. (The place now belongs to Timothy Donovan, who has lived for several years just over the town line in Galen. He is from Waterford, Ireland, his wife, Mary Daly. Their children are John and Maurice, who have contributed no little to their father's success. A daughter, Mary, died in April, 1891, in her sixteenth year. Mr. D. has effectually demonstrated that farming can be made to pay, even in Wayne Co. Before 1894 appears, Mr. D. expects to move to this Rose farm. The town line coincides with the line of fences next south of this home.)

Turning to our right and going toward the west, we come to the early home of the Benjamins. Two brothers, Riley and William, came from Westmoreland, Oneida Co., and took up land from the company, though Riley came first and sold to William. I understand that Riley returned to his former home. William's wife was Nancy Shaver, and both, after long lives of usefulness, sleep in the White School-house burial ground on the Clyde road. They were members of the Methodist Episcopal Church in the Valley. Riley B. built the first log house and William finally replaced it with the cobble stone house, now standing. His children, reared on this site, were nine in number. Maria died young. Henry, who was in the army, has been twice married. His first wife was a Loveless. His home is in Butler. Emeline, also in Butler, married a Calkins. Manly, who followed his father on the home farm, married Jennie Stewart and resides in Clyde. David, a soldier during the Rebellion, married Mary McDougal and lives in the district. Melissa is the wife of Major William Snyder. William, with his wife, Mary Weeks, lives south of Clyde. Eugene died unmarried at the age of twenty-one. Jerome married a Gerald, from Monroe county, and lives in San Francisco. After several changes, between Major Snyder and Manly B., the place passed to the ownership of William Desmond, who now holds a monopoly on cobble stone houses in this district—a good place for one of Mr. D.'s boys to locate when he takes unto himself a helpmeet. (Trueman T. Desmond, having married Mary Shaver of North Rose, has acted on the suggestion and is here installed. The parents are rejoicing over a baby girl, born in July, 1893.)

Opposite is another homestead. long associated with the name of Benjamin. Years ago Nelson Benjamin bought of one Decatur, who was possibly the first settler at this point. Mr. B.'s first wife was a Pressor, who bore him two children—George, who married Mary Loveless, of Butler, and Louise, who, as Mrs. Caywood. lives in Butler. Nelson. who sold to his brother, Alanson, now resides, an aged man, in Clyde. Alanson's pet foible was Scriptural argument, and he would leave work or play any day for his favorite diversion. On his death, Manly, his nephew, purchased. Then came William Benjamin, and. finally, Abner Garlic, who had once lived on the Wright farm further east. Alanson's widow married a Gordon, and is now dead. (As tenant, Jason Cleveland occupies.)

Our western limit is reached when we climb another hill and enter the home of William Finch. The Finches have been identified with this part of the town for many years, and the children went to school in the old wooden building of the Seelye neighborhood long before the old red house of the Town district. Jeremiah Finch, with his good wife. Eunice King, came from Saratoga county. He first took up the farm now held by Eugene Hickok, west of the Valley, but, owing to some informality, lost it. He then came to this place, where he abode until his death, in 1859, at the age of seventy-five. His wife survived him until 1864. when she died at the age of eighty. They are buried in the Seelye district. Their family of children numbered no less than twelve. Their daughters became Mapely Willoughby, of Clyde; Tansey Ann Hastings. who went west; Charity Scott, of Clyde; Sophia Hadley, of Michigan; Jane McCamly. of Lyons; Mary Lape. of Clyde, and Eleanor and Lois, who married in succession John Seaman. of Cortland. Jeremiah, 2d, married a Wilcox and went to Michigan; John has already been named; David married Ann Brush, of Buffalo. and lives on the Bliss farm in Galen; William, who retains the old home, married Clarissa Overton, daughter of Sheldon R., and has two children living—Eva J. and Elvin H. (Eva J. Finch is the wife of Mr. Geo. E. Brisbin, formerly of No. Rose, but now with his father-in-law, and Elvin H. is in the coal business in Clyde. They have one child, James William.) The house opposite is Mr. Finch's tenant house, but the farm was once owned separately. Perhaps Elias Sherman was the earliest proprietor. The house was built, I think, by Mr. Reynolds. Successive owners, or at least occupants, were Joseph Preston, Mr. Wykoff and Henry Decker.

We must now retrace our steps to the road leading eastward from the school-house. A few rods along on the south side is a house many years old and standing on a farm that has had many owners. There may have been earlier ones, but I have no trace of any before Elon B. Andrus, who was a Connecticut acquaintance of Deacon Aaron Shepard's family.

His wife was a Connecticut woman. Of his family I have only scattering facts, but one daughter, Mary Ann, married a Caster and went west. Benham married a Miss Caywood and moved to Huron. Another son married a Cox and went to Huron also. Lydia became the wife of Gerritt Caywood and moved to Michigan. The parents followed their children from the district. Then came Ananias Smith, from Patchogue, Long Island. His wife, Betsey Rose, very aged, is still living with her daughter, Mrs. Horton, in Galen. (Died Nov. 7th, 1887, in her 85th year.) Mr. Smith himself, after selling here, lived many years in Clyde, where he died, in 1872, and was buried in the Seelye neighborhood. The Smith family was noted, far and near, for the remarkable quickness that every member showed in repartee. I can imagine what a circus the devoted school masters of those days must have had with "Wash," "Marsh" and "Tim" Smith, all in school at one time. There ought to be no lack of variety, and the boys and girls who looked on must have had less than ordinary craving for outside shows. When T. R. S. was a small boy, he was sent to one of the Towns to borrow some lard. Being told that the family was out of lard, he says, "Well, I'll take some hog's fat then!" When, in later years, he went to Round Lake camp meeting and there came a time for testimony giving, the speakers would invariably begin by saying, "I am from Syracuse, Albany, New York," or other places, as the case might be. Our Wayne county Methodist thought the form was getting monotonous, and effectually ended that stereotyped preface by saying, "I am from every place in the world but this, and, thank the Lord! I shall be from this in about ten minutes." His mother, in her younger days, was one of the most gifted women in prayer and exhortation who ever tried to draw humanity from its erring ways. But even she could not restrain expressions that would cause the unregenerate to laugh, as, when wishing to illustrate her Christian brightness, she said, "I feel like a newly snuffed candle." She acknowledged the weakness of chewing gum occasionally, but always insisted that when doing so, one should go behind the door. It has been told me by Long Island people that Uncle Ananias once, before moving from the Island, found his cow one night trespassing. He sallied forth in great haste to drive her away, and after chasing around the house two or three times, was amazed at her sudden and absolute disappearance. He could not account for such an effectual vanishing, until the next day, when the poor beast was found in his own cellar, having, in her race, fallen into an open bulkhead. The remarks of the Smith family at this discovery, much to my sorrow, were not taken down, but the readers can imagine what a quick-tongued woman would be likely to say at finding her preserves mixed up, more or less, with cow. Their children married as follows: Washington, Harriet Avery, of Long Island, and lives in North Huron; Timothy, Fanny Roe, and is in Clyde; Marshall, Mrs. Ann Armitage, and also lives in Clyde; and Ellen, John Horton, and lives in Galen. Silas Holcomb followed. He came from Oneida county. After selling to S. R. Overton, he and his wife settled in the Valley and there died, in 1878 and 1875 respectively, and are buried in the Seelye district. His son, Willard, died in 1858, aged 24. There are four daughters living, viz.: Mrs. B. G. Bloss, of New York City; Mrs. S. C. Maxon, of Milton Junction, Wis.; Mrs. F. M. Johnson, of Rose; and Mrs. Jacob St. John, of East Galway, Saratoga county. Mrs. Holcomb's maiden name was Freelove Remington, a distant relative of the Ilion Remingtons, famous the world over for the manufacture of firearms. There are forty-nine acres in the farms. Mr. Overton lived here several years and sold to Horace Perkins, of Gouverneur, St. Lawrence Co., and he, moving to Galen, passed the farm along to Michael Meehan, whose father lived just north of the Lockwood farm, in Butler. (No farm in town has improved more than this under Mr. Meehan's care. He is from Waterford, Ireland; his wife is Annie Finnigan from Lyons. They have children—Thomas, Edward, Martin and Ellen. Could former owners return, they would hardly recognize the fine, white house into which the old wood colored one has been turned.)

Eastward, on the corner, is a very pleasant place that also has passed through many hands. As far as I know, it was first occupied by Uriah Marsh, a brother of Pendar. His wife was a Caster. They had, while living here, no children of their own, but had adopted a girl named Jerusha Knapp. This family, too, took up the line of march for regions further west. One of Ananias Smith's Long Island neighbors, Richard Garratt, followed Marsh. Afterward came Charles Wright, an Englishman and a blacksmith by trade. He was an active, energetic and exceedingly industrious man. There was no loitering when he was about. Just a trifle eccentric, he is still remembered for offering to a neighbor, with whom he had some difficulty, his coat, with the Scriptural quotation, " If thy neighbor sue thee at the law and take from thee thy coat, give to him thy cloak also." His boys were all girls, and he had seven of them. One is Mrs. Selah Finch, living on the Clyde road; another became Mrs. Turner, and still another was Mrs. Scutt, of Clyde. After selling the farm Mr. Wright worked at blacksmithing some years in Clyde, where he eventually died. Mr. Edward Burrill followed, who now lives in North Rose. Then Abner Garlic for a time. His wife is Mary, daughter of Capt. Wm. Graham, who came from Washington Co. to Galen. The place is now owned by George Rodwell, an Englishman, who came from Lincolnshire in 1870. With his brother, he lived for several years near Briggs, and came to this farm in 1883. He long ran a threshing machine, using for this purpose the first portable engine in this section. It is now in use in the mint still opposite. He is unmarried, his mother keeping house for him. He has sixty-nine acres in the farm.

We reach the confines of Rose and the end of the district in the next farm south—that of Horace Hallett. To get to this home we must cross Marsh creek, just below the pond whose water so long ran Briggs' saw-mill. The mill is going to decay, and as the need for one no longer exists, it will doubtless soon entirely disappear. The first mill on the site, I am told, was built by Elias Sherman, one of the pioneers (it is also ascribed to one Barnes), but this went down and afterward Colonel Briggs rebuilt the structure of our own day. The name of Hoag is also associated with this mill. The men who managed the mill had a convenient house near, in which have dwelt a long list of occupants: the only one whom we can mention is Jenner, whose son, James, was killed at Cedar Creek. Mr. Wm. S. Hunt owns the house and pond. The pond itself was a very convenient accessory to the neighborhood. Here the boys swam in summer and skated in winter. Farmers have washed their sheep, and clergymen baptized their converts. One of the saddest events in the chronicles of this neighborhood was the drowning here, long before the War, of Wilbur Snyder, who, having aided in the sheep washing fun, or work, just as you choose to call it, thought he would have a still merrier time on a raft that he had improvised from a barn door. The door tipped him off, he could not swim, and sorrowing forms about a white coffined face, tell the rest of the story. This is one version. Another and more probable one is, that a sheep escaped from the washers and swam out into the pond; young Snyder followed, and being taken with a cramp perished. The Hallett place was taken up by John Caywood, whose name is borne by numerous descendants in the adjoining towns. He lived to be more than a hundred years old. His grandson, Abram, was associated with him in the management of the place. Twenty-five acres on the south part of his farm he sold, in the forties, to George Seelye, but this part with the rest of the farm came into the hands of Josephus Collins. He sold to James Sears, and he, in turn, to Jackson Harper, and he to Wm. Whitehead. Then came Hallett, whose wife is Barbara, daughter of Wm. Aurand. They have two children, William, and Kittie May, the wife of Frank Haugh of Clyde, Galen's town clerk. Mr. Hallett, a native of Wolcott, served in the army during the Rebellion. The farm has ninety-five acres. At this point a high hill confronts us, long known as Briggs'. Colonel Samuel S. Briggs for long years was the most noted man in these parts. Though his residence was in Galen, many of his acres were in Rose. He lived a worthy life and died in 1865. To him succeeded Mr. Wm. S. Hunt, his son-in-law, who for nearly forty years has managed this immense farm of more than three hundred acres. Mr. Hunt has one son, Wm. A., who is in Briggs' Bank. Clyde; a daughter. Martha L., died in 1875, in her eighteenth year. Mr. Hunt is a member of the Clyde Methodist Church, and is about taking up his permanent residence in that village.

Coming back to the cross roads, by the home of George Rodwell, we shall have to go eastward again; crossing a swampy stretch of land and climbing a hill, we are on the Butler line. At our right is a house which marks the former home of Sam. Kilburn, who sold to a Mr. Devoe. One of Devoe's daughters was the wife of John Stringer, whom we have seen as the first occupant of the Dudley Wade farm. My information concerning this family is exceedingly meagre, but I have the impression that the old people died here, and to them succeeded a grandson, John Devoe, who married a Howland, and afterward went to Illinois. The Devoe family was noted far and near for its musical ability; a talent often sought in scenes of country festivity. After Devoe came the Turners, and Charles Wright owned a part of the place. A Mr. Cummings, related to Wm. Haney, was here for a time. His daughter, Libbie, was, for a number of years, a teacher in Rose and Clyde. With her sister Mary, she is now in Chicago. Charles Covell, now county superintendent of the poor, owned the place for a while, and, I think, sold to Buckley, the present owner. John J. Buckley is Irish born, from county Kerry, though coming to Rose from Lyons. His wife is Annie Dwyer. Their children are Mary; Sarah, who is Mrs. Edward Welch of North Rose; Maggie, who married Matthew Kane of Throop; Edward, employed with New York Central Railroad; Michael, John, and Martin. Mr. Buckley has repaired and improved the buildings, moving to this side a house, once standing nearly opposite. The town line runs through his sitting room, so he can take his choice as to the town he stays in. He has about 100 acres in his farm, having added to it the old Austin Roe place, across the way.

Opposite, many years since, there was a log house, in which lived Jonathan Fuller. He was not a careful farmer, but delighted more in roaming about the neighborhood and imbibing hard cider, than in putting in the "big licks" on his land. The story is told that the young men of the vicinity came one very bright moonlight night, cut and bound his very scant crop of wheat and set it up in proper form. Then getting a cow bell, they began to tinkle it. Soon the old man came out with his wife to drive away the intruding kine. But, however fast the old people ran, the cow ran faster, and effectually dodged them. It took the man some time to discover that the wheat had been harvested, but when he did, he nearly convulsed the boys by straightening himself up, and exclaiming: "By the eternal gods, Phœbe, that's no cow." The expression was long a by-word in the vicinity. The place finally came into Austin Roe's possession, and he held it until his sale to John B. Roe. Austin R. retained fifteen acres on the north and south road. A Mr. Harmon owned near this farm once, and I think the places were finally merged. One of the Harmons married Polly Lounsberry. A framed house was built on the north side of the road by a Mr. Irwin, I am told, who was a blacksmith. John B. Roe sold

the whole farm to his son, Merwin S., who, with his first wife, began
housekeeping here. He managed the place for a time, and then sold to
Mr. Buckley, who moved the buildings to the south side, and thus identified the two farms. The writer of these sketches has recollections of work
in Merwin's barn that, to this day, induce waves of heat even to contemplate. It was G. G. R.'s last summer on the farm, and that day's threshing completely dispelled any notions that we may have had of making
farming our life work. The Lockwood boys ran the thresher and they
always made it lively for all concerned. The barley stack was on the
west side of the barn, and old Sol never sent his rays more directly nor
pointedly than he did on that August afternoon. George and I were on
the stack, and it was our duty to keep that voracious, cavernous maw full.
Wellington never longed for Blucher or night as did we for the going down
of the sun or the using up of that pile of barley. Pricked and nettled by
barley beards, dusty beyond recognition, and completely parboiled by the
sun and perspiration, we went home to wash up and to mutually sympathize. What bliss we extracted on the barn floor from those pails of
water! We turned about in scrubbing, and I never shall forget George's
thin voice as he remarked, while undergoing kneading at my hands: "If
there is any easier work than this in the world, I am going to do it. You
won't catch me on the farm another year." He spoke the truth; it was
his valedictory. Though tired as we were, and while going through the
sitting room to bed, we changed our entire plans, and were completely
revived by a communication from Aunt E., to the effect that we were
invited up to F. H.'s to spend the evening. Instead of donning night
garments, we put on our best, and were soon off to spend not only the
evening, but a large part of the next morning. So quickly do the youthful
body and spirit renew themselves.

In this district we have to travel in all directions, and we must now
return to Wright's cross roads and journey northward. Old residents will
readily recall a log house standing on the east side of the road, just opposite
the Marsh place. Some apple trees now mark the vicinity. It gradually
deteriorated until it became a barn and then only an occasional shelter for
animals pasturing in the lot. I cannot name the builder, but in the earlier
years of the century it was occupied by one Knapp, who, selling, moved
to Nunda, Livingston Co. After him came an Allen and perhaps other
occupants. Before this the land had become Austin Roe's. He retained
it until his death, willing it to Austin M. Roe, his son, who sold to John
B. Roe, to whose estate, I think, it now belongs. (Since sold to Wm. H.
Sowls, who has erected a house and purposes to reside here.)

The Marsh place is one of the oldest in the district. Amos Marsh came
from Connecticut, town of New Hartford, early in the century, and marrying Polly, sister of John Q. Deady, reared here his large family. He was

5

a genuine pioneer and experienced all the viscissitudes of life among the Indians and wild animals.   He had his hogs killed by bears and was himself pursued by wolves.   He entertained the vagrant Indian and reclaimed his home from the pristine forest.   His log house was burned and his family had a narrow escape ; but he lived through all these trials till 1866, when he died at the age of sixty-nine.   His wife died in 1873, aged nearly seventy-five.   The children of thirty and more years ago will recall the large orchard which shut out the view of the house.   This a severe storm of some years since, completely leveled.   It not only destroyed the trees, but it nearly wrecked the barn and outbuildings.   So from fire and wind the estate has had its share of suffering.   The story is told of William, the oldest son, that being vexed at something, he one day seized an axe and proceeded to level his father's apple orchard.   He was interrupted in this diversion before he had played George Washington on all the trees, but with unappeased wrath, he joined the " forty-niners " for California, where he has since remained.   (He died June, 1892, in Carson City, Nev.)   Of the other children, Roswell, unmarried, lives on the farm, and this same farm bears excellent testimony to his care and diligence.   On the hillside, toward the west, is, I believe, the only collection of maple trees still devoted to sugar making in this part of the town.   There is hardly an old home near that has not its alder spiles and its old hailless kegs, telling of the sweet times of long ago ; but the trees have gone.   Though not directly interested in the product, I hope this " sugar bush " may long continue to afford saccharine satisfaction to the family.   Nearly all the family bear names that relatives before them had borne in the old Connecticut home. Roswell's great uncle, Roswell Marsh, was the largest land owner in the town of New Hartford.   He was the nearest neighbor there to the Shepards, who, in fact, sold to him when they moved to this state.   Amos was accompanied, on his immigration, by his brothers Uriah and Pendar, who after a time went further west.   Coming back to Amos' family, we find Uriah, Henry and Cornelius—three young men of stalwart frame, good habits and industrious natures, who were for some years the favorite helps of neighboring farmers.   Were John B. Roe living, he would readily add his testimony to these words.   All of them enlisted in Company H of the 9th Heavy Artillery, and all were good soldiers, though Cornelius was discharged before the regiment left the defenses of Washington.   Uriah and Henry stayed through and were discharged with their comrades in 1865.   I remember both the boys at Cold Harbor, and they were then just the same capable help to Uncle Sam that they had been in former years to my Uncle John.   After the War, Uriah, named for his uncle, married his second cousin, Eveline Wadsworth, of Butler, and settled there.   He died in 1890, as patriotic and deserving a son as our town ever produced.   I have stood beside his grave, and with moistened eye have recalled many pleasant memories of my early friend, who, to me, had been in time of need like an elder brother. Henry married Mary, sister of William Desmond, and went to the west. Cornelius took for his wife Mrs. Jane Leaton, and now lives west of the Valley. Garrett, the youngest son, married Addie Clark, and has lived for several years in Clyde. He is a carpenter by trade. Of the daughters, Lydia married William Green of Glenmark ; Rebecca, as already stated, married Martin Saxton ; Lorinda died at home, unmarried, in 1874 ; Matilda is at the old fireside. Amos Marsh's old mother accompanied him in his moving to the then west and narrowly escaped suffocation at the time of the burning of the house. She, too, I suppose, sleeps with her children and grandchildren in the burial ground near.

SCHOOL DISTRICT No. 6, STEWART'S.

Nov. 17, 1887—Jan. 19, 1888.

This district, quite likely the first established within the limits of the town, was originally much larger than at present, including an area now supporting several schools. From the outset it has borne its present name, derived from the early settler, Lott Stewart, whose home was at the cross roads just north of the school-house. For seventy-five years some one of the name has lived on the site, and the corners deserve their appellation. Of the school-house itself, mention was made in earlier letters. This building is a comfortable white structure, succeeding the old red one. Red was the favorite color in our grandfathers' days for school-houses. Doubtless it was cheap as compared with any other ; it made the edifice prominent, and as a logical sequence, I suppose, they thought the pupils might be well read. The red house went back to the log building, in which our grandfathers themselves were instructed. To prevent undo hilarity, probably, on the part of their youth, the early settlers placed their first cemetery just a few steps to the east, and used it till about 1830. *Memento mori*, or remember to die, must have ever been before the children's eyes. Alvin Clark, brother of " Priest " Clark, was one of the teachers in the log school-house, and to illustrate the strictness of rule in those days, he severely whipped George Seelye for making a superfluous mark in his copy-book. Mr. Clark was very severe in school hours, but at recess and noon he could unbend. He snow-balled with the boys and flirted with the girls. It is even told that, one noon, when both arms were occupied in holding upon his knees two girls, he ordered William Kellogg, now of Cattaraugus county, to wipe his (the teacher's) nose, he having no hand to perform this very necessary act. What remark would such a performance nowadays excite ?   By a strange streak of fortune, the nearest house was Lott Stewart's tavern.   This, a double log house, stood at the corner, where is now the home of George Stewart.   Without any authoritative statement, I think we may claim this as one of the very earliest crossings in the town.   The Galen salt road went very near this point, terminating at Port Glasgow, and the rather crooked way leading from the Valley to Wolcott must have followed the early slashing of Jonathan Melvin, Sr.

Lott Stewart was a very early settler from Saratoga county—Ballston Spa.   His tavern was the first one outside of the village, and was long a halting place on the way to Wolcott and Rose.   It stood on the north side of the road, about eight rods east of the corners, where now are the ruins of some Lombardy poplars.   Under later usage, however, the inn would be quite too near the school-house.   At this tavern in "ye olden time," the town meetings were held alternately with those at Wolcott.   It is one of the mysteries of fate that with a tavern, school-house and the town meeting, not to mention the cemetery, this place should not have been the village instead of Rose.   Very likely the division of the town of Wolcott, making Rose Valley the center of the new town, had much to do with its growth.   This, one of the very earliest points to be settled in the town, was occupied by Lott Stewart, of Saratoga county.   His second wife was Mary Harmon, a daughter of Alpheus, his nearest neighbor on the east. He had in all two sons and seven daughters.   Of these, James succeeded him on the home estate, while he himself moved away from the neighborhood, dying in Cattaraugus county, as did his wife also.   His first wife died before he left Saratoga county.   By his first marriage he had a son, James, and two daughters, and by his second, one son, Allen, and five daughters—Hannah, Amanda, Lucy, Betsey and Cynthia.   James Stewart married Fanny Lomis, of Yates county, and had one son, George D., and two daughters—Ann Eliza, who died unmarried in 1842, aged twenty-four, and Lydia, who married Richard Armstrong, of Butler, who went first to Waterloo, Iowa, and afterwards to Dakota.   James Stewart had a good reputation as a farmer and neighbor, and died in April, 1862, aged seventy years.   His wife died in Iowa.   His son, George, who succeeded him on the old place, was one of the earliest converts to Second Adventism in the town, and from the early forties to the present he has been the most conspicuous believer in the doctrine in the vicinity, carrying his faith in the Master's coming, in at least one instance, even to the extent of not putting in seed in the spring—he and his fellow believers thinking they would have other business before harvest time.   His first wife was Sally Bump, who was the mother of Lawton J. Stewart, a young man of much promise, who died in 1861, at the early age of twenty-four.   He lies, with his kindred, in the Collins burial ground.   The mother herself died in 1849, aged forty. Mr. Stewart's second wife was Sally C. Cox.   They have two children living—George H., a teacher in South Butler, and Mary E., who lives at home. Two daughters, Aurelia G. and Lillian E., died at the ages of eight and fifteen, respectively. The present Stewart house was long the wonder of the neighborhood on account of its two wings and its unusual size. It is considerably more than fifty years old. (From Mr. S. this farm passed to the late Mr. Soule of Rochester, and from him to Silas Lovejoy. The latter's son-in-law, Alfred Jones, now lives here. The house has undergone several changes, being much improved thereby.)

Going toward the south from the corners, we find no residence till we reach the home of John Atkinson. Most people, recalling the place at all, will think of it as the former home of "Harl" Wright. The latter was one of those easy-going men who like a good story and who know all about their neighbors. His favorite by-word was "Godies," and many a time, in conversation with his nearest neighbor, J. J. Seelye, have I heard him say, "Godies, Jud, that won't do." His wife was a daughter of Jesse Olmstead. They had one daughter, who is the wife of Charles Reed (subsequently sheriff of Wayne county), of Huron. "Harl," in connection with his small farm, was a carpenter by trade, and did much work in the vicinity. He died some years since and is buried in Wolcott. His father, Daniel, came from Tioga county and bought a small piece of land from the old Stewart estate, though I think he purchased directly from Nathaniel Center. He, too, was a carpenter. His death came in 1854, at the age of seventy-two. His wife, Mary Hyatt, survived till 1872, when she died, aged nearly eighty-two. Both are buried near the Seelye corners. How Mr. Wright's name, Albert, was metamorphosed into "Harl" would puzzle the most skillful philologist. He had seven brothers and sisters, as follows : Sylvanus; John; Henry; Augusta; Elizabeth, who married Eben Rising of the Valley; Mary, wife of Wm. H. Saunders, well known in Wayne county ; and Jane, who became the wife of George Porter of Auburn. Mrs. Saunders has three children—one, George, married Leora, oldest child of Hudson Wood, and resides in New York City; another, Augusta, is the wife of J. J., son of "Ham" Closs. They live in Michigan ; the third, William A., is yet unmarried. Mr. Atkinson is English born, and of excellent reputation. His wife's maiden name was Allie Hield. They have one son, George, at home.

Just a few rods further along is the road taking us to Clyde, and facing this, years ago, was a log house. Very likely there is not a trace of the building now. I believe this was built by Simeon Hendricks, a good old Methodist brother, who was wont to say in meeting that his sins rested on his shoulders like a potash kettle. Both he and his wife were short and very stout, and betrayed in form and speech, as well as in name, their Dutch origin. They came from Herkimer county in 1816 to Galen. To this day people tell of the peculiar speeches that Mr. H. would make in meeting. "When night came, the d—l would whisper to me that I was too tired to go to prayer meeting, but I would take my cane and start slowly for the school-house. The nearer I got, the less tired I felt, till, the meeting over, I would trip it home as lively as a boy." Again, describing an experience common, I guess, to all farmers, he told this story: "The hogs were in the corn. I tried to drive them out, but the more I ran, the more they did, till I knelt down and prayed. When I got up I shouted 'ste-boy,' and away they went, every one of them." He had nine children, but I can trace only a few of them. Barbara married Ralph Fuller, son of Erastus Fuller, living nearer the Valley; Betsey was the wife of Peter Aldrich, a name well known in the vicinity; Katy married William Aurand of Galen. There were other children, whose descendants live in this and adjoining towns. From this place they moved south to the Briggs neighborhood and there died. Delos Seelye and his wife here began housekeeping, and here their oldest child, Angeline, was born. Soon after his leaving, the house fell into decay and finally disappeared.

Keeping the direct road south, on the east side of the road is an old, unpainted house, now unused, and fast falling to pieces. This site was the early home of the Aldriches. The first comer of the name was Micajah, from Chenango county. His wife was an Elliott, a relative of Mrs. George Seelye. In the inevitable log house dwelt, in time, Edward A. Aldrich, son of the preceding. At present I have no data concerning him, but I suppose he took up the line of march for the west. The first Aldrich and wife were buried in the old ground by the Stewart's school-house. After Aldrich, came Deacon David Foster, a gentleman of most excellent repute. He had a son, David. Two of his daughters married brothers named Lyon; and one, Nancy, became the wife of Abram Knight of Clyde. On selling, the Fosters went to Sodus. A brother-in-law, Mr. Davis, bought of Foster a small tract, and built the next house to the south. This, from the start, has borne a red color. Both Davis and Foster were from the east, and were most excellent members of the Presbyterian Church. Then came James T. Vandereof from Orange county. This name most unqualifiedly betrays a Dutch origin. His wife was Martha Post, and their four children were born before leaving their old home. They settled first in Huron. Both are now dead, and lie in the Collins burial ground. The father died in 1870, with his son, William, in the Valley. Both of these people were estimable members of the Methodist Church. The oldest son, Post, married Isabella Hake in Michigan; afterward lived in Lyons, and there died. William and John, as noted in the account of the Town district, wedded Emily and Sarah Town, respectively. William, an excellent carpenter and joiner, lived in the Valley, where he died. John has already been noted as dead also. It has been mentioned in my hearing, as a noteworthy fact, that the sons were married in order, beginning with the youngest and so upward. All had one son each, and each wife had curly hair. The only daughter, Rachel, married James Burt, went west, and has long been dead. After leaving this farm, James T. Vandereof moved to Wolcott. To him succeeded Chester Lee, eldest son of Lyman Lee. His wife, Sally, was a daughter of Jabob Miller, who was Solomon Allen's predecessor on his place. Lee sold to Washington Ellinwood, or, at any rate, was succeeded by him. The latter had married Mary, a daughter of Lyman Lee, who died early in life, leaving a daughter, who became the wife of Philip Turner of the Valley. Both of them are dead. Mr. Ellinwood married again, and has for many years resided in the Valley. Till Mr. Cleveland's administration, he was the postmaster. A second daughter is the wife of Clayton Allen of this district. Lee moved to Ashtabula county, Ohio, where he died twenty years ago. Of his family, Judson J. is a merchant in St. Louis, Mo.; and John W., a contractor and builder in Toledo. Both of these gentlemen retain a lively interest in their native town. To them is due the handsome monument to the memory of Lyman Lee in the Ellinwood burial ground. Next we find here Hudson Wood, son-in-law of Thaddeus Collins. He has been mentioned somewhat at length in former letters. One daughter, Hattie, was born in the red house, which thereafter became the principal house on the farm, the old wood colored one being relegated to the back seat, as it were. In it Wood lived for a part of a year after selling, and before moving to Butler. It might be possible to name each family that has lived in the building, but it wouldn't pay. One family, however, merits more than a passing notice, that of Michael Marsteiner, always known in these parts as "Mike." The honors of his house were fully equally shared by his frau, Rene, whom the neighbors called "Rayner." In hiring them for farm work, the farmers rather preferred the nominally weaker vessel, claiming that she could do more work than her husband. He had been a soldier in the Bavarian army, and as such had received a bad wound in some one of the engagements into which the paternal (?) government had forced its subjects. This breaking out occasionally, made him at times something of an invalid, but "Mike" would work as long as he could stand, and so would his wife. I believe there was no kind of farm work which she could not do with wonderful success. As to her housekeeping qualities, I am not prepared to speak, but certainly her two children, whenever they appeared in public, were clean and neat. Rene had very little time to devote to mere care of her progeny, and when the first one was a week old, the mother was hard at work in the field, while the baby was lying conveniently near on the ground. One day some people passing the house, saw the strange sight of a small child suspended from the door latch by his shirt flap. When the second child came, the first one was promoted to baby tender, while the parents were at work without. It seems that the lad, then two years old, had climbed into a chair for some purpose, and, in turning about, had caught his garment, the only thing he had on, upon the projecting latch. In his effort to release himself, the chair had fallen over and there was the infant in almost as perilous a position as was the youthful Putnam, when only the hem of his trousers leg saved him from a head-long fall from the tree. It is said that the baby balanced very well, and that his frantic arm and leg motions indicated great talent in the swimming line. The passer-by soon liberated the child, much to his own relief and that of his scarcely older sister. The Marsteiners were very saving as well as industrious, and in time owned a farm near Lock Berlin. Louis, the son, now married, lives upon it. "Mike" and his wife and, possibly Mary, the daughter, live near Rochester. Hudson Wood sold to James Sheffield and his son, Kendrick. The latter we have already mentioned as a resident of District No. 7. The father, a brother of Mrs. Geo. Seelye, was born in Northumberland, Washington county. He was a son of Dr. James Sheffield, who afterward moved to Chenango county, town of Sherburne. His wife was Lucy Stevens of Troy, Bradford county, Penn. He was considerably past middle life when he came to this town, but his fervor on all topics in which he was interested, and his eloquence on all religious subjects, few who knew him will ever forget. To me his face was wonderfully suggestive of that of Lafayette, as I have seen the same depicted in print. His stay in the red house was not continuous, he living for a while in the Peter Aldrich house. But, coming back to this abode, he died here in 1859, aged nearly sixty-five. He was a life-long Baptist. "Aunt" Lucy, his wife, did not rejoin him till 1874, at the age of seventy-four and past. Her home was with her sons, Joel and Kendrick, but much of her time was passed with her sister-in-law, Mrs. Deacon Seelye, at whose home she died. Everywhere her sunny, genial nature assured her a most cordial welcome. Their eldest son, Willard, lived and died in New York, but is buried in Rose. The latter's son, James, also a resident of New York, is one of the most devoted of the summer dwellers at Charles' Point. (His wife is Cassie H., daughter of the late Hon. Thos. Johnson of Savannah.) His sister, Sarah, is the widow of Linus Osgood. Beside Kendrick, Mr. S. had other sons—Judson, who died in Chenango county; and Joel, now the postmaster of Rose. The Sheffields sold to Charles Mirick, son of George Mirick, one of the town's oldest and best known citizens. He in time sold, and after keeping a store for a time in Clyde, moved to Adrian, Mich. His successor was Gleason Wickwire from Madison county. He is a relative of the Seelyes; second cousin, I believe, of George and Delos. His second wife is Eliza Chase of Hamilton, herself a sister of the wife of Kendrick Sheffield. Mr. W. has pretty nearly passed the management of affairs over to his son, Jarit, better known as "Jet," who married Ida, daughter of Jairus McKoon of Butler. By his first wife, Mary Brown, he had Matilda, who is now the wife of Lucian Osgood of the Valley. (Mr. W. died Aug. 1, 1888, and is buried in the Rose cemetery.)

On this road it remains only to mention a little event happening some years ago—for the next house, the old home of Joseph Seelye, is in District No. 7. Very near the border line is an old beech tree, on the west side of the way and close to the wall. I doubt whether more scars or initials can be found on any equal amount of surface in the town. That smooth expanse of bark was a greater temptation than any boy with a pocket knife could withstand, and so he cut his own name, and then the initials of the girl he thought he loved, and so on till the devoted tree is like the aged hemlock mentioned by the Indian chief, Shenandoah, "dead at the top." The old tree must soon follow the men who have rested beneath its shade and, like them, moulder back. But I did not stop at the tree to moralize; it was to see two boys coming at a break-neck pace from the north. They are on their father's horses, and are on their way home from Van Antwerp's blacksmith shop, where the old gentleman has renewed the iron shoes while the boys switched flies. Did you ever see two boys who could resist the temptation to race, particularly if they were young, wiry, farmer boys? Who gave the stump I cannot tell; perhaps the boys themselves cannot, but there they are, coming at the top of their speed. They are yelling and lashing their beasts, each determined to reach the swamp first. They run neck by neck. Merwin's "old Doll" is an excellent horse, but "Sol's" white mare keeps well along. Who would have won, I cannot state, for here, right by the tree, Sol's horse stumbled and threw her rider completely over her head. The boy is stunned and unconscious, and friends labored long and anxiously over him. Doubtless as he convalesced, he heard many lectures on the sinfulness of horse racing, and the dangers incident thereto. The boy thus thrown became a major before the close of the Rebellion. Then he sat his steed better.

We must now retrace our steps to the road which turns westward and then twists southward in its peculiar direction, a reminder of the early settlers who laid out roads without chart or compass, and sometimes, one might think, followed a cow. Be this as it may, as we swing around the turn and get well started on the Valley road, if we look sharp through the apple trees, lilac bushes and shrubbery, we shall find a small house, which for nearly or quite thirty years has stood in the name of J. J. Seelye, better known in Rose as "Jud." Some years since, with his son, Ernest, he went to Sully county, Dakota, where he now is. His wife, who was Frank Osgood, remains on the place. Ernest O. married, first, Mattie Chase of Hamilton, niece of Mrs. Kendrick Sheffield, and, after her death, united his fortunes with those of Edith, daughter of Winfield Chaddock, deceased.

Together with her mother, they set forth for their home in the extreme west, and are trying to make the prairie bud and blossom. George S., the younger son, who married Alice Leaton, and for a while lived at this home, has also gone to Dakota. It was here that Mr. Seelye made his first essay at farming and housekeeping. He set out trees, vines and shrubs. He has tried about all the schemes that farming affords ; but now claims to find Dakota a much happier locality. He served during the Rebellion in the 9th Heavy Artillery. His predecessor was his uncle, James Sheffield, who bought of the original patentee, Peter Aldrich. He, a son of Micajah, had married a daughter of Simeon Hendricks. His log house was of the most primitive character, destitute, I am told, of windows. He was a large, vigorous man, and noted in his day for his wood-chopping powers. He once had a fight with Roger Barnum, who lived further west, and in the bout he put out one of Barnum's eyes. Both were in liquor, a not infrequent condition for them, but later B. sued Aldrich for damage, and secured judgment to the extent of one hundred dollars. To pay this, he sold from the south part of his farm to Joseph Seelye, who in time sold to his son, George. So in neighborhood parlance the affair stands as "ten acres for an eye," that being just the amount of land parted with to pay the bill. He had several children, viz.: Maria, who married an Eastman from Sangerfield ; Prudence, Columbus Loveless of Butler ; Polly, Daniel Doty of Butler also. The sons, Walter and Micajah, went to Michigan, as did Peter and his wife. There was a daugh-ter, Barbara, whose name appears in an expression which the old man was heard to utter when his cattle got into his corn. "Hop, Walter; jump, Cager; where the d—l's Barb!" (J. J. Seelye has returned from Dakota and lives in the Valley. George S. also came back, and after several years' struggle with disease, died in June, 1893, at the age of 32 years. He left a son, Joseph Leaton.)

Before we reach the next home, we must pause a moment at the site of a log house on the west side of the road. Here dwelt John Osborn, who came from Lincolnshire, England. He had seven sons, all born in Eng-land, and two daughters, Eliza and Mary A., born after coming to this country. Of these children, Samuel lives on the first road north ; Abner and Elijah live west of the Valley ; Isaac was killed by lightning in the house where Samuel, Jr., lives. The father died in the same building.

Further along, but on the east side, was another log house, which John Osborn once owned. He took it from one Stoddard, who, leaving these parts, became a nurseryman in Rochester. After Mr. Osborn, came Daniel Crampton, who owned thirty-six acres, and who built the frame house, so long situated in the bend of the road. Before him, though, in the log house or shanty, lived at sundry times a Drury, whose wife was in some way related to Alverson Wade's first wife, and by the brothers Jason and Fred Wright, the latter a charcoal burner. I am told that a Mr. Hickok, grandfather of Felton and Eugene, once lived here; but the name most conspicuous among its occupants was that of L'Amoreaux. Certainly, French origin is evident here, and from the names in the Collins burial ground, there must have been quite a family representation in these parts, but no one of the name now lives in town. Peter L. and his wife, Elizabeth, are buried in the cemetery; but Joel, their son, is the one with whom we are chiefly concerned. He had married a widow Baldwin, and had but one son, Sullivan, who, during the War, served in the 9th Heavy Artillery. He enlisted in Company F, from Cayuga county, and came home a brevet lieutenant-colonel. After leaving Rose, Mr. and Mrs. L. lived in Throopsville, Cayuga Co., and there died. Some of Mr. L.'s eccentricities will long be remembered. For instance, calling at a house where the people were accustomed to ask the divine blessing upon the food before eating, and, the man of the house being away, the good lady very innocently asked Mr. L'Amoreaux to perform that duty. The farmer twisted uneasily for a moment and then groaned forth, "Lady, I never did such a thing in my life." I don't know whether the lady asked the blessing herself or whether the food was eaten unblessed. As a story teller, he never had a parallel in Rose. Here is a specimen: "I was mowing one day in that meadow down yonder, when, happening to look up, I saw a big buck deer just a little way from me, and to all appearances about as much surprised at seeing me as I was at beholding him. Well, I wasn't going to lose that chance for venison, so I dropped my scythe and started for him. I never had such a race in my life. I nearly ran my legs off; but he finally got stuck in a snow bank. Without stopping a moment, I grabbed him by his horns and then we had it. All I could do was to hang on, while he plunged and pushed and pawed till he had ripped every rag of clothing off my body. There wasn't a stitch left. What to do I didn't know. If I let go, he might kill me, and I, instead of he, would be fresh meat. Luckily, just then I happened to think of a long knife that I had in my pocket. Drawing this out, I cut his throat just as slick as a mink." Any inconsistency in this yarn seemed never to occur to the narrator. I have wondered whether, as a good Baptist brother in Throopsville, his stories were as interesting as they were when the teller was unregenerate. After the L'Amoreauxs, the place was merged with the farm opposite, and the house, like many others, saw all the degrees of decadence incident to tenant houses, and now nothing remains to mark its location. To show how names change in their daily use, it is interesting to know that the family and neighbors forty years since pronounced the foregoing name "Lummeree."

At the risk of making a bull, I must state that the next place is back of us and on the west side. Here early in the century, came Alverson Wade

from the east. His first wife was Naomi Munger. His second wife, who
survived him, was a widow DeGolyer from Clyde. As Mr. Wade and his
first wife were buried in the Stewart's corners burial ground, and as all
trace of any memorial long since disappeared, it is impossible from any
data at hand to tell just when they died, though it is probable that Mr. W.
died about 1828. Alverson Wade was a brother of Esquire John Wade,
who lived further west, and of Mrs. Deacon Shepard, of the No. 7 district.
It is said that he was born in Penobscot, Me., 1759, and that living near
Boston later, he drove an ox team with supplies to the scene of the battle
at Bunker Hill, where his father, Dr. John Wade, was a surgeon. Later
still, he resided in Springfield, Mass., where his children were born, viz.:
Joseph, 1784 ; Uriah, Naomi, Lovina, Lucy and Mary. All of these went
west. Naomi became Mrs. Jeremiah Chapin ; Lovina, 1st, Mrs. Marcus
Page ; 2d, Mrs. Elihu Drury ; Lucy, Mrs. Zenas Fairbanks ; Mary, Mrs.
Foster Collins. All reared large families.

I have understood that Peter L'Amoreaux, father of Joel L., succeeded
the Wades upon this farm. Concerning him and his wife, I have no data,
save the facts of their deaths as recorded in the Collins burial ground.
John Lee, a brother of Lyman and Joel, came next on this farm. He was
a native of Townsend, Vermont, where he was born, March 7th, 1803. His
wife, Philura Wells, was born in Athens, Vermont, March 5th, 1802.
Marrying in 1825, April 3d, they migrated in November of the following
year to our town and settled on this farm. They here resided and reared
their children till 1850, when they removed to Morgan, Ashtabula Co.,
Ohio. There Mrs. Lee died, April 27th, 1855. In January, 1867, Mr. Lee
removed to Painesville, the same state, and died March 26th, 1881. There
were three sons—Oscar W., who married Laura Lovejoy, of Rose, and now
resides in Painesville, Ohio ; Newton, who wedded Elsie Chaddock, a
sister of Alonzo and Winfield C., and lives in Cleveland, Ohio ; Nelson O.,
the youngest, who married in Ohio, and now dwells in Painesville, that
state. His business is that of wholesale druggist and grocer. We next
find here Philetus Chamberlain, who, a native of Monroe county, has
already been mentioned in the town district. His wife was Julia Barnes,
from the Briggs neighborhood. Of his children, Mary is the wife of George
Graves and lives in Wolcott ; Louisa went to Jackson, Mich., and married
a Dr. Fields ; Philena, married, lives near her father in Mendon, Monroe
Co. His only son, a boy when he moved away, is a prominent lawyer in
Rochester. Mr. C. is remembered as a good farmer. After him came
Milton Town, son of Silas and Polly. He repaired and very much
improved the house. The property is still in the possession of his widow
and son. (Recently Mr. Town has moved the barns to the east side of the
road, much improving the same.)

Standing well back from the road, with capacious barns just east of it, is a comfortable looking house, now owned by Clayton J. Allen. We first find the place in the hands of Joseph Wade, son of Alverson, already referred to. Mr. Wade married Rhoda Rundell in Oneida Co. They had six children, of whom Louisa married James Davenport; Willis S., married Almira Bannister; Lucy, died in infancy; Marcus P., married, 1st, Nerrissa Cranston; 2d, Abigail C. Giles; Uriah, married Lucy P. Giles; Joseph C., married Mary E. Wilson. The family went to Michigan in 1834. All have held places of trust in their respective communities. Following him came Jacob Miller, whom early settlers will remember as a man of stalwart frame, a native of Pennsylvania. His first wife was a May; his second, Amy Dix, born in Ovid, a relative of the John A. Dix family. His family was very large; Sarah, by her first marriage, became Mrs. Chester Lee; Mary married Nathan W. Thomas; Eliza, Samuel Otto; Caroline, Richard Squires, Seville, O.; Harriet, three times married, 1st, ——— Whitesides in Ohio; Emily, ——— Elder, Seville; Melinda, James Quail; 2d, ——— Case, died in Iowa; Louisa married and died in Ohio; Daniel; George C. married, 1st, a daughter of George Stewart in Butler; 2d, a Closs, cousin of the Rose Closses; Rush died young; Jacob B. is in Kansas; Edmund in Seville, O. The Millers, who were staunch Methodists, went to Ohio, and to them succeeded the family of Solomon Allen. The latter was from Tinmouth, Vermont. He always claimed to be related to the family of the famous Ethan Allen; but just how near the relationship was I cannot determine. Mr. Allen was twice married—first to Ziphe Horton, and second to Susan Westcott. By his first marriage, he had Aldula, who married Zadoc Taylor and lives near Carrier's corners; Nathan died in 1842, aged nineteen years; and Noah, who married Elizabeth Playford, of Huron, and moved to Wisconsin. By his second wife, he had Nathaniel, who married Anna Bull, of Huron, and now resides in Cleveland, Ohio, as clerk of the courts; Lampson, who married Augusta Wilson, of Rose; Charles married Amanda Stark, of Wolcott, and as a merchant now lives in that village; Harriet became the wife of Dorr Center, of the same school district, and went to Illinois; and, lastly, Clayton, who married Mary, daughter of Washington Ellinwood. He holds the old farm, and long may it continue in the Allen name. The fact that his only child, Russell, is a boy, insures the succession, unless the fates intervene, for the next generation. Solomon Allen came to Rose in 1833, and purchased the farm now owned by Hudson Wood. When General Adams wished to cut or dig the Sodus canal, he bought Mr. Allen's place, and the latter came to this farm, where he died, in 1870, at the age of seventy-nine. His wife, very aged, still survives. (Died Jan. 26th, 1888, aged 84 years.) Mr. Allen was a man very much respected by all having him in acquaintance, and in 1852 served his fellow townsmen as supervisor. The Allen house, as we now see it, was constructed by him, or its red predecessor was made over and added to until the present result was attained.

Further west, on the south side of the road, is the substantial home of Joel Lee. Here, in the log house days, came "Squire" John Wade, a Connecticut gentleman of the most approved stock. He was, in addition to his farming, a shoemaker, perhaps one of the first in the locality. He certainly displayed taste in the location of his house, near the Rose and Wolcott road ; but they had to bring their water from the spring, under the hill to the southwest. Mr. Wade's wife was Eunice Olmstead, whose relatives we have heretofore noted as living south of Wolcott. Like many of the early settlers, he had numerous children. Perhaps I shall not name them all, but there were : William, who, having married Angeline Lyon, went to Cattaraugus county; Jesse, who married Permelia, sister of Dr. Van Ostrand, of the Valley, and went west also ; Willis G. married Juliette Closs, a sister of Harvey and "Ham" Closs, and, after securing quite a property as a pension agent, died childless, in 1854, aged thirty-three; John, who, from accident and medicine, was a hopeless cripple, and passed the latter part of his life with his cousin, Dudley ; Eliza, who married George Fairbanks and went west, and Eunice, who became the wife of Josiah Upson, a member of one of the oldest families in Huron. As his wife she became the mother of Mrs. Sarah Andrus, Carroll H., Homer J., William and Frank Upson. Dudley Wade, a nephew, and already mentioned, passed his boyhood in the family of John Wade. After selling this farm, "Squire" Wade lived for a while on the Deacon Lyon place, south of the Valley, but finally both he ·and his wife made their homes with Dudley Wade, and in his house died, Mr. Wade, Dec. 24, 1840, aged sixty-five ; Mrs. Wade, Jan. 22, 1847, aged sixty-eight. They are buried in the District No. 7 burial ground.

Lyman Lee followed on the Wade farm, and here passed many years of a long and valuable life. To him we owe the fine house, with its commanding outlook ; but his son, Joel, arranged the farm buildings as they now are, the barns originally being on the north side of the road. Lyman Lee was a Vermonter, coming to Rose from Brooklyn in that state. There were four brothers — Alfred, John, Joel N. and Lyman Lee — all at one time in this town. They were at first nearer the Valley on the west. Alfred, who came first, at one time owned the Elijah Osborn place. He built a saw-mill on the stream which marked the course of Adams' ditch. He sold out and went to Ohio. The other three brothers were interested in a brick-yard, just west of the Valley and near the canal. John Lee we have already mentioned. Joel N. lived north of the Valley, and was the father of Mrs. Chas. S. Wright. All these brothers were exemplary men, and were among the first and most prominent members of the Methodist Church. Lyman was twice married. His first wife, Mary Champion, died in Vermont. She was the mother of Scrotia, who died unmarried, and is buried in the Ellinwood burial ground; also of Chester, who once lived on the Wickwire farm. By his second wife, Betsey Barnes, Lyman Lee had Mary, who married Washington Ellinwood, and died years ago; Joel and Clarinda, who has been named as the wife of Milton Town. Both Lyman Lee and his wife died in 1873, and at nearly the same age; he having been born in 1785, she, in 1786. They are buried in the Ellinwood inclosure. From this epitaph, "Mary, wife of Joel Lee, died February 28th, 1855, aged ninety-three years, eight months," upon a stone near at hand, I conclude that Mr. Lee's mother accompanied him on his migration, and that Joel must have been a family name; we thus seeing three generations of the praenomen. In our account of the Town district, we mentioned Mary, daughter of Silas and Polly Town, as the wife of Joel Lee, who was born before his parents left Vermont, coming to Rose when an infant. They lived for many years in the stone house, a quarter of a mile further west, and here their children — Alice and Clifford — were born. The former, a beautiful girl, died in 1876; Clifford, in 1881. He had married Eva Dodds only a few months before his death. In this part of the town, there is no more thoroughly equipped farm than Mr. Lee's, and the writer has a vivid recollection of the fertility of some of the fields, when he and Uriah Marsh, in ante-bellum days, assisted in garnering the crops. A creamery near the house sends out butter of the choicest kind. Just under the hill is a watering trough, where the traveler may quench both his own thirst and that of his horse, with the purest and coolest water from the spring in the field to the south. In former times, a road crossed from the east and west way, next south, running just east of the spring and along the edge of the hill, but when further settlements were made to the west this road was given up and the one west of Linus Osgood's was opened. It is worthy of note that near the spring, in the early part of the century, was a log house (such houses then sprung up much like mushrooms), in which lived the usual routine of wood choppers, the Bedouins of those days. Here, Samuel Osborn informs me, occurred the only death from cholera in the town. The occupant had been down to Galen, where his son died of the pestilence. Returning to his own hut, he speedily died of the same dread disease.

The last house on this road, belonging to the district, is the one now occupied by Henry Decker. The first resident whom I can find was Elder Smith, a Baptist preacher. After him came Valorous Ellinwood, the father of Valorous E., who married Elnora Seelye, and now lives south of the Valley. The Ellinwood family is one of the oldest in the town, but a full account of it must be reserved till we reach the district next west. Nehemiah Seelye followed, but him and his family we have discussed in our account of the No. 7 district. Very likely there have been other occupants, but the details I cannot give. Henry Decker we have met before in District No. 5, as the husband of Mary Deady. Mr. D. is a native of Dutchess county. Their sons were James and John. The latter kept for some years the hotel in North Rose and died in the fall of 1886. James is in business in Eustis, Nebraska.

From this point our boys and girls went eastward in search of knowledge, and the children who obtained their rudiments of learning, for many years, at Stewart's Corners, knew what it was to walk. To some of them it was a good two miles' walk every day. From the next house the children, like the starry empire, westward took their course and sought their education in the Valley.

We must now retrace our steps to the point near which our lately traversed road began. Almost facing this road there was, until a few years ago, a blacksmith shop, whence rang, early and late, the merry sound of hammer and anvil. Here, in 1844, came Simeon J. Van Antwerp from Rensselaer county; another Dutch settler. He bought an acre of land of James Stewart, put up his shop and house, and was accounted one of the very best smiths in Rose. Visions of that shop will ever be vivid in my fancy. Here the boys of the neighborhood rode their fathers' horses, and what might have been an hour of most restful ease became one of torture, through being compelled to switch flies while the blacksmith renewed the shoes for the hoofs. That old horse-tail switch, with its wooden handle, must ever hold a place in memory. In shape like a cat-o'-nine-tails, while it brought comfort to the steed, it was to the boy swinging it as heavy as a flail. Any falling off in zeal on his part, thereby causing the least restiveness on the part of the horse, brought down upon his head all sorts of objurgations from the irate mechanic. What a hard time for the boy! He wanted to hear all the gossip that the loungers were distributing; he very much wished to see just how the smith's apprentice was making nails and shoes, and he may even have had a little pounding of his own to do at the vise or on the spare anvil; but those cursed flies must be switched. With keen eye, he must detect every vagrant buzzer and thus prevent any movement adding to the workman's labor. If screen doors had been invented in those days, and blacksmiths could have been persuaded to use them, how much happiness might have been added to the life of that greatly abused individual, the boy! The old blacksmith shop, located at the four corners, has had its day. Modern machine-made shoes and nails have driven it out of existence, and where, as in Longfellow's blacksmith,

> "You could hear him swing his heavy sledge
> With measured beat and slow,"

now only cinders and slag remain to mark the site of patient, toilful industry. Mr. Van Antwerp died in 1863, aged sixty-seven. His wife had preceded him into the spirit land in 1857, at the age of fifty-seven.

Both Mr. Van Antwerp and his wife, who was Elizabeth Veley, were born in Schaghticoke, Rensselaer Co. Whether the irritation incident to the spelling and pronouncing of the name of their native town had anything to do with their removal, I am unable to state, but to ordinary mortals the cause would seem sufficient. Their children, eight in all, were born in Rensselaer county. They were: Ann, who married Morgan Dunham, both of whom are dead ; Daniel, a blacksmith like his father, married Margaret Veley and lives in West Butler ; Jane is the wife of Elijah Osborn, of the Valley ; Caroline became Mrs. Perry Barber, and resides in Delta, Delta Co., Colorado ; Lovina married Edwin Van Antwerp, from Troy, N. Y. ; John married Emeline Scott, of Butler, and both sleep the last sleep in the Hubbard burial ground of Butler, the flag over John's grave indicating that, in war times, he responded to the call of duty ; Eleanor Maria married Joseph H. Hemans, and lives in Neosha, Newton Co., Missouri ; Lewis H., the youngest son, died unmarried, at the age of twenty-eight. Following Simeon Van Antwerp, his son-in-law, Edwin, who married Lovina, held the place for a number of years. He had added to it considerably and had a very pleasant and fertile farm. He died in 1879, aged forty-three. His wife resides in the Valley. His children are : Dell, Evelyn, (Ray died early), John Henry and Edwin Elbert. The place is now owned by John Shear, who married Henrietta M., daughter of Stephen Collins. Their children are : Jessie, who married Thomas Gunning of Wilmington, Ill. ; Judson, married Della Veach, and is in Shawville, Ill. ; Arthur, married Mary Joyce of Illinois and lives in Detroit ; Stephen and Thaddeus. (Mr. Shear, who came to this town from Seneca Co., died Nov. 5, 1891, aged sixty-eight years. Stephen, who served three years in the United States navy, is now in possession, having married Maggie Powers, of Butler. Thaddeus served two years in the regular army, and is now in Pasadena, California, and with him his mother will make her home.)

Next west is the place held by Charles Ullrich. The latter was a good soldier in Company A, of the 9th Heavy Artillery. Members of that company will recall "Charlie" as a man always ready to do his duty ; but the hot firing down in front of Petersburg, one day, drew from him this speech, which was taken down by our reporter on the spot, "Uncle Sam might get pretty rich out of dis business if he vas a mind to, for I would give more as one thousand dollars to get out of dis, if I had it." But Charles came home with his regiment like a man, having been made a corporal for bravery at Monocacy. He was from Hesse-Darmstead, a Hessian who came to help, not to destroy, as did the Hessians of the Revolution. He had served in the army of his own country, knew what fighting was, and to avoid further unrequited service there, he had come to this country in 1851. His wife is Catharine Stopfel, and their children

6

are : Charles H., of Wolcott ; Sarah J. Tracey of Weedsport, and Irving
T., at home. Ullrich has had many predecessors, the first occupant,
perhaps, being a Weir, who built a log house. Then came Mr. Freeman,
father of Charles and George F., referred to in the District No. 7 letters.
Thomas Smith lived here, too. He was a cooper by trade, but he was
known familiarly as "Honey" Smith, from his wonderful faculty of finding
bee trees. For many years an old maple stood on the farm of Dudley
Wade, readily recognized as the "bee tree." This "Honey" had found out,
and driving pegs into its side, he easily climbed to the orifice whence toll
could be taken from the honey makers. A man named Sovereign lived
here, too, and I am told the prefix "old" was usually applied to his
cognomen, the fact that, Mormon like, he maintained two wives at the
same time not contributing to his popularity. I am not sure but a Galen
Gardner lived here also for a time. Then came Isaac Doughty, who passed
the property to one Boardman, and he to the present proprietor. The
house, I have heard, was erected just to the east of the old blacksmith
shop and was afterward moved to its present site.

We next reach the farm of the Osborns. John O., we have already
found as a builder of log houses, on the Valley road. The first one is the
home of Samuel Osborn ; but the most of his time is passed in the next
abode, that of his son. I believe that John O. found a log house here,
built by a Mr. Ward, who here had an ashery, where was made potash,
which, in the early days, was a prominent article of commerce. It was
one of the very first houses consumed in this vicinity. The present framed
house was built by the first Osborn, who died in 1853, aged nearly seventy-
three years. His wife, Elizabeth, who, after his death, had married George
Doughty, died in 1860, in her seventy-first year. Samuel Osborn succeeded,
and few men in town are better known. His wife was Elizabeth Oaks, who
died in 1885, aged fifty-eight. She was a daughter of the family living
further west. (Though past four score years, Mr. Osborn is still hale and
hearty.)

The next house is that of Samuel Osborn, Jr. Some rods back of it is
an old log house, standing by a well, which doubtless marks the site of a
spring in the years agone. To the best of my knowledge, it is the very
last remnant of early architecture in these parts. It, too, was built by John
Osborn. In the house of Samuel Osborn, Jr., his uncle Isaac was killed by
lightning, in 1854, at the age of thirty-five years. Mr. Osborn's wife is
Ida M. Ballou, a native of Oswego county. They have five children :
Mamie, Maud, Louella, Corinne and Lizzie.

We find our next house on the south side of the road, the home to which
Lampson Allen took his bride, and here he died in 1878, aged forty-two.
He left two children—Leona, who married Frank Henderson, son of
Eustace, of the northern part of the district, who lives on the farm, and

Florence, who is with her mother in Clyde. Lampson Allen was one of the best of the young men who, thirty years ago, taught school in the districts adjacent, and many men and women of Rose, now nearing middle age, will recall his pleasant yet firm way in the school room. He was a capable farmer and a good citizen. A log house preceded Allen's structure, but I am ignorant as to the builder. It may have been a Green, but I am not certain. (The Henderson children are Helen and Gertrude.)

The western confines are reached when we come to the Oakes farm. Nelson Crisler lives here now; but the place belongs to the family still. Alonzo Mace was the first settler, and after him came Charles G. Oakes, from Vermont. His wife was Sally S. Hills, and their children numbered seven—five boys and two girls. Of these, Joseph and Henry are dead; Samuel is in Michigan; Mary married Harry Valentine, and lives in the Valley; Seth married Mary Lowell, of South Butler, and went to Wisconsin. (He has since died.) The writer remembers him as one of his early instructors in Butler Center. Charles G. Oakes died in 1883, aged eighty-one. His widow is still living in the Valley. (As tenants, John Kellogg and wife, met in the Butler portion of No. 7, have been upon this place for the past five years.)

Coming back to Stewart's corners, and turning to the west, with the exception of an old tenant house on the Stewart farm, we find nothing in the shape of a house till we come to that of Alonzo Chaddock. Reviewing the past history of this farm, there is presented a very confusing array of possessors. The order may be wrong, but, as owners or occupants, I find the names of Murray, E. A. Aldrich, Zenas Fairbanks, who married a Wade, John Lee, Samuel Stevens, Darwin Norton, and many others. Hiram Sprague, whose wife, a Calkins, was aunt to Mrs. George Seelye, came here from Chenango county, but afterward returned. There was also a Donaldson once in possession. It is possible that the above Murray was John N. If so, he had sons, Eron and Halsey, and was tax collector in 1811. It is safe to say that most of the foregoing went to the boundless west, so often named. Alonzo Chaddock, now the owner, is the son of William, one of the very first settlers in town. His wife is Betsey Elwood, of Aurelius, in which town, I believe, Mr. C. was also born. He has six children—John and Marion, both married, and Belle, Dora, Adelle and Eva are at home. (Mr. Chaddock died in 1890. Belle married Mr. Burt Sours, of Huron, and with him manages the farm; Dora is Mrs. Leonard Smith; Adelle and Eva are school teachers.)

Just over the hill is an old house, long used for tenants, and, I think, belonging to Mr. Chaddock, in which once lived Roger Barnum, a brother of Mrs. Benjamin Seelye. He was something of a character in his way. He was a great Bible reader and expounder. Perhaps there was only one thing that he loved better than a Bible exposition, and that was rum.

Fondness for the latter article led to the fight with Peter Aldrich, whereby he lost his eye, and his devotion to the former gave him a measure of respect in the community. His wife was Ann Wheeler. They had several children, viz. : Charles, Van Rensselaer and Mary Ann, who married Abram Wood. All went west. What will migratory people do when the west, completely filled, affords no further place for them to ramble about in ?

Returning to the corners and going north, we pass over a bridge which spans a small stream, the only trout brook in the neighborhood. Having its source only a short distance away, in a large spring east of Mr. Stewart's house, it affords a cool and shady home for the speckled beauties. Up the hill to our left we find a barn, the property of Mrs. Lawson Munsell, received from her father. The place was taken from the land office by Mr. Graves. Several owners followed till we find Abiah Blaine in possession. He sold to the canal company, whence it passed to Mr. Watkins and to Mrs. M. The log house long since disappeared. (Mr. Munsell has recently built here a tenant house.) The Blaines were from Orange county, town of Warwick, where the father was born, on the 17th of June, 1799, and the mother, who was Fanny Baird before marriage, August 4, 1800. They were married December 28, 1820. Mr. Blaine learned the wagon maker's trade in Newburg on the Hudson, and worked at the same while a resident of Orange county, where three of his children were born. In 1826, Mr. B., in true emigrant style, took up his march across the country, having two wagons and three horses. On November 26th he reached the home of Mrs. B.'s brother, Abiah F. Baird, whose home was so long known as the Center place. In the following spring, the family occupied the log house just north of Stewart's brook. He bought of Parmer Lovejoy, father of Silas and William. In 1837, Mr. Blaine sold, as we have seen, to the Sodus Canal Company, and bought of Orrin Moore in Butler, near Whisky Hill, where he died September 23, 1847. His wife, still active in body and clear in mind, lives with her son, William, in Illinois. This son, William, who married a Center, lived on the Butler farm till 1866, when he sold to Hudson Wood, and moved to Illinois, where he is now living in Fairbury. He has two sons—Theron, married, and Nathaniel, unmarried, and at home. His only daughter, Ida W., is the wife of Henderson Fugate. Since moving west, Mr. Blaine has followed to some extent his well-known calling of singing master. In a letter to the writer, he recalls, graphically, his recollections of the old school-house, and of one master, George Seelye, who taught there in 1835. Abiah Blaine had other children, viz.: Sarah Jane, who married Henry Lovejoy. They went to Grundy county, Illinois, where she died January 28, 1887 ; Mary Elizabeth died in Auburn in 1836, and is buried in the Lovejoy burial ground. These three were born in Orange county. Three were born in the old log house.

Cynthia, who married Geo. B. Howland, also went to Grundy county, where she died in 1870; Paulina, who died in Butler in 1842; Christina, who married, in Illinois, Wm. Zeek, and died in Ottawa in 1866. The youngest child, Abiah N., was born in Butler. He went west also, and there died in 1885.

The adjoining place on the north was taken from the land office by Epaphras Wolcott, and after many changes came into the hands of Elisha Brockway. The latter has a fine peach orchard, and a large field of black raspberries, thus entering upon what bids fair to be one of the chief farming interests of the town. In the old land book of Osgood Church, Jonathan Wilson was entered as taking the south part of lot No. 140, where Eustace Henderson is now, April 3, 1811, fifty acres, at 84 per acre. This he must have passed over to the Hendersons, for December 29th of the following year, he is put down as taking thirty-one acres from lot 161, at $4.25 per acre, near where Brockway now lives. Here, on the knoll in the northeast corner of the garden, the Wilson log house was planted. Jonathan was born in Woodstock, Connecticut, and his wife was Damaris Munsell, a sister of Dorman, who lived next, to the north. He came to these parts first in 1810, stopping in Wolcott village. From Rose, he went to Huron, thence to Phelps in 1824; came back to Galen in 1830, and there died, in the same year, a young man, being only forty-eight years old, worn out by pioneer work. His wife survived till 1848. Both are buried in the Collins burial ground. They had numerous children, as Clarissa, who married Stephen Collins; Jonathan, to be met in the Valley; Damaris, the wife of Arthur Dougan, to be met in the Jeffers district; Ephraim B., west of the Valley; Ralph, who died in Waterloo; Henrietta, the wife of Joseph Andrus, now in Huron; Fortescue, who went into the army during the War, and is now buried in the Collins burial ground; and lastly, Walter, who lives in Castleton, having married Louise Whitney. (Mr. Brockway now lives in Ovid, and the place is in the possession of Mr. George Stewart, late of the corners.)

Our road, by which we may reach Wolcott, bears off to the east, and just before reaching a direct turn to the east, we find the home of Lawson Munsell. To this place, as the original owner, came Dorman Munsell in 1813. He was from the east, and came with an older brother, Silas, who settled further north. His wife was Jerusha Lovejoy, of the family living near. His oldest son, Dorman, married Laura Mason, and lives in the adjoining district west; Emeline is the wife of Orlando Ellinwood, and resides in the Valley; Mary married Byron Wells, and moved to Springville, Erie county; Lawson married Lydia Watkins, and has had children as follows: Will, who married Florence Soule for his first wife, and had been for several years in the map and book business in New York, has taken Ida Hamilton for his second wife, and, as a banker, now resides in

Spearville, Kansas (now in Chicago); D. Levern married Emma Falkerson, and is a railroad engineer in Chicago ; Lucien married Mary Housel, and is in Kansas ; the only daughter, Maggie E., is at home. The Munsells were of the very best Connecticut families of English descent. Their home in Connecticut was ancient Windsor. Dorman was born in 1788 and died in 1853. He is buried in the Lovejoy neighborhood. Dorman's brothers, Elnathan and Silas, went to Michigan, and there reared large families. Lawson Munsell and his family have long been members of the Methodist Episcopal Churches of Rose and Wolcott.

Going further north, and almost facing the road we have been traveling, is the home of the Hendersons, long identified with the vicinity. It fronts upon an east and west road, and is the only house on the street belonging to this district. Eli Ward took up the farm, and cleared three acres of land, selling, in 1817, his log house and his improvements to Gideon Henderson, a thrifty young man from New Hartford, Conn. He made his first trip from his native town to these parts a-foot. What grit had our ancestors! Mr. H. was another of those New Hartford people who, early in the century, made what was then Wolcott their home. The town of Rose owes much to their sterling thrift and honesty. It is safe to say that no better blood ever came from the land of steady habits than the family we are now considering. Gideon was long a family name, and our Rose resident was the youngest son of John, the fourth generation, he having a brother Gideon, and we find one, at least, of the name in every generation preceding. He was born in 1789, and married in 1813 the widow of Sherman Goodwin. Her maiden name was Deborah Benham. He was by trade a blacksmith, but the most of his life he was a farmer. He died in 1869, his wife surviving until 1876. Their first child, Evelina, was born in Connecticut, and became, in 1836, the wife of Harvey Closs, and thereby the mother of Frank Henderson Closs, one of the most substantial of the citizens of Rose ; George Wellington, was born in Rose and married, in 1845, Lucy Ann Smith, daughter of Judge Smith of the east part of the district, and a sister of Chauncey Smith, late of Wolcott. He is now a farmer in Hartland, Waukesha county, Wis. The youngest child, Eustace, has always lived on the old place. His wife is Sarah Ann, daughter of the late Jonathan Post of Butler, and, by her mother, grand-daughter of Daniel Roe, 1st, one of the original settlers of the town. They have four children, one of whom, Franklin E., has already been mentioned as the husband of Leona Allen of the western part of the district : Thomas G., who married Georgie Waring ; Daniel W., living in Syracuse ; and Sarah Evelina, at home. The Henderson homestead was built more than sixty years ago. May it see at least another sixty years in the possession of the Hendersons. Mrs. Gideon Henderson had a son, Sherman, by her first husband. This son married Rebecca Brown of Wolcott. He died in Waterloo, Iowa, in 1879.

OLD RESIDENTS.

CHAS. G. OAKS. CHARLES COLLINS. WM. McKOON. JOHN KELLOGG.

GIDEON HENDRICKS. IRA LAKE. STA. JOSLEN.

DANIEL LOVEJOY. JAIRE McKOON. HARVEY MASON. AMAZIAH CORBITT.

Our way through this district takes us to all points of the compass. We must now follow our road a short distance to the east, and there shall take the first turn to the north. A few rods further and at our right is the Salisbury place, with the barns on the west side of the road. This farm was taken from the land office by George Steward, familiarly called "Posey" by his neighbors, on account of his liking for floriculture, a weakness (if such it be) that we might wish many farmers to possess. After Steward came Deacon Miner, and then John Salisbury from Troy, Bradford county, Penn. It ought to be stated that very soon after leaving the Henderson place, we entered the town of Butler.

The next homestead is at the right, and is that of Isaac B. Jones, whom we first met in our account of the Seelye district. He is the son of Irving Jones, who purchased this farm in 1859. Its history is as follows: Wooster Henderson, an elder brother of Gideon, came here in 1809, and made a settlement, taking the land originally. He had little but his axe when he first came; but after making a log house, he went back to Connecticut, whence he returned in 1811 with his wife, Vicey, who was the daughter of Col. Moses Kellogg, of Hartford. He died in 1868, his wife in 1871. They had a family of eight children, two of whom—Mary and Grove—were born in Connecticut, the remaining six in Butler. Mary married Luke Blodgett and went to Michigan; Morgan and Francis J. are farmers in Butler; Vicey married Daniel Roe, of Butler, who died in the past year, i. e., 1887; Sophia became the wife of J. Seymour Roe, brother of the above Daniel, and both were grandsons of the first settler, Daniel; Laura is the wife of the Rev. Daniel Davis, of the Central New York Conference of the Methodist Episcopal Church. In 1836, Wooster Henderson sold to the Sodus Canal Co., when followed a line of tenant farmers, till its sale to Jones in 1859. Mr. Jones built the lime kiln on the west side of the road in 1860. With the exception of passing repairs, etc., the place looks much as it did thirty years ago. Mr. Jones' wife is Eliza Lovejoy of the adjacent district.

Going a very little further north, just beyond the turn to the west, we shall find another lime kiln, the first built in these parts, viz., in 1855, by Alonsworth St. John. It now belongs to the Walker farm, and is, as we must readily see, a valuable accessory to the neighborhood. Freshly burned lime works into a farmers needs in many ways. Just across on the corner is a small house, whose successive occupants, lime burners and others would be as difficult of enumeration as would the guests for a term of years in a given room in a hotel. (Imported lime and cement have quite destroyed the utility of the local kiln.)

Journeying down the west road a little way we are again in Rose, and we find at our left the home of Augustus Lovejoy. This place was first taken from the land office by one David Nichols in 1816. He retained the same after clearing the land and building a house and barn till the death of his wife, in 1831. He then sold to his brother, John, who retained it for seven or eight years. Chester Lee, met before in this district, held it for two years. David Brink was the next owner, from whom it passed to one Forbes, who kept it till 1868, when he sold to David Green. After eight years, Eustace Henderson became the owner. After eleven years, he sold to Halsey Smith, in whose name the farm of something over fifty acres now stands. Mr. Lovejoy is a son-in-law of Mr. Smith.

We reach the western limit on this road in the farm of Burkhart Hurter. This is a part of the Ferris lot and was cleared up by John Drury. Mr. McFarland, a local preacher of the Methodist denomination, probably built the house. He sold to Jacob Bell in 1862. The present owner bought from the heirs of the above. Mr. H. and his wife, Theresa Tait, are natives of Germany. Their son Charles was met in No. 7; Ella Hurter is Mrs. Eugene Akerman of Little Falls; Sophia was killed at the age of seven years, in 1863, by the power rod of a threshing machine; Mary. Mr. Hurter was a soldier in the 90th N. Y.

Again must we return to our corners, and this time journey toward the east. The first place we find is that of Chester Ellinwood. Here was made the very first settlement in the district, if not in the town. Alpheus Harmon came from Ballston Spa, Saratoga Co., as early as 1805. His house was near the large spring, southeast of the present mansion. Of him I am able to state only that he went to Cattaraugus Co., having sold to Abiah F. Baird. Mr. B. was a native of Warwick, Orange Co., N. Y., where he was born September 3d, 1792. He married Lany Farshee, a native of New Jersey, born July 20th, 1800. From Rose they moved to Montezuma, where Mr. Baird died July 18th, 1848. Mrs. B. died November 24th, 1868. There were eight children, of whom Mary Jane married John Morrison, and died near Adrian, Mich., in 1868; Catharine, the wife of Philip Martin, lives in New Hope, Cayuga Co.; John F. married Mary Hicks and died at Walnut Grove, Minn., 1887; Sarah, as the wife of A. J. Sanders, lives in Auburn; David F., who married Isabel Green, resides in Fentonville, Mich.; Thomas B. married Mary Ellen Bachman and lives in Seneca Falls; Martin V. married Cynthia French and dwells in Dexter, Mich.; William B. married Caroline Emorick, and both died in Auburn in 1875. Baird transferred to Moses Wisner, who was a native of Orange county, N. Y.—born August 24th, 1767. His wife was Dorotha Howell, who was born May 29th, 1776, in Southampton, Long Island. Her family has been identified with the island for two hundred and fifty years. Mr. and Mrs. Wisner were married in Florida, Orange Co. They resided for a time in Amity, the same county, where all their children, save Elizabeth, were born. Afterward they moved to the Huron part of the town of Wolcott and thence to Rose. We have already seen them on the Lounsbury farm in District No. 7. From Rose they went to Monroe county, where Mr. Wisner died. His wife eventually died in Rochester, at the home of her daughter, Mrs. Shepard. Of their eleven children, John W., Mehitable, Moses and Amanda died in infancy; Temperance, who became Mrs. Shepard, is now living in Penn Yan; Sarah is the widow of Austin Roe, of Butler, and lives in Wolcott; Charlotte, the widow of Brewster Roe, lives in Penfield; Elizabeth, widow of Willis Roe, died in 1883; James T. died about 1875; Jesse O. is living in Brantford, Canada, while Charles H. died in 1855, in Penfield. A noteworthy fact in connection with this family is that three of the surviving sisters married three brothers, Roe, of Butler. The family was noted, among all acquaintances, for the exceeding good nature of all its members. Then came Nathaniel Center, who dwelt here, or in this vicinity, till his death, in 1845, at the age of fifty-six, leaving a family of three boys and as many daughters. It should be stated that Mr. Center and family left the place for two years, occupying the stone house farm to the northeast, in the town of Butler, where he died. Mr. Center was born in Washington county, N. Y., in 1788, where, in 1828, he married Mary Dewey, who was born in Massachusetts in 1805. They began their married life in Washington county, residing there about nine years, and there their first three children were born. It was in the winter of '36-7 that they came to this town, and fitted into this highly respectable neighborhood. Here three more children were born. After Mr. Center's death his widow returned to the Rose farm and continued there till 1866, when she removed to Ottawa, Ill., where three of her children had preceded her, and there she died in 1885. Of the children, the eldest, Mary Helen, married William Blaine, of Butler, in 1851, living now in Fairbury, Livingston Co., Ill., and having three children. Mr. Blaine was one of the most noted singing masters who ever sang the scale in these towns. The Blaines have already been sketched. The second child, Hallet C., married Harriet Hall, of Huron, and with their two children resides in Pittwood, Iroquois Co., Ill. The third, John H., went to Illinois in 1856, there marrying Sarah Price. He has one son and lives near Ottawa, LaSalle Co. Dorr D. migrated in 1858, but returned to New York to marry an old schoolmate, Harriet, daughter of Solomon Allen. They have four children and are residents of Ottawa. Eliza D. went to Illinois in 1861 and lives in Ottawa. Harriet I. followed her brother and sisters in 1860, and became the wife of C. B. Pendleton, of Grand Ridge, LaSalle Co. Our Centers were relatives of the Butler family of the same name, Leonard, the father of Ganesvoort and Gipson Center being an elder brother of Nathaniel. Charles Allen, son of Solomon Allen, came next in order and lived here some years. As we have already seen, his home is now in Wolcott. Successive owners have been Jotham Post, of Butler, Wm. Southwick, Wm. Niles and the

present proprietor, Chester Ellinwood. Mr. Ellinwood has been one of the
few democratic supervisors whom the town has had. His childhood was
passed on the farm now owned by Ensign Wade. His wife is Mary E.
Phillips of Newark. Their first child, Irene P., died in 1884, aged fourteen years. Their children, living, are Mary Louise, John C., Robert and
Chester E.

The next house, on the north side of the road, was built by Dell Jones.
After him it has had owners or occupants as follows: George Atkinson,
Chas. Reed, Chas. Whitney, George Rote, Edward Boon and Wm. Pitts.

On the south side of the way is the home of Henry Benjamin, built by
himself. He has already received mention in our account of the Town
district. The stream, close at hand, flows from the spring near which
Alpheus Harmon located his log house.

We now come to the place long associated with the name of Smith. It
was orginally taken up by Luther Wheeler about 1810. His wife, Lucy
Rundell, was a sister of Mrs. Joseph Wade. They were from Fairfield,
Ct. They had three daughters and six sons. The youngest, Elizabeth,
married John Harmon, son of Alphens, and lived where Benjamin is.
Another daughter, Anna, was Mrs. Ransom Ward. They went to Cattaraugus Co. The name, too, of Samuel Miller is connected with a part of the
farm, also that of widow Starke. It would seem that the Smiths held what
afterward formed two farms, those north and south of the road. Chauncey
Smith, or, as he was generally called, Judge Smith, was born May 4th,
1785, in Suffield, Conn., and came to Butler, February, 1832. His wife
was Priscilla Pinney. They lived here for many years, having a family
noted for intelligence and worth. Judge S. died on the farm August 8th,
1853. His wife died in Flint, Michigan, December 20th, 1877, at the age
of eighty-six. They were most exemplary members of the Presbyterian
Church in Rose. Their children were numerous. Matilda and Adeliza
died in childhood, and are buried with their parents in the Collins burial
ground. Cordelia married Joseph Crawford and is dead ; Ruth is the wife
of Rev. Thomas Wright, of Fenton, Michigan ; Melissa, the widow of Rev.
Milton Wells, resides in Jamestown, Dakota ; Lucy Ann married George
W. Henderson, of the north part of the same school district, and lives now
in Hartland, Wisconsin ; two other daughters, Sally and Lydia, are dead ;
Chauncey married Martha Wilder, and for many years was the most successful merchant in Wolcott ; he is now in Dakota — a railroad contractor ;
his home is in Jameston, No. Dakota ; Thaddeus took Frank Kingsbury
for his wife, and is a resident of Flint, Michigan (Died in 1889) ; Silas
N. is dead. To the Smiths succeeded one Lampson, then Silas Lovejoy,
Henry Benjamin and John Weeks, who, though still residing there, has
sold to Welthea Talcott, so the two farms are again united.

Our last residence in this direction is the home of Miss Welthea Talcott,
whose parents bought the Elder Daniel Waldo farm. The elder and his

son, Egbert, had bought of Chauncey Smith. This was in the time when clergymen tilled farms as well as preached. Daniel Waldo's history would tell us almost the whole story of the early ecclesiastical history of western New York. A native of Connecticut, he was graduated at Yale in 1788, and from that date to the time of his death was constant in his efforts for good. He was for several years settled over the Presbyterian Church in the Valley. He lived to be more than a hundred years old, dying in 1864, in Syracuse. I heard him preach in Fulton in 1863, he then being more than a century old. He was blind, but when he was led into the pulpit he had no trouble in proving that it was not a case of the blind leading the blind in any harmful sense. For several years he was the oldest survivor of the graduates of Yale. I have understood that he married my great grand-parents, Deacon Shepard and wife, and that he preached at the funeral of the deacon. From Elder Waldo the farm passed to Thomas Forbes, who sold to George Chipman, from whom Mr. Talcott bought in 1854. Both Mr. T. and his wife, who was a Coleman, were born in Coventry, Connecticut. They are both dead and are buried in Huron. Mrs. T. died April 7th, 1881, and Mr. T. June 9th, 1885. Two sons and a daughter are buried with them. This family maintained an excellent standing in a neighborhood famous for the Christian character of its people. The sole survivor of the family, Miss Welthea, holds the old farm, and the house, which is a brick one, was built by the Waldos. It is the only dwelling of this material in the vicinity. (Sold in 1888 to Mr. McIntyre, of Rose.)

As members of this district I ought to include the Freeman family, whose early home was just a little beyond that of Judge Smith. The father, Moses Freeman, came from New Jersey, while his wife, Orinda, was the daughter of Timothy and Orinda Janes, of Vermont. Mrs. Janes died in this place in 1832, and was buried in the Collins burial ground, while Mr. Janes survived to a great age, dying in Illionis, at the home of his grandson, George W. Freeman. The family afterward lived west of Mr. Van Antwerp's, as already stated. Mr. F. died in 1837. Of the children given to Mr. Freeman and wife, there were five boys and one girl. George W. went to Bloomington, Illinois, in 1855, and still resides there. It was at his home that his mother died in 1857. Charles A. married in Iowa, moved to Minnesota, and thence, twenty-five years ago, essayed the overland route to the Pacific coast, and has ever since resided there, his home being in Portland, where he is cashier of the Oregon Railway and Navigation Company. In the account of District No. 7, he was mentioned as having passed several of the early years of his life in the home of Austin Roe. In 1886, passing through Portland, I sought him out, and giving him a letter sent by my father, I found him an exceedingly pleasant and affable gentleman. Timothy J., after the war, settled in Missouri, where he married, and where he now lives. Ephraim died a soldier during the

Rebellion. Moses, the youngest son, is married and living in Nebraska. The only daughter, Charlotte, married Alfred Williams, of Butler, and also lives in Nebraska. The last three of the sons served in the army during the War, all in Illinois regiments, and all served through except Ephraim, who died after about a year's service. Timothy came home with a captain's commission and a wound in the neck. Moses was not scratched, though he was in all the important campaigns from the first one in Missouri to the fall of Mobile.

Facing the brick house we find the road with which we parted company, in our District No. 7 letters, when we left Martin Saxton's home. On this road are two houses belonging to No. 6 district. In the first dwells Daniel Evans, who came to these parts from Palmyra, and whose first wife was Calista Cornell; his second, Carrie Keisler, of Huron. This place also has changed owners frequently. The farm was originally a part of the Woodruff purchase, and here some of the family lived. Charles Allen bought of the Woodruffs. This Mr. Allen was a brother of the wives of Charles Sherman and Chester Ellinwood. He was himself a son of Ezra Allen, of Butler, and, through his mother, own cousin to the Kelloggs. I remember meeting, some years ago, at Patchogue, L. I., a son of this Charles Allen. The gentleman was a commission merchant in New York City, I think; but I shall not soon forget his enthusiasm over the old home on the confines of Butler. Charles Allen's wife was a Miss Leach, of Lyons, and to this place Mr. Allen moved finally, and died there. One son, Willard T., was in the army. After Allen, we find William Sherman on this farm. I am under the impression that we shall not find William again in our journeyings, but this must be the sixth or seventh time that he has turned up in our peregrinations. Then came a Loveless, Newton Moore, Charles Smith. At some time in these years, during the sixties I believe, Jerome Davis held the farm. Jerome is a son of Paul Davis, noted in the history of these towns. His only sister was the first wife of Eron Thomas. His wife, Alice, is a daughter of Jotham Post, of Butler, and so, through her mother, related to the Roes of that town. (Martin Darling now occupies.)

The very last house in the district is one now occupied by Nathan Loveless, son of Ransom Loveless, of Butler. This was the original site of the Woodruff home. The place was long held by the Benjamins, and was well known as the Benjamin farm. Just after the war Henry Marsh held it for a time. Whatever the character of the soil, there certainly are no better farms in Butler or Rose so far as convenience of location and freedom from hills are concerned.

To him who passed any considerable part of his life in this town, all that pertains to any part of the Stewart district, even though it may run over into Butler, is interesting. I only regret that my sources of information have been so few that I could not give the minute description that I wished.

SCHOOL DISTRICT No. 9.

(Nov. 15, 1888—Jan. 3, 1889.)

This school district is known in Rose parlance as the Lovejoy neighborhood or the Lake district, not from its proximity to Lake Ontario, for that is ten miles away, but from the fact that the school-house was built near the home of the Lake family. The name of Lovejoy is readily accounted for from the long residence of Parmer L. and his descendants in the immediate vicinity. We can make no better beginning than to give in detail the facts of this first comer's settlement and life. Parmer (I think it should be Palmer) Lovejoy was born in Sheffield, Mass., and there lived until the beginning of the present century, when he came to our town as one of its pioneers. It was in 1812 that, with his oldest son, Silas, he made the long trip to these western wilds. The lots that he had purchased were originally taken up by one Chapman, a Connecticut man, who had married his wife in Sheffield. He had made a start for this New York home, when the courage of his wife utterly failed. She had heard of bears, wolves and Indians, and she had no heart to brave the dangers before her. She wouldn't go, consequently her husband had to look about for some way out of the dilemma. He didn't wish to lose either his wife or his purchase, and so finally secured Mr. Lovejoy's possessions in exchange for the untilled acres in New York. Eli Ward, who had married a daughter of Lovejoy, was already in these parts, and the Wolcott family was here. In fact, it was "Jim" Wolcott who showed the new comer where his land lay. The farm was one mile long and two hundred rods wide, thus containing just four hundred acres. There were no roads, but winding through the land was a clear stream, having its fountain head near the old log house of Alpheus Harmon. In later years the creek, for its earlier course known as Stewart's, as it grows and gets into Huron, is put down as Mudge. On the north bank of this rivulet, between two unfailing springs, the pioneers cleared away the trees and built a log house. It was not so great a matter to construct a house then as now. Helping hands were found even in this sparsely settled locality, and there was no occasion to build beyond the builder's means. Says one of the first settlers, "Do you know how they laid the floor of a log house?" Of course I was entirely ignorant, till he, resuming, said: "They just took a basswood log and split it up into as thin sections as possible. Then they put down sleepers and cutting into these they put the floor down as even as they could. Then where the women would be most likely to stub their toes they evened the surface, somewhat, with an adze. A hole in the floor let us down into a small cavity where were stored potatoes, etc., while a ladder led up to the attic, where, if he were not too tall, a man might

stand erect under the peak. Here were packed away the boys and girls of
the family, and in those days they were more numerous than they are now.''
A line drawn from the present home of Norman Lovejoy to that of Alonzo
Chaddock would pass very near the site of the old home. An old weather-
worn beech tree stands nearly opposite on the south side of the creek.
Only a few stones and a slight depression in the soil mark the site of this
home in the wilderness. Returning to the Bay State, the father and son
prepared to take their families to their new home. The father was an only
son, though his father's, Timothy, family was a large one, there being
nine daughters in it. Several of these, as we shall find, became migrants
also. Parmer Lovejoy's wife was Esther Butler, a fit consort for a man
who had undertaken to level the forest and to break up the virgin soil.
His own family was very large, there being in it seven boys and five girls.
Of these one boy and one girl died in their old home. The oldest son was
Silas, whom we have already seen as his father's companion in his first
trip hither. Parmer, Jr., married Widow Dolly Sears, *née* Davenport, and
lived for a time in Bristol, Cayuga county, then on the Brockway place.
Afterward he was at the Furnace, town of Wolcott, and then went to
Michigan, where he died about 1850. His children were Norton, Sally,
Lucinda and Harvey Puffer, known among his associates as "Puff." The
whole family had the Michigan fever. William, the third son, married
Sophia Kellogg, from Connecticut, and passed his life on the farm where
now resides Thomas Henderson, half a mile northwest of Stewart's
corners. From the primitive log house his residence progressed to the
commodious house now standing. His children were Henry, who took
Sarah Blaine for his wife, and built and occupied for many years the house
now held by Oliver Bush, just on the confines of the Stewart district; as
we have already seen, he went to Illinois, and had one daughter only;
Wm.'s second son, James, we shall meet later as the occupant of the same
place; his daughter, Laura, we have met as the wife of Oscar W. Lee, a
resident of Painesville, Ohio; Minerva married Darwin Norton, born
in Rose, and resides in Illinois. Parmer's fourth son, Henry, married
Hannah Hicks, and began his wedded life in the old log house first built.
He afterward went to Phelps, Ontario county, and then moved to Michigan,
where he lived and died. He had two sons. The fifth son, Daniel, wedded
Sophia Bassett, who had been brought up by Mrs. Aaron Shepard, of
District No. 7. Him also we shall encounter in our way westward in the
district. The sixth son, Harvey, married Perliette Higgins. His early
home was in Pompey, whence he went to Michigan, where he married
a second time. His children were a daughter, Mary Esther, by his first
marriage and two sons by his second, Charles and Lucien. Parmer's
oldest daughter, Polly, became the wife of Eli Ward, the man who was the
first settler on the Toles place. He also had an interest in the lot which

is now owned by Eustace Henderson. From Rose they moved to Wolcott, where Ward cared for a grist mill. They returned to Rose, but afterward went to that Rose Mecca, Michigan, where they died many years since. They had sons, Henry and Cyrus, and daughters, Adaline, Mary Ann and Maria. Adaline became the wife of Elisha Chaddock, from Cayuga Co. All went to the west. The second daughter, Jerusha, married Dorman Munsell. We have seen them in Stewart's district, and traced all their children. Both husband and wife lie in the Lovejoy burial ground. The third daughter, Maria, married Cyrus Brockway, a native of Castleton, Vt. They settled first in Huron ; then came to Rose and were for a short time on the corner, just south of the John Gillett farm. Soon afterward they moved to the Furnace. There and in Wolcott they lived until Mr. B. died, aged seventy-six, in October, 1876. He was buried in the latter place. Mrs. Brockway is now living with her son Elisha, on the old Wilson place north of Stewart's corners. (Died December, 1891.) Though past eighty, she retains much of the vigor so characteristic of her father's family. Her reminiscences of the early days were especially interesting. She recalled the fourteen days' trip from the old home ; told, laughingly, of the stopping one night, when all washed in an old-fashioned sink, something, I should think, like a modern bath tub, containing several pails of water. "Come," said the energetic mother, "let's be washed," and, ranging from the babe at her breast, now Mrs. Harvey Mason, to the lively boys and girls in their 'teens, all were soundly scrubbed. They brought with them an excellent cow, for, said the father : "I am not going into the wilderness without milk." "Didn't your mother dread such a journey ?" I asked. "Oh, yes ; it was a great undertaking, but she was so anxious to keep her family of boys together. She couldn't bear to think of her six boys being widely separated, and she thought a four hundred acre farm would keep them near her." "But," I say, "they did not stay after all." "Well, the most of them did," she replies. Continuing, she said : "Father brought a supply of provisions to last the first year, such as pork, flour, etc. He and the boys cut off the timber, enough to allow of planting corn the first season, and what big corn they did have among the stumps ! Then they sowed wheat right after, and they raised so much that father was able to sell a little. I remember a man coming to father and he sold two bushels. It was very high and was worth two dollars a bushel. I recall my sorrow at the man having to pay so much, and told mother how badly I felt over such a necessity. I guess the man was glad to get it, though. Yes, we had adventures with the wild beasts. We brought with us a big dog, a most valuable animal, for father said he wouldn't live in the woods without a dog. Well, he followed a deer one day until he tired him out, and luckily drove him near our home. Two of the boys ran out, and Daniel caught the deer around the neck, shouting to me to fetch a knife. I ran for the big butcher's knife and the boys cut the creature's neck. We had venison for some days. At another time we got a supply of bear's meat through the treeing of Bruin near our home. After firing many shots at him, one reaching a vital part, brought him down. It was a bad place to be sick in, this home in the forest. Why, we all had the measles—thirteen of us—not all at once, or we should have died, sure. Some one had to be well enough to gather hemlock boughs, from which we made almost our only medicine. In some way, we all pulled through, though father was never as well afterward as before. It left him with a very bad cough. Father was not a member of the church, but mother, who was reared with the Congregationalists, united with the Methodists under Rev. Wm. McKoon in his early ministrations. Of course she leaned toward the Presbyterians; but there was more or less dissension in their first church in Huron, so she chose the Methodists. Father died in an apoplectic fit, when sixty-three years old, in 1830. He lies in the burial ground near where he built his first house. Mother lived to be nearly ninety years old, dying in 1858." Mrs. Brockway had three children. William and Prudence are both dead. As we have stated, she passed her declining years with her son, Elisha, whose wife was Elizabeth Odell of Junius. They have a boy, Willie, and two little girls. Mrs B. told me that she attended the first school taught in this part of the town. It was kept in Alpheus Harmon's barn and was presided over by Miriam Wolcott, daughter of Epaphras Wolcott, one of the pioneers. Parmer L.'s fourth daughter, Charlotte, married Gowan Riggs of Huron, and is living still; she has a son, Henry, and daughter, Hester Ann, who married Sanford Odell. Parmer's youngest child and fifth daughter, Julia, married Harvey Mason, and is yet living in the district.

Returning now to the first settler and progenitor of all the Rose Lovejoys, we shall find him, in time, leaving his first home by the creek and moving into a new one on the west side of the road, near where Widow Nancy Lovejoy now lives. Here he lived until advancing years prompted him to make his home with his son, William, nearly opposite. And here, as we have seen, he and his wife died. In person Mr. L. was erect and muscular, well fitted for life in a new country. He had a good repute for determination and for reliableness. Like all men of mark he had his peculiarities, and words of his were long repeated in the vicinity. Once when a party was in progress at his home he conceived a dislike for one of the guests, one O——, from the regions south. Perhaps the hard cider jug had been too frequently passed, and to get rid of him he says to his wife: "Weigh him a piece of cake and let him go." The expression became proverbial. He had a notion that women loved to ride about too much, and he sometimes called them "gad-abouts." This doggerel is remembered of him: "Aunt Anna, Aunt Dolly and Old Widow Frolly have all gone to Wolcott with Uncle Parmer's oxen." The first two "aunts" were his daughters-in-law, while " Widow Frolly " was the relict of Elnathan Munsell. He was the first of a numerous race, so numerous, in fact, that when parties were held in the neighborhood, it was customary to say in answer to the question, " Who were there? " "Oh! Mr. and Mrs. So and So and the thousand Lovejoys."

To get our bearings correctly, we must go back toward the east just a few rods, and we shall find a small, weather-beaten house situated in a snug inclosure. Here, for many years, lived the Pattersons. The father came from near Newark, and was a carpet weaver. Though badly crippled, he managed to earn a living. His house was once burned, but the sympathetic neighbors rebuilt it. After his death his wife, Lucy, took up his work, and for a long time was the weaver of rag carpets that cover many a floor in the neighborhood. Always industrious, but never far beyond the door of want, she passed away finally, in 1885, and, with her husband, is buried in Newark. Says a neighbor, " When the folks around here made donation visits to their ministers, I used to take a bushel of potatoes and other things to Mrs. Patterson." She left a son, George, who served in the army, but who now lives in Michigan, and a daughter, Celinda, who is a dressmaker. Since Mrs. P.'s death the house has been without an occupant, some of the neighbors renting the lot. Perhaps the first dweller here was the Widow Lampson, whose husband, a painter by trade, had died in Clyde. She had three children at least. A daughter married James Phillips, and the sons, Edward and Theodore, married Barbara and Phœbe Phillips, respectively. Thus these families were pretty well united. The Phillipses lived on the farm now held by Dorman Munsell. Polly Lampson died in 1849, aged fifty-four years.

Oliver Bush dwells just beyond. Him we found living on the Dudley Wade farm in District No. 7, but in '86 or '87 he made a trade with Sidney J. Hopping, who had occupied this place since 1872. Mr. Bush's wife before marriage was S. Mariette Stone. Their son, Leverrier, married Florence V. Humphrey, and resides in Syracuse ; Fletcher D. married Lottie Hollenbeck, and is in Fair Haven, N. Y.; Lavello S. married Clara Jackson, and resides in Oneida. Mr. Hopping is a native of Elbridge, Onondaga Co., but is remotely of Rhode Island stock. His own father dying when he was two years old, his mother married a Kenyon and finally worked out to these parts. His wife was Jane Cook, of Butler, and his two children, Ada and Darwin, were born here. On coming to Rose he lived four years on the Joel N. Lee farm, north of Rose. This was in 1862. He afterwards went to Chicago, and thence to Sacramento, taking six years for this experience; but ill health drove him back, and in 1872 he bought this place of Alonzo Chaddock, who had held it only a short time, having purchased of Lucian Osgood, whose brief though happy occupancy was

7

cut short by the untimely death, in 1870, of his wife, who was Eudora M. Seelye. Osgood had bought of Henry Lovejoy, already met as the husband of Sarah Blaine and the son of William Lovejoy. He was the original owner and builder.

We are now ready to make a regular peregrination of the district. The next abode toward the north, for here the roads deflect in that direction, is the present Henderson home. As heretofore noted, the house was built by William Lovejoy, and here he died in 1865, aged sixty-seven years. His widow survived until 1878, when she passed away, very nearly eighty-five years old. Here he reared his children, and about him saw beautiful farms appear, where once was the primeval forest. After him, as proprietor, came his second son, James, who married Nancy Lake, of the same school district, and here James died in 1870, at the early age of forty-two. Thus, under the same roof, father, son and grandson passed into the mystery. James had a numerous family, as follows: Fanny, who married John Judge and lives in Wisconsin; Eliza, who became the wife of Isaac Jones and lives on the famous lime-kiln farm in the edge of Butler; Ella, who is Mrs. Seymour Henry, of Huron; Lewis, who married Emma, daughter of William Henry, of Huron; the next two, Augustus and Augusta, are twins. The son took for his wife Lucy, daughter of Halsey Smith, of the same district, and now lives on the first farm west of the lime kiln, on the most northerly road in the town, though his house is in Butler. Augusta married Henry Wellington, of Rindge, N. H., and resides in the old Granite State.

Next came Thomas Henderson, son of Eustace and grandson of that sturdy early settler, Gideon. His wife was Georgie Waring, whom he married in Wolcott: but it is not a little interesting to find that she is descended from the Lovejoys, her great grandmother, who early went to Illinois, having been one of that group of nine sisters whom our pioneer left in Massachusetts. Very aged, she some years ago made inquiries, through Mrs. H.'s mother, about that only brother who so long before had made his home in the wilderness. The inquiries prosecuted by Miss Waring, then a school teacher in the district, resulted in tracing the relationship. It seems very meet that some one of the Lovejoy race should continue to hold the old estate.

The next place, across the road and a little further north, is the home of the widow of James Lovejoy. It is on the old Lovejoy purchase and makes a very pleasant home for Mrs. L. and for her aged mother, Mrs. Tupper, once Mrs. Ira Lake. From this place she can make visits, long or short, as she likes, to her children, whom we have found scattered from New Hampshire to Wisconsin. (Widow Sarah Jones has come back from Illinois, and holds the place. Her son, Alfred, married Nellie E. Lovejoy; Charles, Eva and Frank are at home. Mrs. J. is a daughter of Richard Garratt. Mrs. Lovejoy continues to live here much of the time.)

Proceeding northward, at our right, we shall find the home of Darius Lovejoy, whose father, Daniel, lived nearly opposite, and here his trade, that of a carpenter and joiner, enabled him to erect a comfortable home. His wife is Sally Sampson, a daughter of Gamaliel and Harriet Sampson, formerly of Butler. There are no children to be recorded in this narrative, though one epitaph in the cemetery tells of the loss of a child years ago. The Lovejoy characteristic of large families seems, in this generation, to be in abeyance.

On the corner is a home long conspicuous in the neighborhood. Here, years ago, Daniel Lovejoy, son of Parmer, erected his house, and here brought his wife, Sophia Bassett. The usual transition from log to frame house was had ; the farmer living comfortably and finally dying in 1861, nearly sixty-nine years old. His wife survived him until 1867, when she, too, passed away, at the age of nearly sixty-four years. Of their children we have already accounted for the oldest, Darius. Besides, there were David, who married Parisade, daughter of Horace Peck, of the old Savannah family, and went to Michigan ; John, who married Jane Weeks, from New Hampshire, and lives in Glenmark ; Daniel married Jane Potter, of Rose, and lives in Cayuga county ; and Phœbe, the wife of Martin Darling. After the Lovejoys, the place was occupied for a while by John Briggs, son of Jonathan Briggs, of North Rose. His wife was an Otto, ¦and after the death of her father they moved to the Otto farm, just over the Huron line, and the place passed into possession of Harvey Mason, of whom we have already heard as the husband of Julia, the youngest of the Lovejoy children. Mr. Mason's history is an entertaining one. Long past the four score years of the Psalmist, he says he is not conscious of any pains nor aches, though we are told that such years are to be labor and sorrow. He was born in Castleton, Rutland Co., Vermont. His father, Robert, was from Sheffield, Mass., whence he had migrated to the Green Mountain State, but like many other early New York settlers, he was dissatisfied, and so pushed on to the then west. His wife was Ruth Calender, both names being of most excellent reputation in the Bay State. Here, i. e., in Vermont, Harvey Mason was born, on the 18th of June, 1805. In 1814 the westward march was made, and Robert Mason first settled on the farm long known as the Carrier place, but now occupied by Isaac Cole. He built near here a log house. His companion in this western move was Jonathan Nichols, who lived for a while on the place now held by Halsey Smith. Afterward he lived on the farm known as the Chaddock place, now that of Wm. H. Cole. For a time the elder Masons made their home with Harvey, but they afterward went to Ohio, where their last days were passed with their daughters, Eveline and Delia. Besides Harvey there were children : Amos, who was drowned in Lake Erie, his wife, Susan Wilcox ; Robert, who died in Michigan ; Alvin, who died in Steuben county ; Eveline, who

married Levi Lewis, and Delia is unmarried. The latter two live in
Cleveland, Ohio. Harvey Mason and wife began housekeeping or domestic
life with Mrs. H.'s nephew, Daniel, on the corner, while Mr. M.'s farm
lay further west upon the hill. Here, many years ago, he erected a
commodious house, still standing; but he did not intend to occupy it at
once. His wife, however, was anxious to have a home of her own, and
wanted to move immediately. It was before the days of stoves and Mr. M.
objected that there was no fireplace nor chimney. "I don't care," said
the young woman, "I can cook against a stump." So said the veteran
long afterward, "I thought if she was so eager as that for a home by herself, I would fix up at once for moving in." And fix he did, making this
their abode for many years, until 1871, when they moved to the corners. The
children were three daughters: Laura, who married Dorman Munsell, 2d,
and lives on what was the west end of her father's farm; Almanda, who
was the first wife of Winfield Chaddock; and Lucy, who married Henry
Gillett, and died in Michigan. Both of these daughters are buried in the
Lovejoy burial ground, within sight of the window at which sits many an
hour the aged mother, who, as she knits, no doubt recalls from the buried
past many a pleasant memory of the loved ones to whom she must one day
go. Mrs. Chaddock died in 1859, at the early age of twenty-six. Mrs.
Gillett died in 1880, aged nearly forty-four. In early life Mr. Mason
learned the house builder's trade and so could not only build his own home,
but he was the framer and builder of very many edifices in the vicinity.
As he is prone to state, "It was my trade that gave me a start." Possessed
of a goodly share of this world's goods, and through an upright life having
a lively hope of the life to come, he calmly awaits the inevitable summons.
Both he and his wife have long been members of the Rose Methodist
Church. (D. 1889.) In the battle of life Mrs. Mason has been no ineffi-
cient ally of her husband. Many years since, he made a carpet weaving
loom for her, and on it she has woven many thousand yards of carpet.
During the War, in one year, she wove more than eleven hundred yards;
but the loom is among the "has-beens"—sold and gone; but many a foot
in this and adjacent towns are pressing a surface which is due to the nimble
hands and feet of Mrs. Mason. (Mr. H. W. Clapper, who married Anginette Munsell, Mrs. Mason's granddaughter, now manages the farm.)

Taking the road towards the east, a quarter of a mile along, we come to
the cemetery frequently referred to. Just beyond are the large barns of
the Toles farm, while across the way is the house. One of the first, if not
the very first dweller here was Eli Ward, who had married Polly Lovejoy.
After him came Silas Lovejoy, Polly's oldest brother. He built a log house
somewhere between the Toles house and that of his son, Norman. As near
as I can learn, Silas L. had more experience in log house architecture than
any man of his day. To begin with, he helped his father erect the very

first. Soon afterward, since the parent stock appeared to be very filling, he put up a structure for himself, quite near the original one. Then came a house on the road still further north, near a spring, and still marked by an orchard and some tansy. This third house was succeeded in time by the frame building, which preceded the house now in use. The old house is now Mr. Toles' carriage barn. It was in this vicinity and in these houses that his family grew up. Before leaving Massachusetts he had married Anna Nichols, a sister of Jonathan Nichols, the first man on the Halsey Smith farm. His oldest son, Norman, was a babe of nine months when the long journey was made. To this first farm succeeded Nelson, who married Charity Morey, and for a while lived nearly opposite in the house now occupied by Eson Young, and whose present home is north of Wolcott. He has a son, Eson, and a daughter, Ellen ; William and Harmon died early ; Harriet wedded, first, Elijah Morey, and second, Watson Dowd, of Huron—thus becoming the mother of several well-known citizens of that town ; Perliette married Ira Lamb of North Rose, and moved to Michigan, where she reared a family of three daughters and one son, and there died many years ago. Maria married Albert Preston, of Huron, and died several years since in Minnesota, leaving one daughter ; Alvira became the wife of Warren Stone, of Victory, and died a number of years ago, leaving three daughters and a son ; Sophronia, the youngest, was the second wife of Winfield Chaddock, and is the mother of Winfield, second, and Edith, who married Ernest O. Seelye. With her children she has gone to Dakota. These children, nine in number, I have been told, heard their lullabys while rocked in a sap trough. Highly decorated cribs and cradles could not be afforded then. No doubt childhood's sleep was just as sweet as it would have been if robed in silk and cradled in down ; manifestly, it was more healthy. After disposing of his place to the Toleses, Mr. Lovejoy made his home near that of Mrs. Chaddock, west of the Lake school-house, and finally with her. His death came in 1877, when he was eighty-six years old. His wife had died four years before, when she was in her eighty-first year. Ebenezer Toles, who succeeded Silas Lovejoy on this farm, was born in Otsego county, October 12th, 1805. His first wife was Polly Williams, whom he married in Auburn prison ; said to be the first couple ever wedded there. Mr. T. worked the overseer's farm and the latter was a great friend of the prison chaplain, hence the marriage as above. After bearing him four children, she died in 1838, at the age of thirty-three years, and lies in the North Rose cemetery. He next married in the same year Hannah Vincent, a native of Maine, born November 22d, 1804, who died in this house in 1879. When Mr. Toles came to the town he was first on the farm west of Carrier's corners, once held by C. C. Collins. Selling this, he moved to Wayne Center, but afterward came to this farm, where his earthly days ended in 1883. He and his second wife

sleep side by side in the adjacent burial ground. Mr. Toles was a member
of the Rose Methodist Church; his wife was a Presbyterian. The first
wife's children were Matthew, who married Sarah A. Young, and lives now
in Gratiot, Mich. ; Lucy, whom we met in District No. 5 as the wife of
William Desmond ; Truman, who married Janette Baldwin. He died in
Michigan in 1862, leaving a son, Truman ; Ebenezer, who was a member
of the Ninth New York Heavy Artillery, and who died in February last,
at the age of fifty-one. He was widely known in the town as "Eb" Toles,
having a more extended reputation, perhaps, than many men of greater
wealth and worth. The second Mrs. Toles was the mother of Ezra, who
died at the homestead in January last, at the age of forty-six ; Julia, who
married Henry Jones, son of Erving, and died in 1887, at the age of forty-
four years, leaving a son, Erving ; Orson, who now resides upon the
estate. His wife is Lettie Hoyt, of Weedsport. Their children are three,
viz. : Willie V., Herbert H. and Orson. Mrs. Toles' brother, Adin, a
wounded veteran of the Third New York Light Artillery, makes his home
here. Mr. Toles has just erected a fine dry house, thus taking advantage
of the march of improvement in farming. (Mr. Toles now lives in Wolcott, and the farmer in charge is George Smith, reared in this district.)

The next place east on the south side of the road, is the home of Eson
Young, a son-in-law of Norman Lovejoy. Crossing the road, we are again
on familiar ground, for here we once more meet a Lovejoy, this time
Norman, the oldest son of Silas, the only representative of the third
generation of Parmer's family when they took up the line of march westward. He grew to manhood in sight of his present home, and the evening
of his life is passed on acres every foot of which he has been over again
and again. He went down into the Lyman neighborhood to find his wife
who was Lydia Morey, from Saratoga county, originally. Both she and
the neighbors familiarly refer to Mr. L. as "Dad." I think he doesn't
resent the name. As we have seen, one brother, Nelson, and a sister,
Harriet, married in the same family. He has had three children. His
oldest. Eleanor, (died in 1893), was the wife of Eson Young, a Butler man,
who, on his farm of forty-eight acres, lives opposite, and has one son
named after his grandfather, Norman ; Silas married Eliza Lake, and lives
south of the four corners. The youngest child, Anna, died at the age of
twenty-three, in 1860. These old people have a pleasant home, endeared
by long years of occupancy. "That quince bush," says Mr. L., "is the
most thrifty one in the town." I fully agreed that to beat it, the bush
would have to bear several bushels of fruit. His life can show the usual
progress from a log house to the comfortable frame structure of to-day.
To no other one person is the writer more indebted for family information
than to the veteran farmer, Norman Lovejoy. (Silas Lovejoy and family
have lived here several years. His mother died January 23d, 1892.) Our

trip in this direction is over, for we now reach the farm of Eustace Henderson, whom we met in District No. 6.

To reach our next range of lots north we can go by Mr. Henderson's, and turning to our left, pass the homes of John Salisbury and Isaac Jones. Then reaching the lime kiln, we take the west road, but it is not until we have passed the houses of Augustus Lovejoy and Charles Hurter that we reach once more the confines of District No. 9. If we are on foot we shall save much time when we leave Norman Lovejoy's by going across lots through his lane and pasture to the parallel road north. However, taking the road after passing Hurter's, we find a comfortable house, having a sightly outlook from its position on a hill. The land hereabouts was first taken up by Caleb Drury. Of this particular portion, John Drury, of Huron, gives a very interesting history. He says the land was cleared by a Mr. Ferris, who, with his father and negro slaves, came from Virginia. To pay men for work done, orders were given on a store in Huron, managed by one Mudge. These accumulating, were traded by Mudge with a Williamson in Philadelphia for goods. Ferris was unable to redeem these orders, so the farm passed into W.'s possession, and from him John Drury, first, purchased. Then Mr. Drury sold to that omnivorous Sodus Canal Co. Afterward the place was bought by J. Gurnee, a Huron man, who built the house. Then came Henry Jones, son of John E., who lived here until 1885, when in April Nathan Knapp of Wolcott took possession. Mr. Knapp is a native of Columbia county, but has lived near Newark, and for several years in Wolcott, where he ran the foundry. His wife is Eliza Caton, from the city of Albany. They have only one son, Fred, who manages the foundry in Wolcott.

Going a few rods west we reach the home of Charles Buchanan, standing on the corner of the road leading up or down into Huron, on the west side of which, half a mile away, we should find the home of John Drury, a grandson of the first settler here. Caleb Drury, the first comer, was a native of Eden, Orleans county, Vermont. His wife was Jane Hudson. The first home was, as usual, a log house, under the hill, where an orchard and a well mark the old location. To these people was born a large family. The oldest son, Holloway, we shall meet further west : John married Jane McFarland, of Vermont, and had six children. He went to Michigan in 1843, and there died. Elihu married Lovina, daughter of Alverson Wade, and after living a while near the Wade home, went west ; Anson married Sophia Munsell and lived in Wolcott ; Caroline, the oldest daughter, never moved to Rose, but married in Vermont, Solomon Wood, and went to Pennsylvania ; Sally and Nancy married Alvin and Wallace Buck, respectively, brothers, of Huron, and both migrated to Michigan. John, a son of John, now lives just north, as has been noted, on the Wolcott road. Caleb Drury, at the age of eighty, died in 1843, and was buried in

Huron. From the Drurys the place passed to Wolcott Blodgett, from Connecticut, who married Mary, daughter of Wooster Henderson, of Butler. He had three boys born here, but when they were small, the family went to Michigan. He sold to the Sodus Canal Co. Then for a time came one DeBow, from Canandaigua. His wife died here and he went back to Ontario county. To him succeeded David H. Town, son of Asa, of District No. 5, and in 1857 we find it owned by Marvin D. Hart, who was born in Junius, Seneca county. His wife was Mary Jane Miner, of Butler, but born in Perry, Wyoming county. Mr. Hart made extensive repairs and additions, and as a leading member of the Rose Baptist Church, had a wide circle of friends in the vicinity. The writer recalls one festive occasion in the winter of 1865 and 1866, when a merry load of Rose and Butler young people made the welkin ring until a late hour. Then when we started away, and were going down the hill west of the house, the sleigh tongue fell down, and we were soon landed in the fence, luckily without broken bones. In the farm there are ninety acres, and with buildings in good condition, the place is particularly attractive. Mr. Hart left the farm about eighteen years ago, and after living in Marengo and Clyde, finally located on the Henry Rice place in the Valley, where he died, greatly respected and lamented, on the 21st of June last, aged fifty-eight. His children are Lycurgus S., who married widow Seaman, and lives in Wolcott, and Alice M., who is at home with her mother. Mrs. Hart's father, Isaac Miner, long resident of Butler, also lives with her. He was born the 12th of April, 1792, in Stonington, Conn.; he is probably now the oldest person in town. To the Harts succeeded the Buchanans, who came directly from Huron, but remotely from Rochester. The father, Joseph, died in Galen. His widow, who as a girl was Rebecca Vance, from Pennsylvania, now occupies the old home. (Died February 13, 1890, in her eighty-first year.) Her oldest son, Charles, we have just passed at the corner of the road, where he has erected a house, in which, with his wife, Imogene Prescott, he is rearing his children, Robert and Hattie. Let us hope that this coming Robert may equal the reputation of that other and famous Robert Buchanan, whose verse has pleased so many. Mrs. B.'s second son, Robert, was a soldier in the 111th, and was killed before Petersburg, June 16th, 1864; Mary A. lives at home with her mother, while Louisa is Mrs. Landers, of Sodus.

Down the hill, eighty rods away, on the south side of the road, is a small farm owned now by Charles Peck and George Wellington, son and son-in-law of Betsey (Kellogg) Peck, whom we first met in Butler. The last owner, before them, was David Wood, who, a native of Vermont, dropped dead some years since, when on his way to Clyde. I am told that the house was built for Silas Lovejoy, oldest son of Norman, and that he lived here until he went to reside on the Lake farm. Mrs. Peck, well known to her friends as "Aunt Betsey," and her children have our best wishes in this new undertaking.

The red house, nearly opposite, and well back from the road, is the home of Daniel Lewis. He is a son of P. T. Lewis, who lives further west. Daniel L. married Mary, daughter of Dorman Munsell, and has three children—Lloyd B., Lena and Lester. The alliterative succession of L's will be noted. Whether, had there been more children, there could be found more names beginning with the favorite letter, I can't tell. Mr. Lewis' home is well known in the vicinity as the old "Holl" Drury farm, for here, during a long life, resided Holloway Drury, the oldest son of that Caleb whom we met half a mile back. He was twice married ; once in Vermont, and, second, here, to Prudence Aldrich, a sister of Peter, of Stewart's district. He died in 1877, at the extreme age of ninety-two, and was buried with the Lovejoys. He was, I believe, a member of the Methodist Church. Though for some years residing with the Lewis family, he died with his nephew, John. By his first wife, he was the father of Adaline, now more than seventy-four years old, who has been all her life a most singularly afflicted being. From her childhood, she has had no use whatever of her hands, they and her face having a form of St. Vitus' dance. Had she been taught to read in her childhood, her later years might have been more pleasant, but in spite of all adversities, she has done what seems almost impossible. Seated upon the floor, with her toes she cuts out blocks of cloth and sews them together, having thus made several bedquilts. She threads her own needle, using her toes only. In fine, whatever she does must be done with these members. She cuts out, very deftly, little heart-shaped pieces of papers, which, with the bedquilt blocks, she gives to visitors as mementoes; no pun intended there. Her father's place passed into the hands of Mr. Lewis as compensation for the care of this life-long helpless person.

We next encounter the small house belonging to H. Garlic. For some years this was the home of Alfred Graham, a good soldier of Company A, Ninth Heavy Artillery, who died in 1874. His wife was Kate Eldred, of Rose. He was a nephew of Henry Graham of Rose, though reared in Huron. His father was Zachariah. A comrade of mine, I am glad to know that he was a good citizen as well as soldier. The place came into Graham's hands through his mother, who traded property in Huron with old Captain Sours. There were fifty-six acres in the farm. The house was probably built by a Wood, a relative of "Holl" Drury. H. M. Smith lived here for a while. Mr. Graham had one daughter, Ida, who married Millard Ward and died in Chicago.

Crossing the railroad we find a very fine white house, where lives Philander T. Lewis, a native of the section of country near Rochester. Coming here many years ago, he married Anna, the only child of Daniel

Tucker, the then owner. This farm was taken from the office by one John White, who built a log house. Then came one Murray, who sold to the Sodus Canal Company, and then came Mr. Tucker, a native of Derby, Connecticut. His wife was Anna Ryan, who, more than ninety-one years of age, lives with the Lewises. (She has since died.) Mr. Tucker died October 12th, 1876, and is buried in Huron, where lies also Mr. Ryan, Mrs. Tucker's father, who accompanied her to this town. It is in this house that Adaline Drury finds a home. Mr. Lewis has one daughter only—Anna B., the wife of Benjamin Dowd, formerly of Huron, now of Oswego. (Mr. Lewis died August 15, 1890.)

This east and west road that we have followed for a mile and a half, terminates in one, north and south, and just opposite the end is the home of Halsey M. Smith. This place was pre-empted by Jonathan Nichols, who erected the customary log house. The succession of owners is not clear, but I find the names of Eddy, Havens, Wm. Hallenbeck, who built the framed house. Early in the century Robert Mason must have lived here, for in his own language Harvey M. says: "I have eaten no end of johnny-cake on that farm." It was johnny-cake eating and hard work that enabled the first comers to pay for their farms. After the Hallenbecks came Andrew Pearsall, then Melvin Knights, from Saratoga county, and finally the present owner, who is a son of Solomon Smith, whom we shall meet further north. He married Maria Wilson, of Butler, and is the father of four daughters, viz.: Elva, wife of David Doolittle, of Huron ; Lucy, who married Augustus Lovejoy ; Cora and Retta at home. (Cora is now Mrs. Harvey D. Munsell and Augustus Lovejoy works the farm.)

A few steps north is an old house belonging to the Tucker property, and long used as a tenant house. Of such it would be too great a task to recall the occupants.

There is one house, possibly twenty rods north, which lies or stands just on the line between Huron and Rose, and here I must remark that all the dwellers on the north side of this last Rose road have more belongings in Huron than in Rose. In fact, Mr. Knapp's farm lies in Butler as well as in the other two. If the line had followed the last line of lots in Rose, some of this trouble might have been saved. As it is, for several miles, these farmers are in two towns. This house, which stands on the line, was built by Solomon Smith, and he slept regularly in one town and ate in another. Mr. S. was born in Wallingford, Conn., and married in Wood-bury, Conn., Miss Sarah Ryan, a sister of Mrs. Daniel Tucker. The Ryans were from Southbury, New Haven Co. They came to Wayne county soon after the opening of the Erie canal, and made their first stop at " 'Squire' Daniel Roe's, in Butler, whose family they had known in Connecticut. They soon came to this place, a farm of one hundred acres. Their children were William, who married Betsey, daughter of Jacob Wright, of Butler—

he died a member of a Connecticut regiment, at Hatteras, N. C., on Burnside's expedition ; Harry, who married, first, Elizabeth Graham, and second, Maria Fowler, whose children are Ambrose, who married Cora, daughter of John H. Davis, of Clyde ; Sarah married Edwin McMullen; Helen married Edwin Gulett ; Clarissa and Eliza. Harry Smith was a member of Company H, Ninth New York Heavy Artillery. Solomon's third son was Halsey M.; then came Eliza and Frances, of whom the former was the wife of Albert Graham, of Clyde, the latter of Richard Garratt ; the youngest was George, who married, first, Armene Lake, of Huron, and second, Ida Sedore. His only daughter, Georgie, is the wife of Ed. A. Bradburn, of Clyde. Solomon Smith, who died in 1875, aged 74, was in the War of 1812, in some capacity, and on this account his widow draws a pension. He must have been a very young soldier ; but no one begrudges the stipend which serves to soften some of the widow's rough lines in her old age. She is eighty-nine years old, but quite well and vigorous, and retains her faculties remarkably. Her birthday is the same as that of her sister, Mrs. Tucker. Her home now is with her son, George, on the Robinson place, west of Carrier's corners. (D. 1889.)

Retracing our steps, we pass Halsey Smith's, and there find the pleasant home of Richard Garratt. I think some of his old friends call him "Dick." Mr. G. comes of that Long Island family that we found in District No. 5. He was himself born in Westchester county, and in early life, in spite of home protests, followed the sea, but when, in 1838, his folks came to this town, he came too, and some readers will remember him as the unfortunate victim of the accident at the "horning" given to the newly married Willard and Betsey Peck. In 1846 he married Frances Smith, and for many years has lived where we now find him. He built the house and the barns, and the tidy appearance of everything is owing to his watchful eye and diligent hands. He tells me that his west line marks the western boundry of the original Lovejoy purchase. His daughter, Sarah, married Frank Jones, and lives in Aurora, Ill., while Mary was the wife of Michael A. Fisher, of Clyde. Mr. Garratt showed his devotion to his country by enlisting in Company H of the Ninth Heavy Artillery, at an age when most men thought duty called them to stay at home.

Continuing to Harvey Mason's home at the Four Corners, we turn west and go toward the school-house. Before we ascend the next hill, there are traces at our right of a house, where, in the years long past, dwelt Charles Lake and family. The Lakes were from Rindge, N. H., and Charles had married Betsey Murray, a member of the family that we found in the early days on the now Alonzo Chaddock place. Mr. Lake was a carpenter and joiner, and presumably there are yet standing specimens hereabouts of his handiwork. The children in this home are Miranda, Murray and Byron. The sons went to Michigan, while the daughter married Wm. Ray, and lives in Pittsford, Monroe Co. With her the mother died, while the father ended his days in Michigan. (Geo. Byron Lake died in Northville, Mich., June 12, 1891, in his 58th year.)

The next house was for many years the residence of Ira Lake, from whom the school district takes its name. He was born in Weathersfield, Vt., in 1797, May 29th, and married Adaline Wellington, of Rindge, N. H. She was born in 1806, and is yet living, though now she bears the name of Tupper, having married a second time. Although obliged to use a crutch in getting about, on account of a fall, she yields very little to the infirmities of age, and passes her time in Rose with her daughters, in Oswego with her son, or makes visits to her old home in the Granite State. (Since died.) They came to Rose in 1831, and here reared their family. The oldest son, Henry, married Rosanna T. Deming, of Newark, and now resides in Oswego ; Nancy became Mrs. James Lovejoy ; Eliza married Silas Love-joy; Wellington, who married Emma Potter, of Rose, was a member of the 111th N. Y., and was killed at the Wilderness, May 6, 1864, aged twenty-eight, and a flag upon his grave in the Lovejoy cemetery proclaims his patriotism ; the youngest son, Hermon, married Anna Houston, and lives in Northville, Michigan. During the War Ira Lake went to the south, expecting to secure employment as a carpenter, but illness drove him home, where he died February 5, 1864, aged sixty-six years, eight months and six days. The house is now the home of Silas Lovejoy, born and bred in the district. A citizen of worth and repute, he keeps in excellent condition the acres so long tilled by his wife's father. Here are three daughters—Anna, Florence and Nellie. (Anna is now Mrs. Alfred G. Jones ; Anna, Mrs. David W. Harper : Florence, Mrs. Nelson Graham. The farm is owned by Augustus Lovejoy.)

Opposite is the school-house, whose frame has seen more than fifty years of existence. The covering has been renewed, but the skeleton goes back to the earliest days of many a middle-aged resident of the district. Passing on again we behold the quiet farm house. It is just west of the school house and on the same side of the road. It is on the Harvey Mason farm. It was built by him when he and his wife were young, and here they passed the long years—short in the retrospect—of their married life. After the the Masons moved to the corners, the place has been occupied by a succession of tenants.

Before reaching the old Chaddock place, on the north side of the road, we must go down a hill, at whose foot, on the south side of the road, is a large sulphur spring. I know of no other in the town. A little judicious care would make the place worthy of resort. As it is, many people have carried away barrels of its waters on account of its medicinal qualities. The water is not so heavily impregnated as at Clifton, but unless one is fond of venerable eggs, the water contains sulphur enough. Passing along a pleasant valley and then climbing again, we shall stand where industry has for many years been the prevailing characteristic of man and woman. It is now the home of William H. Cole; but we must go back many a weary year to find the earliest occupant, William Chaddock. He was a Massachusetts man, born in 1786, probably in the town of Rutland. He married there Dorothy Brown, and there they began their life journey. Afterward they moved to Cayuga county in this state, and there some of their children were born. Coming to this town Mr. C. located on lot 136, which I find earliest assigned to Robert Mason, father of Harvey, but I suppose he must have given it up. The first log house was put up in the orchard, or where the orchard is now. This was burned, and then a second one was erected nearer the road, and also near the present framed structure, which came in due time. The story goes that one of these houses, by mistake, was erected over a boundary line, so that a neighbor could claim it. The neighbor forbade his moving it, and proceeded to take legal measures for holding it. But when he came with his process, he was too late, for Mr. C. had gathered his neighbors and, in the night, had moved all the house and a part of the cellar. There was nothing left for him to attach. The most of Mr. Chaddock's Rose life, however, was passed in the primitive log habitation. He died in 1854, October 27th, in his sixty-ninth year— not as old as men and women live to-day. It is noteworthy that the most of the very first comers did not live so long as their children have. They did not become acclimatized, or the excessive labor incident to breaking up a new country broke them down. Chills and fever was a complaint which all suffered from and from which some never fully recovered. Mr. C. was a life-long member of the Baptist Church, and always maintained the respect of his neighbors. It is said that he had to pay for his farm twice, through some rascality. His widow survived him until our centennial year, when she died at the age of 81. As was usual in the olden times, Mr. Chaddock's family was a good-sized one. His oldest son, William, was born in Massachusetts, but accompanying the family to this state, married Miss Lydia Bigelow, of Brockport. Her father was both Baptist clergyman and surveyor, and in the latter capacity surveyed the site of Rochester. The second son, Watson, married Maria Drown, and lives in Huron: Alonzo we have met as a resident of the Stewart district; Winfield we shall return to presently as his father's successor on the farm; Wesley married a Thomas, and lives in Huron. Why a staunch Baptist should name his boy after the founder of the Methodists is more than I can devise. There were daughters, too, viz.: Lydia, who became Mrs. Norman Seymour, of Huron; Mary, wife of Clark Eldred, of North Rose; Caroline, who married successively Francis and John DeLong, of Huron, and Elsie, the wife of Newton Lee, of Cleveland, Ohio. (Mrs. DeLong died July 30, 1893.) Winfield, his father's successor, was twice married. His first wife was Almanda, daughter of Harvey Mason, who died in 1859, at the age of nearly twenty-seven. They had one daughter, Lucetta, the wife of Wm. H. Cole, who now occupies the old homestead. His second wife was Sophronia, youngest child of Silas Lovejoy, and thereby own cousin to Almanda, the first wife. She is the mother of two children—Edith, wife of Ernest O. Seelye, of Dakota, and Winfield, born after his father's untimely death. Winfield Chaddock was one of the town's most substantial and respected citizens. Stalwart in form, he was just as erect in character, and when sudden illness carried him off, in 1873, he left a large void in the Baptist Church, and the neighborhood. His widow managed the farm herself until June, 1883, when she followed her daughter to Dakota. Now in Okobojo, Sully Co., she is with her son, Winfield, waiting for the country to grow up. William H. Cole, having married the older daughter, Lucetta, purchased the farm on Mrs. C.'s departure, and now manages matters in the home of his wife's ancestors. He is himself a son of Isaac Cole, who lives on the old Carrier place, further west. He is a native of Saratoga county, but has lived many years in Galen. Like all the dwellers on this farm, he is a member of the Rose Baptist Church. Just what the peculiarities of the hill lot are, that they should make Baptists of all dwellers, even of those of Methodist antecedents, I can't imagine; for, lo! there is not much water near. One son, Charles S., is growing up, no doubt, to maintain the Baptist traditions of the place. (Mr. Cole evaporates apples extensively, and, with Louis S. Town, is interested in large peach orchards in Georgia.)

Across the road is the pleasant home of Dorman Munsell. As we have noted, he is the second to bear the name—a son of that Dorman who moved from ancient Windsor of Connecticut. The farm itself was the early home of Paine Phillips, who, a half-brother of Mrs. Chaddock and Mrs. Norton, came here from Massachusetts, and here his life was passed. The log habitation was near the present house, possibly a little further west. For his wife he married widow Wood, whom the neighbors called "Aunt Peggy." She had several children by her first marriage, and to one of these, Abner, the farm passed on the death of the old people. I have been told that they are buried in the Briggs or Bishop cemetery. If so, they have no memorial to mark their graves. Abner Wood married Mary Ann Barnum, daughter of Roger, whom we encountered on the western confines of District No. 6. Like all the others hereabouts, he went west. After several short ownerships, the farm was bought by Harvey Mason, who passed it along to its present proprietor. Paine Phillips had several children by his marriage with widow Wood, and three of these we have already met as the consorts of three of widow Lampson's children. She was herself a sister of Roger Barnum's wife. Dorman Munsell married Laura Ann Mason, and has a family as follows :

Josephine; Emogene, who married Byron Brayton, and lives in Hubbard-ston, Michigan; Anginette is the wife of Henry Ward Clapper, and lives with the Masons on the corners: Elnora married Daniel Lewis, and we have seen them on the old "Holl" Drury farm; the only son, Harvey D., and the youngest daughter, Lizzie A., are at home. In common with nearly all the denizens of this town, Mr. Munsell has had the Michigan fever, and in the Badger State lived for some years; but he appears to have survived the attack, and now lives comfortably in the neat house of his own construction, for he is a good carpenter and joiner. (Mr. M. is now in Clyde, and his son, Harvey, manages the farm.)

Going down the hill and across the railroad, we find an orchard on the north side of the road. This marks the site of a former home. There is a shanty standing now, but once a log house held the family of Daniel Norton. The mother was Mary Brown, a sister of the first Mrs. Chaddock. There were sons—Joseph, Elijah and Darwin—and daughters—Emeline and Mary. Mr. Norton, after selling to Zadoc Taylor, moved to Lima, Livingston county. He must have been one of the very first owners of the farm. Eli Garlie may have been there before him. It now belongs to the family of Zadoc P. Taylor.

Further west and on the corners, southeast side, is the home of Isaac Cole; but it was long the home of the Carrier family, and the cross roads are still known as Carrier's corners. The first holder of this farm was Robert Mason, whom we have frequently seen in these parts. A widow Babcock, former wife of Stephen, was the party, who, fifty or more years ago, sold to Amaziah Carrier, and went to the west. When the Babcocks took the place, the father was living. There were five children—Betsey, Jane, Stephen, Willard and Caleb. Mr. Carrier was born in Conquest, Cayuga county, but of Massachusetts stock. His wife was Lois Jane Bottum, born in Conquest also. She was a sister of the late Dr. Bottum of Lyons, but who, years ago, practiced in this and adjacent towns. The name was originally Longbotham, and as such is still a common one on Long Island. Mrs. Carrier's immediate family came from Schoharie county. The wedded life of the Carriers began in Conquest. From there they went to Huron and thence to Rose, where we find them. No people in this town ever enjoyed more thorough respect from their neighbors. Members of the Methodist Church, they gave a permanent respectability to the place of their dwelling. Though only their youngest two children were born here, yet the others were small when the family came, so here all were reared. Their oldest son, W. Seward, was a young man of much promise, who, after several years' study in Fulton, had begun the reading of law; but the war of the Rebellion found him ready to sacrifice all personal ends for the good of his country. He became a member of the 10th Veteran Cavalry, and as such died in Baltimore in 1862—one of the first whose body was brought back from the seat of war to his old home to sleep its last sleep. With his kindred he rests in the Lovejoy burial ground. Mary died in 1859, at the age of nineteen years; Elbert E., after taking a diploma in medicine at Ann Arbor, Mich., began the practice of his profession near Syracuse, but died soon afterward, viz., in 1870, aged twenty-eight years; Ella J. married George Aldrich of North Rose, where they live, having one son, John C.; Lillie Estelle married Burton Partridge from Chautauqua county, and now lives in Wolcott. He is a Methodist clergyman of the Genesee Conference, though not now in the active ministry. Amaziah Carrier himself, after a useful life, died in 1872, at the age of sixty-two. His widow now makes her home in Wolcott. From the Carriers the place passed to David Waldroff of Galen, who sold in a few years to George Fry, from whom it soon passed to its present proprietor. Mr. Cole is a native of Galloway, Saratoga county; his wife is Juliette Northrop. His home for some years before moving to Rose was in Galen. His older son, Wm. H., we have met on the old Chaddock place; Sidney is at home; the only daughter, Harriet, is the wife of John Gillett of Clyde. Mr. Cole is a prominent member of the Free Methodist Church.

Diagonally across the way is the home of the Taylors, but it was here, in the years ago, that the youthful Robinsons sported. Henry Robinson, the first of his family here, was born in Eniskillen, Ireland, in 1797. His ancestors had migrated from Scotland to Erin in Oliver Cromwell's days, and to the last he was a stout champion of Orangeism and all that the name implies. The mother, Elizabeth, was born in the same place, though of English antecedents, in 1799. Together they sought a home in this western world, and first located in Phelps, Ontario county. After coming to Rose, his first work was done for Gen. Adams, on the famous Sodus canal, and on the general's Clyde farm. His trade was that of a stone mason, and a more thorough master of his art never handled a trowel. Many a foundation securely laid and walls compactly built, attest the reliableness of his work. I would defy anyone to find a specimen of Henry Robinson's work that, through any fault of his, was or is imperfect. If devotion to the Orangemen's principles begets such probity and uprightness, let us pray for an increase of the tribe. An exemplary member of the Methodist Church, he finished his course in 1874; his wife in 1875, and both are found in the Rose cemetery. On taking this farm, there was standing on the corner a log house, and in this for several years the family lived. Then they sold to Wm. Underhill from Tyre, and bought of Wm. Chaddock the next place west. Later, in the fifties, he bought of Wm. Havens six acres of land across the road, and having moved the Chaddock house over the way, there he and his wife lived until their deaths, as stated above. The children of these good people were numerous, and some of them are well known in their respective communities. The oldest, James, married a Johnson of Phelps, and resides near Newark ; the second son is the Hon. Thomas Robinson of Clyde. A lawyer of eminence, he has represented his senatorial district at Albany. Always of scholarly characteristics, he taught and worked until he secured a good education. With trowel in hand, he has borne no mean part by his father's side. As a teacher, he is remembered most vividly in Rose, Butler and other towns, where his school was always the best. As county commissioner of public schools, he won additional honors, and as lawyer and senator, he has still further enhanced the luster of the name, always of good repute. His wife is a daughter of Rev. R. N. Barber, whom he wed in 1863. His pleasant home is in the western part of the village of Clyde, the site of Gen. Adams' old residence—a striking illustration of the vicissitudes of fortune in this land. The elder Robinson dug in "Adams' ditch," the younger owns Adams' old home. Who will dare to say that the poor man has no chance in America ? To-day one man drives, another rides. The next generation just reverses the order. The third son, William H., married Lena Hall of Morrisville, Madison county. He died September 30, 1872, and is buried with his parents in Rose. John W. Robinson, as did all his brothers, worked more or less with his father, but he desired an education, and was for a time a schoolmate of the writer at Falley Seminary in Fulton. Teaching and working, he secured an education, fitting him for the place he now holds at the head of the Wolcott union school. His wife, whom he married in Manchester, Michigan, divides with him the honors of the successful management of the school. (Mr. R. is now at the head of the Newark, N. Y., high school.) Another son, Irving J., died in 1875, at the age of twenty-eight years. The eldest daughter, Catharine, was graduated from the Albany State Normal School in the second class fitted there. She died in 1849, at the age of twenty-two. Eliza A. died in 1875, at the age of forty, while Jane, who makes her home with Thomas, is a teacher in Macedon. The family, from the beginning, took an active interest in education. First and last, five of the children were teachers. Three of them taught in the home or Lake district. The only regret, as we end the chapter, is that those in the cemetery are the only ones of this family who remain in the town. It is possible that the first settler here was Orrin Morris. He had children— Hiram and Lucinda. All went to Wisconsin.

Zadoc P. Taylor, who succeeded the Underhills, found the log house still there. He built the frame house and the blacksmith shop on the corner, where he long worked at his trade. His wife was Aldula Allen, oldest daughter of Solomon Allen of the Stewart district. Both husband and wife were natives of Vermont, where the former was born in Pawlet, in 1800. He died in 1881. To them were born three children—Geliza, who now (a Reed) lives in Savannah ; Ruth, who, with her mother, holds the

8

old place; and Allen, who, having married Elizabeth Lund, lives on the Clyde road.   Ruth has been for many years a teacher, having had exceptional early advantages at Oberlin College in Ohio.   She has recently married William L. Brown of Orleans county.   The Taylors also bought the Robinson place north of the road, and there Allen T. built the house now standing.   (Mrs. T. has since died, and to the Browns has come a daughter, Aldula.)

To the next place opposite, we have already had an introduction as the home of the Robinsons, from whom it passed to George Smith, the present owner, and him and his we met when visiting the family of Solomon Smith. William Havens, who once lived here and in other places in the district, came from Cato.   He had two sons and several daughters.   One of these married Elias Wood, who taught the first school in the district.   He afterward became a Baptist minister.   A man by the name of Mandigo also lived here.   He moved over to the Roger Barnum place in District No. 6, and there died.

After crossing the road again, we find the site of the house which Wm. Chaddock, 2d, built many years since, though it succeeded a log house which he constructed after leaving the paternal farm.   He had here twenty acres, and these he held until he bought and built opposite the Grahams, further west.   Subsequently he bought and managed the grist mill in Glenmark.   After selling that he moved to the Valley, and there died, in 1883.   His widow, whom we have met as Lydia Bigelow, lives in the Valley home with her daughter, Mrs. Cephas Bishop.   His children are Sarah, mentioned above as Mrs. Bishop; Jared, who married Miriam Durfee of Marion, and lives on the Samuel Garlic place, west of the village. (Now in the Valley.)   He was a member of the 67th N. Y. during the War.   Judson has been twice married, first to Addie Hoyt of Weedsport, a cousin of Mrs. Orson Toles, and second to Katie Cuyler of Cato, another cousin of Mrs. T.   His home also is west of the Valley.   The youngest, Rosalie, is at home with her mother and sister.   William Chaddock was a reputable, reliable citizen, and it goes without saying that he and his were or are all Baptists.   From Mr. Chaddock the farm passed, first to Henry Robinson, and finally to the Taylors, who now own it.

Only a short distance beyond is the house built years ago by Ebenezer Toles, who, when he took the place, found there a log house, built likely by Joel Mudge.   Of the former I wrote in connection with the Orson Toles farm.   Mr. Toles sold to Josias Vincent, who now lives in Clyde.   After Vincent came Columbus C. Collins, whom we have met repeatedly in District No. 7 and elsewhere.   Collins was a dry joker at times, and to the writer's brother he once said, standing in his porch :   "You see, we have Biblical surroundings.   Over there is Shadrack (Chaddock), yonder is a mere shack (pointing to a log house), and here—well, here to bed we go."

Since Collins' day there have been many possessors, as Ambrose Copeman, who died there. He was a son-in-law of J. Baker, who lives further west. Thomas Robinson came next, then John Barrick, Alonzo Streeter and Robert Jeffers, from whom it passed to John York of North Rose, who still holds it.

Our course is ended in this direction, and we must come back to the corners. Here we shall journey to the north through a valley with a stretch of woods at our left. The road is between the old lots 134 on the west, and 135 to the east. We shall go just into Huron, where the road divides lots 114 and 115; i. e., the lower part of these lots is in the town of Rose, the greater part in Huron. After climbing the hill, we find at our right evidence of industry and thrift in the pleasant home of Edmund G. Smith. The earliest trace of ownership that I can find is that of Darwin Norton, who probably took the place from the land office. Norton has been met as a member of the family west of the first William Chaddock. His wife was a Lovejoy. Then came Alonzo Chaddock, during whose ownership the framed house was built, and with him his brother-in-law, Frank De Long, died. He sold to S. Garlic, and he to Deacon Guthrie. The latter's daughter, Louisa, is the wife of Chas. Deady of District No. 5. Then came Mr. Smith, the present owner. He was born in Nottinghamshire, England, and came to this country in 1850. For some years he traveled with circuses and menageries, among others that of Van Amburg, where I suppose he repeatedly "saw the elephant go round." It was in 1871 that he came to this place, where he keeps things in apple-pie order. No circus around him now. His wife was Elizabeth Livermore, a widow whose maiden name was Parker. Having no children, they give a home to their niece, Eliza, a daughter of Mr. Smith's brother, who died in England. (Married, Sept., '93, to Samuel V. King.)

There is yet one place before we reach Huron. We shall find it a few rods beyond E. G. Smith's, on the west side. There are many years separating us from Orrin Morris, who, I have learned, after selling on the corners, came up here, pre-empted twenty-five acres of land and built his log house, which he sold to the widow of Paine Phillips. Then came names as Hurlburt, C. C. Collins, who joined the farm to his, Turner, then Brunney, an Englishman, whose foster son, James, of the 3d N. Y. Artillery, lies in the Lovejoy burial ground. To Brunney, who went to Michigan, succeeded John Richardson, a native of Queens county, Ireland. He married, long since, Diana Plunket, as good a name as Erin ever produced. They have four sons—John William, Irving, Frank and George—and one daughter, Sarah Jane. At the age of seventy-three, for he was born August 6, 1815, he tills his glebe, and waits the aid that government should give him for injuries sustained in the War. Already passed the age of military duty, he was a soldier in the 3d Light Artillery.

Going across the line into Huron, we come to the home of John Briggs.
He is a son of the late Jonathan Briggs of North Rose. The farm was long
the home of Samuel Otto, whose wife was Eliza Miller. Mr. Otto had rented
his farm and was living in the Valley. In the winter of 1870, while on
the farm, he was killed by his tenant, Walter Graham. The latter died in
Auburn prison years ago. Otto's two sons were in the army; James, of
the 10th Cavalry, died in Andersonville; Guilford, of the 6th Cavalry,
was shot while acting as a scout; one daughter is Mrs. Barrick of North
Rose; the other is Mrs. Briggs. The Briggs children are Eliza, who
married Nathan Turner of Sodus; Olive, who is Mrs. Thomas Welch of
North Rose; and Jonathan F., a lad at home. Mr. Otto was Lyons born,
one of sixteen children born to James Otto, who had moved from Pennsylvania in 1796.

We are not quite through with this district yet, for going south from
Carrier's corners we shall find, on the west side of the road, the farm of
Avery Gillett. As early an occupant as we can find here was Russell
Morris, brother of Orrin Morris, the predecessor of Henry Robinson, at
the corners. The name is all that I have. It was his log house, into which
John Gillett moved when he grew tired of living with his uncle, Asahel.
He was born in Fort Ann, Washington county, and when twenty-three
years old came to this town to live with his uncle, but the combination
not proving a happy one, they separated and the nephew came here. His
wife was Clarissa Jane Rich of the same township. From the log beginning to the present structure, the usual progress was made. Here they
reared their children, and here they lived till war times, when they moved
to the Valley, where Mr. Gillett died in 1866, aged fifty-nine years. During his life he enjoyed the highest respect of all his acquaintances. He
was a devoted and invaluable member of the Baptist Church. He was an
intimate friend of the writer's grandfather, George Seelye, and they were
frequent visitors at each other's home. I can readily recall his cheery
face, and for "Auld Lang Syne," forgive him for calling me "Bub" when
helping him harness his horse. He and grandfather, on one hot August
day in 1863, held the foot of the ladder and cheerfully discussed politics
and religion, while I turned every screw in the blinds of the Baptist
Church—those long blinds that recently came down when the church was
made over. His widow subsequently married Justin Durfee of Palmyra,
the father of the wives of Jared and Jefferson Chaddock. After his death
she became the second wife of Gansevoort Center of Butler. Since his death
she has continued to live in the village. When John Gillett left his farm, his
son, Avery, was left at the head of affairs, and in his hands it still remains.
The children of John and Jane Gillett were Melvin, who married Mabel
Young, a grand-daughter of Benjamin Seelye. He moved to Iowa, and
there died, leaving a daughter, Ella. The writer remembers Melvin as an

excellent teacher, and has great pleasure in paying this inadequate tribute
to his memory. The second son was Avery, who married Augusta Jakeway, and lives in Clyde now. They have one son, John C. Avery was
in the army—the 9th Heavy Artillery. The next son, John Henry, we
have met as the husband of Lucy Mason, and as such a resident in Michigan. Charles married Sarah Bowle of Huron. He was a good soldier in
the 90th New York. He died in 1867, in his twenty-fifth year, and is
buried in the Ellinwood enclosure. Mark, the youngest son, married
Cassie Hoffman of Clyde. For a time he lived on the Van Antwerp place.
He died several years ago, leaving two sons. Southward a grass-grown
depression attracts attention, and I find that thence rock was taken years
since by John Gillett for his adjacent lime kiln, and by the consequent
income was he enabled to pay for his farm. (Marcus Baker, a nephew of
Julius, is in charge now, 1893. He married Mary D. Genung, and
their children are William G., Maud M., Benjamin and a boy baby.)

Still further south and on the same side of the road is a small house
marking the site of the early Crydenwise property. It is probable that the
family came from Saratoga county, where Issac Crydenwise was married to
Eleanor, daughter of John Covey, who took up the old Mirick place on the
Clyde road, now the property of F. H. Closs. Mr. Crydenwise was of
Dutch extraction; his wife of New England stock. They early moved to
Geneseo, where their children were born, and whence the husband enlisted
as a soldier for the War of 1812. He, however, sickened and came home
to die. The children were: Isaac, Jr., who married Sophia Thomas, and
died in 1831, in his thirty-first year. He was buried in the Rose cemetery.
His widow became the wife of Dr. J. J. Dickson. The other children were
daughters, the oldest, Polly, who married Davis Hand, and finally died in
Oakland county, Michigan; Clarissa became the wife of Heman Foster,
and died in Indiana; Abigail married Aaron Foster, and died in Illinois;
Rachel was Mrs. John Fink, and died in Iowa, while Olive, sole survivor,
became the wife of John Sherman in 1827, and lives in Joppa, Calhoun
county, Michigan. Widow Crydenwise, first, married for her second husband Abraham Marsten, also of Saratoga county, and to them was born a
son, Abraham, Jr. Mrs. Amos Dorris was a niece of Mrs. Marsten. This
place was held by Dr. Dickson for many years, and from him or his heirs
it passed to Avery Gillett. Near the John Gillett lime kiln Jos. Boynton,
Sr., built a log house in 1833. He sold to Eli Garlick, who was a blacksmith, and had a small shop near, where work for the neighbors was done.
Through Elder, Marsten, Miner, etc., the place passed to A. Gillett.

The end of this district is reached. In area it is one of the largest in
the town, but like the other outlying ones, it does not have the school
population of years ago. Readers have noticed how the dwellers here, as
elsewhere in town, having gone to school together, there made acquaint-

ances that subsequently ripened into matrimony. Emigration has taken its—I am almost disposed to say—victims to the west, whence, I have no doubt, longing eyes have often been turned to the Lovejoy neighborhood.

SCHOOL DISTRICT No. 3, OR THE LYMAN DISTRICT.

January 24—April 11, 1889.

In our rambles about Rose this is the first school district that we have reached lying entirely in the town, all the others having bordered on adjacent towns. To the dwellers near the location of the district no description is needed, but for those living remote, it may be stated that it lies south of the old Lamb's corners, now North Rose section, west of Stewart's corners, north of the Valley and east of the Covell district. To enter it, we may as well go north from Ensign Wade's, past the old home of Ellis Ellinwood, that of Theodore McWharf, and our first halt will be at the house of the William Welch estate. Like many places in the neighborhood, it has seen many changes. In fact, in the district there are only four estates or parts of original purchases that remain in the families of the first proprietors. This section was taken up by Asahel Gillett, Sr., and Samuel Hand, from whom it passed in turn to Samuel Southwick, Ira and Hiram Mirick and Thomas Bamborough. An early name associated with this place is that of Alonzo Mace, and it is a name only. Ralph Fuller owned it for a while. The land attached was at first scarcely more than a garden spot. Then came Moses Carr as owner, though he lived in the next house north. Thomas J. Graves, a preacher, was an occupant for several years, then August Hetta, Thomas Cullen, and finally the Welches. During the holding of Moses Carr a division of land was made by him and his brother, Lyman, so that the house had twenty-eight acres connected with it, and this is the amount now held, though the family has forty acres north of the next east and west road. William Welch was of Irish birth, and after many years of industrious living died, and was buried in the Catholic cemetery in Clyde. His wife, Mary, survives him and is still on the farm. (Died July 15, 1892, aged 63 years.) There are several children, as Helen, Mary Ann, Katie, Edward, William, deceased, Thomas and Joseph. The latter two maintain a hardware store in North Rose, and one of them is P. M., which is, after the language of the lamented Nasby, postmaster. The farm seems to be well managed and industry is everywhere evident. (Now occupied by Will Shear and family.)

In the next house dwell Isaac Osborne and family. He is a posthumous child of that Isaac who was long since killed by a lightning stroke. His wife is Mary Burkle, a daughter of the man once living on the corner farm now owned by her husband. Their children are three girls and two boys.

Though he lives here his farm is further north, and just at present we are concerned with owners of this place. The place stands now in the name of Wm. Curtis, of Marion, who in some way traded with the late possessor, Philip Fry. Fry moved away three years since, and now resides near Newark. His wife is Catharine Cornell, and they have quite a family of children, as Amy, George, William, Daniel and Belle. They came here from the vicinity of Lyons, and Mr. F. is a brother of the George Fry who owned for a short time the old Carrier farm. Before the name of Fry, I find those of VanAlstyne and James Vanderburgh, who bought of Moses Carr. The latter was from Onondaga county, and went from Rose to Michigan, whence, I understand, he went into the army during the Rebellion. I believe he built the house. His predecessor was Thomas Bamborough, who came to Rose from Lyons and went from this town to Michigan. He had married Widow Gee, and his farm numbered about one hundred acres. Back of Bamborough is chaos, though it is possible that the Mirick belongings covered this estate.

Over the way in the days agone was a log house in which dwelt Lyman Carr, brother of Moses. The two brothers divided the Bamborough property, but finally this Carr formed part of the train westward. Nearly west of this place may be noticed an old apple orchard. The east and west road once ran near it, coming out near the old Ellis Ellinwood home. Here were a log house and barn built by Samuel Hand. He was the father of John Skidmore's first wife. After Hand was James Gordon, a son-in-law of Jonathan Melvin, then John McWharf, Samuel Smith, a relative of the Miricks, and in 1834, Thomas Bamborough. Later came many tenants, till its disappearance in 1845.

To the east of the corners is the old Oakes place, but this was described in the account of the Stewart district. It is the only one belonging to the Lyman neighborhood lying east of the terminus of the north and south road. (In 1893 George H. Ball of North Rose built a barn upon this land on the north side of the road, having purchased the same from the Welch Brothers. He will also erect a house here.) Were the north and south road to continue, it would run over a well covered by a small house on the Osborne property; but to follow the line of the next range of lots, it makes a jog to the west about ten rods, and then runs by Osborne's corners between lots 155 and 156. Just at the turn, on the southwest side or corner, formerly stood an evaporator built by Fry and Welch. This has been moved down to Ensign Wade's, but a small addition to it still remains.

On the northeast corner of our road north, stands a new house built by Isaac Osborne. By-and-by, I presume, he or some other good citizen will occupy it, but just at present a thriving berry patch and a range for a promising pig have sadly encroached upon the dooryard. The barns opposite have long been landmarks and are much as they were years

ago. The house which preceded the new one was old, almost beyond the
recollection of the present generation, though it is probable that it was
built when the place was owned by Dr. Dickson. I can find no trace of
ownership before that of Amos Dorris, and that is well back in the century.
After him for a short time only, Cyrus Brockway held and occupied it.
Then followed Dr. Dickson, but he never lived here. During his ownership there came a long succession of tenants ; among others was our often
found friend, William Sherman. There are other names, as Cornelius
Bamborough, Peter Paine, Thomas Cullen, Mark Gillett, John Lovejoy
and W. Burkle. Just how many of these were nominally owners I have
no means of stating. I am told that Osborne bought of Louis Ebert, a
Clyde glass-blower. In the years to come, it would be pleasant to note a
continued occupancy, one that would develop the resources of the farm,
and bring out the latent possibilities. Thus far it has been a sort of bucolic
hotel. I am told that there have been forty successive occupants. Few
places in the town enjoy a better situation. Amos Dorris, the first owner,
must have been a character, if surviving stories be true. Here are specimens illustrating his extravagance of speech : He lost his cow one day,
the small bell she wore not serving to locate her. Says he : "I wish
she wore a bell as big as that of Moscow. Every stroke of it would
bring her on her knees." Again, the chipmunks made havoc in his corn.
"I wish," said he, "I had a cannon that pointed in every direction; i'd
load it to the muzzle and tech it off." "Why, then," interposed Mr.
Wilcox, a former British soldier. "you'd hit yourself." "I wouldn't
care," says the angry farmer, "if I only killed a chipmunk."

As we progress westward we are on the old Rose and Nicholas purchase
—that lot of 4000 acres, from one of whose owners the town took its name.
Our first stop is at a small house, owned and occupied by Nicholas Powers,
a native of Erin. He is an industrious man, who lays stone wall and does
masonry generally. He has two children—Edward and Alice. Though
there are only ten acres in the place, it has formed the home of a numerous
family, as when held by the McWharfs, who sold it to Abner Osborne, and
he to Mr. Powers. That we may know just who the McWharfs are, it will
be necessary to go back a great many years to John McWharf, who was
born in Providence, R. I. He there married and had two children, one of
whom, James, passed his life in Canada. Coming to Onondaga county,
this state, he married Hannah Skut, a sister of Orrin Skut of North Rose,
and with his wife's father's family came to this town. He located first in
a log house north of Lamb's corners, and near the farm of O. Skut, having
then fifteen acres of land. Here he lived for several years, until he came
down to the Lyman neighborhood, where he bought the small property of
Harvey Gillett. Here, in time, he put up the small frame house now in
existence, and whence he was borne to his still smaller house in the Rose

cemetery, in 1869, at the extreme age of ninety-five. His wife followed in
1872, aged eighty-eight. Of their children, Jane married Cornelius W.
Fairbanks and died on the Alonzo Chaddock place. Fairbanks went to
Wisconsin. Almira married William Lamb of the corners, and once lived
where William Closs now abides. Both husband and wife are dead, and
lie in the Rose burial ground. One of their children, Myron, was a soldier
under Sherman in the Rebellion, and is now in Illinois. Malvina McWharf
married Jerome McQueen; Hayden L. married Mary, daughter of John
Waterbury; Theodore married Mary Stickles of Hillsdale, Columbia Co.
They began their married life in a small building still standing in the
corner of the Powers' dooryard, while attached to it was a still smaller
structure, in which the McWharfs worked at coopering. Mr. McWharf,
who enlisted in Company C, 111th N. Y., was captured at the unfortunate
affair of Harper's Ferry, and was finally discharged on account of disability. He now draws a pension for his services, and lives, still pursuing
his trade, just north of Ensign Wade's. His family was quite numerous
and included John M., who, having taken the degree of M. D. from both
Buffalo and Chicago, lives now at Fort Scott, Kansas. He was for several
years in Dunkirk, in this state, and in that section found his wife, Lucy
Stryker; Jane married Simeon Olmstead, and, a widow, lives in Clyde;
James married Delia Derby, and lives in North Huron, though he once
dwelt in the house opposite; Alice, the wife of Andrew Stickles, is dead;
John J. married Carrie Haugh of Galen, and lives at home; Charles
married Sarah Green of Junius; Marietta is the wife of Alfred Sours of
Galen; while the youngest, George, is a dentist in Ontario, this county.

Harvey Gillett, from whom McWharf bought, was one of the characters
in the early history of the town. He was a cousin of Asahel, settled further
north, and was of Connecticut birth, to which state, in New Canaan, he
eventually returned to care for the closing years of his father's life, though,
as we hear of Harvey, we wonder that he should be put to care for anything. As one neighbor says: "He was too lazy to be dissipated," but
he was always hungry. The death of a child of this man is said to have
been the first in the town. Amos Dorris gave to Gillett a life lease of one-
half acre of ground, upon which he built his log cabin, and here clustered a
brood of little Gilletts, of whom Julia became Mrs. Michael Ryan. Of the
others, at present I can secure no trace. Stories of Gillett's gastronomic
feats still linger after fifty years, and here is one of them: Having eaten a
breakfast before starting for Abner Wood's, he called at Stephen Babcock's,
now the Isaac Cole place, and, being invited, ate a second breakfast. When
he reached Mr. Wood's, though a little late, he accepted a call to eat, and
stowed away his third morning meal. His work was that of scoring
timber; but at ten o'clock in the forenoon he was seen to observe the sun
with interest, saying: "I wonder if it isn't almost noon, for I am darned

hungry." Again, when working for Alpheus Collins, he sat up to the table for a little lunch, and Mrs. C. put before him a quantity of baked beans, just one-half of a mess cooked in the forenoon for the family and several workingmen. The first half had made the dinner, and she had saved this lot for supper, but Harvey made nothing of downing the entire mess, and when asked if he would have anything more, remarked that he guessed he'd top off with a little milk, and actually there and then he drank a pan full of the lacteal fluid. Is there any wonder that a man with such an appetite was always poor ?

Opposite, on the south side, is a small place belonging to Elbert Briggs, he having bought of Michael Londrigan, who went to the part of this district bordering on North Rose. Mr. L. probably bought of H. Metz. The house was built by L. H. Lyman in 1859, a brother of John, next west. (Mr. Briggs has since sold.)

For convenience we will pass the home of John Lyman, and near where the barn of his son William stands, we may fancy the first abode of the Lymans in Rose. The prime comer was Samuel, a son of David and Flavia (Collins) Lyman, of Salisbury, Conn. As Flavia was a sister of the first Thaddeus Collins, her son was first cousin to Thaddeus, 2d, Alpheus and the other children of the pioneer. The first visit was made in the fall of 1817, and in the following spring came the family, in the customary way, viz., by ox team and sled. Betterments had been made on the hundred acre lot by John Drury, a son of the Caleb already mentioned. These were bought and payments were made to the firm of Rose & Nicholas. In the log house the family remained until 1837, when the framed house opposite, and occupied by Charles Lyman, was built. In this Samuel Lyman died, in 1877, aged eighty-three, while his wife had preceded him, in 1870, at the age of seventy-seven. It should have been stated that her maiden name was Clementina Evarts, of the family that has since furnished a United States senator from the state of New York. "Old Mr. Lyman," as he was generally known, was one of the most vigorous Abolitionists in Rose. I am told that the old horse barn, once near the road, has concealed more runaway slaves than any other building in town. He was currently reported to be a station man on the underground railroad. For one, I take no little pleasure in writing these words, for such a record should be a source of pride to his descendants and to his town. The oldest son, John, married Eleanor Griggs, of Seneca county, and made his initiative housekeeping in a log structure standing in the field to the southwest. No trace of this now exists. This particular spot is almost classic in our annals, for here, in the early years of the century, Zenas Fairbanks opened the first store in the town. Here, too, was an ashery, and near, probably the first lime kiln. Charles Lyman's farm barn is very near the site of the kiln. I understand that the Fairbanks family lived first on the Linus

Osgood farm, possibly the very first settlers there. Afterward, I am told, they had a habitation on the Thomas ridge, further south. Zenas married a daughter of Alverson Wade, while George found a wife in John Wade's family, and Cornelius we have seen as the spouse of one of the McWharfs. Northwest of this point, near the present home of Michael McDorman, a bear was slain by one of the early settlers, perhaps Samuel Southwick, whose cabin was a mile or so south. John Lyman afterward bought thirty-four acres of Moses Carr, including the house in which he now lives. The successive owners of this place were the same as those of the next place east, though we shall find near here, as early as 1831, the family of Richard D. Morey. His wife was Sally Harris and they came from Saratoga county, though it is probable that they had lived in Warren county. They afterward lived on the Valley road, south of Shear's corners. Let us now, however, continue with the Lymans. John's oldest child is Caroline. Then follow Charles E., William D., John D., who married Minnie Parslow, (they have one child, Ella); and Samuel H., who, a graduate of the Albany State Normal School, is a successful teacher, being now at the head of the Pulaski union school. (John Lyman died January 14, 1892, aged 72 years.) Samuel Lyman had several other children, as follows : Caroline, who married Cyrus Felt, and died west ; Mary, deceased ; Charles ; David, who married Emma Chalker, and lives in the Valley, though he once dwelt near here ; Lavius H. married Ella Branch, of Onondaga county, and, as we have seen, once lived in the place next east. After the War he migrated to Arkansas, and still lives there ; Frederick, now dead, married in Illinois. He rose to the rank of captain during the Rebellion. Flavia married Levi Chase, from New Hampshire, and once lived on the corner, in the Dr. Dickson house. (Mr. Chase, now living in Sturbridge, Mass., is a genealogist and local history writer of note.) Samuel, the youngest son, married Sarah Vanderberg and lives in the Valley.

Crossing the road we find the new house of William D. Lyman, who married Mary Hoyt, a cousin of Orson Toles' wife. Their children are Maggie, Edith and Benjamin. As the house stands so near the first log house, Mr. Lyman may take a little pride in maintaining the family succession.

Zigzagging to the south side, we have the house built by Samuel Lyman. To be sure, it has been somewhat remodeled, but it is substantially the same. Here resides Chas. Lyman, in a state of so-called single blessedness. But as the Bible has said that it is not good for man to be alone, there must be a contradiction somewhere. Mr. Lyman, in the language of Lafayette, is a lucky dog. The French patriot, at a great party given in Boston, on being introduced to a young married man, shook him vigorously by the hand, saying, " Happy man! happy man!" Soon after, meeting another gentleman and asking him if he was married and getting a negative reply, he slapped him on the shoulder, exclaiming : "Lucky dog." Some one querying as to whom Lafayette intended to say the best thing, a bright listener at once said : "Any one knows that a happy man is better than a lucky dog." Mr. Lyman keeps his property in excellent condition, though many observers are wondering when the fine pear orchard west of his house will begin to bear. The first house on the Lyman farm stood nearly in front of Charles Lyman's barn, and was built by Richard Avery, Sr., who had been a soldier in the French and Indian War and in the Revolutionary. His son, Richard, was in the late War. He was father-in-law of the first Joel Bishop and of Asahel Gillett, Sr. After him were two tenants, one of whom was Davis Hand, who married Polly Crydenwise. The builder sold to Chester Ellinwood, who was here for a while and then traded with Samuel Southwick for the farm where Ensign Wade lives. The succession is Mirick, Bamborough, James Phillips, Moses Carr, John Lyman.

Continuing our zigzag way, we find another Lyman domiciled on the north side. This one is Charles F., a son of John. His wife is Lydia E. Horton, and they have four children—Viola, Ralph, Mary and Ida. The house was built by David Lyman, one of the second generation in these parts. This clinging to the old sod and soil of this family is very pleasant to contemplate, and I doubt not, in storing up this world's goods, they have quite as much to show as they would have had had they, like some others, been constantly on the move.

Our next stop is at a house on the north side, belonging to John Lyman. It stands on the old Lyman farm, which, lacking ten acres, lay entirely on the north side of the road. The site was bought and built upon by one Lancaster. It was also owned by the elder Oaks and by a Mr. Farnsworth, who now lives in Glenmark. Eli Knapp has also occupied it. Without intending to disparage any former occupant, we may be pardoned for feeling glad that another John Lyman, he of the third generation is, living here.

To Charles Lyman I am indebted for many facts, and thanks are especially due for the following incident : Samuel Lyman always braved public opinion when it conflicted with his sense of right and duty, and in the year 1830, being engaged in building a small barn, and having then recently read Dr. Lyman Beecher's "Six Sermons on Temperance," he felt that it would be wrong for him to furnish liquor at the raising, and he determined not to do so. Taking no pains to conceal his purpose, it became noised about that Lyman was going to have a cold water raising, a thing unheard of at that day and age of the world. Consequently a large crowd was attracted—some to lift up and others to pull down, among the latter not only regular old topers, but staid and sedate church members. The builder, a sober man and excellent citizen, was evidently in sympathy with the " hot water " sentiment, as the tone of his commands was wonderfully tame and feeble, the effect of which was apparent when the first bent, after having been started, became stationary, and it seemed certain that the attempt to raise it would end in failure, when a Baptist preacher named Ansel Gardner, who, five years later, built the Baptist Church at the Valley, springing forward with fire in his eye and with the exclamation, "I can raise that bent," rang out his commands in tones so positive and determined that the lifters were animated with new energy, and the bent moved right along to its place. The incident had the effect of shaming the boss into a proper performance of his duty, and the first cold water raising in the town was successfully accomplished. Years after, a neighbor, C. W. Fairbanks, was heard to relate in connection with the foregoing circumstance : " When the first bent was going up, I noticed that some one standing beside me was pulling down, and by a quick movement I shoved the hand of the obstructionist off the beam." The barn alluded to was the one so long standing near the road, and in which numerous Africans afterward halted on their way to liberty. True, the edifice is, in a double sense, a monument. Standing now, well back from the road, it is still a strong tribute to cold water raising.

The Moreys have already been referred to as residents in this section. I have learned that the first Richard D. Morey was a half brother of the first Mrs. Jeremiah Finch. The Morey family came in 1831, having filially remained east until after the death of Mrs. Morey's aged mother. On coming to these parts, Mrs. M. died first, and afterward Mr. Morey married widow Wilcox. With her first husband, she had lived in a log house near where "Ham" Closs now lives. The neighbors say that when Mr. W. was dying, his bed was the floor, and some one calling to ask how he was, his wife cheerfully replied : "Oh, he's slowly wasting away," he getting no more attention than a log of wood. She had a daughter, Julia Ann, who married Jeremiah Finch, 2d, and a son, Richard, both of whom went west. This second marriage, I fancy, was none of the happiest, and going down to Saratoga to visit his oldest son, Mr. Morey died and was buried there. There were ten children, evenly divided as to sex : Jesse, the oldest, remained east ; Elijah married Harriet Lovejoy, who, after his death, married Watson Dowd, and lived in Huron ; William married widow Burch, née Havens ; Richard Derrick, called "Derrick," married Almina Kelsey, who lived at "Holl" Drury's ; and H. Delevan, one of twins. He makes his home with Norman Lovejoy. The oldest daughter, Mapelet, never lived in Rose, for having married John Crapo, went directly west ; Lydia we have seen as the hospitable wife of Norman Lovejoy ; Charity married Nelson Lovejoy, of Wolcott ; Charlotte is Mrs. Philip Thomas, of Huron, while the twin, Nancy Ann, is Mrs. Abram DePew, of Wolcott. Mrs. Norman Lovejoy is my chief informant concerning the

Moreys, and what she doesn't recall concerning her early life in Rose is hardly worth remembering. She says: "I tell you, there was lots of spinning and weaving going on in those days. We had to work the wool for winter's wear and the flax to make linen for summer. I could spin my three runs of tow in less than a day. Laws! the girls nowadays don't know anything about work." On my asking her what constituted a run of tow, she replied: "I guess you don't know much about weaving. Why, twenty knots, of course." Lest I should still further expose my ignorance, I forebore asking the extent of a knot, and to this day can not tell whether the word has to do with the intertwining of strings or is in some way allied to nautical language, as "twenty knots an hour." Continuing, she ran on thus: "Brother Lige got a neighbor to make a broadcloth coat for him, and to pay for it, I had to spin thirty-two run of wool for her. I did it, but I had to work for it. Why, one day, a good many years afterward, a friend came along here and he asked me if I remember the spinning. I told him I did, very well. 'Why,' said he, 'you'd spin two runs before ten o'clock, then go home and get dinner and be back again before one o'clock and spin two more. How you did make things fly.' Oh, I could spin and wash and keep busy. Old Mrs. Mirick, just after we came up here, invited me and my sisters to a party, and we were the only ones in our neighborhood who had an invite. I tell ye, it just sot us way up." Mrs. L.'s conversation gave me a vivid picture of times more than fifty years away. How many boys of today have sisters who would give eight days' hard work to pay for making said boy's coat? I await an answer.

Once more crossing the highway, we may enter the home of Michael McDorman. The latter, though of Irish birth, came hither nine years ago from Canada, and, having purchased a few acres of land, has erected a cosy house near an excellent barn, everything indicating the utmost thrift. His wife is Dillene Quertershan, a lady of the Canadian French. They have a promising family, consisting of Michael, Carrie, John and Edward. Exemplary members of the Rose Methodist Church, they enjoy the highest respect of their neighbors.

Visions of school ma'ams and of pedagogic sway dance before us as we approach the next building, for it is the school-house: the place where the young ideas of the district are taught to shoot, and the edifice itself is highly creditable to those who built it. Painted white, with green blinds, it is no "ragged beggar by the roadside sunning." It is the second building on the site, erected in 1879, though the first school-house in the district was made of logs and stood to the westward over the hill, where Mr. Shear's tenant house now stands. There were two framed buildings there also. The first school-house was burned. I am wondering whether the youth of this neighborhood should be called "hard students" that they managed thus to use up five buildings. From the district school many a boy and girl went to the seminaries in other places, thus securing advantages that were denied to the fathers and mothers. The present location is singularly near the exact centre of the district.

The next move takes us to the four corners, where we may see, facing the setting sun, what was, when erected, the very finest house in Rose. Now the property of Peter Shear, it was built by John Closs before 1828. Though we have the record complete of this farm for more than sixty years, the very earliest history is a little nebulous. If, as I have seen it stated, Oliver Whitmore was located just south of Joel Bishop, then he must have held this place once. Before him may have been a Mr. Belden. "'Squire" Whitmore's son, Seth, was a surveyor, and to him is due the angle in the road near the Lyman farm. Possibly Mr. Closs may have purchased his betterments. John Closs, the progenitor of the Rose family of that name, was of New Jersey birth, very likely of remote Dutch origin, and his name must have passed through an interesting transition, perhaps from Klaus to its present English form. His parents had moved to the vicinity of Lyons, whence our subject moved to Rose. Before coming here, he had held contracts in constructing the Erie canal. However the farm had been held before Closs' coming, his payments were made to the Rose and Nicholas purchase. The place lay on all four corners, and was unexcelled in convenience and fertility. At his coming, in 1825, he dwelt in a log house just below the southeast angle of the cross roads. But Mr. Closs had the means and the disposition to rear for his family a more seemly habitation, and the present structure was the result of his building, though much of the material had to be brought from Jack's Rifts. Perhaps the family moved in in 1827. At any rate, the youngest children, twins, were born here in 1828. The good wife was Hannah Hamel, a native of Verona, Oneida Co. Their children were Harvey, about whom there will be more anon; George, who died in 1848; Lorenzo, who married, in Ohio, a Miss Taylor. He afterward held an appointment in a government office in Washington, and from Georgetown College his two sons, Charles and Frank, were graduated. He now lives in New York City. The fourth son, Caleb Hamel, known familiarly in Rose as "Ham," we shall meet later. There were only three girls in the family, and of these two were twins. The elder sister, Eveline Adelia, died in 1848. The twin sisters, Juliette and Anjenette, were born in 1828, and, if reports be true, they were the light of the household in that, to those rural regions, palatial home. I have heard my mother say, when passing this house, "How many pleasant hours I have passed there with the twins." Juliette became the wife of Willis G. Wade, son of John, the pioneer, but died in 1859. Near her, in the cemetery, lie her husband and infant son. Anjenette died in 1853. The elder Closses died early in life; John in 1832, aged thirty-nine; his wife

in 1831, in her thirty-seventh year. Upon the eldest son, Harvey, cares
were thus thrown very early; but I have never learned that he faltered for
a moment. He married, in 1836, Evelina Henderson, daughter of Gideon,
in the Stewart district, and until 1856 dwelt on the paternal acres. Here
his only son, Frank, was born, and thence two infant daughters were borne
to the cemetery. In 1856 he exchanged with Peter Shear his old home,
taking in part payment the present abode of Wm. Closs, to the westward.   In 1859 he moved into the Valley district, taking the well known
stone house of Hiram Mirick, and here lived until 1876, when, selling out,
he went still nearer the centre of the village, this time to the old Collins
home, and here he dwelt until his death, January 6, 1886. I am sure I
speak within bounds when I state that no resident of this town ever
more deservedly enjoyed the thorough respect of his fellow-townsmen than
Harvey Closs. In 1857 and 1858 he was supervisor of the town, and was
long a prominent member of the Presbyterian Church. To the writer, both
Mr. Closs and his wife have additional interest from the fact that Mr. Closs
went to school to George Seelye, his grandfather, and Mrs. Closs to Catharine Shepard, his grandmother, while their only son was a school-mate
in Falley Seminary. Mrs. Closs, the widow, is passing the evening of
life very pleasantly in the home whence she may overlook the village.
We now come to the present occupant of the old Closs farm, Peter Shear.
He was born in Coeymans, Albany county, his name indicating a Dutch
origin. His wife, Mary, bore the cognomen of Shear before as well as
after marriage. They came to this town thirty-five years ago, living first
on the Van Sicklen farm, near Huron, and they came here in 1859. Mrs.
Shear lives now on another farm, owned by Mr. Shear in Junius, Seneca
county. The husband lives a divided life, managing thus two farms. His
home in Junius he visits weekly, remaining here the rest of the time. He
has long been known as a successful speculator in stock, perhaps more
prominent in this respect than any other man in the town. In this farm
there are 166 acres. His children, all born in Rose, are Stephen, Gertrude,
William, Fred, George and Minnie. With the exception of William they
are in Seneca county, where Stephen married. William we shall see
again. A divided interest necessitating the absence of the gentler portion
of the household, may account for the lack of fix-up ed-ness that once per-
vaded the corner. There are slats wanting in the blinds, and we note the
absence of that intensity of green and white that we like to see in blinds
and house. Mr. Shear's family, I am told, are Progressive Friends. (Mr.
Shear died January 26, 1890, aged seventy years. The place is now owned
by Edward Welch, who has made all the improvements called for in the
home, and more. His wife is Sarah Buckley, and they have one son, William.
Mr. Welch came to this farm in April, 1893. His brothers, Thomas and
Joseph, own that part of the old farm south of the east and west road, and

also some near the school-house. They have this season erected a large, handsome barn near the corner, and will later move the house north of the barn, and, perhaps, make it a counterpart of their brother's fine residence on the other side of the road.)

Still moving westward, we pass at our right a tenement house of Mr. Shear, and soon come to a very pleasant place, the home of William Closs, "Ham's" younger son. Here, too, in antiquarian researches, we are lost in obscurity, for as yet I can go no further back than James Andrews, who was there as early as 1826. He sold to Solomon Whitney, and he to William Lamb, whom we have already noted as the husband of Almira McWharf. As owner, then came Peter Shear, and in 1856, Harvey Closs. Frank Sherman then held it for a time, and to him succeeded Joel Sheffield, repeatedly met in our town jottings. He and his wife, Nannie Osgood, began their married life here, and here resided for some years, until Hamel Closs, desiring a home near at hand for his son, John, bought and located John and his lately wedded wife, "Gustie" Saunders, in this comfortable abode. But John tired of the farm and went west long ago, and is now living in Detroit, Michigan. After a succession of tenants, came the younger son, William, who married Emma Hillman of Webster, Monroe county, and after living with his parents for a while, came hither. He has two children, Ralph and Archer.

Something more than a stone's throw beyond, is the dwelling of Stanton E. Waldruff, who, a native of Galen, married Frances Vanderburgh, and thereby came to this farm, for many years held by William S. Vanderburgh. He was a native of Columbia county, and married Lovina Clapper. For many years he tilled these acres, and, full of years, died about two years since. Both he and his wife, who passed away in 1883, sleep in the Rose cemetery. Sarah, their oldest child, married Samuel Lyman. John W., the next child, and only son, after serving in the 9th Heavy Artillery during the War, went west and has been lost to the knowledge of his friends. The next daughter, Etta, became the wife of James Covell of the adjacent district on the west. Emma married Gideon Barrett of the Jeffers neighborhood. Mr. and Mrs. Waldruff, who hold the paternal roof tree, have three children. Fred, who having taken for his wife Lizzie Harmon, lives in the Valley. (Fred died May 16, 1893, in Allegan, Michigan. Etta was married in 1891 to George W. Rice of Huron, leaving Edna only at home). A much enlarged and improved barn indicates progress. In fact, I am reminded, as I go about, of the great improvement in farm buildings. What would the pioneers say, could they awake and arise, to a barn with matched siding and painted, yes, actually painted? Why, in those earlier days it was rare that paint could be afforded for the house, let alone the barn. Before the Vanderburghs, this was the home of William Havens, twice encountered in the Lake district. He built the house. In

9

the Rose cemetery I find inscriptions to the memory of William V. Havens and Susan, his wife. They died, she in 1848, aged sixty-four, and he, full of years, in 1875, for he had attained the unusual age of ninety-five. The Havens bought of Harley Way, and he of Dr. Peter Valentine, who had helped his brother, Asahel, in paying for the place. The Havens came to this town from Cato. They had two sons—Dexter and William—now living in Weedsport, and several daughters, of whom one became Melesse Lawrence of Weedsport; another, Mrs. Hunt; and Sally married a Drakeford and went to the west; another became Mrs. Elias Wood, already noted in the Lake district.

Continuing toward the west, we find at our right the home of Edwin W. Catchpole, a part of the large Catchpole estate. Here Mr. Catchpole, with his wife, Alice Rich of Marion, and their infant son, George C., takes all the comfort that can come to mortals. (Besides George C., there are now children: Alice A., Rutherford Hayes and Edwin W., Jr.) Mr. Catchpole bought the place of the Klinck heirs; for it was here, in 1877, that Henry Klinck passed from mortality to immortality, a death that to humanity seemed especially untimely, since there was a large family of children seemingly demanding a father's care. There were Henry, who, married, now lives in Shortsville; George, who married a Harper, and lives in the Valley with his mother, his wife having died; Carrie is the wife of George Brown of Chili; William lives in the Valley; Edward; Ellsworth, generally known as "Allie;" and Bert, who, I think, was born here. George and Will are painters. Mrs. Klinck lives in the village, and at her home her aged father, Artemas Osgood, died in 1887. Mr. Klinck bought of John D. Waterbury, who, as was also his wife, Emma Adams, was born in Nassau, Rensselaer county. In 1847 they came to Galen, and the next year to Rose, and here they remained for nearly twenty years, going hence, in 1867, to Huron. He afterward went to Pontiac, Michigan, where he died in 1884, aged seventy-six years. His wife died in 1862, at the age of forty-eight years. Her remains were afterward carried to Michigan also. The living of our town have generally gone to that Peninsular state, but this is the first instance, in my knowledge, of the removal of the dead to that much sought locality. They were respected citizens, members of the Baptist Church. Of their five children, three grew to adultship, viz., Mary E., who married Hayden Lamb of Huron, but a member of our Rose family. They live in Pontiac, Michigan; Hiel Adams married Harriet Williams of Nassau, and resides in Clyde; Emma E. married James Rockwell of Pontiac, and died very suddenly in 1887. William Morey of the same school district, who had married the widow Burch, a daughter of William Havens, was the preceding owner, and he built the framed house. His predecessor was Hosea Howard, a brother of Mrs. Elizur Flint.

Just a little west of opposite is another house, with large barns connected, now the property of George Catchpole, who bought it in 1866 from Mr. Pitcher, who in turn had purchased a short time before from the heirs of Rufus R. Weeks, who was killed in the Valley in 1861 at the raising of a flag pole. This was a very distressing incident. After the injury Mr. Weeks was borne, insensible, into the adjacent hotel, now Pimm's, where, for three or four days, he lay unconscious until death came to his relief. Mr. Weeks was a native of Rensselaer county, but he moved to this town from Galen. Taken away thus in the prime of life, the loss to his family and friends was irreparable. Active and industrious, the raising of a pole seemed small compensation for the loss. The farm of fifty-one acres Mr. Weeks had bought of Alpheus Roberts, now of Huron, and he from Elias R. Cook of Sodus. The latter had not occupied, but had simply rented. At present I can go no further into the past. Mr. Catchpole has added largely to the barns, until now they are among the very largest in the vicinity.

When we come to the next house, that of George Catchpole, we have reached the western limit of the district and one of the landmarks of the neighborhood, for it was to this place that the brothers Pomeroy and Elizur Flint came in 1817. Pomeroy lived only two years, leaving a youthful wife, whom his brother married. The Flints were from Coventry, Conn., and coming here took up one hundred and ten acres, upon which improvements had been made by one Paine and a log house built. Probably the latter came in 1810, and through his betterments, the land cost the Flints nine dollars per acre. The framed house that Deacon Flint in time built was a part of the upright of the present commodious farm house. The wife was Roxy Howard, a good specimen of the go-ahead Connecticut woman, and a model housekeeper. She died many years since, at the age of 70 years. Her husband survived until 1884, being then ninety-one years old. There are few characters standing out more prominently in town history than that of Deacon Flint. In 1812, he shouldered his musket, and, with others, helped man the fort at New London when assailed by the British, and for this service he became eventually a pensioner of the United States. He was once supervisor, and for many years served as a justice of the peace. He was the mainstay in the Presbyterian Church and one of its earliest members. His face, full of decision and will, is not often reproduced. Ever industrious, he rested but little, as some folks understand the word, even in his age. Two children grew up—Calista, who wedded George Catchpole, and Dwight, who married George's sister, Mary. The Catchpoles are of English birth, and George was born in Moulton, Norfolk Co. On coming to this country, they reached Huron by way of Geneva. In Huron, the brothers, Robert and James, located on adjacent farms, and soon won enviable reputations for genuine honesty.

industry and worth. George, having won the deacon's daughter, began housekeeping in Huron, just east of his father's. Dwight Flint soon after contemplated matrimony with Mary Catchpole. For some reason he did not care to take his wife to his old home to live; so one day the deacon rode up to George's, but delayed making known his mission. Something was on his mind, but it was not until a good dinner had lubricated his tongue that he spoke his mind. Then moving back his chair, he said: "I may as well let you know what I came here for. The truth of the matter is, we want you two to come and live with us. Dwight doesn't want to take his wife, home, and I don't see how we can get along without you. There needn't be any fuss about it. When Dwight is ready, just let him come here, taking everything, and you come to the old place." Says George C.: "I don't suppose there was ever quite such a trade effected before nor since. I was satisfied with my place given me by my father. It was well stocked and the house was furnished. I asked my wife what she thought about it, and she replied that we should have to go. Well, one day Dwight rode off and got married. After a short trip, he came up to my place to stay over night. In the morning, wife and I got into his buggy and drove down here, leaving everything of ours there and taking all that we found here. That was in 1859, and there was never a shade of difference or trouble from that day to this over the trade." Calista (Flint) Catchpole died in 1872, and, subsequently, Mr. C. married Mary, youngest daughter of Artemas Osgood. Their home has everything necessary for comfort. Surrounded by great barns to receive the product of the 210 acres of the farm, our farmer friend ought to reign a veritable king on his domain. Five times his fellow townsmen have made Mr. Catchpole supervisor of the town. Fond of travel, he has once revisited England to see the early home, and has in mind to go again at no distant day. His only son, Edwin, we have just passed to the eastward. (Mr. Catchpole later moved to the Valley, and there his wife died in 1893. His son, Edwin, now occupies the farm.)

Having followed this road through the district, we shall avoid turning on our tracks by imagining ourselves transported to the old home of Chauncey Bishop. It is just south from the old burial ground—sometimes called Briggs' cemetery—and opposite. The house is now the home of Elder Anson H. Stearns and his wife, who was Charity M. Bishop, daughter of Chauncey, who found his wife in the present town of Butler, Chloe Wheeler, eldest daughter of Eli Wheeler, one of the earliest comers to that town, then making a part of the old town of Wolcott. She had taught school near in 1817 and 1818, and in the fall of 1818 was married. The groom's party, about twenty in number, went to Butler on horseback. In common with all pioneers, they began their life in a log house, somewhat south of opposite to the site of the present house, built in 1823. A visit to this edifice will repay any one who likes the old. It has been changed very little, if any; large posts and beams, all arranged for strength and convenience. Overhead there is no plastering, but the sleepers are bare, now, of course, being destitute of the nails and hooks which formerly were so handy. From these were suspended many convenient articles for housebould use, as strips of dried pumpkin and beef. Strings of apples were dried by the heat that the wide fireplace afforded. Everything tended toward hospitality, for which the early settlers were noted. The family that grew up here, though not so large as the first generation, was still an extensive one. The oldest, Charles C., is in Manchester, Ont. Co. Charity M. married Rev. A. H. Stearns, a Baptist minister of Massachusetts birth, being a native of West Hampton. He came to this state in 1861, and has been an especially successful pastor in South Butler, Wolcott and elsewhere. Together, they maintain the honors of the old homestead. Candace W. became Mrs. Chester Williams, of Huron. He dying, she moved to Illinois; as did also the next brother, D. Clinton, who married Mary Ann Mead, of Phelps. (Clinton Bishop died Feb. 24, 1892.) The next son, Cicero, was drowned in Stony Lake, Michigan; John Calvin, a civil engineer, married Mary Avery, of Lyons, and now lives at Pilgrimsport; Cephas B., having taken Sarah Chaddock as his wife, dwells in the Valley; Celestia wedded Samuel F. Weaver, of Illinois, while the youngest, Chauncey E., having married Mary Butler, of Weedsport, and after living in these parts for some years, went to Kansas, where he now resides. Chauncey Bishop was another of those devoted men who gave an excellent reputation to the town. One of the constituent members of the Rose Baptist Church, he was for more than forty years its clerk. He died in 1880, in his ninetieth year. His wife, who was born in Cairo, Greene Co., died in 1878, in her eighty-first year.

At one time or another the land near here must have been dotted with the log habitations of the first comers. The small edifice, a little south of opposite, stands near one of the early abodes, that of Samuel Hand; but in recent times it dates from Elbert Briggs, a son of Jonathan. John Groescup came next, then Luman Briggs, Elbert's brother, then S. Wing Langley, who has improved the house. His wife is Mary Brisbin, eldest daughter of James Brisbin, of North Rose. Mr. Langley is a son of Millens L., who once lived on the old Joel Bishop farm across the way. (The children here are Guy M., Eugene M. and Lillian E.) Being on the old Briggs farm, the house belongs to the North Rose district.

Again crossing the road, we may find a new house, an ornament to the street, where lives Michael Londrigan, whom we first met in the Lyman neighborhood. He came originally from Waterford, Ireland. His wife is Bridget Dunn. There are fifty acres in the farm. He has a family of two boys and one girl growing up. James, Willie and Theresa; one daughter,

Mary, is dead. He bought of John Stewart, who held only a short time, having come from Lyons, to which place he returned on selling. Stewart bought from Chauncey Bishop, 2d, who built the new house, the old one, built by his grandfather, having been burned while he was away in Weedsport to get his wife. Though the new house is undoubtedly an improvement, one cannot help regretting the old, especially if of the least antiquarian disposition. Before him was John Briggs, one of Jonathan's sons, whom Myron Langley preceded. Myron was a son of Millens L. His wife was Elizabeth Hibbard, of Butler, a sister of Marshall and Hamilton. The Langleys came from Huron to Rose. Millens' wife was Nancy Mosher. They had several children, as Melissa, Myron, Willard and Wing, then Julia, Emeline, who married a Whiting of Sodus, and Mary, wife of John D. Prosens, of Sodus. Elder John Bucklin, who preceded Langley, was one of the early Baptist preachers. To this place, the first Joel Bishop brought his sons and daughters, at any rate those who were not old enough to make homes of their own. He was an old Revolutionary soldier, born in Guilford, Conn., Oct. 2, 1757, but coming hither from Charleston, Montgomery county, where he had already essayed a pioneer's life. He prospected in the winter of 1810—11, and in the spring his oldest son, Chauncey, and son-in-law, John Burns, came through afoot and began work. Burns was on lot 132, and Chauncey built a log house just where Londrigan's mansion is. The family followed in sections, but all were here in March, 1812. Here he lived for many years until a desire to be with his sons, Elijah and Reuben, prompted him to go to Ohio, where he and his wife, Phœbe Avery, died in Havana, Huron Co. Their family was a large one, so large that the largest modern house, with our notions of comfort, would not hold the young Bishops. Four sons and nine daughters lived to have homes of their own and to add lustre to the family name. Joel Bishop was the sixth in descent from John Bishop, who, in 1639, settled in Guilford, Conn. During the Revolution he was for a time a prisoner of war in New York City. He never had any love for a Redcoat. In 1837, when 80 years old, he went to the Wilderness for the fourth time. He died at the age of 84 years. Chauncey and his family we have already passed, but there was a Joel, Jr., who made his early home on the Bender place. His wife was Zemira Slaughter (a cousin of the famous John G. Saxe), whom I find among the very first members of the Methodist Church in Rose. He afterward went to Butler, somewhere in the forties, and lived many years, finally dying there. Elijah married Jerusha Howard, a niece of Mrs. Flint, and began living his connubial life in a log house just south of his father's. Reuben married Sarah Ann Gardner, of Lock Berlin. He lived with his father until the western fever took both him and the elder Bishops to the state of Ohio. Then come the nine daughters, viz.: Anna, who married, first, Elijah

Bundy, whose children were : Sally, who married George Stewart ; Phœbe became the wife of Thomas Lewis and went west : Joel married a distant relative, also named Bundy, and died forty years since, near Fulton, N. Y. Another brother, Stephen, lived just west of Stewart's corners, in a little house only recently destroyed, and being in the south at the beginning of the War, he is supposed to have lost his life in some way as an enemy to secession : and yet another, Truman, who moved to Missouri and died single. For a second husband Anna married Asahel Valentine, a brother of Dr. Peter. For a while they lived on the Vanderburgh place, then in the Valley. Joel B.'s second daughter, Clara, married John Burns, and was one of the first, if not the very first, settlers on the Benjamin Seelye place, in the North Rose district. He sold either to Henry Graham or Seelye. He also had a good sized family, as Bishop, who took for his wife Olive Fuller, the daughter of Jonathan F., met in District No. 5. Jane Burns was the wife of Asahel Lamb, son of Peter ; Nancy married John Palmington ; Hollister died in 1862, in the army ; then there were Achsah, who married John Ballantine ; Polly, who became Mrs. Sylvester McDerby, and Roxy, who married Jerome Palmington. All of them, old and young, went west. John Burns was a good Baptist, and leader of the singing. It is proper to state that I find John Burns recorded, in 1812, as the purchaser of lot 153, i. e., 108 acres, just opposite the old Dickinson farm. Sally, Joel B.'s third daughter, was the second wife of John Skidmore. His first wife was a sister of Davis Hand, by whom he had a son and a daughter, Sally. He was early on the Ellis Ellinwood place, whence he went to Ohio, and returning bought what is now the Collier place, south of the Valley, and later went to Michigan. His children by second marriage were Truman, Chauncey, George, Catherine, John, Mary Ann, Rachel and Marilla. Like nearly all the Bishops and their affiliated branches, he was a Baptist. Sally Bishop taught the first school in town, in a small log house a mile and a half north of the Valley. Chauncey Bishop has been named. Phœbe Bishop became the wife of Gardner Gillett, a brother of Harvey, and began housekeeping in a log house opposite George Catchpole's, possibly on the Weeks farm. In this town and in Lyons seven children were born to them. Those surviving infancy were Cyrus, who married a Jewell, of Sodus ; Harriet, John, Joel and Cordelia. All went to Illinois. Then came Rachel, the wife of Dr. Peter Valentine, of the Valley. The sixth girl was Roxy, who married David Gates, of Huron ; then Martha followed, the first wife of Lyman Felton, of Red Creek. They went to Ohio. The eighth daughter, Lucinda, wedded Ansel Gardner, of Red Creek, who, a carpenter, lived in the town for a while. In his trade he built the Prosens house, in the North Rose district, and the Baptist Church in the Valley. Becoming a Baptist minister, he went to Illinois and there died. They had eleven children. Last of all was Harriet, who followed her sister, Martha, as the second wife of Lyman Felton. There, that is a galaxy to be proud of. Can a Rose family, during the last twenty-five years, show its equal? Before dismissing the Bishops, I may say that they had their share of frontier adventure. Among many others, Chauncey tells this incident: He and Asahel Gillett once shot a bear, but fearful that the shot was not effectual, they hesitated about approaching the fallen Bruin. They came nearer only to find that their caution had been wise, for his bearship proceeded to arise and to place himself at bay between two trees in a way that he could be attacked in front only. As their last ball had already been sent into the beast, they assailed with clubs, but the beast was smart enough to knock the weapons away in succession, until, finally, going at him simultaneously, they took his life. Bear meat was a luxury for a time. This affair took place on the gravel knoll opposite the residence of Luther Wilson.

Next is found the place long known as the Bender farm, now owned by John York, Jr., of North Rose. As we have seen, Joel Bishop, 2d, was first here and located his log beginning. He sold to Henry Graham. Then came a man named Sweat, then James Weeks, next Mr. Gardener, then Loren Beals, who sold to John Ira Bender. He came to these parts from Manlius, Onondaga county. His wife, Caroline Osborn, was born in Woodbridge, Conn. They have four children—Emily, the wife of James Casler of Manlius; Jacob, Charles E., and Bertha, who, having married Wright McIntyre, lives south of the corners. With her Mrs. B. makes her home, Mr. B. having died two years ago. Since Mr. York's ownership a fine large barn has been constructed. Charles Moore, a native of the Isle of Man, has the next habitation. An industrious citizen, he is rearing a family of six children, Anna, Maggie, John, William, Joseph and Frank, who command the respect of the community. The building was once a tenant house of Peter Shear. Mr. M. has five acres in his holding.

Beyond the corners on the east side is a small house built by Mr. Shear for his son William, and here the latter with his wife, Elnora Monroe, resides. They have an interesting group of children growing up about them. Their names are Perry, Sarah, Harry and Mildred. (The house and farm now belong to the Welch Brothers.)

The possessions of Eliphalet Crisler attract us next. Mr. C. is a son of Adam Crisler, a resident of the north part of Rose. Mr. C. has five acres of land, and in the extreme northwest corner, just on the street, is a little house which was once the dwelling house of the former owners. It was moved here when the new house was erected. Just back of it are the remains of a stave cutting and cooper shop, for Mr. Crisler is a cooper by trade, though latterly he has done more at house-building. Eliphalet's wife was Lucina Lake of Huron, and they have one daughter, Ina. Mr.

Crisler bought of Francis Baker, who came here from Seneca Falls ; before that was from Webster, but remotely was a Long Islander. His son Horatio married a daughter of Leland Johnson. Back of Baker is James J. Vanderburgh, who divided his ten acres, giving half to his daughter, Mrs. Weeks. N. B. Hand preceded, and he went into the army during the War. One Swett also held it for a time, and his predecessor was Elder Andrew Wilkins, one of the most successful of the ministers who have presided over the Baptist Church in Rose. His sons are Hervey, Hartwell, Frank and Fred. All of these young men have proved pronounced successes in life, despite the oft-repeated slander against ministers' sons. The good clergyman died in 1884, at the age of sixty-nine, and is buried with many of his former parishioners in the Rose cemetery. His widow, who was Laurie Barnes, lives now in the Valley, preferring a home of her own to living with any one of her boys. Another minister preceded, Elder Amasa Curtis of the Baptist Church, whose younger two children were, I believe, born in Rose. In those days clergymen apparently found time to till a few acres as well as to attend to the spiritual wants of their flocks. Since the elder performed the marriage ceremony for my parents, his name has always had a special flavor for me. Before the preachers, came John Hyde, who had married the widow of Isaac Gillett, and thereby the mother of Almira Gillett, now of Wolcott. If any one of the feminine gender was ever better known in Rose than the before mentioned " Almi," I should like to know the name. As a peripatetic seamstress, she became the depository of nearly all the secrets in town. Her memory is a pleasant one.

One of the most noteworthy structures on the street, is that which we must cross the street to inspect. It is built of brick, one of the few farm houses in town thus constructed, and is the home of " Ham " Closs, the youngest son of John, the first comer. His wife is Lydia Ann Jones, a sister of the late Mrs. David Ellinwood. Their two sons, John and William, have already received mention in this volume. Everything about and within the premises indicates care and taste. Mr. Closs, in addition to his farm, has given much attention to speculation, and few men in Rose are better known.

We come next to the home of Mrs. Catharine Weeks, widow of Rufus K. We met the name when near the Catchpole farm, and can now learn a little more about the family. She was herself a sister of the W. S. Vanderburgh who lived so long on the Waldruff farm. As Sarah K. Vanderburgh she was born in Greene county. Her maternal grandfather Steinhart was one of those hated Hessians who came to New York with Burgoyne's army. A native of Hesse-Cassel, he had been impressed into the service of his prince, and so came to America. Once here he did not care to return, and marrying on the Hudson passed the remainder of his life there. Her father was James I. Vanderburgh, and her mother Hannah Steinhart. Of a large family of boys and girls, we are interested chiefly in William S. ; Elizabeth, who married Matthew Mackie, the Clyde nurseryman ; Abram D., who once lived east of John Lymans and who married Hannah Finch of District No. 5. Her home she has somewhat improved since buying of Dudley Wade. This was only a small portion, which, joined to the five acres had from the father, makes about six acres. Before Wade, Hamel Closs had owned it. The Vanderburghs were Baptists, while Mr. Weeks had been reared a Quaker.

Our southmost station is attained when we come to the home of George Seager, who, formerly from Huron, having married Jeannette Howland, daughter of George, purchased the property from the Talton heirs. There is a new house here supplanting the old one, which some years since was burned. These people have three children—Claude, Clara and Floy. Mr. Seager's predecessor, John T. Talton, was also known as Williams, there being some mystery about his name, but his tombstone in the cemetery, beside giving his name as Talton, tells us that he was a soldier during the War. It was during his holding that the house was burned. After this the family lived for a time in the barn opposite, and here, in 1882, at the age of fifty-four years, Mr. Talton died. His widow, having married Mr. Walmsley, resides in the Valley. Mr. T. left three sons. There are some more than fifty acres in the farm, and here, years since, Joel N. Lee reared his family. As we have stated elsewhere, he and his family were Vermonters, and no better people ever made their home in this town. Exemplary members of the Methodist Church, they lived and exemplified Christianity. One of their daughters is well known as Mrs. Charles S. Wright, of the Valley, and Lovina we have repeatedly met as Mrs. C. C. Collins, now living in Wolcott : Theresa married Charles Kingsley, son of Harris R., a former Methodist minister in Rose. On his death she returned to the village of Rose, and with her, until their deaths, the aged parents made their home, having given up their farm. Mrs. K. now lives in Batavia. The only son, Addis C., became a soldier during the War. Mr. Joel Lee finished his earthly pilgrimage in 1880, a little more than eighty-three years old. His wife died in 1876 at the age of seventy-five. Mr. Lee sold his farm to his son-in-law, Charles S. Wright, who rented it to different people, among others to Sidney J. Hopping, now living on the Dudley Wade farm, in the confines of Butler. The farm has had many mutations. Taken up by Stephen Brooks, there were at first 115 acres, all but 15 being on the east side of the road. Brooks sold 46 acres from the north side of his farm to Zenas Fairbanks. The remainder was sold to Joel N. Lee in 1826. In 1827 Mr. Z. F. sold ten acres on the road to his cousin, C. W. Fairbanks, and going down to the east end of the lot went into extensive mercantile business, shoe making, lime burning, etc.

OLD AND NEW SCHOOL HOUSE, NORTH ROSE.

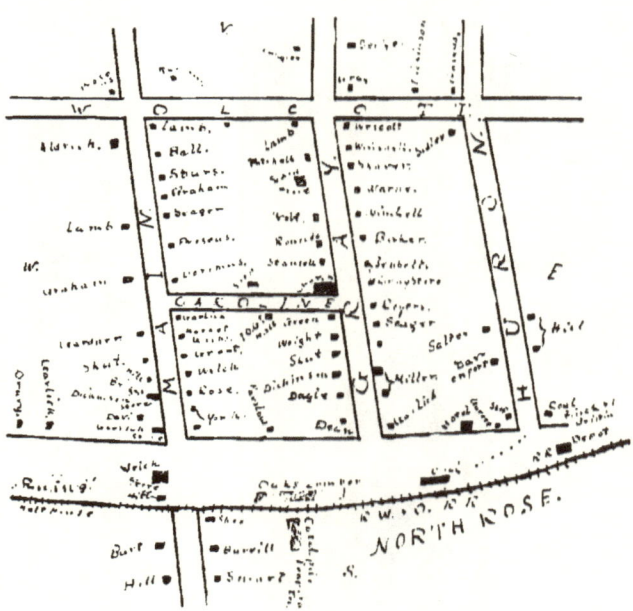

PLAN OF NORTH ROSE.

Later the Fairbankses changed places, and afterward Zenas sold to John Hyde and went to the Covell district. In 1836 C. W. Fairbanks sold to Royal Turner, who also bought out Hyde. Mr. Turner was noted for his law suit tendencies. Both he and his wife lived to be more than 90 years old. Through many changes, the place passed to John B. Lyman and to Crisler and to Mrs. Weeks. (Mr. F. H. Closs now owns the Joel Lee part.)

As the next step will take us to the Valley district, we shall delay that move until we have visited the northern portions of the town, preferring to work from the circumference inward rather than from the heart outward. So then, just under the shadow of the hill, at whose base the Miricks located, we must leave District No. 3.

DISTRICT No. 2.—NORTH ROSE.

April 11—June 27, 1889.

The appellation North Rose is a comparatively new one. To the old inhabitants it was Lamb's corners, and the emigrant who left his native heath in the long ago would gaze in wonderment at our heading, mentally exclaiming : " What *terra incognita* have we here ? " This hamlet of ours is fifteen years old, dating from the opening of the then Lake Shore R. R., now the R. W. & O. R. R.; up to the seventies, where now are houses, gardens, stores and shops, the Aldriches and Briggses raised crops, for the village lies exclusively on land that was once theirs. The railroad went a long distance out of its course to reach as far south as it does, running on one side of a rather short ellipse, almost a circle, but even then, it could not get nearer the Valley than two miles and a half. Locating a station here, known on the time card as Rose, the village is a consequence. As this is the only railroad passing through the town, it will not be amiss to follow its course from entering to leaving. Having nipped off a corner of Huron, it comes into Rose on P. T. Lewis' land, thence, extending southeast, it crosses the Huron road just north of Richard Garratt's ; still continuing thus, it runs diagonally over the next east and west road a few rods west of William H. Cole's. Coming through a deep cut, trains sometimes pick up cattle here. On one of my walks I came along just after a fine cow belonging to Isaac Cole had been thus cut in pieces. (In 1893, Charles Harper lost two.) Crossing Cole's farm and the next north and south road, just south of Carrier's corners, it passes through Avery H. Gillett's possessions and those of Nelson R. Graham. On the latter's farm the grading covered up a fine spring, and on this account the elder Graham, Henry, claimed extra damages, but the company demurred and left the matter out to arbitration. The award was considerably in excess of the amount demanded by Mr. G., thus justifying his claim. Its extreme southern range is reached when it crosses the Sodus road at North Rose, whence it tends northward, with just one variation west of Glenmark, and that a slight one, till a few rods south of the Huron line it runs into Sodus. What might have been is naturally suggested. I understand that neither Rose nor Huron would bond itself to help the enterprise. Had Huron done so and Rose had continued obdurate, naturally the road would have made its Huron station at Port Glasgow, and that place must have regained some of its prosperity destroyed by the building of the Erie canal. Lake navigation and railroad transportation would have made her a no mean rival of Clyde and Lyons, and leaving Wolcott quite in the lurch. Again, had Rose bonded and Huron not, the station could easily have been located as near the Valley as the end of the old Sherman or Merrick Hill, i. e., the present residence of Mr. Isaac Campbell. The Valley would have had the business since located in North Rose and the latter village would not exist. However, our village is a reality, but it is entirely too recent and new to be interesting. Were it placed on a western prairie it would be content with no such modest name as it now bears, but it had long since been Aldrich or Briggs City, or Maltopolis, or some equally sonorous word. Long ago it would have had a race course, half a dozen hotels, so called, a brass band and a national bank. As it is, the neighboring Valley becomes somewhat suppressing, and, perhaps, retards its otherwise more vigorous boom. There is little of the antique in a place only fifteen years old. There are no old houses, no traditions, even the shade trees look new, quite too new for history. We shall find no material here for another Miss Mitford's "Our Village," while the railroad and the immense malt-house quite as effectually prevent a reproduction of George MacDonald's "Annals of a Quiet Neighborhood. The name is a happy one, locating as it does the place. Besides, there was already another Lamb's corners in the state, in Albany county.

Now, then, we will suppose that we have journeyed north from the Valley, have passed through the Lyman district, and leaving the same at the interesting old house of Mrs. Charity Stearns, née Bishop, we shall find our first stopping place, singularly enough, to be the cemetery.

More fortunate than some, we are still able to leave the cemetery, and we halt under a dense cluster of locusts, and find at our right the home of the late Jonathan Briggs, while opposite are the barns in which he stored the products of his fertile acres. We now find as occupants the widow, her daughter, Mrs. Post, and her children. Mr. Briggs was born in Rhode Island, but when only three years old his parents moved to Cincinnatus, this state. His father was John Briggs, who married Margaret Jones, also a Rhode Islander, and sister of Pardon Jones, so well known in Rose.

Mr. Briggs himself early found a veritable helpmeet in Emeline Baker, a sister of Julius, of this same North Rose district, her native place being Watertown, Conn. It was in March, 1844, that Jonathan Briggs moved from Seneca county to this farm. Before the railroad got into it, it numbered, with the accessions that he had made, 213 acres. He was bounded on the south by Bishop and Bender, and on the north by Aldrich. Mindful of the Scriptural injunction to increase and multiply, these good people added to the world's numbers six sons and two daughters. Of these, the oldest, John, married Sarah Jane Otto, and lives, as has been seen, on the old Otto farm just over the Huron line; the next son, George, was drowned some years ago, at the age of twenty-five years; Birney, a carpenter by trade, lives in the adjacent village, and his wife was Anna Terry, of Clyde; Luman and Lyman are twins, and they married twin sisters, Ellen and Helen Doremus, whose father also now dwells in the village, while Luman's home is the Valley, and Lyman lives in Huron; Elbert, having married Nancy Ewing, of Alton, abides in North Rose; Caroline is the wife of William Niles of the Valley, while the youngest child, Sophia, married George H. Post, from Waverly, Tioga county. She has three children—Nellie M., who recently married Julian S. Cross from Broome county; Minnie E. and Alice E. In the same yard with the Briggs homestead is a large house constructed some years ago by Mr. B. for his youngest daughter and her family, but recently she has dwelt with her mother. Mr. Briggs was one of the solid men of the town, not conspicuous in politics, but a man of superior judgment and ability. He was a good representative of the state that gave to the world Tristam Burgess and Nathaniel Greene. Earnest and honest, faithful, liberal and devoted, he was and is sadly missed from his town and church, he having been for many years prominent in the Rose Baptist organization, dying in 1881. He was in his sixty-ninth year. (Mrs. Briggs died August 1, 1891.) Before Mr. Briggs, no one was long identified with the place. He bought of William H. King, of Seneca Falls, who by trade had obtained it. Mr. King never lived here. The last one occupying before Mr. B. was Henry Graham, who here, I believe, made his first essay at farming. One Smith also held, and before him John Brant. First of all was James Leland, who sold and removed to Ohio. Leland had three sons—Lewis, Gale and Isaac. The latter, returning to his old home on a visit, went bathing one day in the Lamb mill pond, and diving, struck his head against something. The injury received resulted in illness, from which he died in about three weeks. (Mr. John Briggs will soon occupy the old homestead.) The next house is that of William Smart. He passed his boyhood in No. 7. His wife is Nellie Perkins, once living in District No. 3. They have one child, Nellie. Mr. S. is employed on the railroad.

Further along is the abode of Edward Burrell, a native of Galen, who came from that town to Rose, and, on the once well tilled acres of Briggs, has planted his vine and fig tree. His home is a pleasant one. His first wife was Charlotte M. Odell, a native of Tyre, N. Y. Their children are E. O., who married Cornelia Hart of Huron, and lives in North Rose; Dorothea, died in infancy, and Cuthbert, who lives in Woodland, Cal. Mrs. B. dying in 1870, Mr. B. married, second, Jane A. (Clark) Mains, in 1872. She died in 1887. Nearly opposite, Mr. William Hill erected in 1889 a very fine residence, and occupies it. He is a house painter and paper hanger by occupation. He came to Rose from Huron, being a native of that town. His wife is Alida, a daughter of Abram Doremus. Eugene Brewster is just finishing a house, next, which in no way suffers by comparison with others in the village. He comes from west of the Valley and finds employment in the lumber yard. (Now the home of Ira Burt, late of Galen, who has left his farm in the care of his two sons, and with his wife has come to this village to reside. They have also two daughters married. Across the street a Mr. Taylor of South Butler is erecting a basket factory [Aug., 1893] and further east is the extensive evaporator of Hill & Quereau, lately sold to Mr. George Catchpole of the Valley.)

This brings us to the railroad, and just over the same, at our left, we must see the immense malt house of John York, Jr. In fact it was visible some time ago, rising much more conspicuously than the single church which the hamlet possesses. To those who can find pleasure in such a presence, this building must be a source of no little pride. As for myself, I allude to it simply as a very striking edifice and illustrative of business enterprise. My birth, rearing and profession, however, lead me to look upon malt houses, brewers and saloons as not indicative of a community's true prosperity. Mr. York is from Huron, a member of the family that has given its name to a portion of the southwest part of the town. His wife is Martha Weeks, a daughter of Caleb, and his home is at the right, the first house on the east corner, north of the railroad. In this part of the town, probably, Mr. York exercises a wider influence politically than any other one individual. The beginning of this structure was made in 1873, and it was simply a grain and fruit storehouse, being enlarged from time to time until, in 1882, it became a malt and storehouse, and assumed its present mammoth proportions. The builders at first were Mr. York and Robert A. Catchpole, of Huron. (The whole structure was totally consumed by fire, Thursday, May 14, 1891.)

Had we glanced to the right, in crossing, we would have met the prosperous lumber yard of Charles Oaks. How desirable that there should be agreement in name and business. Mr. Wise ought to be a school master, certainly Mr. Good would befit the pulpit, and that Mr. Oaks should sell lumber, goes far to preserve the unities so desirable in nature and art. The business was started in 1871 by Straight & Munn. Three years since Mr. Oaks bought out Mr. Straight, who went to Wolcott, and is in the same business there. After one year's continuance with Mr. Munn, the latter sold out entirely to Mr. Oaks and went to Iowa. Since then Mr. O. has run the plant alone. (The office of Mr. John Hill stands nearest the railroad, on the west side of the street. Mr. Hill deals extensively in fruit and agricultural implements.)

The large hardware store of the Welch Bros. is on the west side of the road and north of the way leading to the malt house. Thomas Welch is also postmaster (though he has recently resigned). The building was erected by Lyman Briggs, nearly opposite and on railroad land, and was then moved to its present location. In their line of work the Welch Bros. have no rivals in the town. Early and late they are devoted to their vocation. Naturally, they have been very successful. Back of the stores, facing the most of the malt house, are two dwellings, the first, Harriet Garlick's, the second, Frank Drury's. Lest we should engender confusion we will keep on this side of the street until we get to the Proseus corner.

An Irishman was once sent to count a litter of pigs. He discharged his duty to the best of his ability, though he declared that one little rascal wasn't still long enough to be counted. Since preparing the following article, I have seen in the correspondence of papers, printed in Rose and vicinity, so many statements of movings, that, like a kaleidoscope, the village must have been turned and the harmonies must be entirely different from those seen in August last. I describe the streets as I saw them then.

So then, the next place is the store of Henry Garlick, under the management of his son, Charles. Right here we may as well introduce a little Garlic into our composition, premising that the most anti-Spanish reader will not find the flavor disagreeable. Captain Samuel Garlick, whose body lies in the Rose cemetery, was a soldier in Revolutionary days, having served eighteen months in the patriot army, though very young. He was a native of Huntington, Conn., and when, one Sunday, the good pastor of the church, Dr. Ely, was preaching his usual discourse, there came a swiftly riding herald, who passed in a note to the preacher. Its purport was that the British were devastating the Sound coast. There was no delay for further service. The same God that enjoined prayer, counseled also watching, and fighting, too, if necessary. So pastor and people went into the fray. Young Garlick went with the rest, and thus made a record of which his descendants are justly proud. He was twice married—first, to Sally Lewis and second to Huldah Gilbert. By each of these wives he was the father of four sons and three daughters. The first family embraced Samuel, Eliphalet, Ezekiel, Eli, Sally, Eliza and Abbie. Of these, Eli married Margaret, a sister of Abner Wood, and daughter of that widow

Margaret Wood who became the wife of Paine Phillips. His family was numerous, consisting of Abner, Sidney, who married a Messenger; Samuel, who married a Weeks; Sally, the wife of Henry Garlick, and Barbara. Eli, an aged man, lives now in a small house just back of the Welch Bros. store. He has been an industrious blacksmith all his long life. (Died in January, 1892.) The second group of Capt. Samuel's children was composed of William, David, Henry, Judson, Mary, Maria and Lucy. David married Tabatha Angle, of Rose, while Henry, in whom we are chiefly interested now, took for his first wife Sally, the daughter of his half-brother, Eli. When Captain G. came to these parts, it was to make his home, in 1810, in Galen, on or near the Ketchum place, east of Clyde. He built the old Waldruff house. His father, a very aged man, accompanied him, and lived, I am told, to be one hundred and ten years old. His grave may be found near the old home, east of the village of Clyde. At the time of coming the country was a wilderness, and Henry Garlick says that his mother has ridden her horse by blazed trees from Galen to the old Mudge store in Wolcott, to do a little trading. On the morning after William Garlick's marriage, three inches of snow lay on the bed covering, so many and wide were the crevices in the roof. From Galen the family came to Rose, settling on the Messenger farm, in the western part of the town, buying of one Bacon. Full of years, Capt. Garlick passed away April 28, 1843, in the eightieth year of his age. His son, Samuel, lies by his side. To his father on the farm Henry succeeded, but much of his life has been passed in a grist-mill and in a blacksmith shop. For a long time he ran the mill in Glenmark, and later the blacksmith shop in North Rose. His children are Charles, already mentioned; Frank, a farmer in Huron (now in Coyell's district), whose wife is Clara Terbush; Emmaette, deceased, the wife of Eugene Elwood, and Edith, who is Mrs. Frank Riggs. Romaine Cole built the house in which the Garlic store is kept, just after the railroad was opened, and ran a store for two years. Afterward Irwin Seelye and Lyman Briggs were in partnership here for two years longer, then Seelye had it alone till the Garlicks took it. (Charles Garlick was postmaster during Harrison's administration.)

Somewhat back from the street is a small house, in which lives Frank Davis, a stone mason, who came here from Huron. He is the father of Ellery Davis, of the Town district. The building is noteworthy from the fact that in it was kept the first store in the place. Built by William Dickinson, it originally stood just east of the old school-house, on the site of Robert Andrews' old shoe shop. Here the first place of trade was opened and maintained, till the house itself was moved to its present location, and pretentious structures put it in the shade.

Again we find a store, managed by C. C. Shaw, from Sodus. The house was built by Irwin Seelye, but is now owned and occupied by Nancy Briggs. (In the lower story Jay R. Dickinson now keeps a store.)

John T. Hill lives next. He came here from Huron and is interested in the York storehouse. To him is due the credit of starting the village. His wife is Elizabeth Seager, and his children are Frank and Roy.

Next we find the house of Alexander Skut, but of him and his more anon. (Now the home of his widow and family.)

Then comes the home to which Samuel Gardner came when he left his Huron farm. Mr. G. was a native of Rensselaer county, and his first wife was Hannah Brewster, of Lansingburg, and their only son we shall meet as we journey northward. For his second wife he married Happilona Chatterson, daughter of John P., whose home was in the Covell district, and thereby granddaughter of Betts, whom we saw in the Seelye neighborhood. (Her only daughter is Mrs. S. H. Lyman, and the latter has a son and daughter.)

Murray Becker, a recent comer from Red Creek, resides in the next house, and, for a livelihood, carries the mail to Huron. (In 1893 the home of Mrs. Alfred Graham and mother.) His neighbor on the north, John Lamb, we shall learn more about when we get to the old homestead. Myron Huffman, a brother-in-law, lives with him.

All Rose people have long known the next place as the old Aldrich farm ; but its history goes back many years before these people came hither. It is lot 151 in the old numbering, and hither, in 1813, came Isaac Gillett. He came from Hubbardton, Vt., where he had married Sally Sellick, who was a niece, through her mother, of Isaac Hickok. Though they hailed directly from the Green Mountains, they were originally from Connecticut. Isaac's father, John, came also, and died in Huron in 1819. One of the Gilletts married Rhoda Avery, a sister of Joel Bishop's wife. Perhaps it is as well to trace Isaac Gillett further. To begin with, he was a cousin of Asahel and Harvey. From Rose he went to Huron, and at his death, in 1829, at the early age of forty-five, he was the proprietor of the hotel at Bay Bridge or Port Glasgow. His widow rented this for a time to Henry Graham, well known in Rose. After a while she married John Hyde, a brother of the famous Zenas Hyde, and whom, as a shoemaker, we have seen in District No. 3 as one of the many dwellers in the old house on the present Crisler place. Making a visit to his old home in Massachusetts, he died and was buried there thirty years ago. To Isaac Gillett were born several children, as Isaac Newton and Chauncey H., both born in Vermont and both went to Junius to live ; Prosper, in Missouri ; Moses, in Rochester ; Almira, born on the Aldrich place ; Rhoda, who married E. J. Jackway, an uncle of Avery Gillett's wife, and went to Benton Harbor, Mich.; Sally, who married Charles Kelsey, of Galen, and died in July, 1888. Of these children, Almira and Rhoda were best known in this town. They long lived together in the Valley and took care of their mother, who finally died in Throopsville, in 1862. After the marriage of Rhoda, Almira

10

passed many years in this and adjoining towns as a nurse and seamstress, her services always in request and her presence always enjoyed. If, from the misty past, she could call up all the gossip she has heard, what a recital it would be for the readers and hearers! Failing health now keeps her pretty closely at her Wolcott home. To Gillett succeeded Peter Lamb, a member of the family, whose name has been so long connected with this section. They were from Schoharie county, of good Dutch stock. The wife was Sally —, and the children were : Asahel, who married Jane Burns, Joel Bishop's granddaughter; David, who was an odd mortal; Hiram found his wife west of the Valley, in Diana Cooley, and lived once on the Catchpole farm ; Perry; Ira, who took Perliette Lovejoy for his companion; Lorenzo, Louisa and Laretta. All went to Michigan, and all are dead. Simeon Mott was the next, but how long he remained I can not tell. He had a son, Chauncey, and a daughter, Jerusha, who became Mrs. John Ellsworth ; but it was a sad day for the latter when she took his name. She was a terrible shrew. Says John Lamb : "I was working with Ellsworth in the woods one day when Rusha came along. Her man was stooping down at work, partly under the sleigh. She took up a big knot and was about to hit him on the back. I told her if she did I'd hit her. By this time Ellsworth was out, and, taking the ox gad, he went for her. It was not much of a place for sympathy on either side." In 1833 Amos Aldrich came to this place, succeeding Mott. The house that he found is now George Aldrich's pig pen. He built anew, and with sundry repairs the place is as he made it. His wife was Sally Luce, and they came here from the town of Arcadia, though Mr. A. was born in Rhode Island, where at present one of the U. S. senators bears the honored name of Aldrich. Both husband and wife, after long and respected lives, sleep in the North Rose burial ground. At one time they were members of the Rose Methodist Episcopal Church. Of their children : Joseph lived once west of the corners and then went to Ohio (died in April, 1889); James Benjamin we shall meet east of the corners, while George, who married Ella J. Carrier, retains the old homestead. As they have a son, John C., we may hope that the place will continue in Aldrich hands for another fifty years. The row of houses that we have passed has taken the street front from the farm, but there are still fertile acres remaining. The family has found many queer water-worn rocks on the premises and Indian arrow heads, indicating the early presence of the aborigines. Mrs. A. has also a very fine Indian gonge, found on the farm, and, so far as I know, the only one ever found in the town.

We are now at the corners, the site of the village that was to be, the place near which were the school-house, blacksmith and shoe shops, and several dwelling houses, but the incoming railroad changed it all. The southeast corner was reserved twenty-one years by Fellows & McNab, to be given as a site for a church, but the church didn't materialize, though I understand that Henry Graham and others had spells of trying to raise money to construct it. So, after a while, the inevitable log house came and was occupied by many families, among whom were William Green and John Waterhouse. After a time, Cornelius Van Buren bought and built the house now standing. He was from Dutchess county, and for many years worked at blacksmithing, east of his home and then nearly opposite. He disposed of his lot, and for a while owned the Eldred place. As he and his good wife had no children in these parts, they passed all their possessions over to Henry Garlic for a home to the end of life, and with the Garlics they lived till they passed over the river. Myron Lamb, a son of John, followed. His wife was Anna Weeks, of eastern birth, a sister of Mrs. John Lovejoy of Glenmark. Mr. Lamb is a carpenter by trade, finding here, with wife and daughter, Minnie, a happy home. (The latter is now Mrs. Albert Dagle of Rose.)

Carpenter Birney Briggs, a son of Jonathan, dwells next toward the south, for we will now run down the east side of the street. (In 1893 the home of George H. Ball, born in Cayuga county, who married Sarah, daughter of John Seager of Huron. They have one child, Myrtie. Mr. Ball is interested in raising raspberries, and is about building in District No. 3, near the old Oaks place. Mr. Briggs is in Rochester.)

Martin Sours, a recent comer, lives in the following place, once the home of Burton Partridge.

Then comes another carpenter, Frank Prosens, a son of Mrs. P., on the corner. Certainly, with so many of this profession in the vicinity, there should be no lack of building forces. Judging from his own house, Frank must be a good workman.

Still another carpenter, Warren Morey, follows in "Abe" Doremus' house, and this brings us to Caroline street. (Mr. Dillon, a shoemaker, lived in the Doremus house in 1893.)

Then we find the pleasant home of Henry Garlic, followed by a building in which Myron Lamb and Albert Dagle conduct a meat market (1893). John Weeks owns the building and lives in the upper rooms. In order follow the homes of Fred Grant, Thomas Welch and William C. Rose. In the first of the two houses belonging to Mrs. John York, dwells Mr. C. Halliday, who married Celinda Patterson, of the Lake district. Mrs. York resides on the corner. On Railroad street is the home of Nelson Parslow, who is the father-in-law of Edgar Dean, living on Gray street.

The next street, Gray, runs parallel with the main road; but I can't help thinking that the village had been prettier had it ranged itself around the four corners, thereby escaping the melancholy view of so many rears of houses and their accompaniments. In this respect, the mile-long, single-streeted New England village was far in advance of the more ambitious towns of recent and sudden growth. But moralizing will not take us along the street, which, whether we like it or not, is a verity. On the west side we shall find Samuel McIntyre, a gardener. (Mr. Edgar Dean has built and now occupies a fine house on this site.) Then Mr. Dagle. (Now occupied by Mr. Charles Bowman.) Mr. Charles Dagle, who, in 1893, lives in Huron, is a native of Kingston, Canada: his wife, Adelia Kirwin, was born in Ireland. Their children are Louvinda, the wife of George E. Miller; Ida, who is Mrs. Valentine of Marengo: Charles, died in infancy; Frank, died June 24. 1883, aged 32 years: Addison; Albert; Wallace, died July 14, 1891, aged 22 years; Harvey and Annabelle, at home. Next is Jay Dickinson, whose old home we shall find in our eastward journey; he is a carpenter by trade, and saw service during the Rebellion; his wife was Elizabeth Bovee, and she has borne him a numerous progeny, consisting of William, Robert D., Charles A., Stephen, George, John and Minnie, who is Mrs. Van Sicklen. Mr. Dickinson is a son of the late William Dickinson, and a carpenter by trade. Mrs. Frank Skut, with her daughter May, resides next. (Mrs. Skut is now Mrs. A. H. Mudge of Cortland.) Then John Morey, a carpenter. (Now in Rochester, and the house is occupied by Manly Wright, the Rose station agent.) And next, William Green.

Now we are at Caroline street, and on the corner stands a very pretty edifice, the result of the generosity of the surrounding inhabitants. Where all were generous, it would seem almost invidious to mention names, but it may not be amiss to state that it stands on what was Aldrich land, that it cost $2,000, and that John York, Jr., Nelson Graham, Orrin Skut and others were liberal givers toward this very laudable object.

On Caroline street itself stands the blacksmith shop of G. W. Stansell. The building, an old one, once stood quite near the corners by the school-house, having been moved to that point by Cornelius Van Buren. He, too, had moved it from very near the point where the railroad crosses the main road, it having been the home of one Hudson. Across the way is the unoccupied Good Templar hall, erected in 1889. Returning to Gray street and continuing north, we pass the homes of George W. Stansell, whose house is a new one. John Rounds, Henry Courtermarch (occupied by J. M. Wolf), and Barnard Mitchell.

Coming back on the east side we are attracted by the pleasant home of Everett Slaght. He married Harriet E., daughter of James B. Aldrich. He makes quite a business of berries, raising and dealing in them. (Mr. Slaght's present residence is Rochester, he being employed on the Western New York & Pennsylvania R. R. To him has succeeded Mr. David West-cott, who, a glass-blower by trade, has lived in Clyde and the west. His second wife is Sarah Ann, widow of Christopher Dickinson of Clyde, and oldest daughter of the late William Dickinson, of Rose.)

Southward we find the homes of Wallace W. Winchell, C. M. Shaver, who married the widow of John Hewson, and a house belonging to Samuel Warne; Calvin R. Winchell, who dwells next, is a member of the family met in District No. 10. His son, Wallace W., married Mattie, daughter of Elmer Partridge, of Huron; Frank L. Winchell married Louise A. Cole, and lives in Rochester. Ella Winchell is Mrs. Charles W. Oaks. Marcus Baker owns next, and Elmer Winchell occupies. Dr. T. D. Tibbetts, who keeps a drug store and grocery, follows. He came from Williamson, and married Josephine Derby. They have one child, Ross D. Dr. T. built his own edifices, and also the house of Mr. Henry Garlick. He carries the mail to Lummisville in Huron. Then follow William Rogers, George Seager and Lewis Sours, the house and blacksmith shop owned by George Miller and the abode of Abram Doremus, whose twin daughters married Jonathan Briggs' twin sons. Until he moved here he was a farmer in the western part of the town. (Now the home of Charles H. Garlick, who married Mary R. Travers of Tyre.)

Still further east, there will be eventually another street, and, already on hand awaiting the street, are the homes of Jerome Davenport, David Hill (not the governor), Peter Salter and George Parslow. Beyond these even is the abode of widow Hannah Quackenbush, in a house built by William Dickinson. We must not slight the very necessary hotel, which dates from railroad times, and which was constructed by Thomas Parks, but is now the property of William Roe of Wolcott. It has had numerous landlords, of whom we might name John Decker, who died here, and the present Myron Brant, a son of that John Brant who years ago lived on the Briggs farm. (In 1893 Miss Ara A. Barnum owns the hotel, which is kept by Mr. Guy Beadle. The street to the eastward has been built and changes have been made as indicated in the village plan.)

North Rose as a post office dates from war times. In 1861 "Ben" Aldrich opened the office, and kept it where Mr. Thompson now lives, north of the old school-house. Then David Lyman had it in the little red house, nearly opposite the school-house. Morton Tripp followed in the Eldred house. Jonathan Briggs then had the honor for a while, having the office in the railroad station. Romaine Cole was next, followed by Lyman Briggs, in 1877, who in turn passed the privilege of the place to Irwin Seelye, in 1882. He was postmaster till Grover Cleveland made Nelson Graham postmaster, in 1885. Irwin, however, continued as deputy until recently, when the country was made thoroughly safe by passing the office from an old soldier to Thomas B. Welch, who maintained the same in his hardware store. [Since writing the foregoing, Mr. Welch has resigned.]

The house on the northwest corner of the cross roads is much changed from its former appearance. It was away back in the twenties that Gilbert Miner, a seafaring man, and a bachelor brother of Prentice Miner, already on the ground, was persuaded to erect on this conspicuous corner a tavern. Ansel Gardner was the builder, but before the work of rum selling (in those days the chief business of hotel keeping) could begin, a great temperance wave swept over the country, meetings being held in churches and school-houses, and Othello's occupation was gone. Prentice Miner lived here some years, till, selling out, he went to Michigan. He had three children. I have heard him described as a short man, duck-legged, a sailor in early life, but could out-jump anybody in the neighborhood. The place was owned for a time by a Mr. Simmons, then by a Mr. Young of Geneva. Jonathan Briggs possessed it also, and from him, I believe, it passed to Franklin M. Prosens, who, a native of Dutchess county, came to Rose from Sodus. He enlisted in Company G, Ninth New York Heavy Artillery, and died in 1862, leaving a widow and two children. Mrs. P. was born in Sodus—her maiden name was Anna M. Lake—though the family was of Connecticut extraction. Her maternal grandfather, Horace Terry, died from wounds received at Sodus Point, in the War of 1812. Her son, Allen, married Sophia Andrews, and resides in Huron, while Frank, who married Nellie Tryon, lives in the village. His two children are Frank and Fern.

On the east side of the road, a few rods to the north, two apple trees standing in the field are near the site of the McWharf home, mentioned in the Lake district series. A spring of clear cold water and a consequent stream were doubtless the motives for locating his home thus. He had fifteen acres conveniently near the home of Jonathan Skut, his brother-in-law. The latter's home was over the way and still a trifle to the north of the site of the present house of Orrin Skut. The family was immediately from Onondaga county, but the name is uncommonly suggestive of the Hudson river region, and of those sturdy Dutch burghers, whose stalwart proportions the members of the family still possess. However, the first Mrs. S. was Hannah Rowe, and she was the mother of a large number of children, as follows: Orrin, Charles, David, Andrew, Horace, Mahala, Caroline and Esther. With the marriages of these people we are interested only in that of Charles, who took for his wife an adopted daughter of Eli Andrus, and Orrin's. All the family went to Michigan, but Orrin tired of the country and came back. He says now that he is sorry that he returned. He had learned the cooper's trade, and in the newer regions of the west there was little demand for what he had to give. The elder Skuts, after living for a time on Crusoe Island, in Savannah, went to Michigan and there died many years since. The wood colored house, long prominent here, was built by Jonathan Skut and still remains, though repaired and painted. Here Orrin Skut lived for many years, tilling his forty-eight acres and pursuing his trade. He now lives in the village near. He did not follow his father immediately as owner, having managed it seven years as superintendent for a Mr. Angus, to whom Jonathan had sold. His wife was Almira Lamb, a daughter of Isaac, one of the pioneers. Their children were : Alexander, who, though owning a farm in Huron, has his home in North Rose, and with him his father lives. His wife is Melinda Jones, of Huron, and they have three children—Cora, Annette and Orrin ; the second son, Ira, married Helen Creque of Wolcott, and died in 1881 ; he was a soldier during the War ; Jerome died in 1862 ; Jasper married Frank Park of Wolcott, and went west some years ago. The only daughter, Annette, is the wife of Alexander Ellinwood, of Clinton, Oneida county. Mrs. Orrin Skut died in January, 1886. With both Alexander and Jerome I was well acquainted, having been a fellow pupil with them in Fulton, and know personally of their sterling worth. Jerome was only twenty-two years old at his death. Orrin Skut has been, in one way or another, a town officer for eighteen years, the most of the time a commissioner of highways. (Orrin Skut died May 6, 1892, and June 12, 1892, Alexander died. The place is now occupied by William Dickinson, who married Irene, daughter of Frank Davis, and has children, Forrest, and a baby girl.)

We are pretty near the confines of the town when we reach the next farm, that of Charles G. Oaks, a son of that Charles G. Oaks who lived and died in the Lyman district. He was a soldier during the War, and his wife was Huldah Wilson, a daughter of Robert Wilson, whose home this was for many a year.

One more remove and we reach Daniel Skut, a brother of Jonathan. He, too, had a large family, which also emigrated to Michigan. His children were Robert, Apollos, Daniel, Abram, Truman, Betsey and Hannah, who became the wife of one Sumner, whose father was an early dweller on the Cephas Bishop farm. When the Skuts left, there were only fourteen acres cleared. In the farm, however, there were one hundred acres. The house, as usual, was built of logs, and water was brought from a spring. To this place came, in 1835, Robert Wilson, a native of Romulus, but moving from Dundee. Yates county. His wife was Catharine Raplee, changed, undoubtedly, from the Hudson river name Rapalye. She was born in Dundee. Here these good Baptist people lived and reared their children, building finally the pleasant house now the home of the Oakses. The oldest son, Luther, married Cynthia Boynton, and lives on the next road east, holding a farm formerly a part of the paternal acreage. Mary N. Wilson married Gilbert A. Chapin, and resides now in Denison, Texas. Huldah, the wife of Charles G. Oaks, died in January, 1887, leaving four children, of whom Katie is the wife of James Thomas, of Huron, while Charles W., Marilla and Robert L. are at home. Robert Wilson died in 1868, in his sixty-third year. His widow, quite infirm on account of a fall, makes her home on the old farm with the family of her daughter, Huldah. (C. W. Oaks married Ella L. Winchell, and they have a son, Seth Carroll ; Marilla Oaks is Mrs. Edgar C. Davis, of Central Falls. R. I.)

Our last house faces a road which was once a public way extending down to the Glenmark road, but which terminates now at the home of Ogden Van Sicklen. As laid out many years ago, it led to the property of Isaac Lamb, the first settler here. He was a stirring, enterprising man, and, in 1823, built a saw-mill west of his house, obtaining power by damming the stream which ran through the gully. This mill was in operation more than sixty years, and it fell into decay only when the need of it ceased. It doubtless is responsible for the denudation of the surrounding country, and through said destruction, the stream has dried up so that water power would be quite out of the question. Further up the glen, many years since, the same Ansel Gardner, before referred to, built a mill for carding wool, but it was never utilized. It was just back of Orrin Sknt's home. Fifteen years after the construction of the saw-mill, Mr. Lamb built a grist-mill a half mile down the stream, and the road was correspondingly extended, having, up to this time, terminated at the saw-mill. This must have been a very rough, winding, hilly way, and after the mill went down, I don't wonder that the road was taken up. As we approach from the east, we should have seen, first, the miller's house, in which lived many families, and at one time the Huffmans, with whom the Lambs married. Not a trace of it is now standing. Down under a steep bank, nestled the mill years ago, and many a bushel of wheat was turned into material for the staff of life by the water that long since ran by. It is easy to trace the old dam, and, with some difficulty, I can find indications of the race way, which bore the motive power to the mill, and as the fifty years roll away, in fancy I see the boys of then (the grand-sires of to-day), just as boys will ever do, leaving their clothes on the bank, while they seek happiness in the cooling waters ; or, earlier in the season, trying to secure nibbles from passing minnows by the temptations of a wriggling worm. Perhaps, in winter, our boys of "ye olden time" have bumped their heads in essaying the pleasures of skating. All these fancies float before me on a burning hot day in August, and I, too, sigh for the consolation of the bath or the shade of the glen beneath. Imagination must be drawn upon to call back the old mill, of which there is not a rack left behind. One of the old stones serves Myron Lamb, at the corners in North Rose, for a horse block, and the other is lost to sight and search in the morass near which the building was located. So much for these buildings of old : now let us return to the abodes of men, and pause where Ogden Van Sicklen has his home.

It was many years ago that Isaac Lamb broke into this primeval wilderness and began his living. His cabin and his surroundings were like those of his neighbors. He came directly from Cayuga county in 1820. His wife was Sally Stanley, and they were both Methodists. After many years here, they yielded to their son, John, and, buying ten acres west of

Aldrich's, built a house and dwelt for a time. Mrs. L. died in 1846, aged sixty-nine. After her death the husband went to Lyons, where he died in 1862, at the home of Ira Mirick, his son-in-law, at the age of eighty-six. No trace of his home on the Glenmark road now exists. Both of these good people now sleep in the North Rose burial ground. Their oldest son, Isaac, Jr., married Emeline Hickok, a daughter of Moses, and we shall soon see him again. William married a McWharf, as already noted, and died in Huron. John we shall presently meet; Martha, as the wife of Ira Mirick, must wait till we get to the Valley district; Polly married John Baker, and, after living in Rose, went to Michigan; Almira we have met as Orrin Skut's wife; Jane never married, and died in Lyons some years ago. Somewhat peculiar in manner and speech, she is said to have responded to a query as to why she didn't accept a certain offer of heart and hand : "Do you suppose that I am going to take up with every old jackass that comes along!" Sally Ann became the wife of William Blighton, in Galen, and apropos to this same is suggested a couplet that irreverent youths sometimes sang in "ye good old days :"

> "So glad I come, old Daddy Lamb,
> Oh, won't you give me Sally Ann?"

Isaac Lamb, Jr., and wife succeeded his father. They lived here several years, and had born to them a family, consisting of Munson, named for a brother of Mrs. L.; Munroe, Betsey, Caroline and Almanda. Like scores of others in this town, they took up the westward march and settled in Michigan, where doubtless these Lambs have increased to quite a flock. Lamb sold to Peter Shear, and he to William Hallenbeck, whose name we first encountered on the Halsey M. Smith place, in the Lovejoy district. He was from Coxsackie, Greene Co., and his wife was Rachel Ten Eyck, from the same town—both names betraying unquestionable Dutch origin. It was thirty-six years ago that Mr. H. came to this farm, and here he died in March, 1883, at the age of seventy-one, his widow surviving him a little more than one year, dying in October, 1884, at the age of seventy-three. Their children were not numerous, consisting of Martin F., who died in the army during the War, and Louise, who is the wife of Mr. Van Sicklen. The latter was born in one of the western states, and his father dying when Ogden was very small, his mother, who was a daughter of Elkanah Smith, returned to this town, and here he was reared. They have children, William F., who married Minnie, daughter of Jay Dickinson, of North Rose, and lives at home, and two girls, Belle and Rose. The framed house was built by Isaac Lamb, Jr., and the fine barn by Mr. Hallenbeck. (Wm. F. Van Sicklen and wife have a child, Mildred A.)

On the south side of the road is the estate of John Lamb. The house was constructed in part by Wm. Hickok, who afterward dwelt south of the

Valley, and was completed by John Lamb. John's wife is Jane E. Huffman, a member of the family that once lived a little further west, near the old grist-mill. Like many others, these good people went to Michigan, where they dwelt six years, but came back to this old pasturage, because, Mrs. L. says, "John was homesick." They reared a sizable family here and then went to North Rose to dwell, where "John" may work or not, as he likes. He knows where the biggest blackberries grow. Their children are Myron, Addison, and Mary Annette, whom, as Mrs. John Hetta, we shall meet in the Glenmark district. The place continues to suggest innocence, for Addison Lamb dwells here. His wife is Eliza J. McQueen, from Savannah ; but as people of that name formerly lived in the neighborhood, it is possible that her folks were once Rose inhabitants. They have one child, Cora I. (Now Mrs. Addison Dagle, of Huron.)

Continuing our route across the town line, having returned to the main road, we shall find, first, the valuable farm of Ishmael Gardner. His wife was Sarah Slaght, of Wolcott, and they have two boys to patronize the North Rose school. No one must think that, on account of his name, Ishmael's hand is against every one, for no better nor more highly respected farmer lives on the street. He is an Ishmaelite in name only. Samuel Gardner, who lived here so long, was widely and favorably known. After working his farm up to a commendable condition, he moved down to the village, and there died, the supervisor of Rose, in 1885. Ishmael is the son by his first wife, while Ella, his only daughter, is the child of Happilona Chatterson, his second wife, who now survives him, living in Rose. Joseph Preston was the first settler on this farm. In the local annals, there is also a Hovey Preston, possibly a relative.

Near the corner, on the left, as we continue north, we may see the place where James Catchpole wrought out his fertile and beautiful farm. Robert and James Catchpole came to Huron from Geneva more than forty years ago. They were from Norfolkshire, England, and another brother, George, became a wealthy resident of Geneva. It is quite unnecessary to state that the careful habits of these good people would have made them well-to-do, wherever they were. They were not grinding, grasping folks, but good judgment, backed up by good health, industry and integrity, has given them enviable positions in this lake bordering town. The sequel has warranted us in the thought that their name was from the beginning suggestive, but that wealth, honor and repute might as well have ended it as the commonplace "pole." James, the older, married a widow, Susan Knight, and their children are James, who retains the parent place, and with his maiden sisters, Mary Ann and Matilda, exemplifies how pleasant a thing it is for brethren to dwell together in unity, individually as well as collectively. The next son, Benjamin, married Susan Comstock, of Huron, and has his home a little north of this district ; Robert married Lavina

Tindall ; Susan became the wife of Thomas Smith, of Geneva ; Ann became
Mrs. Edward Thomas, late of Geneva : while Jemima, who married John
Smith, we may meet if we go a few rods to the east and follow a private
road till we find her pleasant home. Of her children, William, with a
wife (who was a Post, from Butler) and two boys, lives at home, as also
does James ; Nora married Fred Kelsey, and lives in Galen ; Maggie, a
beautiful girl, died some years ago. The first James Catchpole and his
wife are dead. Earlier than the Catchpoles, the names of Hiram Lamb and
John Baker may be found connected with this farm.

Across the road from the James Catchpole place, we find Dwight Flint
and his wife, who was Mary, daughter of Robert Catchpole, 1st. The
trade with her brother, George, has already been described. They have
but one child, Augusta, who is the wife of Frank G. Gaylord, of Sodus.
The barns on this place were burned some time since, and have been
replaced with most commodious structures. William Lamb once lived
here, as did also Mr. Parley Lyon.

Our limit in this direction is reached when we come to the home of
Harvey D. Barnes. This place Robert Catchpole bought, away back in
the forties, of Hiram Woodruff, and here he reared his children and developed his farm, and here, too, he remained till advancing age prompted
him to seek a home at the Valley. This was probably twenty years since.
Mr. C. has been dead for several years, but his widow, in remarkable
health and strength, makes her home at the old place. (Died in 1890.)
The family that was reared here consisted of Robert, who lives near Sodus
Bay, in Huron ; George, the present supervisor of Rose ; Ellen, who married Garhardus Watson, of Galen ; Mary A., the wife of Dwight Flint ;
Elizabeth, who is the wife of H. D. Barnes ; and Anna M., who is the wife
of Joel Thorn, of Galen. This is the last farm in the district in this direction, and the last one before making the plunge into the gorge through
which we must pass in going hence to Glenmark ; but the place is a very
superior one, and, as at present conducted, yields admirable returns for
the labor expended. "Harve," as his friends call Mr. Barnes, is an old
friend. We saw him first in District No. 7, the "boy" who lived with
Joseph Seelye ; that outrageous youngster who sorely tried the patience of
the old lady and drew many a satisfactory "ha! ha!" from the old gentleman.
Had we time and place, a book could be filled in detailing the pranks of
this man, who, as a boy, had all the mischief of the neighborhood laid at
his door. But he lived through boyhood, served his country for three
years in the Forty-fourth New York Volunteers, and coming home was
fortunate enough to marry his excellent wife. An admirable pair ; we have
but one regret as we consider their surroundings, and that is, that while
the farm is well tilled and stocked, it has no little Barnes. "Harve" is
the son of Edward Barnes, who had married Hannah Tindall, a sister of

blacksmith "Parm," of the Valley, and also of the late Mrs. Daniel Alexander. Mr. B., senior, lived in several places in this town and in Galen, in which town "Harve" was born. At one time he lived on the Dr. Dickson farm, i. e., the one now occupied by Harlan Wilson, west of the Linus Osgood place. He finally died in Michigan, his wife in the Valley. They had several children, among whom were Harvey; Horatio, who served during the War in the regular army and died afterward at Fort Plain; and Mary, who died at her Uncle Brown's, in Glenmark. In parting with our old friend and his pleasant wife, I must extend sincere congratulations on the evident prosperity of both, and to the Robert Catchpole family for following Scriptural injunctions literally, in that the estate has been gathered into Barnes.

Coming back to the North Rose corners, we are ready for a journey eastward. Mrs. Proseus owns on the north side, and, as yet, her farm has not been cut up into house lots. Very near the angle once stood a blacksmith shop, since moved down into the village and stands on Caroline street.

The school-house is by far the most important building in the vicinity, and now that a new one is so constantly mooted, it will be in place to quote from the early records that have been preserved from 1821. Before the erection of this district, children went to the house down under the hill, west of Peter Shear's. One of the choicest reflections that one has in looking back to the beginning of our town is, that our fathers were so anxious to give to their children educational advantages. These may have been meagre; undoubtedly they were limited enough, but they sufficed to give the young folks a start in life. To me the following extracts seem specially valuable: June 5th, 1820, Joseph Fellows and Andrew McNab leased six rods square of land in the southeast corner of lot 130 in Brother's allotment, for the sum of one dollar and for the term of ten years, to Joel Mudge, Moses Hickok and James Leland, trustees of District No. 14, and to their successors, for the purpose of furnishing a site for a school-house, the lease to be void if the school should not be maintained. October 21st, 1826, Gilbert Miner permanently leased the same site, only a little circumscribed, i. e., it extended five rods back from the middle of the highway, and four rods east and west, but still in the same corner. This was done for the consideration of two dollars and fifty cents. At the rate of holding land then, the price paid was large for a deed in fee instead of a lease simply. This was made to Asahel Gillett, Stephen Benedict and Gale Leland, trustees, and was given shortly after the erection of the town:

"School District No. 14. Beginning at the northeast corner of Nicholas' Four Thousand Tract. Thence west on the north line of said tract three miles and a half, thence north one mile and a half, thence due east until it strikes the west line of District No. two, thence southerly on west line of

Destrict No. two and six to the place of beginning the above. Described Destrict being a part of Destrict number five and three. The above Described Destrict is erected into separate Destrict, and the Clerk of the Town is hereby ordered to Record the same."

MARTIN CARTERIGAT, } *Commissioners of*
ERASTUS FULLER,   } *Common Schools.*

WOLCOTT, June the 27th, 1821.

On the 6th of October, 1826, it was voted to build a new school-house : to begin preparations in the winter; to have it ready in the ensuing June; that it should be 18 x 26. (This was not completed till 1828.) November 1st, 1845, preliminary steps were taken toward building another new school-house. At the adjourned meeting, November 7th, it was voted to build on the old site ; to have Henry Graham, Asahel Gillett and Hovey Preston co-operate with the trustees ; to build of wood with studs and braces and to paint on the outside ; to build 28 x 24, after a model presented by Henry Graham ; to sell the old building and stove to the highest bidder; to levy a tax of $300 to build with ; and to have the edifice completed the first of September next.

Back of the old school-house is a small house in which lives William Thompson, whose business is that of a peddler. Here, before him, dwelt Mr. and Mrs. Thomas Smith, father of E. G. Smith, whom we saw in the Lake district. Before them was Robert Andrews, that merry shoemaker who located first in the Valley, but afterward came here and built a little shop southeast from the school-house, which was long a congregating place for all the male gossips of the vicinity. A Protestant Methodist, he could pray long and loud ; could tell a good story, and was not without interest in a horse trade. Of his children, Kellogg, called "Cal." became a Protestant Methodist minister; Mrs. Colcord lives in North Huron ; Mrs. Phœbe Sherman in Michigan ; Mrs. Dora Thomas and Mrs. Peter Paine are also in the west. From Rose, Andrews went to Huron.

It is possible that Andrews built the red house opposite, or at any rate added to that little school-house that (18 x 26) was the pride of the early settlers, for this was moved off, and, I understand, made a part of this structure. I believe John Lamb owns it now. It was for a time the home of Jay Seelye, and here Michael Prindle, preacher, blacksmith and horse jockey, dwelt. His peculiarities still excite remark among the denizens of the place. I believe that Henry Garlic was here also, and that Elkanah Smith, often met in wanderings hereabouts, dwelt here once. The blacksmith shop, where work was done, and where the small boy languished with switch in hand, was near the shoe shop, and finally melted away. (On the south side also is the second old school-house.)

J. B. Aldrich has opened a new street, or rather has continued Gray street across the road into his orchard, and here, on the east side, Albion M. Gray is building a very fine house. (Mr. Gray was born in Mt. Vernon, Me., reared in Massachusetts and New Hampshire, and learned his carpenter trade in New Jersey. He married Sarah A. Smalley, a relative of Abram Doremus, in New Jersey. Their children are Charles A., John M., Elizabeth L., Otis A. and Alvin M. So far as I know he is the only resident ever given by the Pine Tree State to the town.) Further in the orchard, right among the trees, Irwin R. Seelye has planted his beautiful house. Irwin married Sarah Williams, of Marion, and has one child, Nettie. May they find much pleasure in their home among the apple trees, where annually they must be surrounded by those prettiest of flowers, i. e., apple blossoms. Across from Seelye's is a house owned by Wing Langley. (Robert Dickinson married Emeline, daughter of Birney Briggs, and built, recently, a very pretty home east of Mr. Gray's, and just beyond him. To them in Aug., 1893, a daughter was born. Allen Prosens, having already put up an excellent barn, is erecting an elegant residence. His wife is Libbie, daughter of Joseph Andrews, and their children are Harry I. and Isabelle.)

Here the road leads up to the Huron part of the district, but whose only Rose dweller is Luther Wilson. A visit to him reveals one of the most pleasant homes in Rose. His only child, a daughter, died some years ago. Beyond him, in Huron, we should find Jefferson Chaddock and several others whose affiliations are with Rose.

On the south side of the main road is a red building which years ago Morton F. Trippe bought of the Langleys, it having stood near the cemetery, and having been a tenant house for them, and moved to this site. Here he located his parents. Morton was a soldier during the War, and, it is presumed, filially applied some of his earnings and bounty in this praiseworthy manner. He was graduated at Hamilton College, and became a Presbyterian minister, and is now serving his God in that capacity on an Indian reservation in the western part of the state. The post office was here for a time. Then came Cornelius Van Buren, who deeded the property to Henry Garlic, and he traded it with Katie Graham for the little farm over near P. T. Lewis', in the Lovejoy neighborhood. Here now dwell Katie, the widow of Alfred Graham, and her parents, the Eldreds. Clark Eldred was born in Deerfield, Oneida county, and married, first, Harriet Blanchard of Cato. His second wife was Mary Chaddock, a daughter of that William the first whom we met in the Lake district. His life has been passed principally in Huron and Rose. Now an invalid, he keeps close to his home. Mrs. E. is a good soul, who likes to meet her friends and pass a social hour. They have but two children, Katie and Lydia, who, as the widow Sobers, married Henry Garlic. (Mr. Eldred died August 18, 1889, aged 84 years.)

The home of James B. Aldrich now attracts us, and entering, we shall find not only the head of the family, known among his friends as "Ben," but also his wife, Calista, her mother, Mrs. Julia Dickinson, and an invalid aunt of Mr. A. The home is home-like—and what more in way of praise could be said? Thirty acres of Mr. Aldrich's farm were bought of Darwin Dickinson; the remaining seventy were a part of the old Amos Aldrich estate. As we have seen, Mr. A. has opened a street into his domain, and already houses are going up thereon. The house was built by Emory Roberts thirty-five years ago. Roberts, with his father, John, went to Michigan. They sold to "Dar" Dickinson. They had bought of Henry Graham, and had lived here probably ten or twelve years. The Aldriches have only one child, Harriet E., who married Everett Slaght of the village, though he was formerly from Wolcott.

Crossing to the south side we shall find the house of Morgan Lewis Smith. The politics of Smith's father, Elkanah, and the time of his birth, may be surmised by his Christian name. Mr. S.'s holding is a small one, consisting of thirteen and one-half acres only, and he bought of Jay Dickinson. The latter built the house. Mr. Smith's wife was, as a girl, Florence Jane Commett, from Newark. They have no children. The Smiths came from Delaware county, and the elder Mrs. Smith lies in the Rose burial ground. Elkanah went to Michigan.

James Brisbin has a small holding on the north side of the road, a part of the William Dickinson place. Mr. B. came from Pultneyville, and his wife is Lizzie, a daughter of Mr. Dickinson. Their only son, George, is at home. (Now in Clyde.) Maggie, a daughter of Mr. B. by his first wife, Elizabeth Malcom, is the wife of Wing Langley. Another daughter is Lillian E. Mrs. B. and George are members of the Rose Free Methodist Church.

As we advance eastward we must notice deep excavations on both sides of the road. Hence have been taken many cords of lime stone for building purposes. I should conclude from casual observation that the rock is better adapted to making walls in bulk than to holding them together in the shape of lime. I think no successful effort has been made to burn this stone. Early in the century the quarry was worked by Prentice Miner, but whether he opened it or not deponent doth not aver. From this source material was obtained for the Erie canal locks near Clyde in 1823, and again for the same purpose at the time of the enlargement. Door steps and corner-stones innumerable have been taken thence for use in this and neighboring towns. If Miner (what an appropriate name) possessed any rights in the quarry, they passed to Dickinson, who took articles from the land office. The latter was born near Lake George in 1801 (December 19th), and married first Charlotte Vaughn, by whom he had two children— Sarah Ann, who married her cousin, Christopher Dickinson, a printer, who lived in Albany and later in Clyde. She now lives in this town as Mrs. David Wescott. The son, Robert Darwin, was well known in Rose, where he lived for many years, though he died in New York a commission merchant. His wife, Harriet Ferris, was a daughter of Deacon Ferris of Butler. He left four children—Harvey D., who, having married Clara Colvin, lives now in Idaho; Clarence, since deceased; Merville, in Idaho with Harvey, and Caroline. William Dickinson's second marriage was to Julia Emily Seelye, daughter of Benjamin, and their children were Charlotte L., who married, first, John Partridge, and second, Joseph Boynton. They moved to Napoleon, Michigan, where she died, leaving a son, Merville. Calista Dickinson we have seen as the wife of James B. Aldrich; Eliza is Mrs. James Brisbin; while Isadore Amelia married Philo B. Boynton. They live at Joel Lee's in District No. 6, and have three children—Emily, Joseph and Florence. In the second family of Mr. Dickinson there were only two sons—Judson and Jay R. The latter married Elizabeth Bovee of Rose, and lives in the village, following the trade of a house carpenter. The former, through mental infirmities, was well known in the town, especially in the decade from 1860 to 1870. He died in 1882, and we cannot help wondering what he might have been if nature to him had ne'er been unkind. William Dickinson was always connected more or less with a mill, and in this place erected a structure for fashioning and smoothing stones, but it was not, I think, successful. The pond which supplied his power was immediately at our left as we crossed the bridge going east. Mr. D. was a man of great decision and determination, and it means no disparagement when we state that he was familiarly known in town as " Bill Dick." He was a life-long Baptist, and I would give a great deal if I could settle one question as authoritatively as he, William Chaddock, Jonathan Briggs, Artemas Osgood and other contemporaries used to rule on all matters of state and religion. The lyceum convened immediately after morning services and the place was at the entrance to the church, and here they served up whole chunks of solid wisdom. The world, I fear, will never know just how much it has lost. When Mr. Dickinson raised that oracular finger and emphasized his dictum with "I tell you" so and so, and with a look that Lord Chancellor Thurlow might have envied, there was no gainsaying him. However much one might object to some of his opinions, he was uniformly respected. He died in December, 1879, and is buried in Clyde. His widow was born October 23d, 1799, in Kingsbury, Washington county. In her old age she finds a pleasant home with Mrs. Aldrich. (Died September 3, 1889, in her 90th year.) After Mr. D.'s death, the place passed to James Brisbin for a time, when he sold to Jonathan Briggs, who in time sold to Charles Barrick, and he has lived here for the last seven years. Mr. B. is from Lyons, of a Maryland family long settled there; his wife is Emily Otto, a daughter of Samuel Otto of Huron, but a resident of Rose when he lost his life in 1870. They have two children—Ralph L., who married Sarah Hall of Galen, and is now in Emporia, Kansas ; the daughter, Hattie E., is at home. A small house across the road belongs to the estate. It is surrounded by land belonging to the Briggs property. (Mr. Briggs has recently erected a steam saw-mill south of the road.)

Proceeding eastward we must notice the elegant barn which Mr. John York has erected recently on the old Benjamin Seelye place. Like many farms in this vicinity, this has passed into the hands of the North Rose maltster, and plenty of money is rapidly effecting very noteworthy changes. I do not believe I could enumerate all the people who have lived here as tenants and owners, but going back to John Burns I can give the most of them. In Osgood Church's book of sales, this lot, 132, is assigned to Noadiah Gillett. Of this party, I have thus far obtained no clue whatever. He may have been related to the other members of the Gillett family ; but if so, the survivors do not know it. John Burns certainly lived here and reared his large family. Possibly Henry Graham owned it for a brief time. The period of uncertainty, however, ends when, about 1840, Benjamin Seelye and family came from Washington county and located here. He was an elder brother of Joseph, who, from 1815, had lived in District No. 7. Mr. Seelye had had the care of his aged mother, and after her death he forsook the hills of his native town and came hither. His wife was Eunice Barnum, a native of Shaftsbury, Vermont. She had several brothers in Rose and Butler, as Roger, whom we have seen near Stewart's corners ; Bateman, who married a Richardson, in Butler, and Smith, who married a Mason, in the same town. A daughter of Smith B. married a Leonard, at Spencer's corners. All of " Uncle Ben's " children were born in Washington county, and the oldest we have already met as Mrs. William Dickinson ; Electa married, first, Garrett Clark, whose son, Byron, lives in Savannah ; her second husband was Oliver Millard, and with him she lived for many years in Lockport, finally dying there ; Polly was Mrs. William Farr, of Fort Ann, Washington county, till both went west, to Iowa. Emma was the wife of Jared Young, of Fort Ann, and the mother of Bell and Electa Young, who used to live with the Seelyes, of Rose, Bell married Melvin Gillett ; the youngest child, Caroline, became the wife of David Stanley, who, a miller, for a long time ran the grist-mill in North Huron. She died long since, leaving children, Plumie, who married a Clark, of Waterloo ; Alice, who became Mrs. Michael Vandercook, of Rose ; Elmer and Ellen. Benjamin had two sons, John Jay and Nehemiah. The latter we met two or three times in other districts in Rose. Jay married Minerva Boynton, of Huron, and for many years lived on the old place. Afterward he was in Huron and North Rose, and finally died in Waterloo, in 1887. His burial place is Huron. His children were

11

Irwin, Fred and Burt. Fred married Lottie Sours, of Huron, and died in
Wolcott, leaving a son, Gray P. (Mrs. Seelye married in January, 1890,
Mr. G. F. Smith, of Horton, Kansas.) Burt is a successful teacher in
Waterloo. (Now in Brooklyn.) These Seelyes, Benjamin and Jay, were
entitled to the respect and consideration of all who knew them. Praise-
worthy citizens, they lived beloved and died regretted. As occupants
or owners after this family, we can find the names of Elkanah Smith,
Robert Jeffers, Wing Langley, and finally John York.

Nearly opposite is a dwelling which Henry Graham put up for his
daughter, who married Isaac Maybe. On the north side is a small house
belonging to the Grahams, which was once on the Baker place, the building that William Chaddock found there when he bought. It was sold to
George Smith with one-half acre of land. It now belongs, as stated, to
the Graham estate.

The Graham farm follows, the place where Henry Graham accumulated
his wealth, and where now his youngest son, Nelson, lives. The
latter's wife is Susan Genung, of Rose. The farm was first occupied by
Moses Hickok, grandfather of Felton and Eugene. He probably lived here
several years and reared his family. William, a son, used to tell about
encountering a deer when visiting the spring down by the present site of
the railroad. In this case the boy rather than the animal was hunted.
From relationship, I fancy that the Hickoks were from Connecticut.
Moses' wife was Zervia Felton, by whom he had William, Joseph Munson, Caroline, Emeline, Fanny and Luna M. Fanny, Caroline and Joseph
died young. Luna married John R. Hudson and went to Michigan.

Henry Graham was one of the most noteworthy figures in the history of
the town. He was born in Ulster county, January 19, 1802, and died in
Clyde, October 17, 1878, and was buried there. It is remarkable that at
the time of his death his mother was living with a daughter in Port
Byron, at the wonderful age of 102 years. She lived to be 106. Her name
was Lydia, and with her husband, Henry, moved to Cayuga when our
Henry was only ten years old. He saw the usual round of privation and
adventure. He learned the carpenter's trade, tended lock on the Erie
canal, and was a blacksmith in Canandaigua. His first wife was Roxana
Demure, who died in 1841, in her forty-first year, and was buried in the
North Rose burial ground. In 1831 he moved to Port Glasgow and leased
and kept the hotel owned by Isaac Gillett. Later he came to Rose, to the
Jonathan Briggs farm, and thence came to this, his long-time home. To
begin with, he had 160 acres, but this amount varied from time to time.
His second wife was Eliza Ross, of Auburn, and she survives him, living
in Clyde. (Died July 23, 1892, in her 78th year.) By his first wife Mr.
G. was the father of Henry, who for many years kept the Graham House
in Lyons, whose wife was Jane Lambkin, of Port Byron; he has been dead

OLD RESIDENTS.

LUCY FUCE   AMOS ALDRICH.   WM. DICKINSON.   C   LI BENSON,

S   LE FANNY,   HENRY GOODMAN,   JESSE   BOOD

STEPHEN CURTIS   FRANKLE FINCH.   N   WEEKS.   BENJAMIN SEE

several years; Albert came next, and he married Eliza Smith, as we have seen; Adaline married Welcome Freeman and went to Ohio, and Elizabeth became the wife of Isaac Maybe, of Butler. The present Mrs. Graham is the mother of Nelson; Elmore P., who, having married Nettie Beach, of Seneca Falls, keeps up the old Purdy farm in Butler in fine style; and Archibald, the youngest, married Rose E. Case, of Clyde, he has one child, Louise R. He maintains a large business in running a grist-mill and drug store. Henry Graham was a man calculated to arouse attention anywhere. His business talents were of the highest character, and at his death he was probably the wealthiest man in the town. He was quick and certain in his conclusions and rarely was in error. In personal appearance he was noteworthy, weighing generally about 250 pounds. In stature erect and in motion courtly, he had much of what is styled old time gentility. Though never conspicuous in politics, he had talents fitting him for any position. He built the framed house so long prominent on the farm, but this has been moved to the village. Its predecessor, which Graham found there, is now a barn on the premises. The present well appointed house was built in 1886, and it seems a pity that no youthful Grahams are growing up to utilize so much comfort and elegance. (Mrs. Nelson Graham died April 26, 1892. Mr. G. has since married Miss Florence Lovejoy, of District No. 9. In Sept., '93, was born to them a daughter, Susie E.)

Julius Baker lives on the next place east, and it is a pleasure to talk with so well preserved and active a man, whose years are reaching toward the eighties. Born in 1810, I found him on a hot August day of 1888 using a cradle in an oat field, and full of jovial remark. He says that Dudley Wade used to court a red-headed girl named Goodsell, in Clinton, Oneida county, and that years afterward, when Baker was sawing wood for Mr. Wade, he asked him, as they were sitting down to the table, if he remembered anything about her. "Don't you say a word about that red-haired girl before my wife," says Uncle "Dud," and, says Baker, "I didn't." "Why, Wade hitched up the first horse that I drove when I went courting," continued Mr. Baker. He was born in Watertown, Conn. He was for many years a wagonmaker, and lived in various places, coming to Rose directly from Cayuga county. His wife was Eliza Leonard, who was born in 1811, in Westmoreland, Oneida county. For the last twenty-four years he has lived here. His son, George, lives near Wolcott, and Jerome in Auburn. Nelson is on the farm with his father. Jane married Ambrose Copeman, from Aurelius, who died on the Collins place, east. Nelson's wife is Helen Barrett, a native of Ossian, Allegany county. Their children are Clara and George. Mr. Baker bought of William Chaddock, who built the house, and he followed Hiram Dunn. Unfortunately, I am obliged to leave the farm thus Dunn for.

For a long time I had supposed that the log house on "Sam" Osborn's place, built by his father, was the only one in this part of the town. but I am in error, for going down the hill beyond Mr. Baker's, and just before I begin the ascent of the next one, at my left, I find a log structure slowly settling down and returning to primitive dust. It was built more than forty years ago by "Jim" Phillips, whom we met in the Lake district, but for the most part its history is identified with that of the Feecks, who lived here several years. Nicholas, the father, came here from Aurelius, Cayuga county, and his wife, a Brown, was related to the wife of the first William Chaddock. They had six sons, of whom four went into the Union army, as did Nicholas himself. Alonzo was in Company H of the Ninth Artillery, and was taken prisoner with me at Monocacy. If he ever had any energy he lost it all on his capture, for after entering Danville prison he hardly lifted a hand to help himself. I have seen him lying on the ground and fairly covered with flies. They swarmed over his body and were even on his face and hands. "Feeck, in heaven's name, why don't you brush those flies off," I said to him one day as I passed. "Oh, what's the use ! They'll come again," was the languid response. Such an utter lack of grit could have only one result. He died before the first fall of snow upon our prison pen. William J. Feeck, who was in the 111th N. Y., lives now in Huron. Zadoc Taylor took the place, a small one, after Feeck, and it continues in his family.

Our eastern course is run when we come to the home of Charles Harper, on the south side of the road, but to get at prime facts, let us go back to 1813, where in the books of Osgood Church we may find the following entry : Dr. Asahel Gillett, Cont. No. 102, March 10, lot No. 155, 50 acres. price per acre $4.25. This of course takes us to the land office, and back of Gillett must have been the bears and Indians. This settler was from Connecticut and was one of several Gilletts who have been found in the town. He was a cousin of Harvey of the Lyman district, and likewise of Hosea and Isaac, already seen in this district. His wife was Ruth ——, but unfortunately they were childless. Honest and industrious, they paid for their farm and had money beside. They invited John, a son of Asahel's brother Avery, to come and live with them as heir expectant, but incompatibility of tempers spoiled the plan, and, as we have seen, John set up for himself. Then Alphonso, son of another brother, came to take John's place, but this scheme worked no better than the first one. The old people became suspicious, and they had always been exacting. One misfortune after another followed, till all the savings of many years were squandered, and Asahel finally died in the house of Avery Gillett, son of John, during the War, otherwise he must have been thrown upon the town. After Gillett came Albert G. Graham, Henry's son, and he was followed by the LaRock brothers, Charles and Joseph. Charles married a Hart and Joseph a Seager. At present the former lives near Wayne Centre. Charles Harper came next, and he still holds the property. He is Galen born, being one of a family wherein seven members averaged 214 pounds each in weight. His wife is Clarissa Winchell, born in Rose, and they have two children, David and Minerva. The house remains, without, much as it was in Gillett's day, but the interior arrangements have been altered somewhat. The Harpers are Methodists. (David has recently wed Anna Lovejoy.)

We have now reached the eastern limit, and to get to the other part we must stand again on the corner by Mrs. Proseus'. We shall pass at our right a fruit dryer on the Proseus place, and must then go over a deep glen, along which, years ago, were the saw and grist-mills of Isaac Lamb. Somewhere along here on the south side was the home of Isaac Lamb after leaving the old farm. The first house to be encountered is that owned by Cephas B. Bishop. The latter is a son of Chauncey, so long prominent in the annals of the town, and he married a daughter of the second William Chaddock. I am very sorry that I cannot tell more about Almon Howard, who was one of the first if not the very first resident here. He was prominent in school matters, but like many others went to the west. After him Ebenezer L. Sumner is found, but aside from some marriage connections with neighboring families, we have little save the name. He, too, went west. Then came Dr. Henry Van Ostrand, who finally went to Albion, Michigan. Then succeeded Murray Waterman, who now lives in Lyons. The house was built by Mr. Van Ostrand, but was improved by Waterman. Then followed Henry Clapper, Rose born, but who has lived years in Wolcott. He was his son who married Anginette Munsell, grand-daughter of Harvey Mason. From Clapper the farm passed to Bishop; this in 1863. There are eighty-six acres in it. The owner has not lived on his farm for some years, finding it more convenient to dwell in the Valley, and to thus afford a home to his aged mother-in-law. Cephas is a man of many a joke, and enjoys a good laugh. (Charles Garlick is now the owner.)

The next place, that of Mr. Correll, is a part of a very large farm that was years ago in the possession of a Mr. Young, a wealthy Genevan, whose brother Thomas lived in the Proseus house and managed the estate. One of the first dwellers here was Joseph Aldrich, reared at the corners, being a son of Amos. To him succeeded one of the Lymans, then Alpheus Gillett. Ira Lathrop, and finally the present owner, a German. (Now the property of Mrs. John York.)

Our last place in this district is reached when we come to the long time home of Pardon Jones, though he for many years resided in the Valley. I can find no earlier name connected with the farm than that of James Colborn, the same one who lived so many years in the Griswold district. Though his life more properly belongs to the latter neighborhood, it will not be amiss to state that he was from Pennsylvania, and that his wife was Mary Waters of Alloway, town of Lyons, a sister of Mrs. John Deady of District No. 5. He probably came to this farm in 1816 and helped manage the neighboring saw-mill. Here happened one of those harrowing accidents from which no age nor place is free. His oldest boy, a lad of five or thereabouts, was found dead in the path connecting the house and the place where the father was chopping. There was no mark of violence on his body, and his death was accounted for on the supposition that he had quietly followed his father, and finding a newly fallen tree across the path, had climbed upon this, and was sitting, possibly lying on it, when another tree, falling, struck the fallen tree so violently as to kill the lad by the concussion. Mr. Colburn was here possibly five years, when he was succeeded by Nicholas Stansell, who, in turn, ran the saw-mill. John Fosmire also was a resident for a time, but it is more than forty years since Pardon Jones located and staid. Mr. Jones was born in Rhode Island, and in his ways and sayings retained very much of that quaintness for which New England Yankees have been so long noted. In naming the characters of the town Pardon would come in early. In coming to Rose his first stopping place was near the Lymans, perhaps in that house where John Lyman essayed housekeeping, and then he went to the old Briggs place, afterward and for years that of "Ken" Sheffield. On this farm he lived two years, and then moved to the one so long connected with his name. Mr. Jones had filtered through several states and counties before reaching our town. His wife, Dorcas Burlingame, was a native of Cortland county, and her he had when he came to us. His only son, George H., is a resident of Auburn, where he is developing a very successful invention of his, viz., a turbine water wheel. Pardon Jones died September 5th, 1888, at the age of eighty-four years.

Once more we are at the end of our school district, the second in population in the town, yet were it not for the village at its centre, so great are the changes in modern living, the number of children to attend the public school would not be so large as it was sixty years ago. Unless customs change, no Malthus can inspire us with fear of overcrowding the earth.

SCHOOL DISTRICT NO. 10—"COVELL'S."

Nov. 7, 1889—Jan. 30, 1890.

However much we may obtain from written records, to him who writes there is no satisfaction like that gained from some aged narrator, who, the toils of life all past, passes its evening calmly by the fireside, and, surrounded by loved ones, tells of the events of its earlier and active days. Such a source is had as we come to the district frequently referred to as

Covell's. We enter it by turning to the west at Shear's corners, or if we took the west road, just south of George Stewart's, by continuing due west. This road is the longest straight stretch in the town. Beginning a half mile from the Butler line, it continues parallel with the Rose border and a little less than two miles south of the north edge, to within half a mile of Sodus. It must be, then, about six miles in length. We enter our neighborhood through District No. 3, whose extreme western resident, Supervisor George Catchpole, was mentioned several months since.

Our first stop is at a pleasant farm house on the north side of the road, where we shall find at home a man who, more than sixty years ago, came hither, and in the wilderness laid his hearth-stone. Stephen Collins was born March 8th, 1802—eighty-seven years since—and, with his father, Thaddeus', family, came to Rose from Phelps. Earlier than this he had come in with his brothers, Alpheus and Thaddeus, Jr. In fact, his advent was made on horseback, in some way contributing to the good of his kin. After the coming of his parents and their making their home near where Mrs. Harvey Closs now lives, he led the usual life of boys in these pioneer regions, getting a little schooling in the winter, and having always a pretty definite notion of what hard work was, till his marriage, in January, 1822, to Clarissa Wilson, a daughter of that Jonathan who had made his early home just north of Stewart's corners. They do say that Stephen was a most assiduous courter, and that sometimes the boys would untie his horse, which would result in his late rider's having to walk home. A neighbor says: "His horse was sometimes tied to the fence when I got up in the morning to start the day." Such ardor could have only one ending. So, long before attaining his majority, our friend essayed the yoke of matrimony, thus, it will be seen, never really knowing what liberty is. The full measure of home life, i. e., work at his father's home, was exacted in spite of his marriage. When the full time had been served, or a little after, he came down to this plain and took up his residence in a log house, built by Amasa Andrus. The farm itself was a part of the Nicholas purchase. Two brothers, James and Amasa Andrus, had come with Deacon Elizur Flint, first neighbor east, and Amasa located here. James, who was married, settled first on the farm where Will Closs is now. Afterward he lived in a log house across the road from the present Collins place, built by one Hall. Neither paid anything on their lots, and so, after a while, both went to Huron and thence west. Stephen succeeded to the farm and betterments, paying therefor nine dollars an acre, a sum considerably greater than a new lot would cost. But his hands were young and strong, and with a clear conscience and a willing heart he went to work. He received less from the paternal estate than his brothers; but he succeeded quite as well, a tribute to the zeal and industry of himself and of his excellent help-meet. Could there be embodied in these lines all that this aged man can tell of the days early in the century, we might have veritable pictures of the homes and farms of those times. Let him narrate some of his observations : " Yes, we began in a log house, and began pretty much as others did.   There was no mill near at first and grain had to be taken, at the nearest, to Wolcott.   Then came the one at Glenmark, with saw-mills all along the creek to the eastward.   Roads cut in and across wher-ever the people wished.   Gradually, as the country was cleared up and fences built, it became necessary to lay out and maintain regular thorough-fares : so the temporary ways were closed up.   We lived closely, using much Indian meal and pork.   Game was tolerably abundant.   Everybody thought strong drink necessary, and I bought, soon after coming here, a ten-gallon cask of whisky ; but some how or other I didn't take to the idea, and so never had it filled again.   I had neighbors who were incessantly begging for it.   One man, Solomon Fraly, was a lesson to me.   He lived in the log house, mentioned before, and he drank himself into delirium tremens.   I wanted nothing of the medium that would reduce men to his condition.   There were log houses at frequent intervals, even more com-mon than the permanent homes of to-day.   Quite a ways down there, toward the south, was a log shanty, in which lived a family by the name of Riggs.   They were wretchedly poor, so poor, indeed, that once they were said to have lived two weeks upon leeks.   The Hall already men-tioned had married a sister of Mr. Riggs, who was the father of Gowan Riggs, so recently deceased in Huron.   To put it in the mildest form pos-sible, this early settler was a man of very irregular habits.   He sold to one Bascom.   Then came a Van Wort, and he sold to Henry Ackerman, my son-in-law, and myself.   The house became my barn, and it, in time, fell down.   The Halls, Bascoms and Van Worts went west.   You can not remember the funny way we had to resort to to gather our crops.   Did you ever see grain drawn upon a bush?   No?   Well, this is the way it was done.   We would cut down a small tree or take a branch of a large one and hitching a horse or ox to the end of it, would draw whatever could be piled on it, and we could get quite a deal, too.   Then, too, in cutting grain we had to use the sickle entirely, and it was quite an art.   Men had as much pride in their ability to swing the sickle well, as their sons. in the cradle, and grandsons in the reaper.   We used to make a band of the first clip. then would lay on it enough for a bundle, and so continue across the field.   When we had cut across, we would bind back, rolling our sickle up in our tow frocks, or hanging it on our shoulders.   I used the latter way, generally.   There was more made of the harvest season in those days than now.   Liquor was considered a necessary part of the programme, and here is the refrain of some Pennsylvanians, who came up here to work.   When making their first band, they would sing :

> "'Good Massa Longstraw,
> Bottle at each end,
> But not in the middle of the band, O.'

"This meant, I suppose, that they wanted plenty of drink, but none of drink's results in their hands. Homespun was our chief wear. In the year there might be woven fifty pounds of wool and one hundred of flax. How much money do you suppose I paid out in the making of that barn? Well, you couldn't guess. It was just two dollars and a half. Of course, it cost me more than that ; but grain was our standard and a day's work was rated at one bushel of wheat or two of oats. There were thirteen days' work on the framing of the barn. The house was built in 1839." The marriage of Mr. Collins and Clarissa Wilson, so early consummated, resulted in the birth of several children, as Mary Angeline, who, as the wife of S. Wesley Gage, now lives on the old farm, thus making pleasant the later days of her aged father. Mr. Gage is a native of Cayuga county. They have one daughter, Lillian M., who has had much experience as a teacher, but is now at home. (Now Mrs. J. A. Rose, Hillsdale, Michigan.) Their only son, Thaddeus W., died in 1873, at the age of fourteen. Grace, a niece of Mr. Gage, finds with him a pleasant home. (Married in 1892 W. H. Lassell of Jersey City). Few people are better posted on contemporaneous Rose events than Mrs. Gage. Mr. Collins' second daughter, Damaris Adaline, married Henry Ackerman, and now lives in Huron. His only son, Thaddeus W., is well known in Wayne county, having been for many years a lawyer in Lyons, where he has held many offices at the hands of his fellow citizens. He is a graduate of Genesee College, now Syracuse University, then in Lima, and of the Albany Law School. I was a very small lad when I heard him and John Vandenberg of Clyde address the citizens of Rose in the old Baptist Church on the subject of slavery. I think it must have been my induction into the cause of abolition. He has been three times married. His first wife was Lovina A., daughter of William O. Wood of Red Creek. She was the mother of T. W. Collins, Jr., a rising young lawyer of Lyons. His second wife was Corinthia Bottum of Lyons. Stephen Collins' third daughter, Esther L., married James Winchell, then of Rose, now of Sodus, while Henrietta M. is Mrs. John Shear of Rose, near Stewart's corners, a brother of Peter. John Shear came from Junius. Mr. Collins has been for many years a leading member of the Methodist Episcopal Church. Twice he has gone to Lyons to live with his son, but on the death of his wife late in 1886, he returned to his old home. Though we shall have occasion to refer to him often, we shall have to leave him now, happy, I trust, in the memories of a well spent life, and in the promise of a glorious life beyond. (Died November, 1892. In 1893 the Gages live in the Valley, and Frank Kellogg works the farm.)

The next farm was early taken up by Charles Woodward, who sold his betterments to Moses Foster Collins, another son of that first Thaddeus. He it was, who, when the century was in its teens, went courting with his brother Thaddeus "over east." He was attracted by the charms of Mary, daughter of Alverson Wade, who then lived on what is now the Lewis Town place, while Thad. was enamored of Harriet, daughter of Deacon Aaron Shepard. It was on these expeditions that to protect themselves from wolves, whose howls were alarmingly near, the sparkers armed themselves with stakes from an old wood sled that chanced to be handy. Fortunately for them they didn't have to use them. This story was a favorite one of Uncle Thad.'s, and many a boy's hair has all but stood on end at the recital. Another even better liked by the small boy was about a bear that he and Mr. Beals once treed. They chopped the tree down, and then, by the help of their dogs, killed the animal as he leaped from the fallen tree. When an old man, and when to illustrate, it must have caused him a serious effort, he would get down upon the floor on his hands and feet to show how the bear acted. No circus ever gave one-half the pleasure that that home performance afforded; and when Stephen Collins informs me that Mr. Beals was a Phelps man, that the bear was killed only a little further west, near the home of Francis Osborn, and that he went down the next morning to help skin it, the whole incident becomes a reality. Somehow or other I had grown to think that Mr. Beals and possibly Mr. Bear were only creatures of my good relative's imagination. Foster Collins married Mary Wade, and by her was the father of a numerous family. He was himself a member of the Methodist Church. Like his brothers, his life began in Phelps, May 22d, 1795, and he finished his earthly career July 14th, 1878, in Ann Arbor, Michigan. In addition to the names given here, there were several children not named, who died early and were buried on the farm. His wife was born in Paris, Oneida county, September 18th, 1799, and died in Ann Arbor, August 11th, 1879. They were married July 16th, 1816, in what is now Rose, by the Rev. Mr. Smith, possibly that Elder S. who was the first Baptist preacher in our vicinity. I am under obligations for data to Mr. Collins' oldest daughter, Harriet, who, born July 7th, 1817, is a resident of Ann Arbor, Michigan. She married September 27th, 1838, in Pittsfield, Washtenaw county, Michigan, the Rev. Nelson Eastwood of the Baptist denomination; their one son, John Foster, born December 3rd, 1846, is a Ph. D. from Michigan University, 1887, and an assistant professor of chemistry therein. Foster Collins' next child was Joseph Wade, born in Rose, September 16th, 1818, and he has been twice married; first to Lucy Raymond, of Lodi, N. Y., and second, to Laurie Hines of Michigan; he is a Wesleyan Methodist minister and the father of eight children, all farmers. Next came Franklin B., born September 7th, 1823, an M. D. from Michigan University; he died in 1857, leaving one daughter, Mrs. John Bennett of Ann Arbor, Michigan; his wife was Cordelia Bristol, of Michigan; he practiced medicine in St. Clair and died in Pittsfield. Frederick W. Collins was born

February 14th, 1826; he married Mary McDowell; has been a member of the Legislature; has four children; and is now extensively engaged in grain raising in Dakota; post office, De Smet. Mary L. Collins, born February 11, 1830, became Mrs. Addison McDowell, and died February 11th, 1884, in Middleville, Barry county, Michigan, the mother of nine children. George F. Collins, born March 21st, 1834, married Alvira Hepburn, and a farmer, is in Nebraska; he has one son. Betsey M., the last of Foster Collins' children, and the only one not born in Rose, became Mrs. George Cook, and is a resident of Middleville, Michigan. Her birth-place was Pittsfield, August 9th, 1837; she has one daughter. Truly this Collins-Wade stock was fruitful and of excellent quality. Leaving Rose in 1834, the most of Mr. Collins' following years were passed in Pittsfield. In Rose he was one of the first board of trustees of the Methodist Episcopal Church established in 1832. The Woodward who preceded Mr. Collins on this farm went first to the Valley, where for a time he kept tavern, and then went west. His wife was Clara, a daughter of Captain John Sherman, one of the first settlers. To Foster Collins succeeded John B. Chatterson, a son of that Betts C. whom we found in District No. 7. Before leaving the Hudson river region he had married Cynthia Sours, a sister of Capt. Philip S., long prominent in Huron affairs. His children were all girls, viz.: Happilona, whom we have met in North Rose as the widow of Samuel Gardner; Mary is dead; Emily lives at the old home with her sister Cynthia; Melvina married Newman Finch of Rose; Cynthia married Andrew Andrus of Huron, and lives on the farm whence years ago her parents were borne to their last resting places in the Huron burial ground. The Andruses have one daughter, Eveline May. Mr. A. is a son of Benham Andrus, who once lived on the old Wright place in District No. 5. The farm that Mr. Andrus is managing is a pleasant one, and the house that he has added to and repaired has as fine an outlook as any in this part of Rose. There is every indication of careful, painstaking farming.

The next house toward the west is on the south side of the road, and in it dwells the family of Henry Gardner, a numerous one, for I understand that he has thirteen children, though all are not at home. Several years since, J. Shanker, a German, bought a small lot here and built a modest habitation. He and his wife, adepts in their work, made and sold willow baskets, depending upon several dwellers in Rose for the raw material. They had four children, and are now themselves both dead.

Just under the hill is a still smaller house, in which we may find Charles Ditton, whose wife, Lovina, is a daughter of James Phillips, on whose estate the place is. Down in the vale we may look either way along the site of what was to be the Sodus canal. There is a goodly quantity of water making its way lakeward, just as it has been doing for ages. The century was hardly begun before man, appreciating the power in this stream, began to dam its waters and to erect saw-mills. Stephen Collins thinks that the first mill on the creek was built by one Whitmore, who lived near the Shear corners, and that it was nearly in front of John Phillips'. It was probably put up in 1815 or 1816. A road ran down to it, entering near Mr. Fisher's stone barn. Succeeding owners were Howe and Van Buren. Alfred Lee may have owned it. It went down before the beginning of the ditch. A little further north, one Welch, an early comer, had a mill, and still further down the valley a dam was erected by Samuel Hunn, on which he had two saw-mills. After him came Simeon Barrett, under whom the mills went down, for General Adams prevailed upon him to let him run the water off just for a short time, and the site was not worth a dam afterward. Across the road where we may still see the ridge that formed the dam, Samuel Hunn afterward built a mill on John P. Chatterson's land. Then down about where the railroad crosses the vale, Uriah Wade had his dam and mill. It is only recently that the old frame entirely disappeared. In fact, were we to follow back through this glen we might find traces of all these dams and ponds, where the collected water helped to fashion the material whence came the fences and houses of the early settler. Now the waters flow unvexed, save as sportive, naked boys lash them in juvenile glee, finding in some retired cove no end of the pleasure so dear to the juvenile heart and flesh. To be sure, as when I saw them, the sun may blister their exposed backs, but sweet cream will allay the pain, and to-morrow they will be as fresh for the fun as ever.

Next there is a hill for us to climb and then we stand where two roads cross each other, making a point where the ancient and superstitious buried suicides and drove a stake through their hearts, making a terror for Godly survivors. But no such ghostly vision greets us, for here, rearing its white walls as a bulwark against ignorance and superstition, is a school-house, the one known throughout the town as Covell's, thus commemorating the name of the good people who for so many years have dwelt beneath its shadow. It is the third building on the site.

The old Chatterson farm extended to the northeast corner. On the southeast corner we have the old allotment of the Phillipses. William, the first comer of this family, was from the east, possibly remotely from Rhode Island. He had not that regard for comfort that some of his neighbors possessed, but with his wife, Jane Crandall, reared a large family, and died in 1817, at the age of sixty-three years. He claimed to be a Quaker in faith, a very rare belief in this town. To the best of my knowledge he was the first comer here. The east part of his lot, running from the east and west road which we are traveling to the next one south, he afterward sold to Samuel Hunn, who came to us from Phelps. In time, Mr. P. built his house on the other side of the street, where now Mr. Stopfel resides, and our further discussion of him and his we will withhold till we pass down this road.

On this corner in the long ago Hosea Gillett located, taking up a lot in the Nicholas purchase. To some of the old inhabitants he is yet a veritable figure, but to far the greater portion of Rose readers he is scarcely more than a name. He was said to be a happy-go-lucky man, patterned, perhaps, somewhat after his relative Harvey of District No. 3. I am told that both he and Harvey married Burnhams, sisters, and that Hosea's marriage in January, 1812, was the very first celebrated in town. I am also impressed that these Gilletts were the sons of Nodadiah Gillett, to whom was assigned the old Benjamin Seelye farm east of North Rose. It is said that his wife bore him sixteen children, and yet, when they had migrated to the west, she deserted him for another man. In the rather rough joking of that day it is claimed that she left him for fear that she would die childless. One picture of this pioneer presents him with a pair of breeches, whose warp was coarse swingle tow; the filling was raveling from stocking, woven by his wife and colored by hemlock bark. He came early in the century, and finally sold to the Covells, whose first representative, James, came to Rose from Galen, though he had lived in Savannah and had married in Pompey. His wife was Anna Seymour of that town, and as it was the birthplace of ex-Governor Horatio Seymour, it is more than likely that they were relatives. Their first log house was a little west of where Joseph Phillips now lives. To them were born numerous children, of whom the oldest, James, never resident in Rose, went to Virginia from Clyde, and there died young. Maranda married Silas Brown and lived at Shepard's corners. Their only daughter became the wife of Lewis Barrett of Rose. Both Mr. and Mrs. Brown are buried in the Rose cemetery. Hiram married Huldah Bailey of Galen, went west, and died in Ohio. Seymour, of whom we shall see more, wedded Clarissa Crafts of Wayne Center, and now lives north of the school-house. Charles took for his wife Lizzie, daughter of John I. Smith, then living in the district. They now live in Michigan. After the death of his wife in 1863, Mr. Covell went to Michigan to live with his favorite grandson, James, Seymour's son, and died in 1872. He bore a good reputation among the early settlers of our town. In 1874 and later, this place was the home of W. H. Sutphin, who married an Osborne and now lives in Allegan, Michigan. On this place is now found the home of Joseph Phillips, whose father, William, has already been referred to, and a very pleasant home it is. I only wish that the owner had better health with which to enjoy his surroundings. For a number of years he has been a confirmed invalid, a subject of much sympathy among his friends. Years ago he took for his wife Joanna Waters, one of that family which has furnished helpmeets to the Deadys, Desmonds, and Colborns. Nature to them has not been unkind, for around their hearthstone has blossomed a whole bouquet of juveniles, viz.: Josephine, Jane, Rose, Maranda, Charles, Frank, Anna and Florence. Anna, as the wife of Charles Strong,

lives in the next house west, which was once Charles Covell's home.
Lest the race may become extinct, she carries a babe in her arms as she
answers the knock at the door. (Nearly opposite, Mr. Shoesmith is building a house, August, 1893.)

Francis Osborne lives in a large and commodious brick house. There
is an air of comfort and culture about it pleasing to contemplate. To
reach it, we must leave the Strong place on the south side of the road
behind us; must go down a slight hill, cross a well-bridged creek which a
juvenile Osborne has dammed for purposes useful and sportive, and there,
just at the end of the impending rise, we shall find the home of the
Osbornes. The early history of the farm is even more than usually
obscure. It is probable that it was first taken up by one Dunbar, said to
be a colored man. David Gates, who married Roxy Bishop, daughter of
the first Joel, possibly followed. There was here once a German named
Nierpas, and Judge Hawley of Lyons once owned it. As tenants, were
Broderick and Fairbanks; but the early mists finally clear away, and we
find Francis Osborne, who made this his home in 1836. He was born in
Ireland, one of those unyielding north of Ireland Presbyterians who have
made such excellent American citizens. He came to Rose in 1828, and
settled first on the place just opposite the old Deacon Lyon farm on the
Clyde road. His wife was Martha Cowan, whose parents, James and
Frances, passed their last days in a log house a little west of the present
structure, and after life's battles sleep in Rose cemetery, whither they
were borne in 1842 and 1845 respectively. The elder Osbornes passed
away, the father in 1866, at the age of seventy-seven years, and the mother
in 1856, in the fifty-seventh year of her age. They, too, sleep in the Rose
burial ground. Of their children, William M. married Ruth Foist, of a
prominent Galen family, and now resides in Lyons. He lived for many
years in the Griswold district on the road north of Ferguson's corners,
and was a very prominent member of the Rose Methodist Church. James
married Helen, daughter of Seymour Covell, and is the very next resident
west. For Catharine we must look in the cemetery, where, at the early
age of eighteen, she lies by her parents' side. Martha married William
H. Sutphin, whose former home we lately passed, and who is now in
Michigan. Francis the second occupies the old home, much improved
under his care, where several years ago he brought his bride, Flora Adel
Holbrook of the Valley, a daughter of J. L. Holbrook. They have only
one child, a son, Mervin Marinus, of natural history proclivities. Mr. O.'s
youngest sister, Harriet, makes her home with him. (Mrs. Osborne died
June 1, 1893, aged forty-four years.)

The next place is that of James Osborne, whom we have already
noted as having married Helen Covell. Like his brother, he has built his
habitation of brick, and it is a fine substantial edifice, obviously useful,

and certainly creditable to the street. These good people having no children have adopted two, Carrie and Edna. The former is the wife of John Stopfel and they occupy the next house west, but on the south side of the road. It is the property of Mr. Osborne. These gentlemen, James and Francis, emulate the virtues of their ancestors, and are pillars in the Rose Presbyterian Church.

Still to the west and facing the road running north is the home of Frank Garlick, son of Henry of North Rose. The farm of ninety-two acres was for many years in the possession of Hiram Hart, who came hither from Junius, the farm having been given to him by his father, who probably took the land from the office. The Harts had no children, and after selling to Henry Garlick, eighteen years ago, went to Ohio and there died. Mr. G. has repaired the house and built barns till the place is very much improved. On the east corner is the home of Charles Crisler, whose father, Adam, lives in the northeast part of Rose. His wife is Sibyl Day ; they have two sons, Ernest and Sidney. A cooper shop near by indicates one of Mr. C.'s avocations. From the data in an old Wayne county atlas, I conclude that this location once went under the name of Alvord, for next west, a quarter of a mile away perhaps, was the nominal residence of William and Mary Alvord, whose son, George, dwells next north of Mr. Crisler. His home is on the west side of the road ; his wife is Etta Johnson.

Nearly across, and somewhat back from the road, is the residence of Henry Dunn, whose wife is Nettie Corroll of the Glenmark district. They have one child—Nora. The house was built for him by his father, who lives a short distance north. Before getting to Hiram Dunn's, we must pause a moment at the abode of "Jimmy" Wraight, who is rearing a second family of youngsters with the aid of his much younger wife.

The last estate in this district on this road is on the east side, and here for many years have dwelt Hiram Dunn and family. He was one of Saratoga county's contributions to Rose. His farm was bought of John Adams and Col. Cook of Sodus. The log house found by him has been followed by an ample framed structure. His wife is Jane E. Thompson, and their son, Henry, we have already passed. They have had three daughters—Mary, Hattie and Rosa. Both Mary and Hattie became wives of Monroe Seagar, of the west part of the town. Hattie was first married, and on her death Mary became Mrs. S. Rosa is Mrs. Andrew Brower.

Coming back to the corners, and again going west, we encounter first the house belonging to Eli Riggs. It is, however, occupied by other parties, while the owner resides in the new house of George Wraight. The latter is the son of James, frequently called "Jimmy" W., who, on this spot in our centennial, 1876, in October, was most cruelly set upon and robbed. He then lived in a log house, and it had in some way become known that he was in possession of a large sum of money. Certain parties came to his house in the night, and after nearly killing him, forced from him the location of the treasure and carried it off. The robbers were, however, soon found, and one turning state's evidence, the other was sentenced to a long imprisonment, from which he emerged only a few years since. Jimmy, as we have seen, survived the shock to his nerves and frame, and is now rearing a new crop of Wraights. Eli Riggs married Frances Wraight and has two children, Norman and Hannah, still at home. (Mr. Riggs has since built a new house on his old site. The Wraight house is now owned by the widow of Walter Messenger.)

A little further to the west, were we to look very sharp, we might find the remnant of a blacksmith shop, at whose anvil William Riggs once worked. Beyond it and on the same (north) side of the road, William lived. He came here in 1866, and took up the farm from the land office. Of course there had been many predecessors there; but they had gone, one after the other, he being the first to secure a clear title. Mr. Riggs came here from Lyons, apparently a new family in our midst. His wife was Betsey Purdy of Dutchess county, and it is possible that the Riggses also came thence. Their oldest son, Henry, married Emily Finch, and lives in the north part of Rose; Eli we have just passed; James we shall meet in District No. 11. George died at the age of seventeen. Mr. Riggs has lost five children. He sold to John Creek, an Englishman, but the place is now controlled by Lucy Weeks. In the little house, just a few steps further west, his son Eli once lived. Both houses are now unoccupied and are passing into decay. Mr. Riggs after selling here moved a little south into the Jeffers neighborhood, following Harley Way in the old hill-top home. This place is the last in the district. A few rods further and we should be at the end of our long road in the Wayne Centre district, and very near the Sodus line.

We are once more at the school-house and a few paces to the north bring us to the home of Seymour Covell. To-day there is no man in Rose better known than " Seem " Covell. He has traversed this and neighboring towns in buying stock till his rubicund and merry visage is recognized without introduction. As Mr. C. is an excellent talker, he may tell his own story : " You see, I married a school ma'am, and, with all of her folks, went to Michigan, Oakland county. I had just got things cleared up and was in a good way when I thought I'd come home and visit my folks. After I got here, I found them old and very anxious to have me stay with them. I couldn't refuse them, so back I went to Michigan, sold out and came home." " Yes," says Mrs. C., " and took me away from all my folks. You never thought of that." Mr. Covell is used to interruptions, so he placidly proceeds : " One day, after we had been back some time, some parties stopped, as I was working near the road and asked the location of certain landmarks. Uncle Ira Lathrop, who lived where I do now, remarked : ' I'd sell all I have for so much per acre.' I tell you it set me to thinking. I told him to wait a little while and I'd think about it. I hated to run in debt so much, but I thought it a chance I couldn't afford to lose. After a while I mustered up courage to tell him I'd take the farm. And then I was afraid he'd back out before the writings could be drawn. But he went down to the Valley, and we had the deed drawn there, and I was to have twelve years to pay in. Then the old lady wouldn't sign the deed." " And I don't blame her a mite; I wouldn't if I had been in her place," interrupted Mrs. C. " The idea of signing away one's home. I never would." Taking breath, Mr. C. proceeds : " In spite of the old lady's failure to sign, I got possession, and have been here ever since. The times were good, and the farm laughed. I made big payments. Corn fetched a big price. The hogs were heavy and sold well, and at the end of three, instead of twelve years, I was ready to square up. So I said to Uncle Lathrop, ' I'm ready to pay you if you can get Aunt Jemima's signature.' He managed to get her to sign by giving her a mortgage on certain property in town that had every prospect of running a long time. It did. She never got a cent of interest or principal. I was mighty sorry for her, but what was I to do ? Yes ; they were nice folks, Uncle Ira Lathrop and his wife, who had been Jemima Parrish. They came here from Phelps. They hadn't any children of their own, but they raised three adopted ones, one boy and two girls. The son finally went west, while Ann married Clinton Hart, and for a long time lived up west of the corners. Martha is the wife of George Correll of the North Rose district, and Henry Dunn married her daughter. Somehow or other things didn't go first rate after the Lathrops sold the place. Both are dead now. Uriah Wade was here before the Lathrops, and he built the log house. He was a son of Alverson Wade, over east, and he may have taken the land from the office, but the orchard was planted by a man named King. After leaving here, Wade took up the next farm north and had a saw-mill away down in the glen." So far from Mr. C. himself. Now, I may say, that as the evening shades of life appear, he and his companion have every reason to congratulate themselves on their happy situation. Mrs. Covell was Clarissa Crafts, and her father, Abram, was one of the earliest settlers near Wayne Centre, where she was born. She was the school teacher in the district when her future husband fell in love with her. Their union has resulted in the birth of Helen, the wife of James Osborne ; Charles Henry, whom we shall meet on the next place north ; James Egbert, who married Hannahett Vanderburgh, and is now in Jackson county, Michigan ; Abram Delos, married Helen Griswold and lives south of the Valley ; Irving Seymour, who married Florence Dodge, of Hartford, Connecticut, and is in business in New Haven, Conn.; and Huldah Ann, who is

12

at home. The house, much improved by Mr. Covell, was built by Lathrop.
(Since writing the foregoing, Mrs. Covell has ceased to be interested in
things earthly, and has passed to her reward, dying Saturday, September
28th, 1889. Her health had been steadily failing for some time.) (In 1893
Mr. Covell lives in the Valley, and the farm belongs to Joseph Phillips.)

A large barn, with conveniences equally good, north and south, stands
midway between the homes of Seymour Covell and his son, Charles. The
latter has been for some time the county superintendent of the poor. His
first wife was Jane Haviland of Rose, who was the mother of his only
child, Rose Adele, the wife of Frank Kellogg of District No. 7. He
married, second, Miss Lillian York of Sodus, daughter of Norman York,
who was a sergeant in Company D, Ninth Heavy Artillery. He was taken
prisoner at Monocacy, and never saw the child born to him after his
enlistment. A comrade in Danville, Va., I have seen him walk the floor
hours at a time, talking to all who would listen of the wife and little one
he was never to see. (Mr. and Mrs. Covell have a son, Ross Granger,
born June 19, 1890.)

Our dwellings along this road are all on the west side, facing the gorge,
which was to have been the site of the Sodus canal, an institution whose
building scarcely more than destroyed the mill privileges along the stream.
Below us may be distinctly seen the old dams of Hunn's and Wade's mills.
A short distance north of Charles Covell's is the home of Seth Woodard,
whose father, Charles, bought of Henry Young. The latter obtained of
John I. Smith, who probably took from Uriah Wade. Of the latter we
can give the following facts. He was a son of Alverson Wade, encountered
in District No. 6, and was an exceedingly busy, active man. His wife was
Sally, a daughter of the first Thaddeus Collins. He was born in Chicopee,
Mass., July 30, 1782, and was married in 1807. They had seven children,
and all were born in Wayne county. In 1835 the family went to Michigan,
taking a water route, by canal and Lake Erie, to Detroit. He settled in
Concord, Jackson county. In Michigan he married again, his second wife
being Mary Gates, by whom he had three children. Having been injured
by a train of cars, he died October 11, 1871. Of these Rose children, the
oldest son, Thaddeus, lives in Illinois; the next, Lawson, in Grand Rapids,
Mich.; the next, Clinton, in Dakota; the one following, Chauncey, in Butler, Mich.; the oldest daughter, Paulina, Mrs. Samuel Eddy, in Jamestown,
Dakota; her sister is Mrs. Cordelia Tripp, of Concord, Mich. The
youngest son of the children by the first wife is M. D. Wade, of Indian-
apolis, Ind. Sally (Collins) Wade died in Concord, May 14, 1837. Mr.
Smith was one of the early emigrants, but I understand that he was for
several years a justice of the peace here. Mr. Young had a mill in Glenmark. He, too, migrated. Chas. Woodard came from Ontario county, in
1854. His wife was Caroline Horn, of Lyons, where he now is. His son,

Seth, the present occupant, married Louise M. Messenger, of Glenmark, and their only son bears his grandfather's name, Charles. Levi B. Woodard and wife, parents of the first Charles, came with him, and for several years lived here. They were Canandaigua people. The old house to the north, now unoccupied, was built by Uriah Wade of hewed basswood logs. Clapboarded without and plastered within, no one would suspect it to be a log house were it not for the thickness of the window casings. If I could get all the town history that the successive residents here could recount, I should have little lacking. The most of the dwellers, however, are " beyond the smiling and the weeping."

The very last citizen in District No. 10 is reached when we come to the home of David P. Barnum, whose home we find just south of the railroad. He is a native of Putnam county, but went early to Junius and thence to Wisconsin. His wife is Catharine Burch, of Junius. He came here more than twenty years ago. His children are Laura M.; Mary, who married Albert Ellis, of Glenmark, and Ara, who is at home. In politics Mr. Barnum is an uncompromising democrat. (Mrs. Barnum died December 30, 1889. Mr. B., October 20, 1890.)

Coming back to the school-house, we will journey southward, and near the corners, on the east side of the road, is the home of James Phillips. I think his neighbors more often call him "Jim." He is a son of the first comer, William. Years ago he married Electa Bradshaw. Of his children, Stephen went into the army, served his three years in the 10th Cavalry, and died in 1864, on his return. His grave is one of those decorated by the Rose veterans. George married in Syracuse, and went there to live. He once managed the cider mill just south of his father's, under the hill. Laura became the wife of Charles Hurst, once well known in and about the Valley. Elizabeth married Charles Miner, of that very large family descended from the Baptist elder. Lovina, as Mrs. Charles Ditton, we passed on the road east of the corners.

Near James Phillips' home was the old home of his father, to whom passing reference was made as we went along the east and west road. His log house, one of the most primitive in these parts, covered once the following children : Israel, who, on reaching manhood, went west ; James, already mentioned ; Isaac, who married Louisa Palmer and went to Genesee county ; Mary, the wife of Leonard Lombard, who went to Michigan ; Levi also went to the Badger State ; Hannah, as the wife of Benjamin Snyder, followed her kin to the Peninsular State, as did Lovina, who married John Geer ; William, too, joined the same procession and married west, but, having returned, he lives now in the old Samuel Hunn house. The youngest of the family, Joseph, we encountered west of the corners. After a time William Phillips bought land opposite, and put up the frame of a large house. This, however, was never finished, and finally fell down.

In it old Mrs. Phillips was bed-ridden for many years. Just under the hill is a building used now as a peppermint still ; but it has been a cider mill and possibly an evaporator. It is the property of James Phillips.

Near by, on the west side of the road, is the house of Mr. Stopfel, one of whose sons married the adopted daughter of James Osborne. He has another son, Louis E., and two daughters. Before him was John H. Ruppert, and from a tombstone in the Rose cemetery, I copy this inscription : " John H. Ruppert, born May 29th, 1822, in Willinghausen, Germany ; died April 1st, 1882. Co. H, 148 Regt., N. Y. Vols." One instinctively thinks of that Prince Rupert who came from his German home to the help of his hard-pushed uncle, Charles the First, of England. This German's grave is another of the cherished ones in our cemetery.

Between this house and the next turn to the east were once the homes of Messrs. Hollafolla and Fink. All these names, *i. e.*, these last two and the preceding two, are reminders of that very quiet German invasion which was made in the fifties. George Hollafolla died in 1878, and is buried in the Rose cemetery. His holding was a small one and passed into the large Barrett farm. Christian Fink had a place of twenty acres, but he, too, sold to the Barretts and moved away. Both Fink's and Hollafolla's houses have disappeared, leaving not a vestige on the former sites, though it is proper to state that Fink's abode was moved over the way by Lewis Barrett, and, considerably changed, stands to-day opposite the residence of Jerry Barrett, the property of the latter.

On the east side, a little further north, resides Charles Stephens, whose wife was a daughter of the Mr. Fink just passed. This place is a part of the old Wm. Phillips lot—some ten acres in all. Eli Garlick held it years ago, and built the house. He also had a blacksmith shop near, an invariable accompaniment to any house owned by him. He sold to George Hollafolla, who once lived opposite. Mr. H. passed the place along to LaRock, who in turn sold to Abram Covell, a native of the district, but now dwelling south of the Valley.

Our way southward is ended when we reach the road running east. At our right is a small shop where Simeon I. Barrett formerly wielded his hammer and fashioned iron. Opposite is the house erected by him, and in it he passed the later years of his long and useful life. He was born in Fishkill, Dutchess county, New York, February 22, 1794 ; so, if he lives till next Washington's birthday, he will be ninety-four years old. He came to this town forty-seven years ago, but he left his old home long before that. It was in 1815 that he came to a place south of this. The next season was that of the famous cold summer of 1816. His wife was Matilda, the daughter of a Revolutionary soldier. Ebenezer Pierce, from Massachusetts, and she was worthy of all the affection with which her husband regards her.

Mr. Barrett is of a very active temperament, though he has done very little farm work for the last twenty-four years. Like Isaak Walton, he is a great fisherman, and at least once a week has to go to Sodus bay for his favorite amusement. He reads a great deal and has never used glasses. For many years an anti-Mason, he peruses most diligently the columns of the *Christian Cynosure*, a paper managed in opposition to Free Masonry. His chief delight, however, is in his Bible, and this he reads constantly. He has read it through, consecutively, many times, in addition to the desultory reading that forms his chief occupation. With his faculties unimpaired, he has his opinions on all current topics. He does not, like so many aged people, live only in the past, but he is actively alive in the present. May his good works continue, and may he live to see his fully rounded century! Living with his son, Jeremiah P., he has a happy home. He has had seven children, some of whom have preceded him to the other world. (Mr. B. died in 1887.)

Uncle "Sim's" wife, to whom he was devoted, died July 30, 1863, at the age of sixty-five. Near them, in Ferguson's burial ground, lie Mrs. Barrett's parents, the Pierces, Mr. B.'s mother, Tamar, who died in 1839, and several children. Their children, who survived, were John R. who married Mary Pitcher, and lived on the Wayne Centre road further south. Luman Lewis Barrett married Betsey Brown, of Galen; her mother was Seymour Covell's sister. He formerly lived in Rose, owning, among other places, that on which Jared Chaddock is now, and for a time was opposite the old home place. Till lately, however, he has been in Huron, where his only child, Gardner, who married Alice Bradburn, now resides. In the spring of 1889 he came to the Valley to live, occupying the house north of the corners, owned by Julia Sedore. Mary was the wife of Henry ("Hack") Shepard, and died several years since. They had but one child, "Libbie," one of the merriest of girls, who died some time before her parents. Catharine married Anson Cady, of Galen. The youngest son, Jeremiah, made Anna Collier his wife, and, till this season, ran the farm. He has no children, and now lives in the Valley, leaving Edward Klinck in care of the home acres, one hundred and forty in number. (Mr. B. is again on his farm.) It should be added that Simeon Barrett bought of John Rhea, who, I find, in 1837, selling to Thomas J. Lyman subdivision No. 1, part of lot 425, in Robertson & Howard's tract, three acres, deeded by Fellows & MacNab to Henry Dodds. This covered, I suppose, some part of the old Barrett place. Rhea had a son, Arnold, and his business was largely the care of saw-mills.

The house across the road has already been noted as the old Fink building, moved from the west side of the north and south road. Now it serves a valuable purpose as a tenant house.

Quite a distance back from the road is an old red house, which for many years was the abode of Samuel Hunn and family. He has been referred to before as the purchaser of the eastern part of the old Phillips lot, and as the builder of numerous saw-mills. He came to Rose from Phelps. His wife was Sally, a sister of Samuel Otto. For many years he was a prominent member of the Rose Methodist Church, valuable in all her counsels. He died in 1875, his wife in 1877, and both lie in the Rose cemetery. They had two sons, James and Parsons. The former married a neighbor's daughter, Catharine Winchell. He died in 1861, leaving children—Clayton, now in Indiana; Sally Ann, who married Fernando Miner, and Margaret, the wife of Peter Paine. Mrs. Hunn married, for her second husband, Andrew Andrus, of Huron, and for her third, Albert Harper, a twin brother of Almon H., sons of Daniel Harper. Both were very large men, together weighing more than 500 pounds. Again a widow, she is living in the Valley. Parsons Hunn married Martha Weeks, and had two sons, Jerome and Harrison. After Mr. H.'s death, in 1868, Mrs. H. married David Brower, of the neighboring town of Sodus. The sons went west. I have the impression that the elder Hunns passed their latter days in the Valley. The old Hunn house is a tenant house belonging to Charles Miner. His wife's uncle, William Phillips, lives in it now.

A very pretty white house marks the home of Charles Miner, a son of Riley. His wife is James Phillips' daughter, Elizabeth. The house was built by Parsons Hunn, the place being a part of the old Hunn property. Miner bought directly from Peter Ream. His children are Ada L., James O., and Lydia Jane (and Myrtle). This is a favorite neighborhood for mint stills, and just before reaching the house, on the side of the hill, is one of these tokens of Wayne county's peculiar industry. Mint stills are infinitely better for a section of country than mint juleps.

Mrs. Abram Phillips dwells in the next house, though the same belongs to John Phillips, her son. Our first mention of this family was in connection with the Chatterson farm in District No. 7. They were Hudson river people, and, after living in Huron some years, Mr. Phillips died; so his widow, with her aged mother, Mrs. Tipple, came here to live. The place was first occupied by James Winchell, a son of Riley, who married Esther Collins, and now resides in Huron.

Mrs. Jacob Tipple, on Saturday, the 31st of July, 1887, was congratulated on the one hundredth return of her natal day. She lived with her daughter, Mrs. Abram Phillips, about two miles west of Rose Valley. As Margaret Pultz, she was born in 1787, in Wittenberg, Dutchess Co. She is of good Dutch stock, her father having been Sebastian Pultz, a lineal descendant of the early settlers of New Netherlands. Mrs. Tipple always in her speech betrayed the race from which she sprang. In her father's family there were six sons and three daughters, and though all grew up,

MRS. MARGARET TIPPLE.
Aged 100 years.

none attained remarkable old age. She was next to the youngest child. Her father, who was a farmer, did not live beyond the ordinary span of life, but her mother died at eighty-eight. Those who dwell much on hereditary will see here a reason for the daughter's protracted living. Early in her life her father moved to Kinderhook, where she married Jacob Tipple. Here her children were born, though her family hardly equaled that of her mother. Her daughter, Eliza M., with whom she now lives, married Abram Phillips, who, years ago, worked a farm belonging to one of the noted Van Buren family. A son, Philip, married and lived to middle life, though he has been dead many years. His widow is living now near the lake. Many years since Mr. and Mrs. Tipple moved to Otsego county, and after living there a while, came to Rose, settling first in the Seelye neighborhood. Here Mr. Tipple died in 1853. Afterward his widow went to live with Mrs. Phillips. Years ago, though conspicuous for the neatness of her home and person, she did not consider hers a strong body, and counted perhaps as many ailments as do most persons of sixty and past. She was short and stout, and the word "comfortable" would apply to her appearance as well as any that I am familiar with. What a genial smile always wreathed her face when she greeted her friends. Middle-aged people remembered her as "old Mrs. Tipple" in their childhood.

From an article written by me at the time for *The Clyde Times*, I take the following: "After a hundred years of life we find her in her right mind, vividly recalling the days of old. To a lady past seventy, who recently visited her, she said: 'Why, Mrs. S., I am glad to see you. Do you remember my telling you, thirty years ago, 'You would live to be a fat old woman like me, yet?' She took her visitor's hand in both of hers and pressed the same in sincere pleasure over the meeting. A child of seven years accompanied the visitors, and, kissing the venerable lady, was kissed in return, Mrs. Tipple saying: 'You must always remember that you have been kissed by a woman a hundred years old.' The day itself, Saturday last, was one of the very hottest of an exceedingly hot season: but the friends and relatives were present in large numbers. It was an afternoon of the liveliest kind of congratulations. The chief centre of all this scene of pleasure. Mrs. Tipple, clad in a plain black dress, with the whitest of lace caps upon her venerable head, sat in her favorite chair in the parlor, and received the many hand-shakes and cheering words of her numerous visitors. She recalled with wonderful quickness circumstances pertaining to those whom she had known, but had not seen for many years. My own visit of two weeks since, she immediately mentioned. In person, Mrs. Tipple shows her weight of years. Her form is somewhat bowed, but her hair is scarcely changed in hue from that of youth. She uses no glasses, though she reads but little, and then only in her Dutch Bible.

Her chair is a small, straight-backed rocker with no arms. Here she sits contentedly many hours at a stretch. A year since she walked unaided, but now she requires a helping hand, as when she took a seat on the front porch to sit for her portrait. Had the family of our centenarian been as prolific as those of years ago, she would now count her children and children's children by the many scores. Her son, Philip, had only two children, one of whom has three and the other two children. Mrs. Phillips, her daughter, has six children living. Of these, four were present. Mrs. Phillips herself will be seventy-eight in December; but shows very few traces of infirmities. Her husband, Abram, died in 1884, at the age of eighty-two. The sum total of Mrs. Tipple's living descendants is twenty-six, and of these fifteen were present. John H. Phillips lives in Rose; William resides in Fairhaven; Charles in Rose; Mrs. Amanda Finch in Rose also. These represent the third generation present. One grandson, Nathan Phillips, is in the south, and could not be present." (Died in Maryland, June 3, 1893.)

This fête day was her last, for when the next 30th of July rolled around she was lying by the side of the husband whom death had torn from her thirty-six years before. "Like flowers at set of sun" her eyes had closed in their last sleep, July 7, 1888, and gentle hands performed for her the last sad office. She had no illness. "She simply ceased to live." Mrs. Phillips is above eighty-one years, but she has wonderful strength of body, and may herself attain the great age of her mother. A son, who works for his brother, John, stays with her nights, otherwise she is alone, and she says that she misses her mother sadly. "Her chair sat right over there and she was always in it. I can't tell you how much I miss her." The old lady was placed by the side of her husband in the Collins cemetery. (In 1893 Clarence Phillips and wife are living here with Mrs. Phillips.)

Nearly opposite this house, a road leads southward, passing the home of Isaac Boyce and Horatio Baker, and coming out upon the next east and west road near John Blynn's. Just beyond, and on the south side, lives Darwin Miner, another son of Riley. His wife was Nettie Messenger of the Glenmark neighborhood. He bought of Charles Bradburn, who took from James Hann.

As we go down into the valley, through which flows Thomas' creek, which was to mark the site of Gen. Adams' ditch, we may find a pleasant white house, looking northward out over the mint still, which John Phillips has planted down by the water. This is the Bradburn home. With an eye for the antique, we may be pardoned if reference is first made to an old log house, having two front doors, which stands to the left of the lane leading back to the barns. This is John Winchell's old house; was first put up considerably further back and then taken down and moved to this place nearer the road and just at the point where the road takes a short turn to the north to cross the creek. It may be as well to give a sketch of the Winchell family now, for we are approaching, in fact are in, what was once called Winchellville or Canada. Absalom Winchell was born in Egremont, Massachusetts, though the family was originally from Connecticut, married Byer (Abiah ?) Daly, and, in 1816, moved to the town of Galen, south of Ferguson's corners. His children were Jacob, John, Riley, Russell, Lany (who married Calvin Race, and lived and died in Phelps), Sally, Lucinda, Marta and Lovina. Except Lany, all of these children will be met as we journey through Rose. Jacob, the eldest, a soldier in 1812, settled first in Galen with his father ; his wife was Katie Bradburn, of Massachusetts ; he afterward lived where Leland Johnson now resides, a little east of John Phillips ; he died at the home of David Bradburn, brother of his wife and husband of his daughter Jane. John was twice married, first, to Mary Losier, and with her lived in a log house west of Philander Mitchell's present abode ; she died there ; their children were : John, now living in Huron ; Catharine, the wife first of James Hunn, and last, of Albert Harper ; Sally Ann, married John Almond of Waterloo, moved to Indiana, and there died ; Mary, married a Harper ; Lucretia, a Bennett, and went to Michigan. After the death of his first wife, Mr. W. married again, this time Margaret Ackerman, and moved to the log house near where we now are, on the Bradburn farm. By this marriage his children were : Lovina, who married Isaac Brewster, who died in the army during the Rebellion, leaving two sons—James and Eugene. Sarah Jane married James Van Amburg. John Winchell died in the log house, and was buried at Ferguson's corners. His widow died with Henry Ackerman in Galen. The place passed from the Winchells to Helon Ackerman, and from him through Smith, Van Amburg and Lyman Covell to Andrew Bradburn, who came from Gt. Barrington, Mass., in September, 1846, to the place formerly held by William Pixley on the Wayne Centre road. His wife was Harriet Jones, of New Marlborough, Massachusetts. The Bradburn children reared here were Thomas, now in possession ; Charles, who married Jane Brink of Huron, in which town he now resides ; Alice, who is Mrs. Gardner Barrett of Huron, and Edward, who married Georgie Smith of Rose, and lives in Clyde. Mr. Bradburn died in 1873, at the age of fifty-seven, and is buried north of the Valley. Thomas Bradburn found his wife in the person of Myra Johnson, a daughter of Leland. They have a son, Ray S., a black-eyed youngster, to gladden their fireside. In addition to his farm Mr. B. has long run a threshing machine. Mrs. Andrew B. makes her home with Thomas.

Crossing the brook, we are facing the house of John Phillips, who has, by successive improvements, made his home a very attractive one. As already stated, he is a son of Margaret, who resides a few rods west. The farm is the old German Van Amburg place. His daughter, Eliza Jane, married Mr. Phillips, who in time succeeded to the estate. The Van Amburgs were from Saratoga county, but German's wife was Elizabeth Finch of Yates county. Another daughter, Sarah Caroline, became Mrs. Harvey Clapper, once of Rose, but now of Wolcott. German Van Amburg died in 1878. The Phillipses have only two children—Clarence and Alice. The former married Ina, a daughter of Captain Daniel Harmon, formerly of the Valley, and the latter is Mrs. Luther Waldruff.

The region beyond is known in neighborhood parlance as Minerville, from the many Miners who live in the vicinity. On the outskirts of the Ville is the home of Leland Johnson, who came from Pownal, Vt. His wife was Minerva Goodell, of Williamstown, Mass. Their children are: Benjamin S., who married Kittie Van Gelder ; Edna we shall meet in District No. 11 as Mrs. George Worden, and Rhoda, also, as Mrs. Horatio Baker ; Myra, we just passed as the mistress of the Bradburn home. They have an adopted daughter, Mabel Wooster. Before the Johnsons was Samuel Cox, from whom they bought, and his father, S. D., bought in 1868 of H. P. Howard, now of the Valley. Before him was Forte Wilson, a brother of Ephraim, a resident further east. The latter's holding must go back very near to the land office. By his improvements Mr. Johnson has transformed the house and its surroundings.

The next house has stood in the Bovee name for several years. Stephen was the first name, and his widow is still there. Her sons are George and Herman. The house belongs to Mr. Johnson. These last two places are on the north side of the road.

The Miners on this street are sons of Riley Miner, a son of that Elder Miner who was one of the first ministers of the Baptist denomination in the town. Riley was a stone mason by trade, and was well known in Rose. He had twelve children, eleven of whom were present at his funeral. There are ten sons in the Riley Miner family and, save John and Philo, all live in Rose. John lives in Manton, Michigan ; Philo lives in Summer Hill, N. Y.; and Ursula, Mrs. Knapp, is in Weedsport ; Dora, the youngest, died February 17, 1891, aged twenty-eight years. In the four Miner dwellings we shall find first, William, who married Adaline Richardson. They have children, Ida, Irwin (now in the west), Arthur, Agnes, Flora, Jennie and Leon. In the next resides the widow of Riley. She was, I believe, a Neal. (Here, too, live James Miner and his wife, Jennie Whaley, who was born in Onondaga county. They have one child, Blanche. Mr. Miner is a stone mason by trade.) Then comes Edward, who married Dora Stearns of Sodus. Their children are Augustus, Ezra, Pearl and Sidney. Finally, we have Fernando, whose first wife was Sally Ann Hunn, a daughter of James and Catharine. She died in 1875. His second wife is Mary Hendrick. A neat, new house makes a very comfortable home and an ornament to the street. The children in this family are

Minnie, who married Joseph Bishop of Galen; Margaret, who is Mrs. Chester Plumb, of Clyde, and Samuel. (Lovina died in May, 1893, aged 23 years.)

No part of the district has changed hands more often than these several holdings along this road. On a county map, published in 1858, I find names that to-day have no lodgment here. For instance, beginning on the south side of the road, just east of widow Phillips' home, we find J. O. Hunn, now Darwin Miner's home; then C. N. J. Van Amburg, one of the many owners of the Bradburn farm. "Mrs. Winchell" occurs, possibly the widow of John, and resident in the log house. Then came I. Churchill and J. Greatsinger, about whom I knew nothing. Then is the name of Mrs. Lyman, possibly the widow of Jesse, and finally, R. Winchell, just at the angle of the road, the site of Fernando Miner's house. This was the home of Russell Winchell, who died in 1859, aged forty-seven years. His wife was Lucinda Ackerman, a daughter of John Winchell's second wife, by her first husband. Their children were David, who married an Odell and lives in Galen; Margaret Ann married, first, Alexander Harper, and second, Ebenezer Odell, both of Galen; Clarissa, whom we have seen as Mrs. Charles Harper, of North Rose, and Betsey Maria, who was Mrs. Ebenezer Odell, of Galen.

Going back to Leland Johnson's house, we find there, near it, the names J. Sherman and H. P. Howard. Then D. Bradburn, brother of Jacob Winchell's wife. J. Winchell comes next, and lastly, at the angle on the north side, was Riley Winchell's home. His first wife was Clara Hines, and their son, James, married Esther Collins, Stephen's daughter, and lives in Huron. Another son, Calvin, wedded C. E. LaRock, and dwells in North Rose. Riley's second wife was Mary Alworth, a daughter of the second wife of that "Sammy" Jones whose eccentricities were dwelt upon in our treatment of District No. 7. Their children were: Walter, who married a Blakesley and lives in Michigan, and Sophia, who became the wife of Heman Boyce, a son of Stephen, and the next neighbor west. He married for the third time, his wife being Amanda Swift, of Sodus. Mr. Winchell is living south of Clyde. His house became the property of Ephraim Wilson, who used it for a time as a tenant house, but not liking all the neighbors whom this use brought him, he finally moved it to the back part of his yard, where, as a sort of catch-all, it stands to-day. We have reached the bounds of the district, for the remaining places on this road belong to the Valley neighborhood.

DISTRICT No. 11.—"JEFFERS."

May 1—June 19, 1890.

This district occupies the range south of No. 10, and extends from the Valley neighborhood to that of Wayne Centre. We shall enter it by the road leading to the latter place, turning westward just north of the Presbyterian Church. Our first stop will be at the home of Wilbur Osborn, a son of Abner, who lives in the next house west, and whom we will interview for facts pertaining to him and his. He is a native of Lincolnshire, England, a brother of Samuel, encountered in District No. 6. His wife is Adelia Hendrick, a niece of the late Dr. Hendrick of Clyde. She was, when she married Mr. Osborn, the widow of his brother, Isaac, who, as may be remembered, was killed by a stroke of lightning in the house now occupied by Samuel Osborn, Jr., and in which Abner and his wife began their married life. They came to this location about twelve years ago, buying of Eron N. Thomas. There have been many names here in the past. Originally the land goes back to the old Jeffers purchase, and it was James J. who built the house now standing. Some of the land also was held by William Pixley, who was connected with the Jeffers by marriage. A part also was owned by one of the Clappers. There are now in the farm two hundred acres. Mr. Osborn has improved all the belongings very much, and his barns may favorably compare with almost any in the town. His children are Wilbur, who married Jennie Sherman of the Valley, and John, who married Anna Fredendall, also of the Valley. Wilbur and his wife live in the pleasant white house first reached, which was built expressly for them. Mrs. W. Osborn is a daughter of Henry B. Sherman, deceased. They have one child, Edna, by name, and a boy born August, 1890. John Osborn's home is in the Valley.

Abner Osborn has in his possession a valuable Indian relic in the shape of a stone hatchet. It was found on the farm of Samuel Osborn, and, aside from arrow heads, is the second weapon to my knowledge found in the town. Mr. O. is a very pleasant talker; quite willing to give me all the information desired. Among other items, he told me of a relative who, in 1841 or 1842, came to this town and bought the lot west of the Oaks farm, now belonging to the Welch brothers. This man, an uncle or cousin, had made an unfortunate marriage, and despairing, apparently, of happiness at home, had disappeared. His wife and others on the old English holding finally gave him up entirely, he having last been seen at a public house on his way to town. It was even reported that he might have fallen a victim to foul play at the hands of the unscrupulous bankmen, or those who kept the sea away from the fens. Much to the surprise of his American relatives he appeared among them as above, and abode with them for some years. He was a carpenter and joiner by trade and did some of the work on the McKoon stone house in Butler. His children had grown up, and he heard that two of his sons had emigrated to Quebec. His paternal instinct drew him there on what proved to be a futile search. There was a mystery as to how he had passed the years of his disappearance. He had with him much valuable material, filling certain trunks and boxes. Not finding his sons, he returned to England and there died.

Just beyond Mr. Jeffers' and on the same side of the road is the home of John Jeffers, a son of Nathan, and himself a deaf mute. His wife, also a mute, was Mary Dougan, of New York. She had come to Wayne county to visit the Pimm family, and while thus visiting met her subsequent husband. They have three children, two girls and a boy, all having normal faculties. Before J. Jeffers, this place was in the possession of Joseph Andrus, whose wife was Henrietta, a sister of Ephraim Wilson. They have one daughter, and now live in Huron. In 1858 it was held by Abner Garlick. An earlier resident, George Fisher, who married Betsey Jeffers, would carry us back very near, if not quite, to the Jeffers occupation.

Conspicuous on the south side of the road are the foundation walls of a house, while back of them is a barn. The walls mark the foundation of a house which some years ago was burned. Robert Jeffers is the owner, and it is claimed by some that the structure was burned by an irate applicant for the place on account of his being refused. Be this as it may, the cellar is there and that is about all. The site calls to mind the name of William Pixley, a former owner, whose second wife was Nancy Jeffers, and who long since went to Wisconsin. He had a large family. Before him is the name Pugsley; but it is a name only. There is extant a deed to E. N. Thomas of four acres from William A. Pixley and Nancy, his wife, dated October 16th, 1849, bounded south by David Holmes, west by Ovid Blynn, north by east and west road. Quite likely this is the lot.

Our next stop is at the home of Ovid Blynn, and this we shall find on the north side of the road. We shall be very likely to find the old gentleman at home, for his age forbids his straying far. He was born February 14th, 1803, in Canaan, Columbia county, one of the few who went from rather than to the happy land of Canaan. His wife was Hannah Hadenburg, her name proclaiming her German origin, which she owed to one of the Hessians, whom Britain sent to America during the Revolution. Her father, not liking his hireling business, deserted and became a reputable citizen of this Hudson river country. It was in 1844 that Mr. Blynn sought our town, coming here through his brother-in-law, John Phillips, a paper maker by trade, who had bought not the present home of Mr. B., but one further west of Samuel Way. Phillips never lived here, but his widow is now a dweller with her brother, the latter's wife having died in

1886 at the age of eighty-three. This first home was a log house nearly opposite John H. Blynn's present house west of the corners. It was built by Samuel Way. Mr. Blynn tells me that during his first winter he kept his stock fully a mile and a half away, in the barn of the Ways, on the top of the hill to the westward, where the sky and the buildings apparently meet. There was then only one framed house in the vicinity, that of Robert Jeffers. The whole region was new, left to the very last on account of its low character and the heavy timber covering it. Roads were nearly impassable. In the spring it was a half day's task to drive to Clyde, and another half day's work to get back. In time Mr. B. built or improved his own framed house and barns. These are now in the possession of his elder son, John H., who married Catharine Braman, for some years an invalid. They have one daughter, Mrs. Etta McIntyre of Wolcott. (Ovid Blynn died July 12, 1891 ; Mrs. John Blynn in 1893, and Mr. Blynn has moved from the corners to this place.)

The locality so long unsettled rapidly filled up when the way was opened, and the vicinity became more thickly inhabited than the older portions of the town. About these four corners have dwelt people whose names only remain, and some of whom not even the names can be found. On the southeast corner was Robert Vandercook, a cousin of John and William H., living with his widowed mother in a log house and having twenty-five acres of land. A sister of R. Vandercook married James Ferguson. He sold out to Ovid Blynn and went west. There is now no trace of the house. Just south of the corners is a house built years since by Daniel Wiley for a fanning-mill shop, and I may state here that in this vicinity there were at one time, a long while ago, four places where these useful machines for the farm were made. The house in which John Jeffers lives was erected for that purpose, and in it work was done by Joseph Waring, who married Susan Jeffers, and who kept a toll-gate on the Clyde road, and his son-in-law, George Clapper. Through Henry Garlick this house south of the corners passed into Mr. Blynn's possession, as did also the present home of John H. B., which was built by one Peckham of Balsam fame. Mr. Peckham, on leaving this neighborhood, went east to Johnstown, Montgomery Co. There can be no middle-aged dweller in this part of Wayne county who does not recall the doses of Peckham's Balsam, whereby, in due time, his colds were supposed to be loosened and he restored to health and activity. There were only four acres in the holding. Mr. Blynn bought directly of Jeremiah Bennett, who may have taken from Peckham. After living in this house for many years, Ovid Blynn bought of David Lyman twenty-five acres and the house in which he now resides. To his original farm he also added fourteen acres of William Garlick, which must have joined him in the west. Mr. B. was a Methodist before coming to Rose, and for many years has been a prominent member of the

Rose Church. His second son, Martin H., better known in Rose as " Matt," was one of the best known and most successful teachers in our town. In the fall of 1860, when the writer was just leaving for his first term at Falley Seminary in Fulton. " Matt " Blynn was beginning his winter's work in the old stone school-house in District No. 7. While not necessarily severe, he tolerated no nonsense, and insisted upon strict attention to business. Says one pupil, now a tradesman in Clyde : " He was the best teacher I ever had. He made me learn whether I wished to or not." Certain it was that his schools always stood well in the eyes of the community. Before the War he had studied medicine somewhat, and consequently when the strife came, he was ready to accept a position in the medical department, which he did as hospital steward of the Tenth New York Cavalry. But this place was not adapted to his active temperament, and he was early in 1863 commissioned as second lieutenant in the same regiment. Thence his progress upward was rapid, and he was finally mustered out in June, 1865, as brevet lieutenant colonel. Concerning his service and record as a soldier, I append extracts from a letter written by his comrade, Brevet Lieutenant Colonel N. D. Preston, Pittsburg, Pa. : " Captain M. H. Blynn's record as a soldier was an enviable one. He was one of the most efficient and reliable officers in our regiment. * * * * The first I remember of him he was hospital steward. From this position he rose rapidly, not by favoritism or influence, but by merit, until, as I have said, he came to be looked upon as one of the best officers in the regiment." After the War he finished his medical studies, graduating in New York in the spring of 1866. He then accepted a government medical appointment and was in South Carolina for some time, but coming north, finally he located in Cicero, Onondaga county, where he built up an excellent practice and reputation. He there married Frank Douglas, but his career was suddenly ended December 10th, 1883, by the rupture of the artery of the stomach. He was at the time in his forty-eighth year. (The old Blynn place is now owned and occupied by Mr. Isaac Boyce.)

Our discussion of the Blynn family has led us on all sides of the very comfortable house situated on the northeast corner of the cross-roads. As usual in these parts, we are on early Jeffers ground, and this place was once the property of Mrs. Hannah Dodds. In 1858 it belonged to Judd B. Lackey, who long since went to Michigan. He was a brother of Mrs. Susan Wykoff, of the Valley district, and his wife was Martha Hurlburt, who died in Lanesburg, Mich., January 28, 1890, aged sixty-three years. He was for some time an employee of E. N. Thomas, in the latter's saw-mill. (Mr. L. died in Lanesburg, Nov. 4, 1890.) For some years the place has stood in the name of Fidelus Kaiser, who is German born. His wife was Magdalena Garling, a native of Alsace, one of the long fought for Rhine provinces. Their children were Elizabeth, who, as Mrs. Jacob

Miller, lives in Michigan ; Mary, who is Mrs. William Neilson, of Canada ; Valentine, living in Wayne Centre ; George Philip, in Macedon ; William Henry, in Tonawanda ; John E., who lives in the Valley, and Alfred, who died at the age of twenty-five. Mr. Kaiser settled first in Wayne Centre, but afterward came this way. His faithful wife passed to her reward on the 4th of June, 1889, at the age of seventy years. Since her death Mr. K. has not been much at his old home, but has rather visited about among his children. (Died Feb. 11, 1893.)

Were we from this point to take the south road, we would soon reach the confines of the Griswold district; but there are no more dwellers in District No. 11. Should we go north, which we proceed to do, we would soon find a small house, with pleasant inmates, on the west side of the road, that of Horatio Baker, who came to Rose from Geneva. He bought his farm of twenty-five acres from Julius Smith, who now lives in Sodus. The latter built the house. Mr. Baker's wife is Rhoda, daughter of Leland Johnson, of District No. 10. Three children gladden the fireside—Mabel, Earl and an unnamed girl baby, who was monarch of the cradle when I called.

It should be stated that thirty years since, two houses were found on the east side of the road, between the corners and this point. In one of them dwelt Merrill Pease, of whom more will be said later, and in the northern one, C. V. Smith, of whom I have only the name. There are no traces of habitations now.

Still northward and on the east side Isaac Boyce resides. His neighbors pronounce his name as though it were spelled Bice. His father was Stephen, and the old family home was the place southwest of the Valley, now held by Judson Chaddock. His mother was Mary Ann, daughter of Nathan Jeffers. Isaac came to this place in 1871, buying out Eli Garlick, who, as usual, had a blacksmith-shop hard by. Mr. Boyce's wife is Lany Ream, a sister of Fred Ream, who lives further west. Her family came from Germany thirty or more years ago. There are two boys—Charles and John, who, when I called, were helping their father in harvesting grain. The house was built by Eli Garlick, and there are twenty-seven acres in the farm. A few rods to the north we should find the end of the road, the same terminating in District No. 10. (Mr. Boyce has sold to Burt Haviland, who will occupy in 1894.)

We must return to the corners and resume our westward way. Over the hill, and beyond John Blynn's, were we to look carefully on the south side of the road, we might find a filled up well, the same marking the site of the log house in which once dwelt Merrill Pease and his wife. Being childless, they passed their last years with William Dodds. Mr. P. peddled Peckham's Balsam, and the story is yet told of him that when he sold a bottle, he was wont to say: "After taking the balsam, you had better drink a little water, so as to wash it down on the lungs." Where could he have studied physiology? His acres passed first to William Garlick and then to Ovid Blynn. Before Pease, was one Stewart, whose son, William, married Martha, Mr. Pease's niece.

On the north side, some rods back from the street, is a very pretty cobble-stone house, the very first met on this road. Here, till recently, dwelt Jared Chaddock and family. The earliest resident whom I can find was William Desmond. He was born in Ireland, an uncle of the William Desmond residing east of the Valley. He took up the land from the office and made the usual weary trips to Geneva to make his payments. He built the first log house and lived and died in it. He was only fifteen years old when he came to this country, and his home was with his brother, John, till his marriage, at the age of twenty-two, to Lucinda Winchell. Her brother-in-law, Esquire Mitchell, married them, and she bore nine children to him. He died in 1849, aged forty-two years. His widow subsequently married Edward Horn, and died at the age of seventy-eight. Three of their children died early, but six are still living, viz., John, who resides in Huron; Timothy, in Clyde; Frank, in Missouri; Mrs. Burch and Mrs. Cleveland, both in Rose; William, who lives in Arcadia. To him succeeded William Mitchell, to whom we owe the stone house. He was the second son of Philander, long known as " 'Squire " Mitchell, of District No. 13. He married Jane Grenell, of that family so long identified with Ferguson's corners, and now lives in Lyons. After him came Henry Akerman, Stephen Collins' son-in-law, who built the framed addition to the house and added to the barn. After him came a Mr. Foster; then Lewis Barrett, now of the Valley; next Philander Mitchell, 2d; after him Fred Ream, whose present home is further west; then Samuel Garlick, and lastly, the late occupant, who has made many improvements. In the farm are fifty-seven acres, very pleasantly located. Reference to Jared Chaddock was made in our leaving District No. 9, where he was named among the children of William Chaddock, 2d. His wife, as stated there, was Miriam Durfee, of Marion, a public spirited lady, who is interested in everything that pertains to the good of the town. They have only one child, Maude Evelyn. Mr. Chaddock himself was one of the early enlisted men from Rose, going through the War in the 67th New York, a regiment that began its work at Big Bethel, went through the Peninsula, Fredericksburg and Grant's "Fight it out on this line" campaigns. In his town he is noted for his devotion to the temperance cause and for his unfailing interest in the Grand Army of the Republic. It has been doubted by some whether the Sodus encampment, each August, would be a success if Jared should miss it. He is always first there and the last to leave. Only a few weeks since the farm passed into the hands of Miss Lucinda Mitchell, and Jared has moved to the Valley. (Now owned by Cornelius

13

Marsh, who has rebuilt the barns and house, making them very attractive.)

Our next stop is on the south side of the road, and if our old friend, Cornelius Marsh, is at home, we are sure of a hearty welcome. His name was first given in our rambles as the owner for some years of the Joe Wade farm in District No. 7, and again as one of Amos Marsh's sons in District No. 5. Since leaving the eastern part of the town he has moved about considerably, and we now find him residing on the William Garlick farm. I call his attention to the solitary tree, standing on the very top of the last range of Rose hills to the east, and in the south part of the second lot from the north end of the ridge, and tell him that his birthplace is only just over that tree, a few rods further south. The point is between three and four miles away, but it seems only a brief distance. The house in which the family lives is very old, a log one, yet no one would suspect it, for the squared logs are clapboarded without and lathed and plastered within, similar to the one in District No. 10 built by Uriah Wade. From time to time additions and changes have been made till the structure has many crooks and angles. There are here a son, William, taller than his father; a daughter, Irene, just blossoming into womanhood, and Cornelius, Jr., a black-eyed boy, at the happy and careless age just before his teens. (Irene Marsh was married in March, 1893, to Frank J. Mitchell.) William Garlick, referred to in our North Rose article, formerly owned this place and long lived here. He sold in 1881 to his son, Samuel. His first wife was Caroline Clary, from the northern part of the town. They had but one son, Samuel, who is now a Presbyterian minister, living near Ithaca. Mrs. Garlick died in 1881, aged seventy-two years. Her husband, later, married again, and now lives at Woodmont, Conn., near the old home of the Garlick family. The son, Samuel, took a theological course in the Auburn Seminary. He married Martha Delamatter, of Rose, whose parents have since moved to Michigan. Their children are Lena, who is Mrs. Jay Mack, of Ludlowville, N. Y., and Carrie, at home. (Now Junius, where Mr. G. is pastor of the Presbyterian Church.) Before Mr. Garlick, was John Nelson Pease, who inherited from his father, Alanson. His wife was a daughter of Stephen Boyce, and he long since went to Wisconsin. He was a member of the Methodist Church. Alanson Pease was probably the first holder and the builder of the house. His wife was Nancy, a daughter of the first Robert Jeffers. They had children—John N.; Martha, the wife of William Stewart, and Permillia, who married an Ethridge, in Wisconsin. Mr. Pease was known in town as "Old Honesty," and dying, was buried in the Jeffers ground, further west. His widow accompanied her son to the far west. This farm of fifty acres is on lot 238, and in an old deed, dated January 20, 1850, I find that John N. Pease sold to Eron N. Thomas, who at one time or another had his name connected with very many farms in these parts. He must have passed the ownership to Mr. Garlick. In this deed I find boundaries as follows : North by Samuel Jeffers, east by the same, south by Merrill Pease and Franklin Finch, and west by Henry Wagoner and Frederick Nushikel. What changes have taken place in the intervening forty years, I am unable to state.

Nearly across the way is the home of Gideon Barrett, whose father, John, bought, long since, of Henry Streeter. The latter was the first husband of Maria Winchell, a younger sister of Mrs. Sally Mitchell. Their sons were Alonzo and Jonah. John R. Barrett, as we learned in District No. 10, was the oldest son of Simeon Barrett. He married Mary Pitcher, of Columbia county, a sister of Mrs. William H. Vandercook. This farm, when he took it, was mostly new land, and he found work enough in trying to reduce it to a proper condition of cultivation. For the latter part of Mr. Barrett's life, he was sadly afflicted, being almost helpless for eight years from rheumatism. He died in his forty-ninth year. For many years he was a conspicuous figure at the religious meetings of the town, being one of the first to leave the Methodist Church at the formation of the Free Methodist organization. The children in this family were Gertrude, who became the wife of Harmon Case, recently deceased, a Free Methodist minister ; Gideon, who holds the paternal acres, forty-six in number, and whose wife is Emma Vanderburgh, of the Lyman district : Alice, who died at the age of nine years, in 1865, and Helen, who married George S. Bliss, of Clyde. Gideon Barrett has very much improved the farm, and his father would hardly recognize the house, could he again look at it. In this home are two children—Georgie Emma and Florence May.

Beyond this farm we go past several fertile fields (all the land here is good) and are confronted on the north side of the road by a large, well appointed barn, now the property of George Jeffers, but for many years it stood in the name of Loren Lane ; and here, among the peach trees, was a very pleasant home. He bought of " Little " William Jeffers, son of William, and thereby a grandson of the first Robert Jeffers. It will doubtless be understood why this is called the Jeffers neighborhood. Loren Lane's wife was Fanny M. Van Marter. Their children were Johnson V., to be met later : L. Nelson, who married Rebecca Chidester, of the north part of the district, and who now lives in Michigan, and Elizabeth, who married, first, John Rhea, and second, William Story, living now in Canada. Recently the house has been destroyed, but there is no better building spot in this part of Rose.

Across the way, and for some distance to the south, are the lands of Fred Ream, who lives on the next corner. A very fine apple orchard occupies the field first met and this extends to the next north and south road. In the lots to the south have been, in the years past, one or two mint stills. There is also a spring of sufficient magnitude to find a location in the county atlas.

The next building is the school-house, in some respects the most noted in town. It is called indifferently "Spunk" and "Jeffers." The latter name is readily evident, but to the former there hangeth a tale. This neighborhood was ever clannish. In one way or another the people were related. They did not like to go down to the Griswold district to school, nor to the Covell district north. They were bound to have a school of their own. Old Robert Jeffers gave the land for the building, and willy, nilly, they had their school-house and their school. They were spunky about it, and, lo! the name clings to the building to this day, not only to the first edifice, but to its successor, and bids fair to remain indefinitely. Again, this was the chosen home of the Neversweats. "And who were they?" the interested reader asks at once. Well, if every name and term used in this town had given me as much trouble in looking up, the history of Rose would have required an age like unto that of Methuselah to accomplish it. Everybody knew about the Neversweats; could tell long stories about their meetings; but the one who could tell why they were thus termed could not easily be found. In the history of Wayne county, published in 1877, quite a little space is given to them, but the article really tells us nothing. An aged resident says: "They were good men and women who did not like the forms and ceremonies of the churches and so withdrew and held meetings here in this school-house. They had no organization, but every one did as he thought best." This did not give me the reason for the peculiar name. "Oh," says another. "John Cornwall was there one night, and he, always full of fun and ridicule, just called them Neversweats, and the name stuck." But this did not satisfy me. Cornwall may have given them the name, but why? Finally, my searchings found this good lady, who said that the meetings were often protracted long into the night, sometimes till nearly morning, and that the expression used occasionally ran like this: "We'll hold on till morning and never sweat a drop. We'll never tire; we'll work constantly," and so on in a similar strain. That an irreligious fun lover should catch at the expression "Neversweat" was the likeliest thing in the world, and the people were named just as long as their memory continues. It is stated that one prime cause of the start of the meetings was the desire of one of the near dwellers to preach, he claiming that he had had a "call," but the quarterly conference being quite certain that it was some other sound he heard, refused; hence more "spunk" and the peculiar religionists. By good people, the meetings are recalled as exceedingly spirited affairs, the like of which can hardly be found to-day. To the boys and girls who sat on the writing falls they were very entertaining. There is no doubt that they were productive of good. Though the Neversweats are numbered with other defunct bodies, there are many people in the vicinity who, impressed by the peculiar characteristics of these people, do not affiliate with any church. They claim to be and are, I think, excellent people, but when asked to what religious body they belong, the reply is: "He is, or I am, a stand alone." In all my goings up and down the world, this neighborhood presents to me the first instances of this peculiar religious status. If all were "stand alones," the assembling of ourselves together specially enjoined by the Bible would be rather infrequent. I believe there are some others like-minded in Rose, but this neighborhood seems to have been the birthplace of the notion.

Another remove brings us to the four corners, where the fences are well covered with indications of tradesmen's enterprise, but never a sign to tell whither the roads lead. In that sweet-by-and-by, the few living may see, New England's example will have been followed to the extent of rearing at such a convenient point a guide-board, which will proclaim to the passers-by the distance to Lyons, to Clyde, or to the Valley. Now the manifold virtues of Barnes, the clothier, are frequently set forth: but the traveling public would like to know how far the journey has progressed, how much longer it is to last, and the direction it must take. An excellent location for a guide-board. Neighbor Ream, won't you be the first to set the town a pattern?

Should we turn to our left and go toward the south, we should find no house till we reach the Griswold district, and we are not ready for that yet. On each side of the road we should find the fertile farm of Fred Ream, whose home is on the northwest angle made by these crossing thoroughfares. If interested in indications of prosperity, we will give more than a passing glance at the well built and well painted barn that stands west of the house. The master here enjoys having his belongings well kept. Mr. Ream is of German birth. (His name in German is Rihm), though at his birth, his native city, Strasburg, was on French territory. His father, Peter, came to this country many years since and located on this place, then held by E. Nusbikel, a family that afterward went to Lyons, where members of it are to-day engaged in trade. Before the last named was Matthias Van Horn, whose wife was a Winchell. He went west long ago. Fred Ream's wife is Lovina, daughter of the first Philander Mitchell, and his children are: Alice F. and Edith L., both at home. There are one hundred and three acres in the farm. Mr. Ream was one of the drafted contingent during the War. He says that with others he reported at Auburn and was sent home for a week. On his second reporting, he was told to go home and wait till sent for. He has been waiting ever since. The collapse of the Rebellion rendered his enlistment unnecessary. He tells me that he has not as yet applied for a pension on account of his military services.

Just north of this place and on the same side of the road is the attractive home of Johnson V. Lane, who is a son of Loren, once living to the east of the corner. All these well-appointed buildings are of Mr. Lane's own construction. He is himself an evangelist and not a member of any denomination. Much of his time is thus required away from home. His wife is Sarah Melinda, a daughter of Lorenzo Griswold, once resident further north. They have only one child, Irving J., still at home. Mrs. Lane's mother, now Mrs. Franklin Finch, passes some portion of her time in this place. (Mr. Lane died July 5, 1890. Irving J. married Etha J. Hetta of Glenmark, and lives on the Samuel Garlick place.)

North of and immediately opposite there was once a house occupied by W. Meeks. I think I have heard it stated that he was a shoemaker. Further, I cannot affirm, save to state that to characteristics such as his name implies, has been promised the inheritance of the earth.

From this point northward to the beginning of Covell's district, the locality was known in former days as " Balsamville," all owing to the manufacture of Peckham's Balsam, once made by Selden Borden, and I am told that as many houses have been torn away as are yet standing. Even now the number seems strangely large for a farming community. About each home is a small enclosure, scarcely more than a village lot.

So, then, proceeding on our way, we shall first halt at the home of George Jeffers. South of him there is a noticeable angle in the road, giving it a slight turn toward the east. The farm is old Jeffers' land, and in this house Nathan Jeffers died. In 1858, it is recorded, it was the home of Mrs. J., who is now living in the Valley. Nelson Lane next owned it, and he sold to George Jeffers, who seems to have a faculty of getting all that joins him. His surroundings are becoming more and more convenient every day. For a long time a deputy sheriff of Wayne county, he is well known. There are ninety-eight acres in his farm. His wife is Eliza, daughter of Leonard Mitchell, and thereby grand-daughter of the first Philander. They have three children—Willard, Frank and May. To those whose lot it is to till steep hills and unresponsive swamps, the almost ideal lay of Mr. Jeffers' land must be very inviting. The next house is used by Mr. Jeffers for rental. It was built by John Burt, whose wife was Eleanor, a half sister of the present owner. They went west long ago and died there. Thirty years since it was held by a Mrs. Potter ; fifteen years ago by F. Blake, and now people by the name of Rice occupy it.

Opposite is the home of two very good people by the name of Kamp. Germany itself does not contain ten acres of more Germanized territory than are those belonging to Kasper Kamp. In the fifties this place was ascribed to S. Barrett. John B. once owned it, and he sold to Mr. Kamp. The latter has children residents in other parts of the country ; and they are thoroughly Americanized, but Kasper and his *frau* " can no sprek " English at all. John Chinaman, who does washee-washee in our cities, is not one whit more difficult to assimilate than are these good people to whom Deutschland clings in every particular. (Mr. Kamp has since died.)

Next is the unoccupied house of Melvin Lane. He is a nephew of Loren, his father being Luther. He is now in the west. His house looks desolate and forsaken, as it apparently is. Its remoteness from the stone-throwing village boys has alone saved the window lights. Perhaps we shall not be blamed if we peer in, having pushed our way through branches and burdocks to the side of the house. Truly, the presence of the master is necessary to prevent decay and destruction. Pompeiian ruins could not afford much more in the way of dust and dirt. It is the old Borden place, where Selden made the famous balsam.

The next house was built by John Chidester, to whom Lorenzo Griswold sold two acres of land. He sold to Samuel Clary, a brother of William Garlick's first wife. These people died here. A daughter by the name of Rose is married and lives near Rochester. A son went away long since. Now the place is occupied by William Armstrong, whose daughter, Kate, is the wife of Henry Fredendall of the Valley.

We reach our northern limits when we come to the next place. Here, many years ago, came Lorenzo Griswold, having bought one hundred acres of land with the inevitable log house from William Stewart, who thereupon went west. He had a brother, Solomon, who once lived opposite to Kasper Kamp's home. Mr. Griswold's wife was Betsey, the second daughter of Nathan Jeffers. Their children were: Mary Eliza, who married Nathaniel Weeks, now in Michigan; William H. of the Valley, who made the Weeks account square by marrying Nathaniel's sister Julia; Benjamin Frank, who died when twelve years old; Sarah Melinda, already met as Mrs. J. V. Lane; Helen, who is Mrs. Abram Covell, now south of the Valley; John Willis, who died when twenty years old, and Rachel, who died in infancy. Mr. Griswold himself died in 1851, in his forty-fourth year. It has been stated in these annals that his widow afterward became Mrs. Franklin Finch of the same district. For some time subsequent to Mr. G.'s death the place was held by the family, till it passed into the hands of Arthur Dougan, whose wife was Damaris, a sister of Ephraim Wilson, first, of the Valley district. Mr. D. was from Phelps, to which town he returned when his wife died. They had a son, Jerome, who was prominent in Rose musical matters, and who, I think, enlisted from Rose. The farm is now owned by Simeon Van Buskirk of Ontario county, whose son, Thomas, occupies it.

Reversing our voyage and going southward, it is impossible to repress a wish that we might have every name of the people whose living here was too brief for any record. How many missing genealogical links might thus be supplied, but the search would be fruitless. Even our agricultural town, with its permanent class, has afforded shelter for a brief time to those who have folded their tents, like the Arabs, and as silently stolen away. Only contemporaries can tell to-day where the dwelling places were.

We are again at the corners, and as we walk or ride along the valley we might, had we eyes sharp enough, find traces of former habitations. On the 1858 map, just west of what is now Fred Ream's house, was put down a name, which, after diligent effort, I have given up as undecipherable. It certainly begins with St., then it runs into the delineation of the hill beyond and ends in schif. It is suggestive of something decidedly German, and quite likely some ancient resident in these parts can tell about it. In the 1874 atlas Fred Ream is put down as the owner of both houses, but now I can find only one, viz., the one in which he resides.

Here begins the elegant fence with which the Glens have separated their farm from the road. Made of wood and wire and painted white, it has nothing approaching it in the town. This east and west road of ours is like the young Lochinvar, who "staid not for brake, and he stopped not for stone," for it makes no concession whatever to the hills in its way. Westward it started and it pursues its course remorselessly. As with Sheridan on his famous Cedar creek ride, "hills rose and fell," so here we are uplifted, as on the crest of an ocean billow, and again we find ourselves humbly at the bottom of the trough. Now we must mount upward, till reaching the summit, we may see the final range of Rose hills to the east and are confronted by the final line in the west. Our white fence has been at our right as we climbed, and while the horse takes a merited rest we will alight and call on the Glens. A very pretty marquee is set up in the front yard. That belongs to the "Sam" Glen's children, and if our call is in mid-summer, we may find "Sam" himself happily smoking, taking the *otium cum dignitate* which his New York life will not afford. His figure and bearing will warrant the conclusion that his way through life is not entirely without some of its good things. Again the house and outbuildings all bear testimony to the interest that "Bill" and "Sam" take in the old home. Their mother meets us at the door and invites us to a seat in the front room, and our pleasure at meeting her is more than ordinary, for her son, John, was the writer's chum away back in the early sixties at Falley Seminary. Some folks, Richard Grant White among others, have descanted on the inelegance of the word "chum," but to the old school boy it arouses recollections and brings out old colorings that few other words afford. So, then, elegant or otherwise, John was our chum, and a good one too. If he did rather more than half the small amount of work that we had to do, it was because he liked to work, not that his chum, was I——, well, disinclined. So, then, for the first time in my life, I am talking with John's mother, and she tells me that she and her late husband, William, were Saratoga county born—he in the town of Milton, and she as Nancy Cole, in Galway; that they came to Galen in 1855, and to this farm in 1858. Originally they were members of the Methodist Church, but at the time of the formation of the Free Methodist body, they united with it. Their children are : William, who married Louise Worden, of the western part of the district, and now lives in Lyons, having one son, Willard. As "Bill" Glen, few men ever residing in Rose have a more general county reputation than he. From the farm he, years since, went into Charles Wright's store in the Valley, and there remained for many years. Finally beginning to dabble in politics, he went from one position to another till he became the sheriff of Wayne county, moving then to Lyons. He has since made that thriving place his home. The next son, Samuel, married Cornelia Smith of New York City, and has for some years been in business in Gotham, sending annually his family to the old home, where he passes as much time as he can. John has already been introduced. He married Lucy Bullard of Williamson, and now lives in California. His exceeding goodness—I will not say that he monopolized this trait for the family—could lead him in only one direction, viz., to the ministry. So, very soon after leaving school—he could then make long and most excellent prayers—we find him in the traveling work of the Free Methodist Church. His experience was a varied one in the north and south till failing health forced his removal to the Pacific coast. Elias, the youngest son, married Mary Hill, near Albany, and a teacher, lives in Cortland. The daughters, Harriet, married Wesley Burns, in Alton, and Henrietta died in 1869 at the age of twenty. In addition to the home in which widow Glen resides, there is a tenant house just back of the garden in which lives Orrin Carpenter, whose wife was a Dodds, grand-daughter of Mrs. Hannah D., who lives opposite. They have one child. The Glens bought of David Stanley and Calvin Pease, and before them the place had been owned by Loren Lane and Samuel Jeffers. (Mrs. Glen died June 1, 1893.)

Just over the way, on the south side, is the home of Jeffers Dodds, and now we are surely on Jeffers soil, for Mr. D. is a grandson of the first Robert, and the house is within a stone's throw of the old home. This house, occupying a commanding site, was built for the present occupant. He is the second son of William Dodds and Hannah Jeffers, his wife. His own wife is Jane Fosmire, and their children are : Eva, who married Clifford Lee of District No. 6; the latter's early death left her a very youthful widow ; Florence, who married Frank Lyman : Libbie, who is Mrs. Wells Miller : John and Freddie, boys at home.

Only a few steps further west and we come upon the house built by Robert Jeffers many years ago. In fact, erected in 1818, it may be doubted whether there is an older dwelling house in Rose. The barn, near, was built in 1823. Exteriorly the house stands very much as it was when put up, though I presume its red paint dates from a later period. A knock at the door secures admission at the hands of Mrs. Dodds, now an aged lady, but still the good Samaritan, in that she is caring for a great grandchild, whose mother is very ill at her home in the Valley. Between the pranks of the child and my questions I feared I might drive all memory from her mind ; but she survived and managed to tell me a very interesting story of what was an early home in the wilderness.

Robert Jeffers, with his brother, Nathan, came to this section from Johnstown, Fulton county, in 1813. His location was in a heavily wooded wilderness. No framed nor any other kind of a house was anywhere near. His own log structure was constructed a little further west, in the valley, doubtless on account of the spring near. Convenience with reference to water usually determined the site of the pioneer home. His wife was Christiana Foote. Like many of the early comers, he died comparatively young, in 1844, his wife surviving till 1858. The labor and ailments incident to building up a new country, made havoc in the ranks of men who otherwise would have lived to be octogenarians. Both of these worthy people were buried in the private cemetery on the north and south road, next west. They reared a numerous progeny, and the names are as follows : William, who married Phœbe Wiley, and for a time lived where James Weeks is now, and then went to Wisconsin ; Betsey married George Fisher, who once lived on the corner where George Worden is, but long since went to Michigan : John took Lydia Way, a neighbor's daughter, for his wife, and, after living for a time on the Samuel Garlick, or Jared Chaddock farm, went to Wisconsin : Samuel married Harriet Robinson, and, like others of his kin, went to Wisconsin ; Esther became the wife of John Drown, now of Huron—she once lived near Barnes'; Nancy, after the death of her husband, Alanson Pease, went to Wisconsin ; Susan was Mrs. Joseph Waring, and died in town, while he went west; Hannah married William Dodds, from Lyons ; James married Hannah Rhinehart, and went to Iowa ; Lawson, an invalid, still lives on the old farm and in the old house with his sister, Mrs. Dodds. (Has since died.) William Dodds died September 29th, 1888, aged seventy-five years and one month. He had built a house in the Valley. His family, too, was a numerous one, consisting of Polly, who is Mrs. William H. Thomas, of the Valley, well known for her zeal in religious matters, being a member of the Free Methodist Church : Christiana, who is the wife of Jackson Valentine, also of the Valley ; William Henry, who married, first, Melissa Fosmire, and, second, Louisa Stack ; he once lived south of the Weeks place, but long since went to Michigan. Of his children Hattie married Ira Lamb, of Detroit ; William works for " Bill " Griswold, in the Valley, and Albertine is the wife of Orrin Carpenter, who lives on the Glen farm. James Jeffers Dodds, the youngest son of William and Hannah, has already been noted. Just a little northwest of the old Jeffers home, a small house has long stood, being a sort of receptacle for farm tools. This was once the home of John Jeffers, but during the past summer it was moved to a less sightly locality. It should be stated that Alanson Pease, a Jeffers son-in-law, found a last resting place in the family burial ground. Mrs. Dodds' recollections of olden times are very clear and accurate, and she brings up from the misty past many an interesting relic. She recalls the taking of a pig from his sty by a predatory bear, only a little south of her girlhood home, and her brother, John, with one of the Clappers, captured a wolf in a trap, and received the government bounty for his scalp.

Again we go west, and after crossing a narrow valley, begin the ascent of the last range of hills in the town. Near the summit we reach the cross roads, on whose northeast corner stands the house of George Worden. A well-laden peach tree at the corner of the house told of protection from the north wind, of the warmth of a south exposure, and was a reminder of the days when peaches were as constant a crop as potatoes, perhaps even more so. The house itself dates back to the days of George Fisher, whose wife was Betsey Jeffers. He displayed excellent judgment in locating his house, and I hope his Michigan home was half as pleasant. Fisher sold to George Lapham, who was the first husband of Elizabeth Worden, an aunt of the present owner. To him succeeded his brother-in-law, Constantine Worden. After the latter came his son, George, who, by the way, was born in the house. George Worden has been named already in District No. 10 sketches as the husband of Leland Johnson's daughter, Edna. They have two children—John and Irene—who prove efficient helps in the house and on the farm. The parents are active members of the Rose Methodist Church. Constantine Worden, who lived here for many years, was reared south of the James Weeks home. He married Phœbe Ann Vandercook, now deceased. Their children were: Sarah, who married Allen Robinson, of Huron; George Leonard married Maggie Weeks, and lives east of North Rose; and William, who is north of Wayne Centre. There are sixty acres in the farm.

If we take our way to the north we shall soon finish this part of our district. There is a very steep hill to descend, and we shall need a firm trust in Providence as well as a strong part of the harness on which, it may be remembered, the old lady laid so much stress, and the breaking of which destroyed all hopes of salvation. At the time of my visit the road was much used by those who sought the blackberry said to grow in these parts in great abundance. The road itself was laid out many years ago, and is called the State road. Had it been continued directly to the north, it would have gone very near the house of James Osborne, in District No. 10 ; but fortunately for him it was stopped just at the woods, and though one may go through now, it is not a traveled thoroughfare. Unless after berries, or to call on one of the two families living here, there is no reason why one should risk the going down and climbing back. A trifle north of the foot of the hill, on the west side, is the humble habitation of William

Lambert, who came to these parts from Cayuga county. His family lives in two houses, not because his children are so numerous, though he has several, but because the buildings are so small. (Mr. Lambert was killed by his son, George, Feb. 16, 1891. · For this crime the son was sentenced to life imprisonment.)

Somewhere along these parts, but just where is not clearly placed, an old map locates J. Jenks. Possibly the name is connected with the George Worden place.

Some years ago Peter Hilts, of the Valley, bought seventy-four acres of land in this then wilderness, of Wallace St. John, long known as a Rose and Clyde school-master. There was a small house, which now serves as one of the farm buildings, a much better house having taken its place. Mr. H. came originally from Boonville, Oneida county, and for some time worked for E. N. Thomas, in the Valley. He also served in the army during the Rebellion, in Company H, of the Ninth. His wife is Catherine Stickles. Their children are Frank ; John, who married Jennie Andrews, of Rose ; Louis and Mary. All of these are at home, though a new house is going up for John a little south of opposite. (John and Jennie H. have now two children, Earl and Charles.) In a little shanty near, an old-fashioned occupation is in progress, viz., the making of shingles with a draw shave out of good straight hemlock, and when John gets them laid on his roof, he need give himself no uneasiness as to leaks for the rest of his life, for they will outlast any number of the later sawed variety. This abode of Peter Hilts is on the east side of the road and rather close to the woods, and is quite suggestive of mosquitoes in such seasons as that of 1889. Back of it are numerous small wood lots, owned by different parties, but all affording many blackberries. For several years William Lambert lived in a log house nearly opposite. The sound of a gun in the neighboring woods recalled the days when the sportsman could frequently bring home, for his pains, as many black and gray squirrels as he could comfortably carry ; but all that is past. The big fellows have gone. Only chattering red ones remain. Pigeons, too, that were so common, have flown before the encroachments of civilization.

We must go back to the cross roads and continuing towards the south, will call first on James Weeks. His location is an old one for these parts, and the outlook is grand. Nothing but the final range of Rose hills hides Butler from view, while, north and south, we may look to Huron and Galen. The view from the front porch of this house is unrivaled in this vicinity. Mr Weeks is at home, impaired vision rendering long walks from his fireside impossible. He finds his way to the nearest neighbor, Riggs, on the northeast, but returning he is near his home. Though the outward world is fading, he sees plainly the events and scenes of long ago, and pleasantly recounts to me some of the incidents of his earlier days.

He is a native of Columbia county, and came to Wayne county fifty years since. At one time he owned the Dorman Munsell place in District No. 9, then he owned north of Shears' corners, on the west side of the road. Next he lived on the Hamelink place, south of his present home. Finally he bought of Constantine Worden twenty-five acres, and of Samuel Way fifty, and settled where he now is. Of his family that came up from Columbia county, one brother, Rufus, has already been mentioned in the account of District No. 3, he having been killed in the raising of a liberty pole. Mr. Weeks' wife was Phœbe Waterbury, a sister of the late John D. Waterbury, of District No. 3. Their children are: Nathaniel, who made Eliza Griswold his wife, and went to Michigan; John married Helen Swift, and lives in the Valley; Stephen found a wife in Margaret Grinnell, of Galen, and a home south of the Valley; Julia is Mrs. William Griswold, of the Valley; Mary is Mrs. William Benjamin, and lives south of Clyde; Delia is Mrs. Stephen Miller, now in Iowa; while the youngest, Sarah, married Alonzo Case, from Sodus, and they, living on the old place, make a comfortable home for the aged parents. James Weeks has long been a stalwart, reliable citizen, not prominent in politics, yet always ready to act as he thought right. In religious matters his leanings are toward the Baptist Church, though the Cases are Methodists. His grandfather, it is worth the while to state, died in his 100th year, and voted for Washington and Lincoln. (Mr. W. died June 8, 1892; Mrs. W. two years before.) The present Weeks house was built by a Jeffers. Nathan, a brother of Robert, came to Rose early, and, in this town and in Lyons, reared a very large family. His first wife was Lucy Vandercook, and their offspring were: Sally, who became Mrs. Samuel Boyce, of Rose; Betsey or Elizabeth, who married, first, Lorenzo Griswold, and, second, Franklin Finch, both of Rose; Mary Ann, the wife of Stephen Boyce of Rose; Lydia, who married A. Ira Blynn, once of Rose (Balsamville), but now in Michigan, and who had sons, George and Addison; Eleanor, as Mrs. John Burt, once lived in the house north of George Jeffers', now his property, but both went to Michigan and both are dead; Julia married Adam McMillen, of Lyons; Daniel, who made Malinda Myers his wife, went to Michigan and died; Cornelius, who also went to the Wolverine State and there died; Robert, of the Valley, who married, first, Marie Winchell, and, second, Sarah Holbrook; Nathan, Jr., married Lydia Ann Winchell and lived where George Jeffers is now; he died in 1852, and his children are: Jane, who married Daniel Foster; Ovid, in Galen; Daniel and Lydia. Nathan Jeffers' first wife died in 1837, in her forty-seventh year, having borne him ten children. His second wife was Sarah Dunman, and their children are: John, already encountered near the home of Abner Osborn, at the eastern end of the district; Janette and Jane, twins—the first being Mrs. William Deady, of Lyons, and the mother of six children;

the second, Mrs. Hudson R. Wood, of the Valley; Charles, at home with his mother in the Valley; George, already met in the northern part of the district, and Laura, at home. Two children, James and Lucy, died in infancy. Mr. Jeffers himself passed away in 1854, in his sixty-fourth year. This is the largest family yet met in Rose. There were eighteen children, a number never met nowadays, except among the extremely prolific Canadian French. Had all these children produced as many children as their parents did, and there had been no western vent for this increase of population, this part of the town would have merited in an increased degree its name of Jeffers neighborhood. Mr. J. did not dwell uninterruptedly in Rose, but some part of his life was passed in Lyons on the McMillen place, but he returned to end his days where his son George now is.

Just below Mr. Weeks' home is a new house, erected by Alonzo Case, but used by him now as a tenant house. This marks the site of the first Worden house, where Alonzo Worden dwelt for many years. He, too, came from Dutchess county and died there, years since, at the age of ninety-one. His children were: Constantine; Louisa, the wife of William Glen, of Lyons; Elizabeth, who married first, George Lapham and second, George Porter, now in Waterloo; Delia, who is Mrs. Joseph Shaw of South Sodus; Martha, wife of James Colborn of the Valley, and John V., who married Caroline Hughson and lives south of Clyde. On this spot Nathan Jeffers first lived.

A little south of opposite is a private cemetery, where very many of the early settlers were buried. It is in even a worse condition than some of those in other parts of the town; for there are no headstones, with possibly two exceptions, those of Benjamin Way and his wife, but their inscriptions are illegible. Could I get all the history that the occupants of these graves might impart, my Rose rambles would be much more complete than I can ever expect to make them.

Our southern limit is reached when we come to the next place, where dwells Derrick Hamelink, obviously of German extraction, but who came to Rose from Sodus. His sister Emma keeps his house, while their mother is a frequent visitor. He is an active member of the Rose Baptist Church. In reverse order the dwellers here have been E. Rooke, an Englishman, now in Lyons, James Weeks, Robert Foster and Harry Clapper. This is the old Clapper site, and here, many years ago, Jacob C. settled. He had nine children, at least, but of them I know very little, only one of the name, Henry Ward C., who married Anginette Munsell, being still in Rose. The oldest son was Jacob; then followed Harry, who married Sarah Caroline Van Amburg of District No. 10; David, who married Mary Stewart; George; Ann; Eliza, who became Mrs. John Van Amburg; Clarissa, who married Henry Dunham; Martha, who married Abraham Ferguson in Galen; and a daughter, who became Mrs. Robert Foster.

We are not through with this exceedingly irregularly shaped district yet, for coming through Worden's corners, we must climb a little higher to reach the sightly abode of the Riggs family. It is the old home of the Ways. Benjamin Way was one of the earliest settlers, and Dr. Richard Valentine's first professional visit was made at this early home. The house now standing dates from this pioneer. Both he and his wife are lying in the neglected cemetery south of the corners. They had children—Lydia, who became the wife of John Jeffers, and went west ; Truman, who died at the age of fifteen years ; Samuel ; Harley, and Valentine, who enlisted in the Mexican War and was killed. Harley Way, who succeeded his father here, married Betsey, a half sister of Jesse Lyman. Their children were : David, who lost his life as a soldier during the Rebellion. He was one of those captured, with the writer, at Monocacy, July 9th, 1864, and died in Danville, Va., in the season following ; Elizabeth W., who married Harvey Perkins of Wayne Centre ; Caroline, who was the first wife of William Desmond of District No. 5, and Mary Ann, who married a Preston, went west and died. To Harley Way, on this farm, succeeded William Riggs, who was born in Lyons and came to Rose in 1866, as we have already seen in treating the extreme western part of District No. 10. His family was there discussed, and now we find him living with his son, James, who married Sarah E. Andrews of the north part of the town. The latter has three children—Anna, May and Ida. True to his rearing and habits, Mr. Riggs has a small blacksmith shop near. Across the way we can trace the path made by James Weeks, as he travels to and from his home. The outlook from this point is extensive in every direction.

There is one remove further, and under the hill is the house built long since by Samuel Way. His first wife was Emma, a sister of Robert Foster, and his second, a widow, Mrs. Woolley. He had children—Emma, who married William Blakesley ; Julia, who married a Dennis of Wayne Centre, and a son, whose name I can not give. Some years since he sold to James Weeks, went to Michigan and died there. Mr. Weeks now rents the house. Here ends the district ; a large one in area, but not so populous as formerly. The next step would be into the Wayne Centre district.

DISTRICT No. 8—"GRISWOLD'S."

January 1—January 29, 1891.

The southern boundary of this district is the line between Rose and Galen. It lies directly south of "Jeffers," and its school-house is on the same north and south road and not a mile away. It is not a little interesting to note that this same road has, at its several cross roads, not less than four school-houses, viz. : Griswold's, Jeffers', Covell's and the one at Glenmark. In the district are some of the very best farms in the town, and as a rule, the spirit of thrift appears. There are several roads and our route will necessitate some backward tracks.

In the county atlas of 1874, this district is put down as including a part of Eugene Hickok's farm and R. N. Jeffers' place, but I am told that this is wrong. At any rate, both places are now in the Valley precinct. Accordingly, to enter "Griswold's," we will take the first turn to the left after passing the home of Eugene H., on the road running west from Fredendall's store.

The first abode is on the west side of the road, and it is the home of James Cullen, a brother of the Cullen who was till his death on the old Fuller farm west of the Valley. Mr. C. is from the county of Waterford, Ireland, and he still cherishes the utmost fondness for the "auld sod." "I was born there and I hope to die there," were his words in reference to the place of his nativity. So strong is the hold that childish associations have upon all of us. "Beautiful for situation" has been the burden of many an emigrant's song ever since the days of the psalmist, as his mind reverts to the hills and valleys where, erstwhile, his childish feet essayed to walk ; where they ran the free course of childhood ; where, in later years, he told the tale of love, true the world over, to willing ears, and where, perchance, his sight was gladdened by the coming of his children. Switzers are not the only ones to suffer from nostalgia. The very woes of Ireland have made her doubly dear to her absent sons and daughters. James Cullen married Mary Murray, and their children are Albert, Anna, Joanna, Marelena and Nellie. He bought his place of George Ream, a brother of Fred, of District No. 11, and he in turn took from the estate of C. G. Burton. Ream went to Easton, Maryland. Burton was a Protestant Methodist minister, who never lived on the place. He bought of Johnson Wiley, who had married a Jeffers, and who finally went to Wisconsin. He took from John Jeffers, who also went to Wisconsin. The house dates from the Jeffers ownership, though he never lived in it. Before Mr. Jeffers, was William Dodds, who owned in connection with his farm just south of this. As for tenants and squatters, the place has had fully its share, and time would not suffice to name all those who at times have called the farm home.

On the other side of the road and a little south may be seen the home of Ira Hart. He is a son of Clinton H., once of District No. 10, but now in the northwestern part of Rose. Mr. Hart married early and he has a fine growing family. He and his brother, Marion, just south, do not intend that humanity shall become disheartened through any fault of theirs. His wife is Cornelia Cushman from Oneida county, and they have had six children. Susan, the oldest, is dead. Addie is the wife of William Adsit; then follow Belle, Frank, Charles and Burt. The place stands in the name of S. C. Hart, and came into his possession after the death of Captain (?) Alexander Ready. This man was in his day one of the town notables. His title came from his claiming to have been captain of sundry vessels at various times. During the War interested parties colored his hair and managed to enlist him into the Ninth Heavy Artillery. While on guard one day in the south, a native, noticing his white hair (for the coloring matter had worn off), said : "Ain't you a pretty old man for a soldier?" "Yes," is the Ready answer. "I have served in three wars. I was in the Mexican War and in the War of 1812. Oh, I know how to soldier." During his life Rose never suffered for want of Munchausen stories. Before him was James Watson, and his predecessor was Stephen Boyce, the husband of Mary Ann Jeffers, a daughter of the first Nathan. The family afterward went to the west.

This road of ours must have been started with no definite ending in view, for it comes to an abrupt stand at the north end of one of the drift hills for which the town is noted. The hill will not move, the road clearly cannot climb it, so the thoroughfare has to yield, and it makes a quick turn to the right and goes around, thereby making in the second angle a fine location for a homestead long occupied by a succession of good people. To-day the dwellers are Marion Hart and family. A portion of the latter were helping him unload hay when I called in my neighborhood rambles. He, too, is a son of S. C. Hart, in whose name the place is held. Marion married some years since Salina Cushman, a sister of his brother's wife, and they have numerous children. They are George H., Mary Ann, Clinton M., Ida J., Alice E., Nellie M., John L. and Rose N. Here is a good example for other Rose people to emulate. These little folks form no inconsiderable part of the Rose Baptist Sunday school. Mr. Hart came to this farm in 1875. There are in it ninety-seven acres, seventeen of them only being on the west side of the road. This for years was known as the William Dodds place ; for here Robert Jeffers' son-in-law lived and reared his family. His children were named in the article on District No. 11. Mr. Dodds built this house. The most of the hill farm was bought of John Drown, late of Huron. Parts, however, were bought of Alanson Pease and of William Burt.

Years ago, at the base of the hill, to the northeast, a log house stood, and in it lived Robert Boyce. Further along on the north side, was another log house, where dwelt Emory Boyce. In this first structure an aged Mrs. Winchell died, as did also the first wife of John Drown. Mr. Drown, at nearly ninety years of age, till recently living west of Sheldon's corners in Huron, was a native of Parsonsfield, Maine, then a part of Massachusetts, having come when thirteen years old, with his father, also John, to these parts, and stopped first on the extreme west part of the town—now Mallery's. Taking the road on the west as one line and running south

14

below George Milem's, and then on the east, almost to the Sodus canal, Mr. Drown had two hundred and thirty-seven acres. He cleared away the trees from the summit of the hill and there built his house, just as high up as possible; lest, I suppose, what his name signifies might happen to him and his. His first wife was Esther Jeffers, a daughter of the first Robert; his second, Charlotte Boyce, and his third, still living, widow Mary Ann Whipple. It must have been a wearisome life on the top of this hill, but what a prospect the family had ! The water for family use had to be brought from the spring, still seen just south of the entrance to the Milem place. Naturally, Mrs. D. would occasionally object to the labor necessary to keep the kitchen running. Whereupon her rather easy-going husband would say : " Well, come right out here and show me where you want the well." She would go and tell him, and that is as far as the enterprise ever went. Their first child, Maria, is Mrs. Watson Chaddock of Huron ; the second became Mrs. Dudley Boyce, formerly of this town ; John A., now of Rose, has been twice married, first to Hannah S. Van Horn, a daughter of Matthias and his wife, Roxana Winchell, and second, to Mrs. Louisa (Trask) Sedgwick, but he will be met later in the Valley ; Sanford married first, Emily, a daughter of the late Gowan Riggs of Huron, and second, Artelissa Sedore, a sister of the late Mrs. Enos Pimm. She, too, is dead. The next child, Hester Ann, married Stephen Delamatter, and is in Michigan : Thomas married Jennie Powers, and died in a New York hospital during the War, being a soldier; Napoleon B. married Martha Harper of Galen, and died in Huron : Jane is Mrs. Joseph Thorp of Huron ; Rosette married James Slocum, and moved to Kansas. By his second wife, Mr. Drown is the father of Madison, who married in Kansas. By his third wife he had Huldah, who is Mrs. Lafayette Legg, of the Valley, and Cornelia, who became Mrs. Stephen Brower. On leaving this sightly location, Mr. Drown sold the lower part of his farm to Robert N. Jeffers, and the north portion to William Dodds. Long since, all evidence of the homestead disappeared, save possibly a clump of trees, and were it not for such mousing records as these, in a few years it would be difficult to make any one believe that the hill-top was ever the home of industrious parents and prattling children. Mr. Drown died November 2d, 1890, at the home of his son, John A., in the Valley.

Next we skirt along the base of the hill, having fertile fields and orchards at our right, and the steep hill-side toward the east. When we get to the first west road, we must keep well up lest we go down the descent, whether we will or not. Soon the home of George Milem appears, perched on the ridge of the hill that has now sloped to an accessible altitude. Nevertheless, our horse will have to put forth extra strength as he pulls us up the road cut through the drift gravel of which the hill consists. Reaching the house, Mr. Milem is found putting together a new harvester, and data are imparted as he keeps at his task, for the impending wheat harvest will not admit of any delay. His farm has one hundred and thirty-six acres, fifty of them being in the old Stokes lot, and well back in the level swamp land eastward. This lot was once the property of Captain Stokes of glass factory fame in Clyde, and Walter Harper also owned it once. In former days there were several habitations upon it. The remaining portion he obtained from R. M. Jeffers and William Gillett. Mr. Jeffers bought of John Drown and Robert Vandercook, and they of Garrett Y. Lansing. This must carry the line pretty near to the first owners. The house is on what was the Jeffers portion, and Mr. Milem has enlarged and improved it considerably. The Milems are of English origin. The first, William, and Thirza Sizer, his wife, came from Norfolkshire, England, to this town in 1851, and located just west of the head of this road, where Frank Knapp is now. Mrs. Milem died in 1856 and is buried in the Rose cemetery. Their children were Christopher, who is in East Portland, Oregon ; Sizer Ann, who married Robert Hunter, and lives in Lyons, and George, our resident. Mr. Milem, Sr., went to Ohio in 1866, and is now living in Fowlerville. George M. was a good soldier during the Rebellion, serving in Company F, Ninty-eighth New York Volunteers, and putting in more than four years of service. He married Christina Lang of Galen, who bore him nine children, as follows : Thirza M., George H., Hester A., William B., Minnie M., Elizabeth C., Philip L., Mary E. and Carrie I. This is one of the most encouraging families in Rose. , Would that there were more like him. Mrs. Milem died in 1887, in her fortieth year, and till recently the oldest daughter did the honors of the household. The boys are helps upon the farm. Mr. Milem is a Free Methodist in religion and a Prohibitionist in politics. " And why shouldn't I be ! " he says, " when I have all these boys and girls growing up to be endangered by the rum traffic. I'm down on that all the time." I am pretty much of his sentiments myself. It is impossible to overestimate the danger that alcohol is subjecting us to. In 1890, August 12th, Mr. Milem was married to Miss Julia Sedore of Rose.

South of Mr. Milem's, under the hill, is a fine, unfailing spring, a source of comfort to the stock. Near the road and close to the lane leading up to the house is another one carefully boarded up. Still further along is land belonging to Alonzo Snow of the Valley road, whose possessions extend from road to road.

On the west side is the home of Eugene Converse. The house is considerably south of opposite to Mr. Milem's, and is below the site of the house which once stood in the names of McConnell and Gillett, and in which one Converse killed his wife, several years since, while laboring under *mania a potu*, a tragedy liable to be acted wherever rum may be found. A number of trees still mark the location of the first structure. Mr. Converse has just put up a new barn, and with his growing boys, will doubtless make his farm one of the very best. There are fifty acres in it, and the lads are anxious to help. The place was bought of John H. Barnes, and as already intimated, must have been in the hands of others. The house is the one that Milo Lyman once lived in, and which he gave up when he built his new one. Mr. L. says: "I spent seven hundred dollars in getting the old house in shape, and in fixing up the cellar, and then it didn't suit me, so I just sold it for less than I spent in repairs, and started anew." It was moved down here and makes a very comfortable home for Mr. C. and his family. He is a native of Erie county, but much of his youth was passed in the Valley. His wife is Anna Harper, a daughter of Almon Harper, and their children are Edith M., John D., Ernest E., Arthur J., Flora D., and Daniel E. The family are communicants of the Rose Baptist Church. Mr. C. has been here seven years.

Just below, and on the west side, is the home of Mrs. O'Donald, widow of Patrick. Her children are Joanna, Patrick and James. The belonging, a small one, was bought of H. W. Levanway, and Mr. O'Donald built the house. He once had a log house just under the hill as we turn west to go toward Milo Lyman's.

Still further along, and the last place in the town, situated well back from the street, lives the Pultz family. They are Germans and came here from Lyons, buying the small place from Mr. Levanway. The children here are Emma, Ida and Daniel. They are Lutherans in religious belief.

We must now return to the road leading west, and on the north side just beyond the turn is a red house which once abounded in active life. It is now the property of Milo Lyman, who has turned it into an evaporator. The house was built by Jacob Stack, a native of Strasburg, Germany, who lived and labored here for many a year. He was a cooper by trade, and worked long and faithfully in the Barnes shop, further west. His glebe was small, and he himself built the house. His wife was Eva Strang, a sister of Fred Ream's mother. We met Ream in District No. 11. Their children were many, and as follows: Jacob, who lives in Rochester; Lana married James Lavender; Louis lives with his mother south of Clyde; Lizzie is the wife of John H. Barnes of the Valley; Louisa married Wm. Dodds; Katie married Byron Crandall of Rose; Carrie, who is Mrs. Albert Williams of Clyde; Fred, deceased; George and Helen are at home with their mother. Mr. Stack died several years ago.

The elegant home of Milo Lyman claims us next. This is on the north side of the road, and is the building erected after Mr. L. sold his old house to Eugene Converse. Painted a pure white, the structure is a landmark. If our call is in mid-summer, we shall certainly find Mr. Lyman at work in the field. To reach him, we will follow a lane running back from the road, and will pass a series of large barns conveniently arranged on a gentle slope, thus having that very desirable arrangement in a country of hard winters, viz., underground sheds. Just a little west of front of the barns is the site of the first framed structure on the place, and close by was the log house. The well is there yet, and an avenue of cherry trees leads down to the present abode. Milo Lyman was born south of Ferguson's corners, and at the age of four years was bound out, till he should be twenty-one, to Adam Learn, who lived south of Lock Berlin. Mr. Lyman had very few advantages of the schools. His youth was one of toil, and when the expiration of his time came he had very little to start with save a vigorous body and fifty-eight dollars, a sum coming from the sale of a colt which Mr. L. had given him a few months before. Fortunately Mr. L. turned his face Roseward, and lived for a time in the family of the first John Barnes. Still more fortunate, he secured for his wife Mr. Barnes' daughter, Rebecca, who has been an invaluable helpmeet during all the years of his married life. Their home, before coming to this farm, was south of where the Wykoffs live now, and the place was reached by a lane from the road extending from the Valley to Wayne Centre. They came to this farm just after the War. They have had only one child, John W., who was a most promising young man, a graduate of the State Normal School in Albany in 1878. He had taught two years at Garrisons on the Hudson, when failing health compelled his return to his father's house, where he died May 28th, 1881, at the early age of twenty-three years. With the hope that a change of occupation might improve his health, the fond father had bought for him a store at Lock Berlin, but the young man visited it only once. Life's burdens were scarcely assumed ere he laid them down. Early crowned, he left a desolate household to mourn his departure. The Lymans were of Connecticut origin, no doubt connected remotely with those in the Lyman district, although I have not succeeded in establishing the relationship as yet. The father, Jesse, was long favorably known in Rose, having lived in that town many years. He was once on the old Finch place, near Griswold's school-house. For some years he kept the light-house in Sodus, and finally died in the Valley in 1863, at the age of sixty-nine years, and was buried at Ferguson's corners. His first wife was Betsey Sedgwick, another excellent Connecticut name, who died in 1831, aged thirty-seven years. Their children were Henry, who was for some years a clerk for Eron Thomas in the Valley, and who died in 1850; Lydia married Charles Crafts and went west; Angeline became Mrs. Dr. Robert Copp, of Canandaigua; Milo, already noted; Philander S., who lives in Sodus, having kept the light-house there, as did his father before him, and John B., who lives in Michigan. Jesse Lyman was a shoemaker by trade. After the death of the first Mrs. L. he married the widow of Orrin Lackey. He had two half brothers, once residents in Rose—Thomas, who once lived near the Harley Way place under the hill, and afterward went west and died, and Levi, west of Ephraim Wilson's. The latter has a son, Jacob, now living in the Valley. A half sister of Jesse, Betsey, married Harley Way, while another married one of the Valley Crislers. The Lymans have long been staunch supporters of the Rose Methodist Episcopal Church. The farm includes one hundred and forty-seven acres. The major part of it was bought of John Barnes, first, after the War. The latter had purchased it from James Colborn, Jr., who had traded with John Vandercook. John V. had received it from his father, Michael. Michael Vandercook had taken in part from John Clapper, whose possession goes back to the land office. He built the first log house. Lyman built the present Converse house in 1875. Afterward came the present house, where it is to be hoped Mr. and Mrs. Lyman may take many years of comfort. Though they are childless, they have adopted George, son of Mrs. L.'s youngest brother, James, of Huron. What man has done, man may do. No man in our town had less to start with than had Milo Lyman. Few have done any better. Energy, honesty and perseverance, accompanied by a faithful, devoted and capable wife, have placed him in the forefront of our townsmen, a man to be admired and emulated. (Mrs. Lyman died May 18, 1892. Mr. L. has rented his farm to Frank Mitchell, 1893.)

Next west is the home of William H. Vandercook. This name, once so common in Rose, has pretty nearly disappeared. The farm occupied by Mr. V. is a part of the old Michael Vandercook property, but the original house was on the next road north. Somewhere on these acres Mr. V. has lived for more than fifty years. There are 108 acres in the farm, and the house, a fine brick one, is of Mr. Vandercook's building. Back of his barns, which are on the south side of the road, is an old log house, which was, in olden times, the abode of John Clapper. Mr. C. was a brother of Jacob, who once lived in the Jeffers neighborhood. It is a long time since this family lived here, and memory of them is not over vivid, but I find that there were five children—two daughters and three sons. These married as follows : Polly became the wife of Embury Finch, who once lived south of the old John Vandercook farm, and is now a tobacconist in Auburn ; Sally married James Potter, a son of Godfrey, who once lived as tenant for Bockoven, on the present John L. Finch place, west of the Valley ; George married Eliza Waring, daughter of Joseph and his wife, Susan ; Orrin and Abram both married daughters of this same Godfrey Potter, and all went to the all-absorbing west. Returning to Mr. Vandercook, it is found that he married Helen E. Pitcher, a sister of John Barrett's wife. Their children were John W., who went to the Albany Normal School with Milo Lyman's son, and, like him, died, to human minds prematurely, at the early age of thirty years, in 1887, having married Mary E. Spaulding, of Schoharie county ; Emma Eliza died at the age of nine years ; Mary married Clarence Johnson, of Wolcott ; and Anna M., who is Mrs. Frank Fellows, of Lyons. Like all of the Vandercooks, William H. is a Methodist.

The next place, and still on the north side of the street, is the old John Barnes estate. It is one of the best and most prominent in this part of the town. The century was not very far along when Mr. B. bought out the improvements made by Merrill Pease, and himself settled at the land office for the farm. It was a favorite remark of the old gentleman that when he came into the town, he had only his wife and his axe, carrying the latter on his shoulder. He was Dutchess county born ; but, with his parents, came early in life to Galen. A brother was the father of Harvey Barnes, of Huron, indicated in our North Rose articles. He married Mary Cowan, a sister of Mrs. Francis Osborn, the mother of James and Francis O., of the Covell district. His first stop in Rose was on the present Espenscheid place, a mile further west. Coming to this final site he lived for many years in a double log house, still marked by the large chimney, the latter having been used for many years in the coopering, for which this section was long noted. Finally he built the commodious farm house still standing. After long and useful lives, the aged people passed away, and were buried at Ferguson's corners. They reared a numerous family, as follows : George, who married the widow of Arnold Rhea, and lived, till he went west, where Alvin Barnes resides. At one time he took up land near where Espenscheid is now. George Barnes died in Michigan, leaving one daughter. The oldest daughter, Mary, married William H. Allen, and lived for many years in the Valley, where Mr. A. was a tanner. They afterward moved to Coldwater, Michigan, where Mrs. Allen died Aug. 12, 1888, leaving a son and daughter. Rebecca we have seen as Mrs. Milo Lyman. Alvin married Sarah Finch, and lives in this district. John H. Barnes married Elizabeth Stack, and lives south of the Valley. He has only one child, Jessie May. Elijah married Mary S. Holiday, and lives at Ferguson's corners. Like his brothers, he is a thorough and successful farmer. James married, first, Fanny Griswold, and second, Fanny E. Ferguson, of the corners. They live in Huron, and their children are Eveline, who is Mrs. James Gatchell, of that town : Edwin B., at the Albany Normal School, and George, who lives with his Uncle Lyman ; Margaret is Mrs. Philander Mitchell, whom we shall meet toward the end of the district. Beside these there were James, who died in infancy, and Sarah, who lived to be nine years old. John H. Barnes succeeded to this farm ; but he prefers to live nearer the Valley. His tenant now is James Lavender, a native of Ireland, whose wife was Lana Stack.

The last house to be encountered before reaching the corner is that of Harmon Van Amburg. Harmon has dwelt here many years. The original holding came from his father-in-law, William Griswold. He built the house himself. He is a native of Saratoga county—born in 1812—

whence he came with his parents to Galen when he was quite small. By trade he is a carpenter and joiner. His wife was Emily, the first William Griswold's oldest daughter. She died in 1886. Their children were Deborah M., who died in infancy; Rebecca A., who is with her father; Sarah E., who died in Syracuse, and Ellen M., who married Wesley M. Abbott, of Otisco. She now resides in Syracuse. It is probable that under favorable circumstances, H. V. can beat any man in the town telling stories of the dim and misty past. He once knew all the dwellers west of the Valley and all of their antecedents. He was a brother of German Van Amburg, who formerly dwelt in the Covell district, in that part called Canada. (Mr. V. has since died.)

Just opposite the Van Amburg home is a tenant house, belonging to Alvin Barnes, whose possessions extend southward, and whose home we shall find on the west side of the road. It is a brick structure, and is in excellent keeping with the other farm houses of this locality. As already stated, Mr. Barnes married Sarah Finch. They have two children—Matilda and Willard. I am told that this place was first held by one Green Plum. There is an absurdity in that name that strikes a hearer or reader at once. If it were sweet or ripe Plum, it would be different, but to be always Green is appalling. Well, Green finally sold out, or was forced off the farm and afterward became mildly insane, and thus died. To him succeeded Simeon Barrett, and his father-in-law, Ebenezer Pierce, that Revolutionary veteran. These people were described in our "Covell" sketches. Then came Arnold K. Rhea, who died in 1852, leaving a widow and three children—John, Leroy and Chloe. All of them finally went west. The widow married George Barnes, and the latter managed the farm until John Rhea came of age, when he went to Michigan. John afterward sold to the present holder, Alvin Barnes, better known in Rose as "Alf."

Still further south, and on the east side, is the farm house of James Deady; but it is the long time home of John Vandercook, whose name is indissolubly linked with this locality, for he was the builder of the stately residence. Further back still, I find that this was the old Colborn farm, the place to which James Colborn, first, came when he left his early abode near North Rose. The youth of James Colborn was passed in the extreme western part of the town. His wife was Mary Waters, of Alloway, a sister of Mrs. John Q. Deady, of District No. 5. On this farm their married life was passed and here their family was reared. Beside several children who died in infancy, there were : Lydia, who became Mrs. Charles W. Griswold, of Palmyra ; Margaret, the wife of John Vandercook ; James, whom we shall meet in the Valley; Sarah, who also married a Griswold, William, and went to Missouri; and William, who married Ephraim Wilson's daughter, Caroline, and now lives in Wolcott, though for many years they were Rose dwellers. Another son, Jonathan, lost his life at the siege of Fort Donelson, during the Rebellion. The later years of James Colborn's life were passed in the Valley, where he died in 1871. He and his wife were life-long members of the Methodist Church. John Vandercook, who married Margaret Colborn, succeeded to the old home and place, and to it added acres, till finally he had here about three hundred. In situation and commodious arrangements, Mr. Vandercook's place had no superior in the town, perhaps not in the county of Wayne. He had three children : Mary was educated in Lima, and afterward married Robert Osborn, of Sheldrake, and is now in Indiana ; Frank went to Fulton to school for a time, and then went west, where he married ; Michael, named for his grandfather, married Alice Stanley, and he, too, is in Indiana. After the death of Mrs. Vandercook, a most capable and worthy woman, Mr. V. married again, this time a widow. It was only a short time thereafter that he sold out and went west. At last accounts he was in California. (Died March 13, 1892, in Los Angeles, aged 72 years.) James Deady is a native of Rose, eastern part, Town district. He married Caroline Swift, of Sodus, and has passed the most of his life in Huron. His farm there, now Wride's, was noted for its productiveness. It is claimed that his Huron orchard is the best in the county. He has three children : Charles S.; George L., who married Maggie Murray, of Clyde, and Willig J., who is a printer. He is now in New York, where he has worked on the *Commercial Advertiser*. He is the boy who started a paper in Savannah a year or two since. Mr. D., in buying, did not take all the Vandercook farm, retaining one hundred and seventy-seven and one-half acres. James Deady has boxed the political compass. For years he was one of the few thorough-going Greenbackers. He has probably talked more on that subject than any other man in Rose or Huron. No better view of farm and buildings can be had in Wayne county than that afforded of this place from the next road west.

South of Mr. Deady's are farms belonging to William Glenn, of Lyons, and John Barnes, of the Valley. Both are rented to tenants. In the east place once lived a family of Finches, though not related to the other people of that name in Rose. The mother, a widow, came from West Dresden, Yates county. She had sons—George and Embury. The latter married Polly, daughter of John Clapper. He was lately a resident of Auburn. The place has changed hands a great many times. (In 1893 E. E. Legg is here. He married Dora Wright, from Canada. Their children are Ernest E., Ora and Mary.)

The last dweller on this road, before reaching the Galen line, is Henry W. Levanway. As the name indicates, Mr. L. is of French origin, his birthplace, Clinton county. He was sixteen years old when he came to the town of Macedon. He left home with five dollars in his possession, and became a resident of Wayne county with five cents left. After the

various and usual vicissitudes of childhood, he became a citizen of Lock
Berlin, whence he came to his present home in 1857. He bought of one
of the Van Amburgs, back of whom was a Brink. The farm now held is
not quite the same that he originally purchased. The part opposite, all
save the carriage house, was first sold to Elijah Barnes, from whom it
passed to a Bishop, whose widow, living just over the line, still owns.
Her large barn is on the Rose side of the road. Much of the Levanway
place lies in Galen, but there are still about 100 acres in Rose. It extends
well back and once touched the next road east. On the extreme eastern
part of the farm, Mr. L. is now arranging sheds or barns for hay. Mr. L.
cultivates extensively the osier willows used in basket making. All the
buildings on the place, he either built or considerably repaired. The barns
when he came, were of log, and the house was very old. His wife is Cynthia, neé Curtis, of Galen, but born in Columbia county. They have had only
two children, Alanson, who died in 1857, aged three years, and Edra, who
is Mrs. R. R. Barnes of Clyde—the clothier whose extensive advertisments
are seen all about this section. Mr. Levanway was one of thirteen children,
nine boys and four girls, all of whom grew up. It may be safely said that
here is another of the self-made men for whom this town is noted.

Only a few steps south of the Levanway home, is found the road running west. It is the very first, thus far encountered, which forms a part
of the town line, this time between Rose and Galen. Turning around the
fine barn of Mrs. Bishop, we ride with one wheel in Rose and one in Galen.
The Winchells once dwelt in these parts, and in the olden times there were
log houses hereabouts. To-day there is no house on the Rose side of the
street, but on the Galen side, at the corner, farther west, is one of the
houses belonging to Herman Grenell. Mr. G. was born in Galen, a member of that family formerly so prominent in that town, but now found only
in the burial ground or in the West. He married Marian Greiner of Galen,
and their children are: Eugene, living just north; Lydia, the wife of
Edward Luffman, who is at the old home, and Ada, also at home. Mr. G.
bought of Harvey Warren, thiry-seven years ago, though the place was
once in the possession of John Barnes, the early comer, and Franklin
Finch was also here very long ago. There are in the Barnes place 100
acres. The buildings are of Mr Grenell's erecting. Just north of the west
side is a tenant house belonging to Mr. G. It should be stated that the
home of the family is on the east side of the road, just after turning north.

Going north, we shall find on the west side the 100 acre farm, once
belonging to William Osborn, but now in the hands of Herman Grenell.
His son, Eugene, who married Ida Glover, resides here. (They have one
child, Florence.) Mr. William Osborn is a brother of James and Francis
O., living northwest of the Valley, in the Covell district. He married
Ruth Ann Foist of Galen, to whose father the place formerly belonged.
After leaving this, he was in the Valley for a time, then went to the town

of Lyons, where he now lives, about two miles west of the village. He has but two children: Ida, who is Mrs. Vern Wilson of the Valley district, and Leona, at home. Mr. O. has long been a member of the Methodist Episcopal Church.

The next stop is on the east side of the road, at the home of George H. Green, who was born in Onondaga county. His home for many years was in Wayne Centre. He came to this place in 1879. He married Eliza A. Turner, a daughter of Royal, who formerly lived here. Their children are: Lorani, who married Jacob Barkley of Sodus; Francis, at home; Sarah, married John McMillan of Lyons: Charles, at home: Ada, married J. W. McRorie of Wayne Centre. Mr. Green has been a cooper, also a carpenter and joiner. He repaired the house in which he lives. In the farm there are 34 acres. Royal Turner, whose home was here for many years, came from Vermont, where he married Betsey Cooper. Some of their children were grown up before his coming hither. He lived here about forty years, dying thirteen years since. Mrs. Turner, only recently deceased, lived to be nearly ninety years old. Of their eight children, in addition to Mrs. Green, there were Mrs. S. D. Wilson of Boston, Mass., C. Clark, Elias K., in New York, and Marcus in Rahway, N. J. Mr. Turner bought of one Hoag, and he of Daniel Jeffers. James Colborn, first, many years ago, erected a stave cutting factory on this place, probably the first one in the town. Among so many possessors it is nearly impossible to name all, and equally difficult to preserve the proper order.

William H. Espenscheid is our next resident, and his home is on the west side. Though born in Huron, he is of German extraction, the first of this nationality to be encountered in this western part of Rose, but by no means the last. His father was from Hesse-Darmstadt and has children John, Helen, Derrick and William, whose wife is Mary A., daughter of Henry Steitler of the Wayne Centre district. There are ninety acres in the farm, and Mr. E's. father bought of Philander Mitchell, 2d, who took from Avery Marsh, now south of Clyde, and he purchased from a Foist. Though the Espenscheids have no children, they have most beautiful flowers, on the principle, I suppose, that one must love something. The useful blends with the ornamental in the garden, as beets and onions are crowded by double poppies and sweat peas. All the colors of the rainbow are found in this cheerful corner, just south of the house. This building must date from some one of the earlier occupants. The farm buildings are opposite.

There is no tax on the admirable views that the hill-top affords, and the passing farmer may get what pleasure he can from the same, for air and views are about all he can now get free.

A turn to the west leads down towards Lyons, and on the north side is the place where Joseph C. Crandall has lived for forty-four years. He was born in Dutchess county, but his parents moved when he was small to Chenango county. Thence he came to these parts. His wife was Sarah Brown of Ferguson's corners, who died in 1887. Their children were : Hannah, now dead, who married John Marriott of the Valley ; Byron, who married Katie Stack, and holds the old place; Sarah, Mrs. Thomas Helfer of Newark ; three others died in one week in childhood from scarlet fever. A stone in the burial ground at Ferguson's tells the sad story. When Mr. Crandall came hither, his log house was located quite a distance north of the place where he subsequently erected his dwelling. He bought of John Weigel, who had purchased of John Miller. He had taken from one Shad, or Chad, who bought of John Clapper, who must have bought from the office. There are fifty-six acres in the farm. Though eighty-two years old, I found Mr. C. at work in the wheat harvest, and ready to proclaim his unfaltering Democracy. Byron C., who is now at the head of affairs, and his wife have only one son, Frank.

Henry Lincks dwells nearly opposite. He is Brooklyn, N. Y., born, though his parents came from Alsace. His father, Henry, a furrier by trade, married Mary Simon, and they are now residents of Lyons. Henry L., Jr., who married Carrie Fox, a daughter of the man who long owned the place, came here in 1881. He has greatly improved the plant, having erected one of the best barns in town. Better times will be followed by a new house. (1893—The house is built.) The site of the old building is readily discovered through the rank character of the grain growing over it. Louis Philip Fox lived here for many years, and here reared a family of six boys and six girls. His wife was Lena Horn and both were of German birth. In German the name is Fuchs. Both the parents lie in the Ferguson's ground. The oldest son, George, died in California ; Lena married Cornelius Barton, now in Lyons ; Fred is in Wolcott ; Louis is in Lyons ; Siloma married Ovid Jeffers of Galen ; Carrie married Henry Lincks ; Louisa is Mrs. William Goetzman of Galen ; Charles married Mary Lincks ; Jennie is Mrs. John W. Stewart of Lyons ; William died at the age of nineteen years, and Charlotte died in childhood. The house antedates the Fox family. The farm has eighty-two and a half acres.

On the same side of the street, but a few rods further west, is the holding of William Loryman, a native of Yorkshire, England. He once lived on the Knapp place, north of Philander Mitchell's, but has been here many years. His parents, William and Anna E., came to this country and died with him. William has never known the pleasures nor the vexations of matrimony, his sister Susan having been his housekeeper. He has thirty acres, which he bought of James Wraight, and the latter took from Samuel Wessels. An old log house back of Loryman's abode indicates an era much older than Mr. L.'s days.

Nearly opposite lives Charles Fox, and his residence marks the western limit of the district. As already seen, he married Mary Lincks and they have a numerous progeny growing up. Their names are : Nelson C., Albert H., Mary E. and Godfrey E. There are fifty acres in the place. As owners or occupants before Mr. Fox, were Lampman, Fred Fox, George Fry, Jake Garvey and Henry Wirt.

Returning to the north and south road, we shall soon reach the old home of the Havilands on the west side. As the place has for some years borne the name of Foster, it is necessary to state that Cornelius R. Foster married the widow Haviland and paid off the heirs of the estate. Mr. Foster is a native of Vermont and many years since married Harriet, a daughter of Jacob Clapper. In the sketch of the Jeffers neighborhood, he was found on the old Clapper site, now the home of Derrick Hamelink. His children were : Daniel, who married Jane, a daughter of Nathan Jeffers, and Annabel, who became Mrs. Fred Fox, and is now dead. Daniel's home is just below this place and he works the farm. His children are Chauncey, and Lydia, who is now the wife of Louis E. Stopfel of the " Covell " district. (Chauncey married September 27, 1893, Miss Mollie Ferguson.) An aged man, Mr. C. R. Foster, still is active and alert. Henry Haviland was a native of Dutchess county, but with his family went to Waterloo many years since. He there wedded Jerusha Pierson, of a family that had migrated from Long Island to that point. They came to Rose sixty-four years since. Their first log house was considerably further north, and in the growing corn it is easy to distinguish the old site through the luxuriance of the stalks. The deeper green of the field tells how nature reciprocates the gifts of other days. The family came with oxen and a team of horses, and experienced all the discomforts of the early pioneers. It is said that Mrs. H. once walked to Waterloo where her husband was at work, she being thoroughly homesick. The Havilands built all the buildings. To them were born six sons and as many daughters. Many of them, however, died very young, and on one stone in Ferguson's I read the name of seven children, ranging from the infant to a daughter of twelve years. The death of the latter, Katherine, was particularly distressing, since it was occasioned by the use of an opiate, she being ignorant of its effects. Those who survived were Daniel, who married Charity Dubois and went to Michigan. He there enlisted and died at Memphis during the War. He left three children, of whom Mary is the wife of Henry Jeffers : Burton, who works for William H. Vandercook (he has since married Mary Paine of Huron): and Sarah, who became the wife of Louis Marsteiner of Lock Berlin. Louis will be remembered as the little boy, once living in Stewart's district. The second son, Peleg, though he has been much from home, is now there helping to care for his mother. (D. February 19, 1893.) Sarah is Mrs. George Duell of Marengo : Harriet, deceased, was Mrs. William Mix of the Valley; Jane, also dead, was the first wife of Charles Covell, and thereby the mother of Rose, wife of Frank Kellogg. Mr. Haviland died in 1857, and with him now are all his children, save two. Mrs. Haviland Foster is quite feeble from successive attacks of la grippe. (Mrs. F. died January 2d, 1891, aged about 86 years.)

The road soon takes an abrupt turn to the east and stretches away towards Mitchell's hill. Originally it ran crookedly through the low land, past the old Haviland house, and thence easterly to the brow of the hill. Just before reaching the foot of the hill, we encounter the State road, coming down from the old Jeffers haunts, and we shall have to climb it a little way, till we find away back from the street the house now owned by John Smart, but which has had a great variety of possessors. Taking them in order, it is pretty safe to claim this as the original Ackerman home, for here David A. and his wife lived until his death, about 1821. The Ackermans were from Saratoga county. Mrs. A. was Margaret, daughter of Henry Clapper, and thereby sister of John and Jacob. Their children were: Lucinda, wife of Russell Winchell; Louis, who lived in Victory; Henry C., who married D. A. Collins, a daughter of Stephen of District No. 10, and is in Huron; Helon B., who married Lovina Winchell, and Cyrus, who wedded Mary Loughton and is in California. Mrs. A. afterward married John Winchell, and bore Sarah Jane, who became Mrs. James Van Amburg, and Lovina, who was twice married, first to Isaac O. Brewster, and second to Philo Miner. Mrs. Ackerman-Winchell died with her son Henry in 1876. The place was sold to Daniel Ackley, who built the house and who went west. To him succeeded the Englishman, William Loryman. A pine tree standing near serves as a landmark to the second William L., who lives in the western confines of the district. After him came Hiram Knapp, who was born in Sodus and married Sarah, a daughter of the first Philander Mitchell. The place of twenty-five acres passed from him to Mr. Smart.

Retracing our steps to the east and west road, the hill is climbed, and we look out over the prospect that it has been the lot of the Mitchells to view for many a long year. No name in Rose annals has a more deservedly conspicuous place than that of "'Squire" Mitchell. For many years he was the justice of the peace who adjudicated for this section. Absolutely honest and trustworthy himself, his word was his bond, and his judgment was held in the highest esteem. He was born in Bridgewater, Vermont, and married first, Betsey Ann Andrews. They had four children: Mary Ann, who married, first, John Ferguson of Galen, and second, Nelson Griswold of this same district: Leonard, the oldest son, lived along a mile east on the valley road; William married Jane Grenell of Galen: they now live in Lyons: Barnard married Sally Ann West-

OLD RESIDENTS.

JOHN BARNES.   PHILANDER MITCHELL.   ALPHEUS COLLINS.   ESME WA...

JOEL N. LEE.   SOLOMON ALLEN.   CHAS. SHERMAN.   E. M. LEE

ELIAS SHERMAN.   WM. HICKOK.   DUDLEY WADE.   ADELBERT LEE

brook, and is a resident of North Rose. The first Mrs. Mitchell died and was buried in the long-neglected Jeffers burial ground. His second wife was Sally Winchell of the numerous family described in the Covell district. Born in Egremont, Mass., May 3d, 1800, she was twenty years old when she came to Rose, or Galen. Her first son was Philander, Jr., who, having married Margaret Barnes, retains the old homestead. The second son, John N., was a victim of one of the rural sports long so popular in this town. He was in his seventeenth year, when September 1. 1849, he left his home for a night of cooning, and was brought home a corpse—a terrible blow to the fond mother. A log was to be rolled down a hill, all for fun, and the boy was caught by it and crushed. The first daughter, and Mrs. M.'s eldest child, Lucinda, is still at home, and was the careful attendant of her aged mother until her death, which occurred Monday morning, December 29, 1890, at the age of 90 years, seven months and twenty-six days. Sarah married Hiram Knapp; Lovina is Mrs. Fred Ream of "Covell's" district. "'Squire" Mitchell took up his eighty acres at the Geneva Land office, and he repeatedly walked to that place to pay his interest. He taught school in the Valley, and daily walked backward and forth, attending to home duties as well as to those of the school. The century was well in its teens when Mr. M. became a dweller in these parts. Orrin Lackey and his young family came with him. His first log house was considerably further north than the site of the present structure. As in other cases, there is no trouble in locating the old house, for grass and grain here grow stoutest. His first framed structure was burned, and then came the brick house, so long a landmark from this hill-top. It was in 1870 that, caring for a young horse, he was kicked, and so killed, at the age of seventy-seven years. The Mitchells have long since been devoted members of the Rose Methodist Church.

Philander Mitchell, second, who now maintains the credit of the name, has two children—Darwin P. and Franklin. The former went to South Butler some years ago as the principal of the public school. Afterwards he bought an interest in a store, and has since then conducted a mercantile business in that place. He married Miss Jessie Clapp of South Butler. For a long time he has been the interesting correspondent from that place of the Clyde Times. The younger son, Frank, is a valuable adjunct to his father in the management of the farm. (In 1893 on the Milo Lyman farm.)

It is necessary now to descend one steep hill and to climb another, when we stand at the corners where the school-house is located, and on whose southwest angle is the house built by the first dweller from whom the district is called. The first William Griswold was a native of Saratoga county, but the name certainly betrays a Connecticut origin. He came hither directly from Victory. His wife was Rebecca Barnes, and, like him, was a native of Saratoga county. He here hewed out his home from the wilderness. The usual succession of log and framed houses followed and in them was reared his numerous family. His children were Nelson, whose home was just east of his father, on the Valley road; next was Lewis, who passed his life in Lyons, and was a wire weaver; Charles Wesley married Lydia Colborn, a neighbor's daughter, and is a farmer in Palmyra; William succeeded his father on the homestead, and his wife was Sarah Colborn (died in Starkville, Col., April 10, 1891), another daughter of the neighbor, and he finally went to Missouri. His children were Albert, William, Frank, Nelson, Mary and Anna. There were four daughters in the first Griswold group. Of these Emily became the wife of Harmon Van Amburg; Lydia married Jacob Norris, of Marion; Angeline, now dead, married Byron Bissell. of Syracuse; Melissa married first, Elisha Parsons, of Clifton Springs, and second, Smith Sweezey, of Marion. The Griswolds were God-fearing people and worthy members of the Rose Methodist Church. The second William Griswold sold to Robert N. Jeffers, who passed the place along to another William Griswold, a son of Lorenzo, of the Jeffers district, and from him the farm passed into the possession of the James Deady family. James' second son, George, now lives here—he and his wife and one child, Eva, to carry the name along.

Immediately opposite, on the northwest angle, is the school-house. It is the third in order. The first was built of logs; then came the old stone edifice, long noted in these parts, which, in turn, gave way to the present structure. The corners have been the scene of many excellent meetings.

There is but one home north of the school-house, and this we shall find on the east side of the road. To this point, or near it, Orrin Lackey and Sarah, his wife, came from Vermont, fellow travelers of Philander Mitchell, in the small years of the century. His son-in-law, Amos S. Wyckoff, was subsequently near. Their children were Susan, who became Mrs. Wyckoff, to be met in the Valley district; Lucy Ann, deceased; Judd B., who married Martha Hurlbut, and who was mentioned in the Jeffers series; Sanford married Sarah Ann Wiley, of Rose, and is now in Michigan; Joseph, a soldier in the Mexican War, now dead; Orrin W., who lives in Baltimore, and married there. The senior Lackey died in 1831, at the early age of forty years. His widow became the second wife of Jesse Lyman, who for some time resided on the place, which passed eventually to Franklin Finch. The latter was born in Westchester county, and had married Matilda Harding, a native of Massachusetts, before he came to this town. His advent was in 1830, when he located on the Grenell place, in the south part of the town. He brought the Lyman and Wyckoff houses together and built the house now standing. He had four children, all of whom, except Selah, the youngest, were born in Fishkill, on the Hudson. Newman and John will be found in the Wayne Centre district; Sarah is the wife of Alvin Barnes, of this district, and Selah lives south of the Valley.

Though there is no evidence to substantiate the theory, there can be no doubt that this family is related to that east of the Clyde road. They came from the same portion of the state, and there is a marked family resemblance. The family has been connected with the Rose Methodist Episcopal Church for many years. The property is now in the hands of Alvin Barnes, and he has erected a very large and handsome barn across the road from the house. As his residence is further south, he has had tenants in this the old Finch homestead.

Coming back to the corners, we shall find on the south side of the road leading east, a tenant house, standing on the Deady estate. Just over the ridge of the hill is the long-time home of Nelson Griswold. This was a part of the original Griswold property, and here Nelson built his house and barns, and here he died in 1859. His wife was Mary Ann, daughter of Philander Mitchell, and he was her second husband. Their children were Fanny, who married James Barnes, now of Huron. Salinda, the next daughter of Nelson, is Mrs. Edgar C. Crane, of Eola, Ill.; Edgar lives just east; Philander married Sophia Soper, of Rose, and lives in Galen; John W. married Della Cole, of Lyons, and is with his mother on the farm. He has two children—Nellie and Ray.

Again we must go up and down the hills, and descending a steep incline, we cross a fertile valley, and on the north side of the way, just at the foot of the next hill, Edgar Griswold has erected his home. Like many of the people in this vicinity, he keeps bees, and the air is full of busy hummers. His wife was Anna Hersey before marriage, and their children are Julia and Bessie.

The next hill is very steep, one of the worst in the town. Beyond its summit, on the north side of the road, the relict of Leonard Mitchell has lived in widowhood for many a long year. Leonard, a son of the first Philander, married Mariette, a daughter of Michael Vandercook, and located here on a part of her father's farm. At one time there were 140 acres in it, but now the number is ninety-five. He first built a frame house and then followed it with the commodious brick edifice still standing. Leonard Mitchell was one of the noteworthy Methodists of his day; no one was more zealous than he. Even a short time before his death he had expressed to his wife his conviction that it was his duty to go west and preach. He died in 1865, after an illness of only four days: brain fever induced by a sudden cold. His children were Eliza, who is Mrs. George Jeffers, of District No. 11; Phœbe, who is the wife of Henry Tyndal, now at Iron Mountain, Mich. (a Presbyterian minister reared in Huron), and William A., who lives with his mother on the farm. Two children died unmarried, Frank in 1887, aged 30 years, and Sarah in 1886, aged 25 years. William Mitchell, who now runs the farm, married Eliza York, of

15

Huron, and has one boy, Willie. (Wm. M. died April 22, 1893, aged 40 years.)

Down and up we go again, and at the right is a house fast being dismantled. It is the old home of the Vandercooks. Michael, the first of the name hereabouts, came from the eastern part of the state to Lyons first. He next went to Canandaigua, and thence came to Rose to the farm now held by John Finch, east of Wayne Centre. That place he traded with Samuel Bockoven, of Lock Berlin, for this location on the hill. His family was reared mainly on the Finch place. His wife was Mary Jeffers, a sister of Robert, the first, and Nathan. The Vandercooks and Jeffers were singularly intermarried. Of six Vandercook brothers, three married Jefferses, and one sister became the first wife of Nathan J. Their children were Sally, who was Mrs. Peleg Randall, of Lyons; Lydia was Mrs. David McDonell; Cornelius, who died at the age of thirteen; Elizabeth was Mrs. Adam Fisher, of Clyde, whose only daughter, Sarah, after graduation at Lima (Genesee College), married George Barton, a distinguished teacher of New Jersey; John, whom we have encountered on the present Deady place; Marietta has just been passed as Mrs. Leonard Mitchell; Phœbe, the wife of Constantine Worden, is only recently deceased; William Henry was found in the earlier description of the district. The elder Vandercooks died here and the place now belongs to their youngest son, William H., who began his housekeeping here many years since. Long used as a tenant house, the structure shows the result of neglect, though the brick filling back of the clapboards indicates a disposition once to make the house comfortable and enduring. The barns have gone and nothing works in good shape except the fine smoke house, apparently of recent making. It would seem that Samuel Bockoven was one of the first if not the very first owner of this property. At sundry times Robert and Isaac Vandercook resided in Rose. They were sons of Henry V., who also had married a Jeffers. They went west long ago.

Still journeying toward the rising sun, we come to a modest house on the north side of the road, the home of Andrew Stickles. It was once the property of James Lavender who now lives on the old Barnes farm. I have understood that Mr. L. built the house.

At this point a road leads north, coming out by John Blynn's. The only house near, or in it, is a small one on the east side, the home of Henry Knapp. Here, for some years, lived the Dunham or Donahue family, the head of which was for so long a time one of the blacksmiths in the Valley. The first Milem was also here, long ago.

Old inhabitants tell of a log house still further to the east, where dwelt Nelson Coleman; then one Horn, and afterward the place was joined to the next, or Jeffers farm. Also a log house was on the southwest corner in earlier days, and in it lived Benjamin Johnson. But these are names only.

DISTRICT NO. 12.—WAYNE CENTRE.

June 11—July 9, 1891.

This record of District No. 12 is very incomplete. The removal of the first settlers and their children has left very little source of information. It is a most peculiarly shaped district, extending from the southern line of the town to within less than one mile of the Huron border. It includes parts of both Lyons and Sodus ; but I shall confine myself strictly to our town of Rose. In this district we shall find many Germans, who seemed to have overflowed from Lyons eastward, and to have thus taken the places of the original settlers. To my inquiry as to the reason for this German influx, I was told that many years since, the father of the late Lieutenant Governor Dorsheimer located in Lyons. Naturally others of his race came to a place where he, who had learned English, could interpret for them, and found homes near him. In time they spread out, and the Rose occupancy is the result.

For a long distance this district has the dwellers on one road only. For our purposes it will be as well to enter from the south. To do so, we shall have to go west from Ferguson's corners till we reach this highway. The first house is on the west side of the road, and has long stood in the name of A. H. Mallery. "Captain" Almon H. Mallery was born in Columbia county, though the family was of Connecticut origin. His father, Harvey M., who had married Emma Stone, came to this town more than fifty years ago, and the first home was on the next place north, the original farm being very large. This place, next to the Galen line, and for twenty years occupied by tenants, was bought of Mr. Nichols. "Capt." M. has been twice married. First to Adaline Dunn, who bore him one son, Harvey, a resident of Lyons. His second wife before marriage was Mary Hornbeck, born in Ontario county. Their children are James S., married and living in East Palmyra, and Emma, who is at home. The family many years since moved to Lyons, still retaining, however, the possessions here. The title by which Mr. Mallery is known is purely complimentary. When a lad, in Columbia county, he was the chief boy in a party of twenty or more who trained with wooden weapons. The title was given him then and has clung to date. As he says, everybody but his mother called him "Captain." On an old map where we should expect the initials A. H., I find only C. The maker was obviously *deceived*.

Valentine Goetzman is the owner of the next farm, though he does not at present reside there. He bought of William Espenscheid, who purchased from Oscar Mallery. Oscar Mallery married Anna Ferguson and had three children—Harrison, George and Sarah. He afterward went to Newark, and there died. There are one hundred acres in the farm, which is now in the care of Philip Humbert, who married Carrie Goetzman. Mr. G. is a German by birth, as is also his wife, who was Saloma Hoetzel. Their children are : William, who married Louise Fox, of the family to the northeast : Mary, who became Mrs. Louis Fox, of the same family ; George married Carrie Rinkel, and lives in Lyons ; Sarah, who married Philip Mindel ; Carrie, Mrs. Humbert, and Albert, who married Anna Stell, and is with his father.

Before reaching the next dwelling, we shall pass on the east side a large farm belonging to the Mallery farm, for this almost surrounds the Goetzman place.

John Myers, who planted his house on the west side of the road, purchased a lot of one and a half acres from "Capt." A. H. Mallery, and in 1867 put up his buildings. Like most Germans, he manages to get the most possible from his glebe. He is a native of Baden, and his wife was Margaret Ohl. Aside from tilling his own lot, Mr. M. finds plenty of employment in helping his neighbors. They have had five children, all of whom have gone from home. They are Phœbe, who is Mrs. Henry Christ, of Lyons ; John, who is in Chicago ; Conrad, who married Mrs. Mary (Reynolds) Ferguson, and is in Lyons ; Sophia, who is the wife of Andrew Baker, of Lyons, and Carrie, who also finds a home in the same place.

The next residence north is a handsome white house, the home of Henry Steitler. It is located in the southeast angle of the cross roads. With its convenient surroundings, it is visible from afar in an eastern direction, and is pointed out as the last house on this road toward Lyons. Mr. Steitler is an Alsatian, and his first wife was Mary Weikner, by whom he had Mary, the wife of William H. Espenscheid ; Henry, who is married, and lives in Galen, and William, who married Mary Luffman. Mr. Steitler's second wife was Mary Rankart, who has borne him Charles and Edith, both at home, though Charles has taken to wife Bertha Trask. There are about sixty-seven acres in the farm.

Before leaving this section we must retrace our steps, and place ourselves very near the beginning of the century. Then the road, such as it was, ran along the west ridge, on the preëmption line, and not as now, at the foot of the line of hills. As a consequence, whatever traces of early settlers along that way might have existed, they all long since disappeared. It is more than probable that the first comer to this vicinity was John Drown, first, who came hither in 1813 from Parsonsfield, then District of Maine, erected into a state in 1820. His wife was Sally Ayers, and somewhere on the old ridge preëmption road, south of the east and west one, he located his habitation. He had a large family. He bought of Samuel Hoyt, but paid at the land office. His brother, Solomon, who came in 1812, lived just south of him on the same road, having bought at the office. The last dweller on this road, on the west side, and so in Lyons, was a Mr. Tuck, whose wife was a sister of Josiah Calcott of Huron. Calcott himself married Katy, a daughter of the first John Drown. Ruth, another daughter, became Mrs. Daniel Hayford of Huron. Solomon was twice married. The name of his first wife I have been unable to learn. By her he was the father of John, William, Warren, Charles, Betsey and Solomon. His second wife was Fanny Dennis of the Wayne Centre family, and by her he had eight children. He finally went to Pennsylvania and there ended his days. Several of his children became Mormons, and went off at the time of the excitement and were lost sight of. The first John Drown afterward lived at the foot of the Dodds hill, in the Griswold district, and there his wife died. He, too, went to Pennsylvania and died there. It seems that he had made some extensive purchases of land in that state. When the Drowns left their first settlement, they sold to Aaron Waterbury.

The first settler where Steitler is was Jonathan Colborn, who was a Pennsylvanian. He, too, came very early in the century, having first stopped south of Lyons. His wife was Hannah Hamilton. The farm at first consisted of one hundred acres. Mr. Colborn died at the age of eighty-eight years, in 1857, and his wife followed him in less than three months, aged eighty-one. Both were buried at Ferguson's corners. Their children were James, whom we found in the Griswold district; John, who went to Michigan; Thomas, who married Sally Bowers, from the now Klippel farm, and became a Mormon. He had five girls. Clarinda became a Crippen, and lived near Rochester; Catharine became the wife of Ezra Vincent, and both joined the Mormons. On this farm a Vincent followed Jonathan Colborn, but whether he was Ezra or Josias, I am unable to state. An old map has at this point the name of B. Albough, from whom Mr. Steitler may have purchased. Over this whole section, as far as its early history is concerned, there seems to brood a deep twilight, not to call it night indeed.

After passing Steitler's, should we go east, we should find only the shut-up house of Anthony Turvey, who now lives in Wolcott. This place is now on the north side of the road. Again, were we to go west, our way would soon be met by the boundary between Rose and Lyons. It is the famous new preëmption line; but which every dweller in these parts, young and old, calls "The Preëmption." Were they all Cockney born, they could not insist any more decidedly in putting in that absurd h. Our north and south road runs only a few rods away from this noted meridian.

Fred Trautman resides in the next house, located a little north of the corner, and is on the west side. It was said that a Harvey Gray was first here. Then came Josias Vincent; after him Jacob Mitchell, and next Conrad Young, who sold to the first Fred Trautman. The latter was of German birth and his first wife was Magdalina Baltzel; their children were George, who lives in Buffalo, and Fred, 2d, who, having married Ida, daughter of Ovid Jeffers of Galen, now manages the place. After the death of Mrs. T., Mr., Trautman married again, this time Barbara Smith. He, himself, died in July, 1889, and his widow with their children—Elbert, Philip, Emma and Jessie—resides at the Centre. An older son, Charles, died. There are ninety-three acres in the farm.

The man who holds the next place is, obviously, a careful farmer, for everything is in most excellent condition. This farmer is Henry Klippel, who came to America from Hesse-Darmstadt in 1852. In 1860 he came hither, buying of Lysander Clark, who took from one Bixby, and in time the line runs back to the Colborus. The house was built by Bixby. Mr. K. married Catharine Austerly, and she has been the mother of numerous children. Mr. Klippell has a standing joke, viz. : "I have seven boys and every boy has a sister." Many say at once, "Why, then you have fourteen children." A remark which pleases Mr. K. not a little, and for any one to see through his statement immediately, and to respond, "You have eight children," is just a little disappointing. The sons are : John H., who, having taken Louisa Fox for his wife, lives in Lyons ; George B., in Lyons also ; Philip F., in Chicago ; Edward D.; Sylvester D.; Charles M., and Frank R. The last three are at home, but doubtless they, too, will soon seek more remunerative situations elsewhere. For the rising generation the farm has very little attraction. The only daughter, "every boy's sister," is Isadora. In the place are $117\frac{1}{2}$ acres, much of it timbered swamp land. Mr. K. was one of the very first successful propagators of peppermint in the town.

On the same (west) side of the road, well up and back, is the home of Michael Weeks, though everybody in town pronounces the name Wicks. This is the site of the old Benjamin Craft place. The three brothers, Benjamin, Abram and Thomas, came to these parts from Dutchess county as early, it is said, as 1810. This being the case, they must have been among the very earliest settlers within our present territory. Benjamin Craft died in 1858, at the age of seventy-nine years, and his wife, Elizabeth, survived until 1861, dying in that year, aged 81. Both are buried in South Sodus. It seems certain that Benjamin C. was the first settler here. He had originally 100 acres. His sons were Jonathan Pine and Benjamin, Jr. The daughters were : Deborah who married Abraham VanValkenburg ; Lydia, who married a Ferguson of Galen, and Margaret, who became the wife of Andrew Rhinehart. The latter was killed during the War. J. Pine Craft succeeded his father on the farm. In town parlance, he was generally known as Pine, and this name is the only one attached to the Craft in the South Sodus ground. He died in 1867, at the age of sixty-six years. His wife was Amy, a sister of Michael Weeks, the present proprietor, and she sold to him. His wife was Frances M. Tooker before marriage. Their only child, Ida F., became the wife of Charles O. Baker, a great grandson of Benjamin Craft, the first settler. He resides in Galen. Ida died in 1887. A monument in the South Sodus burial ground tells the story of her early death at twenty-two years, and that of her infant, Frances E., who lived to be only seven months old. The life chapter of mother and child is soon written. There are now only forty acres in the place ; but Mr. W. keeps everything in admirable order. The house was built by the first settler.

The next house, still on the west side, is that of William McRorie. The farm buildings are on the east side. We are yet on the original Craft farm ; for this place of fifty acres the first Benjamin gave to Benjamin, Jr., who built the most of the buildings. His wife was Lucy Ann Goewey. Of their children, Squaire B., an infant, is buried in South Sodus ; Schuyler is dead also, and Betsey Ann went west with her parents, where they died. To the Crafts succeeded Elisha Barton, whose wife was Caroline Warren. Of them my record is very meagre, for I can only mention the death of Elisha in 1879, aged fifty-three, and that of his wife in 1884, at the age of fifty-four years. The present owner, William McRorie, is a native of Missouri. His parents, however, were natives of Galen, whence they went before the War to the west. The father, William, was a Union soldier, and, as such, was killed. The widow came back east, and our citizen was reared here. His wife is Ada, a daughter of the George H. Green met in the Griswold district. Their children are : John W. and Earl F., two as bright little fellows as are often encountered. (In 1883 McRorie is in Lyons, and McMillen is on the farm.)

Whatever there is of the hamlet of Wayne Centre may be said to begin here. The settlement is doubtless the result of the saw and stave mills and cooper shops located at this point. The task is quite too great to trace out all the owners and occupants of the small lots. It is probable that all this land once belonged to the Crafts, and from them passed to their heirs and relatives. The small village has come in the interval of fifty years. There are traces of houses, now destroyed, and of shops that ceased to be remunerative.

Perhaps it will be as well to keep to the west side as we near the corners. After passing a large evaporator, we find the home of Samuel W. Lape, a native of Rensselaer county, though reared in Sodus ; has been postmaster, both in South Sodus and here ; he was a lieutenant in the Ninth Heavy Artillery, Co. D, and is now a justice of the peace. His wife is Julia Ann, a daughter of David J. Seager. In early life Mr Lape was a school teacher. He has twice taken the census of the town ; in 1880 alone, in 1890 the 1st district.

Philip Rodenbach comes next. He is a native of Hesse-Darmstadt, and is one of the most substantial citizens in town. His parents came to Rose for a single year, in 1835, but afterwards went to Lyons. He came again in 1852, and has been here ever since. He has four brothers, and the five brethren average above 200 pounds each in weight. Mr. R.'s wife was in girlhood Margaret Klippel, a sister of Henry, of the same district. There are four children, of whom George H. married Josephine Wilder, and lives in Grand Forks, Dakota; Albert P., now in Rochester, and twin daughters, Carrie E. and Kate M. The former is the second wife of Charles O. Baker of Galen. Mr. Rodenbach bought of William Van Ostrand, and his ten acres are a part of the old Benjamin Craft estate. To his labors as a farmer Mr. R. has added the work of a blacksmith. His shop is still extant, but latterly he has not done much in it. No man in the place enjoys more respect than our friend, who now ranks as one of the oldest inhabitants.

The fine residence of Joel H. Putnam is just north, and it is one of his own building. Before this, was a house in which Jacob Young resided. The saw-mill back was the joint property of the three brothers—Conrad, John and Jacob Young. Jacob, whose home this was once, now lives on a fine farm just north of the Worden place; but is in the town of Lyons. His wife was a Twamley, Martha, a daughter of the family so long identified with this vicinity. Mr. Putnam owns here only six acres, but he has a large farm eastward from the Corners, where his son Hervey lives. At this point he manages an extensive stave factory, a cooper shop and keeps up a very large store-house for barrels. Not the least interesting item about his premises is a fish pond, covering several rods of area, scooped out of the black muck down to the underlying clay, and fed from unfailing springs along the banks. Here he has placed eighty German carp, and they seem to thrive amain. It is worth the time to visit the pond to see the fishes fed. Mr. Putnam was born and reared in Marion, but claims descent from the brave old " Israel Put" of Revolutionary memory. His father was Cornelius, born in Hartford, Conn. His first wife was Happy Miller, and his second, Sophia Harris. His grandfather was Rufus Putnam, Joel H. Putnam married Eliza Alles, a native of the Isle of Guernsey, and they are the parents of Dewey C., who married Nellie Koon, formerly of the Valley, and he lives at home, having three children—Hazel, Olive and Ray. (Also Joel, and a girl, both born since writing the foregoing.) The second son will be found on the east road, and the third son, Wells J., is in Chicago.

The approaches to the cooper shops and mills are passed next, along with the foundations of a house, burned a year ago.

Then comes E. Platt Soper, a native of Smithtown, L. I. His first wife was Charlotte Cady, of South Butler; his second wife was Sylvia Grant, of Butler. The children by his first wife were: Josephine, who married F. Priest Wilcox, of Orleans county, a farmer; and Erwin, who married Nettie Depntron, and lives in Auburn. His second wife is the mother of Elbert

G. and A. Vianna, both young people at home. Mr. Soper has thirty-four acres here, the results of several purchases, representing the names of Craft, Shaw and Barton. Mr. Soper, like many people hereabouts, does coopering also, and his shop and barn are opposite. He is a brother of Egbert and Daniel, once living in the east part of the town.

On the corner is the home of Alfred Spoug, of German birth. He has three children. Before him occurs the name of H. Dunham. Obviously, the site is an old one, but I can not undertake the finding of all those who have lived here.

Crossing the road, on the southeast corner, is one of the oldest houses in the vicinity, associated to some extent with Abraham Van Valkenburg, remembered as the husband of Deborah Craft. There were several children in this family that reached maturity, and are : John, who lives in Leroy ; Benjamin and Isaac, both in British Columbia ; Abraham, who married Dora Barton, of Lyons, and who also lives in Leroy ; Betsey married Andrew Baker, of Sodus, who was killed in logging ; and Margaret, who married John P. Shaw, long a resident on this corner. Mr. Van V. died in 1863, aged sixty-two years, and Mrs. Van V. in 1876, at the age of sixty-eight years. A daughter by the name of Adelaide died in 1881, aged thirty-two years. The Shaws who dwelt here are both dead, and, with their predecessors, lie in the South Sodus burial ground. They died, respectively, in 1880 and 1884, at the ages of forty-three and forty-four years. They left two children—Sheridan, now in California, and Emma, in Leroy. Albert and J. Wesley died in childhood. Mr. Shaw was a member of the 9th N. Y. Heavy Artillery, and Abraham Van Valkenburg, his father-in-law, died in service as a member of the 160th Infantry, rather an old man for soldiering.

Turning to the south, we pass Platt Soper's shop and barn and come to the home of various people, whose residence is more or less transient. Abraham Van Valkenburg's homestead was next. The store and post office are kept by John Trimble, who came hither from the town of Ontario four years since. His wife was Viola Woolsey, of Sodus. He has ten acres of land, having bought from Mrs. Dennis. The post office in Wayne Centre dates from 1863. (?) Joel H. Putnam received the appointment, and he deputized Moses Dennis, who was later made full postmaster. The service was meagre, coming only once a week, gratis, from Lyons. In 1878 the office was put on the route between South Sodus and Lyons, and had mail twice a week. In the days of John Camp, of Lyons, the office began getting a daily mail. After Dennis, as incumbents were S. W. Lape, Augustus Conroe, Joel H. Putnam and Trimble.

Next south is a house erected by Conrad Young, which passed afterward to the father of Dr. J. J. Dickson, late of the Valley, and in it he died. It is now held by Anthony Hebgen. The holdings south of this point are small and have changed owners and occupants many times.

Returning to the cross roads, the school-house is found on the northwest corner. I do not know how many buildings have preceded it, but learn that the first edifice stood to the northward, where a road diverges from that of the preëmption, standing just over the Lyons line. After many years, a site further south was selected. Here are held religious services every Sunday, alternately in English and German. They are Methodistic in character. The point is one on the Lock Berlin charge, though it has belonged to South Sodus and to the Valley. In many respects the latter union seems the more natural and desirable.

Whatever dwellings there may have been in the past, there are no indications of houses till we reach the home of widow Miller. As she says, it has been the widow's abode for many years, since before her for twenty years was the widow Bennett. The site is an admirable one, commanding a wide view to the south and east. Here Philip H. Miller, a native of Alsace, came many years since. His wife was Mary M. Klippel, another sister of Henry. Their children are: Edward, now in Dakota; Wells, who married Libbie Dodds, and lives in Lyons; Frank, married and lives in Lyons; Walter, who is at home; Matilda, the wife of George Wraight, of the Covell district; Carrie E. and Maud C., who are, I believe, teachers. Mr. Miller died sixteen years ago, leaving directions that the place should be managed by his widow for eighteen years, when the property should be divided. She is now nearing the end of her trust, and, apparently, has done her part faithfully. She tells me, however, that the boys of to-day don't like the farm, and she can not get hired help to do as she would like. "Should Miller see those arrow weeds standing in the fence corners, it would make him turn in his grave," was her remark, as she dilated on the decadence of the times and the disposition of the young men of the present to selfishly go for themselves at once. Mr. Miller bought of Jacob Mitchell, who took from the widow Bennett, who had been there for a long time. Before her and her husband are the names of Heldrigel, Vincent and Wm. Morris, the latter of whom probably took up the land from the office.

Our road crooks around toward the west, and on the south side is the most sightly edifice in the vicinity. Tunis Woodruff, who located here many, many years since, was singularly fortunate in his situation. Back of him was only one name, probably that of Lewis Morris, who went west. The Woodruffs, good, God-fearing people, dwelt here many a year, and hence passed to their reward and last resting place in the South Sodus inclosure: Mr. W. dying in 1864, at the age of sixty.

There was once a burial place north of the barn, but who were placed there I have no means of learning. The spot was finally plowed over. The farm has one hundred acres. There were three Woodruffs reared here— George, now in Lyons; Isaac, in the west, and Mary, who once lived in the Valley as Mrs. Anson Waring. After the Woodruffs came Constantine Worden, and this was his home for twenty-four years, he only last spring, *i. e.*, 1890, leaving to live in Lyons. His wife was Phœbe, a daughter of Michael Vandercook. Her death took place four years ago. Their children were: George, of the Jeffers district; Leonard, who married Maggie Weeks, and is east of North Rose, and William, whose home is northeast of Wayne Centre, in the town of Sodus. Mr. Worden still holds the farm, renting it to George L. Reynolds, of Lyons.

This road runs into the town of Lyons, and thence into Sodus, but on the very top of the hill we turn to the north and, for a short distance, follow the thoroughfare that forms for some rods the town line. Just beyond the foot of the hill it crooks abruptly to the right, *i. e.*, east, and our first halt is at a small house, in which resides the widow of Isaac Warren. In 1853 the place was put down as the home of William West, but of him I can give no details. The Warrens were among the very first settlers in Rose, coming in along with or soon after the Craft family. The progenitor was Comstock Warren, who, after the birth of his children, took a load of bark to Geneva and never returned. His leaving was one of the mysteries that afflicted our friends many years ago, and must have been more than a nine days' wonder. No satisfactory explanation was ever made of what could draw a man from his family in this abrupt manner. There may have been home incompatibility, the man's habits may not have always been just correct; but be these suppositions as they may, a woman, practically a widow, was left with small children to maintain. Mr. Warren was from Dutchess county, and only Isaac C. and Caroline, who, as Mrs. Elisha Barton, was many years at the Centre, continued in Rose. The sons, George, Jacob and William, went west; Hannah, who, as Mrs. Abram Morris, went to Michigan; Maria, who married Leonard Brown, of Lyons, and Abbie, who is Mrs. Rufus Rowland, of Michigan. The land taken from the office was paid for by the Warren sons. Upon Isaac early fell the burden of hard labor, and he discharged his duties manfully, till illness prostrated him upon a bed of suffering. His wife was Emeline Bennett, of Sodus. This place was not the old home; that was further along to the north, where Walter White now lives. On that site they lived and here was born their only son, James, to be met later. Isaac Warren, after years of hard work, was afflicted with rheumatism, making him bed-ridden for sixteen years. Nearly helpless during all this time, it seemed a sad sequel to his former life of activity and usefulness. He died in 1883, and is buried in South Sodus. Near him lies his mother, Sarah, who passed away in 1875, at the age of eighty-two. The house in which Mrs. Warren now lives was built by Mr. Morris, and by him sold to Isaac Warren.

Across the way, just where the road takes a northerly course, is a neat house, the home of the Sutherlands. Years ago this bore the name of P.

Bennett. The first of this family was buried in the South Sodus cemetery. There are in the place eight acres, and the occupants of the house are Charles and his sisters, Elizabeth and Rebecca. Mr. S. for some years drove the stage between Wayne Centre and Lyons. Land belonging to the Twamley family surrounds these places.

On the west side of the road, which here is about forty-five points to the east of north, is the place where the Warrens long lived. James, son of Isaac, succeeded his father here, and here he lived with his wife, Ella Lape, till his early death, in 1878, at the age of twenty-five. His taking off was one of those distressing affairs that sometimes end in what began as pleasantry and fun. A party in September had gone out for a night of pleasure in hunting raccoons. The animal had been treed. The tree had been cut down, but a limb had been detached and left hanging to an adjacent tree. This, of course, could not be seen in the night, but its descent was none the less sure, and its stroke none the less fatal. A widow and a fatherless boy were a heavy price to pay for diversion. This boy's name is James Isaac, and he is at home with his mother. She afterward married Walter White, who came hither from Chautauqua county. They have three children—Flora, John and Walter. In the old farm there were one hundred acres. The house built by the Warrens followed the original log house of the pioneer. In the old 1853 map, the name of W. West occurs just south of the Warren place. This farm is on the old allotment, No. 220. Further north, on lot No. 526, was, years since, the name of J. Bowen. I have nothing more.

Across the road is lot No. 517, and on the lower part of it is a house belonging to Charles LaRock, now of Wallingford. He bought of S. W. Lape, who took the land from the office. This part of the town had many acres in the land office till a comparatively recent date.

On the upper or northern part of this lot is the home of Monroe Seager, but years since the name of J. Ellis is found. Mr. S. bought directly from Edward LaRock, who took from S. W. Lape, and he from the land office. On this place Mr. Seager has erected a fine house. He has been three times married. First, to Anna Wraight ; second, to Harriet Dunn, of the Covell district; and third, to Mary (Dunn) Wager, a sister of Harriet. There were two children—Amanda, now deceased, who married Edward LaRock (leaving a daughter, Anna), and Monroe. The latter is by the third wife, the former by the first. There are twenty-eight acres in the farm.

Some ways back from the road, on the west side, are the walls on which stood the Woodruff steam saw-mill. In 1857 this blew up, injuring seriously several men and killing George Grenell. As the trees were nearly all cut off, it did not pay to rebuild, and consequently we have to-day only a history. The owner, however, was anxious to sell, and he succeeded in exchanging the small farm with David J. Seager, who lived next north, for a colt, a pair of oxen and a watch. However good this trade was for both parties, it eventually wrought great misfortune for Mr. Seager, as we shall presently see. The Seagers came from Danbury, Conn., and the first of the family to settle in this vicinity was John K., who, with his wife, Clara Jackson, came first to Lock Berlin, in Galen, and thence to York's settlement, and thereby became the progenitor of the Seagers of Rose, Huron and Sodus. Long since, the first comers found final resting places in the cemetery near York's corners. At present we are specially interested in David J., who was in his seventeenth year at the time of the family migration. In time he wedded Hannah Warner, a daughter of the Asher Warner who was slain in the British attack on Sodus Point in 1813. It may be quite as well to state here the names of the second generation of Seagers. In addition to David there were: John B., who settled in Huron, and was the father of George, living north of the Valley; Harrison, who settled in Sodus; Syrena, who married William Sebring, of Rose, and Clarissa, who became Mrs. Adam Crisler, also of Rose. To David J. Seager and his wife was born a large family, as follows: John, who married Mary York, of the settlement, and formerly lived to the northeast; Julia Ann became Mrs. Samuel Lape of the Centre; Monroe, as we have seen, has been three times married; Benjamin, who was a sergeant of Company D, Ninth Heavy Artillery, married Louisa LaRock, and resides in Huron; Susan, the wife of Warren York, lived and died in Huron; Asher W. we shall meet in the next house north; Daniel, a Huronite, married first, Eliza Hart, a daughter of Samuel C., and second, Lucretia Daly, and has one daughter, Ada; Munson married Emma Dunbar, a daughter of John, and lives in Rose; Clara is Mrs. Charles LaRock, of Wallington, and has four children—Rose, David, Maria and Charles; George W. married, first, Emma Spong, of the Centre, and second, Candace O. Bumpus, of Huron, his children being Maud, Ernest and Earl; Hannah, who married Samuel Davenport, and lives at home with her aged parents. Mr. Seager has done his share of hard work, having taken from the land office his claim and having cleared and nearly paid for it. His claim was north, where Asher is now. He had paid in principal and interest more than the estimated value of the lot, when in trading for the Woodruff lot, he unwittingly violated the terms of his contract, and his lot, improvements and all, were sold from under him. This was a terrible blow, enough to dishearten almost any man, but Mr. S. is not the only man in Rose whom man's inhumanity to man has compelled to pay for his farm twice over. So from the spot where he reared his family he moved to the smaller holding, where he now is, and where he and his wife await the end of life. Mr. Seager has seen many changes on these plains. When he came fifty-three years ago, there were deer to be found, and aside from fifteen acres of improved or cleared land (one Baldwin had been there), his surroundings were those of the wilderness. (Mrs. David Seager died December 30, 1891.)

Passing northward, we find where the longest road in Rose, that going by the Covell school-house, enters this north and south way. Toward the east and also west of us huckleberries abound, and so the respective places are called huckleberry swamps. When David Seager lost his farm, his son, Asher, was only a boy, but he vowed that if he lived long enough, he would yet own the old homestead. The War came, the boy enlisted, served his time in Company D, of the Ninth Heavy Artillery, came home, married Mary J. Weeks, a neighbor's daughter, raised mint, saved his money, and finally realized his boyish dream. To-day he has the old place, and has erected a fine house near the site of the framed building built by the father, and which now forms the latter's home on the Woodruff place. The site of the first log house may also be seen in the door yard. Mrs. Seager is an invalid, and they have no children ; but they have taken to their hearth and hearts the daughter of one of Mr. S.'s army comrades, and Jennie is, to all intents, their own. Mrs. S. died December 1, 1890. (Mr. Seager married, in 1892, Elizabeth A. Klippel, of Lyons.)

Crossing the road and going a little further to the north, we find the home of Abram Wager. There are 117 acres in the place, and he bought in 1855 the contract of John Seager and father, so that, practically, he took his farm from the land office. It should be remarked, in passing, that this locality is known in neighborhood parlance as Seagerville. The house in which Mr. Wager lives was repaired by him, he finding an old one on his coming. Mr. W. has put up one of the largest barns in these parts. Unless struck by a cyclone, there seems to be no reason why it should not long continue a landmark on this road. Close by it, in fact joining it, he is now erecting a carriage house and horse barn of similar model, viz., high studded and with a hip roof. Few farmers in town will be better fitted when this work is done. Abram Wager is a native of this part of the town, and his wife was Hannah Paylor of Galen. Their children are : William P., who married Rosette Phillips, a daughter of Joseph P., of the Covell district, and who now lives in Galen, having two children, Ida and Ada. (Mrs. Wager died August 26, 1891, and Mr. Wager has since married Carrie Raver of Buffalo. Their home is now on the Van Baskirk farm in Jeffers district.) Luther married Ella Potter, and lives just north : Alice E. and Albert are at home. The newness of this part of the town is especially evident, as we reflect that in most cases the children of the original contractors are dead or extremely old, but here we have Mr. Wager in the prime of life, yet he settled with the office for his farm. The Wagers are from the family of David, who was born in Dutchess county, and came to this town long since, locating his lot in York settlement, where the Dixons now live. His wife was Clarissa Dunbar, a sister of Henry Dunbar, a fellow migrant, to be met later. Their children were: Eliza Jane, who died in 1887; Mary Ann; Sarah M., the wife of George Dixon; William Henry, a member of the Ninth Heavy Artillery, Company D., who married Mary Dunn, and died in 1879, and Mrs. Wager afterward married Monroe Seager; Abram, the second child, we have already met.

Beyond the barns, toward the north, is a fine new house, where Luther Wager is tasting the sweets of newly wedded life. This home is the end of our northward journey, though on an old map of the county I find one more name, at the extreme end of the road, i. e., where it terminates in the east and west way. In the southeast angle thus made are the words J. Reynolds, but there is no trace of a habitation there now.

Retracing our steps, we will imagine ourselves in Lyons, and about to reach Wayne Centre by the nearest course. After crossing the preëmption line, there is only one house to be met as we near the hamlet. Indeed, we shall have to look sharp or it will not be seen. A lane reaches up through the fields to the house where lives Samuel Chambers. He came hither from Binghamton. His wife was Nancy Finch of Lyons, and they have one child—Rosa. There are thirteen acres in the holding.

Passing the corners, there is first, on the north side, the house belonging to John Lester, though he is not residing in it. His home is Wallington. Ezra Dunham is the occupant. S. Chambers once owned here. Opposite is the old home of the Van Valkenburgs. Valentine Kaiser is the next dweller. He is a son of the Valentine encountered in our "Jeffers" rambles. He is now the mail carrier between Wayne Centre and Lyons.

There are several reminders of old homes to the eastward—log houses and old framed structures—but they have all been merged into the possession of Mervin Harrington, a native of Savannah, who, coming hither, bought the belongings of Mrs. A. Ridgeway, Geo. H. Green and some of the Thomas Lambert lot. Over his property the cyclone of 1888 passed in all its fury. It strung his barn all over the premises and uprooted many trees. The barn he rebuilt nearer the road, but the trees were pretty effectually done for. His wife is Mary, a daughter of the Lamberts, next east. Mr. H. is a veteran of the 3d Light Artillery, and his latch-string is always out for old comrades. The Lamberts are of English birth, and to the next place east, Thomas L. came many years ago, having taken from the land office a claim of fifty-six acres. He had three children—Thomas, who went out west and died; Mary, who is Mrs. Harrington, and William, at home. Mr. L. died in 1884, and is buried in Rose.

We now come to the farm standing in the name of Joel H. Putnam, but his son, Hervey T., is the occupant. The latter married Hattie, a daughter of Egbert Soper, once of District No. 7. They have four children—Wheeler, Grace, Inez and Victor I. This is one of the oldest locations in the neighborhood. The house and barns, together with the farm, indicate industry and prosperity. There are in all about 200 acres; but the farm represents the former homes of at least two families. On the south side, where the buildings are, was Ebenezer Toles, whose children we encountered in the Lake district, and he bought from Dodds. There are in this part some ninety-six acres. North of the road are indications of earlier residents, very likely one of the Crafts.

Still north of the road, a trifle further east, is an old house, the former habitation of the farm owners. Mr. Putnam bought of James Elmer of Lyons, and he purchased from Thomas Sweet. This is the old Abram Craft place, the spot to which these people came so early in the century. Here the late Mrs. Seymour Covell was born, and here she was married. Thence the family went to Michigan. Abram Craft came from Dutchess county, and took his lot from Fellows & McNab. His wife was Huldah Newberry, and their children were: Joel, James, Thorn, Clarissa (Mrs. Covell), and Charles. The latter married Lydia Lyman, a sister of Milo. The whole family moved to White Lake, Oakland county, Michigan, but the Covells, as we have seen, returned. The continuous migration westward of some families seems almost startling. Alaska offers new opportunities for those who, till its purchase, had to stop at California.

A large brick house, obviously roomy and comfortable, next claims our attention. It is on the south side of the way, some way east of the old wooden structure, in which dwelt for so many years the men and women who called this place home. I am told that Thomas Craft first dwelt here. He was a brother of Benjamin and Abram. I have learned that the name of Van Wort is also connected with it. It is certain that John Dickson was long a resident on these acres. He was from Kingsbury, Washington county, a fellow townsman of the Seelyes, Benjamin and Joseph. Beside the son, Dr. Dickson of the Valley, he had a daughter, Sophronia, who married Thomas Mirick, and after his death married again. She, too, is dead. As we have seen, the first John Dickson died in Wayne Centre. After the Dicksons comes the name of Joel Hall, who went to Palmyra. Succeeding him was William Stanton of Lyons, from whom the present owner, Newman Finch, purchased. There are 101 acres in the farm. Mr. F. built his house in 1880, thus making a very handsome addition to the dwellings of Rose. The old house yet remains, rather a sombre reminder of the days when people worked hard and had few comforts. Mr. Finch married Malvina Chatterson of the Covell district, and they have four children, viz.: Eda, the wife of George Youngs of Lyons; Ina M.; George W., and Lila May, all at home.

I am informed that down in the woods, to the north, lives William Weeks, and that before him was Jerry Lethbridge; but I must take the word of my informant for all this, since, like Chas. Lamb, concerning sunrise, I have had no ocular evidence.

The home of John L. Finch, however, stands out prominently. This house is one of his own building. It is on the north side of the street, some rods west of the old location. With the farm buildings, Mr. Finch has a most delightful outfit for work and pleasure. His wife is Amanda Phillips, a daughter of the late Abram, and so granddaughter of Mrs. Jacob Tipple, who lived to be more than one hundred years old. This place was where Michael Vandercook first located, though his house was further east, and on these acres his children were reared. To him succeeded Samuel Bockoven, who had traded the farm in the Griswold district. The Bockoven house was the one across the vale on the north side, now shut up, but formerly Mr. Finch's home. As we bid good-by to the street and the Wayne Centre district, it is with just a little regret that, unlike the Finch house opposite, there are in this handsome cage no Finches of a younger growth to make it lifeful and musical.

Just a few rods beyond the confines of the district, is the summit of the hill which marks the western limit of "Jeffers," and it is meet to stop and to look backward over the scene. North, south, east and west are the homes of industrious people, and before them were those of former generations. Time speeds along. Many of the former dwellers are in the cemeteries, near and far, and many are yet fighting life's battles on other fields. Born and reared with these beautiful surroundings, let us hope that, whether here or elsewhere, they are worthy representatives of the town, so long conspicuous for honesty and sobriety.

SCHOOL DISTRICT NO. 10.—SODUS; OR, "THE PREËMPTION."

August 13, 1891.

No one has the least idea of the size of the town of Rose till he undertakes, as I have done, a house-to-house visitation. Were this a town in Massachusetts, the frequent convention of her citizens in town meeting would result in familiar acquaintance throughout its limits. As it is, we find here, in the extreme northwestern part, people who have scarcely heard of the first settlers along the eastern border. In fact, as the post office address here is either South Sodus or Alton, in almost every instance, and as going to Rose Valley simply to vote does not necessarily beget intimacy, many of our Rose dwellers in this district are more like Sodus people than Rose citizens. I don't mean to intimate that a stranger would be able to detect any physical characteristics peculiar to either town, but I do mean that their conversation and thoughts are more on Sodus than on Rose.

We shall enter this district by going north from Seagerville, north from Wayne Centre, and I have seen somewhere in the southwest angle, as the
16

road ends, the name of S. Howard, but to-day there is no trace of any dwelling.

Turning to the west, remembering that the boundary between the preëmption and the York settlement district is a line continued north from this road, which ends here, we first encounter, on the north side, the house of Daniel Martin. Mr. M. was born in Lyons, but he was only a small boy when his father came to this farm. His wife was Katie Barnum of Arcadia. They have only one child, Myrtie E. In this farm there are forty-seven acres ; he bought of his father five years ago. Daniel Martin, Sr., bought of DeWitt W. Parshall, the wealthy Lyons banker, lately deceased ; again I turn to an old map, and there I find the name of I. Farr. The early days are thus obscured.

A mint still is passed before reaching the next place, on the same side of the way ; here dwell the Rekuglers, a German family from Wurtemberg ; the first comer, John, is dead, but his sons are yet on the place. The place was bought of D. W. Parshall, who had purchased from E. M. Louis and John Horn. The name of J. Seymour also occurs here earlier. In the original farm there are eighty-eight acres, and to these have been added twelve acres on the north. The first John's wife was Sophia Rinkel ; his sons, Charles and John, are now managing the place, and apparently very successfully. There is a very pleasant house on the corner, northeast, where this road terminates.

Crossing to the southeast corner, we may see where Samuel P. Thompson and family reside. Mr. T. was a good soldier in the 8th N. Y. Cavalry, and his worth is recognized in his holding official positions in Rose. His wife was Emily Burns of Rose ; they have two sons, James P. and Robert L., both at home. Mr. Thompson's father, Robert P., was born in Saratoga county and came hither long since ; his wife was Elizabeth Fulton ; their children are : Albert, living to the northward ; Eliza married Henry Taylor of Sodus, and Samuel. The grandfather, Ezekiel, also came to these parts. The old home was on the Sodus side of the road and to the north, near the site of Mr. Thompson's barns. The well is still in use from which water was drawn in the old open bucket so long ago. It was in this old location that the elder Thompsons died. An earlier name here was that of E. M. Lewis.

To the southward, just where the preëmption road turns off to enter Sodus, at the very angle, on the Rose side, was once the name of E. Lemon, but I have no aid to this suggestive appellation, and so must leave it as it is.

Northward from Rekugler's and Thompson's, keeping to the right, we shall find where, for some time, was F. Myers, but he has sold to the Rekuglers and gone to Michigan. Before him was Geo. Sucher. The house, somewhat ancient, is the home of tenants. Albert Clary lives next, a nephew of the Samuel Clary found in the "Jeffers" district.

Were it not my determination to keep to the right, I have no doubt I could find much of interest in the people who dwell on the west side of the road. There are more Sodus residents than Roses; but I must confine myself to my flower garden. Albert Thompson resides in the next house. As previously stated, he is a son of the Robert Thompson once living to the south. His wife is Sarah, a daughter of Caleb Weeks, who lives on the next road east. Their children are Franklin, Albert, Ernest and Edna E. There are thirty acres in the farm, which was bought of Morris Wager. This gentleman lives now in the Valley district, and will be met there. The place was bought many years since from the widow Sutton, whose husband, presumably, took from the land office. As the old home of the Wagers was on this road, about forty rods north of the old Tindall home in Huron, it will not be amiss to give some data here concerning a name having so many representatives in this part of Rose. John Wager, the first comer, was a native of Dutchess county, and with his wife, Margaret Dunn, came early in the century to Pilgrimsport, the spot of debarking for so many of the early settlers of this region. Afterward he moved to his Huron home, and there died, in 1856, at the age of ninety years. His wife survived him two years, and died, aged eighty-seven. They were buried at York's corners. They had six children, the most of whom will be encountered, either in the flesh or in memory, as we journey through the northwest part of Rose. Jacob lived a little south of York's corners, and had one son, James, who died in 1855, at the age of twenty years; David has been mentioned as the father of Abram Wager, in the north part of the Wayne Centre district; Catharine became the wife of Henry Dunbar, of Rose; Margaret is Mrs. Caleb Weeks; Susan is the wife of Alvah Jewell, both of York settlement; while Charles, the youngest son, now an aged man, dwells on the preëmption road, though on the Sodus side and near the school-house, the old Fellows place. His wife was Mary Alvord, and their children are: Almira, the wife of David McDowell, and lives in Sodus; Nancy, who is Mrs. Charles McDowell, also of Sodus, and Morris. The second child was John, who died during the War at Key West, Florida, a member of the 98th N. Y. Volunteers.

At the left, a few rods south of the railroad, is found the school-house for this district. It is just over the line in Sodus. Nearly opposite was once a home, the abode of N. Utter. The place has been merged in the Tindall farm, and the old home is utterly desolate.

The extreme northwest confines of Rose are reached when, having crossed the railroad, we come to the home of the Tindalls. Charles H. Tindall came here many years ago, from Pilgrimsport, a brother of "Parm," long prominent in the Valley. He was born in New Jersey, and his wife was Polly A. Camp, who was born in Ohio, but of a Connecticut family, long conspicuous in Litchfield county. In her infancy, she was taken back to her New England home, and there she resided till she was fourteen years of age. For this portion of our land she then acquired an affection that years have not been able to efface. Coming on a visit to Pilgrimsport, she met her future husband, and, instead of returning to Connecticut, as expected, she formed a life-long union with him. Eventually, they came to this point, where they have been for more than fifty years. The house, built by Mr. T., stands very near the town line. The Rose portion of the farm was bought of John Wager, who took from the land office. There are in this part some sixty-five acres. Of their children, Louisa married William Gatchell, of Huron; Lovina married Robert Catchpole, of Huron, and both are dead; Lucy married Henry Gatchell; Polly is Mrs. Ralph Palmer, of Sodus; Rosette became Mrs. Philip Weber, of Sodus; Alonzo, deceased, married Sarah Munson; Charles, at home, and Jerome Worth, who, having married Ida Clark, lives south of the Valley. The elder Mr. Tindall died in 1883. His widow, pleasant and retentive in memory, with her son, Charles, still remains on the old place, so fraught with agreeable associations. By a former marriage, Mr. Tindall had one son, Myron P., who married Emeline York, and lives in Huron.

SCHOOL DISTRICT NO. 2.—HURON; OR, "YORK SETTLEMENT."

August 22–29, 1891.

We will enter this district, or that part of it belonging to Rose, from the north, and the first resident therein we shall find in the person of Adam Crisler. Adam, it will be observed, is a good name to begin with. As we enter the premises of this man and observe the cooper shop at the right, we should be justified in thinking that a Crisler dwelt here, even if we did not know the name; for no Crisler ever thinks himself properly equipped till such a shop is added to his possessions. Following a lane, we soon reach one of the cleanest, neatest homesteads that I have found in my Rose rambles. House, barns, yards—everything is the soul of neatness and order. Over all, waves an umbrageous elm, a faithful sentinel, keeping guard over these results of honest toil and industry. The home is on the west side of the road. Mr. C. is a member of the family, for many years identified with Rose. He married Clarissa Seager, a sister of David, of the Wayne Centre district. Their children are: Jared E., who married Rosina Lake, and lives in the Valley; Charles M., who married Sybil Day, and is in the Covell district. Mr. Crisler has been here twenty-four years, but before him the place seems to have had many owners. Of these I can give scarcely more than the names. Mr. C. bought of William Woodward, who bought of R. West. He took from Gideon Wibur; he from William Sebring, and before him was the first owner, Henry Dunbar, to be met in the eastern part of the neighborhood. There are seventy acres in the farm. The name of Stephenson occurs in old records, on the east side, just south of the Huron line, but I have no other trace.

On the east side of the road are fields belonging to Gilbert Brown and to Alvah Jewell. Mr. Brown's extensive berry field is here, some eleven acres being given to this culture.

Next south, we find Samuel C. Hart, who has long been a Rose dweller. He was mentioned in the Covell district article, he having resided many years on the farm now occupied by George Wraight. He was born in Ontario county, and his wife, who died in 1865, was Ann Witherell, from Vermont. Their children were: Mary and Ann Eliza, both dead; Marion and Ira, whom we met in the Griswold neighborhood, and William H., at home. Mary married Geo. Knox, then of Rose, but now in Michigan, and left a daughter, Lillie Ann; Eliza married Daniel Seager of Huron. Mr. Hart came to Rose in 1842, and he tells me that his first place was bought of one Nichols, perhaps the Nicholas property. His present holding of thirty-eight acres he took from the land office. He built the house now used by him. Near it is an old, unoccupied structure, erected by John Weeks, and back of that is a log house, used by some of the line of squatters who, all through this section, preceded the permanent settler. Mr. Hart has long been a member of the Baptist Church.

South of Mr. Hart's, a road begins, which, with many windings, finally runs through Glenmark. On the southeast corner is the fine residence of Frank Weeks, who, a son of Caleb, married Lucy Creek. They have only one child, Jennie.

The next place to the south, and still on the east side, is the old David Wager place. It is now held by George Dixon, who married Mr. Wager's daughter, Sarah. The Dixons were originally from Ireland, where Abel, the immigrant, married Alice Twamley, a native of Wicklow, and a relative of the Twamleys, on the borders of Lyons, near Wayne Centre. Abel must have halted first in New Jersey, for in that state some, if not all, of his children were born. The first Dixon who settled near Glenmark has long been dead, but his widow, at the age of ninety years, died a few weeks since. As the Wagers have already been given, it will be proper to give facts concerning the Dixons. There were several children, namely: Benjamin, who went to Ohio; William is in Michigan: Jane is in New York; Ellen, who married first, John Howard, second, Harry Traher of Glenmark; Hannah, the wife of Monroe Jewell; Mary, deceased, who married James Russell; after Ellen, should have been named George, who lives here, and Abel, who died in War times, a member of Co. G, Ninth N. Y. Heavy Artillery. He sleeps in the burial ground at York's corners. The genesis of this place is short, since it goes back through Dixons and Wagers to the land office.

Still moving southward, we find a house where lives William Weeks, another son of Caleb. The father built this house. William married Lueze Welch, of Sodus, and they have one daughter, Ora.

Opposite dwells Caleb Weeks, who married long since Margaret Wager, a sister, I think, of David, and once a neighbor on the north. Their children are: Frank, living on the corners, north ; Hannah, the wife of Nelson Dunbar, of Huron ; Jane, the wife of Asher Seager; Martha, the wife of John York, of North Rose ; Sarah, who is Mrs. Albert Thompson, of the preemption, and William, the son, dwelling across the way.

At the angle in the road, where it turns abruptly to the west, is a log house, only recently occupied. As late as 1888, a family by the name of Porter lived in it. It was built by one Joe Miles, and among other occupants was Monroe Seager. This house, still well preserved, of hewed logs, with mortar clinking, on the east side of the elbow, is without doubt the last used pioneer edifice in Rose. Similar houses in the eastern part of the town disappeared years since.

Our district, so far as this road is concerned, is ended, but if we ride down into Seagerville, turn to the east and proceed till we come to the house of Frank Garlic, and there turn to the north, we shall again enter York settlement, stopping first at the home of Frank Miner, though I understand that, owing to some differences, his place has been set off to the Covell's neighborhood. Mr. Miner, one of the sons of Riley Miner, married Mary A. Mitchell, and has children ; Jennie, Maud, Franklin, Zenas, Minerva, and John. He succeeded upon these twenty-seven acres P. Brower, who had married a daughter of Philip Marquette, one of the first if not the very first owners. There seem to be several of this name living in Glenmark, whence came Philip, who died in 1861. He had two daughters—Amelia and Elizabeth. The former is dead and the latter is Mrs. George Pritchard of Sodus.

Crossing the railroad, we pass through the Dunbar possessions, whose name the cross roads bear. On the southeast angle there was, long ago, a log house, where dwelt various families. Before that it was the site of many charcoal pit burnings ; for here Henry Dunbar worked many a weary day and night. Bushes and old-fashioned flowers still indicate the haunts of man.

Diagonally across is a small building, where Aaron Dunbar once kept a grocery. On the northeast corner a blacksmith shop once stood, and in it were shod the farmers' horses of this vicinity.

To the west, we shall find but little, only an old house, now nailed up, built by Henry Dunbar's son-in-law, William Chamberlain. Still further west, on the north side, is a small house, where lives widow Daly, once the home of P. Chamberlain.

North from Dunbar's corners, our first stop is at the house of Aaron
Dunbar, and here it was my good fortune to meet Henry Dunbar, the man
after whom the corners were named, and whom I find, despite his ninety
years, a treasure house of early Rose data. He was born in Dutchess
county, and came, with his parents, to the town of Galen in 1809 or '10.
There they died. Since his twenty-third year he has lived in Rose. He
was first on the present Adam Crisler place, which he took from the
office. In 1837 he took this place from the same office, and has been here
since. There were at first some 156 acres. He was an actual pioneer,
and his memory of events, in the long ago, is very vivid—stating months
and days of that period with no hesitation. For instance, it was the 27th
day of January that he came to these then unbroken roads. "Yes," he
says, "there was nothing but woods here. There was plenty of game. I
once followed a flock of deer two days, and shot four of them. Just
below here, where the railroad crosses the road, Andrew J. Sebring shot a
big wolf. There were two of them, and he killed the larger one, and got a
bounty for his scalp. My hearing is poor, but my eyesight is pretty good
for a man who has burned as many pits of charcoal as I have. You know
that is awfully smoky business, and it hurts a man's eyes." His wife was
Catharine Wager, who died in 1870, at the age of seventy years. His
home now is with his son, Aaron. (Died February 13, 1893.) The
children were: John, once living just to the north; Levi, who married
Lucy Day, and lives in Huron; Nelson married Hannah Weeks, and also
lives in Huron; Aaron married Mary J. Burt of Sodus, and has two
children, Benjamin and Cora; Rhoda became Mrs. Wm. Chamberlain,
and is dead; Melissa is Mrs. Chas. Knox, and is the sole dweller in the
house to the east of the corners, and yet in this district. Mr. Chamberlain
was killed by the running away of a team of horses. The original Dunbar
log house stood about where the present house is.

John Dunbar's late home is found next north. He married Harriet
Davenport, who died thirty years ago. Their only child, Emmaette,
married Munson Seager, after whose decease she kept house for her father.
Her children are: Harriet, who married a Pierce of Huron, and Nellie, at
home. Formerly he ran threshing machines, portable saw-mills, and,
obviously, has known what labor is. He had been particularly unfortunate
in certain accidents, which had crippled him considerably. His place is a
part of his father's original purchase. John Dunbar died June 11th, 1890,
aged about sixty-five years. He was buried at York's corners.

No finer farm buildings can be found in this part of Rose than those that
are nearly opposite, yet a little further north. Here is the home of Alvah
Jewell. He was born in Dutchess county. His father, Isaac, who had
married Charity Shaw, came here more than seventy years since. He died
in Lyons. Alvah's wife was Susan Wager, a daughter of John. Their

children are: Henry, who married Sivilla Winget, and is on his father-in-law's place in Huron; Malinda, deceased, married Allen Robinson, of Huron; Alanson married Mary Coats, and died in 1873 at the age of 23 years, and his son, Franklin, lives with Alvah; Elizabeth is Mrs. Thomas Hewson; Franklin married Miranda Barrett. Mr. J. has 170 acres. Of these, he bought twenty-eight of Philip Marquette, forty from his brother, Barney, and eighty-two from General Adams, who took from the office. On the B. Jewell place, opposite, there was formerly a house. Mr. J. is a Republican in politics and Methodistic in religious preferences. His post office is Alton. A few steps to the north is a house where Henry Jewell formerly lived, but which he now lets to a tenant.

Opposite is the home of Gilbert Brown, and when I find that he was a fellow company man with me in the Ninth Heavy Artillery, he seems very much like an old friend. He was badly wounded at Snicker's Gap, at the time Early was trying to get away after his sortie on Washington. Gilbert was born in the town of Marion, and married Arloa Adams of that town. Their children are Clara L. and Elroy G., both at home. Mr. B. bought of Thomas Hewson, who moved to Sodus. He bought of Aaron Winget, and the latter took from the office. The house was built by Hewson. Mr. Brown is a zealous cultivator of berries and has a large dry house. He also has a mint still. There are eleven acres in his place. In religion he is a Disciple.

The house standing out so prominently on the north side of the way, long stood in the name of the widow Shannon. There must have been many of this name here and to the north, years ago. since the name is common in the York's corners burial ground. Samuel Shannon, in solitary bachelorhood. lives on the paternal acres. He has nicely repaired the house, and it is too bad that with so many unmarried women in town he does not take some one to his heart and home. Perhaps he has his reasons. (Died April 8, 1892.) He was a good soldier in the Ninth Heavy Artillery, as was also his brother, Theodore, who died in 1867.

To reach the next house, we shall have to run down a long lane, past an old barn belonging to Shannon, to the end of the lane, where we shall find the residence of the widow of John Seager. She was Sarah York of Huron, a sister of the North Rose maltster. Her children are: Elizabeth, who is Mrs. John Hill, of North Rose; Sarah, who married George Ball, of the same place, and George, Warren, Norman, Oscar, and Jennie. This holding has had some mutations. It is first found under the name of Jacob Wager, and this was more than thirty years since. He had at least one son, who died long since. In old age. Jacob went to live with William Wager, near Glenmark. Also some part of his old age was passed with Mrs. Rhoda Chamberlain. After Wager comes the name of Joanna Phillips, who sold to the widow of John Seager. The latter died just west of Dunbar's corners. There are twenty-five acres in the farm. The old house in which Jacob Wager lived is still standing, an isolated relic.

Still further back, and still more inaccessible, for we must follow a private way from Henry Jewell's house to reach it, is a quite pretty place, held and occupied by John Austin.

Coming back to the road and taking a glance to the north, into Huron, where we may see the elegant buildings of Luman Barrett, now occupied by his son, Gardner, we retrace our way, having thoughts of Green Erin aroused as we pass the home of Shannon, since everybody knows that no finer stream than that flows through the meadows of Ireland.

From Dunbar's corners we ride east, passing the home of Charles Knox, the son-in-law of Henry Dunbar, and when I pass, I find Alvah Jewell engaged in clearing up new land, a labor which took so much of the time of the ancestors here. The pioneer on heavily timbered land had experiences that the dwellers on the prairies know nothing of. It is, however, sad to think of the value destroyed in getting our land ready for cultivation. If the great trees thus cut off could only have been held for subsequent use, instead of being piled in great heaps for burning, what a storehouse there would be for coming time, but that is not the way. The growth of many, many years are felled, rolled together and burned. Fires are kindled around the stumps, and seed is planted at first in what seems to be very uncongenial soil, but great crops have been raised thus. Land that will support great trees will grow immense grain.

The school-house which the York settlement children seek, is found by following the road by Alvah Jewell's, just beyond the Barrett place, on four corners, known as York's. Near here resides Benjamin Winget, and close by, on the north side of the street, is the temple of learning. At any rate, it represents the altitude of knowledge to which the most of the boys and the girls of the settlement attain. The York part of the name comes from dwellers in Huron, though there are several women of the name married in Rose, and John York lives in North Rose. Back of Mr. Winget's is one of the finest chestnut groves in the state. I have never seen a more beautiful collection of these stately trees anywhere. It was a happy thought to allow them to remain and to thrive thus, forming such a charming background to the school-house, and such a playground for the children. Bryant's forest hymn is suggested at once :

" Father, thy hand hath reared these venerable columns."

SCHOOL DISTRICT No. 1.—"GLENMARK."

September 3—17, 1891.

This section was well named. Frequently, names are misnomers, but there is no want of application to this up and down region. Sodus bay has many approaches, many streams running down from the interior. These have worn away the land so that deep glens lead down to the main waters. It is possible that, in remote times, the lake itself occupied a higher level, and that these frequent gulleys represent the bays and inlets of the past. If so, where the farmer to-day raises corn and potatoes, immense fishes once swam in glorious freedom. We shudder at what would happen were the lake to again rise and claim its own. What a submerging of peaceful homes and fertile farms. Just at present, there seems more danger of the still further retirement of the lake. Had General Adams' dream of a Sodus canal been realized, and had the Sodus branch railroad ever been built, our glen-marked region had been to-day much more than the ragged, scattering hamlet that it is. Thomas' creek, whose sandy bed formed so considerable a part of the general's scheme, here has an exceedingly rocky bottom. In fact, I think, at the mill site in Glenmark, there is a cataract, where for untold ages, the waters have plunged over the outcropping limestone. There is not another place in the town where the layers, or strata, are thus developed. The gorge through which the water runs after passing the falls, is a deep, brier-lined chasm, whose depths can hardly be appreciated from the road which winds along the verge, the traveler protected by a rail judiciously placed between him and the abrupt descent. Many a Rose citizen has grown to maturity without dreaming that his native town has broken scenery as rare and engaging as that which people with well-lined purses travel many miles to see. These same people ride over dusty roads to the Bluffs, but they omit this wooded, glen-pierced country, so varied and picturesque. Its beauties and varieties must be seen to be appreciated.

There is not the least attempt at regularity in the roads about this district. They have simply adapted themselves to the glens and streams. In fact, there was no other way to get about. The three roads that lead into the district are merged just below the falls and follow the creek northward. This final gulley reminds one of the neck of a jug, for through it all travel and all water seeking the lake must pass.

Our entrance to Glenmark shall be along the road which leads eastward from Dunbar's corners, and our first farm will be at the home of David Johnson. The line which divides the Glenmark and York settlement districts just misses Mr. J.'s house, but he is in the eastern neighborhood. Huron is his native town, and he was in Company G, Ninth Heavy

Artillery, during the Rebellion. There are thirty-five acres in the farm, which he bought of William P. Angle, who bought from the office. The latter went west some years since. Angle started the house which Johnson completed. It is at this point that the road turns abruptly to the south, though it runs thus only a short way. To the southeast, the woods once standing there afforded shelter to camp meetings in the times when piety, if not more fervent, at least was more demonstrative. Mr. Johnson's wife was Naomi Andrus, also of Huron. Their children's names are : Jennie, who married, first, Herbert Ackerman, second, a Mr. Burch, and Rilla, the wife of Kingsley Clum, who came from Galen to Rose. The Clums live in a house somewhat back from the Johnsons. Mr. C. is of German extraction. They have two sons—Augustus and Claudius.

The next place reached, as we follow the eastern bend of the road, when it turns again, is the home of Calvin Daly. He bought of Samuel Osborn, who took from John Weeks, now of North Rose, and he from Theodore Shannon. The latter followed Charles Angle, whose possessing must have been among the very first.

Then comes the home of Joseph Andrews, whose son-in-law, Asa Potter, lives with him.

Across the railroad, out in the open field to the south, is the place owned by Oscar Weed of Huron. He bought of Abram L. Barnes. When this was covered with heavy timber, Eron N. Thomas owned it, and he sold to Robert Catchpole and others, who cut off the wood and then sold the land. Near at hand was the old Abel Dixon home, where he ended his own life through insanity, on account of the railroad cutting through his farm. This was in 1871. Leman Ellsworth is our next neighbor, or, at least, the place stands in his name, and his son-in-law, James Calkins, lives here. Mr. E.'s wife was a Huffman, of the family once living near North Rose.

Still progressing toward the northeast, we reach the place whose occupants have been sober for many years, for here Jonathan Sober, a native of Pennsylvania, came many years since. There are fifty acres in the farm. Mr. S. died several years since. Of their children, Huldah, deceased, married Albert Baker ; Mahala married George Jewell of Galen ; James, having married Kate Myers, is in Sodus ; Lewis married Alice Wager ; Albert, who married Lydia Eldridge, went west and died ; Eugene, a son of Lewis, lives with his grandmother. The wife of Jonathan Sober was Mary Garlick, the oldest own sister of Henry. Mr. S. took the place from the office, though it is probable that there were contract settlers before him. (Mrs. Sober died February 27, 1893.)

William M. Green, a native of Galen, is found next, on the east side. His holding of five acres runs back to one of the glens for which the region is noted, and it is quite irregular in surface. For twenty-five years Mr. Green has earned an honest living on and from his glebe. He built the house, having bought of David Johnson. Mr. Green is a brother of the George H. Green who was found in the Griswold district. The Green family, of which these two brothers are representatives, moved to Huron, and there the parents died. Early in life, Mr. Green wandered into Rose, and there he found his wife, Lydia Marsh, a daughter of Amos, who lived so long in District No. 5, or Town's. Their children are: Elmer, now in Glenmark; Miss Lelia, at home, and Alice, the wife of Marsden Crisler, of the Valley. (Lelia Green was married June 29, 1892, to Emory J. Weeks of Rose. They have a daughter, Eva L. Mrs. Green died June 16, 1893.)

Toward the north, and having a substantial aspect, is the old Garlick homestead. To-day it is the abode of the widow of Walter Messenger, who died March 30th, 1890. This family is of Sodus lineage, where both husband and wife, who was Jane Jewell, were born. They came hither in 1874. Their children are all married. Polly is Mrs. John Shepardson, of Sodus; Sarah married Sidney Garlick, a son of Eli, and lives next north; Louise is the wife of Seth Woodard, of the Covell neighborhood; Nellie married Darwin Miner, west of the Valley, and Walter married Ida J. Seager, and lives in Huron. The house dates from William Garlick. The original Garlick log house stood considerably further back from the road, where cherry trees now are. Mr. Messenger bought from William Chaddock, who traded his mill property at the falls with Henry Garlick for this. In the hands of sons and father, this was Garlick land for many years. Back of Garlick was Bacon, who followed the Lamberts, a family having numerous representatives, but very little real ownership. They, with other equally irresponsible people, were, more than fifty years since, prevailed upon to accept a free trip to the west. A canal boat was chartered at the expense of several public-spirited citizens, and some sixty or seventy people of both sexes, and of all ages, were loaded on and given this ride toward the setting sun. Save in a few cases where the adage, "A bad sixpence will return," was illustrated, the riddance was effectual. I suppose the donors of that excursion laughed heartily for years over the feelings of the communities among which these bouquets of Roses were scattered. The Garlick genealogy was given at length in the description of North Rose.

The Traher place is next encountered. Here lives Ellen Traher, whose first husband was John Howard, who, a member of the Ninth Heavy Artillery, died in a southern prison. She purchased ten acres of the old Converse farm, and has a small though ample home. (Her second husband, Harry Traher, died last spring, having long been an invalid.)

The road thence, for some distance, is down a steep decline, but the traveler who likes variety will be abundantly pleased with what he finds here. The face of nature is seamed and gashed with cuts so deep that he thinks himself lucky in getting along at all. At the foot of the hill, at the left, is the district school-house. Unhappy, barefooted children are puzzling over their tasks as I pass, and are wondering what schools are made for. We begin to take bitter doses early in life, that we may be happier and better later. The original site of the school-house was just about on the line, in the narrow place, where the road and stream lead out into Huron. The old foundations were visible on John Lovejoy's farm, when he came into possession.

The home of Mr. Lovejoy is built on the hill-side, and he has irregularities of surface wherever he looks. Mr. L. is the son of Daniel, whose home we found in the Lake district, on the corner. His wife was Elizabeth Jane Weeks, born in Rindge, N. H. Her father, Addison Weeks, came to Rose in 1854. His wife was Eliza Wellington, and their home was opposite the present Lovejoy abode. Another daughter is Mrs. Myron Lamb of No. Rose. The Weeks family of New Hampshire has long been one of the best in that state. To the Lovejoys were born these children: Sylvia, who married Frank Soper, of the Valley, and who will be met there; Effie, the wife of Nelson Bush, and Addison, who married Huldah Andrews, and is at home with his father. Addison's children are Frank and Ida. (Also, 1893, Myron J. and Addison Ray.) Mr. Lovejoy built his house, having bought his place of Oscar Weed. The farm is a part of the old Converse estate, and has fifty-two acres in it.

Dwelling nearly opposite is Leman Ellsworth, who occupies the old Addison Weeks place. The house has a water-edged garden back of it. Near this was the carding machine, maintained for many years by Horace Converse and his son. In the long ago, when wool was spun and woven at home, it was necessary to have the fleece worked into long, uniform rolls for the housewife to reduce to yarn. Then the carding machine was busy. Now that is relegated to the great factory, where spinning and weaving have become lost arts. Mr. Ellsworth was born in Phelps, and his only child is Alice, who married James Calkins, living on the farm to the southwest. They have one child, Eva.

The road and the stream are comrades as they lead out to the north. · At the left is the hill-side belonging to John Lovejoy. At the right are the lowlands of Ishmael Gardner. While the Rose part of the district is ended, it will not be amiss to follow on for a while. After a short distance, the road forks, to lead up and out in diverse ways. Should we go toward the east, we will be led along the darkest, most dangerous road in the town. It winds along the steep, densely-wooded hill-side, having on one side the descent so steep and deep that trees, growing in the bottom of the glen, have their tops on a level with the road. Following this to its exit from the woods, the traveler will find himself near the home of Harvey Barnes, the old Catchpole farm, and in the North Rose district. Monday, August 4th, 1890, Thomas Farnsworth, of Glenmark, drove his horse at high speed down this road, till, by some mishap, the whole equipage was launched over the verge and the man was instantly killed: another of the accidents that have from time to time carried sorrow to certain homes in Rose.

The west fork of the road carries us up a steep and winding way, passing several houses belonging to Oscar Weed. By the time we reach his home, the road will have swung around to the west. The large mansion of Mr. Weed is on the north side and is surrounded by shrubbery and trees. Close by are acres of fruit trees, usually the source of large returns. Mr. Weed has made the growing and drying of fruit a specialty. The Weed family came to Wayne county, originally, from Long Island. From it, is said to have come the famous Thurlow, so long the arbiter of New York politics. Oscar Weed was born in Galen, and his wife is Rebecca, née Watson, also of Galen. They came to this place in 1850, and to the 150 acres of the old Peter Paine farm he has added others, till now there are between two and three hundred acres therein. This elegant house he built in 1864. When constructed, there were numerous children at home to make merry its halls and chambers. The mutations of time have removed the most of these from the roof tree, so that now the Weeds find their habitation considerably larger than their needs require. These children are: Watson, who was graduated from Cornell in 1878, and is now a Unitarian minister in Ware, Mass. (now, Scituate); Addison, a graduate from Cornell in 1879, is a farmer in New Hartford, Oneida Co.; Mary, also a graduate from Cornell, is a teacher; Gerhardus, who died in 1878, at the age of eighteen years; Oscar Dillwyn, at home; and Ruth, who died at the age of sixteen years, in 1882, while visiting her brother, Watson, in Dakota. The latter married Frances Wright, of New Hartford, and was preaching in the west at the time of his sister's death. Addison married Ida Cleveland, also of New Hartford. It is noteworthy that both these sons have been the parents of twins.

Returning to the point where the road from York settlement runs into this, we shall find, just south of the bifurcation, the store and residence of Albert E. Ellis. Mr. E.'s wife is Mary, a daughter of the Barnum whom we found in the extreme north end of the Covell district, but who, owing to the death of his wife, lived, till his death, October 26th, 1890, with Mrs. Ellis. The store and home are neat and attractive and betoken thrift.

The site is one of the most noted in the town: for this is where the old Converse Hotel was located, and near here were the shops and mills which once made this an exceedingly busy hollow. The complete genesis of this locality at this late date is almost hopeless, but I will do the best I can. The name of Converse was once very common here, coming from Horace, who migrated hither from Pittsford, near Rochester. While a deal of business seemed to be done here, a class of people was called into the neighborhood whose presence gave all honest people much uneasiness. For instance, one man stole a horse from a clergyman. For this he received a sentence of four years in the Auburn prison. After his release, he became a respectable citizen in a western state. Visits from officers of the law were frequent and necessary, and Rose farmers must have learned that rural quiet is vastly preferable to activity associated, as this too often is, with vice. Converse managed a blacksmith shop, built two sawmills, conducted the carding machine, maintained a grocery, built and ran a hotel. This latter structure, after his death, was allowed to fall into decay. Mr. Converse's wife's name was Abigail. They had three sons and one daughter: Harriet, who married Charles Angle and went west; George married widow Susan Alford; Henry married Rebecca Angle; Charles succeeded his father in the business, and finally died in 1861, at the age of 47 years. It is more than probable that much which was laid at the door of these dwellers in the Glen, they were not guilty of, for the old adage, "Give a dog a bad name and send him to the d—l," applies fully in such cases. It is likely, too, that many instances told to-day are quite legendary.

James Van Auken built the carding mill and he sold his right to the Sodus Canal Co., from whose possession the place passed to Horace Converse. James Van A. was a brother of Simeon, and it is probable that he was the earliest owner. He joined the march to the west. How many other owners there may have been to date I can not state.

The road is narrow, and on the side of the glen, till we pass through and find, at the right, the place whose dwellers, in order, would afford a long list. Thomas Farnsworth, the latest tenant, was killed, as just noted. Mr. F. was born in England. His wife's maiden name was Julia A. Dunham. He bought the place of Sidney Garlick. The small building in which Ira Mirick once kept a store is still standing and yet indicates the purposes for which it was built. Near this place, on the hill, is where some of the first comers buried their dead, and among others Simeon Van Auken's first wife, Olive.

A number of small holdings are found as we pursue the road southward. At first, at the left, is an old blacksmith shop, where Eli Garlick shod horses. His home was the small house just beyond, now occupied by Christian Fink, formerly living south of Covell's. The road goes through a deep cutting and climbs quite an altitude until it emerges on the plain above. At the right is the place where the Marquettes and their descendants have lived for many years. Daniel, the first one, once lived further south on this road, nearly opposite the home of Seth Woodward.

The last farm in the district, on this road, is that of James French, who may be found on the west side of the road, just before reaching the railroad and the beginning of the Covell district. Mr. French was born in Ireland

and came to this place twenty years ago, and bought of John Shear. He married Sarah Bunyea, who was born in Wisconsin, of French extraction. She is a relative of Mrs. Ishmael Gardner, of North Rose, and of Chelsea Deming, of Huron. They have three children—Temperance, Ernest and Wallace—all at home, though Temperance is a teacher. There are fifty acres in the farm. (One of the sons is now in railroad employ in Oswego.)

Coming back to the point where this road emerged from the glen, we may turn to the east. In doing so, it will be necessary to cross a bridge which spans the creek just before it falls over its rocky verge. South of the bridge, there long existed a dam, which retained the waters of Thomas' creek, thus affording power for the mills below it. (Since rebuilt.) Simeon Van Auken was the builder of the dam and grist-mill. He came from Junius, and his wife was Olive Whitney, a sister of Seth Whitmore's wife. The Whitmores—Seth and Benjamin—were mill men from an early date. Mr. Van Auken married for his second wife the widow Wright, née Potwine, and she, too, died here. The Van Ankens were Presbyterians. They long since moved to Michigan and died. They sold to Dr. Peter Valentine, and he to Ira Mirick, who maintained a variety of interests. He sold to the Canal Co., from which Henry Young rented. This man lives now in Ontario. He had a son, Israel.

John Brown, a native of Pennsylvania, married Eveline Tindall, a sister of Chas. H. and "Parm," of the Valley. He held the mill for some time, but finally went to Michigan. Before doing so, he was for a while in Victor, in company with Brownell Wilbur, once of Rose. The Brown children were: Charles, who married Celia Tracy, of Huron, and now lives near Jackson, Mich., and with whom the father died; Juliette and Alfred, both of whom are dead. William Chaddock sold to Henry Garlick, or rather traded with him, and he sold to L. R. Ellis, who came hither from Tompkins county. He was formerly a Protestant Methodist minister. He married Elizabeth L. Yale of Cortland county. Their children are: Albert E., already met further north, and Lydia, who is at home. Mr. Ellis was a member of Battery A, 3d New York Artillery, during the War. The residence of the family is a very pleasant place, on the north side of the road, the same having shared the changes which have come to the mill property.

A private way leads towards the south, along the right bank of Thomas' creek, and in addition to a saw-mill we shall find the home of George T. Ellis. He is a son of Algernon, an Englishman. His wife was Clara Wolff, of Rose, and he bought of Wesley Burns, now of Alton. He purchased from George Correll, who bought of Ira Lathrop, who came here after selling his farm to the south, to Seymour Covell.

Still following this by-path, we gradually mount to the level above and find the abode of Abram Doremus, born in Mentz, Cayugo Co. He once lived where Frank Weeks is, in the York neighborhood. He married

Betsey Featherly, and their children are: George, in Jackson, Mich.; Lydia, the wife of William B. Hill, of North Rose; Adaline, the wife of Douglas Colborn, of the Valley; Jennette, the wife of Darwin Gillet, of Huron, and the twins—Helen and Ellen—who married the twin Briggs—Lyman and Luman. It should be said that these daughters, Helen and Ellen, are the oldest children. This is the old Featherly homestead; and in addition to Betsey there was Lydia Jane, who married Horace Morey. George Featherly was a son of John, one of the most noted settlers of the town. His boyhood's home was where the present Hetta abode is. His wife was Susan Kinkaid, and they bought this Doremus place of James Aldrich. The parents died years since, and this place of fifty-eight acres passed to Doremus, who repaired the house. This and the farm beyond are more isolated than any other places in the town.

Still pursuing a private way, and crossing the track of the R., W. & O. R. R., we find the home of Horace Morey, who married Lydia J. Featherly. His farm he took from the land office. The Morey children are: John, who married Rachel Smalley, and lives in North Rose, and Warren, also in North Rose, who married Carrie Desmond.

Coming back to the road, we turn to the right, and leaving at the corner the home of Mr. Ellis, so long a part of the mill belongings, we climb out of the glen. Years ago the table land beyond marked the beginning of the North Rose district, but in later times the dwellers in the first two abodes belong to Glenmark. The very first home is that in which lives Daniel Jeffers, a son of Nathan, and the place is the old Pardon Jones farm. Note of this was made in the North Rose series, but since then I have learned that the Nicholas Stansell who early settled there was a noted man in his day; a companion of John Featherly, whose sister he married. These two men, with William Stansell, came to Lyons in 1789; the settlers whose coming entitled the county to a centennial in 1889. They located first on what was afterward the Dorsey farm, near Alloway. There was nothing in the way of hardship and privation that these pioneers did not suffer. William Stansell was with Sullivan in his expedition against the Indians in 1779, and the lay of the land charmed him then. He was the leader of the expedition. It is traditional in the family that Featherly was a soldier in the Revolution also. Restless as the waves of the sea, these early hunters worked up into this section, and the name of Stansell is connected with this place, though it seems reasonable that he should have been before rather than after James Colborn, 1st.

With the farm on the south side of the road, the name of John A. Hetta has been connected for more than thirty years. He was born in Germany and found a wife in Mary A. Lamb, a daughter of John, of North Rose. They have only one child—Etha Jane—recently married to Irving J. Lane, of the Jeffers neighborhood. Mr. Hetta has imparted to all his surround-

17

ings many indications of the thrift so characteristic of the Germans. It was to this place that the pioneer, John Featherly, came when the century was young. It is probable that he was of Herkimer or Montgomery county derivation. His wife was Mary Claus, the same name we have found Anglicized as Closs. In his way hither, he had lived in Lyons and Phelps. His final remove was to the cemetery in York's corners. The children were Frederick, who married and died at Three River Point in Oswego county. Then followed George, met in the Doremus place; John, who went to Michigan; Joseph, killed, when young, by a sleigh tongue; Betsey, who moved to Cattaraugus county, and Catherine, who married William Baker, and once lived where the Sobers were reared, in the west part of the district.

DISTRICT NO. 4.—"THE VALLEY."

November 5, 1891—March 3, 1892.

PART I.

Our rambles in Rose have fully skirted the town, and now we approach the heart. For this purpose we will pass toward the west from District No. 6, or what is called Stewart's, and, passing the famous spring at the foot of the hill, we will pause first at the stone house on the north side of the road, for many years the property of Joel Lee. Of him and his, extended mention was made in the article ending District No. 6. It is on this location that one Lincoln is said to have squatted; but his happiness was disturbed by the frogs, that, to his fancy, were perpetually saying: "Don't you want to buy here, Lincoln?" This finally drove him out, when he sought a home further west, and on, let us hope, higher ground. Chester Ellinwood afterward owned, and from him possession passed to his oldest son, Ensign. The latter built the stone house, the material for whose outer courses he drew from Lake Ontario. Henry Robinson of the Lake district was the boss mason in the construction, thus assuring the character of the work. The house was begun in 1841 and finished in 1842. Ensign was twice married, first to Catharine Rifenbach of Newark, and, second, to Mrs. Egbert Brant of Lyons. She, Sarah J. Holmes, was born in Salisbury, Conn. By his first wife, he had two daughters, Jennie and Alice Irene. The latter died in infancy, and the former lived to be a beautiful, accomplished young woman of eighteen years. In October, the 26th day, 1889, Mr. Ellinwood was instantly killed by a train of cars in Newark. He had come down from Rochester, but, by mistake, took a train which ran no further than Newark. There he was killed while on the track of the N. Y. Central R. R. By a singular fatality this accident happened on his birthday, he being seventy-one years old on that day. Mr. Ellinwood, for many years, was one of the most noted teachers of vocal music in Wayne county. An excellent singer himself, he succeeded admirably in imparting his knowledge to others. After leaving the farm, he lived in several places—as Newark, Rochester and Wolcott. I met him last in August, 1889. I took the Clyde and Wolcott stage as it passed the road which enters the post road just east of Ensign Wade's. Mr. Ellinwood was aboard, having taken the stage from his brother Chester's, east of Stewart's corners. Every inch of the land through which we were riding was familiar to him. As boy and man, he had played and worked in every field. As we rode by the Ellinwood burial ground, he leaned out and held the spot in sight as long as it could be seen. I did not mention the subject of his thoughts, but I well knew that in his mind were the wife of his youth, the child that died in infancy, and the daughter who was borne there just as she was budding into womanhood. Into the privacy of such reflections, I would be the last to intrude. Little did I think that before the snows of winter fell, the husband and father would slumber beside his loved ones.

On the south side of the way and some rods to the west, is the abode of Morris Wager, who came hither from the preëmption road in the spring of 1880. His wife was, in girlhood, Ella Silver of Sodus. Their children are: Rose; Iva; Charles; Myrtle, and Willie, all at home. (Rose has since become the wife of Wm. D. Hickok.) Mr. W. makes a specialty of raspberry culture.

My earliest recollections of the place are coupled with the name of Samuel B. Hoffman, who had married the widow of Seth Brainard. She was an Ellinwood, Louise, a sister of Geo. W. and Orlando. The Brainards were from Oneida county, and were exemplary members of the Rose Methodist Episcopal Church. Mr. B. died in 1842. He was the builder of the house now standing. Mr. Hoffman was also a Methodist and prominent in the councils of the church. Mr. Brainard was a pioneer, though he died in his 38th year.

A few rods further west and we find the road leading south, forming the western boundary of Mr. Wager's farm. Men seventy years of age can remember when the trees were cut off to prepare for the road. The trees were used in building a log house for Elder Smith, the Baptist minister, the same being located on the old Valorus Ellinwood farm, or where Henry Decker now lives.

On both sides of the road are fields belonging to Ensign D. Wade. He followed his father, Dudley, on these acres. The father and family were named in full in the account of District No. 7. Ensign, as there stated, married Kendrick Sheffield's oldest daughter, Lucy. They have two children, Lulu and Frank. It is not impossible that Ensign may some day attain to the reputation that his father had in Rose and vicinity.   He certainly will if he will only add auctioneering to his vocation.   Before Dudley Wade's occupation, this was for many years the Chester Ellinwood farm.   He built the house and painted it red.   It was changed very little in his day, and here his large family was reared.   His wife was Sophronia Allen, a daughter of Ezra, of Butler, who had married a sister of Benj. Kellogg.   There were several Allen girls, and, in those early days, extra girls sought service in families where they were not so numerous, so Chester courted his wife in the kitchen of the old Blaine log house, north of Stewart's corners.   When they went to keeping house, it was in a primitive structure, near the present home of John Lyman, in the neighborhood then called "Peth."   This was away back in the twenties, and he carried fruit trees on his back from the Daniel Roe place in Butler to set out here.   It is probable that he was born in Vermont, and there he learned the trade of a tanner, at which he worked to some extent after coming to Wayne county.   He was a soldier in the War of 1812.   This corner farm was bought of Samuel Southwick.   On the south side of the road, it included the cemetery lot and joined the Fuller farm on the west. The original log house was near the southwest corner of this burial ground. It caught fire in the early times and smouldered away two days before it was put out.   Finally it was taken down and relaid, near where the Wade house now is.   In those days there were 140 acres, extending, on the east, to the foot of the hill on Joel Lee's place.   The children born to Chester Ellinwood were: Ensign Warren ; Charlotte M., who became the wife of Gibson Center, of Butler, and is now in Weedsport; Lucy Lemira, who married Peter B. Decker, from Newark, and lived in the Valley.   Her sons, Charles Ensign and Franklin Pierce, died in infancy ; her daughter, Ellen Irene, married in Washington, Penn.   Mrs. Decker died in 1852, at the age of twenty-eight years.   Mr. Decker's second wife was a niece of the famous school teacher, Abigail Bunce.   Mr. Ellinwood's third daughter, Mary, is the wife of Dr. G. C. Childs, long a noted physician in Clyde ; Charles Judson married Helen F. Gildersleeve, of Galen, and died in 1879, in Grand Rapids, Mich., leaving two children, Frederick and Dolly. Ezra Chester, the youngest son, married Mary E. Phillips, of Newark, and, some years since, located on the old Wisner or Center place, east of Stewart's corners.   His oldest child, Irene P., died in 1884, at the age of fourteen years.   His remaining children are: Mary Louise, John Clark, Chester and Robert Ensign.   If there was one characteristic in these Ellinwoods more prominent than another, it was their love for music. As boys and girls, men and women, they excelled in song.   Of Lucy Lemira it is said that on her death bed she picked out those whom she wished to sing at her funeral, not wishing, she said, to have any breakdowns over her.   Late in life, the elder Ellinwood moved from the farm, and died in 1877, at the age of eighty-four years. His wife had died eleven years before. The younger Chester lived here also for a time.

Turning to the north and passing the evaporator of Ensign Wade, we shall find, on the west side of the road, all that is left of the home of Samuel Ellis Ellinwood ; in the town he was generally known as Ellis. He came hither from Oneida county, an uncle of Geo. W. Ellinwood, and for several seasons taught school, among other places, at Stewart's corner. His wife was Submit Southwick, a daughter of Samuel S., one of the pioneers of the town. For many years they dwelt here, prospering, and uniformly possessing the highest esteem of all who knew them. They were among the earliest members of the Methodist Episcopal Church in Rose. Their home passed through the usual changes, from primary simplicity to the comfort of later days. They had only one son—David—who for many years dwelt here with his parents. The elder Ellinwoods died in 1879 and 1866 respectively, and lie now in the Rose cemetery. They were first buried in the Ellinwood ground, but when later their granddaughter, Adele, erected a monument to them and to her parents, their remains were taken up and reburied. David Ellinwood was long prominent in local affairs, a man who liked a good horse and liked to drive him. He married Mary Jane Jones, of the Valley, a sister of Mrs. "Ham" Closs. She was an excellent lady, well worthy of the esteem in which she was held. They had two children—George, who is now in Racine, Wis., and Harriet Adele, who is a teacher in Toledo, Ohio. She was the generous and filial giver of the mortuary tribute standing in the Rose cemetery. David Ellinwood and his wife went west, and died there in 1883 and 1884 respectively.

There is one more house in this district toward the north, that of Theodore McWharf. Him and his I discussed at length in the No. 3. The house was built on lands purchased from Ellis Ellinwood by James Campbell, who died in 1869. His widow, Eleanor, lived in it till she sold to Mr. McWharf. She resided in the Valley till October, 1889, when she died at the age of seventy-five. She had long been an object of tender care and sympathy to the Methodist Episcopal Society of Rose, of which she was a member.

On the leaving of David Ellinwood for the west, he sold to Thomas Cullen, a native of Waterford county, Ireland. His wife was Mary Dunn. Mr. C. died in 1884, but the widow and children are still on the farm. At the time of David E.'s selling, he occupied the house at the top of the hill as we go west from Ensign Wade's. It is proper, in passing, to remark on the excellent care manifested in maintaining the Ellinwood cemetery, as nothing speaks better or louder the character of a people than their care for the resting places of their dead. From the ancestor worshipping Chinese to the dead neglecting Turk, the distance is a long one. While we may not approve the Chinese extreme, we ought to carefully shun the Turkish level. The Cullens, after buying the farm, which included both the old Ellinwood and Fuller places, instituted some changes. The barns on the north farm were moved up to a point nearly opposite the house, and the Ellinwood house was relegated to the use of tenants, a condition that can only have one end, viz., decay and ruin. Nature seemed to object to the new departure, for one day lightning struck the newly-placed structures and destroyed them. Since then a very large and convenient barn has been erected west of the house and on the same side of the road. Recently the family has made quite extensive repairs on the house. Mr. and Mrs. Cullen have had four children—Thomas, William, John and Mary, all of whom are at home. Before the David Ellinwood occupation of the house, was Dudley Wade, who came here from his old home in No. 7. Before Mr. Wade, was Brownell Wilbur, who came, early in the fifties, to Rose from Hamilton. Mrs. Wilbur, before marriage, was Elizabeth Roswell, a native of Washington county. Their children were Marvin A. and Helen A., both prominent in the intellectual and social life of the town. From this farm the family went to the place now owned by William McMurdy, south of the Valley. Thence they moved to Victor, Ontario Co., where the parents died. They were life-long, devoted members of the Baptist Church. In Victor, Marvin married Ida M. Dewey, and has a son and daughter. He was one of the best school teachers ever in Rose. He was once a candidate for the position of commissioner of schools, and had he been on the other side in politics, would have been elected. However, his defeat never seemed to hinder his growth in the least. Helen married also, and went west. She is Mrs. T. T. Maffit of Walnut Ridge, Ark. Erastus Fuller, the first owner of this place, was a native of Connecticut, and probably a descendant of the Mayflower Fullers. During his childhood, he suffered extreme vicissitudes, knowing very little of the pleasures of home; but, as frequently happens, he came out all the stronger for this severe discipline. His wife was Anna Brown, and her children were Ralph, Mary and Almanda. The last we met in District No. 7 as the wife of Delos Seelye. Mary will be seen as the wife of Hiram Mirick. Ralph married, first, Mary Allen, of Butler, and, second, Barbara Hendricks of Rose. His children are Marina, the wife of S. Harrison Ellinwood; William Erastus and Jerome, all of whom live in Fenton, Oakland Co., Mich. Erastus Fuller was one of the first officers in the town and always received the very highest respect and consideration of his fellow townsmen. An anecdote is told which illustrates well the universality of some stories. As a boy, I had heard the following from my father, given as an answer to a question of "'Squire" Fuller, who was desirous of knowing the difference between an owl and a sparrow-hawk: "It is *fuller* in the head, *fuller* in the body, and *fuller* all over."

I have no doubt that many a Rose dweller considered it original, but it really dates from the days of Thomas Fuller, prebend of Salisbury, in the days of Charles the First of England. He was noted for his fondness of punning, and the above was given by a gentleman named Sparrowhawk in reply to the prebend's query, as already told. As the clergyman was very corpulent, the significance of the rejoinder is evident. After a while the management of affairs was given up to Ralph, and in the early fifties, '53 or '54, he sold to B. Wilbur, and the family started west. Ralph, however, was fated not to see the promised land, for he died at Niagara Falls, on his way, after a very brief illness. The parents went on, and died in Fenton.

Where now is the substantial home of the family of Charles Sherman, Jonathan Ellinwood located very early in the century—1818. If there was any one back of him on these acres, it was only some contractor, whose obligation Ellinwood took and carried out. He was a native of Vermont, so said, though it is possible that he was born in Massachusetts, and, like so many others, tried life for a time in the Green Mountain State, and thence emigrated to these western wilds. His wife was Naomi Weeks, and together they saw much of pioneer hardships. They were the parents of Chester, already encountered; Thomas, who was drowned at Newark in the early days of the Erie canal; Lucius, William and Betsey. The last was the wife of William Porter, probably from Oneida county. They lived for a time on the stone house farm, now Joel Lee's. Both are dead. A son, Henry, lives in Lansing, Mich. Lucius, who lived for many years on the farm now held by Harlan Wilson, married, first, Lucy A. Allen, of Butler, who died in 1838. Their children were Thomas Henry, for many years a citizen of Clyde, and S. Harrison, of Fenton, Mich. He was mentioned among the Fullers as the husband of Marina. He has one son, Charles, who lives in Rose, Mich. Lucius married, second, Mahala Davis (a relative of the Butler family), who died in 1864. They had three children, two of whom—William S. and Lucy Ann—died in childhood, and Adelbert D., who married Frank, a daughter of Jacob Seager, of Clyde, the whilom band leader of the old Ninth Heavy Artillery. "Dell," as he was called, died in Lyons in 1889. Lucius died in Clyde in 1884, at the age of eighty-one years. The first comers, Jonathan and his wife, passed away in 1842 and 1840 respectively. It is remembered that the funeral of the former was held in the door yard, which sloped down to the road from the old house, now standing back of the Sherman house. Jonathan was a half brother of the father of Ellis, the nearest neighbor to the northeast. As is frequently the case, William, the youngest son, took the management of the old farm before the death of his parents. He married Clarissa L. Thompson, of Butler. One child of this union, Mary Matilda, lies in the Ellinwood burial ground, and the father himself was laid there before his child, in 1844, at the early age of thirty-one years. The widow married William Sherman, a son of Elias D., and frequently met in our town wanderings. She went west long since. William lies in the Ellinwood cemetery, having died in 1862, at the age of thirty-nine years. To them succeeded Samuel Hoffman, who sold to George G. Wickson, of Lyons, and he, in 1852, sold to Charles B. Sherman.

Of Charles Sherman, extended mention was made in the No. 7 series, and now it is only necessary to make a few additions. Frank's wife was Eveline Moore, of West Butler, and he lives in Rochester. Willard died in March, 1889; his only daughter, Ada P., married Louis F. Lux, of Clyde, and lives in Rochester; George, who died in May, 1889, left a family, to be met in the Valley; Charles, who married Mary Gotier of New York; Lucy, as Mrs. Putnam Sampson, still lives on the Clyde road; Ezra, in Company C, 111th N. Y., was an energetic boy, lost in the wild whirl of war; his folks still preserve letters, written as a soldier. Nothing so well portrays the true farmer's lad as the postscript to a letter sent from Virginia in the winter of 1863. Here it is: "How does my mare look this winter? Good-by." Out of the preparations for killing men, all about him, his mind goes to the peaceful home in the north, and he thinks of the colt which had excited his boyish pride and pleasure. I was a prisoner of war at the same time with Ezra, though not in the same place. He was on Belle Isle, and I have since learned that his father, Charles Sherman, and my grandfather, Col. George Seelye, frequently debated the organization of a crusade, to march through the south to liberate the captives. Perhaps it is quite as well for all that the plans of these well meaning, elderly gentlemen were not undertaken. The parents of Charles Sherman's second wife were from Oneida county, though the family was originally from Connecticut. Their children are: Chester T., Ezra A., and Hattie E. The name Ezra continues that of the boy who perished in the strife. It is claimed, and with propriety, that these young people (Hattie is 22 years old in 1893) are the youngest Revolutionary grandchildren in the country. Chester T. was married in 1892 to Harriet C. Kimberly, of Auburn. It was in 1854, or '55, that Mr. Sherman moved the old Ellinwood house back and constructed the present convenient and commodious edifice. The old house still stands near the corn house, a relic of the long ago. In addition to the Ellinwood farm, Mr. Sherman bought largely from the east and north part of Hiram Mirick's place, thus giving him one of the largest farms in the town. The northwest part of this he sold to his son, George, but of that more hereafter. Born in 1804, in Phelps, Ontario Co., and coming into the town at the early date of 1811 or '12, Mr. Sherman could tell pretty nearly all there was to be told of pioneer life. When young, though not a large man, he was very athletic, and he and Isaac Crydenwise contracted to cut 100 cords of wood for Peter Gordon, of Galen. This they did, averaging six cords per day. Crydenwise was a smaller man than Sherman. When the town lines were run out, Mr. S. assisted in the survey, and it is said that he was one of the first to work on the Erie canal, when this great venture of DeWitt Clinton was started. After paying for several farms by his own work, he at last flagged, and finally passed away in 1883.

The Rose Shermans are all descendants from that Captain John Sherman, of Revolutionary service, who was one of the early comers to the town. His grandson, Chester, now in government employ in Washington, has taken pains to look up his pedigree, and he finds that the pioneer was born in Shrewsbury, Mass., March 27th, 1764, whence he moved to Conway, in the same state. He had a brother, Caleb, born May 14th, 1762, and a sister, Chloe, born August 4th, 1765. He afterward moved to Phelps, N. Y. The first Sherman in America, of this line, was Captain John, who came from Essex, England, to Connecticut, though he seems to have settled in Watertown, Mass. He was a cousin of Samuel, and the Rev. John Sherman, with whom he came to this country. From this cousin branch, descended Senator John Sherman and his brother, General William T. This first Captain John Sherman married Martha Palmer, and died in 1690, January 25th; his son, Joseph, was born in Watertown, Mass., March 14th, 1650, and married Elizabeth Winthrop, November 18th, 1673. He had three sons—John, born January 11th, 1674; Joseph, born February 8th, 1679; William, born June 28th, 1692, who was the father of Roger Sherman, one of Connecticut's signers of the Declaration of Independence. John was in the line leading to Rose, and he appears to have been in Marlborough, Mass.; for there were born his sons—Joseph, 1703; Ephraim, 1710; John, 1713; Samuel, 1718. Joseph married Sarah Perrum, of Sutton, December 25th, 1728; his son, John, born in Shrewsbury, Mass., April 8th, 1737, married Chloe Thayer, of Bellingham, Mass., 1761, who died in 1766, May 26th, at the age of twenty-five years. This brings us again to our Rose pioneer. He married Chloe, daughter of Elias Dickinson, of Conway, who also migrated to Phelps, and died in 1806. The family flight to Phelps appears to have been made in 1790. The further removal to Rose was not until 1811 or '12. A deed is still in existence, stating that John Sherman, in 1810, bought of John and Anne Nicholas part of tract surveyed for Sir John Lowther Johnstone and Lady Charlotte, his wife, by Seth Whitmore, 301 acres, except fifty acres, northwest corner, sold to William Orton, Jr. This location must have been along the west side of the old Block House road, now the main street of the Valley. He early built a log tavern, standing near the present residence of F. H. Closs. The children of Capt. John Sherman were: Claramond, born in Conway, Mass., October 7th, 1791, and who married

Charles Woodard, once residing in Rose; Elias D., born 1794 in Phelps; Wealthy, 1796; Paulexana, 1800; Sarah, 1802; Charles Billings, 1804, and John, always known in Rose as "Jack." Of the Woodards extended mention will be made later. Elias D., with his father, was conspicuous for physical strength, and many an acre of woodland was cleared by their vigorous strokes. He lived in different places in Rose. We have encountered him on the William Finch place, where he cleared a considerable portion of the farm. He was twice married; his first wife was Wealthy Griswold, of Rose; his second, Roxy Neal, who died October 28th, 1871, in Galesburg, Ill. He had a numerous family; by his first wife, there were: William, frequently met in these sketches, born in Rose, as were all of Elias' children; certain data were given concerning him in No. 7; to him and his wife came six sons: William Henry, killed at the Wilderness, a member of the 111th; Charles Eugene, died in infancy; Charles Elvin, now in Carsonville, Mich.; William E., also in Carsonville; Lewis E., Barry, Illinois; George Wallace, died in childhood; Mrs. William Sherman died May 9th, 1887, in Bridgehampton, Mich., and was buried in Forester; Joseph Sherman was born Sept. 27th, 1823, and died in Belmont, Mich., January 15th, 1889; he lost one of his legs in a saw-mill, and it is said was the inventor of rubber cords for wooden legs; Orra was born November 4th, 1825, and lives now in Watkins, N. Y., though he long lived in this town. He was a harness maker, and had a shop on Main street, next door to the house now occupied by Daniel Johnson, though the house is not standing now; he built the houses occupied by Lucien Osgood and by widow Snow; he has been three times married and has three children; Eliza Sherman, born in 1827, died in 1884; Orrin, born in 1829, studied medicine and died in Rose; Levi, born in 1834, is a photographer in Rochester; he served in the cavalry during the War; Franklin N., born in 1836, now in Three Rivers, Mich., also in the Rebellion, from the west; Elias D., born 1839, lives in Watkins; Wealthy died in childhood; Elias D. Sherman, by his second wife, had a son, John, now living in Comstock, Mich. Elias D. died September 28th, 1870. Of the second generation of Shermans, Wealthy married a Mr. Joy, and both lived and died on the lake shore, near Medina, N. Y.; Paulexana married Luther Chapman, in Phelps, though they lived in Buffalo and Adrian, Mich. She died in 1844, and is buried in Buffalo; Sarah became Mrs. Truesdale, and moved to Barry, south of Rochester, where she died. The youngest son, John, or "Jack" in Rose parlance, was a well-known dweller here. His wife was Olive Crydenwise, a sister of that Isaac C. who married Sophia Thomas. The children were: Cordelia, Caleb, Emily, Charles H., Harrison, Harriet. Charles was a Company A, Ninth Heavy Artillery man. When the War was over he went west, married Nancy Keyes, in Michigan, in 1866, and went to Missouri in 1867. He has a large farm.

where he is rearing a family of nine children. John Sherman, on leaving Rose, went to Battle Creek, Mich., where he died, March 23rd, 1891. His Rose home at one time was at or near Minerville, northwest of the Valley. This man, old as he was, was a soldier in the Rebellion. He enlisted in Company H, 111th N. Y., February 6th, 1861, and was discharged September 10th, 1861. His widow, at last accounts, was still living in Joppa, Mich. In addition to Charles, already mentioned, of John's children, Cordelia married Wesley Castor, and died in Oakland county, Mich.; Caleb, married, died at Fortress Monroe, in war times ; Harrison married Mary Copeland ; Harriet is the wife of Ephraim Allen, of Joppa, Mich., while Emily, unmarried, is living with her mother. Going back to Charles B. Sherman, the student of names will be glad to know that Billings, his middle name, is thought to have come from Clara Billings, a friend or distant relative of the family. The first name, Clara, was given to the oldest daughter, and Billings, later, to a son. The first son, Elias D., clearly bore in full the name of his mother's father, Elias Dickinson, the Phelps pioneer.

Back of the Sherman house, the land rises until it reaches the very highest point in the town, said to be 140 feet above the level of the lake. From the pinnacle one may look easily into all the surrounding towns. We stand above the Mirick hill, on the west, and can see the range of hills west of Wayne Centre. Only the foliage of the trees prevents a clear view of the lake twelve miles away. Eastward the Loveless hills and those east of South Butler appear. To the south the ends of many ranges arise, those leading through Galen and beyond. Nearer, the outlook includes all that makes Rose attractive to the native or acclimated foreign born. The road, winding along as the Melvins, Harmons and Stewarts left it ; the farm houses, successors to the humble log houses which supplanted the wilderness ; the fields ripening for the harvest ; the farmers at their useful toil ; while "Round about them orchards sweep,"—the prospect is a glorious one ; but it may be doubted whether a dozen Rose people ever climbed the hill to see what it unfolds. The immediate north view is cut off by the trees still standing, but in my anxiety that the old trees may still remain, I will cheerfully forego any pleasure of the eye, in prospect, that Rose may still include a little of the "forest primeval."

Many people who have traveled this, one of the most crooked roads in the town, will recall a house, I think it was always old, which stood on the east side, just as the road swings around to the south, after passing Sherman's. I understand that it was built by one George Fairbanks, who had married Eliza, a daughter of John Wade. Inclined to the use of the " ardent," he had, nevertheless, quite a local reputation as a horse doctor, butcher and sheep shearer. When " half seas over" he was extremely polite. He and his sought the oblivion that the west afforded to so many denizens of this town. After him came a host of tenants, all of whom seemed to abound in shoeless, noisy children. In time the house disappeared. It is now the barn on the Louis Town place, in the Valley. The well was filled up, and only an extra growth of weeds marks its site.

From this point southward, we are on land that once stood in the name of Thaddeus Collins, 1st, and after him, his sons. Before him, was the famous Nicholas and Rose purchase, and our first halt is at the home of the Harts. To this place Marvin D. Hart, first met in District No. 9, came some years ago, and here he died, June 21, 1888. Mr. Hart was descended from William Hart, who came from England to Rhode Island in the eighteenth century. His son, Samuel, born June 2, 1791, when twelve years old, with an older brother, Rodman, migrated to Seneca county. He served in the War of 1812, and was later a surveyor. He was married December 18, 1817, to Hester Hobrow, born in Liverpool, Eng., June 4, 1791, locating on a farm in Junius. Marvin D., the fifth of six children, and the second son, was born April 5, 1850. In addition to a common school training he was one year at Oberlin. Coming to Rose in 1857, he was married September 23, 1857, to Mary J. Miner. Save four years, from 1871, spent at the old home in Junius, his residence was Wayne county till his death. For generations the Harts were Baptists. Mrs. Hart and her daughter, Alice M., with her aged father, Mr. Miner, maintain a very pleasant and attractive home. Long resident with Mrs. Hart, her aged father, Isaac Miner, is the oldest man in Rose. Born April 12, 1792, in Stonington, Conn., he is very near a century old. His memory recalls vividly the War of 1812. He came with his parents to Winfield, Herkimer county, when young, and there was married to Survilla Gould. Later, he came to Butler, thence he went to Scipio, Cayuga county, and next to Castile, Wyoming county. Finally they returned to Butler. His wife lived till past the seventy-first marriage anniversary. He walks the streets erect, without the aid of a cane. His mind is clear and his memory retentive. (Mr. Miner died just short of his 100th birthday, December 31, 1891, and was buried in Wolcott.)

Years since, a small house on this site was the home of the noted shoemaker, "Johnny" Ogram. This man had a reputation peculiarly his own. No matter how many pairs were promised ahead, one could always have his boots "next Saturday night." If the recording angel took down all the swearing that was done on account of this foible of "Johnny," he must have been kept pretty busy on Saturdays, 'long toward 9 P. M. It is said that Michael Vandercook kept account of the number of his disappointments, and when he did get his boots, he sued the cordwainer and made him pay for all the trouble he had given him. Ogram was said to be a little more careful thereafter. His shop was built of logs and was hard by. Dr. John J. Dickson and Eron Thomas bought quite extensively

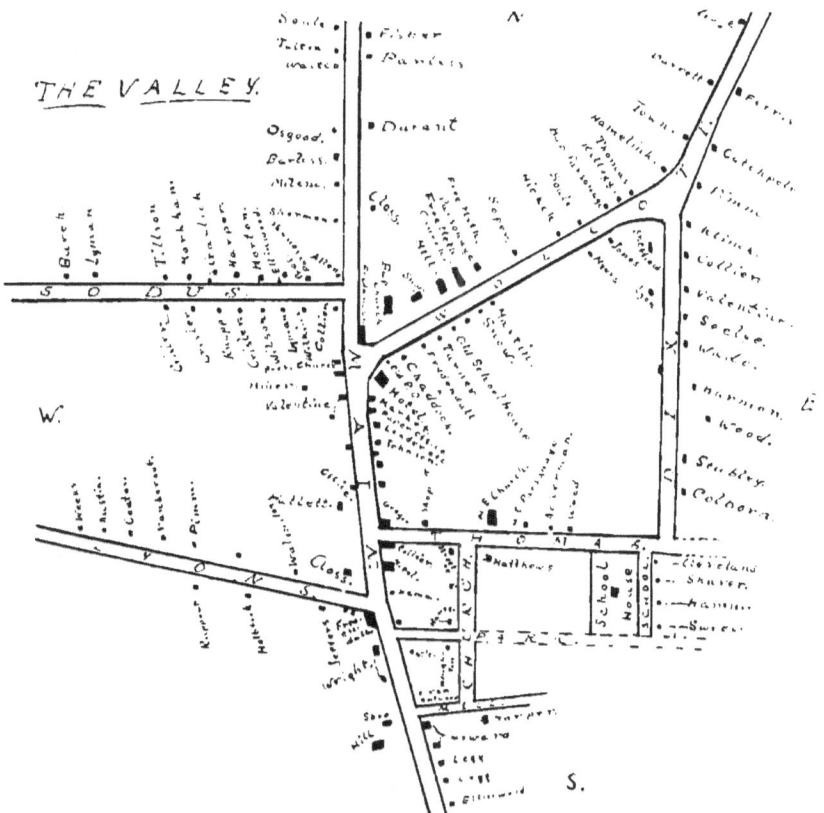

PLAN OF ROSE VILLAGE.

from this point southward, and the old house was rented to many occupants. In it died Richard Deady, a brother of John, 2d, of District No. 5, and grandfather of Ambrose, now in Huron. Dickson sold to Peter Harmon, who erected the house long conspicuous as we approach the village. He sold to Henry C. Rice, a native of Seneca county, the greater part of whose life had been passed in Butler, where he had owned a large farm. He was twice married. The three children by this first marriage—Sarah, Mary and Henry—never lived in Rose, but were married and residents elsewhere, before the moving to this town. His second wife was Catharine B. Ladue, of Butler. Their adopted daughter, Helen, became the second wife of Harvey J. Ferris. Mr. Rice added a little to the land for garden and flower purposes, and always made his home exceedingly attractive. Though ever an attendant, it was not until comparatively late in life that he became a member of the Methodist Episcopal Church, in whose communion he died in 1876. He was buried in Butler Centre. After him came Marvin D. Hart.

More than twenty years since, James Harvey Ferris, who had been a hard working Butler farmer, determined to make Rose the home of his declining years, and so bought here land that ranges back through the hands of Darwin Dickinson, Thomas and Closs, C. B. Collins, Thaddeus Collins, first, etc. There were at first some thirty-eight acres, which, saving the lots of George Sherman and R. D. Dickinson, are now in the Ferris possession. Deacon Ferris built a large house, adapted to two families, and here, in the south part of the structure, with his wife, he lived till his death, in 1885. He was a native of Ira, in Cayuga county : his wife was Esther Terpening, born in Saratoga county. They had six children, who married as follows : Jane, to Christopher Caywood ; Mary, Frank Cobb, of Ouray, Col. ; Harriet, married Darwin Dickinson ; Henry, deceased, who married Lena Albright. She afterward became the second wife of Benjamin Bishop, of Butler. The second son, Cornelius, married Milly Platt, in Michigan, and is a very prosperous resident of Denver, Col. The youngest son, Harvey, married, first, Alice, the oldest daughter of James Armstrong, of Rose, and second, Helen Rice. Their home is in the north part of this large house, and they have a numerous family, bearing the names of Mabel A., Edith M., Nellie R., Edna J. and Harvey L. Mrs. Henry C. Rice makes her home here, while Harvey works the paternal acres. When the road, which turns to the north at Harlan Wilson's, is properly extended, it will enter the village somewhere between the Hart and Ferris houses. The extension cannot come any too soon.

The next house was erected by George Sherman. He had taken what is now the Campbell place, north of the Valley, from his father, Charles, and after some years of industrious labor, most efficiently supplemented by his wife, Sybil Wilson, had retired from it with what seemed a competence for life. He then built this house, and here lived till his death, in 1888. Mrs. Sherman is one of that noted family of Wilson girls, and has ever been a most excellent wife and mother. Her children are G. Adelbert, and Rena, the wife of G. Collins Wood. Since the death of Mr. Sherman, Ephraim Wilson, 2d, a brother of Mrs. S., has lived in the house with her. His wife's name before marriage was Ella Armstrong, daughter of James. They have three daughters, Jessie, Alice and Ruth. Mr. W. is by trade a painter and paper hanger. (This place, with many improvements and additions, is now the home of George Catchpole, formerly of District No. 3, and here, in April 21, 1893, his wife died.)

R. Darwin Dickinson built the next house. We encountered him first in our way through District No. 2, as the oldest son of William D. In that series, the names of his children were given. Harvey and Merville are about leaving Idaho for Fair Haven, Washington, and Carrie, who has successfully passed through the Albany Normal School, is to go to Idaho as a teacher. Her mother will accompany her. (Mrs. Dickinson died August 1, 1892, in Ilaly, Idaho, and her remains were brought to Rose for burial.) John A. Drown resided in the house till recently. Mr. Drown was mentioned in the series on the Griswold district. The Van Horns, whose daughter, Hannah S., he married first, lived once on the place now possessed by Fred Ream. Mrs. Drown died in 1878. She was the mother of Henry, resident in Michigan; Newton A. and George W., both living in Rochester. Mr. Drown is an earnest Christian man, who enjoys a restful life, earned by former years of application to business. Mr. D. lately moved to the west. (Now held by E. T. Pimm.)

As the road once ran along to the west, with no southern continuation, we will follow the old line and notice, first, the home of Joel Sheffield, located on the corner. Here, long since, the first James Colborn built the first stave factory in the village. He sold it to William Sebring, who came hither from Wayne Centre, and went thence to Michigan. Stephen Waite owned afterward, and he built the house. To him succeeded John Gillett, an acquaintance of District No. 9, who died here in 1866. The present owner, Joel Sheffield, has frequently appeared in these sketches. He has been road commissioner, supervisor and postmaster in spite of his being a Democrat in a Republican town. Had his politics accorded with those of the majority of his fellow citizens, it would be difficult to enumerate the positions he might have held. He has long been chorister of the Baptist Church, superintendent of the Sunday school and one of the most important members of that body, i. e., the Baptist organization, much of the musical ability and religious fervor of his father, James, having descended to him. He and his wife, Nannie Osgood, have only one child, Harriet Eudora. In the next house abides the widow of Pardon Jones, whose acquaintance was made in the North Rose district. (Died

January 22, 1893, aged 79 years.) A small turbine water wheel on the porch is an advertisement of the business which her son, George, follows in Auburn. Abel Lyon was before the Jones family, and Stephen Waite built the house. Widow Mary Myers dwells next. She came from Lock Berlin. I might state that though widows abound on this street, it is by no means forlorn. I believe, beginning with widow Cullen and stopping with widow Chaddock, there are sixteen good women who are husbandless. Some one has recently counted up sixty widows in Rose, thus proving, I suppose, that the men work harder than the women. Isaac Race built the house, and his widow sold it. Mrs. Myers has a daughter, who married the late John Decker, of North Rose. Mrs. Jones owns a vacant lot intervening between Mrs. Myers' home and that of the widow of John Gillett, now Mrs. Center.

Across the small run is the house which Howard Foster built. He was interested with the Fredendalls in the mill, east of the Baptist Church. Mrs. Center, who now owns the place, is the widow of Gansevoort Center, of Butler, as well as of John Gillett, of Rose. (Died September 19, 1892, in 79th year.)

The widow of Alonzo Snow, who lives in the next house, has improved it very much since she bought of widow Betsey Peck. Levi Lyman preceded her, and the house was built by Orrin Sherman. Alonzo Snow formerly lived on the Ogram place, south of the Valley. Mr. Snow came here from Madison county. Mrs. Snow was Mary Shattuck, of Poolville, Madison county. They had no children, but their adopted daughter, Carrie, was Mrs. Harlan Wilson, of Rose.

The house in which Frank Blake lives has something of a history. In the long ago, when the old red tavern stood in front of the space occupied by the present Frank H. Closs house, this was a part of it, possibly the bar-room. On the demolition of the tavern, Daniel C. Alexander, the blacksmith, bought this part and moved it back of his shop. Later it took another move and, by Levi Lyman, was planted where it now is. Thus it is probable that the structure dates from the days of Charles Thomas, or Jacob Miller, the pioneer. Mr. Blake, the present occupant, succeeded to the business of Brewster Soper and drives an express between Rose and Clyde.

The old stone school-house follows, but a special chapter will be given to the schools and school-houses of the Centre district.

The daughter of Philip Turner owns the next house. She is a granddaughter of Geo. W. Ellinwood. The building formerly stood on the hill, to the northeast, and it was once occupied by Charles Wright, who bought it of Ovid Allen.

Charles Wright formerly owned the next house also. It then stood on the hill, near the evaporator. One De Golyer bought a lot of the Miricks and moved a part of this present house upon it. He used it as a furniture store-shop. The main upright has been erected since. Hudson R. Wood owned and occupied along in the early seventies, and after him, William Deady resided here with his numerous family. His wife was Janette Jeffers, the twin sister of Mrs. H. R. Wood. Though for some time a resident in Lyons, it will not be amiss to name here the children born in Rose. There were three boys, of whom two were twins: Schuyler Colfax. John Q. and George. The daughters are: Ida H., Florence and Jessie. A Robinson next possessed, and he sold to Jerry Barrett, the present owner. The occupant is George Collier, who married Mary E., daughter of Jackson Valentine.

The corner is reached and the last house, where resides the widow of William Chaddock, 2d. Extended mention was made of her family in the No. 9 series. Peter Decker, Chester Ellinwood's son-in-law, built the house and Willard Sherman dwelt here for some time and, after him, Chester Ellinwood, when he left his farm.

We must return to the northeast entrance to the village and begin again. As usual, we are on old Collins soil and the first house is owned (and now occupied) by S. Wesley Gage, whose wife was a Collins. They were encountered in the Covell district. He built the house, though before him, as owners of the lot, were Sheldon R. Overton and William Chidester.

In the next abode may be found William Kellogg, met in the Butler part of District No. 7. The place is a portion of the estate of Abel Lyon, deceased. The latter was for many years prominent in the counsels of the Methodist Episcopal Church; came here from Red Creek; on his death, his remains were borne thither for burial. There was for many years in his household a grandson, McLane, who is now a successful banker in the west. Mr. McCoy, who came to Rose from Oswego, built the house. He went from Rose to Youngstown, Ohio. (Now owned by Lewis Barrett, whose wife died here May 24, 1893.)

Mrs. Clarinda Town, the widow of Milton, with her son, Lewis S., lives in the next house. Mr. Town, in addition to looking after the paternal acres in District No. 6, is a very successful dealer in dried fruit, going each season to the west for this purpose. The house was built by Charles Deady for the use of his mother, who died here several years since. W. M. Osborne, now of Lyons, once lived here.

Luman Barrett, tiring of the routine of his farm life in Huron, has come to the next house, the property of Elder M. H. De Witt, now of Pennsylvania, but for a short time the pastor of the Rose Baptist Church. He inherited it from W. M. Cole, whose daughter he had married. Another daughter, Angeline, was one of my earliest teachers in District No. 7. Mr. Cole was long a resident of Butler, but he came to this village to pass his last years. The Holcombs also lived here for some time, after leaving their farm in District No. 5. Isaac Race was the builder of the house. (Now occupied by Derrick Hamelink, first met in District No. 11.)

William H., better known as "Bill" Thomas, resides in the next house, of which he is the builder. He married Polly Dodds, a daughter of William, and her aged mother makes her home here. The Thomases had only one daughter, Jennie, who was the wife of John Kaiser. She died October 4, 1891, at the age of 36 years, leaving three children.

Mr. Thomas was a wagon maker and, in company with M. T. Collier, managed the business for many years, further along the street. He died suddenly September 29, 1891, aged 65 years. Mr. Thomas' father was Nathan W., whose old home will be noted when we reach the Free Methodist Church.

The Baptist parsonage is the next house, and, of course, its occupants in all the years have been many. Elder Clemence Shaw has lived in it till recently. He has three children: Herbert, Jennie and Addie. Mr. Shaw came here from Ontario, but he was originally from the northern part of the state. Harrison Valentine built the house which marks the site of William Sebring's cooper shop. (In 1893 the home of Rev. M. H. Cusic and family.)

Ira Soule, who follows, was born in Middleboro, Mass., a descendant of George Soule, who came to Plymouth in the Mayflower. He married Abigail W. Thayer, a daughter of Rose's noted Boniface, and deserted the Bay State and came hither in 1855. After sampling various spots in the village, he settled here in this house, built by William Sebring, but which he bought of George Mirick in 1855. Mr. S. is a shoemaker and keeps a shoe store near Pimm's Hotel. He left the bench in war times, and with his son, Ira T., enlisted in the Ninth Heavy Artillery, and was a member of the band. He has two sons—Ira T. and Stephen W., who married Ottie A. Roe, and lives in Clyde, having one son, Herbert. (Also Roe Thayer, b. in 1893.) The Thayers lost a daughter, Abigail A., in infancy. Lucius Ellinwood was the builder of the next house, and sold to Peter Decker. Frank Sherman was an occupant once. Gilbert V. White, son-in-law of Elder A. Maynard, was here some years. His wife, Frank, died in Lyons, October, 1891. Delos Seelye, when he left the farm, came here to live and die; for it was in August, 1870, that he was borne hence, past the scene of his many labors, to his final resting place, in the Collins burial ground. After his death, his widow, Almanda, lived here for some time, and after her death, in 1883, their daughter, Anna Hickok, and husband, Felton, with their only son, William Delos, came hither and still occupy. Will. is now in the railroad employ in Syracuse.

Brewster Soper for many years lived in the next building, and in it reared a large family. He was of Long Island extraction, and long earned

18

an honest living by teaming between Rose and Clyde. Mr. S.'s wife was Betsey Petty and their children were: Clarissa, who married Leonard Collins, of Clyde; Sarah married John Gage and lives in Brooklyn; Dorenda, the wife of William Waldron, in New York; Catharine died early; Caroline married William Gage, their daughter, Grace, has been met at her Uncle Wesley Gage's; Rua married Lorenzo Terbush, and both are dead; Sophia is Mrs. Philander Mitchell, of the Clyde road, and Frank, who married Sylvia Lovejoy. Brewster Soper died in 1887. His wife passed away in March, 1890, having lived for some time with her daughter, Sophia. This house was built by Mr. Soper more than fifty years ago, and has been changed very little in the intervening time. It is now unoccupied.

Next stands the parsonage of the Free Methodist Church, and this building, too, has known many occupants. The present resident is the Rev. J. B. Newton, who has three children—Earl B., Benjamin T. and Louis A. Mr. N. is a native of Chenango county. The church history will be given in a chapter by itself. (Since the above was written, Mr. Newton was killed, September 3d, 1891, at camp meeting, by the falling of a tent. The present occupants are Rev. F. J. Dunham and family.)

Upon the site of the Free Methodist Church stood the house of Nathan W. Thomas. He was first cousin to Eron N. As Eron had a brother, also named Nathan W., who was a tanner, the latter was called "Red Nate," the former, a blacksmith, was "Black Nate." He came here from Onondaga county, and his wife was Caroline Appleby, afterward Mrs. C. B. Collins. Their children were: William H.; Mary Jane, who lives with Mr. Collins, in Clyde; Maria Antoinette, who died at the age of fourteen years, and Fernando Cortes, who died in California in 1887. He lived first on Valentine's hill and worked for John Bassett. His own shop finally stood near or on the site of the Free Methodist parsonage. His house was afterward moved back and is now the barn for the Soper house. He died in 1838, in his thirty-sixth year.

The wagon shop and blacksmithing of Thomas & Collier come next. William Thomas was the builder, and had long conducted an honest and upright business. In August, 1861, the firm was organized as it exists to-day, and that it should continue thus is creditable alike to the integrity and dispositions of the partners. The business was started on this spot considerably earlier by Chauncey B. Collins and John Lackey, a cousin of Mrs. Amos S. Wyckoff. Since Mr. Thomas' death the business has been conducted by Mr. Thomas Collier.

Beyond is a large building, representing considerable money lying idle. Here, in the remote past, was the first Presbyterian Church. When the new one was built, this was sold to the district, which for a time maintained in it the union school. Then it was sold to Joseph Genung & Co.,

who turned it into a planing mill. After a time, machinery for grinding grain was put in and, by steam power, it was run for a term of years,
coming finally, in March, 1871, into the hands of Jared Chaddock, in
whose possession it was when it burned, December 30th of the same year.
Sympathizing friends raised a thousand dollars to set the mill owner on
his feet again, and the present structure followed. Jared passed it over
to the Fredendalls, and they ran the mill for a time. It is now idle.

For the Baptist chronicles that would naturally follow, the reader must
wait for the chapter on the churches.

We now return to the Thomas triangle and follow Dix street southward.
This way is a continuation of that which Eron N. Thomas laid out in war
times for the purpose of locating the new Methodist Episcopal Church in
the lower part of the village. That or Thomas street did not then extend
further than its present eastern extremity. Later this northerly turn was
taken and the name Dix applied, doubtless in memory of him who said:
"If any man attempts to haul down the American flag, shoot him on the
spot." As John A. Dix was the typical war Democrat. and as Mr.
Thomas was of this ilk himself, it seems probable that my genesis is the
correct one. On the west side of this street, south of Joel Sheffield's,
there is only one house, and this is the pleasant home of Miss Lucetta
Lyon, a niece of the late Deacon Walter Lyon, so long a resident below the
village. Her father was Parley, who came to Wayne county from Wynd-
ham county, Conn., somewhere in the thirties. He lived for a time on the
Dwight-Flint farm, in Huron. His wife was Phœbe Preston, a sister of
Joseph Preston, who formerly held the old Samuel Gardner place. One
of his sons is William H. Lyon, now of Brooklyn, but formerly of Rose.
In early life, the latter taught school in North Rose and in the high school
of Clyde. He married Ellen Gaylord, a daughter of Mrs. Eron N. Thomas.
by her first husband. Parley Lyon died in 1846, and is buried in Rose.
His wife went back to the east, and there died. Miss Lyon is responsible
for the building of this home. To her care was left, in 1866, Willie, the
infant son of her sister, Mrs. Susan M. Lindsley, and to him she gave the
most excellent care, rearing and education; but in 1887, just after his
attaining his majority, he died, and was buried by his mother's side. Mr.
Wm. H. Lyon, in his earlier days, experimented successfully in teleg-
raphy, and invented a system for electrical printing or writing. He,
however, devoted himself to mercantile pursuits, and for more than forty
years was at the head of the oldest and one of the largest importing and
jobbing fancy goods and notions houses in the land. Located at 483-485
Broadway, the business was widely known. Mr. Lyon has traveled extensively; in 1869 was appointed by President Grant a member of the
Board of Indian Commissioners, and in 1889 was still a member. Through
his business knowledge, he has been able to save for the country millions

of dollars. He possesses much real estate in Minnesota, the development of Lake City being largely owed to him.

Beginning with the first house on the east side of the street, we shall find Mrs. Henry C. Klinck. We met the Klincks in District No. 3. Of all the children born to her, only her youngest, or Bert, is at home. This was the home of Artemas Osgood, after his leaving the farm, and here he died in 1887, at the age of eighty-eight years. John Crisler first built here. Mr. Osgood was born in Montague, Mass., Jan. 17, 1799, the son of Samuel and Eunice O. He was descended from John Osgood, born in Southampton, Eng., 1575; came to America in 1638, and settled in Andover, Mass. (Mrs. Klinck died Jan. 15, 1892.)

Mark T., or better known as "Tom" Collier, owns the next house. He bought the lot, having an old house on it, from Lawrence Crisler, and himself built and repaired. He married Sarah F. Zeluff, of Clyde. Their only son is Albert D., who married Grace L. Crowell, of Clyde, and has lately gone into business there, succeeding Henry Ellinwood.

To the adjoining brick residence, reared by himself, Charles G. Oakes came from his farm a long time ago. His old home, in District No. 6, was described in earlier letters. He and his wife encountered very much of the hardships of the pioneer. Mr O. has said that he once went through an entire year with only one dollar in money. Boots and shoes were very dear, and he had heated a thick plank to stand upon in his rag-covered feet, while chopping in the cold snowy winter. Mrs. Oaks, who was born in Pittstown, Rensselaer county, is, at a venerable age, still living, and her mind recalls vividly the vicissitudes of the past. Her home is here with her daughter, Mary, who is Mrs. Harry Valentine. The latter's children are Anna, the wife of John T. Kellogg, of Clyde, and George, at home, (Recently married Alice Rich, of Waupaca, Mich.) Anna has two children —Hattie V. and Clara L. Her husband is a son of William Kellogg, formerly of District No. 7.

Harvey Barnes, of Huron, owns the next house to the south, taking it from the estate of his father-in-law, Robert Catchpole, who came hither when he grew weary of his farm work. It is now occupied by Frank Soper, a son of Brewster, whose wife is Sylvia, daughter of John Lovejoy, of Glenmark. Their children are Bessie E. and John B. Mr. S. follows the trade of a painter. Mr. Soper recently has gone west for a part of the year each season to evaporate fruit. A part of this house is of interest in that it was once the home of Johnny Ogram, on the knoll where Mrs. Hart's house is. It took a journey hither and was worked over. Now owned and occupied by Mr. and Mrs. J. J. Seelye, formerly of No. 6.

Joseph S. Wade follows. Familiar friends call him "Joe," and his face recalls that of his maternal grandfather, Joseph Seelye, whose name he bears. In addition to arduous duties in politics, "Joe" manages his farm.

in the western confines of Butler. The Wade data were given quite fully in District No. 7. His only child is Nellie E., at home. The house was built by William McCoy.

In a brick house, somewhat back from the street, dwells Peter Harmon. He built his own house, for carpentering and joining are his callings. After he had built many houses and lived in some of them, he settled down here. He came to Rose in 1851. His wife was Margaret Moon, from Schoharie county. Their children are Lillie Z. and Ione M. The latter is the wife of Judson J. Sheffield, now in Rochester. This is a good place, in our rambles, to give a sketch of the Harmon family. John Harmon and his wife, Clarissa Abbott, came to Rose in 1852. Mr. Harmon was born in Westfield, Mass., in 1798. His father, Peter, came from England, and was a drum major in the American army during the Revolution. He married in Hunter, Green Co., N. Y., in 1818, and lived many years in Great Barrington, Mass. He was converted under the labors of Rev. John Bangs, and became a devoted member of the Methodist Episcopal Church. For a long time he was prominent in its councils. His wife was born in 1804. They had twelve children, of whom three—Daniel, William and Alfred—were in the army during the Rebellion. The latter years of their lives were passed with their daughter, Mrs. Stephen Waite. The oldest son, Peter, named for the Revolutionary grandfather, has been already mentioned. Daniel P. married first, Nellie Doan, of Newark, who died during the War. Her only child, Ina, is Mrs. Clarence N. Phillips, west of the Valley. His second wife was Jennie Schofield, of Palmyra, where they live and where they have three children. Mr. Harmon was for years a very successful teacher of vocal music, singing being a strong point with the whole Harmon family. I recall a very pleasant winter's instruction from him, that of 1865 and '66. It was just after the War, and my last previous recollection of Daniel Harmon was that of seeing him at Monocacy, Md., trying to rally the men of the Ninth, who were falling back under the galling fire of the rebels. There seemed to be very little order, but a case of every man looking out for himself. The colors were halted just at the verge of the hill and Captain Harmon, of Company H, shouted: "Rally around your flag, men!" A goodly number halted, but our formation and advance were ineffectual. Affliction at home compelled Captain Harmon to resign in 1864. Like nearly all the Harmon family, he is a carpenter and joiner. Latterly he has had a superintendency of canal construction. William Harmon married first, Polly Brewster, by whom he had two sons— Frank, now in Shortsville, and Henry, in Rochester. His second wife was Mary Legg, whose daughter, Lizzie, is the wife of Fred Waldruff, of District No. 3. Mr. Harmon's home is in Rochester. Alfred Harmon, another carpenter, resides in Palmyra; his wife, before marriage, was Mary Forncrook, they have one son and three daughters. John Harmon's daughters were : Hannah, who married Matthew Crisler, of Rose ; Laura, who married Henry B. Sherman, of Rose, and lived in the north part of the village ; their son, John E., a member of the 111th N. Y., was killed in the battle of the Wilderness ; the local post of the G. A. R. is named for him; their daughter, Clara, married James Bowers, and went to Allegany Co.; Lizzie and Flora also married in the same county, while Jennie became the wife of Wilbur Osborn, living west of the Valley. Lydia Ann Harmon married Isaac Race, who, as a builder, has been met several times in the village ; he was born in Egremont, Mass., the same town whence came the Winchells, and died in 1865, in the house now held by widow Myers. Abbie E. Harmon married Stephen Waite of Rose, and Sarah, the youngest daughter of John Harmon, married Samuel Swayne, of Swaynesville, Allegany Co.

Back among the apple trees is the quiet home of G. Collins Wood, but among his friends he is rather known as "Collie." He built this house and the accompanying barn. His vocation during a part of the year is the running of a threshing machine. His wife is Rena, a daughter of George and Sybil Sherman. They have only one child, Ralph. Mr. Wood was born in Butler, at the Centre, when his father, Hudson R. Wood, resided there. (H. R. Wood and wife are now here.)

Near the road is the home of George Stubley, English born, as is his wife, Elizabeth Ranson, both from Lincolnshire. They have two sons and two daughters—William, Fred, Cora and Rose. Mr. Stubley, who is a worker in stone and general laborer, bought of John Gage, a brother of Wesley. William is now with the 10th U. S. Infantry, and Fred is in the employ of the New York Central Railroad. In the brick house near (owned by a Mrs. Brewster of Wolcott), lives James W. Colborn. In the Valley he is better known as "Jim" or "Judge." The Colborn family was met in District No. 8, where James was born and where he lived till about twenty years since, when he moved into the Valley. For some time he was on Main street, near the corner of Thomas. His wife's maiden name was Martha M. Worden, a daughter of Alanson, formerly of the Jeffers neighborhood. Their children are : Irving Worden, married and living in Newark ; Edwin Douglas, who married Adaline Doremus, and lives in North Rose: Rosa Belle, the wife of Arthur T. Barless, of Rose ; Abbie M. and Clarence Clifford, at home. (Douglas Colborn, a painter by trade, lives now in Newark. He has children, Earl and Glen.)

A vacant lot stands in the name of E. T. Pimm and then we find a small structure, used at times for a feed mill, belonging to Collins Wood.

On the corner, for a narrow street runs southerly by the school-house grounds, is Mrs. Mary Cleveland. Alfred Harmon once owned the place and built the house.

Still further south owns the widow of C. M. Shaver. Then comes Thomas Hamm, whose house, formerly owned by Byron Crandall, was partly at one time the shoe shop of Jonathan Wilson, and stood on Main street, three doors south of Pimm's Hotel. Mr. Hamm is from Columbia Co.; his wife was Charlotte Van Dusen. They have two children, William and Augusta. He came to Rose twenty-three years since. Finally, Mrs. Jane Sweet resides, and here the street ends.

Coming back to Thomas street, the school-house is next, to be noticed at length hereafter. No residences intervene till we come to that of William Matthews. This was built by William Holbrook. Mr. Matthews is English born, coming to America forty years since. His first wife he married in England; her name was Sarah Steele. Three children died in the old country, and three came to this land, viz.: William, who married Ida Birdsall, and lives in Clyde; Melicent, who married John Viele, of Rose; both are dead; and Mary, who married William Bolinger, and lives in Clyde. His second wife was Rachel Viele, of Rose, and their children are Richard and Louis, twins, who, with Joseph, the next son, are married and living in Madison county; Charles, in Union Springs, and John, who married Emma D. Hamm, and lives south of the Valley. In addition to this place, Mr. M. owns the house on Main street, in which William A. Mix resides. He will also be met as a former resident in other places.

The street to which we have come is called Church, from the Methodist Episcopal edifice, past which it would run if continued. At present it stops at Thomas street. On the southwest corner is the home of Josiah Streeter, whose mother was a Winchell; his wife a Bovee. He was a soldier during the Rebellion, and has several children. Eron Thomas built the house for a select school, about 1860. Afterward it was made over into a dwelling house, and was occupied by Charles Jennison, a tinner, working for L. H. Dudley. The widow Cummings, a sister of William Haney, formerly of District No. 7, lived and died here. W. R. Winchell also held it, till an adventitious arrearage of pensions allowed Mr. Streeter to purchase.

Returning to the north side of Thomas street, for were we to go beyond Streeter's we should reach Main street, we shall find only vacant lots, till we come to the place now held by William Weed, but was built by a Mr. Blood, who sold to Mr. Weed, who is a brother of Oscar, of the Glenmark neighborhood. He came to this site in 1879, and has kept a livery and horse-training stable. His wife, Anna Walker, is a native of Wyoming county: a brother was the late Rev. Ellis Walker, of the Troy Conference of the Methodist Episcopal Church, and her grandfather, Major James Smith, of Canajoharie, Montgomery county, was a Revolutionary officer. She is herself a writer of no little note, having published, in 1886, a novel entitled " Isadore, or the Day Star of Hope."

A very small house, belonging to C. S. Wright, is found next, and in it lives widow Ackerman, having several children, one of whom is a soldier in the United States army.

In the Methodist Episcopal parsonage, in August, 1890, and for the preceding five years, dwelt Rev. G. W. Reynolds, the first minister to profit by the extension of pastorate made by the General Conference of 1888. Mr. R. is a native of Ulster county; his wife, who was Susan A. Griffin, was born in Orange county. They have three children, a son and two daughters, but only Alma R. has lived with them here, and she was married in the early days of their pastorate. The Methodist Episcopal Church, recently repaired, is next. Rev. George S. Transue is now the pastor.

Crossing to the beginning of Church street, we go down the same, finding, just south of Josiah Streeter's, a small house belonging to John Matthews. He bought of " Deck " Brewster.

East of the angle made by this street as it turns toward the west, are the extensive barns once belonging to the Thomas farm, which ran back and north and south. They belong to William Niles, whose home will be found on Main street, itself the old Thomas house.

On the south side of the way is the home of Postmaster Edgar F. Houghton, a native of Lyons, who came to Rose from Alton in 1876. His wife, Mary E., is a daughter of the late John Becket; they have one child, Blanche E. Beside his post office duties, Mr. H. is a traveling salesman. His wife's parents have lived here for some time. John Becket came from Skillington, England, and had been for more than forty years a resident of this town. Besides Mrs. Houghton, a son, William, resides in Clyde. (Mr. Becket died January 16, 1893, and on the 29th following, his widow followed him. June 4, Mr. Houghton's mother, Mrs. Margery A. Snyder, died at his home.)

Across the way is a small house, lately bought by Mrs. Catharine Harper from Mrs. Viele.

We will next approach the village from the north, leaving behind us District No. 3, or the Lyman neighborhood. The first stop will be made at the home of Isaac Campbell, who was born in Newport, Herkimer county. His wife, Josephine Minott, was born in Schuyler, of the same county. He served during the War in the 34th New York, two years, and later was in the 16th Heavy Artillery, being the first man in Herkimer county to enlist. He came to this place in 1875. There are six children here, viz., Herbert M., Grace, Mabel, Florence, Ross and Nellie. The large cottonwood tree standing near the road is probably the largest in the county. When its twin was standing, they constituted a figure unexcelled in arboreal beauty in the whole section. It was a sad moment when one was cut down. Would that Morris' lines had been read to stay the woodman's axe:

> "Woodman, spare that tree,
> Touch not a single bough."

These trees date back to the time of Samuel Southwick, more than seventy years. Within the memory of the oldest inhabitant, the house has changed little, if any. It is true that George Sherman once drew material for erecting a new dwelling, but nothing came of it. Probably this is the oldest framed building in the town. It certainly goes back to the days of Samuel Southwick, the very first occupant of this section, unless the honor be claimed by William Browning, whose record is lost. Mr. Southwick came originally from Massachusetts, where he was reared among the Shakers till he was sixteen years old. Coming to Seneca county, he married, first, Submit West, in Junius, where she died. Her burial was said to be the first for a white woman in that town. By this marriage, he had only one child, who became Mrs. Ellis Ellinwood, of Rose. It was in 1815 or 1816 that Mr. Southwick came to Rose, buying very extensively from the Rose-Nicholas tract. His second wife was Hannah Brown, also from Massachusetts. By this marriage, he had eight children. After becoming the parent of this numerous progeny, he became convinced that the principles of his early rearing were the correct rules for living, and accordingly sold out his possessions in Rose, and cast in his lot with the Shakers, located in Sodus. All his family went with him, except Lydia, who married William Watkins, a Rose tanner, and the father of Mrs. Lawson Munsell. Southwick's oldest son, Lucius, was engaged to a fair young lady of Rose, but he broke the engagement to go with his father. In 1837 the Shakers went from Sodus to Mount Morris, Groveland, near Rochester. When he was between fifty and sixty years of age, Lucius left the Shakers, having married one of them, and passed the remainder of his life in East Rochester. The family was related to that of Ebenezer Pierce, father-in-law of Simeon Barrett. The Miricks, who succeeded Southwick, were from Saratoga county originally, but they came to Rose from Cazenovia. This name is invariably in Rose pronounced as though spelled Merrick. In Massachusetts, it is pronounced as spelled. Unquestionably the families are allied. Solomon Mirick, the progenitor of the family, had been an extensive contractor and builder. His first wife and the mother of his children was Elizabeth Underwood. His second wife was the widow of Joel Weed, the mother of the widely known Thurlow Weed. He married her in Syracuse, and she was a citizen of Rose till after Mr. Mirick's death, in 1839. After this event, she went to Kentucky, and there died. It was in 1828 that the family came to Rose and bought about 300 acres of land from Southwick and Collins. From that date to the time of George Mirick's going west, few names were more prominent in town

affairs. There were eight children. Ira married Martha Lamb of North
Rose, and till his moving to Lyons was a very important factor in the
business of the town. His headquarters were in Glenmark, where he has
already been named. In the days of the militia, he was the lieutenant
colonel of the regiment of which George Seelye was the colonel. He died
last spring at a great age. His children were: Hiram, Guilford, Jackson,
and three daughters. Hiram, the second son of Solomon Mirick, will be
met soon, in the south: Nelson did not live in Rose, but married and died
in Pennsylvania; George lived long south of the Valley; Thomas married
Sophronia Dickson, a sister of Dr. D., and died in 1841, leaving one
daughter; Henry, the youngest son, was a young man of great promise,
who died in 1841, at the age of twenty-four years. The daughters were
Amanda and Charlotte. The latter married Ebenezer Tyler, and moved to
Ohio. The former became Mrs. David Holmes, and formerly lived west of
the Valley. The orchard, still so prominent on the hill east of the road
north from Rose, is a memory of the Mirick planting. All the Mirick farm
passed finally into the possession of Hiram, on whose going to Lyons,
Charles B. Sherman came into possession, and this north part, including
the old Southwick house, was passed over to his son, George, who had
married Sybil Wilson. They worked here with a will, and finally held it
unencumbered. At a comparatively early age, Mr. Sherman sold to one
Barnham, and moved to the Valley. Barnham, who had grown mentally
unbalanced in trying to keep his work train on the N. Y. Central R. R. out
of the way of the regular trains, did not find farming to his liking, and so
sold to Mordecai Cox. The latter did not hold it long, but sold and went
to Rochester. He died in 1878, and is buried in Rose, as are also his wife
Lovina, who died in 1863, and his son, George, in 1875. After Cox came
Campbell. Over the way, opposite the house, is a field, known by the old
settlers as the stone heap, an outcropping of the limestone ledge that has
been successfully worked in North Rose. In this field was located the first
Rose school-house, a log one, soon afterward burned. David Smith, the
first Baptist minister in town, taught in it. Stephen Collins was a pupil
here.

A few rods south of Campbell's, a road runs toward the west. On the
south side is a building, lately repaired, belonging to Levern Wilson.
For years it was just a little red house, built by Sanford Lackey, who sold
to Joseph Childs, of Ontario county, and he to Joseph Andrus, a brother-
in-law of Ephraim Wilson. The widow of William Desmond owned it for
a time, and in 1871 it was under the name of Edward Horn, whom the
widow, who was Lucinda Winchell, had married. Mr. Horn was English
born, and after leaving this place, lived in Marion.

Ephraim B. Wilson is the owner of the next house on the north side of
the road, and the place is exceedingly interesting, in that Mr. Wilson has

worked out all his possessions from the pristine wilderness. One of the best things that Ephraim ever did was his marrying Calista Flint, from Connecticut, a relative of "'Square" Flint, a neighbor on the north. In all the struggle for a competence, she has done all that could be expected of a wife. It was in 1835 that Mr. Wilson came to the town and bought his lot, one of the last to be taken from the Nicholas purchase. In the fall he put up a log-house. In February following he was married. There were no roads and he went by marked trees. One side of his house was shingled, and when, later, he wished to shingle the other side, so deep was the snow he was able to carry the shingles up the roof, stepping from the banks. Snow lay three feet deep upon the level. The house was built like a cob pile, and the places for doors and windows were cut out afterward. The doors were boards simply, and the windows were not over numerous. There was no fireplace, and for three or four weeks cooking was done by a stump fire. A well was dug, and for curbing or wall Mr. Wilson went to the woods and cut two lengths of buttonwood, hollow, and set them in. A crotched stick was set up for a sweep, and the thing was complete. For a few days the waters may have had the bitterness of those of Marah, but sweetness followed. During the entire summer, he was fixing his house. Sand was found four feet down and this was used in making mortar. Boards for the floor were obtained at Solomon Allen's saw-mill, just south. Partitions and windows followed, having used blankets before. Finally, having obtained some brick, Silas Munsell built a chimney and brick oven. "'Square" Flint came over and arranged the interior woodwork. The first farm work was to plant potatoes. His first lot of fifty-eight acres cost him $5 per acre. The Winchell lot to the west, which he next bought, was the last remnant of the Nicholas tract. Children came to the log house rapidly, and then the girls wanted a new house. It was built, and Mr. Wilson found himself in debt. To raise it, he rented his own place, and went to Lyons and worked Hiram Mirick's farm. When he returned, he had enough to make him square with the world. Surrounded by indications of his energy and honesty, Mr. Wilson is passing a very green old age, his capable and loving wife still by his side. As Mr. Wilson himself says, "she is a smart woman." Among other relics, Mr. W. has a bar still in use, which was hewn from or split from a black ash fifty-four years ago. By "bar" is meant an instrument for stopping a hole or gap in a fence, an abbreviation for barrier. It has nothing to do with hotel or restaurant bars. A total abstainer from stimulants and narcotics, Mr. Wilson has no use for such bars. Doubtless his life-long abstinence accounts for his vigorous age. The children in this family were many, and at one time there were seven of them in the Valley school. Their names are as follows : Sybil has already been met as the wife of George Sherman ; Augusta, also, was mentioned in District No. 6 as the wife of Lampson Allen; Caroline married William Colborn, formerly of Rose, but now of Wolcott; Harlan P. married Carrie Snow, and was encountered in District No. 7; Martha W. is Mrs. Alonzo Post, of Butler; Mary, deceased, was twice married, first, to Joseph Butler and, second, to Chester Ayers, of Clinton, Mass.; Emily, who married Burton Walker, of Lancaster, Mass.; Ephraim B., Jr., who married Ella Armstrong; Theron, unmarried, and a carpenter, lives in Rochester (Davenport, Iowa); Levern, the youngest, married Ida Osborn, a daughter of William, formerly of Rose, in District No. 8, but now in Lyons. They are at the old home and have one child, Mollie. (Now in Levern's house, east.)

The western boundary of the district is reached when we come to the home of the widow of Amos S. Wyckoff. It is a comfortable white house (nearly all houses in the country are painted thus), and it succeeded one of the last occupied log houses in this part of Rose. The Wyckoffs have been mentioned in the Griswold district as once living near the Finch place, north of the school-house. Amos S. Wyckoff was born in Huntington, New Jersey, and the fact that he was a nephew of Jacob Ferguson, of the corners, may have been an inducement for his western migration. He married Susan, daughter of Orrin Lackey. After marriage he lived for a time in New Jersey. Returning, he bought the Milo Lyman lot, back in the fields, between the Wayne Centre and this road. There was a mill on the lot, through which ran the Thomas creek. The log house, back in the lots, will be recalled by many. Objections being made finally to entering the farm from the south, land was bought on the north from the widow of Nathan Jeffers, and the whole farm of ninety-three acres abutted on this road. Mr. Wyckoff died in 1868, at the age of sixty-four years, but his widow is still active in good works. On calling, in 1889, I found her engaged in making cushions for the Methodist Church, then undergoing repairs, and of which she had long been a member. The Wyckoff children were: Orrin, now in Herkimer county, who married Minnie Hughson, of Clyde; Lyman in Lyons, who married Lucy Chambers, of Wayne Centre; Sarah, at home, and William, who married Mary Dewey, of Butler, and now manages the farm. He has one child, Edith. The Lyman lot was taken up by the second Jonathan Wilson, who raised the log house. After him was Henry G. Lyman, whom Milo followed. Wilson traded his interest with Lyman for four acres off the west end of the Bassett lot, on Sodus street, in the Valley.

Returning to the main road and resuming our southerly course, we shall pass, at our left, the well-kept village of the dead, the most considerable cemetery in town. Till recently the old part has been very much neglected, but it now looks as well as the newer portions. This is one of the oldest burial grounds in Rose. At first, interments were made nearly opposite the present residence of Mrs. Harvey Closs. Afterwards these were removed to the grounds now used.

Even at the risk of mingling the grotesque and solemn, the story must be told that right here, years since, when a certain well-known Valley merchant, then young and brave, was courting a lady living just on the confines of the Lyman district, a ghost made its appearance. Possibly it was at the hour when churchyards yawn and spirits do walk abroad. At any rate, lest the love-lorn young man might lose the sight of "ye ghost," a clothes line had been strung across the road, over which the late traveller pitched headlong, and as he (W)righted himself he beheld the spook ; but his fear was not orthodox in the least. He picked up sundry convenient stones and let them fly in a way that put the white sheeted figure to ignominious flight. Then looking about for the rope, the gentleman discovered, by certain marks, that it had been taken from his own store. He put it back in place and then had grace enough to ask no questions of a certain shame-faced clerk, a (s)Lyman, who bore evidence of having been out late the night before.

On the east side of the road, before reaching the stone house, perhaps in the garden thereof, was formerly a small framed house, afterward removed and used as a tool house, opposite. This building is intimately connected with one of the best families ever identified with Rose, viz., that of Alpheus Collins, the eldest son of Thaddeus, 1st, whose purchases were about as early as any in Rose. The farm, of 130 acres, was a part of the large number of acres bought by the pioneer, that he might have his children about him. His sons, some of them, went west, that they might have their children about them, and, in this widening process, descendants have reached Dakota. After all, the sons do not stay as fathers wish and calculate. The age is too uneasy and stirring. Alpheus Collins was born in Vermont, September 30th, 1790. When a boy, his parents removed to Phelps, Ontario county, where in 1811, October 31st, he married Betsey Hall, born in New Jersey, October 5th, 1790. Shortly afterward, they came to this town, where they lived till 1829. Here their children, save one, were born ; one son, born in the west, died in infancy. The oldest son, Selah Baxter, was born November 12th, 1812, and he married Pamela Green, December 26, 1833. He was a farmer, and resided, in 1888, in New Richmond, Allegan county, Michigan. His wife died in 1886. Josiah H. was born May 30th, 1814, and was married December 26, 1835, to Mary Brown, who died several years since. In 1888 he also was a farmer, in Lindon, Michigan. Wellington H., born May 12th, 1816, married Mary Ann Ward, of Butler, September 2d, 1840. Early in life he taught school, was a surveyor, and finally became a Methodist minister. In his denomination he held many important positions. He was twice a delegate to the General Conference, was a presiding elder, a powerful preacher and much beloved by his people. He was presiding elder of the Detroit district at the time of his death, in 1848. His wife died two or three years later. Walter D. was born December 14th, 1817, and became a Methodist minister and a missionary to the Cherokee Indians, in Indian Territory. His wife was Lodoweskei (called Lodi) Baker, a sister of the famous war detective; he returned to Michigan in 1855, and died at his father's the same year; his wife went to Texas, where she had property, and there died, in 1886. Isaac F. was born August 24th, 1819, and was also a Methodist minister and missionary to the Cherokees. December 22d, 1843, he married Mary Wolf, a daughter of the Cherokee chief. Coming back to civilization, he preached in Michigan for several years and then returned to the south, where his wife died. Marrying again, he went to Nebraska and died soon after. The only daughter, Esther D., born June 4th, 1821, was a cripple from birth, although a bright, intelligent girl. She died June 10th, 1849. Judson D., who was born February 12th, 1823, was graduated with first honors from Michigan University, was a professor in Albion College, and became a Methodist minister. As such, he was the first Methodist missionary to China. For five years he was the superintendent of missions in that country, but his health failing, he came back to America, by way of California, in 1851, hoping to regain his health, but he died in 1852, at his father's home. He was never married. William W., who was born May 3d, 1825, has been a farmer, a surveyor and a machinist, and, having been graduated from the medical department of Michigan University in 1852, is now a physician in Albion, Michigan. He married Maria K. Palmer, July 5th, 1849. Being a seventh son, he is very properly a doctor. Sidney A., who was born May 8th, 1828, is a farmer, living in Lindon. His wife is Sylvia A. Reed, whom he married November 15th, 1850. This record has been given thus at length, because I think it one that Rose may well be proud of. What has been the loss of the town in sturdy, manly worth, has obviously been the gain of the country; for we see that the Collins lines have gone out through all the world. On leaving Rose in 1829, Alpheus Collins went, with his family, to Washtenaw county, in the then Territory of Michigan, near Ann Arbor. He took up an extensive farm, and became prominent in town and state affairs, having been supervisor, justice of the peace, etc., and a member of the convention that framed the Constitution for the state. In 1841 he went to a farm in the town of Lindon, on which he died, in 1871. His wife, a most devoted and helpful woman, died in 1870. Both were deeply pious and consistent members of the Methodist Church. To this farm came, after the Collinses, Hiram Mirick; his wife was Mary B. Fuller, of the east part of this same school district. For many years this was his home, and here his children were reared. He was the builder of the stone house and barn opposite.

OLD RESIDENTS.

The latter bears the date "1850." In the gable end of the largest barn may yet be seen the numerals 1817, cut into and through the boards. If these truly represent the date of building, it must be one of the oldest structures in town. The Mirick youths were Nelson, Amelia, Milton, Ira, James and Janette. All went with the parents to Lyons, where Nelson died. All became identified with the interests of that village. The daughters are at home with their mother, who, an aged lady, has survived her husband many years. She has always taken intense interest in politics and passing events. Married to a Democrat, she ever shared with him his views. Well posted, it was a scene to remember when she and her Republican and equally well-posted sister, Mrs. Almanda Seelye, had a friendly set-to on the state of the country. "I am surprised that so sensible a woman as you should persist in such insane ideas," was the sentence with which each ended many a protracted discussion. How much better do masculine disputants make out? After Mr. Mirick's sale to Charles B. Sherman, the farm was divided several times, so that it no longer was the large estate of the Southwicks and Collinses. After Hiram Mirick as dweller in the stone house, came Harvey Closs, who had sold his farm on the corner, north, and had bought of Sherman this part of the old estate. His successor and present occupant, though the name of William K. Rider intervenes, is William Fisher, who came here from Palmyra in 1875. Mr. Fisher is a native of Holland, as was also his wife, Susannah Day. We can't help thinking that names in Holland have grown shorter since the times when that country sent to America her Van Rensselaers and Van Der Hoffens. Mr. F. came to America when a boy, fifty-five years ago. He has made good use of his time and opportunity, and is to-day one of the solid men of the county. Ten children have been born to him, but only five of them have been any considerable time in Rose. These are: Adrian, who married a Miss Koon, of Sodus, and now lives in Butler; James, who married Alice Smith, of Rose, and lives in Palmyra; Charles, still at home; Cornelia, who married Byron Rumsey, and Lizzie, who married and lives in Arcadia. The other children live in the western part of the county. In addition to his regular farm work, Mr. F. maintains a well patronized mint still. Mrs. Fisher died November 23d, 1891, aged sixty-six years. (In 1893 Mr. Fisher married Mrs. Rachel [Beidick] Marshall, of Rochester, who brings with her to the old stone house her daughter Gertrude.)

Still on the east side and going south, we find the house built by Mr. Fisher for his son, Adrian, but now occupied by his daughter, Cornelia Rumsey. Mr. Rumsey is a railroad man, and some time since was unfortunate enough to lose one of his arms. He is now in Connecticut in the employ of the N. Y., N. H. & H. R. R.

Romaine C. Barless and family hold the next place, and the location is
noteworthy as indicating the site of the first home of Thaddeus Collins,
2d, who built a small house here, on his marriage with Harriet Shepard,
and here he lived for a number of years, at any rate past 1829, for in that
year George Seelye's first wife, Mrs. Collins' sister and the writer's grandmother, died here. Years afterward, the building was moved down into
the village and is now the small house on Main street occupied by Daniel
Johnson, a few doors beyond Pimm's Hotel. The present house was built
by Mr. Barless, generally called "Doc," who combines the vocations of
lawyer, dentist and pension agent. I believe that the majority of recipients
of government bounty in Rose had their claims or cases presented by Mr.
R. He was born in Hoosic, N. Y., away up on the Bennington battle field,
though Vermont celebrates the victory as peculiarly one belonging to her.
If once started, "Doc" will tell the whole story of the battle and how New
York's reputation is overborne by the Green Mountain boys. Also when
it comes to narrating the deeds of the Heavy Ninth, Barless is without a
rival. As he was a member of that regiment, Company H, he feels that
the reputation of the organization is, in a measure, in his keeping. Mr.
Barless' wife was Helen J. Thompson, of Saratoga county. Himself a
twin, he has made the record good by being the father of twin boys. His
children are Carrie H., who married Wm. H. Moulton, of Lockport; the
twins, Clayton L. and Clinton J.; Arthur F., and Elmo R. One child, an
infant daughter, died in 1874. Clayton has recently married Lena Markham, of Rose, and Clinton, who prints the *Rose Counsel and Times*, married
Jennie Hickok. She died in 1889. Arthur F. married James Colborn's
daughter, Rosa Belle. Mr. Barless came to Rose in 1858, and, before
building his present residence, constructed several in other parts of the
village.

Joseph Durant, who lives next, married a Tarbell, whose mother is the
owner of the very pretty house. The Durants have one child, George.

Going back to the west side and beginning south of Mr. Fisher's, we
shall find a series of lots extending a number of rods back into the level
region lying westward of the village. Several of these are ten acres in
extent. Ira T. Soule owns the first house, though on his north side
Stephen Waite has a lot of seven acres. Ira is an old friend of the writer,
for they were fellow members of the Ninth Heavy Artillery. After war's
alarms were over, Ira returned to the pursuits of peace, and essayed the
business of painting and paper hanging. He beat a drum in war times,
and has been interested in all the musical enterprises of the village. At
one time his father, his brother and himself were all in the band. He
found a wife in Dr. Dickson's daughter, Rose, who died April 3rd, 1891,
aged thirty-five years. Building a house here on this lot, he has begun the
rearing of his family. This consists of Gilman, Edna, Marvin, and a boy

baby only a few months old. He has lost one child, Wyman. I never envied Ira so much as when, marching along with gun and the inevitable forty rounds, he strolled by my side with only his drum. Ira says that at Monocacy, where we were sacrificed, he just jammed that drum down over a gate post and lighted out. As a drum it was of no earthly use to the Confederate finder. (Mr. S. was married, October 20th, 1892, to Miss Kate Youngs, of Detroit, Mich.)

A vacant lot of ten acres, belonging to Charles Tillson, follows, then the neat home of Joseph Talton, an excellent ditcher and layer of ground tiles. Mr. T. and his wife, who was Catherine Dring, were born in South Witham, Lincolnshire, England. Next we arrive at the home of Stephen Waite. The latter is a native of Massachusetts, coming here from Great Barrington with the Harmons, whose second daughter, Abbie, he married. They have two daughters—Allie, who married George H. Oliver, of Clyde, and lives in Rochester, and Ella. Mr. Waite was a member of the Ninth Heavy Artillery, and was wounded at Cedar Creek. He follows the trade of a painter. This house was the old John Harmon home, and here John Harmon died. Mrs. Waite died in November, 1891.

The next house, in which Lucien Osgood and family live, was built by Orrin Sherman, who sold to Joel N. Lee. It was to this place that Mr. Lee came when he left his farm, a mile or so north. Here he and his wife died. Their daughter, Mrs. Theresa Kingsley, held the place for a time and then sold to Lucien. The latter has been met in different places—in Districts No. 7 and 6. After the death of Eudora Seelye, his first wife, he married Matilda Wickwire, and has a family of five children, viz., Eveline, Herbert, Eudora, Ray and Grace. Mr. Osgood is a son of Artemas Osgood, and he maintains all the traditional uprightness of the family, being a member of the Baptist Church, a justice of the peace, and a straightforward man in every respect.

The next house, built by " Doc " Barless, is owned by James C. Church, of Clyde, and is occupied by Arthur T. Barless.

Chas. Relyea built the adjoining house, now owned by Julia (Sedore) Milem and occupied by Dr. F. H. Hallett. This gentleman is from Huron, though born in Palmyra, and his wife is Katie Scott, from Ontario, Canada. They have a son, E, Bruce. The doctor is a recent comer to Rose, but he is already winning golden opinions. (Mr. and Mrs. Milem are now residing here, 1893.)

George Adelbert Sherman lives in the next house. In Rose, young and old call him " Deb." He combines many callings in his trade, being ready to drive a well, repair an engine, or print an advertisement. His lineage is from George and Charles B. Sherman, already met. He married Hannah Walmsley, of Rose, and has five children—Leon A., Florence E., Nina S.

19

and Charles Ephraim, whose names recall two of his great-grandfathers, and Elsie May. The house and barn are of Mr. Sherman's building.

The next lot marks the site of Chauncey Collins' barn, burned some years ago, and the final place before reaching the corner is the house built by Mrs. Lampson Allen, who, some time since, came hither from her farm in District No. 6. The site is that of the first Methodist Church. Her younger daughter, Florence, having graduated from the Albany Normal School, is a teacher in Massachusetts.

On the east side of the road, a few rods north, is the most desirable building place in the village, and here lives the widow of Harvey Closs. With her, for some time, have resided D. C. Markham, a retired lawyer from Syracuse, and his wife, who is a cousin of Mrs. Closs. To this spot belongs much of the Collins history, so bound up in the early annals of the town. The first Thaddeus Collins was Massachusetts born, and like many of that state, in the latter part of the eighteenth century, sought a home in Vermont, where several of his children were born. But the Green Mountains were not sufficiently inviting, and he brought his *lares* and *penates* to Phelps, Ontario Co., very late in the century. One more move, in 1814, brought him to this his final haven. His wife was Esther Foster, a half sister of Jonathan Melvin, a noted name in Rose history. He was a soldier during the Revolution, and also in 1812. On coming to this wilderness, he bought 400 acres of the Rose-Nicholas tract, located just in the present village. There was only one road then, viz., the one extending from Clyde to Wolcott, and it indicates taste on his part in building his log house near the centre of his purchase and on the most sightly place in it. At this time there was only one building near and that was a log house, near the present home of Frank Closs. My grandfather's notes make this the property of Charles Woodward, but it is elsewhere ascribed to Capt. John Sherman. Mr. Collins placed his son, Thaddeus, Jr., next north, and then Alpheus. Foster was to the northwest, where Andrus is now, on the old Chatterson farm; Stephen in the same direction, but nearer; Chauncey remained at home. There were also two daughters, Esther and Sally; the former married George Wilson, of West Vienna, Ontario Co.; the latter became Mrs. Uriah Wade, and moved to Michigan. This first generation of the Collins family died in 1828 and 1844. Their last home is on the land that was devoted by them to burial purposes. Chauncey B. Collins married Caroline (Appleby) Thomas, the widow of Nathan W. As the village grew, the paternal acres lessened till, on his moving to Clyde, there was little more than the house and lot left. The children of Mr. and Mrs. Collins were Josephine and Louis Dell. The daughter became the wife of Aaron Vanderburgh, of Clyde (now living in Grand Rapids, Mich.), and died in 1879. The son, for some years a resident in New York, has married, and lives near Geneva. Mr. Collins' wife died March 12th, 1874. Mr. C., who is a true disciple of Nimrod and Isaak Walton, flourishes in a vigorous old age, a notable figure in Clyde. Among other dwellers in this house was Dr. J. M. Horne, who, a native of New Hampshire and a graduate of Harvard Medical School, '55, came here as the successor of Drs. Whedon and Neeley. He now resides in Boston.

There is just one building more on this side of the street, and that is the brick structure owed to William Deady. Were it to be destroyed by an earthquake shock or other means, the beauty of the village would not be lessened in the slightest degree. Built as a storehouse, sold to Darwin Dickinson, who continued its use thus, and since occupied as a hardware store, when used at all; its upper story, either empty or employed as a lodge room, latterly for the Good Templars,—there never was a moment when it was not entirely out of place. When Rose gets her village improvement society—and it can't come any too soon— there will be many changes in the topography of this village of ours. In some other place, this edifice would be all right, but where it is, it is like a sore thumb, always in the way. Suppose it were to be removed, and the road entering the Valley from the east to be extended in a direct line past the Baptist Church, thus forming a large triangle, to be enclosed or left as a common, does any one hesitate to say that our already beautiful village would be vastly more interesting? In the centre of this might be the soldiers' monument, which some day should recall the prowess of the sons of Rose in the Rebellion. I would have the old well, long since filled up, dug out and a pump placed in it for public use. When this time comes, and let us hope that I am not portraying a Utopia, the Presbyterian Church will come out from its hiding place, though to accomplish this effectually, one more removal will be necessary, viz., that of the unsightly evaporator, which has too long cut off the south site of the church. I hope I am not misunderstood. Evaporators and storehouses are useful and necessary, but they are better in other places than in those where they hide public edifices and displease rather than gladden the eye.

. On the south corner of Sodus street is the house of Mrs. Emily Vanderoef, whose late husband, William, himself a carpenter, built here. As Mrs. V. says, it was built by inches, beginning forty years ago. The place is the old John Bassett home. His house was further south, nearer the site of the church, and his blacksmith shop was about where the present house is. The old house was moved to the west, and was long the home of Matthew Crisler. The Bassetts sold to Henry Lyman, and he to Vanderoef. Mrs. V. has only one son, Clarence E. (The house is now owned and occupied by George A. Collier.)

Sodus, West or Cooper street, west of Mrs. Vanderoef's, the first house, was begun by Parsons Hunn and finished by Rev. Charles Baldwin, after his retirement from the active ministry. Mr. B. and his interesting family are recalled by many. He died in 1879, at the age of forty-eight years, and was buried in Rose. His daughters—Flora, Mattie and Nettie —all married Methodist ministers, and the mother makes her home with them. The place is now owned by Mrs. Wilkins, the widow of the late Rev. Andrew W., of the Baptist denomination. He was twice the pastor of this church in Rose—first, from 1845 to 1849, and second, from 1881 to 1884. In March of the latter year he resigned the pastorate. In April he moved from the parsonage to this house, and in September he was moved to a narrower one in the cemetery. No one has other than the most affectionate memory of this loyal laborer in the Lord's vineyard. He was born in Eaton, Madison county; his wife, Laura J. Barnes, in Ira, Cayuga county. A faithful, helping wife, the people of her husband's old parish are glad that her home is among them. There are four Wilkins boys, and all save the second are graduates of Rochester University. Hervey D. is a very successful teacher of music in Rochester; Hartwell A. is a business man in New York City, and was a member of the 75th New York Regiment during the Rebellion; Frank is a Baptist minister in Davenport, Iowa (now in Chicago); while Fred. H., the youngest, is in the electric light business. It is noteworthy that the entire record of this house is one of parsons.

Samuel Lyman resides in the next house. He is of that Lyman stock noted in District No. 3. His wife, Sarah Vanderburgh, was from the same district. They have two children—George Frank, who married Florence Dodds, and is in Detroit, and Anna E., at home. Jonathan Wilson built the house and John Nichols once owned it.

Next is a house that was built by R. C. Barless, who sold to Silas Holcomb, and in it both he and his wife died; likewise their daughter, Mrs. Francis M. Johnson. It now stands in the name of the latter's husband. The Johnson sons were three: Frank E., now of Salem, Mass.; William, and George.

The house adjoining Mr. Johnson's was the long-time home of Lawrence Crisler. His widow still holds it. He bought of Julius C. Smith, now of Sodus. We have encountered the name of Crisler frequently in Rose. The father of the family was Martin, who was from Herkimer county originally. He settled first in Savannah, where his wife, Mary Frank, died. He had married her in the same town. He died in Rose. The children were: Matthew, a long resident on this street; Lawrence; Adam, met in York settlement; John, of District No. 7; Mary Ann married George Burch, in Oswego; Jane, in Herkimer county; Margaret; Elizabeth married Edward Dean; Jeremiah, formerly on this street, and Nancy, who married Samuel McIntyre. Lawrence Crisler, like all the men of that name, was a cooper and worked long at his trade. His wife's maiden name was Mary Ann Wilson, a daughter of Jonathan. Their children are : Willis Addie, who is Mrs. Wallace Williams, of Niagara county, and John, at home. Mr. C. died August 18th, 1874. His wife has woven many yards of carpeting, one of the very few to continue the trade once so common in Rose.

Mrs. Sarah Knapp dwells next. She is a daughter of the late " 'Squire " Philander Mitchell. Her husband, Hiram, was Sodus born. They have one son, Fred R. The house has had many owners and occupants. It was built by R. C. Barless, and owned in succession by Jerry Crisler, Abner Osborn, P. R. Tindall, John Winchell and Albert Harper. (Mrs. Lucinda Mitchell now resides with Mrs. Knapp.)

Matthew Crisler, the oldest of the brothers, lived for many years in the next house. This is the old John Bassett residence, standing formerly near Mrs. Vanderoef's house. His wife was Hannah Harmon, and she, with her sister, Mrs. Isaac Race, still occupies the house. Mr. C. died in May, 1890. Near by was the cooper shop where the brothers, Matthew and Lawrence, made many barrels, used in sending abroad the products of this fertile town.

In a house painted dark yellow, lives Willis Crisler. It was built by Jonathan Wilson, a brother of Ephraim B., of this district. Wilson for many years was the most noted shoemaker in town. Quick and racy in speech, his cobbler's bench was usually surrounded by many listeners. It was a favorite joke of his that he had married only one-half of his wife, Mary Ann Caywood, meaning that she weighed twice as much as she did when they were wedded. She was of the Caywood family once living in the extreme southwest part of Rose. Her grandfather was that John Caywood, a Revolutionary veteran, who lived to be more than a hundred years old. The Wilsons had only two children—Mary Ann Crisler, Willis' mother, and Walter, who died in 1860, a young man of twenty-five years. He had married Caroline Genung. Mrs. Jonathan Wilson died about four years since, surviving her husband several years. Willis Crisler, Jonathan's grandson, married Hattie Hughes, of Herkimer county, and has one child, Florence. He is a carpenter by trade.

The next house was built by George Seager, now living north of the Valley. In it died several years since, Daniel Converse, father of Eugene, who lives in the lower part of Griswold's. It is now owned and occupied by John Osborn, son of Abner.

Dwight Bradburn, who married Mary Ann Miller, built and occupies the next house. He is a son of David, who lives next west. Mr. Bradburn is a brother of Andrew, who once lived on the west road, north, in the Covell district. His wife was Jane Winchell, Jacob's daughter, and in her home, her father died. They have only one son, Dwight, though they lost Nelson at eleven, and Louisa Ann at about twenty years of age. The house was built by Daniel Johnson, now on the Main street. Mr. Bradburn died recently.

A very small house owned and built by John Gibbs, now in Rochester, follows. At present it is unoccupied.

When the Chauncey Collins house was fixed over, a part of the back L was moved down to this street, and it is the very next edifice. In it dwells James Johnson, having a very lively family of three sons and two girls. Very few people of the African race have made Rose their dwelling place, but the Johnsons, James and Daniel, belong to this class, and are reputable citizens. (Mr. Johnson has recently erected here a fine residence.)

The expression, "the last ditch," is one with which Americans are familiar, and we reach it when we come to the home of Jacob Lyman. Beyond him is the famous Thomas creek, by the perseverance of General Adams transformed into the beginning of the Sodus canal. Mr. Lyman has five and a half acres of land, a small house, but no children. His wife was Caroline Vanderpool in girlhood, coming from the eastern part of the state. His father was Levi Lyman, a half brother of Jesse. Thereby Jacob is a first cousin of Milo, who lives in the Griswold district. Levi lived further along on the creek, near the old Wyckoff possessions. His wife was Maria Winchell, and their children were : Frank R., now in Michigan ; Catherine, the wife of Jeremiah Crisler ; Ella died in infancy, and Jacob.

Beyond the ditch, on the south side, are fields belonging to Chaddock, Hickok and Jeffers. Crossing to the north side are found several acres, nine or ten, belonging to Jackson Valentine. Then comes, toward the east, a like amount, owned and tilled by the late William Thomas. This brings us to the ditch again, on whose banks Foster Moslein has his abattoir, this being on Thomas' land. (Now Leader.)

Crossing the bridge, we come first to the home which the well-known "Tom" King so recently left for his final one in the Rose cemetery. Few Valley people fail to recall the stalwart form of King, so long in care of horses at the village hotels. During the War, "Tom" was severely wounded during the seven days' fight at Gaines' Mill. It was the reopened wound that finally caused his death. His wife was Hannah Taylor, from Lyons, who continues to live with her children in the old home bought from Calvin Winchell, now in North Rose. Their children are : Ambrose, in Michigan ; Helen, the wife of Fred Goodnow ; Grace, Eliza, and Lena. Mr. King was born in England, and, in the Rebellion, was a member of Co. B, 27th N. Y. S. Vols.

A new but vacant house follows. It belongs to Jackson Valentine, who moved hither the old shop, once near his store, on the north. It is doubtful whether Mrs. Hannah Marriott would recognize it as the place in which she, as Miss Genung, for years sold hats and general millinery.

The widow of "Jerry" Crisler resides in the next house. She was Catharine Lyman, a daughter of Levi. Mr. Crisler was the youngest of the brothers, long famous as coopers. During the War, he served two enlistments: first, in the 33d N. Y., and afterward in the 45th Engineers. He was a very large man, the heaviest in the family. On the 15th of January, 1887, while logging in Seymour Covell's woods, he was killed by the springing back of a tree which he had felled. He was in his fifty-first year. The children are: Marsden, who married Alice Green, of Glenmark; Minnie M., the wife of Albert Shepard, of North Rose; Adam, and Maud. Few would recognize Marsden by that name, for in town he is known as "Manny"; he has one child, Elmer H. Minnie Shepard has two children, Delbert and Frank.

Samuel Bigelow built the next house and sold it to Postmaster Houghton, and he to the present owner, Sally Burch.

It is always a pleasure to meet a member of the Samuel Lyman family, and in the next dwelling is David, of the good old Connecticut stock. His wife was Emma Chalker, from Seneca county. The house was built in part by Philander Winchell. Mr. Lyman bought of Eron N. Thomas, and has extensively repaired the premises.

Charles E. Tillson, our next neighbor, resides in a house built by Peter Hilts, whom we met on the State road, north of George Worden's, in the Jeffers district. Mr. T. is from Camden, and is a carpenter by trade. He has four children—Etta, Stanton, Arthur and Frank. (Etta is Mrs. Geo. D. Johnson, and Arthur died March 30, 1892.)

The widow of Thomas Markham is found in the next place. Mr. M. was from Massachusetts. He left two daughters—Nina, at home, and Lena, recently married to Clayton L. Barless. The house was constructed by Adam Crisler, and by him sold to David Bradburn.

In the cabinet shop near, Judson L. Garlick has made and repaired furniture for thirty-eight years. Like many other trades and industries, cabinet-making by hand has had to yield to machinery, though the need of repairs in machine-made goods has given Mr. G. something to do. He is the youngest son of that large family noted in the North Rose series. His wife was Mary Buckingham, born in Milford, Connecticut. For twenty-four years she was an invalid, and for fifteen years was deranged in mind. Her condition was doubtless induced by the death of her daughter, Emma A., by burning. This sad accident happened twenty years ago. Mrs. Garlick died in 1887, leaving one daughter, Martha Jane. This place Mr. Garlick bought of his brother Henry. No more exemplary member of the Presbyterian Church lives in Rose than our friend, Judson Garlick. The missionary Judson, whose name he bears, could not have been more attentive to religious duties than this Christian, who for long years has not missed, when in health, a meeting in his church.

The house next east was built by John Nichols, sold to Sheldon R. Overton, and then to Mrs. William A. Mix. Alexander Harper is the present occupant. He was born in Galen, one of that family frequently encountered in our Rose rambles. He married Nancy Bivins, and they have five children—Daniel, who married Cora Crisler, a daughter of John of District No. 7, and lives in Rose; Gardner, who works for Joel Lee; Frank married Elizabeth York and lives in Huron; Mary, wife of Aaron Rhinehart, in Huron also, and Charles, who married Esther Terry, and lives near the Hiram Gordon place, in the extreme southern part of the town. Mr. Harper was a member of Company H, Ninth Heavy Artillery.

Judson Lackey was the builder and first owner of the next house. He sold to Charles S. Wright. William O. Horton is the occupant, with his family. He is a Vermonter, a native of Derby; served in the 7th Vermont during the War, and came to Rose in 1866; his wife was Sarah Brewer, and their children are Mary, William, Hattie and Earl. He is a shoemaker, having a bench in Collier's store. (In December, 1892, Mary became Mrs. James T. Harper, and in January, 1893, Hattie was married to Edward Weeks.)

"'Squire'" Ellinwood holds the next residence. It was built by Josephus Collins a long time ago, and by him was sold to the "'Squire.'" The latter was a justice of the peace for more than thirty years. He came to Rose when a little more than twenty years old, and taught school in the Valley and at Stewart's corners. His subsequent wife, Mary Lee, daughter of Lyman, went to his school at Stewart's. For a time after marriage, he farmed on the present Wickwire place. He has been school commissioner and overseer of the poor, and was for many years postmaster. The line of this Ellinwood branch is as follows: Ananias E., was born in Massachusetts, moved to Paris, now Kirkland, Oneida county, where he reared a large family of children; he was a half brother of the Jonathan who lived east of the Valley; His son, Reuben, was nine years old when the migration was made to the Mohawk country. The latter's wife was Emma Hart of Oneida county; he, too, had a large family; but we are interested only in that portion which came to this section. They were Valorous, George W., Orlando and Louise. The first and the last have been met, and Orlando resides in the south part of the village. The first marriage of George W. has already been stated; his only child by this marriage was Ella I.; he wedded, second, Jane Russell, by whom he had Mary, the wife of Clayton Allen, of District No. 6. Ella married Philip Turner, and died in 1873, leaving a child, Nellie, now with her grandfather. Turner's career is worthy of note. Coming from Canada, he was above twenty-one years old before he learned to read. In Red Creek he was fortunate enough to meet the famous teacher, "Nabby Bunce." From her instruction, he passed with marvelous speed to the Red Creek Academy, and was soon a teacher himself. He shouldered a gun during the War as a member of Company H, 96th N. Y. Volunteers, and after the strife he essayed the profession of law ; but death cut him down in 1870, at the age of thirty-five years. He died having the hearty respect of all his fellow townsmen. After Cleveland's administration came in, the " 'Squire " was relegated out of the post office, and since then his time has largely been given to reflection and reminiscence.

Where the Rev. Charles Ray lately resided, the Presbyterians have for some years maintained their parsonage. In the remote past it was held by Samuel Hoffman, then by Hiram Salisbury. For a time it was the Methodist parsonage. After the burning of the church, Stephen Waite owned, then the Presbyterian Society. Rev. Mr. Ray has an interesting history, having been born in Calcutta, India. His father was in the employ of the East India Co., whose name recalls Charles Lamb and his life-long drudgery in the dingy London offices of the company. Mr. Ray came to America in 1838, was graduated at Union College, and from the Princeton Theological School, thereby rendering his orthodoxy above suspicion. Of his college days under the noted Dr. Eliphalet Nott, he retains very striking memories. Some portion of his early life was passed in Middlebury, Wyoming county. His wife died recently, leaving three children— Charles H. Ray, the distinguished lawyer of Lyons ; Mrs. Dr. Silvers, of Youngstown, Ohio, and Ella, at home. Only recently Mr. Ray resigned his pastorate. (In 1893 the home of the Rev. Nathan Bangs Knapp, who, though pastor of the Presbyterian Church now, in his Christian names, bears traces of Methodist origin. He is a graduate of Amherst College and of Andover Seminary ; was born in Rochester, and has been connected with several churches in this state.) This brings us to the residence of Mrs. Lampson Allen and Main street again.

Passing to the south, the Presbyterian Church follows, of which there will be more anon ; next the unsightly evaporator, a veritable fire-trap, owned by William Deady, whose storehouse it was for a time, and then we are confronted by the building that is set upon a hill and cannot be hid. Though now the property of Harmon Miner, it is filled with Valentine memories. When Dr. Peter Valentine erected this, his beautiful house, in 1824, the approaches and surroundings were very different from those of to-day. A gradual ascent led up to it, and the building was not in the dilapidated condition that is noted now. The " bee hive," as it is called, swarms with occupants ; but it is far from being a thing of beauty. The Valentines were from Kingsbury, Washington county. The first of whom I have any note, was Henry, of Hackett, N. J. His son, Jacob, was the Kingsbury father whose sons were Henry, Peter, Asahel, Alexander and Stephen. There was a daughter, Rebecca. Of these children, Henry lived in Galen for a time, while Peter and Asahel only, became residents of

Rose. The latter was met in the western part of District No. 3 ; Peter was the first physician in Rose ; his studies, before the days of medical colleges, were passed with Dr. Richard Sill, of Sandy Hill, and after this doctor, Peter Valentine named his oldest son. The doctor's diploma as a medical practitioner is his certificate of admission to the Seneca County Medical Society. This bears date June 10th, 1820, and is signed by M. A. Bellows, president, and Jesse Fifield, secretary. Dr. Valentine's wife was Rachel Bishop, one of the numerous family to the northward. The children were Richard S., Jackson, W. H. Harrison, Cornelia and Naomi. In this lot there were twelve acres, extending from the Presbyterian Church to the home of the late Dr. Dickson. Peter Valentine was a conspicuous man in the early days of the town. He was the first supervisor and he held the office nine years. During the continuance of the office of town superintendent of schools, he and his son, Richard, filled it every year but one. In person he was short and stout, weighing 198 pounds. In disposition he was gentle and lively, and always left a cheerful impression in the sick room. He died in 1857, and his wife the year following. Richard S. Valentine, M. D. from the Albany School, was associated with his father, but consumption carried him off in 1856, at the early age of thirty years. He had married Ann M. Hickok, who survived him only two years. An only son, Frank H., was graduated from the Albany Normal School, and for some time resided in Galen. He is now editorially employed on the *Rural New Yorker*, published in New York City. Jackson Valentine will be seen in the next place to the south ; Harrison, in Rose, known as "Harry," we have met as the son-in-law of Charles Oakes ; Cornelia married David Town, and moved to Wisconsin ; while Naomi married Oliver Blanchfield, and lives in Wisconsin. The old Valentine mansion is now the property of Harmon Miner, who is a son of the Riley Miner who once lived to the northwest of the village. He is a stone mason by trade, as was his father before him. At present he is running a meat market and has done some farming. He married Lillie Stone, a daughter of Eben and Lucy Stone, of Galen. They have four children living—George S., Mabel, Birdett N. and Louie H. Several years ago they lost two boys, Martin L. and Edward P., in Battle Creek, Michigan. (Recently the "bee hive" was moved back, over the hill, and in time the hill itself will disappear through the digging away of the gravel of which it is composed.)

A small edifice standing at the foot of the hill and a trifle north of Mr. Valentine's store, belongs to Mr. Harmon Miner, and it has harbored a great variety of occupations.

Formerly a small building stood between this shop and the store. Mr. Valentine has recently moved it over to the lower part of Sodus street, and made of it, with additions, a tenement house.

The store so long known as Valentine's was erected in 1836 by Dr. Valentine, and in it Hiram and Ira Mirick, with George Closs, began business. They ran the same for two years and then sold to Wm. S. Worthington. He passed the enterprise to Dr. Peter himself, who undertook, with Chauncey B. Collins, the running of a store. This was in 1839. Both were wholly inexperienced, and after two years of labor, they had the experience and the public the money, for then they failed. For two years the building served as an office for Drs. Valentine and Henry Van Ostrand. The latter is now living in Albion, Mich. In 1844 Hiram Salisbury, who was of New Lebanon, Shaker rearing, filled the store with goods, but in 1846 he sold to Hiram Mirick, and he to Charles S. Wright in 1848. The latter remained till 1853, when he moved into his new building, now Fredendall's. The structure was practically vacant until 1860, when Mr. Valentine opened it again as a general country store, and for thirty years it has been one of the noteworthy features of the village. The village store disputes with the tavern the possession of political discussions and current gossip. Particularly on Saturday nights, it is the headquarters of those who come from the farms to find out what the world has been doing, and at other times the number of idlers in town can be pretty accurately gauged by the representation standing in front of the store or seated on barrels within. As to the contents of such a store, it would be exceedingly difficult to describe their scope, save to say that they include almost everything. Such a store is of necessity a Macy's or a Wanamaker's on a small scale.

In Rose, Jackson Valentine is known as "Jack." This is never an indication of disrespect, for familiar terms are easily applied in country towns. I never heard his children thus address him, nor total strangers, but old and young refer to him as above. When we consider the positions that he has held in town, the peculiarity of the situation becomes all the more curious. While people may have errands at Collier's and Fredendall's stores, they do the same business at "Jack's." I am inclined to think that this condition of affairs is the result of the thorough confidence and esteem in which he is held in his native town. Prominent business men in Rose can not recall the day when his benign face did not beam over the contents of the store. He is by far the best known man in town. Beside, he is a veritable treasure house of information pertaining to Rose, and I hereby acknowledge my obligations. In his earlier days, he was a teacher in the districts near, and in this capacity we may suppose that he met his wife, then Miss Christiann Dodds, a daughter of William, who lived in the Griswold neighborhood. They have four children—Mary E., the wife of George A. Collier, of Rose; Charles A., at home; Marvin J., in Rochester, and Bert, also at home.

The next building, to the south, is Mr. Valentine's house, which he constructed in 1862. There used to be in front of the space a small building, which was moved, first to the north of the store, and then to the Wayne Centre road. This chapter cannot be dismissed until mention has been made of Mr. Valentine's public services. He has been supervisor of Rose for fourteen terms, a length of service exceeded in but one instance in Wayne county, and has been two terms a member of the state Assembly. In no instance has he been other than a painstaking, honest, conscientious public servant. In cases where his wisdom has intervened, his fellow townsmen have been gainers in a marked manner.

The white, square edifice south of Valentine's is the Town or Memorial Hall. By no means pretentious in appearance, it serves a very useful purpose in Rose. (The local post of the G. A. R. has rooms in it now.)

The estate of the late Dr. Dickson follows. It is to-day just as he left it on his death, in 1874. The large barn was erected for the crops raised on the fifteen acres lying back of the road. The stone building next the street was built by the doctor for an office, with a story above for a select school. It would be easier to name the kinds of business that have not been in this building than those that have. At present, from the second story, Clayton J. Barless publishes his *Rose Farmer's Counsel and Times*, for which enterprise all possible success is besought. The house was built more than fifty years ago, but meantime it has undergone extensive repairs and changes. Dr. John J. Dickson, or in popular parlance, Dr. "Dick," was born May 25th, 1807, in Kingsbury, Washington county. At first he was John Dickson, Jr., but later he chose to insert the initial. His medical diploma was from Geneva, and he practiced his profession for many years. He was at times a justice of the peace, and in 1845 was sent to the state Legislature. His wife was Sophia Letitia, daughter of Charles Thomas. She was then the widow of Isaac Crydenwise. A son, Isaac, by this marriage, had his named changed to Dickson. She died in 1848, and for his second wife the doctor married Mrs. Jane (Jones) Bell, a daughter of the "Uncle Sammy" who lived on the Butler confines of District No. 7. By his first marriage, he was the father of Ensign L. Dickson, well known to all Valley people; by his second, he had F. Cora, better known as Ora, who married a Mr. White, of Locke, N. Y. Martha Rose Dickson, the late Mrs. Ira T. Soule, was adopted and made a sharer in his property at his death. The estate is still held in trust and the house is now occupied by Dr. J. E. Bradshaw, from Sodus, an M. D. from Buffalo. His first wife was Jennie Jewell, who died in 1881, leaving a son, George D. He married, second, Alice M. Goewey, who has a daughter, Frances. Dr. B. came to Rose first in 1873. (Dr. F. H. Hallet, who came to Rose from Huron in 1890, now lives here. He is a graduate of Buffalo University. Dr. Bradshaw has gone to South Sodus.)

Coming back to the point where we left Wolcott street for northern rambles, we find a small building, now used by Ira Soule for a shoe shop and store. Originally it was on the hill, nearly opposite, and in it George Howland maintained a shop for years. Mr. Howland's first wife was Harriet, a daughter of Deacon William Briggs, of District No. 7. By her he had two daughters—Josephine, who married Geo. Barless, and Jeannette, Mrs. Seager, of District No. 3. For his second wife, Mr. H. wedded Miss Lucy Town, of District No. 5. He died in 1863, at the age of forty-eight years. " 'Squire" Geo. W. Ellinwood bought the shop and moved it to its present location. Here he kept the post office from 1869 to 1885. As this is the only separate building devoted to post office use in Rose, it is a good place to give the history of the office from the beginning. Dr. Peter Valentine was the first postmaster, appointed in 1827, and the office was known as Valentine's. Soon afterward it became Albion, then Rose Valley, and, in 1834, Rose. As such it has continued to date, though many people persist in adding the superfluous " Valley." Charles Thomas was the second postmaster, appointed June 17th, 1829, and he kept the office in his tavern. After him, came his sons, Nathan W. and Eron N., the latter appointed in 1832, and he held the same till 1841. Next came Hiram Salisbury for four years, going in with "Tippecanoe and Tyler too." With the return of Democracy to office, in the person of James K. Polk, Eron N. Thomas resumed the post office from 1845 to 1849. The Whigs were again successful in electing a president, and with Zachary Taylor, in 1849, came Benjamin Hendricks as postmaster for one year only, when Charles S. Wright took the office to his new store. When the Democrats came back to power in the person of Franklin Pierce, in 1853, Eron N. Thomas once more assumed the position and held it till 1861. Lincoln appointed Charles S. Wright again, and he was the postmaster till 1866, January 1st, when Jackson Valentine assumed the honors and emoluments, but he was not enough of a Johnson man, so he retired in favor of Daniel B. Harmon, a Democrat, and his holding brings us down to the days of G. W. Ellinwood, 1869. During Cleveland's administration, from 1885 to 1889, Joel S. Sheffield held the office, and he went out in favor of E. F. Houghton, who is now in the place. It will be observed that E. N. Thomas and G. W. Ellinwood have held the office the most of the time since its establishment. (With the return of Cleveland to office, George A. Collier became postmaster.)

Pimm's Hotel has been, for nearly a generation, a prominent feature in the Main street of the village. It was seized upon in the thirties, by Ira and Hiram Mirick, as an excellent site for a tavern. To make room for it, the old school-house was moved away and the present structure went up. It has remained unchanged to date, except that the comely piazza has been added and the back wing has been raised. Ira Mirick was the first landlord, and, after his going to Lyons, Hiram took his place. Solomon Mirick, the father, died here in 1839. To Hiram Mirick succeeded Fowler and Woodruff. Both went from Rose to Clyde, where Hiram Fowler still lives. George Woodruff keeps a tavern in the Joppa portion of Lyons. Stephen W. Thayer, so prominent in Rose hotel matters, had his period of keeping this hostelry, and with his efficient wife, we may aver it was well kept. Abram ("Abe") Dratt, Butler born, was land- lord at the close of the War. Mr. Dratt was afterward killed upon the railroad in Lyons. His oldest daughter was the first wife of V. M. Sweeting, the treasurer of Wayne county. Enos T. Pimm, who has been at the helm for so many years, was born in Huron. His wife, who died in 1886, was Martha E. Sedore. Mr. P. was a member of the Ninth Heavy Artillery during the Rebellion, and was elected president, in 1889, of the Wayne County Veterans' Association. For nineteen years this town has voted to not grant licenses, consequently a very enviable condi- tion of sobriety has obtained. In addition to maintaining a public house, Mr. P. until lately ran a line of stages from North Rose to Clyde, and can furnish a team for hire at a moment's notice. (In 1893 Mr. Pimm sold out to Lorenzo Whitney, who came here from Sodus. He has children, Harvey, William, Eva and Birdie. Mr. Pimm was married in 1891 to Mrs. Elizabeth J. Oakes, of Brockport, who has two daughters, Bertha A., wife of S. G. Blythe, associate editor of the *Buffalo Express*, and Bertha A., who is at home. Of course the hotel has been the home of many people, and among these might be named Dr. Nelson Neeley, who years since came to Rose with brilliant prospects. He was of an Oneida county family, had his medical education in Albany, and had married Mary McComb, from Canada. He was assistant surgeon of the 57th N. Y. during the War. He died in Rose. An only son, Clarence, is still in town. Mr. J. H. Woodman, now in Clyde, was a well-known figure here for a term of years.)

Foster Moslein is the village butcher, and furnishes his wares in a new building erected for the purpose. (Mr. M.'s place is now held by Reuben Leader.) The spot, or that near it, has marked a market or grocery for more than twenty years. Dr. J. J. Dickson formerly owned, and in the old building adjoining Moslein's, Eugene Hickok once kept a grocery. The upper part of it is a tenement house. (In the lower story the Barless Bros. print the *Rose Farmer's Counsel and Times*.)

The next place, belonging to Mrs. Ira T. Soule's heirs, is a part of the old Dickson property, and once constituted a portion of the old house, removed by Dr. Dickson when he made over his later residence. It has held a long line of tenants, the latest being Reuben Leader, a native of Canada, whose wife, Mary Head, a sister of Mrs. Edgar Armstrong, was from Madison county. Their children are: Levern, Libbie, Florence and

Etta. (Libbie Leader was married in February, 1893, to Claude Seager: Levern is in Muncie, Ind. Mrs. Wm. Vanderoef and son also live here.)

A house, once ascribed to J. York, was purchased by Daniel Johnson and torn to pieces. Mr. J.'s pretty little house is one that "Parm" Tindall moved down from its old site, south of the cemetery. It is the old home of the 2d Thad. Collins. In it Tindall lived twenty or twenty-five years. Wm. H. Dodds once owned it, and finally Johnson purchased, and has pride in making a very neat and tidy place. His wife died recently, leaving a daughter, Ida. Mr. Johnson, in addition to his duties as sexton of the Methodist Episcopal Church, is a skillful ditcher.

The man familiar with Rose twenty-five years ago, as he visits his old haunts, will look in vain for Alexander's old blacksmith shop, but its site is next south, and the unoccupied building is the old smithery worked over into anything that comes along. Just now it is an ice house, and before that "Joe" Wade and Will Klinck had a meat market in it. What it will be next, only omniscience can tell. It was probably fifty years ago that Daniel C. Alexander built his shop and began shoeing horses on this spot. The open doors and the sooty workmen are familiar memories in many minds. He early associated with himself his wife's brother, "Parm," or Palmer R. Tindall, and this relation was maintained for fifteen or twenty years. Mr. A. was originally from New Jersey, but at the old Tindall haunt, near Pilgrimsport, he had found his wife, Sally Ann. They had children, once prominent figures in young Rose Valley. John B. married a Lounsberry, and went to Michigan. Charles H. is in Kingman, Kansas; Sarah married Leander Mirick, went to Michigan, and there died; Redmond D. also went to the same state. Mrs. A. died suddenly some years since, and Mr. A. died later in Michigan. The Alexander house was built by John Snyder, who came from the east, and afterward went to Michigan. Mr. Alexander bought, added to and fixed over as we see it to-day. If the visitor misses the old shop, his eyes will be gladdened at the sight of the old well in front of the house. The means of getting water may not be those of earlier days; the bucket may have given place to a chain pump, and it to the later suction, but thirsty people continue to slake their thirst as of old. It is not the same tin cup that "Dan" Alexander hung up, but a cup is there and a rill is generally running from this town pump. At present the house is occupied by William A. Mix, who, a native of Washington county, came to Rose in 1860, influenced somewhat by his friendship for the late Dr. John Dickson and father. His first wife was Harriet Haviland; his second a Loveless. His children are: Eunice E., married to J. H. Ackerman, in Brooklyn, and Wm. J., now in Lyons. Though a mill owner, much of Mr. M.'s time is given to moving buildings. (In 1893 Mr. Mix boards at Brant's Hotel.)

Dr. Marcus J. Williams has his office and residence next. The house formerly belonged to the widow of Alonzo Snow, but it was built several years since by William H. Lyon, now of Brooklyn. It was once owned and occupied by James W. Colborn and family. Asa Cook was the first builder upon the site, and in his house dwelt for a time the five sisters of William H. Lyon. Dr. M. J. Williams is a native of Hannibal, Oswego county, born December 14th, 1853. His father, William L., came from Hollyhead, Wales, to America, at the age of twenty years, and married Miss Julia A. Palmer, of Hannibal. Both parents now reside in Clyde. Dr. Williams attended the district school of Hannibal, until he went to Falley Seminary, Fulton, where he passed three years. Afterward he entered the medical department of the Vermont University. He was graduated thence in 1878. His first location was Red Creek, whence he came to Rose seven years ago. He was married November 7th, 1877, to Miss Clara E. Sittson, of Weedsport, who, from the union school of that village, passed to the Auburn high school, where she prepared for college and was graduated from the Syracuse University in 1876. They have one child, Mabel J., twelve years old. The doctor obviously enjoys living in Rose, and has an extensive practice, though the town is called a very healthy one. (Dr. Williams moved to Jordan in 1892.)

The building on the corner of Thomas street was built by Eron N. Thomas as a store for Daniel Harmon, who also had the post office in it. George H. Merritt had a store there afterward. The latter's wife died in Rose. He went from Rose to Red Creek, and thence to Michigan. John and George Collier followed with a general store, remaining until George A. went into the building opposite. An L upon the north side has afforded a pleasant residence for the different occupants of the store. David Gragor now keeps a variety store, and runs a barber shop at the same time. Mr. G. has been in Rose for nineteen years, a considerable portion of the time having a shop in the old stone building opposite. He was born in Montezuma, N. Y., and was a soldier during the War, in the 11th R. I. His wife was Jane Nagle. By a former marriage, he had a son, Joseph. Mr. G. has Indian blood in his veins, coming from the grand old tribe of the Oneidas.

DISTRICT No. 4.—"THE VALLEY."

January 12—March 23, 1893.

PART II.

In accordance with the plan uniformly followed in these letters, of working from the outside to the centre, we will pass to the extreme southern part of the town and follow the Clyde road north toward the village. There are a few farms here that belong to the White School-house district, of Galen; but they are so few that they will be given in connection with the Valley neighborhood, indicating where the sections are separated.

The home of Jeremiah Gatchell, on the west side of the street, is not more than a rod north of the town line. With the place there are thirty-six acres of land, which Mr. G. bought of Ebenezer Odell. The latter repaired the house, which was built by Harry Matthews. James W. Casler preceded Odell. The latter died in 1886. Mr. Gatchell is a native of Huron, though the family is of Massachusetts origin, and his wife is Alice Kanouse, a daughter of the late first neighbor in Galen. They have one child, Grace. The farm is a part of that great plain extending from Clyde to near the northern limits of Rose, and it is not so long since that it was deemed an irreclaimable swamp. General Adams' ditch, if it did nothing more, opened many acres of good land to tillage. (Mr. G. now resides in the Kanouse house over the Galen line, and Gardner Harper and wife occupy the Rose place.)

Hiram Gordon owns the farm across the way. He bought in 1875 from his brother, William. The latter took from Dr. Ely, of Clyde, and he from a Wadleigh. William Gordon built the barns and a part of the house. When Hiram G. bought, he improved and repaired the house. The Gordons are natives of Phelps, but their boyhood was passed in Galen. Mr. Gordon's first wife, Clara D. Kirkland, died in 1855, and his second, Anna Arnold, in 1889. Two children died in infancy, and Martha J., a young lady, in 1861. In addition to the fifty acres in the Rose farm, there are twenty-five in the Galen portion joining. Charles Harper, who works the farm, and with whom Mr. Gordon boards, married Esther Terry, and has two boys, George E. and Selah F. This was true in 1890, but now Mr. Chapin, late of Huron, tills the farm and Mr. Harper lives to the north.

Going northward we find Charles H. Stell, on the west side of the road, living on the Lester Gordon farm. Lester Gordon is a son of William, though in town parlance he was better known as "Bill" Gordon. There are twenty-four acres in the place, and former owners were John Matthews, William Finch, Harmon Miner and many others. Seth Hale once bought this and possibly a part or all of the next farm south, from Stokes, the Clyde glass manufacturer, for 1,000 cords of wood. He failed, however, to keep his contract. Stokes purchased of a Watson.

Still further along, in the same direction, is the farm of Henry Tindall, who married a daughter of the widow of Leonard Mitchell, residing west of the Valley, and here lives Frank Finch, son of Selah, who resides at the next turn to the east. This is the old Bowles place, and the militant minister resided here when he had his famous encounter referred to in the history of the Methodist Church. The house was built by Ebenezer Stone many years since. Tindall bought of Nathaniel Campbell.

20

Frank Finch married Mary Eagan, and they have two children. Albert and a little girl. The house was built by Seth Hale.

This whole section has been subjected to changes innumerable. When the higher acreage, all around, was taken up by permanent settlers, this was deemed almost valueless land, and it was only when General Adams' ditch drained it measurably that it was considered arable. Hence there is no farm along this road for some distance that is identified with any old family name.

The fifty-acre farm of Jerome W. Tindall has seen many owners. Col. Samuel Briggs sold to Henry L. Cole, who passed the right of possession to Charles Howes. The latter went west, though he moved here, for a dwelling, the house that once stood on the Bert Shepard place in Galen, further south. After him came Stephen Weeks, then Abram B. Covell, who now lives in Sodus. The latter married Helen Griswold, a daughter of the late Lorenzo. They have one son, Ernest W. Mr. Tindall came here in April, 1890, from the northwest part of the town, a son of that Charles H. Tindall long identified with the remotest angle of Rose. He married Ida Clark, of Arcadia, and they have one son, Clark. Mr. T., like many farmers along this road, makes a specialty of growing and evaporating the black raspberry.

The Valley district begins with the home of William Steitler, a little north of opposite, i. e., William S. lived there in 1890, but now Charles Harper and family abide. It requires a yearly enumeration to keep track of the dwellers in these parts. The farm belonged to Willis Horton, deceased, and he bought of Samuel Kelsey. Years ago this was the property of Malcom Little, who sold to Morris Conklin, his brother-in-law. The latter was a stone mason by trade, and during the Rebellion was a member of Co. A, Ninth N. Y. Heavy Artillery, a comrade of the writer. He was subsequently accidently killed in the west. There are eighty-four acres in the farm.

Should we turn to the right and take the east road, we should find no dwellers in this district, but should soon enter the confines of the Town neighborhood. Here are still standing parts of the primeval forest, unpolluted by the homes of men, save as vagrant Indians have, from time to time, lived among the trees in basket making expeditions.

On the north side of the corner dwell Selah Finch and wife. He is a brother of the Finches of the Wayne Centre district, and his wife, Melissa Wright, is a daughter of the English Charles Wright who once lived in the extreme eastern part of the town. Their home is an exceedingly neat and pleasant one. They have only one son, Frank, whom we have already met. There are forty-two acres in the farm, and it goes back to Dr. Dickson at least. One Page, of Clyde, once owned and Alonzo Streeter built the house. George Sherman once owned the place, and after him was

Henry Cole, to whom succeeded Isaac Cole, and then came the present owner. The late Brownell Wilbur once owned several acres, east of Finch's farm, the eastern portion of the latter's place, and the writer has distinct recollection of several days' work done thereon, along with Marvin Wilbur, of Victor, all in a summer's "haying." It was there that I first saw a windrow roped to the loading place.

Occupying a commanding site from whatever direction it is regarded, the home of Lorenzo N. Snow is conspicuous on this Rose and Clyde turnpike. Mr. S., a native of Madison county, came here in 1854, succeeding William B. Sears. What was the north part of his farm, he bought from Dr. Henry Van Ostrand. The fine brick house and the roomy barns were all constructed by Mr. S. In the place there are more than 250 acres, extending from this north and south road to the next one west. Much of the land is as level as a floor, occupying, as it does, a large part of the swamp land that the famous Sodus canal of General Adams redeemed from almost hopeless moisture. Mr. Snow is much interested in blooded stock, both horses and cattle. He married Harriet L. Sexton, of Chenango county. Years ago, two brothers, Collins and Isaac Batt, owned the eastern part of the Snow farm with a log house, near where Charles Harper lives, and another near the Snow house. There were other owners before Sears. The latter had one son, Edson, and two daughters by his first wife, Emmaette. These daughters, Sarah and Emily, were successively the wives of a Mr. Reynolds, Emily dying first, leaving two children; Sarah has one child. The second wife, Martha E., survives, and has one child, who is Mrs. Frank Howard of Galen. He afterward lived near the white schoolhouse, and was a member of the Baptist Church. The old Sears house was long a tenant house for Mr. Snow. A recent dweller was "Deck" Brewster, who married Albertine, daughter of Nelson Ferguson. (Benjamin Decatur Brewster, through his mother, is a member of the Butler-Kellogg family; his children are Lena, Nelson and Benjamin. The family is now in Syracuse.)

Opposite, and quite as pretty a figure as there is on this excellent road, is the home of John Collier. If you wish to make the acquaintance of Mr. C., you will have to call on him, for he is not one of those who favor taverns and groceries with their presence. He was born more than eighty years ago in Ireland, in County Carlow, near Dublin, and his people were of the Church of England, longer than memory recalls; he came to Rose in 1845. His wife—wedded in the old country—in girlhood was Hannah Cardiff. She has borne a numerous family, as follows: Alice, at home: John, who died in New York, where the family located on coming to America; Mark T., known as "Tom," of the Valley, who married Sarah F. Zeluff, of Clyde; William, who died before he was twenty-one, having been for some time the favorite clerk of J. C. Atkins, the toy dealer of

Clyde ; Anna, the wife of Jerry Barrett, of Rose ; Eliza (better known as Leila), at home ; John, for some time in business in Clyde, now at home, and George, who married Mamie E. Valentine, and keeps one of the stores in the Valley. Mrs. Collier died April 17th, 1892. Mr. Collier bought his farm of Thomas M. Warn ; but the house then standing has been repaired and improved beyond recognition. There are seventy acres in the farm. John Skidmore, who married Sally Bishop, also dwelt here for a time. It is probable that the farm was taken from the office by Martin Warner. If one delights in pleasant prospects, there is every reason why Mr. Collier should stay at home and enjoy the outlook that the south side of his home affords. He is a pleasant man to meet, with just enough of a brogue to let you know that the curl of his tongue was acquired in Green Erin.

The house which covers George Klinck and wife was old long before they were born. George, a son of the late Henry C. Klinck, and a grandson of the late Artemas Osgood, has been married twice—first, to Lucinda Harper, and second, to Viola Warren, of Walworth. William Matthews, of this village, preceded Klinck, and I have little doubt but the latter wishes that Matthews had retained possession till after the destructive tornado of 1888, which broke the windows of the house and destroyed valuable trees.

Deacon Walter Lyon came before Matthews, and he was the most noted of all the possessors here. He was born in Woodstock, Conn., and came to Rose from Holland, Mass. This township is one of the most sterile in the southern part of the Commonwealth, and the frugality necessary to make a living there followed him to this fertile locality. It was early in the forties that he came among us. His first wife was Lucretia ———, who died in 1846. Their children were Amos, who taught singing schools in Rose, and finally went east, and died ; Lathrop, who went to Gratiot county, Mich.; Winthrop, a wagon maker in Clyde, dying there ; and Emerson, who married a Whittlesey, of Galen, and went to Michigan ; a daughter, Elmina, died in 1850, at the age of twenty-one years. He subsequently married Roxana, the widow of Deacon William Briggs. She survived till 1880, dying then at the age of eighty-five years. Deacon Lyon was long one of the most noteworthy figures in Rose. There are many who can still recall his tall and, as years came upon him, somewhat bowed form. He was as regular as clock-work in going to church, and every line in his face betokened devotion to what he considered right. His title was obtained before coming to Rose. He was extremely careful in his speech, determined to say only good of every man. But even deacons have troubles, and a line fence was a source of much bickering with a neighbor, and things didn't go to suit him at all. Even then he came no nearer a reproach than the following : Speaking of his neighbor's son, he was wont to say: "A fine boy, a very fine boy; very smart. He has an excellent mother, a beautiful woman; but his father—well, we won't say anything about him." If everybody were equally discreet, there would be less suits for slander. He lived to be very aged, and even then passed off the stage by his own hand. He was about eighty-four at his death, and it was the general opinion that he was not in his right mind at the time. The last home of himself, his first wife and daughter is in the neglected burying ground by the white school-house. He was a life-long member of the Baptist Church. John Wade built the house and lived here some years.

Between the Presbyterian elder and the Baptist deacon, came the occupancy of Samuel Jones; he was a native of Albany county, and his wife, Lydia Gardner, was from Hudson. He later kept the south hotel in the village, and finally moved to Williamson. Of his children, Peter went to Sparta, Wis.; Rachel died in Chicago; Elizabeth in Williamson; John is in Adrian, Mich.; Lydia A. is Mrs. Hamel Closs; Mary Jane became the wife of the late David Ellinwood; George is in California, and Abbie, Mrs. Dr. Kimball, resides in Adrian, Mich.

Nearly opposite is a house that has latterly taken on a new lease of life. It belonged to Lyman Legg, and in it his son, DeLancey, resides. His wife is Fanny, a daughter of Nelson Ferguson, once residing in No. 7, and who will be remembered as marrying a daughter of Abram Phillips. (They have one child, Stella.) This place has belonged to many owners, as Lorenzo Snow, Dr. Henry Van Ostrand and Jesse O. Wade. The latter is a son of John Wade, one of the earliest settlers. His wife was Milly, a sister of Dr. Van Ostrand.

Then comes the home of William McMurdy, born in Ulster county. His wife is Mary Wolever, and they came to Rose in 1882. They have only one child, Agnes, recently married to John W. Crisler, of Rose. The farm of eighty-eight acres is entirely of the perfectly flat character so peculiar to this section. Brownell Wilbur and family preceded the present owner, coming here from the Fuller place, and going hence to Victor. The house was built by Mr. Van Ostrand. Before him was Mr. Hoag, a wagon maker, who afterward lived in District No. 8.

The house just to the north, now nearly destroyed, was long the home of John Bassett and wife, they coming here from the Valley. The blacksmith shop was a little south of the house. It yielded to time some years ago. There are twenty-five acres in the place. Truman Van Tassell, a Methodist minister, traded this place with "Uncle" John Bassett for the latter's village lot. These good people were long members of the Methodist Church, but the story goes that "Uncle" John once lost the run of the days of the week and went to work on Sunday in his shop. He was horrified when informed of his profanation. "Uncle" John's old horse was a good

Methodist, too. In the days of the stone church, the beast one Sunday morn grew tired of waiting for the old people and went on up to the Valley alone, stopped at the horse block, and then walked demurely back to his place under the shed. The blacksmith followed in time, proud of the possession of so orthodox a beast. The Bassetts had an adopted son, who strayed away and was last heard from in Australia, writing thence to Eron N. Thomas. Mrs. B. was a sister of the late Mrs. Solomon Allen.

The home of William H. Griswold is one of the oldest houses on the street. In the early matrimonial days of Eron N. Thomas, it was nearly as it is now, only a few additions having been made. The first Mrs. Thomas cooked in the then cellar kitchen. This is still the largest farm in one body in the town. There are 313 acres in it, running back into the eastern swamps, a long ways from the road. In addition to the barns near the house, there is a very large one some rods back, to the east. Extensive young orchards give promise of fruitful wealth in years to come. Eron Thomas took from his father, Charles, who probably bought this farm of John Covey, April 18th, 1826. There were then 100 acres. Mr. Rhinehart now tills the farm. William Griswold is a son of Lorenzo, met in the extreme northern part of the Jeffers district. Lorenzo was a nephew of the first William G., of the district bearing his name. It will be remembered that this William lived for many years on the Griswold corner. He married Julia, a daughter of James Weeks, of the Jeffers district. Their children are Charles E., who has taught school for some time in Idaho; Mary Almeda, now the wife of Dr. Frank S. Barton, of Clyde; and Frank W., at home. The family now reside in Clyde.

Crossing the road, the home of Stephen Weeks is found. He is a son of James Weeks, of District No. 11, and his wife was Margaret Grenell, of Galen. They have only two children—Edith L., at home, and George R., who four years since sought happiness and wealth in California. (Mrs. W.'s mother, Adelia, widow of Henry Grenell, died here January 5, 1892, aged 82 years.) The farm of forty-four acres was bought of Jerome Thomas, who purchased from the Alonzo Snow estate. Here, too, lived once Johnny Ogram, the most famous shoemaker ever in Rose. One old-time owner was Rufus Dann, a college graduate and a most polite gentleman. Ogram went from here to Fulton. Mr. Dann was one of those singular freaks of nature called an Albino.

Ex-Deputy Sheriff John H. Barnes is the motive power in the next stopping place. Since his taking possession, he has instituted many improvements. The location of the outbuildings has been changed, and he has done a deal of "slicking up." He found a wife in Elizabeth Stack, whose family was met in District No. 8, and they have one daughter, Jessie May. Longer than many Rose people remember, this place was called the Austin farm. Ezra Austin was a native of Herkimer county, as was also his second wife, Huldah A. Allen. They were married in 1838, and came to Rose in 1841, buying of Thomas Knight. Mr. Austin died in 1862, his wife in 1885. There were Austin children as follows: by a former marriage, Hubbard, who died unmarried, and Charlotte, the first wife of William Allen, who went west; by his second marriage, Edmund, married Lovina Ingersoll, and was killed at the Wilderness, a member of Company C, 111th N. Y. Volunteers; James died in childhood; Charles Henry, a soldier in the Third Artillery, died at Newburn, N. C.; Mary Josephine, married William Hamm, and lives in the village; Ida E. died in childhood, and Irving, who married Jane Willis, and is a Rose citizen, on Lyons street. It was in the early days of her widowhood that Mrs. Austin allowed some of those rapacious, predacious lightning rod men to mount her buildings, to put on fifteen or twenty dollars' worth of rods. When the men came down, the ridges on the barns resembled nothing so much as elegant picket fences. The bill was $300, and Mrs. A. and her boys had to pay it. Thus the barns became as conspicuous as any on the Clyde road. To be sure, the farmer is not beset by that form of legalized robbery now, but he has to keep his eye peeled lest a greater evil come unto him. The sharper has long considered the farmer his own particular victim. Mrs. Austin sold to Charles Vanderpool, and he to Frank Parkes. This farm, with the one south, is connected with one of the earliest names in the town, viz., that of Milburn Salisbury. It is on record that a child of his was the first one born in the town, in 1812. To him succeeded Abel Lyon, father of the Moses Lyon noted in the annals of the Methodist Church in central New York. Then there was a Caguin, and after him Ezra Dann, brother of the one who lived at the same time on the present Weeks farm. This Dann had a family, and finally sold to Ezra Austin, as stated. The Danns lived together in a house which now serves Stephen Weeks as a horse barn.

Somewhere in these parts was the scene of the following thrilling story, told by an old gentleman, who now lives in Michigan, but was once a Rose boy. The story is due to the kindness of Chester T. Sherman, who is much interested in all Rose matters:

A MURDER STORY.

At the time of the murder in Rose, we lived on the south side of the creek, and west side of the road to Clyde. Our grandparents lived on the north side of the creek, and east side of the road. It was about midsummer—July or August, perhaps—I think, about 1827 or 1828. One evening grandmother came over to our house and said:

"Clara," for so she called mother, "did you hear somebody cry 'murder,' a little while ago, down toward Salisbury's?"

Mother said : "Why, no."

"Well," said grandmother, "when I was milking, I heard some one cry, 'Murder, murder, murder!' just as plainly as I hear you talking here now."

"Oh," said mother, "it was children playing, I guess."

"No," said grandmother, "it was not; and I think there is trouble somewhere."

As no one in the neighborhood seemed to notice it, the matter dropped and nothing more was said about it. About a week after that, mother went to Clyde to do some shopping, and took me along with her. We rode with a neighbor, in a two-horse wagon, since carriages were not much in use in those days. About a mile from where we lived, on the road to Clyde, stood a log house on the west side of the road, and just on the north edge of a thick, heavy timbered, low piece of land, called "the gore." I think the land still belonged to the state or government. As we were coming home from Clyde, about sundown, we came to this log house and were stopped by the man who lived there. His name was Phelps. He was in a terrible state of excitement, and said : "What do you think my dog brought up this evening ?" No one could guess. "Well," said he, "he brought up a man's foot and leg as far as the knee, and here it is." Sure enough, in an hour or two, the whole of quiet little Rose Valley was all excitement, and every man turned out and all night long was looking for the body of the man. Some time in the next day, the body was found away back in the woods, lying on its back, with the throat cut from ear to ear and a razor lying on the ground near his right hand as though he had committed suicide ; but a club was found, near by, with hair on it, showing that it had been used first. The body was, of course, in a terrible state, for it had been lying there some days in the hot weather. A coroner's jury was called, of which my father was one. On examination of the clothes, father recognized them as those of a man whom he had seen at Thomas' tavern a few days before. He and several others happened to be at the tavern, when a stranger came in and asked for a pint of whisky, which Mr. Thomas put up for him in a flask. The man asked if there was land for sale around there, representing that he had means to purchase. Some one told him that there was a piece of land for sale about a mile below, and directed him to go to Mr. Phelps, just on the edge of the land, thinking that Mr. Phelps would go with him and look at the land. The man went out, and nothing more was thought of it until father's discovery.

The jury came to the conclusion that the man came to his death by some unknown person. On his body were found some papers that indicated that his name was Jones, and that he was from some town in the eastern part of the state. I do not remember the name of the place.

They took the body as best they could, and putting it in a rough box, at about midnight buried it in the cemetery, a little north of the village, the same ground in which our grandparents lie, I think. Father wrote to the authorities of the town where it was supposed that the man had lived, asking if such a man had ever lived there, narrating the circumstances of his death as best he could. The answer was that such a man had lived there, and that he was one who liked to have people think him wealthy. Very likely this trait was the cause of his death. I do not remember that his body was ever claimed. Of course, there was a great deal of talk about the matter and some claimed that Phelps was the murderer, or knowing to it. But he had been a prominent member of the Baptist Church, to which mother and grandmother belonged, and he had always been thought very highly of. Mother expressed herself very indignantly against any one intimating such a thing.

I shall remember to the day of my death the night of Jones' burial, as there was a terrific thunder-storm while they were burying him. Nor shall I forget how afraid I was to go along the road after that, as I had been told that "old Jones" might come out after me. Not long after this, it was discovered that the Phelps family had gone, bag and baggage. No one knew when nor where. Some months passed, when, just as suddenly, the family was at home again, claiming that they had been away working on some canal; for they were accustomed to taking contracts for that kind of labor. Soon after their return, mother went down there to make a visit. Just as she was leaving for home, Mrs. Phelps burst out crying. On being asked what was the matter, she said to mother: "You know what the stories are?" Mother was so dumbfounded that she could say nothing, not even to ask what stories, but immediately left for home. Not long after this, Mr. Phelps was taken very ill, and was not expected to live. Mother, with some others, went to watch with him one night, and when she came home in the morning, she declared that she now believed that "old Phelps" was the murderer. "For," said she, "while he seemed about dying, he would spring up in bed and utter the most unearthly screams, and his looks were such as I never want to see again." However, he got well, but no one seemed to wish to take the matter up, and as soon as he was able to be about, he, his wife and two grown-up sons disappeared again, just as suddenly as before, and I think that no one in Rose ever knew where they went.

Years rolled on. We came to Michigan. Some time about 1841, I was teaching a district school in a town eight miles from home, and, as teachers then did, I boarded around. One evening, I was staying at the house of a Mr. Moore. This gentleman was acquainted with my father and mother, when young people, in New York. In the course of the evening, the name of Phelps was mentioned as being that of one of the neighbors. I said: "Phelps! Phelps! where did he come from?" Mr. Moore said: "Why, he came from about where you did, in Wayne county." I was thunderstruck. I said: "Is it possible that that old murderer is alive and so near me?" They asked me what I meant, and I told them the story. It created quite an excitement, and in a few days the Phelps family was missed from that neighborhood, no one knowing where they had gone. One year after that, I was sent as a constable to arrest a man in Shiawasee county. Father went with me, and we were obliged to go to the man's house before daylight in order to catch him. He lived in a lone house in the woods. We arrived at the house just at daybreak, but, to our surprise, the man was just coming home. He saw us and ran into the woods. We went back to the tavern and father and the landlord made up a plan whereby father, who was not an officer, and the man could meet. They met, and the man agreed to go with us, father promising to help him as much as he could consistently. On our return, he told us that he had been watching that night with an old man by the name of Phelps, who, he said, was very ill, but it seemed as though he could not die. He said it was terrible to see the man. We learned a few days after that he was at last dead. So ends the story, as nearly as I can recollect it. The saying that "murder will out," failed in this case.

Chas. Sherman Woodard.

A little more than half the distance between Barnes' and the farm house of Frank H. Closs, long stood the toll house, or gate, an accompaniment of the plank road once existing between Rose and Clyde. On the expiration of the road's charter, the house was sold, and is now a dwelling house, on Lyons street, in the village. The plank road charter existed thirty years, and expired in 1878.

The spacious and inviting buildings of the Closs place follow. The owner and family once residing here, will be met in the Valley. The earlier citizens of Rose knew this as George Mirick's place. He was the builder of the house and barns. He came into possession after the death of his father-in-law, Charles Thomas. The farm in part goes back to John Covey, who sold in 1826 to Charles Thomas. Of the Coveys I know only that John's wife bore the name of Betsey, and that his father, Amos, lived in Fenner, Madison Co. The contract with Nicholas was made by Amos Covey, in 1815, the southeastern part of the Nicholas purchase. George Mirick married Elsie, a daughter of Charles Thomas. They were long prominent in all Rose matters. Their children, also, were all exceedingly bright, active young people. The family, young and old, went to Adrian, Michigan, where Mr. Mirick died, July 31st, 1887. His widow lives in Adrian, with Leander and her younger sons. Sophia Mirick married

Cassius R. Kellogg, and died in February, 1876; Charles married Hannah Foist, of Ferguson's corners, and is in Adrian; Eugenia married Calvin H. Crane, and died November 30, 1871; Mr. C.'s second wife is Emma (Livermore) Kellogg; Leander ("Stubb") married Sarah Alexander, now dead, their only son being William; the three younger sons are George R., Frank and Edward. Few families, in removing, ever took more life and activity from Rose.

The old house in the field north of this place was built by a Walmsley, and is included in the Covey or Captain John Sherman purchase.

Benjamin Genung and his family found a pleasant home in the house a trifle north of opposite, from 1847 to the date of his death, viz., March 23d, 1888. Deacon Genung was born in Fishkill, Dutchess county, and there married Jane Ann Darland. He came to Galen in 1839, and thence to Rose. The place of sixty-four acres was bought of Enoch Knight. Two children were buried in Dutchess county, and the others were: Caroline, who married, first, Walter Wilson, of the Valley, and second, Smith D. German, is a widow, and lives in Clyde; Hannah, Mrs. Marriott, who lives next door north; William D., of the 111th New York, was wounded at the Wilderness, and died in Fredericksburg; Joseph married Julia Wood, of Clyde, and is in the iron business in Chattanooga, Tenn.; Susan, the first wife of Nelson Graham, of North Rose; Mary D., who married Marcus Baker, and Charlotte, who became Mrs. Jessie Heit of Galen, since deceased. Mrs. Genung retains her residence here, though she passes much of her time among her children. Her husband, as man and Christian, left an excellent record. There was once a Devereaux on the farm.

John Marriott (called Merritt), whose house follows, is a native of England. His first wife was Hannah Crandall, of District No. 8. They had children : B. Nelson, who is principal of the South-side school, in Clyde; J. Darwin, of Rochester, employed as fireman on the Western New York & Pennsylvania R. R.; S. Lizzie, a teacher, and Jennie, who is attending the Clyde high school. Mr. Marriott bought fourteen acres of Benjamin Genung and built the house. His second wife was Hannah Genung. (Lizzie Marriott was recently married to William A. Bryar, of Fairville.)

Valorous Ellinwood, whose place follows, was born in District No. 6, the last house on the west. Some data omitted then might be given now. Valorous Ellinwood, first, a brother of George W. and Orlando, was twice married. First, to Sarah M. Turner. By this marriage he had Alexander, who married Susan Ellsworth, of Sodus, and lives in Grand Rapids, Mich. His second wife was Amy Smith, from Ontario county, a sister of the wife of Jester L. Holbrook. Her children were: Valorous, 2d, and George R. The latter married Jennie Greaves, of Clyde, and lives in Adrian, Mich.; his wife is dead, and his little girl has recently found a home with his cousin, Mrs. Adele (Holbrook) Osborn. Valorous Ellinwood, 1st, died in 1853; his widow was married again; this time to Samuel Garlic, and died in 1856. The present Valorous has been town clerk eight years. His wife is Elnora, the youngest daughter of Delos Seelye. Their children are: H. Guy; Raymond S.; Amy B. ("Kittie"), deceased; Mary A. V., Benjamin, and Ruth E.

This farm is the one so long identified with the Hickok name. William, the father, we met in the North Rose district. To him and his wife, Sophia Gunn, were born: Ann Maria, who was the wife of Dr. Richard Valentine; Sophronia died unmarried; William Felton we have already met, and Eugene, to be encountered west of the Valley. After long and valuable lives, the parents now sleep in the Valley cemetery. Part of the farm was bought from the Genung place and part from that of Willis G. Wade. The name of Hendrick is also connected with the farm, and Isaac Tucker built part of the house.

Crossing the street, we find the home of Orlando Ellinwood, a brother of George W., a native of Oneida county. He learned the locksmith's trade early in life, but in Rose he has been a farmer. He has been twice married; first in Oneida county, to Phœbe Ann Cook, who died in Little Falls, and second, to Emeline Munsell, of Rose. They have one son, Edson M., of Clyde, who married Susan Wells, of Springville, N. Y., and has five children, viz.: Hattie Bianca, Lena, H. Ross, Anna Louise and Aurora Blanche; he has been for several years superintendent of the Clyde water works. Orlando and wife have lost two children. This place dates back to Ephraim Wight, of Troy, who, it is said, being alarmed at the undue moisture upon his acres, made haste to sell out. It is also, I think, to some extent mixed up with the Shermans, whose possessions joined. Mrs. Ellinwood suggests that there was a Harvey, whose wife was an inheritor from the Wights, and that he, too, had rights here. At any rate, the old house which Mr. Ellinwood found here, still stands back of the new one, built by Mr. E. It was forty-three years since that he came upon this place of fifty-one acres. A lane leading down to the back portion of his farm has long been thought by many a proper beginning of a road to lead over the hill into the Town district. When the family came to Rose, Mr. E. was for two years on the Hoffman or Brainard farm. Then he was for three years at his trade in Utica. Since then he has been permanently placed in Rose. Returning to the subject of the lane, it should be stated that, years ago, James Cleveland lived at the end of it, at the foot of the ridge. Mr. C. was from Fairhaven, Rutland Co., Vermont. His wife was Sybil (Gibbs) Maynard, whose son by her first husband was also a dweller in another log house here. Only a well marks the old location. The Cleveland children were James, long residing in Butler, whose daughter, Paulina, is Mrs. Newton Moore, of Clyde; Nelson, Charity, Tabitha and

Polly. Nelson married Sally Merrill, and long lived north of Whisky Hill; a son, Jason is now in the Town district. The elder Cleveland died with Nelson. The latter now resides in Wolcott. James was twice married, first to Nancy Wescott, sister of Mrs. John Kellogg, and second, to Miranda Kelly, near Baldwinsville; he is now dead. Charity Cleveland married David Crossman, of Lynn, Mass.; Tabitha, Charles Churchill, and Polly, Lewis Wadsworth.

A deal of history attaches to the next house, where the village begins, found on the west side of the way. Recently it was the home of the widow of Dr. Lewis Koon. A native of Columbia county, he received his medical degree from Albany, and came to Rose in 1865. His wife's maiden name was Lucy A. Carrigan. She was born in Saratoga county. Before coming to this farm, the family lived in various places, among others the old C. B. Collins house. They came to this place in 1878, and here, in 1881, Dr. K. died. The children are: Helen A., who married Dewey C. Putnam, of Wayne Centre; Lewis D. married and lives at Rochester; Cora B. married Charles H. Metts, of Sodus, and Clara W., at home. Before Dr. Koon was Louis Viele, who was from the Hudson river region. He had a numerous family, as follows: Margaret, Betsey, Rachel, Jacob, John, Cornelius, Peter and Stephen. Louis Viele died in Huron. The widow of Dr. Koon has recently moved away. The doctor was well esteemed as one of the long line of physicians who have aimed to keep in order the bodies of Rose dwellers. (Now the home and property of James Coffee who, a native of county Waterford, Ireland, married Anne Cullen and has children, Delia, Nellie, John, William, Mary, Anne and Josie; he was formerly the blacksmith just to the north. He moved here in May, 1891.)

Henry Van Tassel preceded Viele. Mr. V. ran the store in Eron Thomas' building. He came to Rose from Butler, having married a Hibbard, from that town. Hence, he went to Clyde and died there. A daughter, Loretta, became Mrs. William Burnett; and Adelbert L., who married Hettie Ryerson, was a schoolmate of mine, in Fulton. Warren Osborn lived here first. He afterward died in Rochester, from cholera, in 1857 or 1858. Willis G. Wade left his impress on the place in renewing and grouping the barns. Mr. Wade was member of Assembly from this district in 1854. As a pension agent, Mr. Wade was very successful, but death carried him off in 1854, at the early age of thirty-four years. His wife was Juliette, a daughter of John Closs. Their only son died in infancy. Mr. Wade was a son of John Wade, one of the town's first settlers.

The next house is on the east side. It is now the property of Edson M. Ellinwood, but for a long time, his grandmother, Jerusha Munsell, owned and occupied it. She was the wife of Dorman, one of the first settlers in the northeastern part of the town. Before the Munsell occupancy this was the Presbyterian parsonage.

In the next house formerly dwelt Lafayette Legg and family. He married Huldah Drown. They have only one son, Irving. Mr. L. is a stone mason by trade, but latterly has managed a portable saw mill. They now live in Huron. Before Mr. Legg was Mrs. Elizabeth (Parker) Livermore, who afterward married F. G. Smith, of District No. 9. Philip Tindall resided here once, and here his wife died. The house goes back to Eron N. Thomas as original owner.

Another Mr. Legg was formerly found in the next house, Lyman, the father of Lafayette. I can trace the house back to Judd Lackey, who as an employee of Thomas, in his mill, may have bought the lot and put up the house. William Harmon bought from him, and in his name the house now stands. Of Mr. Harmon and family, extended mention was made as we went down Dix street. Mr. Legg was born in Tioga county, and there married Sarah B. Blinn, a distant relative of the family in the Jeffers neighborhood. They came to Rose in the fifties and lived in the village a long time. Their oldest son, Austin, died in the army, a member of Co. C, 111th N. Y. Volunteers; Mary married William Harmon; Lafayette we have just met; Edward, living in District No. 8; Harvey died in infancy; De Lancey married Fanny Ferguson, as was noticed above. Lyman Legg died July 30th, 1892, aged seventy-seven years. (Mrs. L. died August 14, 1893, aged seventy-three years.)

The next house is the home of Henry P. Howard, who was in war times a well-known member of the Ninth Heavy Artillery. For a considerable part of his service, he was regimental postmaster. He came from Manchester, Conn., to Rose, in 1849. For a time he was on the street west of Ephraim Wilson's. His wife was Elizabeth Green, of Windsor, Conn. The house was built by him in 1870. We shall get a better notion of the place and its surroundings by going back to the beginning. The blacksmith and wagon shop so long a feature of this lot, antedate the memory of the most of the people who travel this road. It was in 1854 or 1855 that the old store of Eron Thomas, once on the corner of Main and Lyons streets, was moved down here and placed almost over the creek. The gable end of the store remains as it was, and the hook for the raising of goods, placed there fifty years ago, is still hanging. "Parm" Tindall was the projector of the scheme, and the shop was in his care, along with "Bill" Colborn, whom he later took into partnership. They sold out to Samuel Otto, who sold to Howard. Tindall and Mr. Colborn ran the shop until 1871, when it was rented to James Coffee, who managed it for two years, and then built the shop opposite. Then came Charles Vanderpool for two or three years, and finally Irving Austin. Since his day, Mr. Howard has maintained a wagon repair shop. During all these years, as a workman in the shop, a notable figure was that of James Donahue, or, as he was called later, Dunham. He was born in Cattaraugus county, and married Olive

Morey, of Orleans county. Their children were : Andrew, now in Clyde, who married Frank Vanderpool for his first wife. Andrew, better known as "Drew," was one of the most famous members of Company H, Ninth Heavy Artillery. Till we went to the front he was one of the teamsters, and what he doesn't know about mules is not worth knowing. Olivia Dunham married Henry Knapp, and lives west of the Valley ; Jerome is in Canada ; Ida is Mrs. James Porter, of Wolcott, and Frank married Mary Wetherby, once in the toll gate by the Valley. The Dunham home was in an old house formerly standing just south of the shop. Mr. D., from Rose, went to Hunt's shop in the northeast part of Galen, and finally removed to Clyde, where he died, in December, 1886. His employer, Mr. Tindall, was long a member of his family, his wife, who was widow Nancy Whitmore, having died many years before. She had two grandchildren— Philip and Nancy—who were reared as Tindalls. The former became a second lieutenant in Company H, of the Ninth Heavy Artillery. Mrs. T. was a relative of Aaron Griswold, of Clyde. This same old house in which the Dunhams lived was moved by Mr. Howard back of the shop, into the lane leading to the old saw-mill. This was for some years the home of William H. Allen, whose first wife was Charlotte Austin, and second, Mary Barnes. He was a tanner and worked for the Thomases. He removed to Coldwater, Michigan. Following the Howard possessions around into the lane, we find the small building just described. It is occupied by Daniel Harper, who married John Crisler's daughter, Cora. They have one child, Ruth. Back of this house is the site of the first steam saw-mill erected in Rose. Willis G. Wade was the builder, in 1848. In this mill were sawed the planks for the road from the Valley to Clyde. It was sold to E. N. Thomas, and was burned in 1873. Rebuilt, it was run for a time, but, with the disappearance of timber, its usefulness was ended and it went into desuetude.

Returning to the Main street and opposite Mr. Howard's, we find the steam saw-mill of William A. Mix. Just south of it, in former years, was the home of Winthrop Allen. His wife was Mercy Hall, a sister of Samuel Hoffman's first wife. His children were : Ovid and Oscar, both in the west ; William H., just mentioned as a dweller opposite, and Amanda, who went west also. The parents are buried in the Rose cemetery. Dr. Van Ostrand owned the place afterward, and he had an office near, in which, in later times, the Rose Brass Band met for practice. Elijah Osborn lived here eleven years. It finally passed to Mr. Mix, and was consumed in the conflagration which destroyed the first mill. There a saw and grist-mill was erected in 1866, (the first steam grist-mill in town. After the burning, Mr. Mix rebuilt, but now runs only a saw-mill.

Across the creek is the shop where James Coffee, who came here from Clyde, worked for many a year. The upper story was used for his residence. The

site is that of a house owned by widow Austin, and this was burned in the fire
which destroyed the mill. The shop is now maintained by Mr. Conklin.

A building belonging to Charles S. Wright follows. In former years it
was associated with the name of Smithfield Beaden, a carpenter and general
utility man, who was also a ruling elder in the Presbyterian Church, till
certain home difficulties brought about the withdrawal of fellowship. In
later days he would be called a crank. He didn't like to have his wife
drink tea, nor his family eat certain kinds of vegetables, as green corn.
His overbearing nature in his family was the cause of his church trial.
The name Smithfield is strange enough to arouse inquiry as to how he
came by it. Possibly his parents had read up in Fox's Book of Martyrs,
and so wished to prolong the name of this burning place in London. If so,
their son displayed very little of the martyr spirit, and their naming was
quite in vain. He was a wagon maker and commissioner of deeds. He
and his family went to Michigan early in the fifties. Eli Knapp, a native
of Galen, is the present occupant. His wife, who was Sarah J. Weeks,
died in 1883. Their children are Cora L., Charlotte E. and Florence E.
The first two are successful school teachers.

Crossing to the east side, beyond the lane leading east from the old shop,
is the home of Mrs. Lovina Van Antwerp. We made her acquaintance in
the series on the Stewart district. The first James Colborn, after leaving
his farm, lived and died here. His brother, Jonathan, the manufacturer
of staves, was here before James.

The next house is that of William Niles, from Chenango county, town of
German, who holds some of the late E. N. Thomas' possessions. His wife
was Caroline Briggs, a daughter of the late Jonathan B., of District No.
2. Their children are Florence and William. Florence was recently
married to George W. Wilson, of Butler. The house was once a familiar
figure, on the site of the present Frank H. Closs house. When that mansion was projected, this was moved hither and has been the home of
numerous occupants : among others of Lucius Ellinwood and L. H. Dudley,
now of Rochester, but who kept a hardware store where George Collier is
at present. (Mr. Dudley died Oct. 7, 1893.)

The elegant mansion of Charles S. Wright is just across the road. This
stands where was the former home of Almira and Rhoda Gillett. They
bought of Mr. Bemis, who, as a house carpenter, is met in other places in
the village. Mr. W. built the house in 1855 and 1856, living in the Eb.
Rising house at the time. With its appointments and surroundings, this
is one of the most desirable homes in the village. Mr. Wright, a second
cousin of E. N. Thomas, came to Rose from Pompey, Onondaga county, in
1846. He was for a time in Mr. Thomas' employ, and then began business
for himself, in 1848, in the present Valentine store, continuing there till he
had erected the building on the corner near. Always active and energetic,

Mr. Wright's enterprise covered many miles of the adjoining territory. In 1883 he sold out his business, and since then has had no occupation to take him away from his home. He was supervisor in 1874–5, and was one of the most liberal givers toward the new Methodist Church, of which he had long been a member. A stroke of paralysis, several years since, has incapacitated him for active business. His wife's maiden name was Laurinda E. Lee, a daughter of Joel N. Lee, long a resident north of the Valley. Their children are Irving L., now in the west, and F. Eva, at home. In building his house and store, Mr. Wright removed several buildings, one standing on the corner, which had been used for various kinds of mercantile pursuits, as well as for a wagon shop at one time. Here Benjamin Hendricks kept the post office for a short period. The selection of this site was an indication of Mr. Wright's judgment, and for thirty years, or from 1853, the year of his building, he was vigilant in his affairs. He also had the post office for a time. William Matthews was the successor of Mr. Wright in the store, and, after a couple of years, came the Fredendalls, who are still in the business. Barney M. once ran the grist-mill standing on the site of the old Presbyterian Church, owning also the old stone school-house, where he lived. He has gone back to the Hudson river region. His wife, Sarah H. A., died and was buried in Rose. His second wife was the widow of Mark Gillett. Henry Fredendall married Kate Armstrong, of the western part of the town, and lives over the store. He now manages the business alone. James F. married Mary Relyea, of Albany county, and now keeps a store in the old brick building near the Baptist Church. He formerly lived in the little building west of the corner store, but his home is now on Wolcott street, nearly opposite the Baptist Church. A sister, Anna L., is the wife of John Osborn, who lives west of the village.

Crossing over to the old Rising house, we have a reminder of the man who was for fifty years a familiar form in Rose. He came from the eastern part of the state in 1840, and for many years worked for E. N. Thomas. For some time he had been in poor health and died only a few months since. He married the widow of Royal Van Wort, and left one son, George.

Eron N. Thomas built the next house, and it was for a while the property and home of Lyman Wyckoff, now of Lyons. It is now owned by William Hamm, a son of Thomas, living on the street by the school-house. His wife was Mary Josephine Austin, and their children are: Emma Dora, Ellen and Augusta; a son, Ezra Thomas, is dead. Dr. Draper, once familiar in these parts, formerly had his shingle here.

The next remove brings us to the hotel, long one of the noted sites in Rose. From Lorenzo D. Thomas, the builder, to Myron Brant, the present landlord, there have been many tenants. Among them were: N. W. Thomas, Hiram Salisbury and Samuel Jones, the father of Mrs. Hamel

21

Closs, who kept a temperance house for several years. William H.
("Bill") Saunders was one of the most prominent of these. Mention
was first made of him in the Stewart series as having married Mary
Wright. During his management, a race course was fitted up, inclosing
ten or twenty acres of land back of the hotel barns, and including much of
the territory covered by Thomas, Church and Dix streets. Of course,
there were no such streets there and no buildings east of the Main street.
Another noteworthy landlord was Stephen Thayer, of whom mention was
made in the description of the upper, or Pimm's Hotel. Jacob Conroe, who
preceded Mr. B., came from Savannah. He died December 18th, 1889,
aged fifty-four years, leaving a wife, a son, John, and a daughter, Ada.
Unquestionably, the site is one of the best for a place of public entertainment in this whole section of country. The small grove of trees just north
of the tavern, has been the scene of many animated discussions, when, on
warm, sunny days, the village wisdom assembles here, to settle all
questions of business and state. Myron Brant comes of a Sodus family,
said to be related to that which gave a name to the famous Mohawk chief,
Joseph Brandt. John Brant, son of Peter, began housekeeping on the
Jonathan Briggs farm in North Rose. Myron's wife is Louisa Harris, of
Sodus. Their only daughter, Grace, is the wife of Edwin Weeks, of Rose.

The store of George A. Collier brings us to the corner of Thomas street.
In the second story is the well appointed lodge room of Rose Lodge No.
590, Free and Accepted Masons. The store dates from 1854. The new
edifice, on the corner south, built by Mr. Wright in the preceding year,
had so dwarfed the old building on the Thomas possessions that Eron N.
was prompted to erect this capacious structure. In it he maintained a
store till 1859. To name the young men who, first and last, served Mr.
Thomas in the capacity of clerks, would be to enumerate a large number
of the middle-aged citizens of Rose to-day. Willard Sherman, Felton
Hickok, Carroll Upson, Joel Sheffield and others have sold calicoes and
groceries over these counters. Mr. Thomas was a shrewd man in his
dealings, but always honorable. A certain neighbor and relative had long
made a practice of filling his tobacco box from the store stock, doing this
without leave or license and paying nothing for it. Wishing to stop such
predacious conduct, Mr. T. said to his clerk: "Enter in your account,
Mr. ———, three times a week, one-quarter pound chewing tobacco."
This was done. At the end of the year, a settlement was proposed.
"All right," says the neighbor, "how much does the account foot up?
I'll pay it." "Look over the items," says the merchant. "I don't care
anything about them," is the reply, "only give me the summary." "But I
want you to see the account," was the rejoinder. So they proceeded to
scrutinize the entries. Soon the debtor's eyes rest upon, "one quarter
pound of tobacco." "Hah!" says he. "I never bought any tobacco."

"Oh, yes you did," says Mr. T. "You bought three times a week, and waited on yourself." The account was paid and the lover of the weed never helped himself again. The store stands near where Charles Thomas located his large barn, in which the Methodists held their first quarterly meetings in these parts. It was moved back and became one of the hotel barns. A Mr. Waterman had a store here for a time after E. N. T. Of him the story is told that he alluded to the body at a funeral as a fine looking "core." "Oh," says a listener, "you mean corpse." "No, I don't; I got caught on that word once. I mean just what I say—it's a fine ooking core." Mr. Henry Van Tassel ran the store for a short time, and then Lucius H. Dudley kept a line of hardware goods for several years, maintaining a tin-shop. Mr. Dudley was of the Wolcott family of Dudleys, his brother, Henry, having been the first man wounded in the Ninth Heavy Artillery. Mr. and Mrs. Dudley were regular and valuable attendants at the Methodist Church, the latter being a member. After Mr. Dudley came the Collier Bros., and then George alone.

Again we will transport ourselves to the outskirts, and this time we pause on Lyons street, at the home of Henry Jeffers, whose wife was Mary Haviland. They have one son, Bert. This place is the property of Robert N. Jeffers, and here a considerable part of his life was passed. His first wife was Maria Winchell, who had been twice married before, first to Henry Streeter, and second to John Hellar. His second wife was Sarah L. Holbrook. The son, Henry, is a twin, his sister being Henrietta, who married Bert Wilkinson, and has two children—Dell and Cora. Her home is near the eastern end of this street. The youngest child of Mr. Jeffers is Lina, who married Granville Armstrong, of Butler, and lives in that town. One child was lost in infancy. Mr. Jeffers is a son of that Nathan who lived in District No. 11, and was the progenitor of so numerous a family. Few men in town have owned so many acres of land. During the last fifty years he has stood ready to purchase whatever was for sale. He bought the farm of eighty-six acres from Lucius Ellinwood, who lived here a year. Before him, for many years, was David Holmes, who will be remembered as marrying Solomon Mirick's daughter, Amanda. He was the occupant and owner, almost if not quite, from the beginning. Mr. Holmes reared here six children, who were: Catharine; Alphonso O., for many years a coal dealer in Clyde; Elizabeth; Ira; Lucy, and George G., who died from wounds received in the army. He was a member of Co. A, 111th N. Y. Inf. Mr. Holmes, who built the house, finally moved to Palmyra.

The place opposite, i. e., on the south side of the street, is the property of Eugene Hickok. A man by the name of Lord once owned, and Harrison Ellinwood, a son of Lucius, lived here for a time. In the old lot there were twenty-eight acres.

Mr. Hickok himself lives next east, in a house that dates back to Andrew Healy, who built it. The original log house stood near. Mr. H. married Narcissa Colvin, of District No. 7. They have had two children— Horton E. and Jennie. The former died January 9th, 1888, aged 19 years. The latter married Clinton J. Barless, and died January 8th, 1889, leaving a little girl, Musetta A. Mr. Hickok is one of the most prominent Grangers in Rose, and is an enthusiastic believer in the beneficent possibilities of the organization. His brother, William Felton, preceded him here, and this takes us back to war times. The farm belonged to the father, William. As stated, Andrew Healy was the one before Hickok. He was an Irishman, who always was held in the highest respect by his neighbors. Himself a Roman Catholic, he brought his wife, Sally, and son, Andrew, to the Presbyterian Church in the village, while he went down to Clyde for his services. Mrs. Healy died in 1857, at the age of 58 years. Mr. Healy and son went to Michigan, where the latter married a daughter of Marcus P. Wade, a relative of the family so long identified with this town. Mr. Hickok has made a specialty of raising pop or tucket corn. This town has become noted in agricultural specialties, and this one has only just popped in.

Still moving eastward, we may find the home of Judson Chaddock, a son of William, the second mention of whom was made in the No. 9 series. His first wife was Addie Hoyt, and his second Katie Cuyler. A daughter, Myrtie, by his first marriage, lives with her aunt, Mrs. Cephas Bishop. There are fifty-two acres in the farm, which extends northward to the next road. William Matthews was here before Mr. C., and he bought of Eion N. Thomas. Stephen Boyce and James Packard took the farm from the office. The old log house was near the southeast corner of the lot. Matthews repaired the present house.

The place next east, on the south side, was occupied in 1890 by James Van Amburgh, a brother of Harmon, late of the Griswold district. Mr. Van A. married Sarah Jane Winchell, a daughter of John D. They have two children—John and Ida. (Philander Griswold, who married Sophia Soper, of the Valley, now lives here. The place is owned by Nelson Morgan, of Newark, who bought of W. O. Gillett. "Bill" Saunders built the house. About 110 acres are in the farm. The Griswold children are Agnes S., Jennie E. and Nelson B.)

The small house on the south side of the way, to the east, is now occupied by "Colley" Wood. He recently bought from the Conroe estate. The house was built away back in the woods and there occupied by the builder, Mr. Walmsley. To get at the farm proper, we must follow the lane back to the large barn, near which is a tall wind-mill, conspicuous from afar. There are forty-seven acres in the place, once owned by E. Walmsley, and later by Wm. H. Saunders. For some time, the place has been known as the Saunders farm. Dr. Peter Valentine owned a lot in back of this, long known by his name.

The clean, white house belonging to R. N. Jeffers next appears. It was built by Harry Valentine, who sold to Charles White. Valentine bought of Holbrook. There are twenty acres in the farm, bringing us to the old canal or ditch. (In 1893 occupied by Bert Haviland.)

Crossing the road, we find the abode of Elijah Osborn, whose family name we encountered in District No. 6. Excepting the people who held the place on contract, Mr. Osborn had no predecessors here. A Mr. Ingersoll cut off the timber, thereby depriving it of just so much value. There are seventy-five acres in the farm, which Mr. O. keeps in a high state of cultivation. His wife was Jane Van Antwerp, of that same School District, No. 6. They have only one son, Edward, found just over the stream, east. Mr. Osborn sells many agricultural implements along with his farming, and Mrs. O. cultivates the beautiful, in the shape of many and varied flowers. All the buildings on the place have come from Mr. Osborn's energy and industry.

A bridge carries us safely over the creek, a favorite bathing pool for the boys, and was long the Baptist place for immersion, where, just at our right, is the house of Hudson R. Wood, now occupied by Mrs. Nathan Jeffers, her son, Charles (who recently married Augusta Hamm), and daughter Laura. Mrs. Jeffers is the mother of the present Mrs. Wood. Mr. Wood has been met repeatedly in our town rambles. His first wife was Catharine Collins, daughter of Thaddeus, 2d, and his children were named in other series. I repeat them here. Leora married George Saunders, and, having a son and daughter, lives in Toledo, Ohio ; Frank, the wife of George G. Roe, of Clyde, has one child, Edra ; Harriet married, first, a Leonard, and married a second time, she now lives in the west : the youngest, G. Collins, has been met in the village. Many proprietors have been here, as Emanuel Walmsley, who bought of Alonzo Snow. An Ingersoll lived here, while cutting off the wood from Elijah Osborn's place. The large house was started by Solomon Allen, when he came down from Vermont. Before it was finished, Gen. Adams had begun his famous canal and the consequent loss inflicted serious damage, much to Mr. Allen's advantage. The log house identified with the lot stood over the creek, near the white house on the south side of the road. Tradition here does not go back of the name of Alfred Lee, one of the Vermont quartette of brothers who were prominent in Rose affairs in its early history. He was one of the constituent members of the Rose Methodist Episcopal Church. From his son, Luther L., I learn that Alfred Lee was born in Dudley, Mass. His birthday was January 30th, 1783, and it would seem reasonable that his parents were among those who took advantage of cheap Vermont lands, and so moved north, as did very many other farmers in Connecticut and Massachusetts. He was married December 3d, 1806, to Miss Aseneth Harwood, in Brookline, Vermont. She was a native, November 28th, 1781, of Walpole, N. H. He moved from Vermont to Waterloo, Seneca Co., in 1820, and came to Rose in 1822 or '23. His children's names were Anson, Laura, Marantha, Emeline, Maria, Alfred C., Joel N., Aseneth J. and Luther L. The latter was born in Rose, May 13th, 1824. As he was the youngest, it would seem as though the other children were born in Waterloo or Vermont. The family moved from Rose February 28th, 1833, to Jefferson, Ashtabula Co., Ohio, and there Alfred Lee died May 26th, 1868. His wife died November 22d, 1872, very nearly ninety-one years old. The saw-mill, of which Alfred Lee was the proprietor, was located to the north of the road, nearer Sodus street. Like other indications of the early settlers, it long since disappeared. Mr. Lee has kindly furnished other data, as follows: Anson Lee was born November 1st, 1807, in Brookline, Vt.; married, December 28th, 1831, in Hopewell, N. Y., Sarah A. Church. He died April 10th, 1844, in Jefferson, Ohio. His wife died in Iowa. They had three sons—John C., Orchard, Mitchell Co., Iowa; Julius A., in Dakota; and Joel in Jefferson.

Elijah Osborn's son, Edward, who married Emma Ellsworth, lives opposite. He bought of the Dickson estate and built the house. He is a skilled mechanic.

Now follow several houses, all on the north side, unless otherwise specified. In the first dwells John Weeks, a son of James, in District No. 11. He married Ellen Swift, and they have six children, viz.: William Henry; Alice E., a recent graduate of Geneseo Normal School; Nellie L., John W.; Charles H., and Lena V. As in all cases on this side of the street, the lot formerly belonged to Dr. Dickson.

Irving Austin and his wife, who was Iva J. Willis, have two children— William T. and Anna May. They have lived here for several years, buying from Thomas Hamm, who built the house ten years ago.

William Coates dwells next, he having bought of William Hamm. Mrs. Coates was Margaret Burkle.

In the next house east, we shall find James Vanderoef and family. He bought of Mrs. Sarah Williams, and the house was built by George Seager. Mr. V. is a son of the late John Vanderoef and Sarah Town, his wife. Mrs. Vanderoef is a daughter of Emanuel Walmsley. They have three daughters—Nellie, Alice and Maud. Nellie was recently married to J. H. Van Antwerp, another time-honored Rose name.

Close by is the old Rose toll gate, somewhat added to. Frank Soper once held it, and it is now in the charge of Landlord E. T. Pimm. At last account it was unoccupied.

In the small cottage opposite, lives Mrs. John H. Ruppert, a widow of German nativity. She once lived in District No. 10, or Covell's. With her is her nephew, Foster Moslein, who once kept a market in the village. Philip Stopfel once owned and traded with the widow. Harris Bemis lived here years since, and Robert Jeffers remembers that from him he borrowed a broad axe, when, a young man, he undertook to score and hew out the timber for his barn, on the present Milem place. It is probable that the house was built by Robert Andrews, noteworthy in "ye olden times" as the first shoemaker, and as fully maintaining the reputation for sportive jest of those who pound the lapstone. The story is told of Harris Bemis that he was once very ill, so much so that watchers had to sit up with him. "Uncle" John Bassett and George Howland were acting in this capacity, when their patient proclaimed that he wanted something to eat, insisting that he should not die hungry. They asked him what he would like. Much to their astonishment, he looked away over an ill man's regimen, and chose pudding and milk. They got it for him, and, being a great smoker, they propped him up in bed and gave him his pipe, after he had finished his lunch. When he had fallen asleep, as he soon did, the watchers discussed the ill man's condition. "Well, what do you think of him, Uncle John?" says Mr. Howland. "Oh," replies the worthy blacksmith, "give him a little more pudding and milk, and I guess he'll get well."

Across the way is a house owned by Mrs. John Phillips. Here live Ephraim Wilson, Jr., and his family. They were met when living on Wolcott street. Mr. Wilson is now town clerk. The house was built by Harmon Miner.

The next house is the home of Emanuel Walmsley, long the careful and diligent keeper of the Rose cemetery. A native of Lincolnshire, England, he came to this country when young, yet his speech will ever betray him as one whose vernacular is from beyond the seas. He has been met before, as a dweller further west. His wife was Elizabeth Wilkinson, but for more than twenty years she has lain in the cemetery, so long her husband's care. They had eight children, of whom Louisa married James Vanderoef, living near, and Hannah is the wife of G. A. Sherman. Born in 1810, Mr. Walmsley bears his years with remarkable vigor. His second wife was the widow of John T. Talton.

Advancing toward the east, we find, on the south side of the road, the house long identified with the name of Holbrook. Jester L. Holbrook was born in Townsend, Vermont, and his wife was Margaret Smith, a sister of the second wife of the first Valorous Ellinwood. It was about 1835 or 1836 that he came to Rose and purchased the tannery, long maintained near. He bought of N. W. Thomas. Traces of the tannery may still be seen, but ere many years all indications of the vats will have vanished, and nothing will be found to mark where once was a flourishing industry. The site was just to the west of the house. Back of it may be found the creek or stream which General Adams fancied might be transformed into a water highway. The Holbrook children were: Sarah L., now Mrs. R. N. Jeffers; Frances M. and Franklin, twins; William A.; Jester H., and F. Adelle. The latter is Mrs. Francis Osborn, of the Covell district (lately deceased); William A. married Sarah Frear, a Pennsylvanian, and lives in Rochester, having four children—Webster C., Ella, Frances and Willie; Jester H. learned his father's trade. The sisters, Sarah and Frances, were for twenty years the milliners for the village, having their store in one of the small buildings near the corner store. Miss Frances M. Holbrook still lives in the old home, the parents having died several years ago. In their lives they were substantial members of the Methodist Church. Miss Frances Holbrook, of Rochester, was married September 6th, 1892, to James Crumbie, of that city. For some years, "Aunty" Harriet Stevens, who once lived on the Alonzo Chaddock place and who is in her 95th year, has lived here.

Should we call at the next house, we should find Mr. and Mrs. Robert N. Jeffers, of whom extended mention was made at the first home as we entered the district from the west. (Mr. J. died June 11th, 1893.) There are two small buildings yet remaining before reaching the corner. In one of these the Misses Holbrook long had a millinery store. Here died "Aunty" Campbell, so long a loving charge and care of the Methodist Church.

The last home to be noted, in this extended series of rambles through Rose, is that of Frank H. Closs, the large brick house on the northwest corner, where Lyons street enters Main. In many respects, it has long been the most important spot in town. Here was held the first town meeting, and about it, in one way or another, revolved much of the town history. In 1815 Capt. John Sherman built a double log house, somewhat back of where the brick structure now stands, using one end for a dwelling, the other for a tavern, the first in this part of the then town of Wolcott. Later the plant passed into the hands of Capt. Sherman's son-in-law, Charles Woodward, who sold to Jacob Miller, and from him it became the property of Charles Thomas. This was in 1825, and from that date it has been in the possession of some member of the Thomas family. Mr. Miller built the first framed building here, which, enlarged, stood for many years a conspicuous object on the corner. About thirty years ago, it was removed to the east side of Main street, where we find it to-day, the abode of Mr. Niles. Upon the old site was reared the elegant house now standing.

The Thomases came originally from Massachusetts, though Charles Thomas moved from Pompey, Onondaga county, to Rose. His wife was Polly Wright, and no pioneer ever had a more earnest or determined helpmeet. Both of them were prominent in the early days of Rose Methodism. After Mr. Thomas' death, which took place in 1830, she

married a Mr. Clark, of Canistota. Her latest years were passed with her
daughter, Mrs. George Mirick, dying in 1863. The children of Charles
and Polly Thomas were: Nathan, born in 1807, who married Mary,
daughter of Jacob Miller, having four children—Polly, Harriet, Dan C.
and John. The second child was Sophia, whose first husband was Isaac
Crydenwise, and second, Dr. J. J. Dickson. Her son, Isaac Crydenwise,
took the name of Dickson ; her other son, Ensign Dickson, has long been
well-known in Rose. Elsie O. Thomas became Mrs. Geo. W. Mirick, and
of her mention was made as we passed along the Clyde road. Eron Noble
Thomas was older than Mrs. Mirick, but I have purposely withheld his
name for the very last mention in this list of Rose residents, for to him
and his family these final words belong. In boyhood Mr. Thomas was an
invalid, so much so that long months were passed in bed, yet not so weak
that he could not read and study. An object thus of tender solicitude to
his parents, means were found to gratify an inquiring mind till he became
one of the best posted young men of the vicinity, and his fund of general
information was always noteworthy. His illness finally necessitated the
amputation of one of his legs, but its artistic substitute was so serviceable
that, in subsequent years, he was able to move quite as quickly as those
to whom nature had been kinder. What might have been to some a great
loss, was to him really a blessing in disguise, for he, with excellent mental
attainments, became an active and useful man. One of his first essays in
work was that of clerking for John Barber, Jr., later of Clyde, who kept
the first store in Rose Valley. This was about 1831, and to Barber's
business Mr. Thomas succeeded. From that date to the time of his death,
there were very few great interests in the town in which he had not a part.
His first wife was Lucy Ann Davis, of Butler, and their only child who
survived infancy is Paul Jerome, now of New York City, but for many
years one of the most noted men in the town. Mrs. Thomas died in 1843,
and, second, Mr. Thomas married, in 1844, Mrs. Rachel (Elton) Gaylord.
The latter was born in Burlington, Conn., and her first husband was
Marvin J. Gaylord, of Bristol, Conn., by whom she was the mother of
three children—Ellen M. (Mrs. William H. Lyon, of Brooklyn), Josephine
and Marvin E. The latter two are not living. To Mr. Thomas she bore
Zadora G., who is Mrs. Frank H. Closs, and Corinne R., who married J.
Henry Morrow, of Waterbury, Conn. Mrs. Thomas was a woman of
commanding figure and inspiring presence. Though nearly eighty years
of age at the time of her death, in 1891, few would suspect her to be more
than three score and ten. After Mr. Thomas' death, she had lived much
in Brooklyn and Connecticut, with her daughters. Many will remember
Corinne, the younger daughter, as a school girl with hair ever in glossy
ringlets. Her husband was for some time editor of the *Waterbury Republican*, but a few years since the family removed to Los Angeles, Cal.

They have four children. Mr. and Mrs. F. H. Closs have a pleasant family of seven children, whose names are Nellie T., M. Josephine, Fred William, Wilbert H., Ellen H., Rachel E. and Frank H. For this interesting group, the parents have provided excellent educational advantages, and the eldest daughter is now a musical director in Wisconsin. To the observer who only occasionally visits the old scenes, it is delightful to note that one modern home is brightened by the presence of many children.

Returning to Eron N. Thomas, it should be stated that, irrespective of politics, he always stood high in the opinions of his fellow citizens. They elected him to about all the offices in their gift that he would accept, including a year in the Assembly, the winter of 1862. In Albany he was highly esteemed, as is evident from letters sent to him by Governor Horatio Seymour. It is told of him that, during an exceedingly cold and dreary winter, when many men in the Valley were out of work, he deliberately sat down and considered what he could do to give them employment, and he entered upon a scheme of getting out stave bolts, saying: "I shall not make one cent, but I shall have the satisfaction of keeping the wolf from many a poor man's door. I don't like to think of hungry children." How would that do for an epitaph? Mr. Thomas' figure is very familiar in memory, though it was in 1874 that friends bore his remains to the Rose cemetery. He was below the average stature, rather heavy in build. His face betokened generosity, while his heavy lower jaw told of giant firmness. His countenance lighted up easily, and no one enjoyed a joke or a song better. There were few gatherings of the people wherein he was not found, if time and health would permit. Many of the Rose citizens lived longer lives in point of years, but few crowded more into their periods of existence; and when we consider the physical difficulties under which he labored, the record seems little less than wonderful.

Here, then, the record ends. With me, the readers have gone over every highway and through some of the byways of our good town of Rose, so redolent in names. Since we began our journeyings, many who started with us have fallen out to repose in the various burial grounds encountered in our progress. May they rest in peace, and may we, too, fight a good fight and keep the faith, and may we never lose any of the interest due to the town in which we were born.

> "Breathes there the man with soul so dead,
> Who never to himself hath said,
> This is my own, my native land!"

ROSE AND WAYNE.

AN ADDRESS DELIVERED IN ROSE, N. Y., JULY 4TH, 1889,

BY ALFRED S. ROE.

"Man, through all ages of revolving time,
Unchanging man, in every varying clime,
Deems his own land of every land the pride,
Beloved by heaven o'er all the world beside ;
His home, the spot of earth supremely blest,
A dearer, sweeter spot than all the rest."
—*James Montgomery.*

1789—1889.

A hundred years ! In that interval generations of men have come, have played their brief part and have gone. Then France, awakening from the lethargy of centuries, was girding herself for the destruction of the Bastile ; for the liberation of the masses, and for the guillotining of crowned heads. The Napoleonic battles, called by Hugo the readjustment of the universe, were yet to be fought ; for the being who prompted them was still scarcely more than a boy, a subaltern at Valence. England, just recovered from the struggle with her colonies, was breathing more rapidly over the eloquence of Edmund Burke, as he impeached Warren Hastings in the name of heaven and humanity. America, adjusting herself to her new condition of freedom, had accepted a Constitution for the United States of America, and, under the presidency of George Washington, was pushing out into the unexplored territory of the west.

Now France celebrates the centennial of the destruction of the Bastile and, escaped from kings and emperors of whatever line, smiles, a republic. England, under her Victorian Queen, forgets the animosities of Bunker Hill and Yorktown, and, in the van of nations, disputes with America only the leadership in thought and liberty. America, a universal refuge, has repeatedly accomplished the nominal impossible—for a teeming populace fills the Great American Desert, making it bud and blossom as the rose ; an iron road-bed crosses the Rocky mountains, over which loaded trains ascend and descend as easily as did angels in the patriarch's vision the ladder reaching heavenward ; away above the East river shipping, apparently as stable as earth herself, a mighty arch binds the twin cities of New York and Brooklyn—a bow rivaling in promise that which spanned the firmament when the receding waters released the prisoners of the Ark; for one gave assurance of no more deluge and desolation, while the other forecasts the infinite possibilities of science and art ; five hundred and fifty feet above the base, at times among the clouds, shines the aluminum tip, whose refulgence tells of the gratitude of the republic to him whom all call the Father of his Country ; the Washington monument eclipses all similar structures, and, standing in the national capital—itself a growth of the century—it may look back over the contests of the hundred years; over the liberation and enfranchisement of a race : over the waxing and waning of reputations ; over high officials slain in office ; over the development of the country and the almost utter annihilation of the impossible.

Till March, 1789, what is now Wayne county was virgin soil. Southward a line of settlements had led to the west, and, even in Revolutionary days, the Indian whoop and scalping knife had proclaimed the presence of adventurous whites, along what we call the southern tier. Water-ways had borne the exploring French over vast areas to the Mississippi. On the north, the waters of Ontario had for ages laved the beach, as yet untrodden by the feet of white men. Oswego, a strategic point, had long been held, and hostile arrays had moved up and down the Oswego river ; but what this country possessed in the way of civilization was still in the far east. As when the English rulers gave a charter to a colony, they made the western limit the setting sun, or the very nearest, the Pacific ocean, so the earliest formed county, west of the Hudson, was named Albany and included everything in the state to the westward. This was in 1683, and while Mohawk, Oneida, Cayuga, Onondaga or Seneca roamed at will over this vast domain, the name remained unchanged till 1772, when Tryon county was organized, embracing all that territory west of a line running north and south, through the middle point of Schoharie county, and was thus called from William Tryon, then governor of the province. The Revolution speedily followed, and at its end, the patriotic inhabitants could not endure the name of a loyalist governor and so changed it to Montgomery, thus recalling the thrilling scene before the gates of Quebec. But the star of empire was steadily moving westward, and in 1791 the setting off of Herkimer county permitted the application of the name of the hero of Oriskany. The area included all between the present eastern boundary of Herkimer county and the eastern line of Ontario, erected in 1789, this running along the eastern side of Lyons and Sodus. Of that part of Wayne county we will speak later. Now we will trace the further changes in that part of the county where we meet to-day. In 1794 there was another slicing off, and one portion became a part of Onondaga ; again a division in 1799, and we became a part of Cayuga.

In 1804 another tribal name came to us, through the creation of Seneca county, whose extreme northern town, Junius, included the present township of Huron, Wolcott, Butler, Rose, Galen and Savannah.

Thus we continued until April 11th, 1823, when the above part of Junius from Seneca and Sodus, Lyons, Williamson, Palmyra and Ontario from Ontario county were united to bear the cognomen of that glorious veteran of the Revolution, "Mad" Anthony Wayne. The leader at Stony Point had been sleeping more than a quarter of a century on the shores of Erie when he was thus remembered in this shire of ours, and the creation of Marion township, in 1826, from Williamson, gave the hero Revolutionary company. There is a whimsical jumble of names in our county that will bear a moment's contemplation. The word Wayne is melodious, terse and suggestive; Marion, too, arouses a host of memories, and Williamson, on the north, is quite in place as the name of the first agent of the Pulteney estate, but on the south we step into the past and Palmyra. One naturally looks for Thebes hard by, for the names are so commonly joined in story, but instead, if we go west, we are in the domain of Philip and Alexander, or Macedon, while, should we journey east, our way will lead into Arcadia, the land so often praised by poets as the abode of peace and innocence. The name of the bordering lake fitly appears in one division, while just below it is the town named from Chancellor Reuben Hyde Walworth. From Arcadia we make only a step and Grecian reminders cease and we are in France, "sunny France;" at any rate, the town is Lyons, and all school children will tell you that Lyons is the second city in France. Just one, and one only, reminder of Indian occupation is had in Sodus, but that must go back to Assorodus, before we find the aboriginal for "silvery water." Possibly Huron may be of American origin, in its recalling of the great northern tribe of savages; but east of it is Wolcott, a loyal tribute to the memory of Gov. Oliver Wolcott, of Connecticut. The origin of Butler is probably in that Richard Butler, who, with Oliver Wolcott and Arthur Lee, was appointed by the government of the United States to negotiate with the Six Nations in 1784. Rose comes from a purchaser of a large tract of land, including that on which we now are gathered. Galen owes its title to so queer a notion as the ascribing that part of the military tract, covered by the township, to the medical department, and in its annals, who so prominent as him of Pergamus? The jumping-off place is reached when we get to Savannah, along the Seneca river, and the name of the town explains itself. So then, in these fifteen towns, we have ancient history and geography drawn upon along with those of modern times, beside an occasional reference to individuals and to the aborigines.

The first settlements were made within the bounds of the present towns of Palmyra and Lyons, and through these settlements the exercises of to-day partake of a centennial character. The venturesome pioneer from

Connecticut or New York sailed up the Hudson to the Mohawk ; then by means of a pole he pushed his craft up that stream till he reached the site of the present city of Rome, when his boat and effects were carried across the country, a mile and a half, to Wood creek, down which he floated to Oneida lake. The wind might propel him the length of that body of water, and down its outlet, Oneida river, to its junction with the Seneca to form the Oswego. Then he turned his prow southward, travelling the sluggish stream till he entered the Clyde river, up which he went till he dropped anchor at Lyons or Palmyra. This journey, under favorable circumstances, covered twenty-eight days. Among the many changes of the one hundred years, no one is more marked than the improvement in locomotive facilities. Yesterday your speaker breakfasted within forty-four miles of the city of Boston. It was not till nearly ten A. M. that he took the cars for the Empire State, yet at nine P. M. he was landed at the station on the very banks of that river along which, a century since, our ancestors pushed their clumsy bateaux, at scarcely more than a snail's pace.

Of the events incident to the towns of Palmyra and the old area of Lyons, it would be interesting to speak, for in Palmyra, Mormonism had its origin, and in Arcadia, set off from Lyons, the famous Fox sisters set the world to thinking about the phenomena of Spiritualism ; but it will be better for us to confine ourselves to a " pent-up Utica," and to tell of those narrower bounds that inclose what to the majority present is our native town.

" With what a pride I used to walk these hills." They first beheld the tottering steps of my childhood, and now look solemnly down upon the graves of my grandsires, and, though more than half of my life has been passed out of my native state and only a small fraction in this, the town where I first saw the light, there has never been a moment when I could not reproduce at will " many a path beloved of yore and well remembered walk." In our company there is no one with soul so dead that he hath not o'er and o'er said, " This is my own, my native land." No boy nor girl, however mischievous, has ever climbed these steep hills, to roll down stones in summer and snow-balls in winter, without pausing to drink in great draughts of inspiration from the grandeur of the scene. From several points in this town may be seen the waters of the lake, while in other directions we may gaze beyond the borders of our own township. When nature gives an extra turn to her kaleidoscope, and, in a mirage, throws upon the sky the lake shore, can anything be more glorious ? These hills, left by the melting glaciers of an early age, are a peculiar feature of our landscape, and nowhere in our country is there better evidence of water and ice action in the formation of the earth's surface, and in no town in the county are the results better marked, than here in Rose. It was Auerbach who said that on every height there lies repose. Though we may be tempted to spend hours in visual feasting as we scan the scene from their summits, certain it is that nothing tends more to thrill the soul of man than the sight of lofty eminences. Though these of ours do not approach the mountains in height, yet I believe they have so impressed themselves on the youth of this town that from whatever station, looking back to their old home, no fancy would be complete without the familiar contour of the north and south ranges of hills.

> "Ye hills of Wayne! ye hills of Wayne!
> In dreams I see your slopes again—
> In dreams my childish feet explore
> Your daisied dells, beloved of yore.
> In dreams, with eager feet, I press
> Far up your heights of loveliness,
> And stand, a glad-eyed boy again,
> Upon the happy hills of Wayne."

The earliest settlements in our county were sixteen years old when, in 1805, the pioneers turned northward from the Clyde river and pushed out into the wilderness, following, possibly, pretty nearly the direction and location of the present Clyde and Wolcott road. Before that date our section had been the hunting ground of the savage. This part of the state seemed to be held in a sort of joint ownership by the Cayugas, Onondagas and Mohawks, of the Six Nations, and they were the tribes that signed away their rights, when a grateful nation determined to pay in land a part of the debt owed to those who had fought during the Revolutionary war. Of this Indian occupation we have very little trace. Occasionally the farmer turns up an arrow head in his plowing, and Mrs. George Aldrich, of North Rose, has an excellent gouge or scoop; but to my knowledge there is no other utensil of the kind among us. There are no traces of burial places nor villages, but that game was abundant, thus affording the savage a reason for roaming over this part of the country, all early settlers agree. Even after the coming of the white man, his red brother was a frequent guest as he flitted phantom-like over the region which he once called his own. I sometimes wonder if the Chief [Logan, to whose memory those patriotic words, engraved upon the pyramidal structure in Fort Hill, Auburn, "Who is left to weep for Logan?" may not have followed the chase hither, or whether, in the remoter past, hostile Hurons may not have skirted the lake and Assorodus bay to the point of debarking in our own town as they preyed upon the more peaceful Iroquois. But all this is fancy, for long since the Indians "slowly and sadly climbed the western hills and read their doom in the setting sun." The sword of the white man has swept them away. The land they left was devoted to the soldiers of the Revolution; but very few of them ever occupied the lots assigned to them. They sold their claims to speculators who may or may not have realized upon them. In the vicissitudes incident to the Phelps and Gorham purchase, whose new eastern line ran along the western part of this town, the state gave to the successors of the original purchasers of the Pulteney estate, certain parts of the military tract, and in this way our location came into the care of Captain Williamson as agent, and from him, finally, the Geneva land office passed under the direction of Messrs. Fellows & McNab, whose names may be found upon the deeds of all the original farms in our vicinity. Osgood Church, one of the first settlers of Wolcott, father of that worthy veteran, Hiram Church, was a sub-agent for the estate, and his old sale book, still in existence, is a precious relic of the early part of the century.

It was in 1805, then, that, armed with their deeds of sale from the patentees, Caleb Melvin, Alpheus Harmon and others made the beginnings in our town. Melvin's location was on or near the Thomas place, south of the Valley. He was a relative of the first Thaddeus Collins, who was another early comer, the father of probably the latest survivor of those who moved into Rose. I refer to Stephen Collins, our aged and revered fellow citizen. But 4,000 acres in this very centre of the present town had been bought by Major Robert S. Rose and Judge Nicholas, both Virginians, but then of Geneva ; so the giving of titles was still further mooted. Alpheus Harmon located his log hut near a spring, still flowing, a little east of Stewart's school-house, and there remained till the moving spirit carried him further west. A granddaughter, Mrs. Ambrose Lockwood, of Butler, only recently died. A near neighbor on the west was Lot Stewart, who came to the then Wolcott from Saratoga county. We of to-day can have little conception of the nerve necessary to carry our ancestors over their long and tedious march hither. In this gathering, to-day, are descendants of those who first walked, with knapsacks upon their backs, to this wilderness to inspect and locate their purchases. Coming from Massachusetts, Connecticut or the Hudson river counties of our own state, we can properly rate the distance traveled. Then, returning, they fitted up a vehicle, to serve as wagon and house, and often, with slow moving ox team, started, in some cases with a numerous family of small children, on their journey of hundreds of miles. Roads as we know them had no existence. Streams must be forded, ferried, or " gone around," and then after weeks of shaking and jolting, following blazed trees, camping by the side of some spring or creek, the home is reached. And what a home ! Let the cultivated fields and comfortable houses of to-day disappear. In their places stands the primeval forest, and close by the perennial fountain, furnished by nature, is the early settler's home. In his first visit he had cut down and piled up certain trees, covering the enclosure as best he could, and into this abode the weary mother and fretful children are ushered. Food has been brought with them till the first crop can supply them. When this is grown, there is no mill near by to grind it, so the inventive pioneer hollows out the top of a stump, and for this he will not have to go far, and in this primitive mortar brays his first fruits. Fancy, if you can, the agony of friends when disease came among them and singled out its victims. The old and the young, the weak and the strong were alike liable. The facilities of the old home were not to be had, and only patience, and faithfulness in the use of such medicines as the forest afforded, were of any avail. And should death, always terrible, take from the circle the aged matron, who had joined the migration, or the tiny baby, whose coming had speedily followed the settlement, where was the minister who should speak the usual words of consolation ? When the grave was dug, in the newly cleared vicinity, and the body of the loved one was laid away for time and eternity, who can portray the desolation that must have been felt in the scantily furnished home !

In spite, however, of all hindrances, population poured in till, in 1810, the original town of Wolcott possessed 480 inhabitants. Immigration was rapid, and the difficulties of assembling for town meetings, alternately at Wolcott Village and Stewart's corners, resulted in the dismemberment of the old town and the creation of three new ones, viz., Rose, Huron and Butler. We may be pardoned a morsel of pride as we reflect that the year of our separation was the semi-centennial of the Declaration of Independence, though we made our start in February rather than July. Had it occurred to the good people of this town to celebrate, in 1876, the nation's centennial and their own half century, what a goodly array of those who came to the wilderness as boys and girls might have been brought together !

This town of ours has been and still is eminently agricultural. The arts and manufactures so prominent in some sections have never been located here ; while this fact may account for the lack of large fortunes in the possession of any one individual, it is not without its agreeable features. As a rule, vast holdings presuppose the proximity of the very poor. Many doubtless have said : "If the Sodus canal or General Adams' ditch had only been put through, this town would have been much more flourishing." Location upon water-ways or trunk lines is not without its drawbacks. The man who grumbles thus may reflect that the crime and pauper average is correspondingly lower. The saw-mills which cut up the timber once standing here did not give place to the hum of the loom nor the rattle of the shoe factory, but the population has remained honest and homogeneous. Go to the churches in this village next Sunday and you will find the descendants of those who first broke into this primeval forest ; not so in the east, where ten years will nearly transform the personnel of a manufacturing village. There are many worse surroundings than a farming community ; but what would the fathers say could they return and see the

22

methods of to-day? Those good old men who cleared away the trees, turned over the soil and sowed wheat which grew so heavy that it would scarcely bend as the farmer threw his heavy wool hat upon it; what would they say were they to walk forth some fine day and see acres given to the growing of onions, where they devoted a few feet only! Wouldn't they think that the habits of the people in the way of food had wonderfully changed? And when they saw an adjoining field covered with a rank growth of peppermint, what would be their reflections on the popular stomach-ache! As they passed large enclosures given to the growth of raspberries, may we not fancy some patriarch saying: "Well, I do declare, if these folks don't beat all! In my day these things grew wild all over the back lots, and the boys and women folks had no trouble in finding all they wanted, but here are whole acres just covered with bushes, and it does look as if they had run cultivators through them, too. I wonder if folks have given up eating bread and have taken to berries? Strange times!" Should he continue these investigations, he would find, on some farms, as much land given up to potatoes as to corn, and I can fancy him wondering if there is a greater percentage of Hibernians in the country now than there was in his day. Should his visit come in the autumn, he would be filled with wonder as he saw great loads of fine apples, not the crab apple kind, which grew on the trees that came from seeds of his planting, but large, smooth Greenings and Baldwins, carried—to the cider-mill? not at all, but to this queer building, one of whose most prominent features is a big chimney and which seems to be a great devourer of fuel. Here, should he look in, he will see the fruit speedily transformed into the whitest of dried apples, not in the least like the results of patient paring, quartering, coring and stringing of his time. Do you not think he would draw strange conclusions as to the likings of the present generation for dried apple pie? In harvest what would be his wonderment at following one of those machines which cuts the grain and, binding it, drops it ready to be put into the shock. A few weeks earlier, would not his bones ache with very envy as he saw horses drawing a cutting bar, which did what it took many a sweep of his brawny arm with snath and blade to accomplish, and then when down, a machine, which, kicking like an exaggerated grasshopper, stirred out the grass. Soon afterward, a man, boy, or perhaps a woman, comes riding along on a skeleton-like contrivance, which speedily gathers the hay into windrows. If away up in conveniences, the wagon and rack which follow will have a loader attached, and what cost him many a weary tug will now be done by horse power. He goes with the load to the barn, and just look at his eyes as he sees a large fraction of that mass, at the will of the party on the mow, put just where he wishes, with no more effort on his part than merely to direct it. The horse down below is doing the lifting, and the boy who, in his grandfather's day, sweat and suffered under the roof, with more or less hay seed down his back, cursing the day he was born, is driving the horse. Do you believe this visitor from the cemetery would sigh to any great extent for the old times ? But since he is out, let's take him further and show him some of the utilities never dreamed of when he walked the earth. A creaking sound up aloft attracts his ears, and his eyes wonderingly behold the arms of an immense wind-mill. "Well, I vum ! What's that for ? That beats all the contrivances of my day. We used to make little ones for fun, but this looks like business." "My revered ancestor, this is to pump water for the stock and to force it, when necessary, to all parts of the house and barn." "Do tell ! But I don't see any well for the water to come from, and I think that you folks of this centennial spell must be trying to live without work. In my day, we thought it the proper thing to drive the critters to the creek, summer and winter, and when it was real cold, it was somebody's job to keep the hole through the ice open. But just tell me where the water comes from. What ! you don't say that they just drive a pipe right down into the ground, and then set this 'ere thing to going ! If I had only known all about that, what a pile of digging and tugging I might have saved when I dug that forty-foot well, near the house, and stoned it up. But say, what's this about forcing water all over the house ? You don't mean to say that you have a cistern away up under the roof, and that you can let water run from it to every room in the house ? What's that ? Water runs into the bath-room ! You don't tell me that you've got a room where you can swim summer and winter ? Say ! let's get along toward the house. I want to look in. Bath room ! Well, I'm beat now ! When I was in my prime and the work was done, 'long toward night, we used to hitch up and all the men and boys went down to the pond and jumped in and splashed around till we'd had enough, but in the winter, why, we sort of waited till summer again : but here you tell me that you can go in all the year around, and with warm water, too ! Now, just hold on : that's going it a little too strong. I can believe a good deal : but warm water to swim in in winter ! That won't do." However, our doubter enters, and where the capacious fire-place once devoured cords of wood, he beholds the modern "air-tight," consuming only a tithe of the matter, yet sending out vastly more heat, and as for convenience, as far beyond the fire-place as that was better than a stump fire. He soon understands how water may be heated and sent to the bath or any other room in the building. He beholds carpeted floors, where in his day they were, at the best, sanded. From the parlor or sitting-room come the notes from piano or organ, and his ears are delighted with sounds that were never heard in life. The tables are strewn with books and papers, telling of the doings of the outer world. Letters come from hundreds of miles away, yet have occupied only a few hours in coming. A relative enters,

who, twenty-four hours before, had left a point so remote that at the
beginning of the century, to reach it would be the event of a life-time. A
telegram is received, and the ghostly visitor will not credit the time and
distance involved, and when the tinkle of the telephone bell calls him
to the receiver and he hears distinctly the voice that must be miles away,
his wonderment reaches its climax and he retreats to the quiet and
seclusion of his grave.

Our ancestors were eminently sober and God-fearing men. They early
organized their churches, though they were first identified with the Presbyterian Church of Huron. In 1825 the Rose Presbyterian Church was
organized, and its first settled pastor was the Rev. Jonathan Hovey.
Over it have ministered men not unknown to fame; among others that
William Clark, known to the old inhabitant as "Priest" Clark, who
could think out his sermons "at the tail of his plough." His son, Colonel
Emmons Clark, has just resigned his twenty-five years' command of the
famous New York Seventh Regiment. Daniel Waldo was here two years,
from 1837, a man who survived his one hundredth year. The Baptist organization has long served its day and generation, a type, in its inflexible
principles and purposes, of that rock on which it is founded. Its pastors
have been men popularly identified with all that conduced to the good of
the town. The Methodists owed their planting to that horseback ride in
1812 of Daniel Roe, from his home, near Wolcott, to the session of the
Genesee Conference in Lyons, and, although the session was over, he
prevailed upon Bishops Asbury and McKendree to send a supply to this
section. These roving Methodist bishops have left us very pleasant
impressions of our country. In his journal, dated Thursday, July 2d,
1807, Asbury says: "This is a great land for wheat, rye and grass; and
the lakes, with their navigation of vessels and boats and moving scenes,
make the prospects beautiful." Meeting in barns, homes and school-
houses till 1824, the society in Rose was formed and has continued steadfast to date. Perhaps no one in this gathering is more closely connected
with all these bodies than myself. My great grand-parents, Aaron
Shepard and wife, were constituent members of the Presbyterian Church,
and Mr. S. was its first deacon. By its pastors the funerals of my ancestors were conducted. One of the first deacons of the Baptist Church was
George Seelye, my grandfather, and for more than fifty years he went in
and out among you. In the pews of the building every Sunday were
gathered more immediate relatives than often falls to the lot of one mortal.
By the Methodist Church my paternal grandfather was long licensed as an
exhorter and local preacher, and from it my own father, who to-day sits
beside me, went forth to his long ministry. As a member and as a worker, my beloved uncle was long identified with it. By its pastor his funeral

sermon was preached, and now, in our cemetery near, he awaits the resurrection. Beyond that range of hills, to the eastward,

"Under the sod and the dew,
Waiting the Judgment day,"

Deacons Shepard and Seelye, with "Father" Roe, were laid by gentle hands, to sleep the last long sleep with their kindred till God shall bid them rise.

Our forefathers were foremost in all that pertained to the good of mankind. As early as 1829, a temperance society was organized, which included nearly all the citizens of repute in the town, and they subscribed to this pledge: "We, the undersigned, do agree to abstain wholly from the use of ardent spirits, except for medical purposes; not to furnish them as a part of hospitable entertainment, nor to laborers in our employ; in no case to give or vend them either by large or small measure, so as knowingly to countenance the improper use of them, etc." Who can tell how much this society may have prompted the sober record of Rose for the intervening sixty years! Its first president was that sterling settler from Connecticut, long known to us as Deacon Elizur Flint. Of the first board of managers only Stephen Collins survives, but among his associates were Dr. Peter Valentine and Samuel Lyman, of course.

These fathers of ours early became convinced of the total depravity of slavery, and abolition was long a popular doctrine. That barn of Samuel Lyman, the first framed structure raised in town without the use of liquor, became the fit harboring place of the escaped bondman, and by Lyman and his neighbors he was helped on to Canada. Such principles constantly instilled into the minds of the youth of this town, made it a good recruiting place when the war of the Rebellion broke out. The farmers' boys were among the first to put on the blue and to wear it till death came or the Rebellion was ended. Were there in our village a soldier's monument (how devoutly I hope the day may come when it may be a reality), and upon it were to be inscribed the names of the battles participated in by those who called Rose their home, the list would include almost every one during the War—from that terrible defeat at Bull Run, through the Peninsular Campaign, Fredricksburg, Gettysburg, the Wilderness, the Valley, the Gulf, to Appomattox itself; in every one of these, Rose boys were present, and if in lasting granite we could tell the story to our children, what a lesson it would be!

My friends, the Fourth of July, ever sacred, ever memorable, never has a more fitting observance than when, as to-day, "Auld Lang Syne" is renewed. While pealing bell and roaring cannon recall the days when battles raged, let us rather think of those patriots who, with resolute intent, pledged to each other their lives, their fortunes and their sacred honor that liberty should ever be maintained on this continent; and as they were faithful to their promises, so let us, of a later day, pledge anew our fealty to all for which the fathers suffered, and, like them, make our lives well rounded and useful.

However many are here to-day, there are places we would like to see filled. How would it gladden our hearts if, from his resting place, Deacon Flint could look upon us. Simeon Barrett, so lately departed, would shed lustre on this hour. Thaddeus Collins would, as of old, rub his hands together and say: "I feel that it is good to be here," and, Mr. President, what would we not give could your honored father, Harvey Closs, be a part of our exercises in person, as he is in memory? Can you not fancy the merriment that would follow were the cheery voice of Dudley Wade to resound in our midst? What an outburst would ensue should Eron Thomas arise to address you, or Dr. Dickson come among us! We would willingly be ailing if, from his tomb, we could draw our first physician, Peter Valentine, whose son has so long and so honorably served his town. Chauncey Bishop, Jonathan Briggs, Henry Graham, John Gillett, the Lovejoys, Chaddocks, Lees, Merricks, Kelloggs, Smiths, Hendersons, Seelyes, Munsells, Lambs, Jefferses, Roes, Aldriches, Mitchells, Stewarts, Vandercooks, Griswolds, Deadys, Covells, Towns, Collinses, Vanderoefs, Colborns, Dickinsons, Hickoks, Shermans, Osgoods, Phillipses, Fullers, Chattersons, Ellinwoods, Oakses, Osbornes, Allens, McKoons, Andruses, Benjamins, Catchpoles and Finches—all these and the many more who have made the town what it is, would we gladly welcome here to-day. And though we may not see them face to face, yet may our spirits join with theirs in devotion to this home of ours, pledging ourselves to the maintenance of its fair name and our undying love for the town of Rose and for the county which is now in its second century; and when fifty or a hundred years hence our descendants celebrate, may they, as truthfully as we to-day, repeat these words:

> "Ye hills of Wayne! ye hills of Wayne!
> Ye woods, ye vales, ye fields of grain!
> Ye scented morns, ye blue-eyed noons!
> Ye ever unforgotten moons!
> No matter where my latest breath
> Shall freeze beneath the kiss of death—
> May some one bear me back again
> To sleep among the hills of Wayne!"

THE ROSE M. E. CHURCH—1824-1889.

READ AT ITS RE-OPENING, AUGUST 27TH, 1889.

BY ALFRED S. ROE.

" Nor heeds the sceptic's puny hands,
While near her school the church-spire stands."

—*Whittier.*

The territory now covered by the Rose Church was included within the bounds of the Philadelphia Conference from its organization till 1810, when the Genesee Conference was formed, with the exception of the single year, 1808, when it formed a part of the New York Conference. From July 20th, 1810, to 1829, it continued as Genesee territory. Then came eight years of connection with the Oneida Conference, or till 1836, when the Black River Conference was organized, and as a part of it, we find ourselves till 1869, when the Central N. Y. Conference was begun. Again, in 1873, when the new adjustment came, Rose fell under the former or latest name and so continues to date.

Were we to mention the districts upon which our vicinity has been located, they would be in Albany, till 1803; then Genesee till 1808, when it was Cayuga one year; from 1809 to 1811, inclusive, the Susquehanna; from 1813 to 1814 it was once more the Genesee, and then, viz., in 1814, it became the Chenango, and so remained till 1820, when it passed into the Black River limits. Again, in 1825, it is the Chenango, but in 1828 it returns to the Black River, and there remains till 1833, when it forms a part of the newly constructed Oswego district. There is no further change till the new conference lines, in 1869, threw it into the Auburn bounds, and there it is to-day.

As to circuit names, the very first, in the least looking this way, were Herkimer, Otsego and Seneca, which appeared toward the end of the last century. Oneida and Cayuga are found in 1799. In 1803 appears Ontario, and in 1806 we have the very neighborly name of Lyons. The moving into that town of Methodists from Maryland, gave the denomination an early start there. Sodus is the next name in which we are interested, and this is in 1813. In 1817 a division occurs, and we form a part of Cato, and so continue till 1821, when we take the significant title,

Victory. O'er all victorious we remain till 1832, when we assume the Rose, and thus crowned, remain to this year of grace, 1889.

We can only conjecture as to who of the early itinerants passed this way. In 1793 the Rev. Thomas Ware was appointed to the Albany district, and he states that his ride included Herkimer county, which then extended to the western line of this town. Grand old Revolutionary soldier that he was, we would like to think that our soil had borne the impress of his feet, and that the forests once standing here had resounded with his voice as, in passing through, he chanted the praises of God, a frequent diversion of these almost homeless wanderers. Freeborn Garrettson was one of the earliest appointed ministers to the circuits, which may have included our bounds, but during all these years we have no knowledge of our present town limits holding any permanent settlers. There was, however, a semi-nomadic population that was here to-day and there to-morrow, forerunners of that stable class, which, following, cleared up the land and built for themselves comfortable homes. But there was no habitation too primitive for our Methodist pioneer, and I love to believe that at the very earliest date he sought out the settlers here. In 1807 Bishop Asbury records his pleasant impression of Lyons, where he was the guest of his Maryland friends, the Dorseys, and in Esquire Dorsey's barn, in 1810, the first session of the Genesee Conference was held.

From notes contributed to a Wayne county paper by C. S. Jewell, now of Fleming, N. Y., I learn that regular Methodist ministrations in our vicinity were indebted to Daniel Roe, of what now constitutes the north-west corner of Butler. A native of Brookhaven, Long Island, he had begun his married life in Connecticut, where his Methodist zeal was apparent, for I find that he is accounted the founder of our church in the town of Derby of that good old land of steady habits. Revolutionary troubles had compelled his father's family to take up their abode across the Sound, and it is more than likely that his start in Methodism was had through the preaching of Jesse Lee, who first penetrated the chosen field of the "Standing Order." At any rate, when, in 1812, he became a central N. Y. pioneer, his latch string was always out to anybody who could bring tidings of great joy. His learning of the session of the Genesee Conference at Lyons, July 29th, 1812, was somewhat late, but he hastened away upon horseback to that place and secured the appointment of a preacher who would restrict his wanderings to a range embracing what is now several counties. His own house was the chosen scene of preaching services at times, while the school-house near was often called into use. On such considerable occasions as quarterly meetings, no less commodious structure than his recently constructed framed barn would suffice. That building is still standing. The story is told that a certain minister, noted in the annals of another denomination, when told that Mr. Roe had secured the coming of the Methodists, said: "Well, let them come; we'll soon root them out." To this, Daniel Roe responded: "If he is a mind to be a hog and root, why, let him root." From results, one may conclude that the rooting scarcely more than loosened the soil, thereby rendering our growth all the more vigorous. The preachers who rode this great circuit, Zenas Jones, Ebenezer Doolittle, John Rogers, Joseph McCreary and Joshua Beebe, have their names written not only in our record of Methodism, but we trust in the Lamb's Book of Life. Theirs were names long revered in a section of country covering nearly the whole extent of the Middle States. Their purses did not wax plethoric at the expense of their people, for we find that their average support was $84.65 per year. In 1816 Joseph McCreary received items as follows: Five and one-half bushels of wheat, $1.75; thirteen pounds of pork, 12½ cents; sugar and lard, 12½ cents; ten pounds of venison ham, 0.4; six pounds of flax. If, however, the preacher fared poorly, so did his people. Money was a rare article, scarcely to be had at all. The first local preachers were Samuel Bentley, John Seymour, Jacob Snyder and Joshua Beebe, who afterward entered the traveling connection. Daniel Roe, Thomas Armstrong and Stephen Sprague were the first class leaders.

Under the name of Cato circuit, matters progressed till 1821, when Victory began, and during its eleven years of existence, societies were organized as follows: Conquest, October 19th, 1822; Hannibal, March 23d, 1825; Butler, April 8th, 1826; Rose, September 21st, 1827; Clyde, January 22d, 1831. The society at Daniel Roe's in 1812 finally became the foundation of the Wolcott Church. The foregoing dates refer to the holding of the first quarterly meetings. Classes, as we shall find, were organized much earlier.

So much for the nebulous portion of our church history. Now follows a period when the sun glimmers through the clouds and we can obtain some definite knowledge. Probably the first permanent Methodist within the confines of our present town was Alfred Lee, the forerunner of the other brothers—Lyman, Joel and John—who came down to us from the Green Mountain State. He came early in the century, and we may suppose that his Methodist start was had up among the rugged scenes of Vermont, through the labors of Garrettson, Hull and others. In 1818 or 1819 Caleb Mills, a local preacher and a carpenter by trade, used to conduct prayer meetings in the log school-house, which stood on or about the site of what was so long the post office. There are those who still retain a recollection of his wide-brimmed white hat and quaint attire; for in those days dress and walk as well as conversation proclaimed the Methodist. In 1824 Charles Thomas and family moved into the town from Pompey, Onondaga county. He and his active, vigorous wife were trophies of the preaching in that section, begun as early as 1803. With them came, in their employ, Zemira Slaughter, who was born in Willington. Conn, Sept. 11th, 1802.　Though young when she came hither, she had been six years a member of a class, having been converted under the preaching of Daniel Barnes, who was a presiding elder in these parts in 1823-4.　She was baptized by Abner Chase, a man long held in reverence by those who knew him.　With this reënforcement our founders proceeded to organize a class, and in 1824 this very important step was taken.　The names were Charles Thomas and Polly, his wife, Alfred Lee, William Watkins, Abigail Bunce and Zemira Slaughter.　Mr. Lee was the first leader, and he has been described to be as talkative, energetic and a great worker in every way.　Charles Thomas was an active business man, but it may not disparage him in the least to state that "Sister" Thomas was more often referred to in matters spiritual than her husband.　She was short of stature, somewhat stout, very early married, the mother of a numerous family, but the very embodiment of zeal and energy in all respects.　She frequently led the class herself, and her home was the chosen abode of the itinerent in passing.　William Watkins, of Welsh birth, came with the Thomases, and was a tanner by trade.　Abigail Bunce was the most noted teacher the old town of Wolcott ever knew.　Renowned in her schools, she was equally worthy of recollection in the church.　Of a tall, commanding stature, she was sure of a hearing whenever she arose.　Of all these beginners, only Zemira (Slaughter) Bishop remains this side of eternity.　As the wife of Joel Bishop, who was of Baptist rearing, she went with him to his church home, though she accounted herself a Methodist for fully eighteen years.　Though her name may not appear on our books to-day, we are none the less sure that she can read her title clear, and we rejoice that bodily she can be with us after all these many years of pilgrimage, and on this occasion with us be glad at the sight of what God hath wrought.　From the diminutive log school-house to this church, truly the step is a long one.　Charles Thomas died in 1830, comparatively young.　His wife, as Polly Clark, died in 1863.　"Aunt Nabby" Bunce finished her journey in September, 1875, at Red Creek, at the age of eighty-two.　William Watkins, the father of Mrs. Lawson Munsell of the Wolcott Church, died in Portland, Oregon, November 3d, 1882, having left Rose about 1827.　Alfred Lee joined the procession westward to Ohio, and there died May 26th, 1868, aged eighty-five years.

The first meetings of these people were held in the log building, erected by the first settlers for school purposes ; but even this was sometimes closed to them, whether on account of their noisy ways or through accident, I cannot state.　However, if the door was locked, they were in no way cast down, for they would have their meetings somewhere, and have been known to adjourn to logs, lying at right angles to each other, back of the school-house, and upon such improvised seats to conduct their religious classes. They had not long to wait for increasing numbers, since a revival speedily followed, and before the fall of snow their class numbered thirty. Early in the twenties, extreme measures in the collection of church dues among the Presbyterians of the Port Bay, now Huron, Church caused many withdrawals, and the consequent increase of the Methodist Society. Owing to a misapprehension of the terms of their subscription, many had refused to pay, and hence had been sued. Naturally they felt aggrieved.

In their first summer Ellis Ellinwood and wife, who came up from Oneida county, joined them and remained steadfast to the end of their long and useful lives. Till 1832 there is not a written word to chronicle the work of this small band of Chistians, yet by their fruits we may conclude that they delved well in their Master's vineyard. The first quarterly meeting, in 1827, was held in Charles Thomas' barn, then standing where now is the store of George A. Collier. As George Gary was then presiding elder, we may suppose that he was present. Mrs. Bishop retains a pleasant memory of some of the early pastors, having vividly in mind Revs. Jones and Doolittle, and can yet tell of the sermon preached by Charles Giles at quarterly meeting, proclaiming it both eloquent and good. I should state that her recollection of these men is coupled rather with the Pompey circuit than with that of Rose.

Later, when the Collinses had become connected with the church, meetings were held, at times, in the barn of Thaddeus Collins, 1st, and Alpheus, his son, standing somewhere near the residence of Mrs. Harvey Closs. The quarterly occasions were made much of and large congregations assembled, sometimes coming from great distances. Our venerable brother, Stephen Collins, has told me of their going to Daniel Roe's, in Butler, and even to Victory, saying: "I have made more acquaintances at one of these meetings than I made during an eight years' residence in Lyons." Our founders were eminently a social people. I would that our later representatives might emulate them.

We have only the barest glimpses of the ministers who passed through in these early days. Brother Stephen Collins, though eighty-seven years of age, was not of our body in his youth. His parents went to the Port Bay Presbyterian Church, while he first heard Baptist doctrine as expounded by Elder Smith, but later he cast in his lot with us, and here abides to-day. He says that regular preaching was had at Stewart's corners earlier than in the Valley. He recalls Joshua Beebe, 1818, Palmer Roberts, 1819 and 1820, while Wm. W. Rundell, 1821, used to put up at his father's house. Presiding Elder Renaldo M. Evarts, 1820 and 1822, lingers also in memory's gallery, while Enoch Barnes was to him like a brother. Seth Youngs and J. M. Brooks, 1823, are remembered as active, go-ahead men, the latter considerably the younger. James P. Aylsworth was the pastor in charge of Sodus circuit in 1824, and once, when asked his age, he ran his fingers through his hair, thus giving it a stand-up condition, and replied: "Now guess." He it was who told of his experience in the food line, when making his rounds. His appetite was equal to anything that was set before him, save in one instance, when he saw the good wife prepare the johnny-cake and set it to bake in the out-of-doors fire. That was well enough, but when he beheld the interest and proximity of a number of goslings, whose investigations considerably affected the cake, he concluded to forego eating for one day, though the woman and her family seemed in no way disturbed by the admixture. William McKoon was four times a laborer on the Victory and Rose circuits. Of him, Brother Collins says: "He did as much good as any man the circuit ever had. No man in these parts could equal him as a preacher of funeral sermons." He spoke the final words over the first Thaddeus Collins and Esther, his wife. Samuel Bebins, in 1831, was the last rider of the Victory circuit, leaving it with a membership of 1,200 people. He is remembered as wearing a red bandanna on his bald head, and as being a man of a lively nature. It was a six weeks' circuit, or one requiring that time to make the complete round : so one day, in leaving his Butler charge, he said: "Brethren, I don't like this six weeks' business. The devil gets around before I do." Perhaps he was active in securing the change, for in 1832 there was a subdivision, and Rose circuit appeared with a membership of 531. The first ministers over the new circuit were Elijah Barnes and John Thomas. The latter was an Englishman, and in a country where the latch string was always out, his conventional ways seemed very strange. Says one : "Why, he would knock at a door all day, or till some one opened it for him, never heeding the old-fashioned 'come in,' and I don't know as he would ever get off his horse unless bidden to do so."

In 1832 our people were still worshiping in school-houses, though the Valley log building had given place to a framed structure. With the new circuit, a movement was made for the building of an edifice, and hereafter are copied verbatim the first written records of our Rose organization :

"At a meeting of the inhabitants of the town of Rose, held in the school-house in Rose Valley on Monday, the 27th day of August, 1832, pursuant to publick notice, for the purpose of adopting measures for building a chapel for the use of the Methodist Episcopal Church in Rose.

"1st. RESOLVED, That Elijah Barnes be chosen Chairman, and Eron N. Thomas act as Secretary.

"2d. RESOLVED, That the name of this Society be 'The First Methodist Episcopal Society' in the town of Rose.

"3d. RESOLVED, That there be nine trustees, and Jacob Miller, Abel Lyon, Chester Ellinwood, Samuel E. Ellinwood, Geo. W. Mirick, Robert Andrews, Thaddeus Collins, Isaac Lamb and Moses F. Collins be said trustees.

"4th. Resolved, That Eron N. Thomas be the clerk of said Society."

Here we have something definite, and, as corner-stones of our structure, we find certain representative names. Of the man whose name appears as clerk, I may state that he retained the office till his death in 1874. "Sister" Polly Thomas was well represented during these more than forty years by her capable, determined son.

September 8th, 1832, at an adjourned meeting, Brothers Miller, Chester and Ellis Ellinwood, Mirick and Andrews were appointed a committee to agree on a site for a church and to circulate a subscription. The 19th of October, it was resolved that the site of said house be on the hill, north of Mr. Bassett's shop. It was further resolved that Thaddeus Collins, Joel N. Lee and Chester Ellinwood be a committee to build said house, and further, that it be 32 x 45 feet. The form of organization already given was certified to before Judge Arne, and September 13, 1833, was recorded in the clerk's office in Lyons.

In 1836, February 26th, there was a reorganization of the church, and the number of the trustees was reduced to three, who were Ellis Ellinwood, Joel N. Lee and Geo. W. Mirick. We may conclude that proper measures were at once taken to build the church, whose site, given by Thaddeus and Chauncey Collins, was where the house of Mrs. Augusta Allen now stands, at the corner of the street leading to Wayne Centre. Owing to the abundance of cobble stones in the vicinity, I suppose it was thought the builders could use them cheaply and, at the same time, have a substantial edifice. John Hannahs was the carpenter, and, as usual, "Sister" Thomas was a mighty power in the progress of affairs. Once, when the builder had fallen short of material and had gathered up his tools and departed, he was surprised at hearing a great clatter in his rear, and, turning, saw a woman standing up in her wagon and shouting to him to stop. It was Mrs. Thomas, who, fearful that if the carpenter went away it would not be easy to get him back, had followed to tell him that she had sent her men into the woods for timber, and that he might return and go to work. The masonry was done by John Layton. The most liberal contributor to the "chapel" was Polly Clark—our "Sister" Thomas—who gave $100; Thaddeus Collins gave $65, and other sums were given, ranging down to those of one figure only. Of the fifty-five givers recorded, only three are yet on this side of the grave, viz., Brother Stephen Collins, a brother of Thaddeus; Chauncey B., the youngest of the family, now living in Clyde, and Ira Mirick, of Lyons. In this way, $743.15 was subscribed, but, as the building cost over $1,200, there was quite a debt to begin with, in this way being too much in keeping with custom, the country over. The building was roofed in and seated temporarily before it was dedicated. In fact, my great-aunt, Mrs. Mary Wade, tells me that she attended revival meetings in the church just after the first corn hoeing in 1835, and that the seats were boards laid upon the end of logs of wood sawed off at the proper length. There is extant a contract between Geo. W. Wainwright and the trustees to complete, *i. e.*, finish the church, bearing date of December 1st, 1835, and the work was to be completed on or before the 1st day of May following. July 13th, 1836, he acknowledges receipt of payment in full, viz., $375, on which day the pews, forty-eight in number, were advertised to be sold. Ensign Ellinwood, with his sisters, Charlotte and Lemira, were singers at the dedication. One of the selections sung was, "How Lovely are Thy Dwellings." This church long maintained the exceedingly quaint custom of separating families, the males sitting on one side and the feminine portion demurely occupying the other part of the room. When completed the "chapel" was a comfortable one, the second church edifice in town; the Presbyterians being a short time ahead. The pulpit was an old-fashioned, high-perched, box-like affair, between the two main entrance doors on the east end. There were galleries on the other three sides.

This building was for nearly twenty-five years the temple whither resorted the Methodist tribes at least one day in the week. Built, however, of cobble stones, and not, perhaps, supported as dwelling-houses are, it was deemed insecure, and people grew afraid of it. There was one unsuccessful attempt to burn it, but in 1859 it was again fired, this time to its destruction, and the edifice which had occasioned so many prayers, so much anxiety and work, was only a smouldering heap of stones. In those days the parsonage was just a little west of the church: now somewhat changed, it is the home of the Presbyterian ministers. Between it and the church was a row of horse sheds. It is a fitting commentary on the fears of some as to the security of the walls, that when the fire was over and the woodwork burned, it took the united work of many to pull and push down the pile of stones so long deemed dangerous. Truly, the temple was well built, a strong tower to those who feared Him.

The true story of this quarter of a century it would take too much time to tell. There were the regular warfare against sin, the revivals where many were gathered into the fold, the marriages and the deaths, when the aged and the young were borne hence to their final resting places. The ministers who followed each other in these years were Burroughs Holmes, who became a prominent figure in his conference: Joseph Cross, who, Brother Stephen Collins says, was the first minister he ever knew to wear whiskers, and they were kept well back under the chin and on the throat. Another has described him as a regular jumping-jack in the pulpit. His career was an eventful one—going south, and to the Methodist Episcopal Church, South, he became the chaplain of the famous Black Horse Cavalry, and after the War returned to become a minister in the Episcopal Church. He was of English birth, which may account for his ready donning of

Confederate gray. In his Rose days, he was quite young, and before the War was done went to Clyde. Humility was then one of his strong points. How strange it seems to us that one's garb, or way of wearing hair or whiskers, should be thought worthy of special attention. When my father first ventured to let his beard grow, his father said : " Wear a very modest beard, my son, a very modest one." On his own face no one ever saw more than the stubble of a week's growth. Anson Tuller was a conspicuous figure, and, with his colleague, in 1837 and 1838, conducted one of the most extensive revivals in the history of the church. Tuller lived a long life of usefulness ; Kilpatrick, who was a man of great eloquence and effectiveness, located in 1846, and went west. From our Rose Church Moses Lyon went out to his mission, terminating last spring. He was a son of Abel Lyon, one of the first trustees. He was noted throughout this section as a sweet singer in Israel. John W. Armstrong came down from Red Creek, and by our quarterly conference was recommended to the traveling connection. Anson Tuller was the presiding elder, and after the young man, who was a teacher in the Red Creek Academy, had withdrawn, he said : " That man has a long head, and it appears to be well filled," a statement well borne out in subsequent years. Austin M. Roe was sent hence, owing much, perhaps, to the promptings of William Peck, a brother of the subsequent bishop. He, doubtless, is well remembered to this day for his tobacco pipe and his horse, Selim.

The membership was a substantial one, and a glance at the names of those who helped build the first church shows many of the best persons in the town. Time would not suffice to sound the praises of all these excellent people. That first Daniel Roe, who lived to be nearly ninety years of age, I can remember as he rode about on his cream-colored horse, keeping to his saddle almost as long as he lived. In his garb and appearance he made a picture in my memory not unlike that of John Wesley. His youngest brother, Austin, my grandfather, came to Rose in time to help build the stone church. A Long Islander, he was a convert at those meetings conducted early in the century by Ezekiel Cooper and William Phœbus. Thaddeus Collins, I have heard my father say, used to yoke up his oxen and take the whole neighborhood to Stewart's corners to attend the meetings in the winter of 1833-4. There could be nothing good in progress in which he did not have a part. But in those days our meetings were not conducted without opposition. To many the fervor and zeal of the Methodists were a stumbling block. My great-grandmother said to my mother : " No, Polly ! you can't go to those meetings. They'll scare you to death." However, she seemed to have survived more than forty years of living as the wife of a Methodist minister, tolerably unscared.

Again, as to ministers, were Jairus McKoon living, I wonder if he would be amused as he was, years ago, when Joseph Byron told of the " he-she

bears." Sitting on the writing falls of the school-house, which was long
the home of Joseph Tipple, he almost lost his centre of gravity over the
sad lapsus of the minister. William Mason located to become the steward
of Red Creek Seminary, a position which he long honored. He used to
tell this story of himself, laughing as heartily as any one at the joke. In
settling accounts once on leaving a charge, a sixpence too much had been
paid him. "Well," said he, "I'll come along and preach you a sermon
for that some day." "Oh, no," said the careful steward, "we've had
enough of six-penny sermons." Nearly all, however, preachers and people,
have passed over. As we recall those times, we cannot help wishing that
once more on this side the River, we might see the Lees, Thomases, Hoff-
mans, Barretts, Griswolds, Wyckoffs, Mitchells, Winchells, Toleses,
Vandercooks, Kelloggs, Lymans, Collinses, Miricks, Ellinwoods, Allens,
Holbrooks, Roes, Lyons, Hunns (there were no Vandals) and all those
who did valiant battle during all these primordial years. It cannot be;
but though they cannot come to us, we may go to them.

From the burning of the old "chapel" to the present, may properly be
termed a new era in the history of our society. Successive divisions and
cuttings off had made the numbers of the organization vary considerably.
Then, too, the spirit of migration had its weight in the membership, but
through all this the church and the neighborhood kept up their proverbial
reputation for regular attendance at meeting. Said William Haney, who
came to us in the sixties from Boonville, N. Y. : "Why, this disposition
to go to church astonishes me. When I get up on a hill-top and look
forward or back on a Sunday morn, the road has the appearance of a long
procession. I verily believe that everybody, religious and irreligious,
goes to meeting." The spirit imparted by our long line of church-going
New England ancestry will not die in a generation, and our hope is that
the succeeding generations will keep up the practice and spirit.

However, the old house, with its memories of revivals, the preaching
and singing for nearly twenty-five years, was a thing of the past. What
should be done next? Measures were taken at once to rebuild—but
where? Shall it be on the old site, or will a new one be selected? Many
said the hill was too cold and breezy, and that there was not room in its
vicinity for horse sheds, while the newly opened street leading eastward
from Eron Thomas' house, would be just the place. Really, the new street
was opened for the church. Arguments, pro and con, were had, but
finally the new streeters prevailed, and the present structure was the
result.

No sooner were the Methodists without a home than the Presbyterians
kindly opened their doors, and, till the basement was finished, more than
a year later, these people worshiped together, apparently to the edification
and profit of all. In fact, Deacon Flint said he didn't care to hear any

better preaching than that given them by Mr. Salisbury. The debates and conferences of the fall of 1859 and following winter resulted in the breaking of ground in the following spring—perhaps in May—and the framing was started in July. Rev. Mr. Brown, of the Clyde Methodist Episcopal Church, was noted for his church building proclivities, and he submitted a plan to our brethren, which was, in the main, adopted ; but Brother Peter Harmon, the builder, was not entirely satisfied. So, broaching the matter to the trustees, they unanimously approved his suggestions—changes which make this edifice practically a home affair, in that the architect and builder was a member of the church.

In December of 1860, the basement was completed and Brother Salisbury came from Wolcott to preach the first sermon in it. The room above the audience room was inclosed and floored and afforded a good place for banquets during the stirring war period, a time when the basement or lecture-room frequently resounded with patriotic appeals. So time passed along. The original cost estimated at $4,000 had swollen to near $7,000. Brothers Wells and Skeel had had their pastorate in the basement, but the coming of Brother Charles Baldwin started the era of finishing, and the work was pushed along to completion. The bell was in place, and on March 3d, 1864, the long houseless congregation assembled to dedicate their edifice. Peter Harmon, the builder, at the suggestion of Elder Dunning, then in charge of the Oswego district, got together an excellent choir, in which was prominent Chester Ellinwood, whose elder brother, Ensign, had led the singing when the old house was set apart. Seated here by the pulpit was "Father" Austin Roe, in a little more than a month to be gathered to his rest, the oldest man in the membership of the church. The sermon was preached by Dr. J. M. Reid, then president of Genesee College, while in the evening Rev. Samuel Clark, of Weedsport, officiated. Rev. B. I. Ives, the noted debt raiser, was also here, and his honeyed utterances succeeded in extracting something more than $2,000 from the audience to raise the debt.

The old church was burned Monday night, April 18th, 1859, during the pastorate of Geo. II. Salisbury, and the new one, building through several years, was dedicated March 3d, 1864, while Charles Baldwin was minister. The very day of the burning of the Rose Church, the corner-stone of the new one in Clyde was laid, a coincidence worth noting. From that date to the present there have been very few changes. It and the parsonage adjacent have been convenient, comfortable places for service and the pastor's abode. To the majority of the membership to-day, it is the only building recalled. In this room, could a phonographic record have been made and to-day we were to set the cylinder back, there would come to us the tones of Dr. Reid in the opening address, and then would be heard the mild words of the pastor, Charles Baldwin, who, when he felt life sinking

23

apace. made his home among us, and finally, went from our church militant to that triumphant, his body lying with many of his church associates in the cemetery near. No one would mistake the voice of S. B. Crosier, who was prominent in many things in our village. Of him it is told that W. H. (better known as "Bill") Saunders, showing to him the appointments of his newly fitted up hotel, he pronounced everything excellent if he would only keep the "critter" out, referring to that bane of civilization, alcohol. As the vibrations continue, there would come the beginning of a talk to the Sunday school children; but the inexorable five minutes' rule cut the speaker off completely and he concludes with "I wish I hadn't begun." But there were pleasanter affairs to bring back our genial old friend, Royal Houghton, who gave two sons, Ross and Oscar, to the ministry. He was Houghton to the end, though his sons are now called Howton.

Many ears will listen more intently when the next preacher's tones are heard, and we rejoice that they may be heard to-day. He was the first minister to stay the possible three years, from 1868 to 1871, Rev. Phineas Wiles. Revs. Curtis, Edson and Day all arouse trains of familiar memories. Could our recording phonograph tell all the good things about those whose tones have been preserved here and elsewhere, it would render back to us the somewhat hesitating reading of an Old Testament chapter, wherein hard, double-jointed names abounded. Noticing the obvious amusement of his congregation at some of his efforts, the reader coolly remarks: "If any of you think you can do better than I am doing with these names, why, just come up here and you may have a chance to try." But the active Christian industry of D. D. Davis needs no story to recall it. By the way, the fact that the prominent initials precede his name does not prevent the important truth that he is the only D. D. ever stationed in Rose. Revs. Hoxie and Beach recall long and successful pastorates, and of the latter, I will state that he kept the church record better than any I have ever seen. Were he to give lessons in this respect to his brother preachers, he would confer a priceless boon upon the future mousing chronicler. Brother C. E. Herman's interim of a single year brings us to a voice that, improving the possibility to remain beyond the old three years' bounds, is now, in its fourth year, able to speak for itself. All will know that I refer to him who has so long and so faithfully served this people, and whose zeal, in and out of season, has brought about so much that to-day gladdens our sight. Under the pastorate of Brother G. A. Reynolds, our church has taken a new lease of life. While the membership of the parent church remains much as usual—subject to the fluctuations of removals and lukewarmness—a growing daughter is found in the North Rose organization, where thirty-five probationers form an excellent foundation. May the enterprise increase and prosper.

While mention has been made of the later pastors, we would not forget those who earlier toiled here. There was Harlow Skeel, who was preacher in a trying period and who is still a standard bearer in the Northern New York Conference, and I doubt not that many here remember his family as well as himself. Frank and Clarence both were graduated from Wesleyan in 1874. The former is now a physician in New York. The latter found an early grave while following in his father's footsteps. It was during Brother Skeel's stay that the Rev. George Bowles, a local deacon, was expelled. He was an Englishman of massive frame and persuasive eloquence, as all who recall him will testify. In early life he must have been "an awkward hand in a row." He had been much abused and provoked by a neighbor, nameless here. So long as the latter's taunts were confined to Brother B. personally, he did nothing, but when the man assailed the character of the preacher's family, he said: "You may talk about me, but my children never," and pitching in he gave the sinner one of the best thrashings ever administered by a representative of the church militant to one of Satan's crew. It was, of course, very unchristian, but carnal man cannot repress a feeling of pleasure that the militant Methodist was also triumphant. In the eyes of the community, he was very much of a hero, having given what all considered a fully merited punishment. But the church must free itself from such odium, and so expelled, but on profession, readmitted, and in a few years reinstated. The example is not the best possible, but sometimes fire must be fought with fire. The presiding elder was Chas. A. Dunning, and I have wondered whether he may not have had a fellow feeling for Mr. Bowles, since of him the story is told that, in his earlier life, he knocked down an impious jackanapes, who, in reply to the query as to whether he would not like religion, had answered: "Yes, I guess I'll take about three cents' worth." Contrition and repentance had accomplished for him the same end gained by our erring brother of Rose. M. D. L. B. Wells. Does anyone wonder that the bishop once referred to him as Alphabet Wells? Geo. H. Salisbury. What a career of usefulness was cut short when death claimed him! Having much of his father, Nathaniel's, ability he had vastly more tact and suavity, yet can anyone believe that, twenty-five years ago, there were those in the Rose Church whose righteous souls were vexed because he had patent leather tips on his shoes? William Morse, O. C. Lathrop, so recently gone home; Harris Kingsley, Cyrus Phillips, William Jones—all these names will have a familiar sound to some.

But the past is past. From the insignificant beginning in numbers of six Methodists, sixty-five years ago, to the present, there has been a practical confirmation of the promise that where two or three are gathered together in His name, He will be in the midst of them, and that to bless. Through divisions or changes, through dissension within, through considerable secessions, through removal and death, through our discriminating Baptist and Presbyterian brothers seeking here fair partners for life's journey,—through all these hazards the church has survived, and there have been found those who have kept the altar bright, the fires burning. If there be Pharisees, so also there are strong, faithful souls, who know no such word as fail, whose hand once placed to the plough continues firm to the end. Here, then, are the stages: A class in 1824, but no abiding city till 1836. Then a comfortable home till destroyed by fire in 1859. Again shelterless till March, 1864. Then twenty-five years in this structure, to-day renewed, beautified, it becomes more fitly than ever the place of worship, the abode of the Most High. May God in His wisdom sanctify and keep it.

ACCOUNT OF MONEYS PAID IN BUILDING STONE CHURCH.

Jacob Miller, $31 ; Abel Lyon, $25.75; Sol. Whitney, $15.50; Matthias Van Horn, $11 ; Moses F. Collins, $13.62; William Griswold, $6 ; John N. Chidester, $5 ; Lorenzo C. Thomas, $25 ; John J. Dickerson, $30 ; John Bassett, $20 ; Eron N. Thomas, $27 ; Chester Ellinwood, Joel N. Lee, $31.63 ; Samuel E. Ellinwood, $33.63 ; Robert Andrews, $29 ; Geo. W. Mirick, $31 ; Samuel N. Welch, $5 ; Moses Lyon, $13.38 ; Polly Clark, $100 ; Solomon Allen, $8 ; Thaddeus Collins, $65 ; Stephen Collins, $12 ; Joel Bishop, Jr., $3.50 ; Merrill Pease, $2 ; Samuel Hunn, $8 ; Samuel Jones, $5 ; A. F. Baird, $5 ; S. H. Brainard, $10 ; Enoch Knight, $5 ; William Mitchell, $2.26 ; E. D. Sherman, $2 ; Abram Van Tassel, $3 ; Orrin Moore, $10 ; Samuel Bucknam, $5 ; Ira Lathrop, $3 ; Uriah Wade, $5 ; Joseph Wade, $1 ; Nicholas Stansell, $12 ; James Aldrich, $2.50 ; Isaac Lamb, $12 ; Stephen Babcock, $6 ; Charles G. Oaks, $2 ; Orrin Morris, $2 ; John McWharf, $2 ; Chauncey B. Collins, $38 ; John W. Lee, $2 ; Wm. McKoon, $1 ; Willis Roe, $2.50 ; Paul H. Davis, $.50 ; Daniel Roe, $2 ; Hiram and Ira Mirick, $5 ; Austin Roe, $10 ; John Q. Deady, $5 ; John Springer, $— ; John Ogram, $3.63. Total, $743.40.

Wm. Lord, $—— ; — Benedict, $2.50 ; Peter Valentine, $—— ; — Twiss, $—— ; S. Munsell, $4 ; H. Drury, $3 ; D. Munsell, $3 ; Wm. Walmsley, $2 ; Joseph Seelye, $10 ; W. Allen, $—— ; Nathan W. Thomas, $——.

SLIPS AND OCCUPANTS IN OLD STONE CHURCH.

No. 1. Robert Andrews. No. 2. Stephen Babcock. No. 3. Solomon Allen. No. 4. John Bassett. No. 5. Jester L. Holbrook. No. 6. John W. Lee. No. 7. Abel Lyon. No. 9. Charles G. Oaks. No. 10. Lorenzo C. Thomas. No. 17. John Ogram. No. 18. Dorman Munsell.

No. 19. Stephen Collins. No. 20. Eron N. Thomas. No. 21. Samuel E. Ellinwood. No. 22. Geo. W. Mirick. No. 23. Thaddeus Collins. No. 24. Chester Ellinwood. No. 25. Seth H. Brainard. No. 26. John J. Dickson. No. 27. Polly Clark. No. 28. Joel N. Lee. No. 29. Chauncey B. Collins. No. 30. Austin Roe. No. 31. M. A. Cornwell. No. 38. Solomon Whitney. No. 39. Moses Lyon. No. 40. Polly Clark. No. 41. Joel Bishop, Jr. No. 42. John A. Chidester. No. 43. Thaddeus Collins. No. 44. Stephen Collins. No. 45. Jacob Miller. No. 46. Lyman Lee. No. 47. Matthias Van Horn. No. 48. Chas. G. Oaks.

OFFICERS OF THE ROSE METHODIST EPISCOPAL CHURCH.

STEWARDS.—Eron N. Thomas, from 1853 to 1874—Recording Steward, twenty-one years; Ovid Blynn, from 1853 to 1879 and 1885; S. Ellis Ellinwood, from 1853 to 1867; Samuel B. Hoffman, from 1853 to 1869; Thaddeus Collins, from 1853 to 1861; John Vandercook, from 1853 to 1867; Wm. Benjamin, from 1853 to 1864; Geo. W. Mirick, from 1857 to 1865; John Harmon, from 1857 to 1861; Wm. Osborne, from 1861 to 1867 and 1871; Wm. Haney, from 1861 to 1867; G. L. Munsell, from 1863 to 1871; James Armstrong, from 1865 to 1871; Henry C. Rice, from 1867 to 1876; Oliver Bush, in 1867; Stephen Kellogg, from 1867 to 1879; Oscar Weed, 1867 to 1889; Wm. H. Vandercook, from 1867 to 1889; E. Toles, 1871 and 1872; Philander Mitchell, 1875; Wm. Desmond, from 1875 to 1881; John Crisler, 1875; John B. Roe, from 1875 to 1885; Clayton J. Allen, from 1879 to 1881 and 1885 to 1889; D. Finch, 1881 and 1882; P. Soper, from 1881 to 1885; Abram Covell, from 1882 to 1889; Selah Finch, from 1885 to 1889; E. Burrell, from 1885 to 1889; James Armstrong, 1885; C. Barrick, 1885; Milo Lyman, 1888 and 1889; Edgar Armstrong, 1888 and 1889; Daniel Foster, 1888; Alonzo Case, 1888 and 1889; J. Morey, 1888 and 1889; C. Shaw, 1888 and 1889.

TRUSTEES.—Jacob Miller, 1832; Abel Lyon, 1832; Chester Ellinwood, 1832; Samuel E. Ellinwood, from 1832 to 1851; George Mirick, from 1832 to 1850 and 1860 to 1866; Robert Andrews, 1832; Thaddeus Collins, 1832; Isaac Lamb, 1832; Moses F. Collins, 1832; Joel N. Lee, from 1833 to 1848; Samuel B. Hoffman, 1849 and from 1860 to 1872; Charles S. Wright, from 1859 to 1875; John B. Roe, from 1859 to 1873; Eron N. Thomas, 1859 to 1874; John M. Vandercook, from 1860 to 1870; Harvey D. Mason, from 1860 to 1865; Lucian Dudley, from 1865 to 1874; G. L. Munsell, from 1870 to 1872; Wm. Osborne, from 1875 to 1878; Oliver Bush, from 1875 to 1888; H. Perkins, 1875; Peter Harmon, from 1875 to 1886; James Armstrong, from 1875 to 1878; Milo Lyman, from 1875 to

1881 and 1888 ; Clayton J. Allen, from 1878 to 1888 ; Wm. H. Griswold, from 1878 to 1885 ; Philander Mitchell, from 1883 to 1888 ; David Finch, from 1883 to 1886 ; J. Crisler, from 1884 to 1886 ; Wm. Desmond, from 1884 to 1886 and 1888 ; Edgar Armstrong, from 1884 to 1887 ; Stephen B. Kellogg, 1888 ; Abram Covell, 1888 ; Daniel Foster. 1885.

CLASS LEADERS.—Alfred Lee, from 1824——; Orrin Lackey, ——; Joel N. Lee, from 183- to 1880 ; Samuel B. Hoffman, 1853 and 1854 and from 1857 to 1863 ; Thaddeus Collins, from 183- to 1854 ; Samuel Hunn, from 1853 to 1875 ; Nelson Griswold, 1853 ; Jester L. Holbrook, 1853 and 1854 ; John B. Roe, from 1855 to 1885 ; David Ellinwood, from 185- to 1856 ; C. D. Hinman, 184- to 1856 ; G. W. Mirick, from 1857 to 1863 ; J. B. Barrett, 1857 and 1888 ; C. C. Collins, from 1857 to 1863 ; Henry Young, from 1857 to 1863 ; Leonard Mitchell, 1858 ; Orrin Sherman, 1860 ; John M. Vandercook, 1861 ; Wm. Osborne, 1862 and from 1872 to 1874 ; G. L. Munsell, from 1865 to 1872 ; Wm. Haney, 1865 and 1866 ; Philander Mitchell, 1865 ; Abel Lyon, from 1867 to 1872 ; Milo Lyman, from 1869 to 1885 and 1889 ; Edgar Armstrong, 1872 and from 1885 to 1889 ; Charles C. Relyea, 1875 ; Ebenezer Toles, from 1875 to 1883 ; Wm. Harmon, from 1875 to 1885 ; Stephen B. Kellogg. from 1878 to 1885 and 1889 ; J. L. Finch. from 1878 to 1884 ; George Ream, from 1881 to 1884 ; Selah Finch, from 1884 to 1889 ; C. More, from 1885 to 1889 ; J. D. Morey, from 1885 to 1889 ; S. H. Lyman, 1885 ; Edward Burrell, 1888 and 1889 ; Stanton Waldruff, 1888.

OFFICERS SINCE 1889.

STEWARDS.—Milo Lyman, 1889-'93 ; Stephen B. Kellogg, 1889-'91 ; Clayton J. Allen, 1889-'93 ; William H. Vandercook, 1889-'93 ; Edgar A. Armstrong, 1889-'93 ; A. Covell, 1889 ; Selah Finch, 1889-'93 ; Alonzo Case, 1889-'91 ; Edward Burrell, 1889-'92 ; John Morey, 1889-'90 ; Oscar Weed, 1889-'91 ; Daniel Foster, 1890-'93 ; E. Brewster, 1890 ; E. P. Soper, 1891-'93 ; M. N. Sours, 1891-'93 ; George Worden, 1891 ; C. E. Tague. 1891-'92 ; Roswell Tracy. 1892-'93 ; E. A. Griswold, 1893 ; David Wescott, 1893.

TRUSTEES.—Edgar A. Armstrong. 1889-'93 ; Daniel Foster, 1889-'93 ; Milo Lyman, 1889-'92 ; John Crisler, 1889-'91 ; Clayton J. Allen, 1889-'93 ; William Desmond, 1889-'93 ; H. S. Perkins, 1889-'93 ; Alonzo Case, 1889-'93 ; Oscar Weed. 1892-'93 ; Edward Burrell, 1892 ; M. N. Sours, 1892 ; E. Thomas, 1892 ; William Lyman, 1892-'93 ; William H. Vandercook, 1893 ; Roswell Tracy, 1893 ; C. E. Tague. 1893.

CLASS LEADERS.—Stephen B. Kellogg, 1889–'93 ; Edgar A. Armstrong, 1889–'93 ; John Morey, 1889–'90 ; Edward Burrell, 1889–'92 ; E. Thomas, 1891 ; George Worden, 1892–'93 ; John L. Finch, 1892–'93 ; S. E. Waldruff, 1892–'93 ; C. E. Tague, 1892–'93.

MINISTERS IN THE VICTORY AND ROSE CIRCUITS.

Wm. Rundell, Levi Brown, 1821. Enoch Barnes, Jos. Williams, 1822. Seth Young, J. W. Brooks, 1823. James Aylsworth, Mark W. Johnson, 1824. James Aylsworth, Wm. Jones, 1825. James B. Roach, James Hazen, 1826. Anson Tuller, Benson Smith, 1827. Anson Tuller, Mattison Baker, 1828. C. Northrop, Wm. Johnson, 1829. C. Northrop, Wm. McKoon, 1830. Samuel Bebins, Wm. McKoon, 1831. Elijah Barnes, John Thomas, 1832–'3. Wm. McKoon, Lewis Bell, 1834. Burroughs Holmes, Joseph Cross, 1835. Burroughs Holmes, Joseph Byron, 1836. Anson Tuller, Joseph Kilpatrick, 1837. Anson Tuller, Benj. Rider, 1838. Benj. Rider, Wm. McKoon, 1839. Wm. Mason, Josiah Arnold, 1840. Isaac Hall, John W. Coope, 1841. Isaac Hall, Isaac Turney, 1842. Rowland Soule, J. F. Alden, 1843. Rowland Soule, Moses Lyon, 1844. J. M. Park, Moses Lyon, 1845. Geo. G. Hapgood, Joseph Kilpatrick, 1846. John W. Coope, 1847–'8. Wm. Peck, 1849–'50. Hiram Nicolls and supply, 1851. Wm. Jones, 1852. Cyrus Phillips, 1853. Harris Kinsley, 1854–'5. O. C. Lathrop, 1856. Wm. Morse, 1857. Geo. H. Salisbury, 1858–'9. M. D. L. B. Wells, 1860. Harlow Skeel, 1861–'2. Charles Baldwin, 1863–'4. S. B. Crosier, 1865–'6. Royal Houghton, 1867–'8. Phineas H. Wiles, 1869–'71. Wm. H. Curtis, Philip Martin, 1872. J. L. Edson, 1873. J. H. Day, 1874–'5. D. D. Davis, 1876–'7. E. Hoxie, 1878–'80. C. J. Beach, 1881–'3. C. E. Hermans, 1884. G. W. Reynolds, 1885–'90. G. S. Transue, 1890–'93. W. H. Rogers, 1893.

THE ROSE BAPTIST CHURCH.

It is not a little strange that a bishopless church should have had its origin, and for some years almost its maintenance, in a family of Bishops. for had the people of this name settled elsewhere, our Rose Baptists had waited longer for their beginning. It has been stated that the church was organized January 3d, 1820. Be this as it may, the first date recorded in the church book is March 4, 1820, just in that era of "good feeling" which characterized President James Monroe's administration. The fly-leaf of this book of records is inscribed thus : "A book of the records of the Second Baptist Church in Wolcott." The church, then antedates the town of Rose, which was not known till 1826. The sixteen names given later were those of people representing various parts of the eastern portion of our country, but by far the majority were in some way allied to the Bishop family, which came from Montgomery county. Earlier than this, churches of this denomination had been formed in Wolcott Village and in Sodus. It is reasonable to suppose that these early comers had made regular journeys, when roads and weather permitted, to these remote places. In fact, the late Deacon George Seelye was wont to state that in his boyhood, he and his mother had ridden horseback to Sodus, crossing the floating bridge at the Bay on their way. They came to the new settlement in 1815, and Mrs. Seelye early connected herself with this church in the wilderness. The books of record are in the handwriting of Chauncey Bishop till July 7, 1855, when, July 14th, the familiar script of Deacon George Seelye appears, and continues till September 3d, 1881. Then Lucien H. Osgood was elected clerk, and in his hand the books have been kept to date. From these books, whatever data recorded here are taken. Kept with the punctilious correctness of a good brother of the old school, the earlier volumes contain much that seems strange to our modern eyes and ears. Those founders tolerated very little nonsense, and if the member did not walk in the way prescribed, his brethren proceeded at once to know the reason why. "Voted that Brothers —— and —— serve as committee to *labour* with Brother or Sister —— for disorderly walk," is of frequent recurrence. It must not be inferred, however, that this often mention indicates more irregularity then than now, but rather that the people then were more particular, and that they had, seemingly, more time to look into the ways of their neighbors. Nor must the term "disorderly" be taken in its usual

TOWN HALL.   FREE METHODIST CHURCH.

BAPTIST CHURCH.

NORTH ROSE CHURCH.   PRESBYTERIAN CHURCH.

·acceptance to-day, for then, in religious parlance, it meant usually nothing worse than failure to attend Baptist meetings or, possibly, a little family or neighborhood brawl. Of course, it might mean worse, and it did have a significance, in one or two cases, that brought much sorrow to the church. However, through evil as well as good report, the church has persevered and long has been one of the agencies for good in which our town has abounded.

Probably no denomination is more democratic in its creed and government than the Baptist. Neither diocese, presbytery nor conference confines it.   While holding to the prime tenets of the church, each body adopts its own rule, and herewith is given the "Church Covenant" of our Rose Baptists :

"Having been baptized upon our profession of *Faith* in *Christ*, and believing it to be our duty to walk in all the ordinances of the *Gospel*, which we cannot be in a situation to do without being united together in the order of a Gospel Church ; and that we may with one mind and one mouth glorify God, even the *Father* of our *Lord Jesus Christ.* We do, therefore, in *sincerity* declare the following Covenant to be a summary of Christian duties, which we look upon ourselves under the highest obligations to embrace, maintain and defend, believing it to be our duty to stand fast in one spirit, with one mind striving together for the faith of the Gospel, and not to countenance any of the vain, unscriptural tenets, traditions or customs of men.

" We are very sensible that our conduct and conversation, both in the church and in the world, ought to be such as becometh the Gospel of Christ, and that it is our incumbent duty to walk in wisdom and prudence towards all them that are without, to exercise a *conscience* void of offense towards God, and towards all men, by living soberly, righteously and godly in this present world, endeavoring by all lawful measures to promote the peace and welfare of this particular church, and the prosperity of the Redeemer's Kingdom in general.   As to our regards to each other, in our church communion, we esteem it our duty to walk with each other in all humility and brotherly love, to watch over each other's conversation, to stir up one another to love and good works, not forsaking the assembling of ourselves together, as we have opportunity, to worship God according to his revealed will and, when the case requires, to warn, entreat, exhort, rebuke and admonish in the spirit of meekness, according to the rules of the Gospel.

" Moreover, we think ourselves obliged to sympathize with each other in all conditions, both inward and outward, which God in his providence may bring us into ; also to bear with one another's weaknesses, failings and infirmities, so much as the law of Christ requires us to do ; at the same time to be careful not to suffer sin one upon another, or to have fellowship with any one that is immoral in conduct or heretical in principle. Furthermore, we view it to be highly necessary for our peace and prosperity, and for the honor of God, to be careful and keep up a strict Gospel discipline among us, and to be careful in receiving members not to refuse the weak, nor to admit any unbaptized person to our communion, or any one but such as make a good profession of repentance towards God and faith in our Lord Jesus Christ, and also to cut off or reject and put away any one member from our communion, fellowship, watch or care, whose conduct is such that the word of God requires us to do it, but in no case to be heedless, slothful or rash, but in all matters endeavoring to act in the fear of God, with a Christ-like temper of mind, that God in all things may be glorified in the church ; and particularly to pray for one another and for the spread of the Gospel, the increase of Christian knowledge, and the prosperity of Zion universally.

" Now all these and every other duty held forth and enjoined on a Gospel church in the Scriptures of truth, we desire and engage to be in performance of, through the *gracious assistance* of the Lord, while we both admire and adore the grace that has given us a place and a name in God's house, better than that of sons and daughters.

" In testimony of our full agreement and unanimous consent to the aforesaid Covenant, each one of us has voluntarily subscribed his or her name. (Signed) : Hosea Gillett, John Skidmore, Peter Lamb, Joel Bishop, Chauncey Bishop, Phœbe Bishop, Clarry Burns, Hannah Miner, Sally Skidmore, Rachel Bishop, Lydia Fuller, Martha Bishop, Simantha Lealand, Nancy Ticknor, Hannah Gillett." Just one-half of these names belonged to the Joel Bishop family. " Father and mother," Joel and Phœbe Bishop, were dismissed by letter July 3d, 1836.

This covenant has received an almost monthly renewal of fealty from 1820 to the present. While these covenanters have had no such trial of their faith as had those of Scotland, few would presume to affirm that they had not the courage of their convictions, and that they, too, would not seal their devotion with their blood, as have done the faithful in all ages of the church. The carefully kept records appeal to the reader, just in keeping with his own spirit. Does he look for material for merriment, it may be found in abundance, but should he turn to these pages for the long roll of duties carefully and regularly performed, for indications of a disposition to obey God's commands in the best way possible, he will find what he seeks in equal abundance. To err is human, and our common humanity has no startling exception in Rose. While we may pause over the name of the delinquent whom the committee visits to secure a renewed " travel " with the church, let us not forget the many more whose names are never found in such connection. The prodigal son is ever of more mention and importance than that elder brother who never strayed. Of course, it is natural that we should smile over some of the "labours" of the many visiting committees. For instance, it seems a little queer, and possibly a trifle indicative of the original Adam, when a certain ex-deacon is received by letter, and in only a few months has to be "laboured" with because of his refusal to pay his assessment toward defraying the gospel bill. Doubtless he believed in *free* grace as well as election. However, as he soon paid up, he was restored to fellowship. One brother was called upon to have his many shortcomings set before him, and, according to common report, he was deserving of the severest censure, but he, suspecting the nature of the errand, quite forestalled his visitors by telling them that the church had become so corrupt, he desired to withdraw from it. There was nothing left to do but to grant his wish. One sister was the subject of long and serious consideration, since she attended the ministrations of another denomination at the instance of her husband, who was not a Baptist. Among other reports presented, was one wherein it was stated : "She, wishing to cultivate friendship at home, thought it best for the present not to meet with the church, and the church voted to exercise Christian forbearance towards her for the present."

The men and women who made up this first roll of membership were the sturdy pioneers of the town. They worked hard in clearing the way for later generations, but they found time to attend divine service better than some of their descendants. They were seldom absent from the covenant meeting on the afternoon of each first Saturday of the month. Then was transacted the regular business of the church, and on the Sunday following, alternate months, came the baptisms and receptions of members. In the early days the ordinance was administered in Thomas' creek, west of the Valley, and occasionally in Lamb's pond, near our present North Rose, but for some years the church has had a well appointed baptistry.

The list of those who were faithful to the end is a long one, and were it made out, in it would be found the names of several hundred of the town's worthy citizens. They had their peculiarities of voice, manner and thought, and the expression of these characteristics often rendered meetings memorable, that otherwise would have been forgotten years ago. An old lady, now gone to her reward, has told me of one of the early worthies who was always on hand at all the means of grace, but who had a stereotyped form of ending his remarks. It was something like this, accompanying his words with a very vigorous scratching of his head, "Finally, brethren, I hope you will all prove faithful, and that you will persevere to the end, and as for myself, I mean to keep digging." His suiting the action to the word produced an impression that years could not efface.

The story was long told with infinite gusto of one good brother, who was accused of the exceedingly ungallant act of pulling his wife out of bed in the morning, a charge that he indignantly repelled, saying : "I had called her repeatedly, and as she failed to appear, I just took her by her lily-white foot and gently drew her from the couch." However clear the distinction was in the brother's mind, it never struck his fellow members as particularly vivid.

The first meetings of the church were held at the house of Joel Bishop, and April 15, 1820, it was voted to request the churches of Wolcott, Galen and Lyons to constitute a council, "to examine into our situation, and if they see fit to show their fellowship of this conference as a sister church of Christ." April 27th, 1820, it was voted to present to the council as their views of doctrines and practice the confession of faith and platform of the Ontario Association. Moreover, it was voted that Brothers Chauncey Bishop and Hosea Gillett be a committee to represent the conference to the council. The record of this council is in the handwriting of John B. Potter, of Galen, who was clerk. Joel Blakeman, of the same town, was chairman. The council convened at the house of Joel Bishop, Wednesday, May 3d, 1820. Wolcott sent Elder David Smith, Jacob Purdy and Charles Sweet. From Galen came Brothers Potter, Blakeman and John Flint, while Lyons sent William W. Brown, Ebenezer M. Pease, and James Bryant. Visiting brethren, John Burns, from Wolcott, James Beard and Alanson Richmond, from Lyons, were invited to a seat in the council. After the proper examination and deliberation, it was voted to fellowship the conference as a "church of Christ in sister relation." Those who constituted this assembly long since passed on, but the object of consideration flourishes in perennial youth. May 20, 1820, Chauncey Bishop was made clerk, and September 20, 1820, it was voted to apply for membership in the Cayuga Association, sending Chauncey Bishop as delegate. The request was granted. In 1834 the church became one of the Wayne Association Baptist Churches. The first minister was Elder David Smith, whose name appears in the council of recognition as a delegate from Wolcott. His letter was accepted January 8, 1821. The list of preachers from that date to the present is a long one. It includes names that have been very familiar throughout the western part of the state. While few of them have been sounded by the trump of fame, by far the larger number are those of men who worked long and faithfully in the Master's vineyard. The second incumbent was ordained here. William B. Brown was called May 5, 1821, and the council which acted upon his case met at the house of Joel Bishop, August 29th, of the same year. Participants in this council had been invited from Wolcott, Victory, Cato, Ira, Mentz, Brutus, Aurelius, Galen, Lyons and Sodus, while the local representatives were Zenas Fairbanks, Hosea Gillett and Chauncey Bishop. How many responded to the invitation is not stated, but at the council Rev. John I. Twiss preached ; Rev. John Jeffers prayed the prayer of ordination ; and with Revs. Twiss,

Smith and Davis, laid on hands : Rev. David Smith gave the charge ; Rev. George B. Davis gave the right hand of fellowship and made the concluding prayer. As many of the ministers continued to preach here after they had received letters of dismissal, it is possible to approximate only to the dates of their ministrations. During the intervals between regular pastorates, many candidates were heard, but no effort has been made to secure their names. It is possible that the following list may include some names whose owners were merely birds of passage, but the frequency of their appearance in the records is the warrant for their appearance here.

Elder Brown was dismissed February 2d, 1822, but he was in and about the church for some years afterward. In fact, his name, with those of Luther Goodrich, Isaac D. Hosford, William Moore, Ezra Chatfield and A. Barrett, fill the gap till 1834, when Rev. Martin Miner appeared and remained till 1836. Then, in order, we have Revs. Issac Bueklin, H. B. Kenyon, Luke Morley and Hezekiah De Golyer, to 1837. The next four years were occupied by Revs. B. Putnam, —— Dodge and John Fairchild. From 1841 to 1845, in which time Rev. Amasa N. Jones was ordained, Rev. Amasa S. Curtiss filled the pulpit ; and from 1845 to 1849, the Rev. Andrew Wilkins had his first pastorate in Rose. Elder Anson Graham came in 1850, and continued two years. January 1st, 1853, Butler Morley was received by letter, and the churches of Clyde, Lyons, Butler, Wolcott, Red Creek, Marion, Sennett and Sodus were invited to participate in a council of ordination, which met and ordained the candidate January 20th, of the same year. Elder Morley remained till 1854, and June 11th, of that year, the Rev. Thomas T. St. John came and remained three years. After him, 1857–'59, the church had as pastor the Rev. Nelson Ferguson, and then, 1860–'62, the Rev. John Halliday, though between these two, the Rev. Leander Hall was ordained here, in March, 1860, remaining only a short time. Then followed Elder Ira Dudley, who went away in 1865. Rev. George Butler, an Englishman, was here one year, 1866, and the Rev. Abner Maynard followed till 1870. In 1871 we have Elder L. P. Judson, and in 1872 Elder W. O. Gunn. Rev. Thomas J. Seigfried is assigned to 1873, and the only settled minister till 1876 is the Rev. Russell Collins, though some part of the time was occupied by the Rev. Reuben Burton, now of Syracuse, but then in the Rochester Seminary. Then came the Rev. Thomas F. Smith, and his pastorate held till 1880. He was succeeded by the Rev. Andrew Wilkins, December 11, 1881, who continued till his ministrations ended with death, and his body was borne to the neighboring cemetery. The Rev. M. H. De Witt came next, going away in 1885. Elder L. G. Brown continued till 1887, and then Elder Clinton Shaw till 1890. The Rev. N. C. Hill presided for a single year, 1891, and then followed the Rev. Maxwell H. Cusick, the present incumbent.

To the older members of the church, each one of these thirty-three names will arouse many memories, not always pleasant, but, in the main, bearing out the usual proportions of the bitter and the sweet in this life of ours. The most of these preachers had families, and their wives and children bore their part in the annual routine of church and town existence. Comparisons would be invidious, but if one man was not liked by some, he was so much more popular with another faction that a good average was maintained. One man was conspicuous for his success in revival services, while another could preach the best doctrinal discourses. Another was noted for the zeal of his pastoral labors. Thus while no one man had in perfection all the ministerial graces, a glance over the whole array finds much to admire. While only one minister was called back to a second pastorate, it is highly to the credit of the church that very many of the former pastors have been willing to take up the lines again. Many will recall the bright faces of ministers' children who here grew to maturity. The Wilkins boys, two of them, had here their early boyhood. Wallace St. John became one of the most noted schoolmasters in the town. Clark Ferguson became himself a clergyman, and his sisters contributed no little to the life of the church. Elder Maynard's only daughter, Frances, married Gilbert White, and for some years lived in town, and the widow of Elder Wilkins is still a highly esteemed resident of the village.

For many years the ministers have lived in the Valley, but in the earlier days they resided out of the village, and not infrequently tilled several acres of land, thus conferring a deal of pleasure upon some parishioners, who thought sermons constructed at the "tail of the plow" much more efficacious than those which "smelled of the lamp." Elder Fairchild and his family occupied a log house, afterwards owned and used by Egbert Soper, standing on the side of the hill, just east of the present residence of Charles Osborn, in the east part of the town ; and Mr. O.'s home was the habitation of Elders Graham and Ferguson. Elder Bucklin's home was the old Joel Bishop place. Elders Curtiss and Wilkins, in the latter's first pastorate, lived a little north of opposite to the abode of Hamel Closs. The first minister, David Smith, dwelt in a log house erected for him on the site of Henry Decker's home. Elder St. John resided on the road east of the white school-house in Galen ; Elder Halliday in the bee hive ; Elder Dudley, while he did not keep a hotel, did live for a time in the south tavern. One shot from Elder Gunn did memorable execution, for he raised the money to pay for the parsonage where subsequent pastors have been domiciled.

Though organized in 1820, it was not till 1836 that a building was erected for divine worship. Before this, the people had used the school-houses at the Valley, and at Lamb's corners, along with private houses, particularly the home of Joel Bishop. Evidently they counted well the cost before beginning. Very little data can be found as to the building of the edifice, but it appears that the architect and builder was Ansel Gardner, a son-in-law of Chauncey Bishop. Items concerning the building period are scarce, but November 11, 1834, the trustees appointed Chauncey Bishop, Ira Mirick and Peter Valentine a building committee. As the annual business meeting of 1836 was held in March, in the school-house, and that of 1837 was held in the same month in the meeting house, it must be inferred that the edifice was completed in the interval. I have not been able to find any data as to cost. The site was bought of the late Hiram Mirick. Whatever changes have been wrought in subsequent years in covering and in refitting the interior, the old frame-work has not been altered. Nothing but fire or tornado could harm these timbers, so securely and honestly laid. The edifice made very little pretension to architectural beauty, but it answered well the purposes for which it was constructed. Within, the way of life was made plain. Without, between services, the vexed questions of the day were discussed with as much zest and fervor as the time and place would permit. Few problems of politics, political economy, agriculture and other science escaped weekly solutions at the hands of these sapient farmers. No chief justice, wig-covered and wool-sack seated, ever gave expression to more oracular utterances than every Sunday fell from the lips of those who leaned up against the south side of the building and talked. Had plans, developed here, been followed, who knows but that the Rebellion might have been suppressed years before Grant wore it out ?

In 1861 there was a reformation of the interior, changing the pulpit to the north side, so that the preacher might face, not only his people seated, but all late comers, and blinds were placed upon the windows. Of the latter improvement, I have not the least doubt, for I drove every screw, while Deacon George Seelye and John Gillett held the foot of the ladder and discussed the War. At this time, also, a bell was placed in the church steeple.

In 1885-6 a very thorough renovation of the structure, within and without, was effected. The outlay of $4,400 was well expended, and the result has so metamorphosed the original structure that the early worshipers would pass it without recognition. The galleries disappeared, singers' seats were placed at the pulpit's right, a baptistry was constructed beneath the pulpit, and new entrances were devised, considerably adding to the capacity of the church. The basement has kitchen and dining-room, so essential to modern churches. The roof is covered with tin, but the old church sheds remain as in days of old. Good Baptist horses instinctively turn towards them whenever driven through the Valley.

During these seventy-two years of existence, the Rose Church has elected to the office of deacon many men who have merited and enjoyed the highest respect of their fellow citizens. The first appointed were William Briggs and George Seelye, who were ordained to their office July 16th, 1835. Again, in 1843, September 19th, John I. Smith and James H. Ferris were ordained deacons. Elder John Mitchell, of Clyde, preached, and was also chairman. The pastor, Elder A. S. Curtis, prayed, and with Elder Mitchell and Deacon George Seelye, laid on hands. Deacon Seelye, also, gave the hand of fellowship. These were the only cases of ordination, but other deacons were appointed, as Benjamin Genung, William Guthrie, Luther Wilson and Jefferson Chaddock.

The church has always been well supplied with musicians. The Holmeses, Genungs, Ellinwoods, Osgoods and others well maintained this part of worship. When, in 1835, Mrs. Deacon George Seelye appeared, she was the first of a long line of singers, for the Sheffields have contributed no little to the church music. Her son, Judson, at one time led, and after him Joel S. Sheffield came, and he held the leadership till 1892. Eudora M. Seelye played the melodeon, both before and after her marriage to Lucien H. Osgood. Her sister, Estelle (Mrs. M. G. McKoon), followed her, with Mrs. Frances (Maynard) White, till Lucy (Sheffield) Wade took the place. Joel S. Sheffield's daughter, Hattie, is the present instrumentalist. William B. Kellogg and Felton Hickok were long singers in the choir.

The incorporation of the church took place March 17, 1834, with David Holmes, Ira Mirick, Chauncey Bishop, Joseph Seelye and Peter Valentine as first trustees. This was entered in the county clerk's office, April 15. The annual meeting comes the third Thursday in February.

THE ROSE PRESBYTERIAN CHURCH.

The old yet well preserved first volume of the records of this church has upon its first page the following interesting entry: "Records of the Third Presbyterian Church in Wolcott, February 17th, 1825. The Reverend Francis Pomeroy and the Reverend Benjamin Stockton, members of the Presbytery of Geneva, met at the school-house near Mr. John Closs' in Wolcott for the purpose of setting off certain members of the first Presbyterian Church in Wolcott, and organizing them into a church by themselves. Opened by prayer. The following members were set off and formed into a church, viz.: Males, John Wade, Aaron Shepherd, Simeon Van Auken, Rufus Wells, Moses Hickok. Females, Eunace Wade, Polly Shepherd, Lydia Van Auken."

Then follow the articles of faith and the covenant. At the same meeting, John Wade and Moses Hickok were set apart as elders in the church, and Aaron Shepherd was made the first deacon. Several of these constituent members, having come from New England, must have been Congregationalists, but Presbyterianism had the stronger hold in this locality, and a matter of church government was not enough to estrange those who accepted the prime tenets of English dissent. Of these first eight members, all died in Rose, worthy members of their church, save three, who took letters of dismissal to churches in other localities. These were Simeon Van Auken and wife and Rufus Wells. Till his death in 1840, December 24th, Elder John Wade missed very few meetings of the session. Deacon Aaron Shepherd passed away in 1840, and Moses Hickok in 1826. Polly Shepherd, as the widow of Asel Dowd, of Huron, died in 1858. The student of local history finds much to admire in these names, representing men and women who followed blazed trees to their new homes in the wilderness. Pioneers, when the century was in its teens, they had first cast in their religious lot with the church originally located at Port Bay, since known as the First Church of Wolcott. It was a long ride for the Wades and Shepherds from their home in the south part of the town to this early church, but all of them were God-fearing people and, in their old Connecticut home, had been used to all-day sessions of worship in the edifice on Town hill, New Hartford. However, all must have hailed a church nearer home with no little satisfaction. "The school-house near John Closs'" and that "near Charles Thomas'" long served these people

24

in lieu of an edifice of their own. Session meetings were held usually at private houses. March 8th, 1825, Elizur Flint applied for membership, and was received, and during the many subsequent years of his long life as elder, deacon and clerk, he went in and out before his fellow citizens, holding their highest respect. In April of the opening year, Mrs. Chloe Bishop united with the church and during their long lives she and her Baptist husband, Chauncey, walked in the most "orderly" manner their respective religions ways. Occasionally they would go together, but as a rule they separated as they left the vehicle which brought them to the village. In another world, they are beyond sects and creeds.

The Presbyterians had trouble with faithless members, as have had all churches from the beginning and, recorded in Deacon Flint's accurate and conscientious manner, the stories are entertaining reading, but as erring and weak humanity is not a product of any particular age or place, it is best to draw the mantle of oblivion over the deeds of those controlled by debasing appetite or unruly tempers. The membership of the church has never been large, but it has always included many of the best people in the town.

As already indicated, its meeting places were migratory till 1833, when a place of worship was dedicated on the site of the mill just east of the Baptist Church. It was not showy, but built after the notions of church architecture then prevalent, it long answered the needs of the society. In or about 1862 it was sold to the village for a school-house and a new edifice of brick was erected on its present location. The old structure, from its school uses, became a mill, and as such was burned several years ago. The new one was dedicated in 1865. A commodious building, put up at a cost of about $8000, it is a highly ornamental feature in the north part of the village. The site was purchased of William Vanderoef; that of the first edifice from Hiram Mirick. Though sold for secular purposes, Sunday services were held in the old structure till the dedication of the new.

The most interesting items in the records of the church are those pertaining to temperance and slavery. In the early days of Rose Presbyterianism, several men united with the church who were no temporizers in reform measures. Though no names are given as the writers of several resolutions, it is quite obvious to long-time observers of Rose matters that the man who first put up a frame for a barn, without the use of intoxicants, and who subsequently helped many a negro refugee towards a Canadian home, had much to do with the display of principles set forth upon these pages. The following statement was much to the credit of Rose people, irrespective of denominational lines: February 27, 1831. "The church unanimously resolved that they would hereafter receive to church fellowship no person who would not agree to abstain from the use of ardent spirits as a drink." The church had suffered much from a bibulous member, and dropped him only when thoroughly discouraged as to his reformation.

The church's most serious trouble, however, arose over slavery, and the following is on record : March 1, 1844. "At a meeting of the church to consider the subject of slavery, therefore

"*Resolved*, that slavery is a heinous sin against God and man—in the language of the General Assembly, utterly inconsistent with the law of God, and totally irreconcilable with the spirit and principles of the gospel of Christ, and we therefore believe Christians are bound to oppose the sin wherever it is intrenched, whether in church or state.

"*Resolved*, that the church of Jesus Christ has no right to sustain a permanent church relation to so vote a sin.

"*Resolved*, that we are unable to see why, if the church can safely sustain a church relation to this sin, and permanently tolerate the sum of villainies in her body, why she may not safely associate with and tolerate any other known habitual sin by the same rule.

"*Resolved*, that we cannot consent, with our views of the exceeding sinfulness of slavery, to remain in a permanent church relation to it, and we believe if the whole Presbyterian Church will continue to connive with and fellowship this sin, despite the remonstrance of her members, and her acknowledgment of its inherent guilt; then it will become the duty of the minority to do right if the majority will not.

"*Resolved*, that we as a church will hold no fellowship or communion with slaveholders or their avowed apologists.

"*Resolved*, that the above resolutions be entered on the church records."

But these resolutions, however comprehensive and pertinent, did not satisfy the minds of the agitators, for that they continued to agitate is evident in that the church even determined to go out of the Presbyterian fold, hoping thereby to retain them. Accordingly, January 5. 1846, appears the following entry :

"*Resolved*, with the concurrence of Presbytery, that the Presbyterian Church of Rose adopt the Congregational form of government."

February 5, 1846, Deacon Flint writes : " Presbytery accede the right to the church to practice the foregoing resolution." Accordingly our Presbyterian became a Congregational body, and for some years there were no meetings of the session. To us of this day, these concessions seem to be all that any man or class of men could ask, but April 4. 1846, E. Flint and S. Lovejoy were appointed a committee " to visit those persons which have left the church informally and ascertain the reasons of their leaving." July 4, 1846, a good day for liberty sentiments, the committee reported the following letter :

"May 12th, 1846.

"To E. Flint:

" Sir—We cheerfully comply with your request in giving our reasons in writing for seceding from the Presbyterian Church of Rose, in order that they may be recorded in your church records. And we give for our first and great reason that we do not believe the Presbyterian Church to be a true church or, in other words, a church of Christ. And we found our belief on the following facts: First, because she does not teach or practice the first great principle of Christianity, viz., the inviolability of human rights, but suffers unrebuked one portion of her members to chattelize and traffic in the souls and bodies of another portion of her own members, thus virtually reducing the image of God (in the persons of many thousands of her own acknowledged members in her church for whom Christ died) to the condition of things, to property, and by impiously robbing them of their inalienable rights, have reversed the great law of love, this distinguishing feature between a true and a false church, and have completely annihilated the distinction which God has established between the nature and condition of immortal man and the beasts that perish, thus sanctioning crimes in her communion, which is utterly subversive of a church of Christ.

Second, that said church, with a full knowledge of these facts before her, did declare through her representative in her highest judicial capacity at the meeting of her last General Assembly, not only to the shame and disgrace of Christianity, but to our common humanity, that it was not for the edification of the church to take action on the subject. Thus, in effect, reversing her former decisions (though she never complied with them in practice), and sanctioning by that and subsequent acts in her lower judicatories, in refusing to bear witness against slavery, most of the crimes she charges against the church of Rome, and for which she does not hesitate to call her a church of anti-Christ, thus we are forced to the conclusion that she must and does necessarily partake of the character of the church of Rome in an exact proportion as in her practice she approximates towards her, and we have not arrived at this conclusion in a hasty or precipitate manner ; we have long and faithfully examined this subject, as in the light of eternity, and are fully established in the belief, not without evidence, but from facts which cannot be denied, that the Presbyterian Church, in consequence of her participation in and by the position she has assumed, does, while sustaining such position with regard to American slavery, stand as truly convicted before high heaven and the world as does the Romish church of withholding the Bible from a portion of the laity. Of abrogating the institution of marriage at pleasure, compelling thousands of her members to live in adultery or in a state of forced concubinage, that she governs and holds her church together, not by the law of love, but by physical force, by the power of the sword and by pains and penalties—we cannot, therefore, in the light of divine truth, by the most favorable construction, believe the Presbyterian Church in the United States of America sustains the character necessary to constitute her a true church, or church of Christ. Samuel Lyman, Gideon Henderson, Daniel Lovejoy, Wm. Lovejoy."

Whereupon the church adopted the following :

"*Resolved*, that the report be accepted.

"*Resolved*, that the report be adopted.

"*Resolved*, that the names of Gideon Henderson and Deborah Henderson, Daniel Lovejoy and Wm. Lovejoy, Samuel Lyman and Clement Lyman and Caroline Lyman be stricken from our roll."

While deprecating such a disintegrating course, one cannot repress a feeling of admiration for people in whose breasts love of oppressed humanity had too strong a lodgment. Rose never had more reputable citizens.

As the cause of leaving the Presbyterian Church no longer existed, it is not surprising to find the following action :

April 18, 1851, at the instance of Elizur Flint, the following preamble and resolution were voted by a church meeting: "Whereas, this church obtained leave of Presbytery to withdraw from its care and assume the Congregational form of government for the purpose of reconciling difficulties that existed between it and certain members, that harmony in views and actions might be promoted for the glory of God and good of man, and whereas after the lapse of five years, having tried the result of that action in vain, therefore, resolved, that this church ask Presbytery to receive us under their care and restore us to our former privileges, that we may enjoy the ordinances of God's house." Vote 21.

Protest. Rose, April 18, 1851. "We, the undersigned, disbelieving in and wholly abhorring the cruel and wicked system of American slavery and wishing to maintain no voluntary connection whatever with it, now send our earnest protest against uniting with or putting ourselves under the care of any Presbytery that holds any connection with that portion of the Presbyterian Church that holds slaveholders in its bosom. And we now ask the members of the Congregational Church of Rose, assembled on the 18th of April, to consider a proposition to put themselves under the care of Presbytery, to take this protest into consideration, and if they vote in favor of the proposition thus to unite, to consider us as no longer holding church connection with them. Vote 11.

From that date to the present, the church has continued in the Presbytery. No religious body in the town has come up through greater tribulation, but it stands, to-day, a tribute to the sterling worth of its founders and fosterers and the cause which they loved.

The list of ministers is a long and honorable one. The Rev. Jabez Spicer seems to have remained only a short time, and was followed by Revs. Jonathan Hovey and —— Hubbel. In 1827-'29 Rev. Nathan Gillett filled the pastorate. One of the most notable clergymen of any denomination ever in the town was the Rev. William, better known as "Priest" Clark. He was here from 1829 to 1835, and the impression left was lasting and salutary. Then came Rev. Jesse Townsend, 1836; Rev. Solon G. Putnam, 1837, and Rev. Joseph Merrill in the same year. The Rev. Daniel Waldo, another remarkable figure in the history of the town and state, was here from '37 to '39. Rev. —— Burbank was pastor till 1840, and was followed till January, 1847, by the Rev. Beaufort Ladd. Then came four years of the Rev. O. Fitch, and next the Revs. James Gregg and E. Everett to 1853; Rev. Chas. Kenmore, '54; Rev. B. Ladd, '59; Rev. Wm. Young, '65; Rev. Martin B. Gregg, '67; Rev. J. J. Crane, '70; Rev. Wm. Young, '75; Rev. J. A. Phelps, '77; Rev. E. G. Cheeseman, '82; Rev. J. McMaster, '85 to '88; Rev. Chas. Ray, '91; Rev. Nathan B. Knapp, 1893.

The deacons have been Aaron Shepherd, David Foster, Elizur Flint, Francis Osborn, Wm. Garlick, Judson Garlick, Charles E. Tillson.

The roll of elders includes John Wade, Moses Hickok, Rufus Wells, Smithfield Beaden, Elizur Flint, Martin Warner, Simeon Van Auken, David Foster, Gideon Henderson, Chauncey Smith, Wm. Lovejoy, George Wickson, Jesse O. Wade, Lorenzo N. Snow, James Osborn, Lampson Allen, H. K. Lovejoy, Harvey Closs, Eustace Henderson, Frank H. Closs, Ira T. Soule.

The first clerk was James Van Auken and he served till November 9, 1829. Then Smithfield Beaden kept the records till November 2, 1834. Next Elizur Flint took up the pen and he used it faithfully till October 24, 1882, when the following entry is found, "I, Elizur Flint, clerk of sessions of the Presbyterian Church of Rose, resign the office on account of the infirmities of age, being eighty-nine." To him succeeded Harvey Closs till September 13, 1885, and then the latter's son, Frank H. Closs, became clerk and still holds the office. The church belongs to the Lyons Presbytery.

FREE METHODIST CHURCH.

This body is an offshoot of the M. E. Church and dates from about 1860. Bishop Matthew Simpson, in his Cyclopædia of Methodism, gives the date of the organization as August 23 of the above year, and states that its origin was within the confines of the Genesee Conference, dissatisfaction having arisen among certain ministers concerning the administration of affairs. This unrest had been growing for several years, and 1860 was simply the culminating date. In doctrines it differs in no essential respect from the parent body. It retains conference boundaries, Rose being in the Susquehanna; instead of bishops it has a general superintendent, and in place of presiding elder, it maintains a chairman of the district.

Probably the chief cause for the beginning of the Rose Free Methodist Church may be found in the discussions incident to rebuilding the place of worship of the old church after its burning in 1859. Naturally there was much diversity of opinion as to the form, location and cost of the new structure. At any rate, in 1860, the seeds of the new church seem to have been sown. In the formation and maintenance of this church, none was more prominent than Thaddeus and Josephus Collins, father and son, and for more than thirty years the latter has remained steadfast at his post. Probably no name in the state, in the ranks of this body, is better known than that of F. J. Collins. By his presence, speech and purse, he has made for himself a foremost position among the faithful. His home has ever been open to the ministers, and once a camp meeting was held in a grove upon his farm. His only daughter is the wife of one of the successful clergymen of the denomination, the Rev. Wm. Winget, now of Buffalo, chairman of that district.

Like so many other religious bodies in Rose, this began its worship in the Valley school-house. Soon after, the present house of worship, on Wolcott street, was begun; though added to in various ways, the original structure stands to-day, and just to the eastward is the parsonage. In no way pretentious, these buildings answer well the purposes for which they were erected. The edifice was dedicated January 8, 1863, sermon by the Rev. J. Travis, of Rochester.

Rose first appears on the minutes of the Free Methodist Church in 1861, when it was to be supplied by Revs. Burton and J. W. Stacey. Wm. Cooley came in 1862 and remained one year. During his stay, the church was dedicated. M. N. Downing served from October, 1863, to October 12, 1865 ; J. Olney and D. A. Cargil, from October 15, 1865, to October 6, 1866 ; M. D. McDougal preached from October 6, '66, to October 6, '67. McDougal served the next year with L. Graham. John Glen and D. Dempsey were pastors from October 6, '68, to October 11, '69. Next, J. B. Freeland and G. Eakins, from October 12, to September 19, 1870; M. N. Downing, September 20, '70, to September 15, '72 ; W. Southworth, September 15, '72, to September 12, '74; T. Whiffen, September 13, '74, to September 16, '76 (T. Ross supplying the last year); O. M. Owen, September 17, '76, to September 15, '78 ; G. T. Sutton, September 16, '78, to September 14, '79 ; Y. Osborne, September 15, '79, to September 20, '80; J. Odell, September 21, '80, to September 11, '82 ; J. D. Osmun, September 11, '82, to September 15, '84; T. Whiffen, September 16, '84, to September 6, '86 ; George Stover, September 7, '86, to September 10, '88 ; J. B. Newton, September 11, '88, to August 24, '90; A. F. Curry, August 24, '90, to September 24, '92 ; T. J. Dunham, September 24, '92, to September 19, '93. The latest appointee is the Rev. D. C. Stanton.

Wm. Finch, Philo Miner, the late Wm. H. Thomas, as well as F. J. Collins, have long been prominent in the councils of the church. The present clerk is George Milem.

From this church, John Glen went out to his life of ministerial usefulness and Thirza M., the oldest daughter of George Milem, has recently entered upon a similar work, and is now in Weedsport. Happily, in this denomination, sex is no barrier to Christian activity. The Rose Church is associated with Clyde, making one charge, and both belong to the Clyde district.

THE "VALLEY" SCHOOL.

" Nor fears the blinded bigot's rule
When near her church-spire stands the school."

—*Whittier.*

The proximity of the village school-house to the Methodist Church suggests the above words from New England's beloved poet. It was a favorite scheme of the late Eron N. Thomas to have his church and the school near each other, and both on the street that he opened above thirty years ago, through his meadow land. There have been four stages in school-house building in the Valley. First, the log structure, next the red school-house, then the stone, and finally the brick building now in use. Mr. Thomas claimed that the first regular school in town was taught by Sally Bishop, near her father's home, and that Maria Viele, from Butler, followed her. David Smith, the Baptist minister, also taught in the same place, and, according to Mr. Thomas, he was the first teacher in the Valley, in the old log house standing near the present North Hotel. The same authority names as subsequent teachers, Abigail Bunce ("Aunt Nabby"), Catharine Robinson, William H. Lyon, Gibson P. Center, John S. Roe (Butler), George W. Ellinwood ("Squire"), George Paddock, Jackson Valentine, Wallace St. John, John and Isaac Robinson.

The first written data that I have been able to find is an almost illegible (through the faded ink) scrap, which reads as follows :

"At a meeting of the freeholders and inhabitants of school district number thirteen, in the town of Wolcott, held pursuant to adjournment at the school-house, on the 4th day of October, A. D. 1819, Milburn Salisbury was chosen moderator, and Jeremiah Leland was present as district clerk.

"1st. *Resolved*, Unanimously, Jeremiah Leland shall serve as clerk the ensuing year.

"2. *Resolved*, That Alpheus Collins, Erastus Fuller and Samuel Southwick shall serve as trustees.

"3. *Resolved*, That Thaddeus Collins, Junior, shall serve as collector.

"4. *Resolved*, To furnish a book to keep the district records.

"5. *Resolved*, To raise a tax of six dollars to repair the school-house, and to purchase the aforesaid book."

Apparently the book was not procured till 1823, for only scraps of data appear. Possibly the six dollars did not suffice. October 24, 1820, Jeremiah Leland is directed by Ebenezer Fitch, one of Wolcott's commissioners of common schools, to notify the residents of said District No. 13, of a school meeting to be held November 4, at 3 P. M. The annual meeting for 1821, October 1st, made Thaddeus Collins, Jr., Moderator; Jeremiah Leland, Clerk; Jacob Miller, Samuel Southwick and John Skidmore, Trustees; Thaddeus Collins, Collector. Parents were to provide a half cord of wood for each pupil by the 15th of ensuing January. In 1822, Leland and Thad. Collins, Jr., were continued in respective offices. Alfred Lee, Milburn Salisbury and Elias D. Sherman were made trustees. Parents had an option of a half cord of wood for each pupil or pay thirty-seven and a half cents instead. The well-kept book appears in 1823, and the very first entry is to the effect that Lee and Salisbury, trustees, received of Elizur Flint, in cash, $28.17, which they paid to C. Salisbury, $18.17, and to A. Bunce, $10, teachers. Teaching was done in those days, probably, for the love of it. October 6, 1823, it was voted to build a school-house 22 x 26 feet. It was also voted to "vandue" said house to the lowest bidder, to be paid in grain: wheat at one dollar per bushel, and corn at fifty cents; the same to be paid in two installments. The trustees were voted power to select a site. Obviously, objections were raised, for December 20, the same year, the district met again and rescinded the vote as to grain, and voted to raise a tax of "twenty dollars, cash, to procure glass, nails, etc., for a school-house," and voted further to raise by tax two hundred dollars for the new house, said tax to be paid in work or building materials, at the discretion of the trustees. Work was rated at six shillings, or seventy-five cents per day for a man, and four shillings, or half a dollar, for his team. Should a citizen delay unreasonably in doing as directed, the trustees were to collect cash. Should the above levy prove insufficient, the trustees were to impose enough more to complete the structure. Considerable confidence was indicated in the trustees, Messrs. Southwick, Salisbury and Alpheus Collins. The building was to be completed the first day of the next November.

The school book contains the indenture, or rather copy, between the trustees and Thaddeus Collins, whereby the latter sells or leases to the trustees and their successors, for the consideration of one dollar paid, and the annual rental of two peppercorns, if lawfully demanded, twelve rods of land bounded as follows: "Beginning at the N. W. corner of the log school-house, thence south four rods, thence east three rods, thence north to the Adams road, thence west to the place of beginning." It is stipulated that the land shall be used for school purposes only.

November 24, 1824, the house was not finished, for the fathers then voted to complete it, and let the job to Thaddeus Collins, Jr., for $16, to be raised from the district by tax, and the old building was sold at auction to Elias D. Sherman for six dollars and thirty-one cents. At the annual meeting, December 25, 1824, it was voted to paint the school-house red, with corner boards white, and a tax of six dollars for paint and oil was levied. In 1825 the freeholders voted to have "a man school four months the ensuing winter season and six months woman school in the summer season." Among other duties, the teacher had to measure the wood sent for each pupil. October 16, 1826, was the first meeting after the formation of the town of Rose, and the new school-house was not paid for, it being resolved that the trustees collect arrearages. Nov. 15, boundaries for the new No. 4 district were specified, covering all the territory now included in the Valley district, and considerably more on the east, south and west. A special meeting was held April 25, 1827, to vote the use of the school-house for religious meetings. Also, voted to procure a bolt-lock, and that John Bassett be "saxten" to keep the key, etc. In October of the same year it was voted that each proprietor pay fifty cents a cord for wood, if he fail to deliver his quota when called upon by the trustees. In 1829 came the first report to the commissioners of common schools by the trustees, and it is noteworthy that the clerk spells the important word thus, "Commishoners." October 3d, 1831, Eron N. Thomas first appeared as clerk, and the spelling and penmanship improved at once. At this time it was voted to raise five dollars for repairs to the school-house. The year also marks the advent of a stove, for October 24, at a special meeting, it was voted to raise by tax $25 for a stove. The chimney was sold to Abel Lyon for $4.50, the andirons to Samuel Batt for fifty-six cents. The report for the year 1831 sets forth that the school had been kept eight months, that the public money amounted to $43.44, and the amount raised above this was $20.56, making an aggregate easy to average for the months taught. Teachers certainly did not get rich in those days. There were eighty-five pupils at school, but the whole number in the district between the ages of five and sixteen years was seventy. Old boys and girls went to school then. In 1832 it was resolved, "That the writing falls be lowered and made not so steep." February 8, 1833, at a special meeting, twenty-one votes were cast for and four votes against a change of school-house site. August 6, 1833, it was voted to raise twelve dollars for repairs, and for building a certain necessary small building. As this is the first mention of the same, curiosity is naturally excited as to whether any had existed previously. The report for 1835 gives 110 children taught, and 109 of school age. Not much for a truant officer to do. In 1837 matters had progressed to the extent of supplying wood by one person, he securing the job by bidding. The bills were to be paid pro rata, according to children sent. Lucius Ellinwood secured the contract at "75 cts. per cord two ft. wood." The first mention of a library is in 1839, when five dollars was voted for it.

But the new school-house had become an old one.   To accommodate the builders of the hotel, now known as Pimm's or Whitney's, the building had been moved to the site of the old stone school-house.   Ira Mirick and his wife, Martha, executed a deed for the land in September, 1845.   The stone edifice was in process of erection, the contract therefor having been made in March preceding with William Dickinson and Henry Robinson "to build a good and substantial cobble stone school-house, to be 26 by 36 feet inside in the clear, to be divided into two rooms and an entra."   The rooms were to be ten feet high and the walls sixteen inches thick.   "The corner stones to be as good as those of Wm. Benjamin's House."   (The present home of Truman Desmond, in Town's district.)   The specifications throughout are very exact, and the structure was to be ready for occupancy the 15th of September following.   The cost, complete, was to be $400.   Like all of Henry Robinson's work, this was well done, and the stones laid by his diligent hands are yet in place.

This building also had its day, and bills for repair became so frequent that either a new house or very thorough overhauling became imperative. June 26, 1861, Brownell Wilbur, moderator, it was voted to adjourn to the Presbyterian meeting house, and also voted to adjourn to E. N. Thomas's school-house, which latter vote seemed to be the effective one, for on the 29th of June, the district thus met, and by a large majority voted to purchase the unused Presbyterian edifice, and in this old-time structure, Rose Valley young ideas were nurtured for several years.   Of course, this was only a tiding over till the people were ready to build a substantial edifice. The matter was so momentous that many meetings were called and many votes taken, till it was finally decided in 1867, March 28th, to build on the present location, on Thomas street.   The total outlay for site, materials and construction was to be $4,000.   Peter Harmon drew specifications and was the builder.   As it was voted October 8, 1867, to put the wood for the year in the basement of the new school-house, it may be inferred that the winter term for 1867–8 was begun in the new edifice.   To-day, the same, surrounded by trees, is a shrine of learning loved and esteemed, as a rule, all the more as the years increase, separating the pupils from it. The school has a good, local standing.   It may be of interest to state that the annual bill for wood grew to be more than $80, and in 1878 a coal stove was bought for one room, and the next year another stove of the same kind followed.   Among later teachers may be named Messrs. H. E. Thornhill, George H. Stewart, and Misses A. M. Colburn, Cora and Lottie Knapp.   The present principal is George D. Sprague, of Butler.   His assistant is Miss Ara Barnum, of Glenmark.

TEMPERANCE IN ROSE.

Doubtless this town has had as little drunkenness as any in the state. Of course, there have been those who lingered long over their cups and who found pleasure in strong cider, still they were the exception, and now more than a score of years have elapsed since there was a legal sale of an intoxicant in Rose. May such abstinence continue, even till the end of time.

The town was just three years old, lacking seven days, when a meeting was called to see what could be done in behalf of temperance. That first record book is still extant, commencing with the handwriting of James S. Showers and ending with that of George Seelye, secretaries. The date of beginning is February 18, 1829, and the last entry is October 18, 1836. Just what caused the society to cease, it would be difficult to tell at this late date, certainly not for lack of material to be reformed. At the first meeting of the inhabitants of the town called to consider the subject of temperance, Doctor Peter Valentine gave an address, James I. Woolsey was made chairman and Smithfield Beden was secretary. To us of to-day, the pledge taken is of the most consequence, though there was a long and somewhat flatulent preamble, apparently the result of the combined wisdom of all the town's teachers and preachers. The organization was named "The Rose Temperance Society for the Promotion of Temperance," and here is the pledge: "Article 3d. Any person may become a member of this society by subscribing the following pledge': We, the undersigned, do agree to abstain wholly from the use of ardent spirits, except for medical purposes; not to furnish them as a part of hospitable entertainment, nor to laborers in our employ, in no case to give or vend them either by small or large measure, so as to knowingly countenance the improper use of them, in particular in no case to violate the laws of the land regulating the sale of ardent spirits, and also to give our patronage to those merchants and keepers of public houses who by their example and influence bear a decided testimony against the sin of intemperance."

It was also stipulated that erring members should be labored with and held in line if possible; if not, they should be excluded. To the above pledge, above three hundred names are attached, representing the best people in Rose at that time. The late Stephen Collins was one of the last survivors. Possibly C. B. Collins, of Clyde, is the only one now living whose name was officially connected with the society, he having been one of the last board of managers. Now and then a name was dropped for failure to observe the constitution, and it seems not a little queer that a man should have been prominent in his church and still could not abide by the requirements of the society. One party, long an influential citizen west of the Valley, wrote asking to have his name removed from the list, saying, "My reasons are I do not like the conduct of some of the members as such and also that, in my opinion, it will lead to tyrannical government." 'Twas ever thus. In resisting the tyranny of a temperance society, many a man forged yet more strongly the links binding him to absolute degradation and woe.

The first president was Elizur Flint; Vice-President, Chauncey Bishop; Treasurer, Smithfield Beden; Secretary, James S. Showers; Managers, John Burns, Isaac Fulton, Stephen Collins, Peter Valentine, John Skidmore, Samuel Lyman. Deacon Flint continued to be president to the end, and he was ever ready with tongue and pen to promote true sobriety. At various times addresses were delivered by the Rev. Wm. Clark, by Deacon Flint, Smithfield Beden, Rev. Wm. McKoon and others. In a table of data, December 2, 1829, apparently for the year, we find that Rose used 700 gallons of distilled liquors; that there were twenty habitual drunkards, eight cases of poverty, two crimes, one death, presumably owing to drink, and also the pleasing statement that the use of drink had diminished one-fourth. Had the same ratio of decrease continued, our town had become, long ere this, the most abstemious in the country.

It is in place to recall other officers as follows: Chauncey Bishop continued to be vice-president till 1832, when he was succeeded by Jacob Miller, then Dorman Munsell, Joel N. Lee, and finally Chauncey Bishop again. The treasurers were Smithfield Beden, Peter Valentine, Alfred Lee and Gideon Henderson. Secretaries, James S. Showers, Smithfield Beden, Truman Van Tassel, C. B. Collins and George Seelye. In addition to the first board of managers, already given, were Alfred Lee, George Seelye, Elizur M. Ballard, Samuel Lyman, Caleb Mills, James S. Showers, Thaddeus Collins, Samuel Buckman, L. Leland, Anson Lee, Martin Warner, Jacob Miller, Samuel E. Ellinwood, Wm. Lovejoy, Chauncey Bishop, Wm. Griswold, Joel N. Lee, E. N. Thomas, C. B. Collins and Dorman Munsell. These more than fifty years old records have a wonderfully sincere appearance. The people who made them were in earnest. Their society became auxiliary to that of the county, the members met, listened, discussed and did what they thought their best to suppress a ruinous practice. They appointed parties to labor in their respective school districts for the good of the cause; still the evil lived on and, like the master of all evil, is rampant to-day. The meetings were held in the various school-houses of the town, and were regularly opened and closed with prayer.

Names are always significant and here are those of the people who signed the constitution of the society. Those who were expelled or wished to have their names erased are here with the others. In the dim light afforded by so many years, all are much the same. For the sake of convenience, they have been arranged alphabetically. Possibly, had women been admitted to management, the society had lasted longer, for it is the feminine contingent that keeps the temperance cause in the forefront to-day. The names of officers are not repeated in the list and the family name is given but once: Aldrich—Amos, Asahel; Allen—Aldula, Betsey, Mercy, Rebecca, Winthrop; Andrews—Clarissa, Lydia; Andrus—Elizabeth, James; Matilda Baker; Lany Baird; Maria Baldwin; Barber—John, Jr., Laura; Ann Barnum; Barrett—Simeon I., Tamar; Lydia Bassett; Batt—Amanda, Collins, Samuel G., Wm.; Beden—Amanda, B. G., Rebecca, Seth N., W. M.; Bishop—Candace, Charles, Charity, Chloe, D. W. C., Eliza H., Harriet, Jerusha, Joel, Jr., Reuben, Zemira; Blaine —Abia, Fanny, Mary E., Sarah J., William; Blodgett—Luke W., Mary; Cynthia Boyd; Boynton—Abigail, Benjamin, Hannah, Minerva; Rufus C. Brainard; Maria Briggs; Brown—James, Mercy, Nancy M.; Clarissa Buckman; Bundy—Eliza, Phoebe, Sally; Burns—Achsah, Ann, Clara, Elisha, Olive; Maria Busby; Chaddock—Caroline, William; Chapin— Ferzah M., Harriet; John Chidester; Harvey Closs; Colborn—James, Jonathan; Collins—Catharine, Clarissa, Esther, Harriet; Craft—Clarissa, Jacob, Lydia; Cyrus Crippen; Elizabeth Deady; Dean—Daniel, Prudence J.; Ellinwood — Charlotte, Chester, David, Ensign, Lucy L., Mary, Sophronia, Submit; Ellsworth—Jerusha, Jonathan; Fairbanks—Cornelius W., George, Jane; Fisher—Elizabeth, Rebecca; Roxy Flint; Foster— Abigail, David, David, Jr., Emma; Fulton—Hannah, Mahala, Margaret I., Martha, Robert, Peter; Gardner—Ansel M., Esther Ann, Polly; Gillett—Abram, Gardner, Hosea, Moses, Phoebe; Sherman Goodwin; Graham—Henry, Roxeany; Grant—Benjamin, Patty; Gray—Deborah, Eleanor B., Harvey; Griswold—Lewis, Rebecca; George Hamilton; Hand—Clarissa, Mary; Henderson—Charlotte, Deborah, Eveline, George W.; Julia Hillcox; Hinman—Enos, Mary; Hoag—Elisha, Losina; Holmes—Amanda, David; Elizabeth Horne; Howard—Esther, Happy, Hosea, Mary Ann, Wm. C.; Catharine Hultz; Aurilla Hush; Jonathan Hutchinson; Hyde—John, Mary Ann, Sally; Jeffers—Nathan, William; Knight—Eliza G., Enoch; Sylvanus Lackey; Lake—Adaline W., Betsey, Charles, Ira; Lamb—Asahel H., Hiram, Ira, Jane, Lorenzo, Lorilla L., Louisa L., Perez, Peter, Sally; Polly Lampson; Lee—Alfred C., Betsey, Laurissa, Mary N.; Perus Leland; Angeline Lonne; Lovejoy—Anna, Daniel, Esther, Harriet, Maria Jane, Norman, Perliette, Silas, Sophia;

Lumbert—Jabez, Rachel ; Lyman—Caroline, Clementina, Levi A., Sally Thomas J. ; Lyon—Frederick, Moses; B. F. McCumber ; Marietta McKoon ; McQueen—Clarissa Ann, Orena ; Mason—Harvey, Julia, Rhoda D. ; Miller—Amy, Caroline, Daniel, Eliza; Mills—Betsey, George W., Huldah; Miner—Harvey, Prentice J.; Mirick—George W., Mary, Thomas ; Mary Mitchell ; Moore—Orrin, Sally; Morris—Lewis, Lovina ; Sarah Morse; John Mosier ; Anna Mott; Munsell—Emeline, Gavin L., Jerusha ; John Ogram ; Osborn—Edwin, Martha, Warren ; Samuel Otto; Pease—Alanson, Charlotte, Merrill ; Preston—Joseph, Nabby, Tabitha; Lucy Proctor; Zena P. Rich ; Relief Richardson ; Riggs—Charlotte, Gowan ; Roe—Austin, Catharine, Daniel J., Sarah ; Seelye—Delos, Elizabeth, Louisa ; Benjamin Severance; Patty Seymour ; Shepherd—Aaron, Polly; Simmons—G. F., Lydia F.; Truman Skidmore ; Charles Skut ; Smith—Chauncey, Melissa; Sarah Squier ; Stewart—Ann Eliza, Lydia ; Swift—Anna, Selam; Thomas—Caroline, Wm. H. ; Town—Asa, Emily, Hannah ; Nancy Tucker ; Twomley—George, Martha, Mary Ann ; Valentine—Anne, Asahel I., James Van Auken; Van Horn—Matthias, Proxena ; Elizabeth Vandercook ; Van Tassel—Abraham, Jerusha ; Van Valkenburgh—Abram, Deborah ; Vary Van Vleck ; Minerva Van Zile ; Wade—George W., Jesse O., John, John W., Wm. D. ; Barbara Walker; Ward—Eli, Esther M., Mary, Mary Ann ; James C. Warn ; Warner—George L., John, Nancy, Sally B. ; Whitney—Caroline, Lucy L., Sarah, Solomon ; Luana Wilder; Wilson—Henrietta, Jonathan ; Eve Winchell; Wisner—Charles, Elizabeth, Jesse, Moses ; Solomon Wren ; Susannah Wyckoff.

SOCIETIES.

GOOD TEMPLARS.

There is to-day a lodge of Good Templars in Rose Valley, and its members are zealous for good. Organized in June, 1888, the first chief templar was Jared Chaddock, and to him have succeeded Thirza Milem, Rose Stubley, Truman Desmond, Florence Niles, George Harper, George Chatterson and Almon Harper. From the beginning, there have been in all 175 members of the order. The good that has been done can never be told. Many young people have here received a stimulus to active opposition to the drink curse.

NORTH ROSE.

The lodge, in this village, No, 696, I. O. G. T., was organized April 17, 1887, by Dr. Diamond, special deputy. Mrs. Sarah Seelye was the first chief templar, and Ara Barnum was deputy. Since then the following have filled the office of C. T., viz., 1. R. Seelye, Cora Skut, C. W. Oaks, E. E. Brewster, Wm. Thompson, Charles Barrick, E. J. Weeks, T. J. Chaddock and Bert Oaks. The maximum membership was reached in 1890, when the lodge numbered 109 persons. In 1890 it built, at a cost of $700, the hall on Caroline street, an ornament to the village.

ROSE BRASS BAND.

Our town was ever musical. Church music of excellent quality has been a distinguishing characteristic of all the denominations. It is no wonder, then, that a band should have been formed early. In 1857, August 14, an organization was effected with Daniel B. Harmon as leader, E. C. Ellinwood, clerk, Joel Sheffield, secretary and treasurer. In the following September, the 15th, Mr. Sheffield resigned, and C. A. Lee was chosen to fill the vacancy, and he continued in it till his enlistment in 1862. Z. P. Deuchler, of Lyons, was the first instructor, and after one year became a member. After him, for a year, E. B. Wells, then of Lyons, taught. From 1857 to August 20, 1862, when the band enlisted, the membership was as follows : * Daniel B. Harmon, Carroll H. Upson, Eugene Hickok, E. C. Ellinwood, * Alfred B. Harmon, * Charles A. Lee, * Ira Soule,

25

Walter A. Wilson, * W. F. Hickok, Andrew Healy, *Ira T. Soule, Z. P. Deuchler, E. B. Wells, * R. C. Barless, John Fosmire, Joel Sheffield and * William Harmon. The starred names indicate enlistments.   At this time Jacob Sager of Clyde enlisted and joined, and our boys became the nucleus of the famous Ninth Heavy Artillery Band, and how they could play " Belle Brandon ! "   'Tis said that " Jake " once started Old Hundred as a marching tune at a funeral and switched off into " The Dead March in Saul," only when the surgeon, unable to make his horse keep step, shouted back : " What kind of a tune do you call that ? "   Then he was overheard saying : " I thought I could march to anything, but I'll be d—d if I can catch on to the Doxology."   The War over, the " boys " came home, having escaped all the perils of the deadly fray.

In 1870 five members of the old band formed with others a new organization, which continued till 1884, and then disbanded after the Presidential contest. So many members went away from Rose, it was found impossible to continue.   In 1870 Captain Daniel B. Harmon was leader, and he was succeeded in 1874 by Andrew J. Dougan. The members from 1870 to 1884 were A. B. Harmon, Ira T. Soule, Stephen Soule, Duane Armstrong, Ira Soule, James Race, Eugene Hickok, William Felton Hickok, Valorous Ellinwood, Levern Wilson, A. J. Dougan, Edson M. Ellinwood, Fletcher Bush, Lycurgus Hart, Charles Benjamin, Seymour Benjamin, Henry Turner, Judson Sheffield, Mortimer Leach, G. A. Sherman, I. L. Wright, E. B. Wilson, George Fry, Constance Kunkel, George McWharf, W. D. Hickok, Charles Redding, Frank Proseus, Charles G. Oaks, Frank Mitchell and Emil Kunkel. Of this list Race and Dougan were in the army, and in the former list, Fosmire and Deuchler also were soldiers. The memory of the Rose Band is a pleasant one. From first to last, it had forty-one different members. Thirty-six are now living. Of the original nine members of the first organization, all are living save Walter A. Wilson.

MASONIC.

Freemasonry in Rose dates from 1865. Previous to this time members of the order had gone to adjacent towns for lodge meetings. The warrant of Rose Lodge, No. 590, is dated June 22, 1866, issued to certain parties who had worked under dispensation for one year. The charter members were James M. Horne, M. T. Collier, Lucius H. Dudley, John J. Dickson, George Catchpole, Seymour Covell, Eugene Hickok, Seymour Woodard, James Covell, Samuel Gardner and P. Jerome Thomas. The first meetings were held in the brick building on Thomas street, now a shop. Subsequently excellent quarters were arranged for the lodge over E. N. Thomas' store, and the same are still retained. They are commodious and comfortable,

and many scores of Rose dwellers have here taken the first three degrees.
The first W. M. was James M. Horne, and few men have ever filled that
position with more grace and dignity. He continued to adorn the office
till 1870, when James W. Colborn was inducted, and was W. M. for two
years. Henry Klinck, of ever pleasant memory, followed for the year
1872. Then came Mark T. Collier for four consecutive years, and again in
1879. George Catchpole presided in 1877–8; Edson M. Ellinwood in 1880;
Valorous Ellinwood, in 1881–2, and again in 1891–2; Alfred Lefavor held
the first office in 1883-4-5-6, and Enos T. Pimm was W. M. from 1887 to
1890, and again in 1893 his name heads the list. For many years Eugene
Hickok has been the careful and efficient secretary.

ODD FELLOWSHIP.

North Rose possesses an organization of I. O. O. F., known as Bay Shore
Lodge. The present N. G. is Elmer Mitchell. It is said to be in a very
flourishing condition.

GRAND ARMY OF THE REPUBLIC.

Very soon after the close of the late War, there was organized in Rose a
Post of this beneficent order, but it suspended a long time ago. In 1883,
September 28th, a new Post was started, having eighteen charter members,
and was named the John E. Sherman Post, No. 401, after a Rose member
of the 111th, slain in the Wilderness. The first commander was E. H.
Cook, M. D., a member of the 75th. Then in 1884–5–6, E. T. Pimm
followed, a member of the 9th Heavy. H. P. Howard of the 9th, also,
followed in 1887. Jared Chaddock of the 67th commanded in 1888.
Harvey D. Barnes, a 44th veteran, was at the head in 1889–'90. In
1891 and 1892, E. T. Pimm again led, and W. F. Hickok was installed
commander for 1893. For many years the Post meetings were held in
Pimm's Hotel, but in 1892 the Post was given quarters in the Memorial
hall.

SONS OF VETERANS.

A Camp of Sons of Veterans, known as the Nelson Neeley Camp, was
instituted March 15, 1893, with C. J. Barless as captain. Meetings are
held in G. A. R. hall.

This farmers' organization, No. 148, was organized in March, 1874, with Henry C. Klinck, master, and Linus P. Osgood, secretary. It flourished for three years, surrendering its charter April 1, 1877. Oscar Weed was the second master, and Henry Klinck, second secretary. The other masters in order were : W. F. Hickok and Eugene Hickok ; the secretaries, Eugene Hickok and Frank H. Valentine. The total membership was thirty-eight. Many of these people now belong to the Clyde Grange. In a community so agricultural in its characteristics, it would seem that a grange ought to have a permanent home.

ROSE NEWSPAPER.

The Rose *Times* was started September 15, 1886, by Burt E. Valentine, this being the first venture of the kind in town. It was a modest sheet, two columns, four pages, semi-monthly. December 15, 1886, the young editor enlarged his paper to four columns and eight pages, having his office over his father's store. His paper flourished, and a larger press was bought, and March 1, 1887, he moved into the old post office building of " 'Squire " Ellinwood. The paper then had seven columns and four pages, weekly, the subscription being one dollar per year. A little before this C. J. Barless had started the *Farmer's Counsel*, and January 1, 1888, a union of the two papers was effected under the name of the *Farmer's Counsel and Times*. March 1, 1889, Mr. Valentine went out, and with G. A. Sherman, set up a job office. The paper continued in the hands of Mr. Barless, who still publishes it. The press upon which this paper is printed is specially noteworthy, since it is the very one on which John H. Gilbert worked off the first edition of the Book of Mormon. The identity of the press is established beyond a question. Let us hope that it is now doing better service than when sending out the delusions of Joe Smith.

CENSUS GLEANINGS.

These data are given to show, to some extent, the growth and development of Rose. Unfortunately, after 1840, the national census was not collated by towns, but by counties, thus rendering it impossible to secure the desired facts, and in 1830, the government sought only population items. Again the omission to take the state census in 1885 left a large defect in our data; that of 1892 was only an enumeration of people. However, some interesting items are brought out in the figures presented. The croaker about old times finds that crops have not particularly changed in quantity. My own regrets are entirely over what is not shown, rather than on account of what is. The development of berry culture does not appear. The evaporating of apples and other fruits has no place, and the growing of onions, one of the town's chief industries, has no mention whatever. Tobacco, also, would come in as a great factor. The state census of 1895 will be a valuable supplement to these facts. In 1864, the town paid out $244.31 for manures and fertilizers; in 1874, the amount paid for the same object was $2,367, and I am told by competent informants that in 1892, the amount must have been more than double the latter sum. Some of the gleanings of the early census takings, while not appearing in the tabulations, are very interesting. Thus, in 1835, the first state enumerating after the town was organized, I find that Rose had one grist-mill, and that it ground grain to the value of $11,250. In 1845, there was still but one mill and its work was only a trifle greater. In '35, there were seven saw-mills, cutting up logs worth $2,172, to make lumber worth $4,450. In '45, there were eleven mills, sawing $2,400 worth of logs into $4,900 value in product. One fulling mill, in '35, turned $2,625 worth of wool into $5,250 worth of manufactured goods. In '45, the same mill's work was $2,000 raw into $4,000 manufactured. One carding machine, in 1835, rolled $3,000 worth of wool into $3,750 worth of spinning material. In '45, the record was $3,000 and $3,500 respectively. One iron working plant, in '35, transformed $2,000 in ore into $5,000 in product. In the same year an ashery worked over $350 worth of wood ashes. One distillery is said to have changed $2,700 in solids into $4,300 in liquids. A tannery, in 1835, worked over $600 worth of hides into $1,200 worth of leather. In '45, the record was the same. In 1835, there was not in Rose, a deaf and dumb, blind, idiotic nor lunatic person. In 1845, there were one deaf and dumb, two idiotic and two lunatic. In 1845, Rose had two inns, two stores, 330 farmers, 63 mechanics, five clergymen, whose total salaries were $1,150, and three doctors. In 1838, Rose had 166 militiamen, her schools numbered 11, and there were 629 pupils, for whom the town drew $173.53 public money. In 1893, the amount drawn from the same source is $1,946.50. In 1830, the town had 29 people of foreign birth and 573 children between 5 and 16 years of age. In 1845, there were 56 foreigners and 615 children, as before. In 1855, Rose had 329 owners of land and 435 in 1865. The record of illiteracy has always been excellent. In 1840, there were 101 persons above 21 years of age who could not read nor write. In 1855, this number was reduced to 34, and 1865 showed but 28. In 1840, the value of orchard products was $1,504. In that year dairy products yielded $6,054. In 1875, there were sold 214,195 lbs. of pork, while in 1865, 7,550 lbs. of tobacco are reported raised. Turnips appear only once and then in 1845, when 11¼ acres produced 2016 bushels. In 1840, there were reported made 180 lbs. of wax, presumably beeswax, and in the same year the people sold 2,122 cords of wood.

The population record of the town is as follows :

1830—1,641	1850—2,264	1875—2,215
1835—1,715	1855—2,115	1880—2.244
1840—2,031	1860—2,119	1890—2,107
1845—2,060	1865—2,209	1892—2,002
	1870—2,056	

The maximum, it is observed, was reached in 1850, or just 53 years ago. There are more families in Rose, to-day, than then, but they are not so large. The children do not appear. While the number of people is not so large as in some towns of less area, it must be borne in mind that with crowded masses there is also corresponding misery.

In the following scheme, I have not attempted to glean valuations from the assessors' returns, for these, subject to the changes of the Board of Supervisors, fluctuate too much.

CENSUS TABLES.

	1835	1840	1845	1855	1865	1870	1875
Voters.	324			469	438	566		
Families.					419	473		536
Improved land, acres.	6913			10477	13272¾	13199½	14444	17042
Unimproved land, acres.					8577			4938
Cash value of farms.					$831771	$1051268	$1497800	$1496065
Cash value of stock.					$125870	$154295	$191245	$164852
Cash value of tools and implem'ts.					$18091	$26663	In farm	$53141
Apples, bushels.					28535	39284		76117
Cider, barrels.					399	739		1118
Barley, { acres.				54½	311	429¼		386
Barley, { bushels.			383	222	6013	3558		7368
Butter, pounds.				71697	66330	98242		83061
Cheese, pounds.				16257	7075	12046		1285
Milk, gallons sold.								46236
Corn, { acres.				1065½	15046½	1805		1601
Corn, { bushels.			20866	22700	40035	41767		50498
Flax, { acres.				131½		4½		
Flax, { pounds.			2500	2869				
Hay, { acres.					1908½	2437		
Hay, { tons.			1863		1724½	2308	2901	3909
Hops, { acres.						5		5
Hops, { pounds.						3400		3109
Honey, pounds.					4722	1964		4804
Maple sugar, pounds.			5904		446	442		6
Oats, { acres.				821	1760½	1888½		1765
Oats, { bushels.			17588	25477	44266	25708		58012
Potatoes, { acres.				255½	1844	204½		284
Potatoes, { bushels.			27078	28455	13246	20355		29574
Rye, { acres.				84½	72	44½		34
Rye, { bushels.			391	687	885	140		466
Stock, { cattle.	1545	1878	1905	2057	1816		1539
Stock, { horses.	473	519	556	754	750		894
Poultry, value sold.		$830			$1050	$2265.25		$3136
Eggs, value sold.					$2503	$3789.97		$4111
Sheep.	2405	4385	4702	3727	4583		1644
Swine.	1733	1950	1381	1241	1395		1709
Wheat, { spring, { acres.					10	1		
Wheat, { spring, { bushels.					138	45		
Wheat, { winter, { acres.				2272½	907½	1524½		1759
Wheat, { winter, { bushels.				20376	23700	8893	19101	30981
Wool, pounds.				6656	10736	11856	18794	8679
Buckwheat, { acres.				219	311½	151		289
Buckwheat, { bushels.			1957	3677	3270	2531½		4168
Beans, { acres.				16				21
Beans, { bushels.				117				296
Peas, { acres.				125				12
Peas, { bushels.				1174				170
Value of all productions.							$2245.10	
Home made fulled cloth, yards.	2433			2453	134	12		
Home made flannel, yards.	2407			2994	559	175		
Home made linen, yards.	2611			3757	57	225½		
Home made cotton and mixed goods, yards.					95			

OFFICERS OF THE TOWN OF ROSE.

" An act for erecting the southwest part of the Town of Wolcott into a separate town by the name of Rose in the County of Wayne. Passed February 25, 1826.

" Be it enacted by the people of the State of New York, represented in Senate and Assembly, That from and after the first Monday of April next, all that part of the now town of Wolcott, in the County of Wayne, comprehended within the following boundaries (viz.) beginning at the southwest corner of said town and running from thence east, on the south line thereof, seven miles; thence north five miles, thence west seven miles, or until it strikes the division line between said town and the town of Sodus; thence south, and along the east line of the town of Sodus, to the place of beginning, shall be, and the same is, hereby erected into a separate town by the name of ROSE, and that the first town meeting, to be holden therein, shall be held on the first Tuesday of April next, at the house of Charles Thomas, in said town."

The above is a true copy of records.

Attest,   D. SMITH, Town Clerk for 1826.

MEMBERS OF ASSEMBLY.

John J. Dickson, 1845 ; Willis G. Wade, 1854 ; Eron N. Thomas, 1862 ; Jackson Valentine, 1877-8.

WAYNE COUNTY OFFICERS.

Sheriff, William J. Glen, 1879, '80, 81.

School Commissioner, 1st district, Wayne county, Thomas Robinson, 1863, '64, '65.

Superintendent of Poor, Philander Mitchell, 1860, '61, '62: Charles Covell, 1883 to 1889.

OFFICERS IN OLD TOWN OF WOLCOTT.

Assessor and Collector, John N. Murray, 1810-11 ; John Wade, 1813.

Commissioner of Highways, Joseph Wade, 1812-13 ; John Wade, Eli Andrus, 1814.

SURVIVING SUPERVISORS.

E. C. LITTLEWOOD,   W. H. GRISWOLD,   C. S. WRIGHT,

M. G. McKOON,   W. J. OTT,   J. S. SHEFFIELD,

W. GAGE,   J. M. HORNE,

GEO. CARROLL,   J. VALENTINE,

SUPERVISORS.

(Years Inclusive.)

Peter Valentine, 1826, '27, '28, '29, '36, '37, '38 '39, '42; Philander Mitchell, 1830, '31, '32, '44, '45, '48, '49, '50, '56; Dorman Munsell, 1833, '40, '41; Thaddens Collins, 1834; Ira Mirick, 1835; Eron N. Thomas, 1843, '51, '53; Elizur Flint, 1846; Hiram Mirick, 1847; Solomon Allen, 1852; Thaddeus Collins, 1854; Jackson Valentine, 1855, '59, '60, '61, '62, '63, '64, '65, '66, '67, '68, '69, '74, '75; Harvey Closs, 1857, '58; James M. Horne, 1870, '71; Charles S. Wright, 1872, '73; Joel S. Sheffield, 1876; William J. Glen, 1877 and part of '79; S. Wesley Gage, 1878; George Catchpole, part of 1879, '82, '83, '84, '87, '88, '89, '90; William H. Griswold, 1880, '81; Samuel Gardner, part of 1885:-- Chester Ellinwood, part of 1885, '86; Merritt G. McKoon, 1891, '92, '93.

TOWN CLERKS.

David Smith, 1826, '27, '28; Philander Mitchell, 1829; George Seelye, 1830, '31; Eron N. Thomas, 1832, '33, '35, '36, '37, '39, '40, '41; Chauncey B. Collins, 1834, '38; Elijah F. Thomas, 1842, '43; Samuel Jones, 1844, '45, '46; Henry G. Lyman, 1847, '49; Richard S. Valentine, 1848; William Hickok, 1850, '51; Jackson Valentine, 1852, '53, '54; Willard Sherman, 1855, '56, '57, '58, '59, '60; J. B. Alexander, 1861, '62; B. Frank Sherman, 1863, '64; James M. Horne, 1865; W. H. H. Valentine. 1866, '67, '68; Romaine C. Barless, 1869; Ira T. Soule, 1870; Valorous Ellinwood, 1871, '75, '76, '86, '87, '88, '89, '90; Lucien Osgood, 1872; Frank H. Closs, 1873, '74; Stephen W. Soule, 1877, '78, '79, '80, '81, '82, '83; Edgar F. Houghton, 1884; Judson J. Sheffield, 1885; Ezra A. Sherman, 1891; Ephraim B. Wilson, Jr., 1892, '93.

COLLECTORS.

Thaddeus Collins, Jr., 1826, '27, '28; Harley Way, 1829; Orrin Lackey, 1830, '31; John S. Cornwall, 1832; Asahel Gillett, 1833, '35; David Closs, 1834; Jesse Lyman, 1836, '38, '42; Nathan W. Thomas, 1837; Nelson Griswold, 1839, '43; James Clapper, 1840; Not found, 1841; Abraham Fergnson, 1844; James W. Jeffers, 1845, '46; Cyrus Root, 1847; James W. Page, 1848; Charles S. Wright, 1849; William Vanderoef, 1850; Judd B. Lackey, 1851; William H. Thomas, 1852, '58, '59; Palmer R. Tindall, 1853; B. Frank Sherman, 1854, '55, '56, '57; Lampson Allen, 1860; John H. Barnes, 1861; James Winchell, 1862; Jerome Thomas, 1863, '65, '66; Philander Mitchell, Jr., 1864; William J. Glen, 1867, '68, '69, '70, '71, '72; George Jeffers, 1873, '74, '78, 79; Henry P. Howard, 1875; Joseph S. Wade, 1876; Valorous Ellinwood, 1877; Frederick Ream, 1880; A. J. Dongan, 1881; Levern Wilson, 1882, '83; Ensign D. Wade, 1884; Jared Chaddock, 1885; John Hill, 1886, '87, '88; Merritt G. McKoon, 1889, '90; Edward Welsh, 1891, '92; Orrin Carpenter, 1893.

ASSESSORS.

James Colborn, 1826, '27, '28; Jeremiah Leland, 1826; Dorman Munsell, 1826, '27, '28, '35; Milburn Salisbury, 1827, '28; Thaddeus Collins, 1829, '30, '31, '32; Nathan Jeffers, 1829, '30, '31, '32, '36; Jacob Miller, 1829, '30, '33; Moses F. Collins, 1831; Elizur Flint, 1832, '39, '50; Ira Mirick, 1833; Thomas Colborn, 1833, '35, '37, '38, '40; Philander Mitchell, 1834, '39, '41, '42, '43, '46; Gideon Henderson, 1834; Joel N. Lee, 1834; George F. Simmons, 1835, '36; William Briggs, 1836; Dudley Wade, 1837; Chester Ellinwood, 1837, '38, '40, '41, '42, '44; Henry Graham, 1838, '40; George Seelye, 1839, '46; Valorous Ellinwood, 1841, '43, '45, '48; Hiram Mirick, 1842, '43, '46, '51; Nelson Griswold, 1844, '45; Tunis Woodruff, 1844; Ovid Allen, 1845; George W. Mirick, 1847; Embury Finch, 1849; Seymour Covell, 1852, '59, '62, '65, '80, '83; Harvey Closs, 1853, '55, '56, '64, '73, '76; Charles B. Sherman, 1854; Ephraim B. Wilson, 1855, '58; Artemas Osgood, 1856, '57; Jonathan Briggs, 1857, '61, '67, '70; Gavin L. Munsell, 1860, '63; Lampson Allen, 1866; H. W. Levanway, 1868; William F. Hickok, 1869, '72; John M. Vandercook, 1871, '74, '77; Oliver Bush, 1875, '78; Orrin Skut, 1879; Eustace Henderson, 1881; Lucien H. Osgood, 1882; Clayton J. Allen, 1884, '87; William H. Cole, 1885, '88, '91; Asher W. Seager, 1886, '89; Chester T. Sherman, 1890; Joel H. Putnam, 1892; Frank E. Henderson, 1893.

COMMISSIONERS OF HIGHWAYS.

Elizur Flint, 1826, '27; Robert Jeffers, 1826, '27; William Lovejoy, 1826; Benjamin Haviland, 1827; Jacob Miller, 1828; John Tuck, 1828; Charles Thomas, 1828, '30; John Closs, Jr., 1829; Jacob Clapper, 1829, '39, 44; Asa Town, 1829; Dorman Munsell, 1830; Samuel Smith, 1830; Gideon Henderson, 1831; Joel N. Lee, 1831, '39; Michael C. Vandercook, 1831, '32; Uriah Wade, 1832; John Bassett, 1832; Abia F. Baird, 1833; Andrew Longstreet, 1833; Abner Wood, 1833, '35; Charles B. Sherman, 1834, '39, '41, '42; Nicholas Stansell, 1834; Harley Way, 1834; Tunis Woodruff, 1835, '36, '37, '38, '40, '41, '48, '51; William Briggs, 1835; Isaac Mills, 1836, '37; James Covell, 1836, '37, '38, '40, '41; John Q. Deady, 1838, '40, '44; Nathaniel Center, 1840; Harvey Closs, 1842; William Sebring, 1842, '43, '50; Ephraim B. Wilson, 1843; George D. Stewart, 1843; James Colborn, 1844; George Seelye, 1845, '49, '58; William A. Stewart, 1845, '47; John Jeffers, 1845, '54; George W. Mirick, 1846; William Dodds, 1846; Orrin Skut, 1846, '56; Dudley Wade, 1852, '55; William S. Woodard, 1857, '60, '63; James E. Ferguson, 1853; James O. Hunn, 1854, '58; Eustace Henderson, 1861, '64; Henry P. Howard, 1862; George Catchpole, 1863, '66, '69; Charles Covell, 1865; Samuel Osborn, 1867; Joel S. Sheffield, 1868; John B. Roe, 1870; James

C. Osborn, 1871, '74 ; Henry C. Klinck, 1872 ; Sidney P. Hopping, 1873, '76, '79 ; Thomas Bradburn, 1875, '78 ; Asher W. Seager, 1877, '80, '83 ; Linus P. Osgood, 1881, '84 ; Valorous Ellinwood, 1882 ; Fred'k Ream, 1885, '88, '91 ; Samuel P. Thompson, 1886, '89 ; Ensign D. Wade, 1887, '90 ; Jay R. Dickinson, 1892: Andrew Andrus, 1893.

OVERSEERS OF THE POOR.

John Skidmore, 1826, '27, '28 ; Aaron Shepard, 1826, '27, '28 ; Alpheus Collins, 1829, '30 ; Jacob Miller, 1829 ; Alfred Lee, 1830, '31, '32 ; Chauncey Bishop, 1831, '32, '34 : David Foster, 1833 ; Harvey Gray, 1833 ; Simeon I. Barrett, 1834 ; James Colborn, 1835 ; Henry Graham, 1835, '37 ; Asahel Gillett, 1836 ; Stephen Ferguson, 1836 ; Nathan Jeffers, 1837 ; William Griswold, 1838, '41, '42, '43 : Abner Wood, 1838 : (1839 wanting) ; Austin Roe, 1840, '44, '45, '47 ; Jesse Lyman, 1840, '47, '51, '52, '53 ; Abraham Ferguson, 1841 ; Seth H. Brainard, 1842 ; John P. Chatterson, 1843 : Alanson Worden, 1844, '45 ; Benjamin Seelye, 1845, '46 ; Tunis Wooodruff, 1846 : William A. Pixley, 1848, '49 ; George Seelye, 1848, '55, '56 ; Elizur Flint, 1849, '55, '56 ; Charles B. Sherman, 1850 ; Thaddeus Collins, 1850, '57 ; Arnold K. Rhea, 1851 : Amos Aldrich, 1852 ; George W. Mirick, 1853 ; Amaziah T. Carrier, 1854 ; George W. Ellinwood, 1854 ; John Barnes, 1857: Samuel B. Hoffman, 1858 ; Charles Woodward, 1858 ; Solomon Allen, 1859 : Charles B. Sherman, 1859, '60, '61, '66, '67, '68, '69 ; Dudley Wade, 1860, '61, '62, '64, '65, '67, '71 ; George Catchpole, 1862 ; N. Kendrick Sheffield, 1863 : William Osborn, 1863, '64 ; Henry Levanway, 1865, '66 ; Philander Mitchell, Jr., 1868, '69, '70, '71, '72, '73, '74 ; William Vanderoef, 1870, '78 ; Alonzo Snow, 1872, '81, '82 ; William H. Thomas, 1873, '74, '75, '76, '77, '83, '84, '86, '87 : Frederick Ream, 1875, '76, '77 : William Chaddock, 1878 ; Joseph S. Wade, 1879 ; Alvin Barnes, 1879 : John H. Winchell, 1880, '81 : Henry Garlick, 1880 : Harvey Closs, 1882 ; Charles Jeffers, 1883, '84, '88, '89, '90 ; Abram Covell, 1885 ; Birney Briggs, 1885 ; August Hetta, 1886 ; Jay R. Dickinson, 1887, '88, '89, '90 ; Judson Chaddock, 1891 ; Darius Lovejoy, 1891, '92, '93 ; James E. Vanderoef, 1892, '93.

JUSTICES OF THE PEACE.

Previous to 1830 appear the names of Erastus Fuller, Elizur Flint, Philander Mitchell, Charles Richards, Dorman Munsell and Peter Valentine. Alpheus Collins, 1830 ; Thaddeus Collins, 1831, '37 ; Elizur Flint, 1831, '34 ; Philander Mitchell, 1832, '36, '43, '47, '59, '63 : John Barber, Jr., 1833 ; John J. Dickson, 1835, '38, '41, '48, '52 ; Dorman Munsell, 1835 ; Wm. Briggs, 1836, '40 ; Chauncey B. Collins, 1838, '42, '53 ; (1839 wanting) ;

Orrin Skut, 1844; Harvey Closs, 1844; Hiram Salisbury, 1845: George W. Ellinwood, 1845, '56, '64, '69, '73, '77 ; Henry E. Youngs, 1846, '50 ; Truman Spencer, 1851, '55; James Shipman, 1852; Peter Shear, 1854, '58, '62; Nelson Griswold, 1856; Palmer R. Tindall, 1857, '61; R. Darwin Dickinson, 1865, '71 ; Joel H. Putnam, 1866, '70, '74; James B. Aldrich, 1867, '71; S. Wesley Gage, 1868: Wm. M. Osborn, 1872; George Aldrich, 1872; Romain H. Cole, 1875; Romain C. Barless, 1876, '80, '93; Samuel W. Lake, 1877, '78, '90; Robert C. Taylor, 1877 ; Irwin Seelye, 1879; Charles G. Oaks, Jr., 1879, '83 ; Joseph S. Wade, 1881, '85, '89 ; E. Platt Soper, 1882, '87 ; James W. Colborn, 1884 ; Eugene Davis, 1885 ; Lucien H. Osgood, 1888 ; Alexander Skut, 1891: Frank E. Soper, 1892 : Thomas B. Welch, 1893.

CONSTABLES.

Thaddeus Collins, Jr., 1826, '27, '28 ; Lewis Leland, 1826; Harley Way, 1827, '28, '29 ; Samuel Johnson. Jr., 1827, '30, '33 ; Charles Lake, 1828, '29; Warren Osborn, 1829 ; Orrin Lackey, 1830 ; Asahel Gillett, 1830, '33, '35 ; John D. Winchell, 1831, '32; Cornelius W. Fairbanks, 1831, '32: John S. Cornwall, 1832 ; Dudley Wade, 1833 : David Closs, 1834 ; Joel Bishop, 1834, '36; John Springer, 1834 ; Henry H. Ferris, 1835 ; Jesse Lyman, 1835, '36, '37, '38, '41, '42, '43 : Lewis H. Lownsbury, 1836, '37 : Nathan W. Thomas. 1837, '38 : George F. Caguin, 1838; (1839 wanting) : James Clapper, 1840 ; David West, 1840, '46 : Palmer R. Tindall, 1840, '41, '44, '53 ; William Vanderoef, 1840, '50 ; Harrison D. Reynolds, 1840; Nelson Griswold, 1841, '43; Abraham Ferguson, 1842, '44, '45 ; William Ellsworth, 1842, '54, '57 ; Daniel C. Alexander, 1843, '44, '45, '60 ; James W. Jeffers, 1845, '46, '48; Amaziah T. Carrier, 1846 ; James W. Page, 1847, '48 ; Cyrus Root, 1847 : John M. Town, 1848, '49; Orrin J. Wiley, 1849; Martin Rhinehart, Jr., 1849 ; James Shipman, 1850 ; Truman Spencer, 1850 ; Columbus Collins, 1850 ; Judd B. Lackey, 1851 ; Seymour Covell, 1851; William H. Thomas, 1851, '58, '59 ; Henry Garlick, 1852 ; George Woodruff, 1852 : Albert H. Wright, 1852, '53 ; Eli Garlick, 1853 ; John H. Blynn, 1853 : B. Franklin Sherman, 1854. '55, '56, '57 : John F. Jenks, 1854, '55 : James R. Winchell, 1854, '55, '60, '61, '62, '63, '64 ; Daniel B. Harmon, 1854 ; Henry P. Howard, 1856, '72, '73, '74, '75, '76 : Darwin Dickinson, 1856 : Joseph A. Waring, 1857 ; John H. Barnes, 1858, '59, '60, '61, '71, '72, '76, '77, '78 ; Andrew Bradburn, 1858, '62, '68 ; Lampson Allen, 1859, '60 ; George W. Sherman, 1859, '70, '78 ; Isaac Race, 1861, '64 ; William A. Snyder, 1860 ; Lyman Wykoff, 1862 ; Stephen Weeks, 1862 ; P. Jerome Thomas, 1863 ; Philander Mitchell, Jr., 1863, '64 : Robert Jeffers, 1863; James H. Barnes, 1864, '70, '79 ; William J. Glen, 1865, '67, '68, '69, '70, '71, '72, '73 ;

Edward Horn, 1865, '66, '67, '68; Frederick Ream, 1865, '66, '80; Alonzo Streeter, 1865, '66; Henry Goss, 1865; John Mabb, 1866, '67; George W. Streeter, 1866; E. Platt Soper, 1867; Jay Dickinson, 1867; Rollin C. Barless, 1868, '69; George Jeffers, 1868, '70, '71, '72, '73, '74, '75, '76, '77, '78, '79, '80, '81; Samuel W. Lape, 1869; Albert Sober, 1870; Jared Chaddock, 1871, '85; James H. Brisbin, 1872; H. Kenyon, 1873; George Langley, 1873; Joseph S. Wade, 1874, '75, '76; Eliphalet Crisler, 1874; William H. Griswold, 1874; Luman Briggs, 1875, '76; Philander Griswold, 1875; Valorous Ellinwood, 1877; Cassius M. Shaver, 1877, '82, '83, '84, '87, '89; Valentine Kaiser, 1877, '78, '79, '80, '81; Jacob L. Lyman, 1878, '79, '80, '88, '90, '91, '92, '93; Albion M. Gray, 1879; S. W. Dunham, 1880; A. J. Dougan, 1881; Leland Johnson, 1881, '91; Eugene Davis, 1881, '82; Levern Wilson, 1882, '83; John F. Decker, 1882; C. S. Dennis, 1882; Charles E. Sutherland, 1883; Myron J. Lamb, 1883, '84, '85, '86, '87, '88, '89, '90; Harmon Miner, 1883, '84, '91; Ensign D. Wade, 1884; Charles La Rock, 1884; Joseph Talton, 1885, '87; William Miller, 1885; Frank E. Soper, 1885; John T. Hill, 1886, '87, '88; J. H. Winchell, 1886; Orrin B. Carpenter, 1886; Charles Miner, 1886, '89, '90; William A. Holbrook, 1887, '88; Samuel Davenport, 1888, '89, '90, '93; William H. Weed, 1889, '90; Edward Welch, 1891; George E. Seager, 1891, '92; James E. Miner, 1892; Dell E. Van Antwerp, 1892, '93; Charles Seager, 1892; Edward A. Weeks, 1893; William B. Hill, 1893.

INSPECTORS OF ELECTION.

Thomas W. Warn, 1844, '45; Ezra Dann, 1844, '45; Nelson Griswold, 1844, '45, '46, '49, '51; Joel N. Lee, 1845; Matthias Van Horn, 1845; Eron N. Thomas, 1846; Samuel Lyman, 1846; Harvey Closs, 1847, '48, '52; David Holmes, 1847; Philetus Chamberlain, 1847; Elizur Flint, 1848; Benjamin Hendricks, 1848; William A. Sebring, 1849, '55; Ephraim B. Wilson, 1849; Daniel C. Alexander, 1850, '51, '52, '53, '54; Robert K. Andrews, 1850; Chauncey B. Collins, 1850; James Shipman, 1851; Jonathan Briggs, 1854, '55, '56; John Brown, 1856; Lorenzo N. Snow, 1856; William H. Thomas, 1857, '66; Henry C. Klinck, 1857, '59, '60, '65, '69, '71; Peter Harmon, 1857, '58; Jackson Valentine, 1858; Whiteman Brown, 1858; R. Darwin Dickinson, 1859, '60; S. Wesley Gage, 1863, '65, '66; Avery Gillett, 1864; Joel S. Sheffield, 1864; John M. Town, 1866; Henry C. Rice, 1867; Romain C. Barless, 1867; George F. Merritt, 1868; William F. Hickok, 1868; George Aldrich, 1868; Frank H. Closs, 1870, '72, '76, '77, '78, '82, '84; William Harmon, 1870, '83; Orrin L. Wykoff, 1870; Lampson Allen, 1871, '72; Ira T. Soule, 1873, '74, '75, '77, '80; Lucien H. Osgood, 1873; Valorous Ellinwood, 1874; Linus P. Osgood, 1875; Edson M. Ellinwood, 1876, '80,

'81 ; John A. Smart, 1878 ; Ephraim B. Wilson, Jr., 1879, '85 ; Lyman
Legg, 1879 ; Oliver L. Bush, 1879 ; Harvey J. Ferris, 1881, '83, '86, '87,
'92 ; Jarit L. Wickwire, 1881, '85 ; Adelbert Sherman, 1882, '91, '92 ;
Darwin P. Mitchell, 1884 ; Eugene Hickok, 1885 ; Eugene Davis, 1885 ;
Nelson R. Graham, 1885 ; Samuel H. Lyman, 1885 ; Levern Wilson, 1886,
'87, '88 ; Eugene Brewster, 1886, '87, '88 ; George Miller, 1886 ; Merritt
G. McKoon, 1886, '88 ; Andrew Andrus, 1886, '89, '90, '91 ; William J.
Klinck, 1887 ; J. Darwin Marriott, 1887 ; James C. Osborn, 1887 ; Ezra A.
Sherman, 1888 ; Seth C. Woodard, 1888, '89, '90, '91 ; Darius Lovejoy,
1888 ; George L. Deady, 1889, '90 ; Dewey C. Putnam, 1889, '90 ; Frank
Kellogg, 1889, '90, '91 ; William B. Hill, 1889, '90 ; Clarence N. Phillips,
1891 ; Clayton B. Barless, 1891 ; Charles H. Garlick, 1891, '93 ; George
L. Klinck, 1891 ; John Van Antwerp, 1891 ; Fred G. Goodenow, 1892,
'93 ; Albion M. Gray, 1892 ; Stephen J. Shear, 1892 ; Charles W. Oaks,
1892 ; Edwin A. Weeks, 1893 ; Tunis D. Tibbetts, 1893.

COMMISSIONERS OF EXCISE.

William M. Finch, 1877, '81 ; William F. Horton, 1878 ; William H.
Vandercook, 1879, '82, '85 ; James A. Armstrong, 1880 ; Frank H. Closs,
1883 ; Jeremiah H. Barrett, 1884 ; Ephraim B. Wilson, Jr., 1886 ; John L.
Finch, 1887 ; Jackson Valentine, 1888, '91 ; Chester T. Sherman, 1889 ;
Joel S. Sheffield, 1890, '93 ; Harvey J. Ferris, 1892.

INSPECTORS OF COMMON SCHOOLS.

Alpheus Collins, 1826 ; Peter Valentine, 1826, '27, '28, '29, '30, '31, '32,
'34, '37, '42, '43 ; David Smith, 1826, '27, '28, '29 ; Samuel E. Ellinwood,
1827, '34 ; Luman Putnam, 1828 ; Joel N. Lee, 1829, '30, '31, '32 ; Truman Van Tassel, 1830 ; Chauncey B. Collins, 1831, '32, '34, '38 ; John J.
Dickson, 1833, '35, '36, '37, '38, '40, '41, '43 ; Nathan W. Thomas, 1833 ;
John Barber, Jr., 1833 ; Eron M. Thomas, 1835, '36, '37, '40, '41 ; Ralph
Fuller, 1835, '36, '38 ; (1839 wanting) ; William B. Williams, 1840 ; Edward Lampson, 1841 ; Hiram Salisbury, 1842, '43.

COMMISSIONERS OF COMMON SCHOOLS.

Jacob Miller, 1826, '27, '28 ; James Colborn, 1826, '27, '28, '30, '37, '38 ;
Milburn Salisbury, 1826, '27, '28 ; Elizur Flint, 1829 ; David Smith, 1829 ;
Alpheus Collins, 1829 ; Dorman Munsell, 1830, '37 ; Peter Valentine,
1830 ; John Wade, 1831, '32 ; Stephen Babcock, 1831, '32 ; Lewis L. Mor-
ris, 1831, '32 ; Hiram Mirick, 1833, '35 ; Tunis Woodruff, 1833 ; Abia
Blain, 1833, '36 ; George Seelye, 1834, '43 ; Samuel Lyman, 1834 ; John D.

Winchell, 1834; William Lovejoy, 1835; Michael C. Vandercook, 1835; Ira Mirick, 1836; Ralph Fuller, 1837; William Briggs, 1838; George W. Mirick, 1838, '41. '42; (1839 wanting); John Q. Deady, 1840; Harvey Closs, 1840; Samuel Chamberlain, 1840; Lorenzo Griswold, 1841; Joel N. Lee, 1842; Orrin Skut, 1842; Henry E. Youngs, 1843; Matthias Van Horn, 1843.

SUPERINTENDENTS OF SCHOOLS.

John J. Dickson, 1844; Peter Valentine, 1845, '46, '47, '48, '49, '50, '51; Richard S. Valentine, 1852, '53, '54, '55; Henry Van Ostrand, 1856.

TOWN SEALERS.

John Bassett, 1830, '31, '34; Henry Graham, 1833; Joseph Seelye, 1835, '36, '37, '38, '40, '44, '46; (1839 wanting); Elijah F. Thomas, 1841; Winship Allen, 1842; John Harmon, 1843; Fred. Ream, Jr., 1845; Levi A. Lyman, 1847; James T. Jeffers, 1848; Jester L. Holbrook, 1849; Charles S. Wright, 1850; Palmer R. Tindall, 1851; Thomas H. Ellinwood, 1852; Henry R. Riker, 1853; Matthew Crisler, 1854, '55, '56; George W. Sherman, 1857; Judson Garlick, 1858, '65; William Vanderoef, 1859; Dudley Wade, 1860; C. H. Closs, 1861; P. B. Decker, 1863; Riley Miner, 1864.

TOWN AUDITORS.

Lucien H. Osgood, 1876, '77, '78; Lorenzo N. Snow, 1876, '77, '78.

GAME CONSTABLES.

Joseph S. Wade, 1872, '73; Dudley Wade, 1874, '75; Daniel C. Alexander, 1876; Riley Miner, 1877; Cyrus A. Winchell, 1878, '80; W. K. Rider, 1879; Jeremiah Crisler, 1881, '82; William Holbrook, 1883, '85; Rollin C. Barless, 1884; Daniel Johnson, 1886, '89, '90; John Rounds, 1887; Richard Smith, 1888.

ROSE IN THE REBELLION.

Our town, in the great conflict, bore her part well. Her farmers' boys willingly forsook home and put on the blue. Many of them did not come back, but in national cemeteries, or in unknown graves, await the resurrection. Our own burial grounds contain the remains of those who have passed away since the War was ended, save where the moving spirit of the age has taken the veterans to other sections. The small flag, above the mound in the cemetery, is a perpetual reminder of the patriotism and devotion of him who slumbers beneath it.

The basis of the following list is the Rose part of Mr. Lewis H. Clark's enumeration of Wayne county soldiers, in his "Military History," and I hereby render grateful acknowledgment for his kindness in permitting me to thus use it. In addition, I have certain lists prepared during the War, and through these I have ventured to vary, at times, from Mr. Clark's showing. I also have the record, prepared for the census of 1865, by Mr. Chauncey B. Collins. The adjutant general of the state says that Rose is credited with 218 enlistments, but the names of those thus enlisting are not given. From my papers I am able to secure nearly all of them; such are designated by a star. All other names are those of parties who had been residents of Rose before the War, or who have come to the town since the strife was ended, and thus have a right to be included in our enumeration. Having access to the muster rolls of New York, and also those of several other states, I have been able to fill out certain records otherwise incomplete. The history of the individual, i. e., his wounds and career since the War, I do not attempt to give. Such facts, if properly presented, would make a book of themselves. Where I have been unable to secure the desired data, I have left the story untold, preferring a blank to a possible error.

It is due the town to state that no name is borne on this list against whose owner was laid the charge of bounty jumping or of desertion. In western regiments many a soldier did valiant service, whose early days were spent in Rose, but I have tried to indicate all of them. The page of illustrations is made of faces long since forgotten by many, but cherished fondly in one or more households. They are copies of copies in some cases, and that heart must be almost calloused that does not beat more rapidly at the sight of these features, recalling the boys who, nearly or

WAR MEMORIES.

quite thirty years ago, went down in the terrible storm of war. Such boys as these made the rank and file of our army, and such as they won the victory. Can the nation be grateful enough? They died in the flush of youth; we, their schoolmates and comrades, can only recall their heroism and pass the lessons of their deeds on to our children.

> "The hand of the reaper grasps the ears that are hoary,
> But the voice of the weeper wails manhood in glory;
> The autumn blast rushing, wafts the leaves that are serest,
> Our flower was in flushing when blighting was nearest."

EXPLANATORY.—All regiments, named, are from New York, unless otherwise specified. In complete records, the first date is that of enlistment, the second of discharge; *d.* stands for died, *k.* for killed, *r.* for reënlisted, *sub.* for substitute, *trans.* for transferred, *w.* for wounded, *H. A.* for Heavy and *L. A.* for Light Artillery, *V. R. C.*, Veteran Reserve Corps. A star [*] indicates enlistment from Rose.

*Albaugh, John, Aug. 15, '62; D, 9th H. A.; Dec. 28, '63.

Alexander, Charles H., Aug. 22, '62; E, 15th Penn. Cav.; June 21, '65.

*Andrews, Joseph, Aug. 23, '62; H, 9th H. A.; July 6, '65.

Andrews, Rowland B., April 25, '61; B, 27th Inf.; w. June 27, '62, Gaines' Mill; d. July 2, '62, Savage Station.

*Angle, George W., Sept. 5, '61; D, 90th Inf.; d. Tortugas, Sept. 25, '62.

Angle, Lathrop, Dec. 15, '63; A, 9th H. A.; Sept. 29, '65.

*Austin, Charles H., Sept. 3, '64; 3d L. A.; d. Newbarn, N. C., Nov. 2, '64.

*Austin, Edmund G., June 30, '62; C, 111th Inf.; k. Wilderness, May 5, '64.

*Babcock, Edward L., Aug. 12, '62; B, 111th Inf.; June 4, '65.

*Barless, Romain C., Aug. 21, '62; H, 9th H. A.; May 29, '65.

Barnes, Abram T., Dec. 15, '63; G, 9th H. A.; trans. 2d H. A., June 27, '65; Sept. 29, '65.

*Barnes, Harvey D., Sept. 23, '61; K, 44th Inf.; Sept. 25, '64, from V. R. C.

*Barnes, James, Sept., '62; D, 9th H. A.; July 6, '65.

*Benjamin, James E., July 22, '62; B, 111th Inf.; June 4, '65.

Bennett, William H., Aug. 5, '62; C, 111th Inf.; June 4, '65.

*Berg, Miles P., July 30, '64; sub. for G. Lawson Munsell.

Birdsall, William A., Feb. 24, '64; D, 111th Inf.; Oct. 22, '64.

*Bishop, Chauncey E., Sept. 4, '64; E, 3d L. A.; June 23, '65.

*Blackman, Wallace, Sept. 25, '61; D, 8th Cav.; d. Feb. 19, '62.

*Blood, Newton S., Sept. 7, '64; E, 3d L. A.; June 23, '65

*Blynn, Martin H., July 23, '62; 10th Cav.; Lieutenant, Captain, Major, Brev. Lieut. Colonel; June 17, '65.

*Bovee, Edward H., July 17, '62; D, 111th Inf.; trans. to V. R. C.

*Bovee, George S., Nov. 13, '61; I, 98th Inf.; r. Jan. 1, '64; Mar. 29, '65.

Bovee, Heman, Jan. 16, '62; F, 105th Inf.; r. Jan. 1, '64, and attached to 94th Inf.; July 18, '65.

*Bovee, William H., Aug. 15, '62 ; K, 9th H. A.

Bowles, Frederick J., Feb. 18, '64 ; 111th Inf.; d. Washington, June 17, '64.

*Bowles, James A., Aug. 21, '62 ; H, 9th H. A., 2d, 1st Lieutenant ; Mar. 29, '65.

*Bowles, John A., June 20, '61 ; D, 67th Inf.; r. '65.

*Bowles, Jonadab J., June 8, '61 ; 67th Inf.; trans. to G, 2d U. S. L. A.

Boyce, Dudley W., Sept. 15, '62 ; K, 9th H. A.; July 6, '65.

*Boynton, Judson C., June 20, '61 ; D, 67th Inf.; Jan. 1, '63 ; r. Sept. 1, '64 ; H, 9th H. A.; July, '65.

*Boynton, Philo D., June 20. '61 ; D, 67th Inf.; Aug. 19, '65.

Bradburn, Peter W., Sept. 3, '64 ; unassigned, 9th H. A.; d. Feb. 5, '65, Frederick City, Md.

*Brewster, Benj. D., Aug. 12, '62 ; H, 9th H. A.; June 28, '65.

Brewster, Isaac O., Aug. 28, '62; C, 160th Inf.; k. Winchester, Sept. 19, '64.

*Briggs, Birney, Aug. 25, '64 ; E, 3d L. A.; June 29, '65.

*Brown, Byron, Aug. 12, '62 ; D, 9th H. A.; July 6, '65.

*Brown, John, Aug. 30, '62 ; H, 9th H. A.; July 6, '65.

*Brunney, James, Aug. 31, '64 ; 3d L. A.; '65.

*Brunney, John, Aug. 9, '62 ; A, 9th H. A.; Dec. 4, '63.

Bunyea, Francis M., May 10, '61 ; B, 27th Inf.; May 21, '63 : r. Aug. 11, '63 ; Co. C, 21st Cav.; July 6, '66.

Burns, George E., Dec. 14, '63 ; 9th H. A.; July 6, '65.

*Burns, James W., Aug. 14, '62 ; D, 9th H. A.; July 6, '65.

Campbell, Isaac G., April, '61 ; G, 34th Inf.; June 30, '63 ; r. 16th H. A.

Carrier, Seward W., Oct. 22, '61 ; E, 10th Cav.; d. Baltimore, Aug. 21, '62.

*Chaddock, Jared, May 10, '61 ; D, 67th Inf.; June 20, '64.

Chatterson, William Henry, May 2, '61 ; B, 27th Inf.; May 31, '63 ; r. E, 3d Wis. Inf.: '65.

Church, James C., Oct. 8, '62 ; B, 8th Mich.; trans. Sept. 7, '63, V. R. C.; March, '64.

Colborn, Jonathan, May 25, '61 ; E, 17th Ill. Inf.; k. Fort Donelson, Feb. 13, '62.

Collins, Leonard, Oct. 4, '64 ; H, 9th H. A.; July 6, '65.

Colvin, Asahel, '64 ; 111th Inf.; lost arm at Petersburg, July, '64.

Colvin, Sidney T., Sept. 23, '64 ; K, 44th Inf.; r. Aug. 14, '62 ; H, 9th H. A., 2d Lieut.; Dec. 19, '64.

Conklin, Morris, Dec. 24, '63 ; A, 9th H. A.; trans. 2d H. A.; Sept. 29, '65.

*Conroe, John, Aug. 8, '62 ; B, 111th Inf.; w. Wilderness, May 6, '64 ; d. May 26, '64, Fredericksburg.

Correll, Nicholas, Aug. 1, '61 : C, 12th Ill. Inf.; r. Jan. 1, '64 ; Oct. 6, '64.

*Coster, Joseph, July 30, '64 ; sub. for William H. Dodds.

*Coventry, William A., July 9, '63 ; C, 21st Cav.; June, 1865.

Crisler, Jeremiah, May 4, '61 ; K, 33d Inf.; June 2, '63 ; r. Sept. 5, '64 ;
   M, 15th H. A.; June 13, '65.

*Darling, Daniel. Aug. 15, '62 ; C, 111th Inf.; June 4, '65.

*Dawson, John W., July 31, '62 ; H, 111th Inf.; d., Washington, Nov. 5, '64.

*Deady, Henry, Sept. 5, '62 ; H, 9th H. A.

*Deady, William N., June 20, '61 ; D, 67th Inf.; '62.

*Delamater, Merrill. Aug. 12, '62 ; C, 111th Inf.; July 3, '65.

Delamater, Stephen J., Sept. 25, '62 ; 25th Inf.; r. Sept. 13, '64 ; 91st Inf.;
   July 3, '65.

*Desmond, William H., Aug. 5, '61 ; C, 111th Inf.; June 20, '65.

*Deuel, Albert E., May 1, '63 ; H, 9th H. A.; July 6, '65.

Devereaux, Spencer, Dec. 11, '63 ; G, 9th H. A.; trans. June 27, '65, to
   2d H. A.; Sept. 29, '65.

*Dickinson, Jay R., Aug. 3, '64 ; E, 3d L. A.; June 23, '65.

*Dickson, Ensign L., Sept. 18, '62 ; 26th Ind. Bat.; Sept. 12, '65.

*Dickson, George, July 30, '62; B, 111th Inf.; k., Wilderness. May 5, '64.

*Dixon, Abel, Jr., Aug. 22, '62 ; G, 9th H. A.; d., Washington, April
   29, '64.

*Doremus, Abram, Aug. 30, '64 ; F, 111th Inf.; June 4, '65.

Dougan, Jerome, Aug. 29, '64 ; I, 148th Inf.; June 23, '65.

*Dowd, John, July 30, '64 ; sub. for Francis Osborn.

Drown, Napoleon B., Oct. 19, '61 ; E, 10th Cav.; July 19, '65.

*Drury, Frank, Aug. 23, '64 ; K, 111th Inf.; June 4, '65.

*Dunbar, Levi H., Aug. 15, '62 ; D, 9th H. A.; July 6, '65.

*Dunham, Andrew H., Aug. 25, '62 ; H, 9th H. A.; July 6, '65.

*Dunn, Hiram. Given by Mr. Clark as in the 98th Inf.

*Edwards, Charles, July 23, '64 ; sub. for M. T. Collier.

Ellinwood, George E., Sept. 5, '64 ; 3d L. H.; June, '65.

Ellis, L. R.; A, 3d L. A. Did not enlist from Rose.

Feeck, Alonzo, Dec. 10, '63 ; H, 9th H. A.; d. Nov. 12, '64; Danville, Va.,
   prisoner of war.

*Feeck, William, Aug. 30, '64 ; 111th Inf.; June 3, '65.

Ferris, Harvey J., Sept. 1, '64 ; K, 3d L. A.; June, '65.

*Finch, Benjamin, July 27, '62 ; D, 111th ; April 21, '64.

*Finck, Christian, Sept. 1, '64 ; F, 111th Inf.; June 6, '65.

*Fitzgerald, Nicholas, Aug. 5, '62 ; C, 111th Inf.; d. July 19, '64. Ander-
   sonville, Ga., prisoner of war.

*Fosmire, John, April, '61 ; B, 27th Inf.; June 2, '63.

*Fosmire, William H., June 20, '61 ; D, 67th Inf.; July 4, '64.

Fox, Philip, Feb. 4, '62 ; F, 98th ; March 29, '63.

*Francis, John, July 30, '64 ; sub. for Lorenzo N. Snow.

*Francisco, Jeremiah, Aug. 5, '62 ; C, 111th, Inf.

*Fuller, David L., Aug. 5, '62; C, 111th Inf.; k., Wilderness, May 6, '64.

*Garratt, Richard, Jr., Aug. 21, '62; H, 9th H. A.; March 10, '63.

*Genung, William D., Aug. 6, '62; B, 111th Inf.; w. at Wilderness; d. May 13, '64, at Fredericksburg, Va.

Gildersleeve, Porter, Dec. 30, '63; G, 9th H. A.; trans. 2d H. A.; Sept. 29, '65.

*Gillett, Avery H., Sept. 3, '64; N, 9th H. A.; June 15, '65.

*Gillett, Charles, Sept. 9, '61; D, 90th Inf.; r. Feb. 20, '64; Feb. 9, '65.

*Gillett, William B., Aug. 24, '62; H, 9th H. A.; July 6, '65.

*Gillen, John, July 30, '64; sub. for Merwin S. Roe.

Gragor, David G., Nov., '63; L, 14th R. I. H. A.; Oct. 2, '65.

*Gregory, William, July 30, '64; sub. for Jackson Valentine.

*Gross, John, July 30, '64; sub. for Jerry Barrett.

Hall, Melvin, Dec. 16, '63; A, 9th H. A.; trans. 2d H. A.; Sept. 29, '65.

*Halley, Joseph, July 30, '64; sub. for William Desmond.

*Hallinbeck, Martin F., July, '62; H, 9th H. A.; not heard from since enlistment.

Hallinbeck, Richard I., Aug. 25, '62; H, 9th H. A.; May 23, '65.

*Hand, Nathan B., Aug. 1, '62; C, 111th; r. Jan. 1, '64; May 15, '65.

*Harmon, Alfred B., Aug. 21, '62; H, 9th H. A.; July 6, '65.

*Harmon, Daniel B., Aug. 25, '62; H, 9th H. A., 2d and 1st Lieut., Captain; Nov. 16, '64.

*Harmon, William J., Aug. 21, '62; H, 9th H. A.; May 23, '65.

Harper, Alexander, Sept. 1, '64; H. 9th H. A.; July 6, '65.

*Hart, Thomas R., Nov. 18, '61; K, 98th Inf.; Dec. 5, '62.

*Hickok, William F., Aug. 21, '62; H, 9th H. A.; trans. '64, C, 7th V. R. C.; June 28, '65.

*Hill, Erastus L., Aug. 19, '62; G, 9th H. A.; July 6, '62.

*Hilts, Peter, Aug. 22, '62; H, 9th H. A.; July 13, '63.

Holbrook, Jester L., March. '64; 111th Inf.; June 3, '65.

Horne, Charles V., Aug., '64; H, 188th Inf.; July 21, '65.

*Horne, William, Aug. 24, '62; G, 9th H. A.; July 6, '65.

Horton, William O., April 25, '61; 7th Vt. Inf.; r. same reg.; July 20, '65.

*Howard, Henry P., Aug. 25, '62; H, 9th H. A.; July 14, '65.

*Howard, John. Sept., '63; 111th Inf.; d. on road from Salisbury, N. C., March 4, '65.

Howes, Orrin. Aug. 16, '61; D, 44th N. Y.; May, '62.

Hudson, Enos. Aug. 15, '62; D, 9th H. A.; July 6, '65.

Hunn, Samuel C., Aug. 30, '64; 111th Inf.; June 3, '65.

Hurd, George L., Aug. 22, '64; 3d L. A.; June, '65.

Hurd, Norman R., Aug., '64; 3d L. A.; June, '65.

Hurd, William H., Aug. 18, '64; B, 111th Inf.; March 13, '65.

*Hurst, Charles R., April 19, '61 ; 3d L. A.: r. June 4, '63 ; H. 9th H. A.; Dec. 5th, '64.

Hurter, Burkhart, Sept. 9, '61 ; D. 90th Inf.: r. Aug., '61 ; Feb., '66.

*Ingersoll, John J., Aug. 19, '62 ; G, 9th H. A.; July 8, '63.

*Jenner, James J., May. '61 ; D, 67th Inf.; July 4, '64.

*Jenner, Van Rensselaer, July 30, '62 ; B, 111th Inf.; Dec. 17, '63.

*Johnson, David, Aug. 25, '62 ; G, 9th H. A.; July 6, '65.

*Johnson, Robert, Sept., '61 ; E. 10th Cav.: July 19, '65.

Kellogg, Ethan B., Aug. 25, '62 ; H, 9th H. A.; March 10, '64.

Kimpland, Rufus H., Sept. 7, '61 ; F, 98th Inf.: r. Feb., '64 ; Aug. 31,'65.

*King, Thomas, Nov. 26, '61 ; B, 27th Inf.; Jan. 1, '63.

Knapp, Henry. Mr. Clark has him in H, 22d Cav.; fall of '62 ; dis. April, '65.

*Kneely, Michael, Aug. 25, '62 ; H, 9th H. A.; July 6, '65.

*Knox, Charles E., Aug. 15, '62 ; D, 9th H. A.; July 6, '65.

*Lake, Wellington, Aug. 12, '62 ; C, 111th Inf.: k., Wilderness, May 6, '64.

*Lambert, Thomas, Jr., Oct. 25, '62 ; I, 98th Inf.: r. 1864 ; Aug. 31, '65.

Lamoreaux, Sullivan B., Aug. 22, '62; F, 9th H. A., 2d, 1st Lieut., Captain, Major and Brev. Lt. Colonel ; Sept. 29, '65.

*Lampson, Theodore, Aug. 15, '62 ; C. 111th Inf., 2d Lieut.; Nov. 7, '62.

*Langley, S. Wing, Aug. 19, '62 ; G. 9th H. A.; July 6, '65.

Lape, Samuel W., Aug. 15, '62 ; D, 9th H. A., 2d Lieut.; Oct. 8, '64.

*La Rock, Charles, Oct. 19, '61 ; E. 10th Cav.; r. Dec., '63 ; July 19, '65.

*La Rock, Joseph, Oct. 19, '61 ; E. 10th Cav.: r. Dec., '63 ; July 19, '65.

*La Rock, Leonard, March 4, '63 ; G, 9th H. A.; trans. 2d H. A.: Sept. 29, '65.

NOTE.—A younger brother of the La Rock family, William H., enlisted at 17 years in the regular army, and was slain with Custer, June 25, 1876, at the Little Big Horn.

*Lee, Charles A., Aug. 21, '62 ; H, 9th H. A.; trans. 2d H. A.: Sept. 29, '65.

*Legg, Austin A., July 20, '62 ; C, 111th Inf.; d. Chicago, Oct. 2, '62.

Lethbridge, Jeremy, Oct. 7, '61 ; D, 90th Inf.; r. Sept. 15, '64 ; 3d L. A.; Feb. 9, '66.

*Lyman, Jacob L., July 26, '62 ; C, 111th Inf.; trans. to V. R. C.: March 6, '65.

*Mabb, John, Aug. 31, '64 ; H, 9th H. A.; July 6, '65.

*McBeth, William L., July 30, '62 ; B, 111th Inf.; thought to have been drowned in Lake Erie.

*McCoy, William G., Aug. 5, '62 ; C, 111th Inf.; d., Washington, Aug. 29, '63.

*McDonald, Charles, Aug. 15, '62 ; D, 9th H. A.

*McGinnes, Daniel, Aug. 18, '62 ; H, 9th H. A.; d., Washington, July 31, '63.

*McKenny, Thomas, July 30, '64 ; sub. for Thomas Robinson.

*McWharf, James, Sept. 1, '64 ; 3d L. A.; June, '65.

*McWharf, Theodore, Aug. 6, '62 ; C, 111th Inf.; Sept. 22, '63.

*Mariquette, Daniel, Sept., '62 (?); 111th Inf.

*Marsh, Cornelius, Aug. 15, '62 ; H, 9th H. A.; May 2, '64.

*Marsh, Henry, Sept. 25, '61 ; D, 8th Cav.; afterward, Sept., '62, in H, 9th H. A.; July 6, '65.

*Marsh, Uriah, Aug. 23, '62 ; H, 9th H. A.; July 6, '65.

*Milem, Christopher, Nov. 14, '61 ; I, 75th Inf.; r. Jan. 24, '64 ; Aug. 31, '65.

*Milem, George, Oct. 28, '61 ; F, 98th Inf.; r. Jan. 1, '64, 1st Lieut.; Aug. 31, '65.

Miller, Cornelius, Dec. 14, '63 ; H, 9th H. A.; July 6, '65.

Miner, Philo, Jan. 18, '64 ; C, 111th Inf.; trans. 4th H. A.; June 3, '65.

Morey, Edmund W., Sept., '63 ; H, 9th H. A.; k., Cold Harbor, June 3, '64.

*Morey, George N., May, '61 ; B, 27th Inf.; d., Alexandria, April, '62.

Morey, Horace M., Dec. 10, '63 ; G, 9th H. A.; trans. 2d H. A.; Sept. 29, '65.

*Murphy, Cornelius, April 25, '61 ; B, 27th Inf.; June 2, '63.

Murphy, John, July 30, '64 ; sub. for Philander Mitchell, Jr.

*Murray, July 30, '64 ; sub. for E. C. Ellinwood.

*Neeley, Nelson, Aug. 29, '62 ; Asst. Surgeon, 57th Inf.; June 29, '64.

*Nichols, Francis M., Aug. 5, '62 ; B, 111th Inf.; Jan. 27, '64.

Oaks, Charles G., Jr., Sept. 15, '64 ; E, 5th Wis.; June 20, '65.

*O'Brien, John, July 30, '64 ; sub. for Marvin Wilbur.

Odell, Lorenzo, Feb. 25, '63 ; G, 9th H. A.

Paine, Daniel M., Aug., '64 ; 111th Inf.; June 3, '65.

Paine, Peter C., Aug., '64 ; F, 111th Inf.; June 3, '65.

*Paine, Smith R., Aug. 31, '64 ; F, 111th Inf.; June 3, '65.

*Patterson, George, Oct. 19, '61 ; E, 10th Cav.; r. Feb. 25, '64 ; July 19, '65.

Perkins, Charles, Jan. 3, '64 ; 111th Inf.; d. July 13, '64.

Perkins, Charles W., Sept. 5, '61 ; D, 90th Inf.; d. July 15, '62.

Perkins, Harvey, Aug. 15, '64 ; E, 61st Inf.; July 14, '65.

Perkins, John L., Aug. 19, '62 ; D, 9th H. A.; d., Danville, Va., Aug. 18, '64, prisoner of war.

*Phillips, George, Oct. 19, '61 ; E, 10th Cav.; Oct., '64.

Phillips, James H., May, '61 ; 2d Mich.; d. June 3, '62.

*Phillips, Stephen, '61 ; E, 10th Cav.; also enlisted March 13, '63, in G, 9th H. A.; d. Dec. 14, '64.

Pimm, Enos T., Sept. 3, '64 ; H, 9th H. A.; July 6, '65.

*Pitcher, George A., Aug. 31, '64 ; H, 9th H. A.; July 6, '65.

Prosens, Franklin M., Sept. 2, '64 ; 9th H. A.; d., City Point, Va., Dec. 9, '64.

*Purchase, Lewis, Sept. 2, '64 ; E, 3d L. A.; June 23, '65.

*Ready, Alexander, Aug. 22, '62 ; H, 9th H. A.; March 10, '63.

Reed, John A., Nov. 20, '61 ; G, 75th Inf.(?); k., 2d Bull Run, Aug., '62.

*Rhinehart, Andrew, Aug. 22, '62 ; D, 9th H. A.; k., Winchester, Va., Sept. 19, '64.

Richardson, John, Feb. 15, '64 ; 3d L. A.; July, '65.

*Ridegway, Sylvanus, Aug. 12, '62 ; D, 111th Inf.; June 4, '65.

*Ridgeway, Sylvester, Aug. 12, '62 ; D, 111th Inf.

*Roach, Patrick, July 30, '64 ; sub. for James C. Osborn.

Roe, Alfred S., Jan. 21, '64 ; A, 9th H. A.; trans. L, 2d H. A.; Oct. 16, '65.

Rounds, John, May 25, '61 ; C, 32d Inf.; June 19, '63.

Ruppert, John H., Aug., '62 ; H, 148th Inf.; June 22, '65.

*Seager, Asher W., Aug. 19, '62 ; D, 9th H. A.; July 6, '65.

*Seager, Benjamin, Aug. 19, '62 ; D, 9th H. A.; July 6, '65.

Seager, George W., Sept. 12, '61 ; D, 90th Inf.; Feb. 9, '66.

*Seelye, Alfred, Aug. 31, '64 ; H, 9th H. A.; July 6, '65.

Seelye, Irwin R., Sept. 1, '64 ; H, 9th H. A.; July 6, '65.

*Seelye, J. Judson, Aug. 22, '62 ; H, 9th H. A.; June 12, '65.

*Selcor, Conrad, June, '61 ; D, 67th Inf.

Shannon, Samuel L., Aug. 15, '62 ; D, 9th H. A.; July 6, '65.

*Shannon, Theodore, Jan. 4, '64 ; G, 9th H. A.; May 24, '65.

*Shaw, John P., Aug. 22, '62 ; D, 9th H. A.; '64.

*Sherman, Charles, April 25, '61 ; B, 27th Inf., 2d Lieut.; May 21, '63.

*Sherman, Ezra A., July 30, '62 ; C, 111th Inf.; d. in rebel prison, Richmond, Va., March 24, '65.

Sherman, Franklin N., served in a western regiment.

*Sherman, John E., July 26, '62 ; C, 111th Inf.; k., Wilderness, May 6, '64.

Sherman, Levi, Aug. 8, '63 ; C, 21st Cav.; July 3, '66.

*Sherman, Robert, Dec., '61 ; E, 98th Inf.; later in G, 9th H. A.

*Sherman, W. Harrison, Aug. 5, '62 ; C, 111th Inf.

*Sherman, William Henry, Aug. 16, '62 ; C, 111th Inf.; k., Wilderness, May 6, '64.

*Shoemaker, John H., July 30, '64 ; sub. for Robert N. Jeffers.

*Silver, Benjamin C., Oct., '61 ; E, 10th Cav.; July 19, '65.

*Silver, John, Oct., '61 ; E, 10th Cav.; July 19, '65.

Skut, Ira, Nov. 6, '61 ; E, 10th Cav.

*Smith, George, Fall, '63 ; A, 9th H. A.

Smith, James, Aug. 29, '62; H, 9th H. A.; July 6, '65.

*Smith, Leonard A., Oct. 1, '61; F, 75th Inf.; r. Jan. 1, '64; Aug. 31, '65.

*Smith, Lewis W., Aug. 19, '62; G, 9th H. A.; July 6, '65.

*Smith, Sidney L., Aug. 11, '62; 9th H. A.

*Snyder, Harvey H., Oct. 13, '61; E, 10th Cav.; r. Dec. 18, '63; July 19, '65.

*Snyder, John W., Aug. 14, '62; B, 111th Inf.; Dec., '62, at Chicago.

*Snyder, William A., Oct. 14, '61; E, 10th Cav., 2d, 1st Lieut., Captain, Major, Brev. Lt. Colonel; July 19, '65.

*Soule, Ira, Aug. 21, '62; H, 9th H. A.; July 6, '65.

*Soule, Ira T., Aug. 21, '62; H, 9th H. A.; July 6, '65.

*Staffen, Jacob, Sept. 13, '61; D, 90th Inf.; March 4, '65.

Starkey, David, Oct., '61; E, 10th Cav.; July 19, '65.

*Starkey, Edward H., Oct. 19, '61; E, 10th Cav.; July 19, '65.

Stewart, William H., Sept., '64; 3d L. A.; June, '65.

*Stickles, Andrew, Aug., '62; B, 111th Inf.

*Streeter, Josiah W., Aug. 5, '62; C, 111th Inf., June 4, '65.

*Sullivan, Michael, Aug. 21, '62; K, 9th H. A.

Sutherland, David W., Aug. 7, '62; D, 111th Inf.; June 4, '65.

Thomas, Fernando C., Sept. 6, '61; 1st Cal.; r. Sept. 3, '64; E, 3d L. A.; June 23, '65.

Thompson, Reuben S., Oct. 5, '62; E, 10th Cav.

*Thompson, Samuel P., Sept. 16, '61; C, 8th Cav.; June 27, '65.

*Tindall, Philip P., Aug. 22, '62; H, 9th H. A., 2d and 1st Lieut.; June 27, '65.

*Toles, Eben W., Sept. 5, '64; H, 9th H. A.; May 25, '65.

Tompkins, Henry, Feb. 22, '64; D, 111th Inf.; '65.

*Trippe, Edward M., Oct. 19, '61; E, 10th Cav.; July 19, '65.

Trippe, Morton F., Feb. 22, '63; A, 9th H. A.; April 1, '64.

Turner, Philip, March 21, '65; H, 96th Inf.; Feb. 6, '66.

*Ullrich, Charles, Aug. 6, '62; A, 9th H. A.; July 6, 65.

*Utter, Uriah B., July 6, '62; D, 111th Inf.

*Van Antwerp, John, Aug. 25, '62; G, 9th H. A.; d. April 17, '65.

Vanderburgh, John W., Dec. 11, '63; H, 9th H. A.; March 5, '65.

Van Valkenburgh, Abraham, Aug., '62; 160th Inf.; d., Baton Rouge, Aug. 22, '63.

*Van Wort, James L., Aug., '62; H, 9th H. A.; July 6, '65.

*Viele, Aaron, March 25, '63; H, 9th H. A.; trans. to V. R. C., May 14, '64.

Wager, Stephen, Oct. 15, '61; D, 90th Inf.; trans. to 1st U. S. Arty. Lost an arm at Cold Harbor.

*Wager, William, Aug. 15, '62; D, 9th H. A.; July 6, '65.

ROSE NEIGHBORHOOD SKETCHES. 393

*Wait, Stephen M., Sept. 3, '64; H, 9th H. A.: May 18, '65.

*Wallace, Henry, July 30, '64; sub. for John H. Barnes.

Walmsley, Albert, Dec. 23, '63; D, 9th H. A.: trans. M, 2d H. A.; Sept. 29, '65.

Walmsley, Henry, Dec. 23, '63; D, 9th H. A.; trans. M, 2d H. A.; Sept. 29, '65.

*Watson, George, July 30, '64; sub. for Peter Harmon.

*Way, David, Aug. 16, '62; D, 9th H. A.; d., Danville, Va., prisoner of war.

*Weaver, Chester, Oct. 21, '62; B, 8th Cav.

*Weaver, Spencer C., April 30, '61; B, 27th Inf.: Oct., '62.

Weed, William H., March 9, '65; C, 193d Inf.: Jan. 18, '66.

Weeks, De Witt M., Dec. 17, '63; F, 2d Mounted Rifles; May 26, '65.

Wescott, Daniel C., July 31, '62; B, 111th Inf.: lost right arm at Petersburg; June 4, '65.

*West, Alonzo, Aug. 26, '62; K, 9th H. A.: July 6, '65.

*Westbrook, Charles, Aug. 18, '62; D, 9th H. A.

*Whedon, George D., Dec. 23, '61; Asst. Sur., 10th Cav.; Nov. 1, '62.

*Wilcox, Jack, July 23, '64; sub. for George Woodruff.

*Williams, Alexander, Oct., '61; E, 10th Cav.; July 19, '65.

Wilson, Fortescue W., Oct. 18, '61; C, 105th Inf.; d. 1864.

*Winchell, Calvin R., Aug. 15, '62; G, 9th H. A.; trans. 11th V. R. C., April, '64; March 19, '65.

*Wood, Ira, Aug. 9, '62; A, 9th H. A.; d. July 28, '64.

*Woodard, Seymour, Aug. 24, '62; H, 9th H. A., 2d Lieut.; Feb. 25, '65.

*Woodruff, Isaac, Aug. 9, '62; D, 9th H. A.; July 6, '65.

Wooley, Charles M., Sept. 2, '64; 9th H. A.; July 6, '65.

Worden, John V., Jan. 2, '64; 9th H. A.; July 6, '65.

*Young, Edmund, Aug. 20, '62; H, 9th H. A., 2d Lieut.; July 6, '65.

Young, James A., Aug. 6, '62; H, 126th Inf.; June 3, '65.

EPITAPHS FROM THE BURIAL GROUNDS OF ROSE AND ADJOINING TOWNS.

In copying these inscriptions I have made no effort to reproduce peculiar orthography, lettering, arrangement nor poetic effusions. I have secured the facts in the briefest and most comprehensive manner possible. As the copying has been done at intervals during the last six years, it is more than probable that inscriptions of later years, in the more remote inclosures, have not been secured. All epitaphs were taken in the Rose and other cemeteries, save those of South Sodus and York's corners, where only those pertaining to Rose were copied. A strictly alphabetical order is followed, save where the members of a given family are involved. In such cases the names of wife and children follow that of the husband and father. Unless otherwise specified, the first date refers to birth, the second to death ; age is indicated in order of numerals—years, months days. The final letter is the initial of the cemetery where the epitaph is found.

The following explanation should be carefully read :

A. stands for Aurand's burial ground, located in Galen, about two miles south of Town's district; *B.* indicates Briggs', immediately south of the southeast corner of Rose and nearly opposite the residence of William Hunt; *C.,* abbreviation for Collins, the cemetery in District No. 7; *E.,* Ellinwood's, a mile east of the Valley; *F.,* Ferguson's, in Galen, a mile south of southwest corner of Rose; *H.,* Hubbard's, in west part of Butler; *Hu.,* Huron, southeast part of that town; *L.,* Lovejoy's, in District No. 9; *N. R.,* North Rose; *R.,* Rose, or the Valley burial ground, and the largest in the town; *S. S.,* South Sodus, in southeast part; *W.,* White school-house, on the road from the Valley to Clyde, a mile-and-a-half south of the town line; *Y.,* York's corners, in southwest part of Huron.

Louisa A. Ackley, June 16, 1884 ; 22, 0, 11.	R.
Charles G., her son, Sept. 11, 1884 ; 3 months, 6 days.	R.
Ede Alden, Dec. 2, 1870 ; 82, 11, 2.	S. S.
Mary Alden, June 25, 1842 ; 22d year.	S. S.
Amos Aldrich, April 3, 1875 ; 81, 5, 12.	N. R.
Sally, his wife, Aug. 30, 1859 ; 64, 4, 5.	N. R.
Harriet, their daughter, Dec. 21, 1850 ; 31, 9, 4.	N. R.
Orin, their son, March 12, 1849 ; 26, 9.	N. R.
John W., their son, March, 1833 ; 7 weeks.	N. R.
Clarissa, their daughter, May, 1833 ; 2 years.	N. R.

Their infant, died 1835. N. R.

Willie, infant son of George and Ella Aldrich, April 21, 1865. L.

James Alexander, Nov. 30, 1849 ; 67 years. Hn.

Charlotte A., wife of William H. Allen, Feb. 8, 1859 ; 30, 4, 18. R.

Eve, wife of Asa L. Allen, March 14, 1871 ; 66, 2, 10. W.

Ezra Allen, June 26, 1836 ; 69 years. H.

Lucy, his wife, April 30, 1852 ; 78, 9, 18. H.

James Allen, Co. K, 9th N. Y. Heavy Artillery, Aug. 4, 1863 ;
  57, 3, 9. F.

Solomon Allen, May 26, 1870; 79 years. R.

Susan Allen, his wife, Jan. 26, 1888 ; 84 years. R.

Lampson Allen, June 24, 1833—March 24, 1875. R.

Nathan Allen, April 13, 1842 ; 19 years. R.

Winthrop Allen, Sept. 22, 1854 ; 72, 0. 2. R.

Mercy, his wife, Sept. 14, 1853; 57, 3, 24. R.

Ann, wife of Joseph Andrews, March 29, 1876 ; 43, 6. Y.

Charles M., their son, March 3, 1860 ; 2, 9, 7. Y.

A. J. Andrus, June 21, 1879; 46, 3, 29. R.

Eli Andrus, April 5, 1846 ; 65th year. Hn.

Henry E., son of J. and A. H. Atkinson, June 11, 1862 ; 1, 6. F.

William Aurand, Nov. 16, 1803—Sept. 15, 1884. A.

Catherine, his wife, April 12, 1808—April 29, 1884. A.

Harriet, their daughter, March 1, 1855 ; 16, 10, 22. A.

Ezra Austin, May 3, 1861 ; 66 years. R.

Ida E., daughter of Ezra and Huldah Austin, Jan. 8, 1858 ; 4, 4, 18. R.

Hubbard T. Austin, March 1, 1852 ; 26, 10, 5. R.

Stephen Babcock, April 22, 1837 ; 48 years. N. R.

Huldah, wife of Almon Baker, and daughter of J. and Mary Sober,
  July 17, 1863 ; 28 years. R.

Ida E., wife of C. O. Baker, and daughter of William and Margaret
  Weeks, March 3, 1887 ; 22, 4. S. S.

Frances E., their daughter, Sept. 15, 1887 ; 7 months. S. S.

Rev. Charles Baldwin, Sept. 10, 1831—March 12, 1879. R.

Samuel A., son of T. W. and S. Barber, Oct. 26, 1850 ; 4, 0, 16. A.

Infant daughter of Romain C. and Helen J. Barless, June 29, 1874. R.

Arnold A., son of Elijah and Mary Barnes, March 12, 1865; 11
  months, 16 days. F.

Emily, wife of Benjamin Barnes, Nov. 27, 1860; 31, 8, 11. A.

John Barnes, June 10, 1874 ; 78, 2, 5. F.

Mary, his wife, April 10, 1871 ; 75, 10, 12. F.

Sarah, their daughter, July 15, 1842 ; 9, 0, 3. F.

D. P. Barnum, Oct. 20, 1890 ; 79 years. R.

Catherine, his wife, Dec. 30, 1889 ; 59 years. R.

John R. Barrett. April 1, 1872; 48, 5, 26.   F.
Alice C., his daughter, September 26, 1865 ; 9, 5, 25.   F.
Simeon I. Barrett, Nov. 22, 1887 ; 93, 9.   F.
Matilda A., his wife, July 30, 1863 ; 65, 10, 8.   F.
Simeon O., son of above, April 1, 1833; 10 months, 17 days.   F.
Simeon J., son of above, April 20, 1841 ; 3 years.   F.
Tamar, wife of Elder Simeon Barrett, April 21, 1839 ; 75th year.   F.
Elisha Barton, Oct. 7, 1879 ; 53, 11, 11.   S. S.
Caroline, his wife, Oct. 9, 1884 ; 54, 5, 5.   S. S.
John Bassett, Dec. 26, 1870 ; 77 years.   R.
Lydia, his wife, June 2, 1869 ; 74 years.   R.
Peter Becker, Jan. 10, 1843 ; 64, 6, 14.   W.
Elizabeth, his wife, Jan. 7, 1851 ; 71, 11, 7.   W.
Seth Becker, Dec. 29, 1843 ; 30, 3, 28.   W.
Philip Becker, July 1, 1850 ; 43, 1, 8.   W.
Diana, daughter of Smithfield and Rebecca Beden, June 18, 1822 ;
    2, 0, 11.   W.
Calista, daughter of same, April 15, 1822; 3, 6, 28.   W.
William Bedient, Sept. 1, 1828 ; 58 years.   F.
Mary, his wife, Sept. 14, 1828 ; 60 years.   F.
Hannah, wife of Harris Bemis, May 5, 1849 ; 50, 10, 16.   H.
Frank, son of Henry and Phœbe Benjamin, Aug. 27, 1863 ; 1, 9, 11. W.
Manly, son of A. and C. J. Benjamin, Oct. 16, 1864 : 20, 1, 13.   A.
Ruth, wife of Nelson Benjamin, Aug. 9, 1839; 27, 5, 4.   W.
William Benjamin, Jan. 28, 1864 ; 63, 4, 10.   W.
Nancy Shaver, his wife, Nov. 25, 1863 ; 54, 9, 11.   W.
Mariah, their daughter, Sept. 22, 1844 ; 13, 6, 27.   W.
Deborah, wife of Rial Betts, Oct. 6, 1840 ; 33, 3, 21.   B.
Matilda, their daughter, Dec. 24, 1851 ; 17, 0, 20.   B.
Lydia, wife of Samuel Bigelow, Dec. 15, 1843 ; 61, 1, 26.   N. R.
Chauncey Bishop, June 29, 1791; Aug. 5, 1880.   R.
Chloe W., his wife, May 27, 1797 ; Feb. 24, 1878.   R.
Children of Joel and Z. M. Bishop :
    Eron D., Jan. 25, 1854 ; 19, 4, 4.   N. R.
    Antha, Aug. 12, 1849 ; 5 weeks.   N. R.
    Emma, June 3, 1848 ; 8 months.   N. R.
E. Wallace Blackman, Feb, 19, 1862 ; 21, 1, 4.   E.
David L. Blackslee, April 13, 1854 ; 18, 0, 21.   E.
Abiah Blaine, Sept. 23, 1847 ; 48, 3, 6.   L.
John L. Blauvelt, March 11, 1864 ; 27, 8, 26.   W.
William G. Bliton, Co. G, 9th H. Arty., Feb. 1, 1864 ; 36 years.   A.
Diana, wife of E. W. Bliton, April 8, 1850 ; 59th year.   A.
Catharine A., wife of John Blynn, Dec. 1, 1817 —— ——, 1893.   R.

Ovid Blynn, Feb. 14, 1803 ; July 12, 1891.   R.
Hannah, his wife, May 20, 1803 ; Feb. 3, 1886.   R.
Selden Borden, May 16, 1849 ; 51 years.   F.
William H. Bovee, Aug. 28. 1874 ; 35, 10, 15.   R.
Mary A., his daughter, Nov. 15, 1864 ; 19, 5, 28.   R.
Dudley W. Boyce, June 6, 1871 : 56 years.   N. R.
Andrew Bradburn, Nov. 3, 1873 ; 57, 2, 23.   R.
David Bradburn, Jan. 13, 1892 : 72 years.   R.
His children :
    Nathan F., March 4, 1855 : 9 months, 5 days.   R.
    Benjamin D., Jan. 22, 1857 ; 7 months, 29 days.   R.
    Nelson, March 29, 1872 ; 11, 10, 21.   R.
Lewis Braden, Dec. 11, 1851 ; 22, 1, 9.   F.
Jennie L., wife of J. E. Bradshaw and daughter of G. and M. Jewell,
    Jan. 29, 1881 ; 29, 7, 18.   R.
Seth H. Brainard, May 29, 1842 ; 38th year.   E.
Louise, his wife, also wife of Samuel Hoffman, Nov. 22, 1878 ; 71
    years.   E.
Henry Brewer, March 1, 1874 ; 74 years.   A.
James E. Brewer, Jan. 30, 1861 ; 25, 5, 19.   A.
Thomas Brewer, Co. K, 9th N. Y. H. Arty., Feb. 11, 1874 ; 63 years.   W.
Addison C., son of I. O. and L. Brewster, Oct. 5, 1858 : 2, 1, 20.   F.
Jonathan Briggs, July 20, 1881 ; 68, 9, 17.   R.
Emeline, his wife, Aug. 1, 1891 ; 80 years.   R.
George Briggs, June 8, 1878 ; 25, 9, 5.   R.
Samuel Briggs, Oct. 17, 1831 ; 64th year.   B.
Sarah, his wife, April 17, 1833 ; 68th year.   B.
William Briggs, March 19, 1844 : 58th year.   R.
Roxanna, his wife, also relict of Walter Lyon, July 20, 1880 ; 85,
    10, 15.   R.
Georgie, son of James and Lizzie Brisbin, Sept. 18, 1865 ; 1, 0, 11.   R.
Prudence, daughter of Cyrus and Maria Brockway, March 24, 1846 ;
    17 years.   L.
Asa Brown, July 22, 1851 ; 55, 6, 22.   N. R.
James, son of Silas and Maranda Brown, April 26, 1837 ; 70, 0, 21.   A.
Ponclah, wife of George Brown, Jan. 17, 1860 ; 76, 9, 14.   F.
Silas Brown, Nov. 15, 1884 ; 77, 0, 21.   R.
Maranda, his wife, May 22, 1877 ; 65, 10, 5.   R.
Seth Brown, March 20, 1850 ; 67th year.   A.
Betsey, his wife, June 24, 1840 ; 58th year.   A.
Catharine, daughter of Seth and Emma Brownell, April 4, 1858 ;
    19, 6, 8.   W.
Ira, her brother, same day : 17, 10, 4.   W.

Emily Brownell, June 24, 1867 ; 18, 11, 24,   W.

Mary, daughter of J. and E. Brownell, Feb. 4, 1844 ; 2 years.   W.

James Brunney, 1865 ; 21 years.   L.

Gustave Buhler, Dec. 25, 1870 ; 21 years.   L.

Chloe, wife of Benjamin Burgess, Nov. 5, 1799 ; Dec. 16, 1883.   L.

Alzina, wife of Daniel W. Burgess, March 3, 1852 ; 22, 0, 21.   C.

Phœbe, wife of Daniel W. Burgess, June 19, 1864 ; 45, 7, 23.   C.

Horatio Bush, Nov. 22, 1866 ; 86, 5.   C.

Elenora Byce, April 28, 1851 ; 5 months 21 days.   F.

Hudson Calkins, July 30, 1840 ; May 23, 1872.   H.

Insign Calkins, April 19, 1844 ; 23d year.   H.

John Calkins, Aug. 11, 1851 ; 66 years.   H.

Phœbe J., his wife, Jan. 26, 1863 ; 76 years.   H.

John W. Calkins, Oct. 29, 1886 ; 70, 7, 15.   H.

Hannah, his wife, Sept. 7, 1818 ; Feb. 21, 1881.   H.

Mary J., daughter of William W. and A. Calkins, June 4, 1863 ;
   4, 7, 20.   H.

James Campbell, March 5, 1814 ; Dec. 22, 1869.   E.

Eleanor, his wife, Wicklow, Ireland, April 17, 1814 ; Oct. 28, 1889.   E.

Loiza, daughter of William Campbell, Aug. 11, 1827 ; 1, 5, 20.   F.

Roy, son of A. B. and H. A. Campbell, April 11, 1883 ; Sept. 26,
   1886.   F.

Stephen Cane, Nov. 26, 1860 ; 46, 9.   A.

Infant son of Stephen and Elizabeth Cane, July 29, 1852.   A.

Jacob Carkner, May 5, 1871 ; 69, 1, 15.   B.

Stephen Carr, May 6, 1854 ; 70, 7, 7.   R.

Amaziah T. Carrier, June 15, 1872 ; 62, 7.   L.

Mary, Nov. 6, 1859 ; 19, 9, 1.   L.

William Seward, Aug. 3, 1862 ; 24, 0, 28.   L.

Elbert E. (M. D.), Aug. 19, 1870 ; 28, 0, 18.   L.

Elizabeth, wife of Abner Carter, Feb. 22, 1855 ; 52, 10, 13.   H.

Mary A., daughter of Henry and Huldah Carter, Feb. 22, 1848 ;
   1, 2, 13.   H.

Sarah E., their daughter, July 3, 1849 ; 7 months, 29 days.   H.

Willie, son of W. and J. Casselmore, Feb. 27, 1862 ; 2, 1, 27.   W.

Calista, wife of George Catchpole, Oct. 17, 1872 ; 39 years.   R.

Susan, wife of James Catchpole, Feb. 25, 1866 ; 77, 1, 2.   R.

Nathaniel Center, May 18, 1845 ; 56 years.   C.

Addie, wife of Judson Chaddock, March 20, 1874 ; 29, 8, 10.   R.

Alonzo Chaddock, July 22, 1822—Dec. 12, 1890.   L.

Wesley Chaddock, Dec. 17, 1861 ; 26, 8, 23.   L.

Knowlton W., his son, Jan. 1, 1866 ; 5, 2, 25.   L.

William Chaddock, April 1, 1883 ; 72, 0, 23 ;   R.

Mercy E., daughter of William and L. Chaddock, May 4, 1849 :
    5, 2, 20.   N. R.

Winfield Chaddock, Dec. 28, 1873 ; 47, 8, 16.   L.

Amanda Mason, his wife, March 8, 1859 ; 26, 9, 10.   L.

William Chaddock, Oct. 27, 1854 ; 68, 7, 10.   L.

Dorothea Chaddock, his wife, July 9, 1876 ; 87 years.   L.

Nettie, wife of Rev. D. O. Chamberlayne, and daughter of Rev.
    Charles Baldwin, 1860—1891.   R.

Abby, wife of James Chambers, Nov. 11, 1882 ; 77th year.   F.

Flavia E., wife of Levi B. Chase, May 31, 1833—Nov. 9, 1856.   R.

John P. Chatterson, Oct. 20, 1849 ; 56, 0, 12.   Hu.

Cynthia, his wife, July 15, 1859 ; 58, 10, 10.   Hu.

Mary, daughter of above, Dec. 25, 1870 ; 42, 8, 10.   Hu.

Mary, wife of Betts Chatterson, July 16, 1846 ; 85 years.   C.

James Clapp, Sept. 18, 1828 ; 50, 3, 11.   F.

Elizabeth Clary, Oct. 3, 1887 ; 82 years.   R.

Samuel Clary, May 20, 1845 ; 66th year.   S. S.

Christina, his wife, April 28, 1846 ; 65th year.   S. S.

Harvey Closs, April 25, 1815—Jan. 16, 1886.   R.

Children of H. and E. H. Closs :
    Mary, Aug. 31, 1837—Aug. 31, 1837.   R.
    Ellen H., July 19, 1845—Aug. 16, 1846.   R.

John Closs, Feb. 18, 1793—Feb. 16, 1832.   R.

Hannah, his wife, April 30, 1794—Sept. 26, 1831.   R.

Children of J. and H. Closs :
    E. Adelia, Dec. 25, 1825—Jan. 16, 1848.   R.
    Anjenet, Dec. 28, 1828—Oct. 30, 1853.   R.

Rebecca A., daughter of David and Polly Closs, Oct. 6, 1833 ; 2, 3, 8.   F.

Calista L. Cobb, Feb. 14, 1827 ; 13, 6, 18.   W.

Fanny, wife of John M. Cobb, June, 1826 ; 43d year.   W.

Jonathan Colborn, March 14, 1857 ; 88 years.   F.

Hannah, his wife, June, 22, 1857 ; 81 years.   F.

Catharine, daughter of James and Mary Colborn, April 29, 1832 ;
    14, 1, 18.   F.

Charles W., son of same, March 13, 1851 ; 9, 3, 17.   F.

Jonathan, son of same, fell at siege of Fort Donelson, Feb. 13, 1862 ;
    29 years.   F.

Simeon Colborn, July 4, 1855 ; 18, 11, 15.   F.

John H. Cole, April, 1841 ; 1, 6.   R.

Minerva, daughter of William and Susan Cole, May 23, 1844 ;
    9, 7, 20.   C.

Thaddeus Collins, Sept. 4, 1828 ; 65th year.   R.

Esther, his wife, July 27, 1844 ; 78th year.   R.

Thaddeus Collins, Oct. 27, 1865 ; 72, 10, 26.   C.
Harriet, his wife, July 25, 1874 ; 74, 6, 16.   C.
Angeline, wife of David E. Converse, Jan. 31, 1886 ; 54 years.   R.
Charles Converse, May 30, 1861 : 47, 7, 16.   Y.
Daniel E. Converse, Nov. 19, 1826—May 30, 1889.   R.
Horace Converse, May 28, 1847 ; 63 years.   Y.
Horace, son of H. and Abigail Converse, Aug. 15, 1844.   Y.
Charles H., son of same, Feb. 10, 1853.   Age of both obscure.   Y.
Amanda, daughter of G. H. and S. A. Coon, Feb. 7, 1857 ; 6 months,
    26 days.   A.
Marilla, daughter of same, May 14, 1857 : 10 months.   A.
Martha, daughter of same, Oct. 14, 1849; 9 months, 1 day.   A.
Charles, son of same, Sept. 15, 1853 ; 8 months, 18 days.   A.
Jacob I. Coon, July 10, 1852: 70, 6, 8.   A.
Catharine, his wife, Sept. 6, 1865 ; 78, 2, 24.   A.
Sophia, wife of Hiram Coon, Feb. 24, 1859 ; 40 years.   A.
Bertie, their son, Sept. 17, 1858 ; 1, 6.   A.
Mary G., their daughter, Jan. 12, 1855 ; 9, 10, 19.   A.
John S. Cornwall, Sept. 28, 1854 ; 54, 4, 19.   F.
Anna, his wife, and daughter of Alexander and Sarah Harper, Sept. 3,
    1859 ; 50, 2, 26.   W.
Rebecca Cornwall, July 22, 1851 ; 37th year.   F.
Solomon Cornwall, Aug. 27, 1852 : 65 years.   F.
Shubail H. Cornwall, son of Solomon and Lucy, Dec. 23, 1849 ;
    24, 7, 16.   F.
Clarissa Covell, Sept. 28, 1889 ; 76 years.   R.
Ida, daughter of Abram and Helen Covell, Sept. 27, 1870 ; 3 months,
    3 days.   R.
James Covell, April 15, 1872 ; 82, 10, 10.   R.
Ann, his wife, May 6, 1863 ; 74, 4, 8.   R.
Jane R., wife of Charles Covell, April 23, 1884 ; 42 years.   R.
James Cowan, June 21, 1842 ; 72 years.   R.
Frances, his wife, Sept. 9, 1845 : 73 years.   R.
Mordecai Cox, Sept. 17, 1878 ; 60, 0, 17.   R.
Lovina, his wife, May 11, 1863 ; 34, 8, 14.   R.
George F., their son, July 30, 1875 ; 12, 8, 10.   R.
Willie A., son of M. and Stella Cox, July 20, 1884 ; 5 months, 15
    days.   R.
Benjamin Craft, Nov. 23, 1858 ; 79, 5, 1.   S. S.
Elizabeth, his wife, Sept. 9, 1861 ; 81, 6.   S. S.
Pine Craft, Sept. 23, 1867 : 66, 3, 1.   S. S.
Squaire B., son of Benjamin and Lucy Craft, Jr., March 17, 1849 ;
    7 months, 14 days.   S. S.

Daniel Crampton, Sept. 14, 1832 ; 47 years.   W.

Sarah Ann, daughter of Joseph C. and Sarah M. Crandall, May 29, 1842 ; 5, 3, 29.   F.

Helen, daughter of same, June 5. 1842 ; 2, 6, 17.   F.

Mary, daughter of same, June 2, 1842 ; 2 months, 21 days.   F.

Clarissa, wife of Adam Crisler, Aug. 11, 1876 ; 54, 1, 1.   R.

William A., son of Jeremiah and Catharine Crisler, Sept. 26, 1865 ; 5 months, 28 days.   R.

Isaac Crydenwise, Aug. 28, 1831 ; 31st year.   R.

Isaac, son of Isaac and Sophia Crydenwise, Sept. 17, 1830—Oct. 27, 1850.   R.

Isaac Curtis, Dec. 7, 1845 ; 31, 5.   C.

Melvin D., son of Prentice and Margaret J. Cushman, May 31, 1846; 2 months.   B.

Anna Maria, wife of Peter Darling, Sept. 24, 1860 ; 50, 11, 28.   A.

David C. Day, Co. B, 160th N. Y. Inf., Feb. 13, 1879 ; 49 years.   W.

John H. Deady, killed by the running away of a span of horses, May 5, 1848 ; 17, 3, 18.   C.

John Q. Deady, Sept. 28, 1856 ; 62, 0, 19.   C.

Thomas Deady, Feb. 1, 1847 ; 27, 1, 6.   C.

Lucy Lemira, wife of P. B. Decker, May 3, 1852 ; 28 years.   E.

Charles E., their son, July 30, 1847 ; 1, 11, 27.   E.

Francis L. DeLong, July 19, 1851 : 58, 9, 15.   Hu.

Sarah, his wife, Jan. 14, 1884 ; 88, 9, 27.   Hu.

Francis DeLong, March 18, 1853 ; 35, 1, 17.   Hu.

John DeLong, 9th N. Y. H. A., at Winchester, Va., Oct. 14, 1864 ; 32, 3, 14 ;   Hu.

Alonzo H., son of Henry L. and Amanda L. Demsin, Aug. 22, 1847 ; 1, 5, 2.   W.

Caroline, wife of William Desmond, Feb. 24, 1859 ; 26, 5.   F.

James, their son, March 23, 1860 ; 4, 7.   F.

John Desmond, June 23, 1859 ; 67 years.   F.

Catharine, his wife, March 29, 1835 ; 42d year.   F.

John, their son, Aug. 1, 1836 ; 1, 4, 6.   F.

Mary, wife of John Desmond, Jan. 10, 1845 ; 43d year.   F.

Martha A., their daughter, May 30, 1844 ; 3, 8, 3.   F.

Charles, their son, June 28, 1852 ; 5, 9, 10.   F.

Eliza A., their daughter, Aug. 13, 1852 ; 14, 1.   F.

Michael Desmond, Oct. 2, 1848 ; 52d year.   F.

Norah, his wife, July 2, 1863 ; 70 years.   F.

Mary, their daughter, Oct. 9, 1848 ; 13 years.   F.

William Desmond, Dec. 21, 1849 : 42, 8, 21.   F.

Michael, son of William and Lucinda Desmond, Sept. 28, 1852; 3, 1, 7.   F.

27

Catharine, their daughter, Oct. 1, 1852 ; 5, 4, 6.   F.
Charles, their son, Oct. 2, 1852 ; 9, 7, 20.   F.
William L., son of William and Lucy Desmond, March, 11, 1873 ;
   13, 2.   F.
Charles H., son of George and S. M. Deuel, Feb. 8, 1863 ; 7, 5, 21.   F.
Peter, son of Peter C. and Eveline Devoe, July 5, 1842 ; 2, 1, 12.   H.
Safety, wife of Joseph Dexter, July 15, 1858 ; 80, 11.   W.
Martin C., son of George and Lois E. Dickinson, Jan. 11, 1849 ;
   10 months.   R.
Son of R. D. and H. F. Dickinson, Sept. 23, 1861 ; 3, 2, 7.   R.
John Dickson, April 25, 1788—Jan. 15, 1863.   R.
Betsey, his wife, Nov. 27, 1797—Feb. 28, 1849.   R.
John J. Dickson, M. D., May 25, 1807—Feb. 15, 1874.   R.
Sophia L., his wife, Feb. 10, 1811—April 7, 1848.   R.
William Dinsmore, April 13, 1861 ; 57, 4, 10.   A.
Mary Tibbets, his wife, July 24, 1878 ; 72, 1, 26.   A.
William Arthur, their son, at Sutler's Creek, Cal., May 11, 1873 ;
   43, 1, 17.   A.
Mary Jane, their daughter, Aug. 17, 1855; 22, 1, 1.   A.
Abel Dixon, Co. G, 9th N. Y. H. A., April 29, 1864 ; 23 years.   Y.
Albert, son of G. and S. Dixon, March 31, 1877 ; 13, 0, 17.   Y.
George S. Doolittle, March 22, 1866 ; 53, 1.   H.
Stephen Doolittle, May 4, 1816 ; 62 years.   H.
Polly, his wife, Nov. 4, 1850 ; 65 years.   H.
Stephen S., son of George and T. C. Doolittle, July 4, 1856 ; 11
   months, 15 days.   H.
John Doty, Oct. 11, 1809—Oct. 29, 1881.   Hn.
Emmeline B., his wife, Oct. 9, 1829—Sept. 2, 1883.   Hn.
Sarah Doty, June 25, 1813—April 15, 1860.   Hu.
William W. Doty, Oct. 5, 1864—April 17, 1886.   Hu.
Asahel Dowd, Jan. 25, 1855 ; 80, 5, 21.   Hu.
Archie Dunbar, Dec. 4, 1876 ; 80 years.   Y.
Catharine, wife of H. Dunbar, May 5, 1877 ; 70 years.   Y.
Harriet C., wife of John Dunbar, March 16, 1860 ; 27 years.   Y.
Charles H., their son, March 5, 1860; 10 years.   Y.
Aldice C., their son, May 28, 1862 ; 2, 2, 20.   Y.
William Dunbar, June 25, 1864; 51, 2, 4.   Y.
Ann, wife of Morgan Dunham, June 30, 1861 ; 39 years.   R.
Elmore E., son of H. C. and L. Dunham, March 17, 1853—July 13,
   1860.   F.
Emeranca, daughter of H. C. and C. Dunham, Feb. 25, 1846 ; 3
   months.   F.
Eveline, daughter of S. W. and S. M. Dunham, Nov. 2, 1883 ; 5, 1, 27.   R.

Thomas Drakeford, July 11, 1849 ; 26, 4, 7.   R.
Elizabeth, wife of John Dratt, July 22, 1854 ; 82, 5, 23.   B.
Artelissa Drown, Aug. 31, 1885 ; 47, 5.   R.
Hannah S., wife of John A. Drown, July 14, 1878 ; 52, 3, 4.   R.
Napoleon B. Drown, Sept. 13, 1875 ; 38 years.   Hu.
Thomas J. Drown, Co. D, 67th N. Y. Inf., U. S. General Hospital,
    David's Island, N. Y., Nov. 15, 1862 ; 28, 6. 11.   Hu.
Holloway Drury, July 15, 1864 ; 79 years.   Hu.
Holloway Drury, Nov. 26, 1879 ; 92 years.   L.
Alexander Edmonds, Dec. 31, 1856 ; 70, 4, 3.   H.
Clark Eldred, Feb. 5, 1805—Aug. 18, 1889.   Hu.
Elsie J. Eldred, adopted daughter of M. C. and M. Vandercook,
    Aug. 23, 1851 ; 16th year.   F.
Charlie O., son of E. M. and S. A. Ellinwood, April, 1886 ; 1, 2, 4.   R.
Chester Ellinwood, April 1, 1877 ; 84, 3, 10.   E.
Sophronia, his wife, Aug. 26, 1866 ; 67, 0, 1.   E.
David Ellinwood, Nov. 30, 1883 ; 60 years.   R.
Mary Jane, his wife. June 15, 1884 ; 62 years.   R.
Ensign W. Ellinwood, Oct. 26, 1818—Oct. 26, 1889.   E.
Catharine R., his wife, May 3, 1822—April 17, 1888.   E.
Jennie, their daughter, Oct. 3, 1861 ; 18, 9, 28.   E.
Alice Irene, their daughter, Aug. 4, 1847 ; 1, 8, 19.   E.
Irene P., daughter of E. C. and M. E. Ellinwood, July 23, 1870—
    Oct. 27, 1884.   E.
Jonathan Ellinwood, Aug. 3, 1842 ; 76, 3, 28.   E.
Naomi, his wife, April 28, 1840 ; 72, 10, 3.   E.
Lucius Ellinwood, Feb. 26, 1884 ; 82 years.   E.
Lucy, his wife, Dec. 20, 1838 ; 34 years.   E.
Mahala, his second wife, Sept. 27, 1864 ; 49, 7, 16.   E.
William S., their son, July 23, 1847 ; 2, 0, 18.   E.
Lucy Ann, their daughter, July 27, 1847 ; 4, 2, 24.   E.
Mary, wife of G. W. Ellinwood, Sept. 9, 1849 ; 29th year.   E.
Jane, his second wife. Jan. 26, 1881 ; 66, 0, 4.   E.
Mary E., daughter of O. E. and E. E. Ellinwood, April 27, 1851—
    Sept. 29, 1854.   R.
Infant son of same, Feb. 4, 1857—Feb. 21, 1857.   R.
Samuel Ellis Ellinwood, April 18, 1879 ; 82 years.   R.
Submit, his wife, May 21, 1866 ; 64 years.   R.
Valorous Ellinwood, Dec. 26, 1853 ; 48, 4. 4.   F.
Sarah M., his wife, April 14, 1845 ; 40th year.   E.
Amy, his second wife, also wife of Samuel Garlick, July 2, 1856 ;
    16, 6, 4.   E.
William Ellinwood, April 11, 1841 ; 31, 8, 27.   E.

Mary Melissa, daughter of William and Clarissa L. Ellinwood,
    Aug. 26, 1846 ; 3, 1, 14. E.
George Ellsworth, March 28, 1840 ; 84 years. R.
Sarah, his wife, April 2, 1849 ; 79 years. R.
Jane, wife of Zechariah Esmond, March 13, 1838 ; 31, 11, 19. C.
Jane, wife of C. W. Fairbank, April 11, 1841 ; 34th year. R.
Eber, their son, drowned June 12, 1853 ; 17th year. R.
Francis M., son of C. W. Fairbank, Jan., 1843 ; 21 months. R.
Thomas D. Farnsworth, Aug. 4, 1890 ; 64 years. R.
Augustus Featherly, Co. G, 3d L. A., April 2, 1886 ; 40 years. Hn.
John Featherly, died about 1843. Y.
Mary, his wife, July 29, 1840 ; 81 years. Y.
Mary A., daughter of N. and E. Feek, Sept. 6, 1847 ; 1, 3, 9. N. R.
David Ferguson, Oct. 24, 1867 ; 75, 8, 25. F.
Sarah, his wife, July 9, 1873 ; 84 years. . F.
Their infant, Jan. 28, 1811. F.
Stephen, their son, Aug. 13, 1826 ; 3, 8. F.
Charles, their son, Aug. 18, 1821 : 1. 7. F.
Sarah, their daughter, Feb. 20, 1831 ; 9 months, 2 days. F.
Deborah, wife of Nicholas Ferguson, and daughter of J. and S. Van
    Amburgh, Oct. 14, 1831 ; 33, 7. F.
Eliza, wife of Abraham Ferguson, Sept. 13, 1859 ; 52, 2, 1. F.
Jacob Ferguson, Nov. 12, 1852 ; 63, 1, 13. F.
Fanny, his wife, Dec. 24, 1870 ; 72 years. F.
John Ferguson, Nov. 12, 1842 ; 25th year. F.
John Ferguson, Nov. 30, 1840 ; 75 years. F.
Martha, wife of Stephen Ferguson, Sept. 21, 1833 : 36th year. F.
Sarah Ann, wife of Charles Ferguson, March 11, 1847 ; 21st year. F.
Alice M., wife of H. J. Ferris, May 11, 1874 ; 27, 2, 11. R.
James H. Ferris, May 27, 1885 ; 80 years. R.
Franklin Finch, July 3, 1876 ; 72, 1, 5. F.
Matilda, his wife, March 16, 1851 ; 40, 9, 10. F.
Jeremiah S. Finch, Dec. 13, 1859 ; 75, 2, 9. C.
Eunice, his wife, Oct. 24, 1864 ; 80, 2, 10. C.
John Finch, Jan. 29, 1874 : 58, 10, 27. C.
Mary E., daughter of J. and Diademia C. Finch, Feb. 8, 1859 ; 15, 0, 8. C.
Louisa J., daughter of D. S. and M. A. Finch, Sept. 23, 1855 ; 4, 11, 3. B.
Martha, wife of John Finch, Oct. 28, 1847 : 86th year. F.
Reynolds Finch, June 20, 1870 : 75th year. F.
Phœbe, his wife, Aug. 18, 1868 ; 69th year. F.
Children of William and C. A. Finch : C.
    Della G., Jan. 10, 1865—Oct. 6, 1867.
    Elvina M., April 26, 1871—Nov. 19, 1871.

Children of Christian and Frances Finch :   R.
    Alice F., Oct. 27, 1878 ; 10 months.
    James F., Oct. 16, 1881 ; 17 days.
    John H., April 15, 1875 ; 3, 1, 20.
    Rosa, Sept. 22, 1874 ; 6 months, 7 days.
Susannah, wife of William Fisher, Nov. 23, 1890 ; 66 years.   R.
Dalinda C., wife of William B. Fletcher, Jan. 26, 1832 ; 23, 0, 28.   B.
Rachel Caroline, daughter of Russell and Rachel Fletcher, Jan. 30,
    1826 ; 6, 6.   B
Elizur Flint, Feb. 1, 1884 ; 91 years.   N. R.
Roxy, his wife, May 16, 1865 ; 70 years.   N. R.
Roxy M., their daughter, June 16, 1828 ; 1 year.   N. R.
Pomeroy Flint, Nov. 3, 1819 ; 29 years.   N. R.
Sarah M. Flint, Sept. 12, 1824 ; 25, 3, 12.   W.
Elizabeth Ford, adopted daughter of W. and C. Pease, March 21,
    1851 ; 11, 2, 29.   F.
Phœbe M., wife of J. S. Forncrook, and daughter of D. and B. Pettys,
    July 25, 1858 ; 23, 11, 25.   W.
Henry Fosmire, July 16, 1840 ; 50, 4, 27.   R.
Hannah, his wife, April 3, 1817 ; 46, 7, 22.   R.
Maria H., their daughter, June 7, 1854 ; 15, 9, 21.   R.
John Fosmire, Dec. 20, 1863 ; 56, 9, 24.   R.
Anna B., wife of Frederick Fox, Aug. 22, 1867 ; 23, 8, 28.   F.
Delbert, son of Louis and Mary Fox, April 30, 1877—May 27, 1877.   F.
Edward, son of Louis and Mary Fox, April 30, 1877—June 15, 1877.   F.
Louis P. Fox, Nov. 15, 1877 ; 69, 10, 21.   F.
Magdalen A., his wife, March 17, 1880 ; 68, 3, 25.   F.
William, their son, Oct. 12, 1875 ; 19, 11, 28.   F.
Levine, wife of Jared Frazier, Sept. 25, 1849 ; 67 years.   H.
Sarah H. A., wife of B. M. Fredendall, Sept. 9, 1884 ; 38, 3.   R.
David Freer, April 24, 1848 ; 79, 4, 10.   W.
Fanny, wife of Benjamin Frink, Oct. 18, 1834 ; 52 years.   F.
Mary, wife of Ralph Fuller, Aug. 19, 1829 ; 28 years.   E.
Mary, wife of John Fullmer, Jan. 7, 1841 ; 39, 4, 19.   E.
Thaddeus W., son of S. W. and M. A. Gage, March 17, 1873 ; 14,
    1, 14.   R.
Samuel Gardner, May 3, 1885 ; 64, 6.   R.
Hannah, his wife, July 19, 1860 ; 40, 5, 6.   R.
Pearley E., their daughter, Sept. 30, 1855 ; 1 year.   R.
Caroline, wife of William Garlick, May 10, 1881 ; 72 years.   R.
Emma A., only daughter of J. L. and M. T. Garlick, Dec. 6, 1863 ;
    3, 8, 13.   R.
Ezekiel Garlick, June 4, 1832 ; 37 years.   R.

Lydia, his wife, Sept. 3, 1828 ; 31 years. R.

Sally G., wife of Henry Garlick, Feb. 10, 1872 ; 42 years. R.

Frank, their son, Oct. 17, 1860 ; 4, 7, 5. R.

Captain Samuel Garlick, April 28, 1843 ; 80th year. R.

Huldah, his wife, Nov. 15. 1878 ; 88, 6. R.

Samuel Garlick, Sept. 24, 1871 ; 81 years.' R.

Ida, daughter of L. B. and B. Garrison, April 22, 1859 ; 7, 7, 2. A.

Jeremiah Gatchell, April 12, 1859 ; 41 years. Y.

Marion E. Gaylord, son of Mrs. R. M. Thomas, April 13, 1840—
    July 23, 1850. R.

Benjamin Genung, Aug. 20, 1806—March 23, 1888. R.

John S. Gildersleeve, April 17, 1865 ; 59, 11, 14. W.

Melinda, his wife, Nov. 7, 1866 ; 58, 6, 25. W.

William S., their son, Sept. 16, 1848 ; 5 months. W.

Antoinette E., their daughter, July 15, 1850 ; 3 months. W.

Asahel Gillett, March 26, 1826 ; 75th year. N. R.

Mrs. B. Gillett, July 29, 1874 ; 79, 5, 10. Hu.

Charles Gillett. Co. D, 90th N. Y. Inf., Aug. 19, 1867 ; 24, 5, 11. E.

Isaac Gillett, Nov. 28, 1829 ; 45, 2, 1. Hu.

John Gillett, Aug. 30, 1819 ; 71, 1, 14. Hu.

John Gillett, Feb. 5, 1866 ; 59 years. L.

Lucy Mason, wife of John Henry Gillett, Dec. 7, 1880 ; 43, 9, 9. L.

Marquis N. Gillett. Oct. 3, 1847—July 27, 1876. L.

Eliza, wife of William Gordon. Nov. 5, 1865 ; 53 years. A.

Phœbe, their daughter, March 2, 1852 ; 7, 4, 6. A.

Phœbe, their daughter, Nov. 30, 1842 ; 2, 7, 5. A.

Alfred Graham, Co. A, 9th H. A., Dec. 27. 1871 ; 35 years. Hu.

Roxany, wife of Henry Graham, Dec. 9, 1841 ; 41st year. N. R.

Their infant daughter. N. R.

Susannah, wife of Nelson Graham, March 10, 1847—April 26, 1892. R.

Zachariah Graham, July 11, 1852 ; 51, 5, 18. Hu.

Lydia, his wife, Dec. 31, 1807—Dec. 11, 1886. Hu.

Naomy, wife of John B. Gray, Nov. 1, 1856 ; 29, 8, 3. F.

Bertha, daughter of William H. and Hannah Green. May 2, 1883 ;
    1 month, 11 days. Y.

Roswell Greene, May 30. 1862 ; 106, 1. 29. Hu.

Abel Grenell, Mar. 30. 1881 ; 89, 0, 3. F.

Rebecca, his wife, July 21. 1828 ; 28 years. F.

Polly M., his wife, Sept. 20, 1856 ; 50, 9, 16. F.

Rebecca Ann, their daughter, July 7, 1842 ; 2, 8, 9. F.

Andrew M., their son, Aug. 12, 1852 ; 10 months, 3 days. F.

George W., their son, July 8, 1857 ; 19, 8, 25. F.

Ada L., daughter of Abel and Rhoda Grenell, March 3. 1881; 23, 3, 9. F.

Mary, wife of Israel Grenell, June 22, 1873 ; 31, 8.   F.
Eva J., Sept. 22, 1868 ; 4 months, 7 days.   F.
Pearl A., Nov. 10, 1872 ; 2 months, 22 days.   F.
Mary, wife of Henry Grenell, Dec. 30, 1825 ; 26th year.   F.
Catharine, their daughter, Aug. 17, 1824 ; 10 months, 24 days.   F.
Sally, their daughter, July 17, 1826 ; 11 months, 7 days.   F.
Lucretia A., their daughter, Dec. 22, 1840 ; 18, 11.   F.
Ruth Ann, daughter of Henry and Adelia Grenell, June 5, 1852 ;
    19, 9, 24.   F.
Napoleon B., Feb. 21, 1829 ; 3 months, 7 days.   F.
Oliver J., Nov. 18, 1845 ; 2, 0, 3.   F.
John, Aug. 31, 1830 ; 8 months, 25 days.   F.
Napoleon B., Feb. 23, 1841 ; 1, 9.   F.

NOTE.—Abel and Henry Grenell were from Connecticut. The latter, who had three children by his first wife, Mary Patterson, and ten by his second, died Oct. 8, 1879, aged 84 years. Of these children, only two survive, one being Mrs. Stephen Weeks, of Rose. His son, Owen, died at 50, in 1885, in Phelps ; William, who died at 63, April 17, 1891, is buried here with his kin.

Lorenzo Griswold, March 4, 1852 ; 43d year.   F.
John W., son of Lorenzo and Elizabeth G., July 20, 1868 ; 20, 4, 13.   F.
Benjamin F., son of same, March 13, 1851 ; 11, 1, 25.   F.
Richard L., son of same, May 27, 1851 ; 1, 2, 9.   F.
Nelson Griswold, April 1, 1859 ; 48, 1, 16.   F.
William Griswold, Jan. 5, 1852 ; 65, 2, 25.   F.
Rebecca, his wife, Sept 22, 1868 ; 76, 9, 18.   F.
John Groeskopt, Co. K, 86th Inf., Dec. 16, 1884 ; 36 years.   W.
Amy, wife of Joseph P. Hall, Feb. 25, 1857 ; 22, 3, 14.   H.
Deborah, wife of Stephen Hall, June 19, 1839 ; 36 years.   H.
Deborah, their daughter, May 15, 1839 ; 1 month, 15 days.   H.
Elias Hall, Dec. 7, 1836 ; 45 years.   H.
Jane, his wife, July 22, 1854 ; 57, 6, 4.   H.
Elias T. Hall, Aug. 12, 1846 ; 26, 1, 29.   H.
Joshua Hall, Aug. 29, 1830 ; 44th year.   H.
Margaret Hall, June 28, 1854 ; 66, 5, 11.   H.
Mary C., daughter of A. S. and T. M. Hall, March 21, 1853 ; 14, 9, 24.   R.
Thomas Hall, Dec. 2, 1843 ; 80th year.   H.
Amy, his wife, Sept. 18, 1829 ; 64th year.   H.
Matilda, daughter of Alonzo and Marilla Hamilton, Oct. 18, 1877 ;
    1, 2, 27.   W.
John Harmon, Jan. 19, 1887 ; 88 years.   R.
Clarissa, his wife, May 30, 1876 ; 72 years.   R.
Almon Harper, June 3, 1828—April 3, 1884.   R.
Sally Ann, his wife, Aug. 1, 1832—Jan. 30, 1887.   R.

Everett B., their son, June 11, 1869—April 11, 1883.   R.
Buel Harper, April 10, 1855 ; 56, 9, 25.   W.
Daniel Harper, April 13, 1855 ; 61, 3, 23.   W.
Ameriah, son of Daniel and Mary Harper, Dec. 24, 1844 ; 21, 7, 13.   W.
Sarah, wife of A. Harper, March 22, 1842 ; 72, 5, 15.   W.
William H. Hart, Nov. 1, 1863; 22, 8, 2.   R.
William V. Havens, April 24, 1875 ; 95, 8, 21.   R.
Susan, his wife, March 12, 1848 ; 64, 4, 19.   R.
Henry Haviland, July 22, 1857 ; 57 years.   F.
His children :
 Charles, Aug. 29, 1830 ; 4 months, 7 days.
 Charles, March 30, 1840 ; 5 months, 26 days.
 John, Aug. 14, 1845 ; 4 months, 7 days.
 Katharine, Sept. 27, 1848 ; 12, 5, 29.
 Elizabeth, March 15, 1851 ; 7, 10. 14.
 Emma E., June 27, 1852 ; 1, 1. 9.
 John, Feb. 28, 1854 ; 5, 8, 1.
Daniel Hayford, Feb. 21, 1841 ; 54 years.   Hu.
Ruth, wife of Daniel Hayford, March 5, 1852 ; 56 years.   F.
L. Jenette, widow of B. W. Hazard, April 8, 1843 ; 40th year.   C.
Sally, wife of Andrew Healy, June 9, 1857 ; 58 years.   R.
Gideon Henderson, Sept. 12, 1869 ; 79, 11, 11.   L.
Deborah, his wife, May 5, 1876 ; 84, 9, 6.   L.
Rodney, son of Benjamin and Catharine D. Hendrick, April 11,
 1848 ; 1, 9, 3.   E.
Simeon Hendrix, Oct. 4, 1844 ; 69, 8, 2.   A.
Lovinia, his wife, Aug. 14, 1849 ; 75, 7, 10.   A.
Addison L., son of J. A. and M. A. Hetta, Feb. 10, 1866; 1, 7, 21.   R.
Martha I., daughter of same, Oct. 23, 1869 ; 1, 4, 9.   R.
Mary, wife of Thomas Hewson, Jan. 11, 1871 ; 62, 4, 26.   Y.
George H., their son, June 23, 1857 ; 15, 0, 28.   Y.
Moses Hickok, Dec. 6, 1826 ; 56, 8.   N. R.
Zervia Felton, his wife, Nov. 1, 1819 ; 39, 6.   N. R.
Joseph M., their son, Aug. 14, 1822 ; 20, 1.   N. R.
Caroline, their daughter, Sept. 3, 1819 ; 14, 6.   N. R.
William Hickok, Aug. 25, 1871 ; 71, 7.   R.
Sophia Gunn, his wife, July 12, 1881 ; 77, 0, 25.   R.
Sophronia, their daughter, June 18, 1868 ; 39 years.   R.
Esther, wife of Uriah T. Hill, July 17, 1867 ; 60 years.   R.
Mary S., wife of Curtis Hill, and daughter of Reuben and Hannah
 Sears, Feb. 2, 1794—Sept. 22, 1866.   R.
Ina S., daughter of C. D. and S. A. L. Hinman, Aug. 13, 1863 ; 3,
 3, 29.   R.

Jester L. Holbrook, Nov. 8, 1808—Aug. 27, 1882. R.
Margaret, his wife, April 9, 1814—May 1, 1887. R.
Franklin J., their son, Sept. 3, 1841—Dec. 8, 1842. R.
Silas Holcomb, Feb. 7, 1878 ; 81, 8. C.
Frelove R., his wife, Jan. 26, 1875 ; 80, 5. C.
Willard S., their son, April 17, 1853 ; 24, 6. C.
George Hollafolla, Feb. 5, 1878 ; 44, 6. R.
Lydia, wife of Jesse Hopping, Sept. 11, 1868 ; 89, 10, 5. R.
Martha Ann, wife of Jesse Hopping, Dec. 2, 1877 ; 70, 2, 11. R.
Edward Horn, Dec. 22, 1889; 88 years. R.
Lucinda, his wife, March 15, 1886 ; 78 years. R.
Anna Bell Horton, Aug. 28, 1881 ; 5, 9, 18. R.
Betsey, wife of Barzilla Howard, July 17, 1846 ; 70 years. H.
Frankie, son of F. R. and Carrie Howard, Sept. 20, 1882 ; 21 days. R.
William Howard, Jan. 8, 1818—May 14, 1891. R.
William H. Howard, March 20, 1855 ; 63, 2, 20. A.
Martha, his wife, Jan. 3, 1866 ; 67, 4, 20. A.
George Howland, Oct. 30, 1869 ; 48 years. R.
Harriet, his wife, May 24, 1850 ; 26, 3, 15. R.
Almira, wife of Alonzo Hubbard, and daughter of John and Betsey
    Kellogg, Jan. 31, 1856 ; 27, 3, 4. C.
John M., son of Alonzo and Almira Hubbard, July 18, 1853 ; 1
    month, 18 days. H.
Coral, daughter of A. and C. Hubbard, Sept. 15, 1864 ; 2, 9. H.
Jennie May, daughter of Civilian and Louisa Hubbard, Feb. 15,
    1874 ; 3, 7, 2, H.
Orestes Hubbard, Feb. 20, 1865 ; 74, 9, 14. H.
Sally, his wife, July 30, 1879 ; 85 years. H.
Phœbe, wife of Nodadiah Hubbard, May 27, 1821 ; 63 years. W.
Thankful, wife of same, Feb. 1, 1828 ; 75 years. W.
Amy, wife of Samuel B. Huffman, Aug. 9, 1847 ; 43, 0, 26. H.
Deborah, daughter of John and Eunice Huffman, May 17, 1834 ;
    1, 2, 25. B.
Jacob C. Huffman, Sept. 12, 1862 ; 73, 5. R.
Catharine, his wife, Dec. 18, 1869 ; 75, 4. R.
Eliza J., daughter of M. N. and S. Humphrey, Oct. 18, 1844 ; 2, 9, 5. W.
James O. Hunn, Aug. 14, 1861 ; 39, 4, 23. R.
Parson A. Hunn, June 10, 1868 ; 40, 9. R.
Harrison K., son of P. A. and M. A. Hunn, April 27, 1879 ;
    18, 10, 18. R.
Samuel Hunn, Aug. 16, 1795—May 28, 1875. R.
Sally, his wife, Nov. 16, 1803—Aug. 8, 1877. R.
Sophia, daughter of B. and T. Hurter, Aug. 16, 1863 ; 7, 1, 17. L.

Andrew Hutchings, Co. H, 9th H. A., Sept. 26, 1877 ; 72 years.   F.

Lydia, wife of Asa Hutchins, Dec. 16, 1862 ; 71 years.   R.

Loranda, daughter of John and Rohala Hyde, Dec. 31, 1835 ; 21
    years.   R.

Chester S. Irish, Oct. 23, 1839—Sept. 23, 1873.   C.

Lydia, wife of Bartlett James, March 20, 1838 ; 37, 0, 25.   A.

Nathan Jeffers, May 23, 1854 ; 63, 1, 23.   F.

Lucy, his wife, Feb. 21, 1837 ; 47th year.   F.

Lucy, daughter of Nathan and S. M. Jeffers, March 30, 1864 ; 12, 4, 6.   F.

James, son of same, Feb. 24, 1866 ; 18, 5.   F.

Nathan Jeffers, Jr., Oct. 2, 1852 ; 34, 5, 10.   R.

Eleanor, his daughter, Oct. 30, 1851 ; 1, 6, 2.   R.

Robert N. Jeffers, April 22, 1820—June 11, 1893.   R.

Mariah, his wife, Oct. 1, 1814—May 22, 1863.   R.

Robert, their son, Aug. 26, 1854—July 28, 1857.   R.

Roby, son of Henry and Mary Jeffers, May 14, 1879.   R.

Ira S., son of Theodore and Mary Jenkins, Jan. 27, 1854 : 1, 4.   H.

Alanson, son of A. and S. Jewell, Dec. 4, 1875 ; 23, 5, 5.   Y.

Maranda Barrett, wife of Frank Jewell, Dec. 6, 1887 ; 24, 4.   H.

Margaret D. Holcomb, wife of Francis M. Johnson, July 8, 1889 ;
    62 years.   C.

Harriet, wife of Samuel Jones, Nov. 28, 1832 ; 40th year.   C.

John E. Jones, April 12, 1812—Jan. 30, 1877.   C.

Frances H., his daughter, Feb. 20, 1864 ; 9, 7, 20.   C.

Peter F. Jones, Nov. 28, 1857 ; 51, 5, 18.   C.

Lieut. William Jones, Co. K, 44th Inf., May 14, 1862 ; 23, 4.   Hu.

Wyan Kanouse, May 16, 1824—Aug. 20, 1891.   R.

Benjamin Kellogg, July 6, 1779—Nov. 16, 1829.   C.

Pamelia, his wife, also wife of Ebenezer Pierce, Jan., 1862 : 83 years.   C.

Charles B. Kellogg, Feb. 11, 1854 ; 41, 0, 8.   C.

Elmer Lavern Kellogg, Oct. 29, 1860—July 25, 1887.   C.

John Kellogg, May 25, 1876 ; 74 years.   C.

Betsey, his wife, Oct. 14, 1807 —Aug. 11, 1886.   C.

Paulina, their daughter, Aug. 23, 1851 : 16, 6, 20.   C.

Lewis B. Kellogg, Oct. 28, 1835—Dec. 3, 1875.   C.

Mary A., daughter of E. B. and S. M. Kellogg, June 9, 1843 ;
    4, 7, 2.   C.

Charles Kelsey, Oct. 7, 1857 ; 75, 9, 24.   W.

Thomas King, Co. B, 27th Inf., Dec. 4, 1889 ; 54 years.   R.

Meigs Kirkland, Oct. 16, 1865 ; 71 years.   A.

Henry C. Klinck, Oct. 5, 1831—Sept. 28, 1876.   R.

Caroline A., his wife, June 30, 1831—Jan. 15, 1892.   R.

Amos, son of A. M. Knight, April 10, 1854 : 4, 9, 24.   W.

Alfred, son of A. M. Knight, Oct. 15, 1862; 11 months, 16 days.   W.
Erwin, son of A. M. Knight, Feb. 28, 1870 : 3, 9, 13.   W.
Hannah, wife of Simeon Knight, June 24, 1834 ; 63d year.   W.
Sarah, wife of George Knight, Oct. 29, 1878 ; 26 years.   W.
Orrin Lackey, Dec. 26, 1831; 40, 10, 4.   F.
Sarah, wife of Orrin Lackey, also of Jesse Lyman. Dec. 21, 1869 ;
   76 years.   R.
Lucy Ann, daughter of Orrin and Sarah Lackey, March 6, 1859 ;
   43, 9.   R.
Judd B., Jr., son of Judd B. and M. G. Lackey, Oct. 15, 1865 ;
   9, 8, 21.   R.
Sarah A., wife of Sanford G. Lackey, Nov. 2, 1849 ; 29, 4, 2.   F.
Mary L., wife of Rev. B. Ladd, March 26, 1848 ; 40th year.   R.
Ira Lake, Feb. 5, 1864 ; 66, 8, 6.   L.
Mary J., wife of Allen Lake, Feb. 4, 1861 ; 25, 9, 13.   F.
Wellington Lake, killed at the Wilderness, May 6, 1864 ; 27, 5, 12.   L.
Della, daughter of John and Jane E. Lamb, Oct. 17, 1864 ; 11. 10, 18.   R.
Fidelia, daughter of William and Almira Lamb, Sept. 10, 1848 ;
   6 months.   R.
Harvey M., son of same, March 10, 1843 ; 9 months. 10 days.   R.
Zenette, daughter of same, Aug. 24, 1849 ; 3, 0, 28.   R.
Isaac Lamb, May 22, 1862 : 86, 5.   N. R.
Sally, his wife, July 4, 1846 : 70th year.   N. R.
Thomas Lambert, Oct. 11, 1818—March 9, 1884.   R.
John Lamoreaux, Nov. 29, 1860 ; 75, 1, 20.   C.
Martha, his wife, March 8, 1865 ; 76, 4, 7.   C.
Susan, their daughter, June 19, 1854 ; 30, 10, 21.   C.
Peter Lamoreaux, Dec. 22, 1850: 89, 6, 20.   C.
Elizabeth, his wife, Sept. 6, 1845 : 84th year.   C.
Barbara A., wife of Edward D. Lampson, June 6, 1816—Aug. 8, 1891.   R.
Margaret I., daughter of H. P. Lampson, May 10, 1858 ; 11, 3, 15.   R.
Polly, wife of David F. Lampson, April 5, 1846 ; 54, 1.   R.
Frankie, son of J. and S. M. Lane, April 27, 1880 ; 4 months.   R.
Johnson V. Lane, Sept. 21. 1840—July 5, 1890.   R.
Frankie, his son, Dec. 19. 1879—April 27, 1880.   R.
Nancy, wife of Myron Langley. June 15, 1849 ; 40, 4, 7.   R.
Julia, their daughter, Oct. 1, 1850 ; 16, 0, 8.   R.
Franklin Lee. Oct. 9, 1853 : 20, 7, 5.   E.
Joel N. Lee, March 5, 1807—Oct. 20, 1880.   R.
Laurissa A., his wife, Jan. 20. 1801—Dec. 7, 1876.   R.
Lyman Lee, April 18, 1785—Jan. 1, 1873.   E.
Betsey, his wife, Aug. 3, 1786—Jan. 13, 1873.   E.
Serotia, daughter of Lyman and Mary Lee, Jan. 6, 1846 ; 36, 1, 11.   E.

Mary, wife of Joel Lee, Feb. 28, 1855 ; 93, 8, 13.   E.
Harvey, son of L. and S. Legg, Aug. 23, 1854 ; 1, 9.   R.
Leonard Lerock, July 4, 1859 ; 55, 9, 21.   R.
Rosetta Lerock, Jan. 4, 1890 ; 71 years.   R.
In memory of William H. Lerock, killed in the Custer Massacre,
    June 25, 1876; 22, 10, 11.   R.
Susan M. Lindley, April 14, 1832—Oct. 23, 1866.   R.
William H. L. Lindley, July 9, 1866—July 23, 1887.   R.
Eunice W., wife of James Livermore, Aug. 15, 1870 ; 74, 2, 26.   C.
Hannah, wife of William Loryman, Nov. 22, 1858 ; 76 years.   F.
Anna, daughter of N. and L. Lovejoy, Dec. 24, 1860 ; 22, 9, 1.   L.
Daniel Lovejoy, Feb. 24, 1861 ; 58, 8.   L.
Sophia, his wife, Sept. 20, 1867 ; 63, 8.   L.
Catharine, their daughter, June 26, 1833 ; 2, 10, 10.   L.
Dwight B., son of Darius and S. S. Lovejoy, Nov. 18, 1853 ; 3, 1, 8.   L.
James Lovejoy, March 23, 1870 ; 42 years.   L.
Parmer Lovejoy, Oct. 4, 1830 ; 63 years.   L.
Esther, his wife, Oct. 7, 1858 ; 88, 3, 5.   L.
Silas Lovejoy, April 7, 1877 ; 86, 1, 5.   L.
Anna, his wife, Dec. 20, 1873 ; 80, 7, 2.   L.
Marion, their daughter, July 9, 1833 ; 2, 4, 24.   L.
Herman, their son, May 10, 1831 ; 1, 5.   L.
William, their son, Feb. 7, 1830 ; 7, 11, 7.   L.
William Lovejoy, May 16, 1865 ; 67, 6, 16.   L.
Sophia, his wife, April 4, 1878 ; 84, 9, 9.   L.
Selecta, their daughter, Sept. 30, 1831 ; 1, 3.   L.
William B., son of H. R. and S. J. Lovejoy, March 13, 1853 ; 2, 7, 13.   L.
Egbert, son of same, June 15, 1849 ; 1, 7, 9.   L.
Mary L., daughter of Hiram and S. M. Loveless, Aug. 19, 1850 ; 4
    months, 20 days.   C.
Harriet, wife of H. Lovett, Feb. 20, 1839 ; 27, 10, 14.   A.
Ella D., daughter of J. and E. Lyman, March 26, 1874 ; 17, 10.   R.
Ellen H., daughter of L. A. and M. Lyman, Jan. 21, 1851 ; 11
    months, 23 days.   F.
Henry G. Lyman, March 10, 1850 ; 30, 6, 12.   R.
Jesse Lyman, Aug. 17, 1863 ; 69, 9, 11.   F.
Betsey, his wife, May 4, 1831 ; 37, 10, 20.   F.
Levi A. Lyman, Sept. 27, 1851 ; 38, 9, 15.   F.
Rebecca, wife of Milo S. Lyman, Nov. 15, 1826—May 18, 1892.   R.
John W. Lyman, their son, Feb. 11, 1858—May 23, 1881.   R.
Samuel Lyman, Aug. 10, 1794—May 28, 1877.   R.
Clementine, his wife, July 7, 1793—June 25, 1870.   R.
Mary Lyman, May 16, 1821—March 27, 1885.   R.

Darwin A., son of Lothrop M. and Lois P. Lyon, July 22, 1846 ; 1, 3, 4.   W.

Parley Lyon, March 17. 1846 ; 57, 6, 29.   R.

Philo F., his daughter, July 20, 1849 ; 27, 6, 21.   R.

Deacon Walter Lyon, Sept. 8. 1874 ; 84, 0, 19.   W.

Lucretia, his wife, Nov. 8, 1846 ; 59th year.   W.

Elmira, their daughter, Nov. 29, 1850 ; 21, 6, 10.   W.

Jane A. McCamby, Sept. 3, 1853 ; 38, 4, 22.   W.

Charles G. McCarthy, Sept. 16, 1852 ; 31, 1, 2.   A.

Leonora F., his daughter, Jan. 8, 1854 ; 3, 9, 22.   A.

William G. McCoy, Co. C, 111th Inf., Aug. 29, 1863 ; 24 years.   R.

Elijah McGraw, June 23, 1851 ; 47, 2, 5.   B.

Jeremiah, son of Elijah and Phœbe McGraw, July 20, 1847; 18, 11, 10. B.

Franklin, son of same, Nov. 14, 1847 ; 7 months, 10 days.   B.

Isaac McIntosh, March 13, 1838 ; 25, 2.   A.

James McIntosh, Sept. 23, 1828—April 28, 1892.   R.

Jairus B. McKoon, June 25, 1823—Sept. 3, 1885.   C.

Martin W., son of J. B. and R. M. McKoon, Aug. 17, 1855 ; 3, 5, 11.   C.

William McKoon, June 14, 1870 ; 78, 7, 21.   C.

Lucy, his wife, June 11, 1854 ; 64, 9, 22.   C.

Emeline, wife of D. McMullen, and daughter of Minoris and Margaret Smith, July 21, 1849 ; 26, 8.   W.

John McWharf, April 5, 1869 ; 95 years.   R.

Hannah, his wife, Nov. 3, 1872 ; 88 years.   R.

Alonzo A., son of D. A. and E. A. Mallery, Sept. 27, 1851 ; 2, 5, 19. F.

Thomas Markham, April 10, 1884 ; 70, 6.   R.

Daniel Marquat, Co. F, 111th Inf., May 20, 1877 ; 34 years.   Y.

Henry Marquat, March 9, 1814—April 17, 1887.   Y.

Philip Marquat, March 11, 1861 ; 48, 6, 7.   Y.

Caroline A. A., his wife, July 4, 1851 ; 23, 2.   Y.

Chester, their son, Nov. 21, 1852 ; 1, 6, 26.   Y.

Verma J. Marquat, June 24, 1881 ; 3, 10, 21.   Y.

Leaman H. Marquat, May 30, 1882 ; 2, 0, 29.   Y.

Hannah J., wife of John Marriott, Nov. 20, 1871 ; 36, 2, 14.   F.

Amos Marsh, Nov. 9, 1866 ; 69, 10, 9.   C.

Polly, his wife, Dec. 27, 1873 ; 74, 10.   C.

Lucinda, daughter of, June 19, 1874 ; 32, 9.   C.

H. D. Mason, June 18, 1805—Dec. 24, 1889.   L.

Elizabeth, wife of Daniel Martin, March 29, 1827—May 30, 1884. S. S.

Sarah, wife of Fernando Merrill, Jan. 25, 1870 ; 19, 2, 25.   H.

Hattie, his son, May 23, 1872—Sept. 19, 1872.   H.

Christina L., wife of George Milem, Sept. 27, 1887 ; 39, 10, 24. R.

Thirza, wife of William Milem, Aug. 26, 1856 ; 34 years.   R.

John Miller, Sept. 25, 1827 ; 71, 8, 15.   W.
Laura Millias, Oct. 28, 1844 ; 39th year.   B.
George H., son of John and A. E. Millias, Jan. 31, 1857 ; 3 months.   B.
Anna May, daughter of Charles and Elizabeth Miner, March 10, 1881;
    2, 2, 25.   R.
Martin Miner, Oct. 25, 1841 ; 56 years.   L.
Ami, his son, Dec. 31, 1839 ; 20 years.   L.
Sally A., wife of Fernando Miner, April 22, 1875 ; 31, 4, 7.   R.
Henry B. Mirick, Sept. 11, 1841 : 24, 8, 17.   R.
Horatio, son of Hiram and Mary B. Mirick, Feb. 16, 1835 ; 3 months,
    8 days.   R.
Pollyette G., daughter of George W. and Elsie O. Mirick, Dec. 22,
    1818 ; 2, 0, 19.   R.
Solomon Mirick, Aug. 11, 1839 ; 67th year.   R.
Thomas M. Mirick, Nov. 7, 1841 : 28, 5, 10.   R.
George O., son of Thomas M. and Sophronia Mirick, March 3, 1841 ;
    11 months.   R.
Jane, daughter of William Mitchell, June 24, 1867 ; 35, 9.   F.
John Mitchell, Jan. 3, 1855 ; 71, 6, 6.   F.
Permelia, his wife, March 7, 1873 ; 81 years.   F.
Leonard T. Mitchell, June 28, 1819—March 8, 1865.   R.
Sarah, his daughter, May 10, 1886 ; 25, 8.   R.
Frank A., his son, Sept. 20, 1887 ; 30, 1.   R.
Lydia G., daughter of B. and S. A. Mitchell, Feb. 14, 1866 ; 1, 3, 14.   F.
Philander Mitchell, Nov. 24, 1870 ; 77 years.   F.
John, his son, Sept. 1, 1849 ; 17th year.   F.
Sarah, daughter of William and N. J. Mitchell, Aug. 9, 1861 ; 5, 2, 20.   F.
Conklin, son of Joseph and Harriet Moon, Jan. 27, 1848 : 1 month,
    21 days.   A.
May E., daughter of same, Jan. 10, 1852 : 1, 0, 14.   A.
John, son of same, Sept. 19, 1856 ; 5, 10.   A.
Wilbur A., son of same, Sept. 17, 1856 ; 1, 9.   A.
Cornelia, wife of John Moon, Oct. 7, 1843 ; 74 years.   A.
Joseph Moon, Oct. 26, 1858 ; 48, 1, 6.   A.
Hope W. Moon, Feb. 8, 1882 ; 84 years.   A.
Elijah Morey, April 8, 1836 ; 26th year.   R.
Martin Morse, March 2, 1851 ; 68, 6, 10.   F.
Dorman Munsell, Feb. 4, 1852 : 61, 8, 16.   L.
Jerusha, his wife, May 11, 1881 : 88, 3, 22.   L.
Emily S., wife of Alonzo H. Mudge, Sept. 11, 1891 ; 45 years.   R.
C. W. Murphy, Sept. 3, 1867 : 25 years.   R.
Henry Near, March 28, 1861 ; 86th year.   W.
Hannah, his wife, Oct. 17, 1861 : 82d year.   W.

Nelson Neeley, M. D., Assistant Surgeon 57th Inf., May 26, 1879 ;
    44 years.   R.
Anna, wife of Jonathan Nichols, Dec. 17, 1884 ; 77, 6.   L.
Roxy V., wife of John Nichols, Dec. 25, 1848 ; 29th year.   R.
Charles G. Oaks, Jan. 12, 1802—March 21, 1883.   R.
William H., his son, Aug. 10, 1839—April 23, 1857.   R.
Joseph B. Oaks, Aug. 20, 1885 ; 48 years.   R.
William H., son of J. B. and E. J. Oaks, Dec. 10, 1865 ; 4, 5, 19.   R.
Elizabeth, wife of Samuel Osborn, Jan. 13, 1885; 58 years.   R.
Ella, daughter of E. and J. Osborn, April 5, 1866 ; 2, 9, 23.   R.
Infant son of E. and J. Osborn.   R.
Francis Osborn, June 4, 1866; 77 years.   R.
Martha, his wife, Aug. 14, 1856; 56, 6.   R.
Catharine, their daughter, June 2, 1850 ; 18 years.   R.
Isaac Osborn, Sept. 3, 1854 ; 35, 1, 16.   R.
Alvira, his wife, May 16, 1851 ; 22, 3, 12.   R.
Sarah A., their daughter, Nov. 15, 1849 ; 9 months, 20 days.   R.
John Osborn, June 22, 1853 ; 72, 10, 9.   R.
Mary, his wife, also wife of George Doughty, Feb. 2, 1860 ; 71st year.   R.
Elizabeth, their daughter, Nov. 6, 1847 ; 25, 10, 25.   R.
Mary Ann, their daughter, April 17, 1849 ; 21st year.   R.
Joseph Osborn, Jan. 19, 1845 ; 34th year.   R.
Artemus Osgood, Feb. 21, 1887 ; 88 years.   C.
Harriet, his wife, March 7, 1870 ; 66, 4, 4.   C.
Eudora M., wife of Lucien H. Osgood, Nov. 20, 1870 ; 28, 3, 10.   C.
Samuel Otto, Nov. 2, 1807—Jan. 14, 1870.   R.
Eliza, his wife, Feb. 3, 1813—April 7, 1857.   R.
Sarah M., also his wife, Aug. 13, 1830—Oct. 26, 1866.   R.
J. Guilford Otto, Sept. 13, 1836—July 1, 1863.   R.
James S. Otto, Aug. 1, 1839—April 24, 1864, at Andersonville, Ga.   R.
H. Rufine Otto, Sept. 30, 1846—Aug. 19, 1848.   R.
Fremont B. Otto, Dec. 22, 1861—April 16, 1882.   R.
Sheldon R. Overton, Dec. 10, 1800—April 27, 1887.   C.
Catharine Roe, his wife, Dec. 22, 1811—Jan. 30, 1891.   C.
Harriet S., their daughter, Aug. 12, 1850—Aug. 19, 1868.   C.
E. Everett, their son, Nov. 28, 1852—Jan. 7, 1875.   C.
Mertie Bell, daughter of George and Catharine Parslow, Sept. 5,
    1889 ; 1, 5, 10.   R.
James H. Patten, Nov. 5, 1859 ; 37, 9, 9.   W.
Sidney Patten, Feb. 1, 1856 ; 49, 7, 6.   W.
Benjamin W. Patterson, March 24, 1853 ; 29 years.   W.
Peter Payler, June 2, 1849 ; 32, 9.   F.
Alice H., his daughter, March 20, 1848; 2, 7.   F.

Alanson, son of Asahel and Mary Peck, Jan. 3, 1828 ; 30, 2, 7.   H.
Frances E., daughter of Harlow and Betsey Peck, Sept. 9, 1855 ;
   1, 9, 14.   H.
George F., son of same, June 22, 1865 : 4. 1, 19.   H.
Horace Peck, Nov. 15, 1865 ; 76, 5, 22.   H.
Anna, his wife, Aug. 1, 1880 ; 87, 4.   H.
Willard Peck, Dec. 22, 1855 ; 34, 2, 22.   C.
Franklin P., his son, Dec. 14, 1853 ; 10 months, 16 days.   C.
Horace B, his son, Oct 5, 1850 : 1, 11. 9.   C.
James O. Perry, March 5, 1851 ; 16th year.   R.
Abram Phillips, Jan. 11, 1884 : 81, 1. 8.   Hu.
J. H. Phillips, June 3, 1862 : 25 years.   R.
Stephen Phillips, Co. E, 10th Cav., Dec. 14, 1864 ; 23 years.   R.
William Phillips, Sept. 17, 1847 ; 63d year.   R.
Ebenezer Pierce, a soldier of the Revolution, March 11, 1854 ; 91 years. F.
Mary, his wife, Sept. 26, 1831 ; 67th year.   F.
Mary, daughter of A. and D. Pierceall, March 26, 1851 ; 10, 3, 7.   B.
Josephine, daughter of O. and J. A. Piersons, Sept. 28, 1848 ; 2, 7, 16. H.
Martha E. Sedore, wife of E. T. Pimm, March 26, 1886 ; 50, 5, 8.   R.
Nancy C., wife of William A. Pixley, Oct. 9, 1848 ; 40th year.   R.
Absalom D. Potter, Feb. 18, 1858 ; 49, 10, 28.   F.
Lucy, his wife, May 15, 1863 ; 49 years.   F.
Lillie A., daughter of Levi and Miranda Potter, Oct. 11, 1865 ; 3, 8. L.
Clarence L., son of same, March 3, 1869 ; 3 years.   L.
Caroline E., daughter of Sardis and E. Preston, Oct. 4, 1845 ;
   1, 4, 26.   N. R.
Joseph W., son of same, Aug. 17, 1847 : 1, 3, 14.   N. R.
Nabby, wife of Joseph Preston, June 9, 1843 ; 62, 9, 17.   N. R.
Wealthy Preston, July 4, 1848 : 67, 2, 26.   R.
Elizabeth, daughter of Daniel and Rebecca Price, Sept. 11, 1831 ; 1, 2. F.
Merritt Purdy, Jan. 16, 1874 ; 65 years.   H.
Almanda, his wife, Oct. 11, 1869 ; 51 years.   H.
Elizabeth, wife of Peter Rage, Sept. 12, 1859 ; 54, 1, 25.   A.
Peter, their son, Sept. 24 ; 7, 6, 4.   A.
Allie, daughter of C. and M. Relyea, May 18, 1872 ; 1, 10, 16.   R.
Jerusha Reynolds, Oct. 31, 1846 ; 73d year.   C.
Martin J. Reynolds, Feb. 12, 1854 ; 38th year.   A.
Rebecca, wife of J. Reynolds, Oct. 18, 1840 ; 57, 4, 9.   A.
Susan Reynolds, Jan. 20, 1871 ; 51, 0, 16.   A.
Arnold K. Rhea, Nov. 14, 1852 ; 32, 3, 16.   F.
Allen B., his son, Dec. 17, 1846 ; 3 months, 17 days.   F.
John Rhea, March 31, 1847 ; 69 years.   F.
Bahama, wife of Elijah Rice, Sept. 7, 1847 ; 70, 7, 7.   B.

Franklin J., son of J. G. and L. H. Rice, Aug. 19, 1858 ; 8, 0, 16.   H.
Levine, daughter of S. D. and L. J. Rice, April 16, 1859; 7 months,
    10 days.   H.
Lydia M., daughter of Hand C. Richmond, Sept. 27, 1847; 10 months. N. R.
Ellen L., daughter of H. and O. Riker, June 1, 1854 ; 1, 9, 2.   R.
Margaret, wife of Andrew Rinehart, Feb. 4, 1868 ; 51, 11, 26.   S. S.
Silas B., their son, Nov., 1857 ; 5 years.   S. S.
Caroline, wife of Alpheus Roberts, Sept. 15, 1852 ; 28, 10, 15.   L.
Alice M., their daughter, July 16, 1851—Sept. 8, 1889.   L.
Emmet A., son of Emery and Maria Roberts.   L.
John Roberts, April 7, 1855 ; 83, 5, 10.   L.
Dorcas S., wife of A. E. Robinson, Nov. 17, 1831—Nov. 17, 1887.   R.
Henry Robinson, Oct. 13, 1874 ; 74 years.   R.
Elizabeth, his wife, May 22, 1875 ; 73 years.   R.
Catharine, their daughter, Oct. 21, 1849 ; 22 years.   R.
Eliza, their daughter, March 24, 1875 ; 40 years.   R.
William H., their son, Sept. 30, 1872 ; 33 years.   R.
Irving J., their son, Nov. 24, 1875 ; 28 years.   R.
Austin Roe, April 20, 1864 ; 81, 6, 2.   C.
Sarah, his wife, Sept. 29, 1863 ; 73, 8, 18.   C.
John B. Roe, Dec. 9, 1818—May 8, 1885.   R.
Roxana, his wife, Dec. 3, 1847 ; 30, 4, 18.   Hu.
Emeline, wife of Elder E. B. Rolf, June 12, 1861 ; 48, 7, 26.   A.
Francis M., son of John C. and Caroline Rounds, Jan. 3, 1892 ; 13,
    7, 2.   R.
Ann, wife of Israel Roy, July 14, 1882 ; 70 years.   F.
Alexander, their son, March 24, 1847 ; 1 year.   F.
John H. Ruppert, Co. H, 148th Inf., May 29, 1822, Willinghausen,
    Germany—April 1, 1882.   R.
Ambrose Ryon, April 3, 1855 ; 84 years.   Hu.
Gamaliel Sampson, March 4, 1870 ; 75 years.   C.
Minnie B., daughter of A. P. and L. L. Sampson, Sept. 26, 1869—
    Nov. 11, 1887.   R.
Martin Saxton, Feb. 18, 1891 ; 63, 0, 18.   C.
Rebecca A., his wife, Jan. 12, 1877 ; 44 years.   C.
Artemas G., son of A. and L. Scott, Aug. 7, 1857 ; 33, 3, 10.   H.
Ebenezer Scott, Aug. 22, 1851 ; 62d year.   B.
Charles E., son of E. and C. Scott, Sept. 19, 1848 ; 1, 3, 18.   B.
Ezekiel Scott, Sept. 13, 1848 ; 90 years.   H.
Olive, his wife, Oct. 3, 1835 ; 73 years.   H.
Hester Scott, Aug. 9, 1859 ; 18, 10, 23.   H.
Jesse D. Scott, Sept. 9, 1844 ; 24 years.   H.
Phœbe L., wife of A. Scott, March 11, 1875 ; 63, 10, 20.   H.
    28

Zelina, wife of Ira Scott, July 20, 1796, Winsted, Conn.—July 8,
 1871.   H.
Almeda, their daughter, Oct. 8, 1824 ; 6, 3.   H.
Anna, wife of Monroe Seager, June 6, 1871 ; 31st year.   Y.
Harriet, wife of same, April 23, 1877 ; 26, 11, 5.   Y.
David L., son of Benjamin and Louisa Seager, Aug. 6, 1872; 6
 months, 7 days.   Y.
John Seager, March 10, 1882 ; 50, 5, 27.   Y.
John Seager, Jr., March 31, 1887 ; 23, 4.   Y.
Mary Jane, wife of Asher W. Seager, May 30, 1843—Dec. 1, 1890.   R.
Annie, wife of Orange Sears, Sept. 17, 1841 ; 59 years.   H.
Charlotte A., daughter of Oscar and Mary Sears, July 4, 1845; 2, 8, 13 H.
Mehitable, wife of James Sears, March 11, 1826 ; 45th year.   B.
Reuben Sears, April 27, 1773—May 13, 1850.   R.
Hannah, his wife, Dec. 23, 1772—Jan. 16, 1856.   R.
Wellington, son of J. W. and A. Sears, April 7, 1863 ; 7, 6.   A.
William B. Sears, Oct. 27, 1801—July 3, 1883.   R.
Emmarett, his wife, March 3, 1821—Jan. 23, 1858.   R.
Clara E., daughter of William A. and Syrena Sebring, Sept. 5, 1847;
 5, 4, 1.   Y.
Amos J., son of same, Feb. 1, 1845 ; 1, 2, 20.   Y.
Conrad Sedore, Jan. 14, 1872 ; 70, 2, 10.   R.
Maranda, his daughter, Dec. 19, 1848 ; 15, 10, 11.   R.
Captain Benjamin Seelye, April 15, 1854 ; 81, 1.   L.
Eunice, his wife, May 27, 1863 ; 84, 2.   L.
Delos Seelye, Aug. 27, 1870 ; 54, 2, 19.   C.
Almanda, his wife, Dec. 11, 1883 ; 65, 6.   C.
Sarah L., their daughter, Sept. 14, 1842 ; 8 months, 27 days.   C.
Hermon G., their son, Jan. 5, 1853 ; 23 days.   C.
Deacon George Seelye, Nov. 12, 1806—Dec. 30, 1885.   C.
Polly Catharine, his wife, June 5, 1807—Sept. 19, 1829.   C.
Heman Ensign, their son, July 4, 1829—Aug. 25, 1829.   C.
Joseph Seelye, Feb. 9, 1854 ; 77, 11.   C.
Elizabeth, his wife, Sept. 10, 1833 ; 53, 10, 7.   C.
Ensign, their son, killed by a falling tree, April 1, 1818 ; 9, 8, 15. C.
Bertie J., son of L. H. and F. H. Shannon, Dec. 3, 1885 ; 1, 9, 15.   Y.
George M. Shannon, Aug. 2, 1868 ; 67, 9, 16.   Y.
Rhoda, his wife, Jan. 15, 1884 ; 79, 7, 7.   Y.
Lydia, their daughter, Nov. 26, 1848 ; 17, 4, 23.   Y.
Margaret, their daughter, Nov. 10, 1848 ; 9, 9, 21.   Y.
James B., their son, Oct. 16, 1860 ; 30, 6, 15.   Y.
Theodore, their son, Aug. 22, 1867 ; 15, 3, 8.   Y.
Margaret, wife of G. S. Shannon, Feb. 2, 1845 ; 63, 0, 3.   Y.

Mary L., wife of A. R. Shannon, Feb. 11, 1849 ; 32d year.   Y.

John P. Shaw, Dec. 11, 1880 ; 43, 2, 4.   S. S.

Margaret, his wife, Dec. 15, 1884 ; 44, 4, 7.   S. S.

Bertie N. and J. Wesley, their sons.

James Sheffield, Dec. 14, 1859 ; 64, 10, 14.   C.

Lucy M., his wife, July 12, 1871 ; 74, 4, 12.   C.

James W. Sheffield, Dec. 31, 1821—Dec. 7, 1882.   C.

Melissa A., his wife, Dec. 7, 1826—Oct. 27, 1889.   C.

Lucy D., their daughter, April 7, 1861—Oct. 18, 1866.   C.

N. Kendrick Sheffield, March 21, 1823—July 10, 1892.   C.

Kennie Sheffield, Oct. 1, 1887 ; 20, 1, 10.   C.

Deacon Aaron Shepard, Aug. 25, 1840 ; 65 years.   C.

Polly, his wife, also wife of Asahel Dowd, Dec. 18, 1858 ; 80th year.   C.

Harry Shepard, Oct. 28, 1867 ; 62, 0, 19.   A.

Clara Ann, his wife, Jan. 3, 1850 ; 21, 1, 11.   A.

Elder Heman Shepard, Dec. 28, 1847 ; 48, 6, 7.   A.

Nancy, his wife, Oct. 7, 1884 ; 77, 3, 18.   A.

Silas Shepard, Dec. 7, 1887 ; 74 years.   A.

Lovina, wife of Silas Shepard, May 13, 1824 ; 60, 4, 15.   A.

Albert M., son of O. and D. Sherman, Sept. 19, 1854 ; 1, 11, 9.   R.

Elmer, son of same, Oct. 26, 1863; 4, 6, 28.   R.

Alcena B., daughter of Orra and Charlotte Sherman, Dec. 5, 1852 ;
1, 3, 7.   R.

Charles Sherman, Co. B, 27th Inf., April 20, 1839—June 19, 1884.   R.

Charles B. Sherman, Dec. 21, 1804—Feb. 9, 1883.   R.

Lucina, his wife, June 20, 1809—Feb. 19, 1858.   R.

John Sherman, a Revolutionary soldier, March 28, 1764—Nov. 28,
1832.   R.

Chloe, his wife, Nov. 5, 1860 ; 91, 11, 14.   R.

Orrin Sherman, Feb. 4, 1830—Oct. 31, 1863.   R.

Wealthy, wife of Elias D. Sherman, May 28, 1846 ; 43, 9, 26.   R.

Wealthy Sherman, Sept. 6, 1854 ; 8, 4, 11.   R.

William Sherman, Feb. 27, 1862 ; 39, 10, 20.   E.

William V. Sipperly, Oct. 1, 1886 ; 60, 4, 20.   R.

Almira, wife of Orrin Skut, Jan. 22, 1814—June 15, 1886.   R.

Jerome, their son, July 26, 1862 ; 22, 5.   R.

Ellen A., daughter of Conrad C. Skut, March 1, 1859 ; 2, 6, 15.   N. R.

James, son of Jonathan and Hannah Skut, March, 1835 ; 6 months,
2 days.   N. R.

Benjamin Slater, Sept. 25, 1853 ; 78, 7, 11.   B.

Elizabeth, his wife, April 8, 1852 ; 77, 7.   B.

William N., son of J. and E. Smart, Dec. 30, 1853 ; 3, 2.   R.

Amanda, wife of Elkanah Smith, Jan. 8, 1861 ; 72 years.   R.

Ananaias Smith, March 15, 1793—March 21, 1872.   C.
Desire, his mother, Brookhaven, L. I., Aug. 20, 1770—Dec. 30, 1850.   C.
Frank M., son of T. R. and F. M. Smith, June 15, 1854 ; 3, 1, 6.   C.
Infant daughter of G. W. and H. Smith, June 12, 1855 ; 12 days.   C.
Ann, wife of George Smith, Nov. 30, 1863 ; 36, 2, 6.   L.
George D., their son ; 3 months.   L.
Robert G., their son, April 22, 1863 ; 3, 2, 3.   L.
Charles M., son of C. N. and I. Smith.   W.
Chauncey Smith, May 4, 1785—Aug. 8, 1853.   C.
Priscilla, his wife, March 31, 1791—Dec. 20, 1877.   C.
Matilda, their daughter, March 25, 1830—April 19, 1832.   C.
Adaliza, their daughter, April 2, 1824—April 27, 1832.   C.
Elijah Smith, April 27, 1892 ; 67 years.   R.
James E. Smith, Nov. 20, 1856—Oct. 14, 1890.   R.
Linwood J., his son, March 30, 1890—Aug. 31, 1891.   R.
Lana, daughter of O. A. and P. A. Smith, April 12, 1880 ; 1, 6.   W.
Lucy V., wife of Julius C. Smith, Feb. 8, 1876 ; 38 years.   R.
Mary, wife of Jeremiah Smith, March 18, 1873 ; 45, 0, 12.   R.
Mary Jane, wife of Carlton E. Smith, June 2, 1871 ; 33, 6, 7.   A.
Minoris Smith, April 15, 1863 ; 70, 8, 17.   W.
Margaret, his wife, Feb. 15, 1878 ; 82, 2, 2.   W.
Morgan H. Smith, July 15, 1865 ; 38, 2.   W.
Eliza J., their daughter, Aug. 24, 1841 ; 21, 10, 6.   W.
Moses H. Smith, June 10, 1858 ; 72, 10, 26.   A.
Lovina L., his wife, Dec. 14, 1843 ; 56, 0, 2.   A.
Solomon Smith, Jan. 1, 1869 ; 74, 6.   Hu.
Sarah R., his wife, Aug. 15, 1889 ; 89, 10, 7.   Hu.
Solomon S. Smith, Oct. 14, 1834 ; 73d year.   W.
Mary, his wife, Aug. 12, 1843 ; 59th year.   W.
Thomas Smith, Aug. 10, 1879 ; 86 years.   L.
Elizabeth, his wife, Jan 29, 1882 ; 75 years.   L.
Alonzo Snow, Feb. 14, 1815—July 31, 1885.   R.
Charles E., son of E. M. and S. Soper, Dec. 14, 1854 : 1, 11, 20.   C.
M. Rose, wife of Ira T. Soule, April 3, 1891 ; 36, 3, 7.   R.
Hannah, daughter of Tunis and Mariah Sours, June 8 ; 75, 6, 8.   Hu.
Joseph Southwick, Sept., 1848 : 56 years.   H.
Frederick L. Spencer, April 25, 1853 ; 32, 8, 3.   H.
Pelegg Spencer, Dec. 12, 1830 ; 66 years.   H.
James P. Springer, Dec. 23, 1828 ; 8, 9, 18.   C.
Mary B., wife of Edward H. Starkey, Oct. 22, 1871 : 48, 9, 3.   R.
Alice, wife of Andrew Stickles, Oct. 3, 1883 ; 35, 1, 23.   R.
Joseph Stickles, Co. K, 1st Cav., April 10, 1886 ; 68, 6.   R.
Pearsie, son of J. L. and J. A. Stickles, Aug. 21, 1886 ; 5 months.   R.

Mary, wife of Henry Steitler, March 11, 1863; 33, 4. 26.   F.

Philip, their son, July 17, 1858 ; 5, 4, 23.   F.

Jacob L., their son, July 12, 1858 ; 1, 1, 5.   F.

Martha B., wife of George Stevenson, April 20, 1877 ; 28 years.   A.

James Stewart, April 8, 1862 ; 70 years.   C.

Ann Eliza, daughter of James and Fanny Stewart, Jan. 24. 1842 ;
    24 years.   C.

Sally, wife of G. D. Stewart, June 6, 1849 ; 40 years.   C.

Lawton J., their son, July 9, 1861 ; 24 years.   C.

Aurelia G., daughter of G. D. and S. C. Stewart, May 21, 1863 ;
    8 years.   C.

Lillian E., daughter of same, April 8, 1879 ; 10 years.   C.

Carrie V., wife of William H. Stiegelmaier, Nov. 2, 1868 ; 29, 2. 22.   H.

Rena, their daughter, Oct. 11, 1868 ; 8 months, 12 days.   H.

Betsey E., wife of Joseph Stone, Nov. 27, 1856 ; 63, 1, 18.   W.

Elvira Lovejoy, wife of W. J. Stone, March 5, 1870 ; 44, 5.   L.

Hiram W. Stone, May 26, 1867 ; 24, 6.   C.

Lucy J., daughter of Joseph D. and Charity E. Stone, July 11, 1849;
    3, 8, 27.   W.

Ansel Strong, Sept. 26, 1788—Aug. 24. 1866.   W.

Betsey, his wife, March 13, 1802—Nov. 19, 1881.   W.

Asa Strong. Dec. 18, 1829—Sept. 15, 1847.   W.

Fready B. Strong, Sept. 24, 1864—Jan. 4, 1866.   W.

Wallace, son of Henry and Emeline Stuck, Oct. 30, 1860 ; 8, 4, 27.   A.

Infant son of same, March 8, 1862 ; 10 months, 20 days.   A.

William H. Sutherland, June 2, 1867 ; 64, 1. 12.   S. S.

Maria, his wife, Oct. 17, 1872 ; 65, 4, 17.   S. S.

Eliza J., their daughter, Feb. 17, 1868 ; 37, 10, 4.   S. S.

Michael Sweet, Co. E. 81st Inf., Nov. 27, 1889 ; 65 years.   R.

George Swift, Co. B, 100th Inf., Feb. 13, 1864 ; 24 years.   R.

Palmedia, wife of N. Sylvester and daughter of Eli and Jennette
    Murdcck, March 25, 1839 ; 41 years.   H.

Thomas Taber, July 7. 1849 ; 61, 5, 26.   F.

Dotha, his daughter, Oct. 8, 1850 ; 11, 5, 8.   F.

John T. Talton, May 30, 1882 ; 54 years.   R.

Henrietta, daughter of B. and Maria Taylor, Dec. 5, 1846 ; 1, 0, 22.   R.

Zadoc P. Taylor, Aug. 30, 1806—July 23, 1881.   R.

Alfred D., son of W. and Emily Thayer, July 29, 1861 ; 19, 1, 9.   R.

Charles Thomas, Aug. 28, 1830 ; 53, 6, 2.   R.

Polly, his wife, June 14, 1863 ; 77, 4, 24.   R.

Eron N. Thomas, May 9, 1809—Aug. 20, 1874.   R.

Lucy A., his wife, Feb. 26, 1818—Nov. 26, 1843.   R.

Julia, their daughter, April 12, 1840—April 12. 1840.

George B., their son, March 7, 1843—March 17, 1843.

Rachel M., wife of Eron N. Thomas, Jan. 5, 1812—April 10, 1891.   R.

Charles Roscoe, their son, Jan. 27, 1845—Jan. 23, 1847.   R.

Nathan W. Thomas, April 29, 1838 ; 36th year.   R.

Marie Antoinette, his daughter, Nov. 7, 1847 ; 14, 5, 21.   R.

Edward J. Thompson, June 16, 1822, Red Hook, N. Y., Nov. 22,
1851.   B.

Samuel Thompson, Oct. 3, 1852 ; 58, 3, 11.   C.

Abigail, his wife, March 18, 1851 ; 52, 1, 3.   C.

Elmira Tice, April 15, 1876 ; 76, 3, 15.   C.

Delia, wife of Philip P. Tindall, Nov. 4, 1861 ; 23, 7, 19.   H.

Emeline, wife of Myron P. Tindall, June 6, 1829—Sept. 3, 1857.   Y.

Jacob Tipple, April 1, 1853 ; 66, 2, 15.   C.

Margaret, his wife, July 7, 1888 ; 100. 11, 7.   C.

Lucy, wife of E. Toles, 1st, Sept. 11, 1858 ; 83 years.   N. R.

Ebenezer Toles, Nov. 30, 1883 ; 78, 0, 18.   L.

Polly, his wife, May 31, 1838 ; 36 years.   N. R.

Hannah, also his wife, Sept. 29, 1879 ; 74, 10, 6.   L.

Ezra Toles, Jan. 29, 1888 ; 46 years.   L.

Mary, wife of Benjamin Tougat, Sept. 20, 1865 ; 25 years.   L.

Asa Town, May 25, 1848 ; 66, 1.   C.

William W., his son, March 6, 1833 ; 5, 8, 27.   C.

Lucy A., his daughter, Feb. 2, 1832 ; 2, 11, 10.   C.

Eugene Town, Aug. 20, 1841—Jan. 28, 1881.   C.

Lewis S. Town, May 29, 1853 ; 24, 0, 17.   C.

J. Milton Town, March 4, 1882 ; 59, 10, 16.   E.

Silas Town, Sept. 17, 1873 ; 87, 7, 27.   C.

Mary E., his wife, Jan. 19, 1882 ; 80 years.   C.

John F. Towns, Oct. 10, 1838 ; 32, 2, 24.   F.

George Adelbert, son of John A. and Sarah A. Towns, Jan. 19,
1870 ; 20, 1, 9.   F.

Benjamin Tucker, M. D., Aug. 28, 1833 ; 66 years.   H.

Eve, his wife, Feb. 22, 1834 ; 55 years.   H.

Daniel Tucker, Jan. 1, 1796—Oct. 12, 1876.   Hu.

Ellen, wife of A. W. Tucker, June 11, 1844 ; 44, 6, 9.   B.

William W., their son, Oct. 1, 1841 ; 1 year.   B.

Emma, daughter of A. W. and L. Tucker, Feb. 18, 1874 ; 1, 0, 28.   A.

Philip Turner, April 3, 1870 ; 35 years.   E.

Ella L., his wife, Feb. 12, 1848—Jan. 17, 1873.   E.

Pliny H., son of A. W. and S. A. Tucker, June 13, 1853 ; 2, 4, 19.   B.

William H., son of same, March 13, 1850 ; 10 months, 5 days.   B.

Roderick C., son of S. B. and S. H. Tucker, Jan. 2, 1849—Nov.
18, 1849.   H.

Benje Ann, daughter of same, April 29, 1845 ; 1, 7.   H.

George Twamley, July 30, 1862 ; 80 years.   S. S.

Mary, his wife, Aug. 18, 1854 ; 63d year. Both from County Wicklow, Ireland.   S. S.

Peter Valentine, M. D., April 1, 1857 ; 63, 11, 8.   R.

Rachel, his wife, May 7, 1858 ; 62, 7, 2.   R.

Richard S. Valentine, M. D., May 5, 1856 ; 30, 8, 1.   R.

Ann M., his wife, July 13, 1858 ; 33, 8, 8.   R.

Washington, son of Asahel and Anna Valentine, Jan. 26, 1833 ; 2, 3, 13.   R.

Emily, wife of Herman Van Amburgh, Sept. 16, 1815—March 15, 1886.   F.

George H., son of Nathaniel and Sarah Van Amburgh, Aug. 26, 1812 ; 1, 7, 20.   F.

Fanny E., daughter of same, April 28, 1834 ; 1, 5, 5.   F.

German Van Amburgh, April 22, 1878 ; 78, 8.   R.

James Van Amburgh, Dec. 29, 1862 ; 90, 11, 13.   F.

Sarah, his wife, Nov. 16, 1864 ; 87, 7, 20.   F.

John L. Van Amburgh, April 28, 1864 ; 44, 2, 8.   F.

Jacob, his son, April 28, 1864 ; 16, 9, 15.   F.

Henry Van Amburgh, Dec. 22, 1872 ; 67, 3.   F.

Sarah M., daughter of J. and S. J. Van Amburgh, Jan. 25, 1858 ; 2, 5, 7.   F.

Daniel Van Antwerp, Oct. 29, 1844 ; 43, 0, 15.   C.

Isaac Van Antwerp, Dec. 1, 1843 ; 36, 5, 5.   C.

John Van Antwerp, Co. G, 9th H. A., April 17, 1865 ; 27, 7, 11.   H.

Emeline, his wife, July 31, 1861 ; 21, 2, 20.   H.

Little son of Edwin and Lovina Van Antwerp, Feb. 4, 1870 ; 3, 5, 6.   R.

Simeon J. Van Antwerp, Nov. 12, 1863 ; 67 years.   R.

Elizabeth, his wife, Sept. 6, 1857 ; 57, 6, 3.   R.

Lewis H., their son, May 21, 1866 ; 22, 11, 18.   R.

Charles, son of M. J. and H. C. Van Buren, May 3, 1834 ; 1 month, 8 days.   C.

Lovina, wife of William S. Vanderburgh, June 16, 1817—Dec. 5, 1883.   R.

Emma E., daughter of William H. and H. E. Vandercook, Feb. 7, 1863 ; 8, 7.   F.

John Willis Vandercook, June 8, 1887 ; 30 years.   R.

Lucy M., wife of R. H. Vandercook, Aug. 26, 1842 ; 25 years.   F.

Michael C. Vandercook, Jan. 16, 1862 ; 81, 11.   F.

Mary, his wife, Dec. 18, 1858 ; 73, 6, 26.   F.

Cornelius, their son, June 23, 1831 ; 19, 6, 1.   F.

John W. Vanderoef, March 6, 1861 ; 39, 11.   C.

Andrew Van Leuven, Feb. 20, 1836 ; 67th year.   F.
Phœbe A., his wife, Jan. 25, 1845 ; 38th year.   F.
William Z., their son, Aug. 26, 1845 ; 7 months, 9 days.   F.
Sally Van Leuven, May 26, 1864 ; 66, 0, 14.   F.
Charles H., son of Henry and Sarah Van Ostrand, Aug. 4, 1850 ;
    2 months, 2 days.   R.
Abraham Van Valkenburg, Aug. 22, 1863 ; 62, 10, 13.   S. S.
Deborah, his wife, Sept. 19, 1876 ; 68, 9, 20.   S. S.
Adelaide, their daughter, March 17, 1881 ; 32, 3, 9.   S. S.
Lydia, their daughter, Sept. 27, 1837 : 2, 2, 28.   S. S.
Lovina Veley, July 6, 1801—Nov. 22, 1877.   C.
Edwin Vincent, May 28, 1830 ; 32d year.   W.
Eleanor Vincent, Nov. 11, 1831 ; 27th year.   W.
Jonathan Vincent, March 18, 1852 ; 86th year.   W.
Elizabeth, his wife, Oct. 3, 1839 ; 69th year.   W.
Oscar, son of Joshua and Lorena Vincent, April 16, 1842 ; 3, 1, 2.   W.
Ovid Vincent, May 16, 1836 ; 24th year.   W.
Hannah, daughter of John and Christiana Vosburgh, Jan. 7, 1849 ;
    1, 10, 6.   A.
Catharine, daughter of same, July 2, 1845 : 14, 8, 2.   A.
Dudley Wade, Feb. 26, 1876 ; 70 years.   C.
Mary E., his daughter, Feb. 19, 1842 ; 4, 11.   C.
Frank D., his son, Nov. 8, 1875 ; 20, 4, 8.   C.
John Wade ; no date.   C.   Eunice Wade : no date.   C.
Willis G. Wade, June 7, 1854 ; 33, 5, 7.   R.
Juliette, his wife, March 26, 1859 ; 30, 2, 28.   R.
Willie Edward, their son, Nov. 7, 1853 : 3 months, 20 days.   R.
David Wager, Feb. 19, 1879 ; 82 years.   Y.
Clarissa, his wife, April 23, 1865 ; 56 years.   Y.
Eliza J. Wager, Dec. 18, 1887 : 54 years.   Y.
Freelove, wife of George Wager, March 25, 1850 ; 27 years.   Y.
James Wager, Jan. 26, 1855 ; 20, 3, 27.   Y.
John Wager, Aug. 25, 1856 ; 90 years.   Y.
Margaret, his wife, April 3, 1858 ; 87 years.   Y.
Mary, daughter of George and F. Wager, Jan. 16, 1846 ; 10 months,
    5 days.   Y.
Rosie, wife of William P. Wager, Aug. 25, 1891 ; 27 years.   R.
Stephen Wager, Co. D, 90th Inf., Dec. 31, 1869 : 26 years.   Y.
William Wager, Co. D, 9th H. A., May 5, 1879 ; 40 years.   Y.
Henry Wagner, July 13, 1867 ; 74, 9.   F.
Mary, his wife, Oct. 5, 1850 ; 60 years.   F.
Abbie, wife of Stephen M. Waite, Feb. 3, 1830—Nov. 28, 1891.   R.

In Memory of Mr. Jonathan Walker, who died Oct. 19, 1813, in the
34th year of his age.

> His days are spent, his glass is run,
> Oh see, how soon his work was done,
> His body in the tomb doth lie,
> We hope his soul's with Christ on high.

This, the oldest inscription in Rose, is upon the only stone left in the
Stewart's burial ground, without doubt the very first in the town.

Elizabeth, wife of Emanuel Walmsley, Jan. 1, 1813—Jan. 6, 1873.   R.

George, their son, Aug. 12, 1851—April 29, 1873.   R.

Isaac Warren, April 10, 1821—Feb. 12, 1883.   S. S.

Sarah, his daughter, May 31, 1845—Feb. 1, 1862.   S. S.

Sarah Warren, Feb. 6, 1875 ; 82, 1, 18.   S. S.

James W. Warren, May 3, 1853—Sept. 8, 1878.   S. S.

Betsey Ann, wife of Harley Way, March 18, 1871 ; 63, 9, 18.   N. R.

Jane, daughter of Samuel and Aveline Way, June 19, 1842 ; 17th
year.   F.

Lizzie, their daughter, July 15, 1861 ; 1, 7, 15.   F.

Addison Weeks, March 28, 1881—71, 3, 25.   R.

Eliza G., his wife, June 22, 1884 ; 73, 6, 2.   R.

Frances Augusta, daughter of M. D. and S. Weeks, Aug. 16, 1851 ;
1, 0, 2.   R.

Francis W. Weeks, Nov. 1, 1861 ; 73, 2, 15.   Y.

Hannah, his wife, Feb. 16, 1870 ; 76, 5, 4.   Y.

Freddie, son of John and Helen Weeks, Dec. 26, 1876 ; 6, 6, 8.   R.

Georgie, son of same, Dec. 31, 1876 ; 2, 1, 4.   R.

Margaret, wife of William Weeks, June 8, 1886 ; 73 years.   S. S.

Marsal P., son of David and Mary West, May 3, 1848 ; 3, 11, 17.   R.

Mary E., wife of N. Weeks, Feb. 12, 1869 ; 33, 1, 11.   F.

Moses Weeks, Jan. 21, 1853 ; 26, 5, 14.   R.

Eli Wheeler, Jan. 12, 1770, N. Fairfield, Conn., Aug. 10, 1847.   H.

Grizel, his wife, Jan. 17, 1776, N. Fairfield, Conn., March 28, 1868.   H.

Cynthia, their third daughter, July 12, 1826 ; 24th year.   H.

Laura Jane, their fourth daughter, Jan. 12, 1828 ; 15th year.   H.

Phineas Whittier, June 1, 1833 ; 22 years.   Y.

Barbary, wife of John Wikel, Aug. 1, 1846 ; 56 years.   F.

Selah B. Wilder, June 16, 1803—July 26, 1829.   W.

Tamer, wife of Erastus Wilder, July 14, 1828 ; 50, 6, 24.   W.

Andrew Wilkins, Dec. 7, 1815—Sept. 4, 1884.   R.

Alfred, son of Charles and Joanna Willard, July 1, 1853 ; 5, 3, 11.   B.

Aaron F., son of N. and P. A. Williams, July 16, 1853 ; 10 months,
25 days.   A.

Katy Ann., daughter of Thomas and Sarah Williams, April 27,
1871 ; 1, 4, 22.   W.

Matthew Willis, May 1, 1853 ; 79 years.   W.
Sarah H., his wife, Oct. 13, 1854 ; 82 years.   W.
Birdie Bell, only daughter of M. L. and C. B. Wilson, May 17, 1868;
   8, 2, 4.   R.
Fortescue Wilson, Co. C, 105th Inf., 1864 ; 48 years.   C.
Henry, son of A. J. and M. Wilson, March 19, 1874 ; 30 years.   W.
Jonathan Wilson, Aug. 25, 1830 ; 48, 10, 17.   C.
Damaris, his wife, May 14, 1848 ; 66, 4, 23.   C.
Robert Wilson, July 31, 1868 ; 62, 6, 6.   R.
Zephaniah, his son, Aug. 16, 1841 : 3 days.   R.
Walter D. Wilson, Nov. 10, 1860 : 25, 0, 18.   C.
Hattie, daughter of C. R. and C. E. Winchell, June 11, 1875 ; 3, 9, 19. R.
Lana, daughter of J. and G. Winchell, May 18, 1828 : 2, 5, 3.   F.
Russell Winchell, Sept. 8, 1859 ; 47, 0, 5.   F.
James T. Wisner, Nov. 30, 1877 ; 72, 8.   Hu.
Abner Wood, Sept. 10, 1852 ; 66th year.   Hu.
Tunis Woodruff, Nov. 12, 1864 ; 60, 8, 7.   S. S.
Harvey L. Worden, March 7, 1856 ; 20, 5, 12.   F.
Johnny, son of J. V. and C. Worden, May 26, 1876 ; 3, 9, 26.   F.
Frances, wife of James Wraight, March 10, 1877 ; 67, 6, 4.   S. S.
Daniel Wright, March 3, 1854, 72 years.   C.
Mary H., his wife, April 10, 1872 ; 81, 9, 7.   C.
Jacob W. Wright, April 13, 1863 ; 69, 11, 8.   C.
Mary E., wife of Charles H. Wright, April 4, 1876 ; 30, 9, 15.   F.
Mary Bell, their daughter, Jan. 10, 1860 ; 3, 6, 12.   F.
Charles B., their son, April 1, 1886 ; 16, 3, 27.   F.
Amos S. Wykoff, Dec. 27, 1868 ; 64, 5, 4.   R.
Charlie, son of Lyman and Lucy Wykoff, Sept. 23, 1872 : 11 months,
   13 days.   .R.
O. L. Wykoff, May 10, 1866 ; 28, 7, 12.   C.
Catharine, wife of Conrad Young, July 22, 1854 ; 75, 3.   F.
Mary, daughter of Conrad and C. Young, May 23, 1872 ; 13, 0, 14.   F.
Robert R. Young, Aug. 15, 1860 ; 30th year.   W.
Mary E., his daughter, Aug. 23, 1859 ; 2, 0, 3.   W.
Charles D. Zeluff, July 4, 1859 ; 28, 1, 25.   H.

INDEX.

— —

This index was started with the intention of entering every proper name given in the text, with every page indicated, but it was soon found that this would necessitate almost the reproduction of the entire matter. Accordingly, as a rule, the names of heads of families are given; in most cases, the maiden names of wives, and generally, those of the men who have taken Rose life partners. Wherever names are already alphabetically arranged, they are not repeated in the index. This applies to those in the Rose Temperance Society, the list of Rose soldiers and the chapter of epitaphs. Of Rose town officers, there are given in this index only the names through and including the list of collectors.

Abbott, Clarissa, 261

Ackerman, David and family, 206; Eugene, 72; Helen, 169; Henry, 153, 169, 177; Margaret, 169

Ackley, Daniel, 206

Adams, Arloa, 232; Emma, 114

Adams' Ditch, xvi, 96, 97, 156, 289

Adams Land Co., 21, 61, 234, 321

Albough, B., 213

Aldrich, Amos and family, 130; Benjamin, 130, 133, 142, 143; Edward, 54, 67; George, 96, 130; Joseph, 130, 149; Micajah, 54, 58; Peter, 53, 56, 58, 68; Walter, 58

Alexander, Daniel, 140; family, 287; J. B., 377

Allen, Aldula, 61, 97; Charles, 61, 73, 76; Clayton, 55, 61; Ephraim, 251; Ezra, 76; Harriet, 61, 73; Lampson, 61, 66, 67, 274, 377; Nathaniel, 61; Noah, 61; Ovid, 255, 303; Solomon, 55, family, 61, 97, 309, 377; Willard, 76; William, 199, 303; Winthrop, 303

Allis, Eliza, 216

Alvord, William, Mary, George, 159

Andrews, James, 113; Joseph, 235; Robert and family, 141, 311

Andrus, Amasa, 151; Andrew, 155; Benham, 45, 155; Betsey, 206; Eli, 376; Elon, 44; James, 151; Joseph, 69, 173, 266; Lydia, 45; Sarah, 62; Sophia, 134

Angle, William, 235

Annin, Joseph, xiv

Annin's Gore, xiv

Armitage, Ann, 45

Armstrong, Edgar, 7, 8, 12; Granville, 307; James, 4, family, 12; Richard, 52; William, 183

Atkinson, George, 53, 74; John, 53

Aurand, George, 42; William, 47, 53

Austin, Ezra and family, 294, 295; Irving and family, 310; John, 233

Austerly, Catharine, 214

Avery, Harriet, 45; Mary, 117; Phœbe, 118; Rhoda, 129; Richard, 108; Thomas, xv

Ayers, Sally, 212

Babcock, Stephen and family, 95, 105

Bachman, Mary E., 72

Baird, Abiah, 68; family, 72

Baker, C., 28; Charles, 214; Emeline, 125; Francis, 121; George and family, 147; Horatio, 120, 170; John,

139; Julius, 98, 147; Marcus and family, 101
Baldwin, 59; Rev. C., 275; Janette, 86
Ball, George H., 103, 131
Ballard, Mary, 29
Ballou, Ida M., 66
Baltzel, Magdalena, 213
Bamborough, Thomas, 102, 103
Baptist Church, History of, 344; Preachers' Names, 349
Barager, Delilah, 20
Barber, Perry, 65; R. N., 97
Barless, Arthur, 262, 273; C. J., 272, 308; C. L., 272; R. C. and family, 272, 377
Barnes, Abram, 235; Alvin, 199; family, 200; Betsey, 63 ; Edward, 139 ; Elijah, 199; Harvey, 139; Horatio, 2, 140; James and family, 198, 199; John, 198, family, 199, 202; John H., 199, 201, 294, 377 ; Julia, 60; Laurie, 121; Margaret 199, 207; Mary, 140; R. R., 202; Rebecca, 197, 207
Barnum, Ara, 133; David and family, 163; Eunice and brothers, 145; Katie, 226; Roger, 58, 67; family, 68
Barrett, Gardner, 165, 233; Gideon, 113, 179; Helen, 147; Jerry, 164, 165; John, 165, 179; Lewis, 164, 165, 177, 256; Mary, 42; Simeon, 29, 156, 164, 200; William, 37
Barrick, Charles, 144 ; John, 99; Ralph, 145
Barton, Elisha, 215; Dr. F. S., 294
Bassett, John, 277, 293; Sophia, 78, 83
Batt, Isaac, Collins, 291
Beach, Nettie, 147
Beaden, S., 304
Beadle, Guy, 133
Becket, John, 264
Bell, Jacob, 72
Bemis, Harris, 311
Bender, John and family, 120
Benham, Deborah, 70
Benjamin, Alanson, 44; David, 42, 43; George, 44; Grant, 36; Henry, 74; James, 8, 36, 37, 42; Manly, 42, 43; Nelson, 44; Riley and family, 43; William, 42, 43, 189
Bennett, Merritt, 37; Jeremiah, 174
Bigelow, Lydia, 93
Bishop, Calvin, xiii, 117; C. E., 117; Cephas, 98, 117, 149; Chauncey, 116;

family, 117; Joel, 26, 108, family, 118; Joel, 2d, 118; Joseph, 171
Blackman, E. Wallace, 21
Blaine, Abiah and family, 68; Sarah, 78; William and family, 68, 73
Blake, Frank, 255
Blanchard, Harriet, 142
Blodgett, Luke W., 71, 88
Bloss, Mrs. B. G., 46
Blynn, John, 174; Ovid, 173; Martin, 22, 175
Bockoven, Samuel, 210
Boon, Edward, 74
Borden, Selden, 182
Bottum, Lois J., 95
Bovee, Elizabeth, 132; George, 170; Herman, 170, 171; Stephen, 170
Bowers, James, 262
Bowle, Sarah, 101
Bowles, Rev. George, 339
Bowman, Charles, 133
Boyce, Charles, 176; Charlotte, 193; Emory, 193; Isaac, 175, 176; John, 176; Robert, 193; Stephen, 176
Boynton, Cynthia, 135; Joseph, 101, 144; Minerva, 145; Philo and family, 144
Bradburn, Andrew, 12, 169; Charles, 168; Dwight, 277; E. A., 91; Edward, 169; Thomas, 169
Bradshaw, Electa, 163; Dr. J. E., 284
Brainard, Seth, 243
Braman, Catharine, 174
Branch, Ella, 107
Brant, John, 125; Myron, 133, 305, 306
Brass Band, History and names, 369
Brayton, Byron, 95
Brewster, 6; Decatur, 6, 291; Eugene, 126; Hannah, 129; Isaac, 169, 206; Joseph, 31; Rebecca, 29; Samuel, 6
Briggs, Birney, 125; Elbert, 106, 117; Jonathan, 100, 124, family, 125; John, 10, 83, 100, 118, 124, 125; Samuel, 42, 47; William and family, 10
Brink, David, 72; Jane, 169
Brisbin, George, 44, 143; James, 44, 117, 143; Mary, 117
Brockway, Cyrus, 79, 104; Elisha, 69, 79
Brower, David, 166
Brown, Betsey, 165; Dorothy, 93; George, 114; Gilbert, 229, 232; John and family, 240; Mary, 57, 95; Rebecca, 70; Sarah, 204; William, 96

Browning, William, 265
Brunney, James, 99
Brush, Ann, 44
Bryar, William A., 299
Buchanan, Charles, 87, family, 88;
Joseph and family, 88
Buck, Alvin, Wallace, 87
Buckley, John and family, 48, 49
Bucklin, Rev. John, 118
Bull, Anna, 61
Bullard, Lucy, 185
Bump, Emma, 26; Sally, iii
Bundy, Elijah, Joel, Stephen, Trueman, 119
Bunyea, Sarah, 240
Burch, Ædna, 29; Catharine, 163;
Sally, 279
Burgess, 42; Daniel, 24, 27
Burke, Edward, 27; Ella, 27; James, 27; John, 27; Patrick, 26, 27, 32;
William, 27
Burkle, Mary, 102
Burlingame, Dorcas, 150
Burnham, 266
Burns, Emily, 226; John, xv, family, 118; Wesley, 185
Burrill, Edward, 46, 126; E. O., 126
Burt, Ira, 126; James, 55; John, 182;
Mary, 231
Bush, Edward, 5; Fletcher, 5, 81;
Lavello, 5, 81; Leverrier, 5, 6, 81;
Oliver, 5, 78, 81
Butler, Esther, 78; Mary, 117; Richard, ix
Buttonwood Tavern, viii
Cady, Charlotte, 216
Calender, Ruth, 83
Calkins, 67; James, 235; Mortimer, 24; William, 29
Calm, George, 40
Camp, Polly, 227
Campbell, Isaac and family, 264;
James, 245
Carpenter, Orrin, 185, 377
Carr, Lyman, Moses, 102, 103, 107
Carrier, Amaziah, 95; Elbert, 96;
Elizabeth, 1; Ella J., 96; Lillie, 96;
Seward, 95
Case, Alonzo, 189, 190; Harmon, 179;
Rose C., 147
Casler, 289
Caster, Mary Ann, 45

Catchpole, Benjamin, 138; Edwin W., 114, 116; George, iii, 11, 115, 116, 126, 139; James, 115, 138, family, 139;
Robert, 115, 126, 138, family, 139
Caton, Eliza, 87
Cavanaugh, Mary, 41
Caywood, 44, 45; Abram, 47; Gerrett, 45; John, 47, 277
Census Gleanings, 373
Center, Dorr, 61, 73; Eliza, Hallet, John, Mary, 73; Nathaniel, 53, 73
Chaddock, Alonzo and family, 67, 78, 99; Elisha, 79; Jared, 98, 177, 259, 377; Jefferson, 142; Judson, 98, 308;
Watson, 93; Wesley, 93; William, 67, 93, 96, 98, 256; Winfield, 57, 84, 85, 93
Chalker, Emma, 107
Chamberlin, Hamlin, 39; Philetus, 36, 42; family, 60; William, 230
Chambers, Samuel, 223
Champion, Mary, 62
Chapin, Delademie, 41; Gilbert, 135;
Jeremiah, 60; Stephen and family, 36
Chapman, 77
Chappel, Lina, 21
Chase, Eliza, 56; Levi, 107; Mary A., 10; Mattie, 57
Chatterson, Abram, 4; family, 17;
Betts, 17; George, 18; Henry, 17;
family, 18; John P., 129, family, 155; Laney, 17
Chidester, John, 183; Rebecca, 179;
William, 256
Childs, G. C., 244; Joseph, 266
Chipman, George, 75
Church, Hiram, viii, xiv; Osgood, viii, xii, 69
Clapp, Jessie, 207
Clapper, George, 174; Harvey, 170;
Henry, 149; H. W., 84, 95; Jacob and family, 190; James, 377; John and family, 198
Clark, 145; Addie, 51; Alvin, 51;
Darius, 22; Emmons, 22; Garrett, 145; Lorinda, 3; Lysander, 214;
" Priest," 22, 51
Clary, Albert, 226; Caroline, 178;
Samuel, 183
Claus, Mary, 242
Cleary, Maurice and family, 41
Cleveland, James, 300; Jason, 44;
Mary, 262; Nelson, 300

Closs, David, 377; Frank, 70, 298, 312, 377, family, 314; Hamel, 111, 121; Harvey, 111, 113, 271, 274, 377; John and family, 111; John J., 53, 61; Will and family, 113

Clum, Kingsley, 235

Coats, William, 310

Cobb, Emeline, 31

Coffee, James and family, 301, 303

Colborn, Edwin, 262; James, 149, family, 200; James W., 200, family, 262; Jonathan, 200, family, 213; William, 200, 302

Cole, Angeline, 256; Charles, 94; Isaac, 83, 94, 95; Lucy, 32; Romain, 133; Nancy, 184; William H., 83, 93, 94, 123; W. M., 256

Coleman, 75; Nelson, 210

Collier, Albert, 260; Anna, 165; George, 275, 306; John and family, 291, 292; M. T., 257, 260

Collins, Alpheus, 106, 269, family, 269, 270; C. B., 258, 274, 377; C. C., 5, 16, 26, 85, 98, 99; Flavia, 106; Foster, 60, 153, family, 154; Harriet, 17, 154; Ida, 16; James, 17; Josephus, 12, 15, 16, 33, 40, 47; Julian, 26; Newton, 17; Sally, 162; Stephen, 65, 69, 151, family, 153, 331; Thaddeus, 1st, xv, 16, 106, family, 274, 331; Thaddeus 2d, 5, 12, 15, family, 16, 34, 41, 106, 272, 377; Thaddeus W., 153

Colvin, Asahel, 7, 30; Nathan, 30; Oliver and family, 30: Pitt, 30; Sidney, 30

Commett, Florence, 143

Comstock, Mary, 36; Susan, 138

Conklin, 304; Morris, 290

Conroe, Jacob, John, 306

Converse, Charles, 239; Eugene and family, 195, 196; Horace, 238; family, 239

Cook, Elias, 115; Jane, 81

Cooley, Sloan, 22

Cooper, Betsey, 203

Copeman, Ambrose, 99, 147

Cornell, Calista, 76; Catharine, 103

Correll, Nettie, 159; Nicholas, 149

Cornwall, John, 180, 377

Coutermarch, Henry, 132

Covell, Abram, 161, 164, 290; Charles,

48, 161, 376; Helen, 158, 161; Irving, 161; James, 1st, and family, 157; James, 2d, 113, 161; Seymour, 160; family, 161

Covey, John, 101

Cowan, Martha, 158; Mary, 199

Cox, 45; George, Mordecai, 266; Sally, 52; Samuel, 170

Craft, Abram, 161, family, 224; Benjamin and family, 214; Clarissa, 157, 161; Thomas, 224

Crampton, 42; Daniel, 58

Crandall, Byron, 204, 263; Jane, 156; Joseph and family, 203

Cranston, Nerissa, 61

Crawford, Joseph, 74

Creek, Lucy, 229

Crisler, family, 276; Adam, 228; Charles and family, 158; Eliphalet, 120; Evander, 33; Jerry, 279; John, 12, family, 33, 260; John W., 293; Lawrence, 276; Marsden, 279; Matthew, 262, 277; Nelson, 33, 67; Willis, 277

Cross, Julian, 125

Crydenwise, Isaac and family, 101; Isaac, Jr., 101, 249; Polly, 108

Cullen, James and family, 192; Thomas, 102, 245, 246; William, 256

Cummings, Libbie, Mary, 48

Curtis, Rev. Amasa, 121; Cynthia, 202; Isaac, 36; William, 103

Cushman, 5; Cornelia, 192; Salina, 193

Cusic, Rev. H., 257

Cuyler, Katie, 98

Dagle, Addison, 132, 138; Albert, 131; Charles and family, 132; Frank, 132

Daly, Byer, 169; Calvin, 235; Mary, 43

Dann, Ezra, 294; Rufus, 295

Darling, Chauncey, 12, 33; Martin, 76, 83

Davenport, Harriet, 231; James, 61; Jerome, 133

Davis, Daniel, 70; Edgar, 135; Ellery, 38; Frank, 128; Irene, 135; Jerome, 76; John, 91; Paul, 76

Day, Lucy, 235; Sibyl, 159

Deady, Ambrose, 253; Charles, 9, 36, family, 37; Elizabeth, 37; George L., 201, 208; James, 9, 37, family, 201; John Q., 9, family, 37; Margaret, 9; Richard, 253; William, 37, family, 256

Dean, Edgar, 131, 132
Decker, Henry, 11, 37, 40, 44, 63; James, 64; John, 64, 133, 255; Peter, 244, 257
Delamatter, Martha, 178
DeLong, Francis, 93, 99; John, 93
Deming, Rosanna, 92
Demure, Roxana, 146
DePew, Abram, 109
Derby, Delia, 105; Josephine, 133
Desmond, Agnes, Albert, Charles, 39; Mary, 51; Truman, 39, 43; William, 39, 42, 43, 86, 177; family, 177
Devoe, 48; John, 48
Dewey, Mary, 73
DeWitt, Rev. M. H., 256
Dickinson, Christopher, 143; Darwin, 143, 144, 254; Harvey, 30; Jay, 128; family, 132; Robert, 132, 144; William, 128, 143, family, 144; William, 132; family, 135
Dickson, Ensign, 313; Dr. J., 7, 12, 20, 101, 104, 140, 217, 253, family, 284, 376; John, 224: Sophronia, 224
Ditton, 131; Charles, 155
Dix, Amy, 61; John A., 61
Dixon, Abel and family, 229, 235; George, 223, 229
Doan, Nellie, 261
Dodds, Albertine, 186; Christiana, 186; Eva, 63; Jeffers, iii, family, 185; Polly, 186; William, 185, 193; William H., 186
Donaldson, 67
Donovan, John, Maurice, Timothy, 43
Doolittle, David, 90
Doremus, Abram, 133, 240, family, 241
Dorris, Amos, 101, 104
Dorsheimer, Lieut. Gov., 211
Doty, Daniel, 58; Isaac, 66
Dougan, Arthur, 69; Mary, 173, 183, 377
Douglas, Frank, 175
Dowd, Azel, 15; Benjamin, 90; George, 24; Watson, 15, 85
Drainage, vii
Draper, Doctor, 305
Drown, Huldah, 194; John, 1st, and family, 212; John, 2nd, and family, 193; John A., 194, 254; Maria, 93; Solomon, 212, family, 213
Drury, Adaline, 89; Anson, 81; Caleb, 87, 106; Elihu, 87; Frank, 127; Hol-

loway, 87, 89; John, 72; Marcus, 60; Warren, 41
Dudley, L. H., 304, 307
Dunham, Andrew, 303; Ezra, 223; Rev. F. J., 258; James and family, 302; Julia, 239; Morgan, 65
Dunman, Sarah, 189
Dunn, Adaline, 211; Bridget, 117; Catharine, 27; Henry, 159; Hiram, 147, 159; Margaret, 227
Durant, Joseph, 272
Durfee, Justin, 100; Miriam, 177
Dwyer, Annie, 48
Eastman, 58
Eastwood, Foster, Nelson, 154
Eaton, 4, 12
Ebert, Louis, 104
Eddy, 90
Elder, 61
Eldred, Clark, 142; Kate, 89, 142; Lydia, 142
Elmer, James, 224
Ellinwood, Adele, 245; Alexander, 135; Chester, 108, family, 244; David, 245; E. Chester, 72, family, 74, 244, 377; Edson, 300, 301; Ellis, 103, 245, 331; Ensign and family, 247; George, 245: Harrison, 247, 307; Jonathan and family, 242: Lucius, 11, 247, 257, 304, 307: Mary, 61; Orlando, 69, 300; Valorous, 63, 299; Valorous, 2d, 9, family, 299, 377: Washington, 55, 61, 245, 280
Ellis, Albert, 238; George, 240: L. R., 240
Ellsworth, John, 130; Leman, 235, 237
Elwood, Betsey, 67
Emorick, Caroline, 72
Epitaphs, 394
Esmond, Zechariah, 8
Espenscheid, William, 203, 211
Evans, Daniel, 76
Evarts, Clementine, 106
Fairbanks, Cornelius, 105, 109, 122: George C., 62, 107, 251: Zenas, 60, 67, 106, 107, 122
Fairchild, John, 9
Falkerson, Emma, 70
Farnsworth, Thomas, 237, 239
Farr, William, 145
Farshee, Lany, 72
Featherly, Betsey, 241: John, 241, family, 242

Feeck, Nicholas and family,   148
Fellows, Frank, 199; Joseph, xii, xvi, 140
Felt, Cyrus,   107
Felton, Zerviah,   146
Ferguson, Abraham, 377; Clark, 105;
    Nelson,   10
Ferris, 87; Harriet, 144; Harvey, 12;
    family, 253; Henry, 41; J. H. family, 253
Fields, Dr.,   60
Finch, David, 44; Elvin, Eva, 44; Em-
    bury, 201; Frank, 41, 290; Franklin,
    182, 208; George, 201; Jeremiah, 1st,
    41, 44, 109; Jeremiah, 2nd, 44; John,
    41, 44; John L., 225; Nancy, 223;
    Newman and family, 224; Sarah,
    208; Selah, 46, 290; William,   21, 44
Fink, Christian, 167, 239; John,   101
Finnigan, Annie,   46
Fish, T. S.,   28
Fisher, Adam, 210; Adrian, 271;
    George, 173, 186; Mary, 27; Michael,
    91; William,   271
Flint, Augusta, 139; Calista, 115, 116;
    Dwight, ix, 116, 139; Elizur, 115, 377;
    Pomeroy,   115
Foist, Ruth,   202
Foote, Christiana,   186
Forbes, 72; Thomas,   75
Forncrook, Mary,   261
Fosmire, Jane, 185; John,   150
Foster, Aaron, 101; Cornelius, 205;
    Daniel, 205; David, 54; Esther, 274;
    Heman, 101; Howard, 255; Nancy,   54
Fowler, Hiram, 286; Maria,   91
Fox, Charles and family, 205; Louis
    and family,   204
Fredendall, Anna, 172; Barney, 304;
    305; Henry, 183, 305; James,   305
Freeman, Charles, 20, 66; George, 66;
    Moses and family,   76
Free Methodist Church, History of,   359
Free Methodist Preachers,   360
French, Cynthia, 72; James, 239;
    family,   240
Fry, George, 96; Philip and family,   103
Fugate, Henderson,   68
Fuller, Almanda, 8; Erastus, 8, 54;
    Jonathan, 48; Mary, 246; Ralph, 54, 246
Fulton, Elizabeth,   226
Gage, Lillian, 153; S. W.,   153, 256, 377
Gardner, Ansel, 109, 119, 134, 136;
    Ella, 138; Ishmael, 138, 237; Henry,

155; Samuel, 129, 377; Sarah,   118
Garlick, Abner, 44, 46, 128, 173;
    Charles, 127, 133, 149; Eli, 101, 127,
    128, 164, 176, 239; Frank, 128, 159;
    Harriet, 127; Henry, 89, 127, 128, 131,
    141; Judson, 128, 279; Samuel, 99,
    family, 127, 128; Samuel, 178; Sid-
    ney, 128, 236; William,   174, 178, 289
Garling, Magdalena,   175
Garratt, Esther, 37; Mary, 91;
    Richard, 29, 46, 82, 91, 123; Sarah, 91
Gatchell, Jeremiah,   289
Gaylord, Ellen, 313; Frank, 139;
    Marvin,   313
Genung, Benjamin and family, 299;
    Joseph, 258; Mary, 101; Susan,   146
Geology and Topography,   vi
Gilbert, Huldah,   127
Giles, Abigail, 61; Lucy,   61
Gillett, Almira, 121, 129, 304; Asahel,
    xv, 100, 102, 108, 141, 148, 377; Avery,
    100, 101, 123; Charles, 101; Gardner,
    119; Harvey, 104, 105; Henry, 84,
    101; Hosea, 157; Isaac, 121, family,
    129; John, 100, 148, 255; John C.,
    101; Julia, 105; Mark, 101; Melvin,
    100; Nodadiah, xv, 145; Rhoda, 129,
    304; W. O.,   308
Glen, Elias, 184; Harriet, 185; John,
    184; Samuel, 184; William, 184;
    William J.,   185, 201, 376, 377
Glover, Ida,   202
Goetzman, Valentine, 211; family,   212
Goeway, Lucy,   215
Goffe, Ruth,   17
Goodell, Minerva,   170
Good Templars,   369
Goodwin, Sherman,   70
Gordon, Hiram, 289; James, 103;
    Lester,   289
Gould,   8, 36
Gragor, David,   288
Graham, 10; Alfred, 89, 129; Archi-
    bald, 147; Eliza, 91; Elmore, 147;
    Henry, 89, 123, 125, 129, 141, 146,
    family, 147; Nelson, 92, 123, 133, 147;
    Walter, 100; William,   38, 46
Grand Army of the Republic,   371
Grange,   372
Grant, Fred, 131; Sylvia,   216
Graves, 68; George, 60; Thomas,   102
Gray, A. M., and family,   142

Green, David, 72; Elmer, 236; George, iii, family, 203; Isabel, 72; Sarah, 105; William, 51, 131, 132, 235

Grenell, Abel, 407 ; Eugene, 202 ; George, 220; Henry, 294, 407; Herman and family, 202; Jane, 177

Grenier, Marian, 202

Griggs, Eleanor, 106

Griswold, Charles, 294; Edgar, 209; Helen, 183; Lorenzo, 182, family, 183; Nelson, 206, 208, family, 209; William, 1st, 207, family, 208; William, 2d, and family, 208; William H., 183, 208, 294, 377

Gunn, Sophia, 300

Gunning, Thomas, 65

Gurnee, J., 87

Guthrie, Deacon, 99; Louise, 37, 99

Hadenburg, Hannah, 173

Hadley, Sophia, 44

Hake, Isabella, 54

Hall, Harriet, 73; Lena, 97

Hallenbeck, Martin, 137; William, 90, 137

Hallett, Dr. F. H., 273, 284; Horace, 47; William, iii, 47; Kittie, 47

Halliday, C., 131

Hamel, Hannah, 111

Hamelink, Derrick, 190, 257

Hamilton, Hannah, 213; Ida, 69

Hamm, William, 263, 305

Hand, Davis, 101, 108; N. B., 121; Samuel, 102, 103, 117

Haney, Albert, 21; Anna, 21; William and family, 21

Harmon, Alfred, 261; Alpheus, xv, 52, 72, 74, 77, 80; Daniel, 170, 261, 288; John, 74, 261, 273; Peter, 10, 261; William, 261

Harper, Albert, 166; Alexander, 280; Anna, 196; Charles, 123, 148, 280, 289; Daniel, 33, 280; David, 149; D. W., 92; Gardner, 280, 289; Jackson, 47; Minerva, 149

Harrington, Mervin, 223

Harris, Sally, 107

Hart, Alice, 88; Clinton, 161; Hiram, 159; Ira and family, 192; Lycurgus, 88; Marion and family, 193; Martha, 161; Marvin, 88; family, 252; S. C., 229

Hastings, Tansey, 44

Haugh, Carrie, 105; Frank, 47

Havens, 90; Dexter, 114; William, 96, 29

98, 113, family, 114

Haviland, Burt, 176, 205, 309; Henry and family, 205, 206 ; Jane, 162 ; Mary, 307

Healy, Andrew, 308

Hebgen, Anthony, 217

Heermans, H. C., xii

Hemans, Joseph H., 65

Henderson, Daniel, 70 ; Eustace, 66, 69, 70, 72, 79 ; Eveline, 70, 112 ; Frank, 66, 70; George W., 70, 74; Gideon, 70, 71; John, 70; Thomas, 70, 78, 82; Wooster and family, 71

Hendrick, Adelia, 172; Mary, 171

Hendricks, Barbara, 54; Betsey, 53; Frank, 6; Katy, 53; Simeon, 53

Henry, Emma, Seymour, William, 82

Hersey, Anna, 209

Hetta, August, 102; John A., 241

Hibbard, Elizabeth, 118

Hickok, Eugene, 30, 44, 59, 307, 308; Isaac, 129; Moses, 146; Will, 257; William, 137, 300, 377; William F., 9, 59, 257

Hicks, Hannah, 78; Mary, 72

Hield, Allie, 53

Higgins, Perliette, 78

Hill, David, 133; John, 127, 129, 377; William, 126

Hillman, Emma, 113

Hills, Sally S., 67

Hills of Rose, vii

Hills of Wayne, 319; 326

Hills, John, 188; Peter and family, 188

Hines, Clara, 171

Hoag, 47

Hoetzel, Saloma, 212

Hoffman, Cassie, 101; S. B., 243, 248

Holbrook, Jester, 311; family, 312; William, 263

Holcomb, Elizabeth, 28; Francis, 26, 28; Harrison, 26, 28; Hattie, 28; Mary, 12, 26, 28; Silas, 46, 256; Willard, 46; William H., 28

Hollenbeck, Lottie, 81

Holloway, John, 8

Holmes, 1; David, 266; family, 307; Demarkus, xv

Hopping, Sidney, 5; family, 81, 122

Horn, Caroline, 162; Edward, 177, 266

Hornbeck, Mary, 211

Horne, Dr. J. M., 275, 377

Horton, 45; Ellen, John, 46; Lydia,
108; William, 280; Ziphe,   61
Houghton, E. F.,   264, 377
Housel, Mary,   70
Houston, Anna,   92
How, Elijah,   xv
Howard, Frank, 291; Henry, 170, 302,
377 ; Hosea, 114 ; Jerusha, 118 ;
John, 188 ; Roxy,   115
Howell, Dorothy,   72
Howlaud, George, 38, 69, 122, 285;
Jeannette,   122
Hoyt, Addie, 98; Adin, 86; Lettie, 86;
Mary,   107
Hubbard, Alonzo,   32
Hudson, Jane, 87; John,   146
Huffman, Jane, 138; Myron,   129
Humphrey, Florence V.,   81
Hunn, Clayton, Harrison, James, Je-
rome, Margaret, Parsons, Sally, 166;
Samuel,   156, 166
Hunt, William A., William S.,   47
Hunter, Robert,   195
Hurlburt,   99
Hurst, Charles,   163
Hurter, Burkhart, 72, family, 72;
Charles, 20; Willie,   20
Hyatt, Mary,   53
Hyde, John,   121, 129
Indians and Relics,   viii
Irish, Chester and family,   5
Irwin,   48
Jackson, Clara,   81, 221
Jakeway, Augusta,   101
Janes, Orinda,   75
Jeffers, Betsey, 173; Charles, 190, 309;
Daniel, 241; Esther, 186; George
and family, 182, 377; Hannah, 185;
Henry, 307; James, 377; James J.,
172; Jane, 189; Jeannette, 37; John,
173; Mary, 210; Nancy, 173; Nathan,
182, 186, family, 189; Ovid, 189;
Robert, 99, 173, 185, family, 186;
Robert N.,   208, 307, 312
Jenkins, James,   25
Jenner, James,   47
Jewell, Alvah, 227, 229, 231 ; Barney,
Henry, 232; Isaac,   231
Johnson, Benjamin, 170, 210; Clar-
ence, 198; Daniel, 287; David, 234,
family, 235; Edna, 170; Etta, 159;
Frances, 46; sons, 276; James, 278;

Dr. Lawrence, vi, 15; Leland, 121,
169, 170; Myra, 169; Rhoda, 170;
Thomas,   56
Jones, Adelbert, 24, 74; Alfred, 53, 82,
92; Betsey, 183; Frank, 91; George,
150, 255; Henry, 24, 86, 87; Isaac,
24, 71, 82; John E., 24, 71; Lydia,
121; Margaret, 124; Mary, 24, 245;
Melinda, 135; Pardon, 124, 149, 150,
241, 254; Perry, 26; "Sammy," 20;
Samuel and family, 293, 305, 377;
Sarah and family,   82
Jordan, Mary, 41; Ransom, 9; Wil-
liam,   43
Joyce, Mary,   65
Judge, John,   82
Kaiser, Fidelus and family, 175; John,
176, 257; Valentine,   223
Kamp, Kasper,   182
Kanouse, Alice,   289
Keisler, Carrie,   76
Kellogg, Allie, 32; Almira, 32; Ben-
jamin, 24, 27, 29; Betsey, 29, 32;
Charles, 26, 29, 32; Ethan, 26, 27, 29;
Experience, 6; Frank, 15, 153, 206;
Harriet, 29; John, 6, 11, 29, 30, 32;
John, 2d, 32, 67; John C., 27; Levern,
15; Lewis, 29; Lucy, 27; Maria, 29;
Permilla, 11, 32; Moses, 71; Rebecca,
29; Sophia, 78; Stephen, ix, 6, 12,
13, 15, 17, 32; William, 29, 51; Wil-
liam, 15; William B., 29, 32, 256;
Vicey,   71
Kelsey, Almira,   109
Kenyon,   81
Ketchum,   29
Kilburn,   48
Kimberly, Harriet,   248
King, Eunice, 44; Samuel, 99; Thomas
and family,   278
Kingsley, Charles,   122
Kingsland, Edward,   xii
Kinkaid, Susan,   241
Klinck, Bert, 114; Carrie, 114; Ed-
ward, 27, 114, 165; Ellsworth, 11,
114 ; George, 292 ; Henry, 114 ;
Henry C., 7, 114, 260; William,   114
Klippel, Elizabeth, 222; Henry and
family,   214
Knapp, 22, 49; Eli, 108, 304; Fred, 87,
277; Hiram, 206; Jane, 27; Jerusha,
46; Nathan, 87; Sarah,   277

Knight, Abram, 54; Susan, 138;
  Thomas, 295
Knights, Melvin, 90
Knox, Charles, 231
Koon, Dr. L. and family, 301
Lackey, John, 258; Judd, 175, 280, 377;
  Orrin, 207, 377; Sanford, 208, 266;
  Sarah, 208; Susan, 208
LaDue, Catharine, 253; Duane, 32;
  Mary, 30
Lake, 77; Anna, 134; Armene, 91;
  Byron, 91, 92; Charles and family,
  91; Eliza, 86, 92; Henry, Hermon,
  92; Ira, 82, 92; Lucina, 120; Nancy,
  82, 92; Wellington, 92
Lamb, Addison, 138; Almira, 135;
  Cora, 138; Hayden, 114; Hiram, 139;
  Ira, 85; Isaac, 136, family, 137; Isaac,
  Jr., and family, 137; John,
  129, 136, 137; Mary, 138; Minnie,
  131; Myron, 105, 131, 136, 138; Peter
  and family, 130; William, 105, 113, 139
Lambert, Thomas, 223
L'Amoreaux, Elizabeth, Joel, 59;
  Peter, 59, 60; Sullivan, 59
Lampson, Edward, Polly, 81; T. J.,
  25, 81; Theodore, 81
Lane, Irving, 182, 241; Johnson, 179,
  181; Loren, iii, 179; Melvin, 183;
  Nelson, 179
Lang, Christina, 195
Langley, Millens, 117, family, 118;
  Myron, 118; S. Wing, 117, 118, 142
Lansing, G. Y., 195
Lape, Ella, 220; Mary, 44; S. W., 215, 217
Lapham, George, 187
LaRock, family, 148, 164; Edward, 220
Lathrop, Ira, 161
Lavender, James,   .   199, 210
Leader, Reuben and family, 286
Leaird, 40; Charles, 40; Ida, 40
Learn, Adam, 197
Leaton, Alice, 58; Jane, 25, 51
Lee, Addis C., Alfred, 62, 156, family,
  309, 310, 329; Arthur, ix; Chester,
  55, 61, 63, 72; Clarinda, 36, 39, 63;
  Clifford, 63; Henry, 20; Joel, 38, 62,
  242; Joel N., 16, 62, 63, 81, 122, 273,
  329; John, 60, 62, 67, 329; John W.,
  55; Judson, 55; Laurinda, 305;
  Lovina, 16, 122; Lyman, 9, 36, 55,
  62, 329; Mary, 55, 63; Nelson, 60;

Newton, 60, 93; Oscar, 60, 93;
  Theresa, 112
Legg, DeLancey, 293; E. E. and
  family, 201; Lafayette, 194, 302; Ly-
  man and family, 293, 302
Leland, Gale, Isaac, James, Lewis, 125
Lemon, E., 226
Leonard, 21; Sarah A., 27
Lester, John, 223
Lethbridge, Jerry, 224
Levanway, Edra, 202; Henry, 201
Lewis, 7; Anna, 90; Daniel and
  family, 89; E. M., 226; Levi, 85; P.
  T., 89, 123; Sally, 127; Thomas, 119
Lincks, Henry, 204
Lindley, Susan, Willie, 258
Livermore, Elizabeth, 99, 302; Emma,
  29, 299; Eunice, 20; Polly, 16; Ruth,
  12; Wesley, 12
Lockwood, 49; Burt, 33; George and
  family, 21; Isaac, 13, 21; family, 33
Lomis, Fanny, 52
Londergan, Michael, 106, family, 117
Loryman, William, 203, 206
Lounsberry, xv; Daniel, 17; Isaac, 21;
  Polly, 48
Loveless, Columbus, 58; Crandall, 26;
  Nathan, 76; Ransom, 28, 76; Wash-
  ington, 26
Lovejoy, Addison, 237; Alvira, 85;
  Anna, 86, 92, 149; Augusta, 82;
  Augustus, 71, 82, 90; Daniel, 78, 79,
  83, 84; Darius, 29, 83; David, 83;
  Eleanor, 86; Ellen, 85; Eliza, 24, 71,
  82; Eson, 85; Florence, 92, 117;
  Harvey, 78; Henry, 68, 78, 82;
  Jerusha, 69, 79; James, 78, 82, 92;
  John, 83, family, 237; Julia, 80, 83;
  Laura, 60, 78; Lewis, 82; Lucetta,
  94; Minerva, 78; Nancy, 80; Nellie,
  92; Nellie E., 82; Nelson, 85, 109;
  Norman, 78, 84, 86, 109; Parmer, 68,
  77; Parmer, Jr., 78; Silas, 53, 74, 84,
  86, 88, 92; Sophronia, 85, 94; Wil-
  liam, 78, 82
Lowell, Mary, 67
Luce, Sally, 130
Luffman, Edward, 202
Lumbert, George, William, 188
Lund, Elizabeth, 98
Lyman, Charles, 106, 107, 108; David,
  106, 108, 133, 174, 279; Flavia, 107;

Frederick, 107; George F., 276; Henry, 377; Jacob, 198, 278; Jesse and family, 197, 208, 377; John, 106, 107; John D., 107; John W., 197; Levi, 198; Lavius, 106, 107; Milo, 196, 197; Samuel, 106, 107, 276; Samuel H., 107, 129; William,   107

Lyon, 54; Abel, 255; Angeline, 62; Lucetta, 259; Parley, 139, 259; Walter and family, 292; William H.,   xvi, 258

McCamly, Jane,   44
McCoy, William,   261
McDorman, Michael and family,   110
McDougal, Mary,   43
Mace, Alonzo,   67, 102
McFarland, James,   87
McIntyre, Ella, 174; Samuel,   132
Mack, Jay,   178
McKoon, Charles, 33; Hattie, 33; Ida, iii, 33, 57; Jairus, 32, 33, 57; Mairetta, 32; Merritt, 4, 19, 21, 33, 377; William,   27, 32, 33, 80
McMullen, Edwin,   81
McMurdy, William,   295
McNab, Andrew,   xii, 140
McQueen, Eliza, 138; Jennie,   105
McRorie, J. W.,   203, 215
McWharf, Almira, 105; George, Jane, 105; John, 103, 114; John M., 105; Theodore and family,   105, 245
Maffit, T. T.,   246
Mains, Jane A.,   126
Malcom, Elizabeth,   143
Mallery, A. H. and family, 211; Oscar,   211
Markham, D. C., 274; Thomas,   279
Maroney, Walter,   27
Marquette, Philip,   230
Marriott, John and family,   299
Marsh, Amos, 19, 49, 50; Cornelius, 25, 27, 50, 51, family, 178; Garrett, 51; Henry, 50, 51, 76; Jonathan, 14; Lorinda, Matilda, 51; Pendar, xv, 19, 42, 46, 50; Rebecca, 27, 51; Roswell, 1, 50; Uriah, 46, 50, 63; William,   22, 50
Marsteiner, Louis, 56; Michael and family,   55
Marsten, Abraham, 1st and 2d,   101
Martin, Daniel, 226; Edward, 37; Philip,   43
Mason, Alvin, Amos, 83; Laura, 69;

Harvey, 79, 83, family, 84, 90, 92; Robert and family,   83, 90, 93, 95
Masonic,   370
Matthews and family,   263, 292
Maxon, Mrs. S. C.,   46
Maxwell, Hugh,   xiii
Mayho, Isaac,   146
Mead, Mary A.,   117
Meehan, Michael and family,   46
Melvin, Jonathan,   52, 103
Merritt, George H., 288; Rachel,   32
Messenger, Louise, 163; Nettie, 168; Walter and family,   236
Methodist Church burned,   337
Methodist Church dedicated,   337
Methodist Church, History of,   327
Methodist Church officers,   340
Methodist Preachers' names,   343
Metz, H.,   106
Mflem, Ann, Christopher, George and family, William,   195
Millard, Oliver,   145
Miller, George E., 132; Eliza, 100; Jacob, 55, family, 61, 312; Philip and family, 218; Sally, 55; Samuel, 74; Stephen,   189
Mills, Isaac,   17
Miner, Charles, 163; family, 166, 170; Darwin, 168; Deacon, 71; Edward, 170; Fernando, 166, 170; Frank, 230; Gilbert, 133; Harmon, 281; Irwin, 170; Isaac, 88, 252; Mary, 88; Philo, 170, 206; Riley and family,   170
Mirick, Charles, 56, 298; George, 56, 266, family, 298; Hiram, 102, 246, 266, family, 271, 285, 377; Ira, 102, 266, 285, 377; Leander, 298; Solomon, 265, 285; Thomas,   266
Mitchell, Barnard, 132, 206; Darwin, 207; Eliza, 182, 209; Frank, 178, 207; Jacob, 213, 218; Leonard, 206, 209; Lovina, 181, 207; Lucinda, 177, 207; Mary, 230; Philander, 177, 206, 376, 377; Philander, 2nd, 207, 377; Phœbe, 209; Sarah, 207; William,   177
Mix, William,   206, 287, 303
Monroe, Elnora,   120
Moon, Margaret,   261
Moore, 11; Abram, 25; Charles and family, 120; Eliza, 42; Newton, 76;

Orrin, 68

Morey, Charity, 85, 109 ; Delevan, Derrick, 109 ; Elijah, 85, 109 ; Horace and family, 241 ; Lydia, 86; Richard, 107, family, 109 ; Warren, 131

Morris, Hiram, 97 ; Lewis, 218 ; Lucinda, 97 ; Orrin, 97, 99 ; Robert, x ; Russell, 100

Morrison, John, 72

Morrow, Henry, 313

Mosher, Nancy, 118

Moslein, Foster, 286, 311

Mott, Chauncey, Jerusha, Sumner, 130

Munger, Naomi, 60

Munsell, Anginette, 84 ; Damaris, 69 ; Dorman, 69, 70, 377 ; Dorman, 2d, 81, 84, family, 95 ; Elnathan, 70, 81 ; Emeline, 69 ; Harvey, 90, 95 ; Lawson, 68, 69, family, 70 ; Levern, 70 ; Lucien, 70 ; Mary, 69, 88 ; Silas, 69, 70 ; Sophia, 87 ; Will, 69

Munson, E. Y., 25

Murder Story, 295

Murray, 67 ; Betsey, 91 ; John N. and family, 67, 376 ; Maggie, 201 ; Mary, 192

Myers, John and family, 212 ; Mary, 255 ; Rhoda, 29

Neeley, Dr. N., 286 ; Clarence, 286

Newberry, Huldah, 224

Newspapers in Rose, 372

Newton, Rev. J. B., 258

Nicholas, John, xi

Nichols, Anna, 85 ; Daniel, 71 ; Jonathan, 83, 90

Niles, William, 73, 264, 304

Norris, Ellen, 38

Northrop, Juliette, 96

Norton, Daniel and family, 95 ; Darwin, 67, 78, 99

Nusbickel, Margaret, 41 ; E., 181

Oaks, Charles G. and family, 67, 260; Charles G., 2d, iii, 126, family, 135; Charles W., 133, 135; Elizabeth, 66; Marilla, 135

Odd Fellowship, 371

Odelle, Charlotte, 126; Ebenezer, 289; Elizabeth, Sanford, 80

Officers of Rose, 376

Ogram, James, 6; John, 6, 252, 294; Polly, 6

Ohl, Margaret, 212

Olmstead, 15, 42; Eunice, 62; Jesse, 53; Millard, 42; Simeon, 105; William, 18, 24

Onions, Growing of, viii

Osborn, Abner, 58, 104, 172; Caroline, 120; Charles and family, 10; Edward, 308, 309; Elijah, 58, 65, 303, 309; Francis and family, 158; Isaac, 58, 66; Isaac, 2d, 102, 103; James, 158; John and family, 58, 66; John, 2d, 172, 277; Mervin, 158; Samuel, 58, 63, 66; Samuel, 2d, 56; family, 66; Robert, 201; William, 158

Osgood, Artemas, 4, 5, 11, 114, 116, 260; Caroline, 7; Emma, 5, 25; Frances, 4, 11, 57; John, 260; Linus, 11, family, 11, 63, 107; Lucien, 4, 11, 81, family, 273, 377; Mary, 11, 116; Nannie, 11, 113

Otto, Emily, 144; Guilford, James, 100; Sally, 166; Samuel, 61, 100

Overton, Clarissa, 36, 44; Emily, 9, 19, 21; Howard, 21; Laura, 21, 36; Lucilla, 21; Sheldon, 7, 8, 19, family, 21, 36, 46

Ownership of land, ix

Page, James, 377

Paine, 115; Mary, 205; Peter, 166

Palmer, Abram, xv

Parrish, Drusilla, 27; Jemima, 161

Parslow, George, 133; Minnie, 107; Nelson, 131

Partridge, Burton, 96, 131; John, 144; Mattie, 133

Patterson, Celinda, George, Lucy, 81

Paylor, Hannah, 222

Pearsall, Andrew, 90

Pease, Alanson, 178, 186; John, 178; Merrill, 176, 178, 199

Peck, Arvine, 22; Betsey, 88, 91, 255; Charles, 88; Harlow, 29; Horace, 31, 83; Parisade, 83; Willard, 29

Peckham and his balsam, 174

Pendleton, C. B., 73

Peppermint, Growth of, viii

Perkins, Horace, 46; Nellie, 125

Petty, Betsey, 258

Phelps & Gorham purchase, x

Phillips, Abram, 18, 160; Alice, 170; Barbara, 81; Charles, 168; Clarence, 168; Frank, Horace, 18; Isaac, 18; James, 81; James and family, 163;

John, 168, 169; Joseph, iii, family, 157, 162; Mary, 74; Paine, 94, 95; Phœbe, 81; Rosetta, 222; William, 156, family, 163; William, 168

Pierce, Ebenezer, 28, 200; Elizabeth, 29; Eugene, 9; Harriet, 11; Jeremiah, 29; John, 9; Matilda, 29, 164

Pimm, Enos T., 254, 286

Pinny, Priscilla, 74

Pitcher, 115; John, 24; Helen, 198; Mary, 165

Pitts, William, 74

Pixley, William, 169, 172

Playford, Elizabeth, 61

Plum, Green, 200

Plumb, Asa, 38; Chester, 171

Plunkett, Diana, 99

Pomeroy, 29; Samuel, 27

Porter, Asa, 235; George, 53

Post, Alice, 76; George and family, 125; Jotham, 70, 73, 76; Martha, 54; Sarah, 70

Postmasters in Rose, 285

Potter, Emma, 92; Jane, 83

Powers, Edward, 104; Electa, 30; Maggie, 65; Nicholas, 104

Preëmption Lines, x, xi

Presbyterian Church, History of, 353

Presbyterian Preachers, Names of 358

Prescott, Imogene, 88

Preston, Albert, 85; Hovey, 138, 141; Joseph, 44, 138

Price, Sarah, 73

Prindle, Michael, 141

Pritchard, George, 230

Proseus, Allen, 134, family, 142; F. M., 134; Frank, 131, 134; John, 118

Pulteney Estate, x

Pultz, Margaret, 166

Purdy, Betsey, 160

Putnam, Dewey and family, 216; Hervey, 216, 223; Joel, 216, 217

Quackenbush, Hannah, 133

Quail, James, 61

Quertershan, Dillene, 110

Race, Isaac, 257, 262, 277

Rankart, Mary, 212

Raplee, Catharine, 135

Raver, Carrie, 222

Ray, Rev. Charles, 281; William, 92

Ready, Alexander, 193

Ream, Fred., 177, 179, family, 181,

377; George, 192; Lany, 176; Peter, 181

Reed, Charles, 53, 74

Rekugler, John and family, 226

Remington, Freelove, 46

Reynolds, 44; Rev. G. W., 264; John, 27

Rhea, Arnold, 165, family, 200; John, 165, 179

Rheinhart, Andrew, 214

Rice, Charles, 12, 25; Decatur, 25; Frank, 6, 25; George, 25, 32; Geo. W., 113; Hattie, 25; Henry, 88, 253; Jared, 25; Jonathan, 6, 12, 25, 27; Lavina, 26

Rich, Alice, 114; Clarissa, 100

Richards, Charles, 15

Richardson, John and family, 99

Ridgeway, A., 223

Riggs, Eli, 159; Gowan, 80, 112; Hannah, 160; Henry, 80, 160; Hester, 80; James and family, 191; Norman, William and family, 160

Rinkel, Sophia, 226

Rising, Ebenezer, 305

Roads, Public, xv

Roat, Joseph, 8, family, 9

Robinson, Catharine, Eliza, 97; Henry, 96, 98; James, 96; Jane, John W., 97; Thomas, 97, 98, 376; William H., 97

Roberts, Alpheus, 115; Emory, John, 143

Rockwell, James, 114

Rodenbach, Philip, 215; family, 216

Rodwell, George, 46, 48

Roe, Addie, Alfred, 15; Alice, 20; Austin, 4, 19, 21, 36, 48, 49; Austin M., 4, 15, 20, 22, 49; Austin, 2d, Brewster, 17; Catharine, 19; Charles, 15; Daniel, 70, 71, 90, 128, 335; Daniel J., 19; Eliza, 19, 22; Fanny, 20; George, 16, 20, 309; John, 18, 19, 20, 23, 48, 49, 50; Mrs. J. B., 5, 12, 29; Merwin, 20, 21, 49; Mortimer, 15; Ottie, 20; Sarah, 19; Seymour, 71; Willis, 17; William, 133

Root, Cyrus, 377; R., 29

Rose and Wayne, an address, 315

Rose and Nicholas, xi, 320

Rose in the Rebellion, 384

Rose, Betsey, 45; J. A., 153; Margaret, 41; William C., 6, 131

ROSE, ROBERT S., xi

Rose churches, 324
Ross. Eliza, 146
Roswell, Elizabeth. 246
Rote, George, 74
Rounds, John C., 132
Rundell, Lucy, 74; Rhoda, 61
Ruppert, John H., 164, 310
Ryan, Anna, 90; Michael, 115; Sarah, 90
Sager, Frank, 37
St. John, Alonsworth, 71; Jacob, 46; Wallace, 188
Salisbury, Hiram, 283, 315; John, 71; Milburn, 295
Salmon, George, 22
Salter, Peter, 133
Sampson, Ethan, Gamaliel and family, 29; Putnam, 11, 29; Sally, 29, 83
Sanders, 30; Clark, 32; A. J., 72
Saunders, Augusta, 113; George, 53, 309; William H., 53, 305, 308
Saxton, Albert, 27, 28; Alzina, 27; Drusilla, 26; Jane, Lucy, 27; Martin, 6, 27, 28, 51; Mary, 27; Phœbe, 27; Philo, 6, 24, 27
Schofield, Jennie, 261
School District No. 1, 234; School District No. 2. 123; School District No. 3, 102; School District No. 4, 242; School District No. 5, 36; School District No. 6, 51; School District No. 7, 1; School District No. 8, 191; School District No. 9, 177; School District No. 10, 150; School District No. 11, 172; School District No. 12, 211, School District, Preëmption, 225; School District, York's, 228
Scott, Charity, 44; Emeline, 65
Seager, Asher, 222; Clarissa, 228; Claude, 122; David and family, 221; Elizabeth,, 128 George, 122, 277; Jacob, 247; John, 232; John K. and family. 221; Julia, 215; Monroe, 220; Munson, 231
Seaman, 88: Eleanor, Lois, 44
Sears, Dolly, 78; James, 47
Sebring, William, 229, 254, 257
Sedgewick, Betsey, 197
Sedore, Ida, 91; Julia, 195
Seelye, Alfred, 9; Alice, 30; Angeline, 8. 54; Anna, 8; Benjamin, 9, family, 145; Burt, 146; Caroline,
145; Delos, 1, 3, 8, 9, 30, 35, 36, 54, 56, 257; Elnora, 9, 63; Ensign, 2; Ernest, iii, 57. 94; Estelle, 4, 33; Eudora, 4, 11, 82; Fred, 146; George, 1, 2, 3, 5, 6, 10, 22, 30, 34, 47, 51, 56, 68, 98, 112, 272, 377; Mrs. George, 5, 10, 11, 54, 67; George S., vi, 25, 58; Irwin, 128, 133, 142, 146; Jane. 30; Jay, 141, 145; Joseph, 1, 2, 38, 57, 139; Judson, 4, 33, 37, 38, 260; Julia, 144; Lewis, 38; Mary, 3, 5; Nehemiah and family, 9, 63, 145; Polly, 38
Sellick, Sally, 129
Settlements, First, xiv
Seymour, Anna, 157; Norman, 93
Shanker, J., 155
Shannon, Samuel, Theodore, 232
Shattuck, Mary, 255
Shaw, Charity, 231; Rev. Clemence, 257; John P., 217
Shaver, C. M., 133, 263; Mary, Nancy, 43
Shear, Arthur, 65; John and family, 65, 153; Judson, 153; Peter and family, 111, 112; Stephen, 65; Thaddeus, 65; Will, 102, 112
Sheffield, Dr. James, 4, 56; James, 10, 56, 58; James, 2d, 10; James C., 56; Joel, 10. 11, 56, 113, 254, 377; Judson, 10, 261, 377; Kendrick, 5, 9, 10, 56; Lucy, 5, 10; Mattie, 10; Sarah, 11, 56; Willard, 56
Shepard, 73, 75; Aaron, 4, 5, 6, 12, 13, 44, 78; Harriet, 15; Harry, 42, 165; Heman, 10; Jerusha, 23; Polly C., 4, 112; Seth, xv, 13, 19
Sherman, Adelbert, 254, 273: Charles, 11, 248; Charles B., 10, family, 11, 248; Chester, 11, 248; Clara, 155; Elias, 24, 44, 250; Ezra, 11, 248; Ezra A., 11, 248, 377; Frank, 11, 113, 248, 377; George, 11, 248, 253, 265, 290; Harrison, 251: Henry, iii, 21, 250: Henry B., 262; Jennie, 172; Capt. John and family, 249, 250, 274, 299, 312; John, iii, 101, family, 250; John E., 262; Lucy, 11: Orra, 250: Orrin, 250, 255; Willard, 11. 248, 377; William, iii, 21, 24, 26, 31, 36, 76, 104, 248, family, 250
Silver, Ella, 243
Sizer, Thirza, 195

Skidmore, 103; John and family, 119, 292
Skut, Alexander, 129, family, 135;
    Annette, 135; Charles, 134; Daniel
    and family, 135; Frank, 132; Han-
    nah, 104; Ira, Jasper, Jerome, 135;
    Jonathan and family, 134; Orrin, 132, 134
Slaght, Everett,   132, 143
Slaughter, Zemira,   118
Smalley, Sarah,   142
Smart, George, 9, 11; John, 9, 206;
    Mary, 9, 11, 40; Newton, 41; Thomas,
    9; William, 9, 41,   125
Smith, Ambrose, 91: Ananaias, 41, 45,
    46; Byron, 27; Charles, 76; Chaun-
    cey and family, 70, 74, 75; Cornelia,
    185; David, 63, 243, 377; Duke, 20;
    Edmund, 99, 141; Eliza, 91, 99;
    Elkanah, 141; George, 86, 91, 98; G.
    F., 146; Georgie, 91; Halsey, 72,
    83, 90; Harry, 91; John and family,
    139; John I., 162; Leonard, 67;
    Lucy, 70, 74, 82; Marshall, 45; Mor-
    gan, 143; Samuel, 103; Solomon,
    90, family, 91; Thomas, 66, 141;
    Timothy, 20, 45; Washington, 45;
    William,   90
Snow, Alonzo, 12, 195, 255; Carrie, 12;
    Lorenzo,   iii, 291
Snyder, Amariah, Azro, Charity,
    Charles, 42; Harvey, 42; Henry, 41;
    John, 42; Wilbur, 42, 47; William,
    40, 42.   43
Sober, Jonathan and family,   235
Soil and products,   vii
Sons of Veterans,   371
Soper, Alfred, 9; Annette, 9, 10;
    Brewster, 7, 257, family, 258; Dan-
    iel and family, 7, 30, 32; Egbert, 9,
    36, 37; Frank, 237, 258, 260; Hattie,
    223; Platt and family, 216; Robert,
    7; Sophia, 209; William,   7
Soule, 53; Florence, 69; Ira, 257, 272;
    Ira T., 257, 272, 377; Stephen, 20, 257, 377
Sours, Alfred, 105; Burt, 67; Cynthia,
    155; Lottie, 146; Martin, 131; Rox-
    ana,   20
Southwick, Samuel, 102, 107, 265; Sub-
    mit, 245; William,   73
Sowls, William H. and family,   40, 44
Spaulding, Mary E.,   198
Spencer, Elihu,   32
Spong, Alfred,   217

Sprague, Hiram,   67
Springer, James, 23; John,   5, 23, 48
Squires, 22; Richard,   61
Stack, Jacob and family,   196
Stacy, Hannah,   38
Stafford, George, 20, 22; Sarah,   20
Stanley, Alice, 201; David and family,
    145; Plumie, 145; Sally,   136
Stansell, G. W., 132; Nicholas, 150,
    241; William,   241
Stark, Amanda,   61
Stearns, A. H., 116; Charity, 124;
    Dora,   171
Steinhart, 121; Hannah,   122
Steitler, Charles, 212; Henry, 203, 212;
    William,   290
Stell, Charles H.,   289
Stevens, Charles, 164; Harriet, 312;
    Lucy, 56; Samuel,   67
Stewart, Allen, 52; George, 52, fami-
    ly, 53, 61, 69, 71; James and family,
    52, 64; Jennie, 43; John, 118; Lott,
    51, 52; William, 177,   183
Stickles, 8, 40; Andrew, 105; Catha-
    rine, 188; Edward, 4, 17; Mary,   105
Stone, 5; Homer, 7; Mariette, 81;
    Mary, 33; Warren,   85
Stopfel, 164; Catharine, 65; John, 159;
    Louis,   .   164
Strang, Eva,   196
Streeter, Alonzo, 98, 179; Henry, 179;
    Josiah,   179, 263
Strong, Charles,   157
Stryker, Lucy,   105
Stubley, George and family,   262
Sumner, Ebenezer,   149
Surveys of Rose,   xiii
Sutherland, Charles,   220
Sutphin, W. H.,   157
Swart, Henrietta,   37
Swayne, Samuel,   262
Sweet, 12; Jane, 263; Thomas,   223
Swift, Amanda, 171; Carrie, 37, 201;
    Helen,   .   189
Tait, Theresa,   72
Talcott, 75; George, 28; Welthea,   74
Talton, John, 122; Joseph,   273
Taylor, Allen, 98; Elias, 25; Eliza, 26;
    Geliza, 97; Lydia, 26; Ruth, 97, 98;
    Vesta, 26; Zadoc,   61, 95, 97
Tebbetts, T. D.,   133
Temperance in Rose,   365

Ten Eyke, 137
Terbush, Clara, 128; Effie, 27; Jackson, 26, 32
Terry, Horace, 134; Jennie, 33
Terwilliger, Melville, 33
Thayer, Stephen, 286, 306
Thomas, 93; Charles, 42, 294, 312, family; 313; Elijah, 377; Eron, xiv, xvi, 76, 285, 288, 294, 305, 306, family; 313, 314, 376, 377; Jerome, 313, 377; Lorenzo, 42, 305; Nathan W. and family, 258; N. W., 61, 311, 313, 377; Philip, 109; Sophia, 101, 284
Thomas & Collier, 258
Thompson, Albert, 227; Camilla, Clarissa, Cordelia, Edwin, Elijah, 31; Ezekiel, 226; Jane, 159; Robert, 226; Samuel, 31; Samuel P., 226; William, 141
Thorn, Joel, 139
Thorpe, Joseph, 194
Tillow, Ann, 19
Tillson, Charles, 273; family, 299
Tindall, Charles and family, 227, 228; Hannah, 139; Henry, 289; Jerome, 228, 290; "Parm," 140, 302, 377; Philip, 302, 303
Tipple, Eliza, Philip, Jacob, 18, 167; Mrs. Jacob, 166
Titles and Agents, xii
Titus, Rev. Anson, viii
Toles, 84, 85; Ebenezer, 85, 86, 98, 224; Ezra, 86; Julia, 24, 86; Lucy, 39, 86; Matthew, 86; Orson and family, 86; Truman, 86
Tompkins, N. W., 25, 26
Tooker, Francis M., 214
Town, Absalom, 37; Asa, xv, 37, 38; David, 38, 88, 282; Emily, 38; Eugene, 38; Hannah, 38; Henry, 38; Lavinia, 37; Lewis, 36; Lewis S., 38, 94, 256; Lucy, 38; May, 38; Mary, 38, 63; Mary A., 39; Milton, 8, 36, 38, 60, 63, 256; Norris, 38; Polly, 39; Sarah, 38; Silas, xv, 36, 37
Town Names, Reasons for, 317
Tracy, Sarah J., 65
Traher, Ellen, Harry, 253
Transue, Aurilla, 39; Rev. George, 264
Trask, Pamelia, 29
Trautman, Fred, 213, family, 214
Traver, Asa, 43

Travers, Mary R., 133
Trimble, John, 217
Trippe, Morton, 133, 142
Troup, Robert, xii
Tucker, Anna, 89; Daniel, 90
Turvey, Anthony, 213
Turner, 46; Philip, 55, 255, 280; Royal, 123, family, 203
Twamley, Alice, 229; Martha, 216
Tyler, Charlotte, 11; Eliza, 32
Ullrich, Charles, 65; family, 66; Irving, 66
Underhill, William, 96
Underwood, Elizabeth, 265
Upson, Carroll, Frank, Homer, Josiah, William, 62
Utter, N., 227
Valentine, 281; Anna, 32; Asahel, 119; Bert, Charles, 283; Cornelia, 39; Frank, 282; George, 260; Harry, 67, 257, 309, 377; Jackson, 39, 282, family; 283, 376, 377; Marvin, 283; Dr. Peter, 240, 281; Dr. Richard, 282
Valley School, History of, 361
Van Amberg, Eliza, 170; German, 169; Harmon and family, 199; James, 169, 308; Sarah, 170
Van Antwerp, Dell, 65, 304; Edwin and family, 65; Evelyn, John, John H., 65; Simeon J., 64, family, 65
Van Auken, James, Simeon, 239, 240
Van Buren, Cornelius, 131, 142; Martin, 41; Peter, 27, 114, 377
Van Buskirk, Simeon, Thomas, 183
Vance, Rebecca, 88
Vanderburg, Abram, 41, 122; Elizabeth, 122; Emma, 113, 179; Etta, Frances, 113; James, 103, 121; John, iii, 113; Sarah, 107, 113; William, 113, 122
Vandercook, Frank, 201; John, 174, 198, 200, 201; Lucy, 189; Michael, 198, 210; Michael, 2d, 201; Phœbe, 187, 219; Robert, 174, 195; William, 174, 198
Vanderoof, Clarence, 38, 275; James, 41, 54, 55, family, 310; John, 38, 54; Post, 54; Rachel, 55; William, 38, 54, 275, 377
Vanderpool, Charles, 302
Van Dusen, 37; Hiram, 40
Van Horn, Matthias, 181
Van Marter, Fanny, 179
Van Ostrand, Henry, 149, 291; Per-

melia, 62
Van Sicklen, Ogden, 136; William and family, 137
Van Tassel, Adelbert, 301; Henry, 307
Van Valkenburg, Abraham, 214; family, 217
Van Wort, 224; Royal, 305
Vaughn, Charlotte, 143
Veach, Della, 65
Vedder, Richard, 40
Veley, Elizabeth, Margaret, 365
Viele, Louis and family, 301
Vincent, Ezra, 213; Hannah, 85; Josias, 98, 213
Voorhees, George, 24
Vought, Eva, 6
Wade, Alverson, 58, 59, 60, 87, 107; Dudley, 3, 5, 6, 24, 31, 48, 62, 66, 81, 246; Eliza, 62; Emily, 5; Ensign, 5, 32, 243, 377; Eunice, 62; Frank, 5; Imogene, 5; Jesse, 62; John, xv, 24, 60, family, 62, 293, 376; Dr. John, 5, 13, 60; Joseph, 61, 376; Joseph C., 61; Joseph S., 5, 25, 27, 266, 377; Louisa, 61; Lovina, 60, 87; Lucy, 60, Marcus D., 162; Marcus P., 61; Mary, 60; Naomi, 60; Polly, 13; Uriah, 156, 161, family, 162; William, 62; Willis G., 62, 111, 300, 301, 376; Willis S., 61
Wadsworth, Eveline, 50
Wager, Abram and family, 222; David and family, 223; Jacob, 232; John, 227; Luther, 222; Margaret, 230; Morris, 227, family, 243
Waite, Stephen, 254, 255, 262, 273
Wainwright, Abigail, 31
Waldo, Daniel, 74, 75; Egbert, 74
Waldron, Addie, 18
Waldruff, David, 96; Fred., 113, 261; Luther, 170; Stanton and family, 113
Walker, Anna, 263
Walmsley, E., 308; family, 311
Ward, 66; Eli, 22, 70, 77, family, 78, 79, 84; Jacob, xv; Millard, 89; Ransom, 4, 74
Waring, Georgie, 70; Joseph, 174
Warne, Samuel, 133; Thomas, 292
Warner, Martin, 292
Warren, Caroline, 215; Charles, 31, 32; Comstock and family, 219; Harvey, 202; Isaac, 219; James,

220; Viola, 292
Waterbury, Aaron, 213; Emma, Hiel, John, Mary, 214; Phœbe, 189
Waterman, 307; Murray, 149
Waters, James, 37; Joanna, 157; Mary, 150, 200; Susan, 37
Watkins, 68; Lydia, 69; William, 265, 330
Watson, Gerhardus, 139; James, 193; Rebecca, 238
Way, Benjamin, Caroline, David, 191; Harley, 114, 377; Josie, 10; Lucy, 38; Lydia, 191; Samuel, 174, 191; Valentine, 191
Weaver, Samuel, 117
Weed, Addison, Dillwyn, 238; Oscar, 235; family, 238; Thurlow, 265; William, 263
Weeks, Addison, 237; Alexander, 39; Amy, 214; Anna, 131; Caleb, 126, 230; Catharine, 121; Delia, 189; Emory, 236; Frank, 229; George, 294; Ida, 214; James and family, 189; Jane, 83; John, 74, 131; John, 2d, and family, 310; Julia, 189; Martha, 126, 166; Mary, 189; Mary J., 222; R. R., 115; Robert, ili; Stephen, 290, 294; William, 224, 230
Weikner, Mary, 212
Welch, Edward, 48, 102, 112, 377; Joseph, 102, 112; Lueze, 230; Thomas, 100, 102, 112, 130; William and family, 102
Welch Brothers, 127
Weller, Lillie, 24
Wellington, Adaline, 92; Eliza, 237; George, 88; Henry, 82
Wells, Byron, 69; Lorinda, 22; Milton, 74; Philura, 60
Wescott, Betsey, 30; David, 132; Susan, 61; William, 6
West, Submit, 265; William, 219
Westbrook, Sally, 206
Wheeler, Ann, 68; Anna, 74; Chloe, 116; Eli, xv, 116; Elizabeth, 74; H. H., ix, xi; Luther, 74
Whipple, Mary, 194
White, Gilbert, 257; John, 90; Walter, 219, 220
Whitehead, 25; William, 47
Whitemore, Benjamin, 240; Oliver, 111; Seth, 111, 240

Whitney, Charles, 74; Louise, 69;
Solomon, 113
Wickwire, Gleason, 10, 11, 56; Ida,
iii; Jarit, 33, 57; Matilda, 11, 57
Wight, Ephraim, 300
Wilbur, Brownell, 240, 246, 291, 293;
Helen, 246; Marvin, 22, 291
Wilcox, Julia, 109; Susan, 83; widow, 139
Wilder, Martha, 74
Wiley, Daniel, 174; Johnson, 192
Wilkins, Rev. A. and family, 121, 276
Wilkinson, Bert, 307
Williams, Alfred, 76; Chester, 117;
Harriet, 114; Dr. M. J., 288; Polly,
85; Sarah, 142
Williamson, Charles, x, xii
Williamson's Patent, xi
Willoughby, Mapeley, 44
Wilson, Augusta, 61; Clarissa, 69, 151;
Damaris, 69; Ephraim, 69, 171, 266,
family, 267, 268; Ephraim, Jr., 12,
family, 254, 377; George W., 304;
Harlan and family, 12, 140, 255;
Huldah, 135; Jonathan, xv, family,
69, 276; Lewis, 12; Levern, 203, 266,
377; Luther, 135; Maria, 90; Mary,
61; Mary N., 135; Robert, 135;
Walter, 69
Winchell, Absalom, 169; Calvin and
family, 133, 171; Catherine, 166;
Clarissa, 149, 171; Giles and family,
30, 31; Jacob, 169; James, 153, 171,
377; John, 168, family, 169; Lovina,
169; Lucinda, 169, 177; Maria, 179;
Riley, 169, 171; Russell and family,
171; Sally, 169, 207; Sophia, 171
Wing, Abel, 27
Winget, Benjamin, 233; William, 16, 17
Wisner, Charles, Charlotte, Elizabeth,
James, Jesse, Moses, Sarah, Tem-
perance, 17, 73
Witherell, Ann, 229
Wolcott, Epaphras, xv, 69; "Jim,"

77; Miriam, 80; Oliver, ix
Wolf, J. M., 132
Wood, Abner, 94, 105; Abram, 68;
Collins, 254, 262, 308; David, 88;
Elias, 114; Frank, 16; Hattie, 55;
Hudson, 5, 10, 16, 21, 55, 56, 61, 68,
190, 256, 309; Leora, 53; Solomon,
87; widow, 94
Woodard, Charles, 163; Seth, 162
Woodman, J. H., 286
Woodruff, Charles, 25; George, 218,
286; Jesse, 24, 25, 28; Lambert, 25;
Tunis, 193, 218
Woodward, Charles, 153, 250, 274, 312;
Charles S., 298; William, 228
Wooster, Mabel, 170
Worden, 42; Alonzo, 190; Constan-
tine, 187, 219; Elizabeth, 187; George,
187; Irene, John, 187; John V., 190;
Leonard, 187, 219; Louisa, Martha,
190; William, 187, 219
Wraight, Frances, 160; George, James, 159
Wright, Augusta, 53; Betsey, 90;
Charles, 28, 46, 48; Charles S., 62,
122, 255, 264, 304, 377; Daniel and
family, 53; Fred, 58; "Harl.," 53;
Irving, 305; Jacob, 28; Jason, 58;
Manly, 132; Thomas, 74
Wyke, John, 40
Wykoff, Amos, 208, family, 268; Ly-
man, 305; Sarah, William, 268
Yale, Elizabeth, 240
York, Eliza, 209, 230; John, 99, 126,
131, 145; Lillian, Norman, 162
Young, Bell, 145; Conrad, 213, 216,
217; Electa, 145; Eson, 85, 86; Hen-
ry, 162, 240; Israel, 240; Jared, 145;
Jacob, John, 216; Mabel, 100; Nor-
man, Sarah, 86
Youngs, Kate, 273
Zeek, William, 69
Zeluff, Sarah, 260

www.ingramcontent.com/pod-product-compliance
Lightning Source LLC
Chambersburg PA
CBHW032021110726
47901CB00004B/1160